KINGMAKER

Books by MARGARET WEIS and ROBERT KRAMMES

DRAGON BRIGADE

Shadow Raiders

*Storm Riders**

*The Seventh Sigil**

DRAGON CORSAIRS

*Spymaster**

*Privateer**

*Kingmaker**

*A TOR BOOK

KINGMAKER

Margaret Weis
and Robert Krammes

TOR

A TOM DOHERTY ASSOCIATES BOOK / NEW YORK

KINGMAKER

Copyright © 2019 by Margaret Weis and Robert Krammes

Dragon ornament © 2014 by Jeff Easley

Map and family tree by Ellisa Mitchell

A Tor Book
Published by Tom Doherty Associates
120 Broadway
New York, NY 10271

www.tor-forge.com

Tor® is a registered trademark of Macmillan Publishing Group, LLC.

The Library of Congress Cataloging-in-Publication Data is available upon request.

ISBN 978-0-7653-8111-8 (hardcover)
ISBN 978-1-4668-7797-9 (ebook)

Our books may be purchased in bulk for promotional, educational, or business use. Please contact your local bookseller or the Macmillan Corporate and Premium Sales Department at 1-800-221-7945, extension 5442, or by email at MacmillanSpecialMarkets@macmillan.com.

First Edition: August 2019

Printed in the United States of America

0 9 8 7 6 5 4 3 2 1

We dedicate this book to one of our characters, Sir Henry Wallace, Queen's Spymaster. Henry was a villain in the first series, Dragon Brigade, but he endeared himself to us with his love for his family and his loyalty to his friends and his country. We wrote the series Dragon Corsairs to continue Henry's story, and thus it is fitting that the last book, *Kingmaker,* should be his.

—Margaret Weis and Robert Krammes

King Lionel II

Ester of Travia (D)   Blanche Hunsman

Osric (D) — Frederick (M) Elizabeth   Oswald I (M) Caroline
Died with
Queen Ester

Victoria (M) Michael   Bridgett   Oswald II (M) Ann

Richard (M) Margaret   Mary (M) Oswald III   Phillip (M) Martha
                                    (K)

Lucia (M) James I (K)   Oswald   Mortimer   Alfred I (M) Susan
                             (K)   (K)

Vincent (M) Evelyn   Margaret   Thomas   Marjorie (M) William I   Jonathan   Richard (D)
                              Died
                              as a Baby (D)

Elanora (M) Henry   George I (M) Caroline

Giovana (M) Joseph   Anne (M) George II   Bastard Line

Constanza (M) Alistair Oberlein   Godfrey I (M) Jane   Godfrey (M) Honoria

                                                          Elise (M) Hugh
Thomas Stanford   Michael Owens (M) Mary I   Elinor   Martha (M) Claire (M) Jeffrey
(Prince Tom)   Susan

                        (D) Osric   Jonathan   Henry F. (M) Ann

                                                          Henry E.

House Stanford   House Chessington

(M) Married
(D) Died
(K) Killed

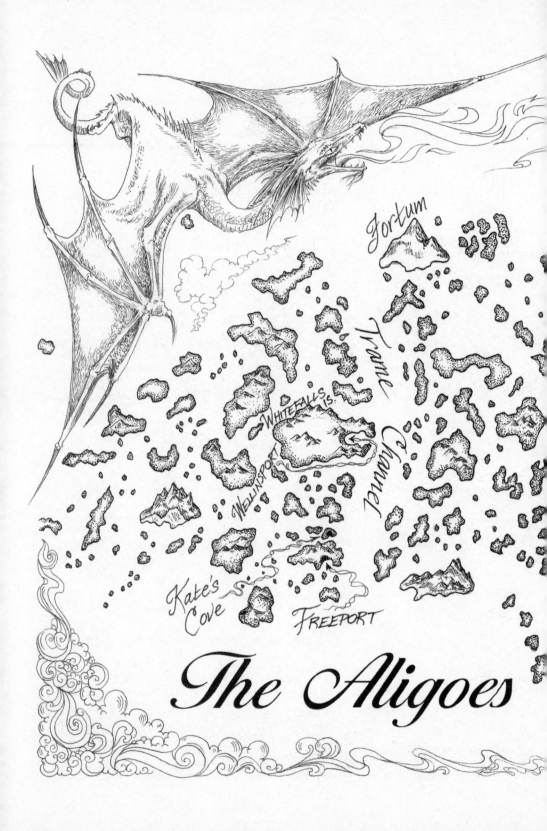

Fortum

Trame Channel

WHITEFALLS IS.

WELLINSPORT

Kate's Cove

FREEPORT

The Aligoes

Maribeau

Imperial Channel

Sornhagen

100 Miles

KINGMAKER

ONE

Captain Alan Northrop and Admiral Randolph Baker of the Freyan Royal Navy were sitting down to a late supper in the dining room of the Naval Club when the club steward came to inform them they were both wanted in the Visitor's Room.

"Now?" Randolph demanded, shocked. "I'm to be interrupted in the middle of my goddamn dinner?"

"I am afraid so, Admiral," said the steward apologetically. "The gentleman said the matter was one of urgency."

"Who the devil is it?" Randolph asked, scowling.

"The gentleman did not provide his name, sir. He handed me this."

The steward gave Randolph a note. Randolph read it, frowned, and tossed it to Alan.

Alan glanced at it. The note contained a single word, scrawled in all capital letters, EMERGENCY. The note was not signed, but Alan knew immediately who had sent it.

"Simon." Alan glanced up at the steward. "Is the gentleman who delivered this note extremely tall and built like a bear?"

"I have never seen a bear, sir," said the steward. "But I would say that is an apt description."

"That would be Mr. Albright," said Alan. He looked troubled. "This summons is not like Simon. He never wants to be disturbed in his studies. What is the time?"

"Just coming up on nine of the clock, sir," said the steward.

Alan rose to his feet. "We better go see what is so urgent, Randolph. Perhaps we're going to war with Rosia."

Randolph irritably yanked his napkin off from where he had tucked it beneath his chin and threw it on the table. "We bloody well better be!"

The two men had returned to their rooms in the Naval Club after spending the past fortnight as guests of Lord Alfred Winterhaven, who owned an estate in southern Freya. The party had also included Lord Alfred's charming niece, Annabelle.

The Winterhavens were attempting to promote a match between their niece and Alan. The handsome, dashing Captain Northrop, in his midforties, had thus far avoided matrimony, but he had found himself spending most of their time during dinner talking to Randolph about the lovely and spirited Annabelle Winterhaven.

"I find her completely captivating," Alan had said.

"'Captive' being the appropriate word," Randolph had said with a chortle. "She's out to hook you like a trout."

"I really don't think I should mind," Alan had said with a smile.

The Naval Club was a private club for officers in the Freyan Royal Navy and for highly placed government officials, such as Sir Henry Wallace, who was in the foreign office and dealt in matters related to the Royal Navy, as well as the defense of the nation. Club rules stipulated that only members of the club or invited guests were permitted beyond the Visitor's Room.

Alan and Randolph found Mr. Albright holding his hat in his hand, gazing out the window. He turned when he heard them enter.

"What is the matter, Albright?" Alan asked. "Is Simon all right?"

Simon Yates had what Henry Wallace termed a "giant brain." He also called him "Freya's secret weapon." Simon had been felled by a bullet more than twenty years earlier and now spent his days in his wondrous floating house, seated in his specially designed floating chair, using his giant brain to gather information, ferret out criminals, and foil plots against his country.

Mr. Albright appeared to be of two minds regarding whether or not to answer the question regarding his master. He was a taciturn man by nature, which suited Simon perfectly. One of the terms of Albright's employment was that he should go about his duties with as little speech as possible. In this instance, he decided the matter was important enough to respond, for he spoke.

"The master is agitated," said Mr. Albright.

Alan and Randolph exchanged alarmed glances. In more than twenty years of friendship, they had rarely known Simon to be "agitated."

"We will come at once," said Alan.

Since the late autumn night was chilly, the two navy men both wore their boat cloaks. Albright had traveled in Simon's magic-powered carriage, which he had designed himself. Mr. Albright opened the door, and Alan started to climb inside, but paused.

"Are we to meet Henry there?" he asked.

Albright simply shook his head. He ushered Randolph and Alan inside, then mounted the box. Placing his hand upon the helm, he sent the magic flowing to the lift tanks and the airscrews. The carriage left the ground and sped through the darkness, bound for the famous floating house known as Welkinstead.

"What the devil do you suppose is going on with Simon?" Randolph wondered aloud. "Agitated, my ass. This had better not be more goddamned theorizing on the possibility of anomalous liquid Breath pools in the Aligoes."

"I just hope it doesn't have to do with the discovery of some new type of bug," said Alan.

Randolph laughed. "Like that bug he named after you! What did he call it? Northrop's Weevil?"

"I have no idea," said Alan. "I took care to forget it as soon as possible. You cannot imagine the humiliation I endured. I was attending a party and having a confidential chat with a lady when we were quite rudely interrupted by some blighted bug enthusiast asking me questions about weevils!"

Randolph's laughter soon died and the men rode in silence, both of them pondering Simon's unusual summons.

"Can you see the house?" Randolph asked Alan after some time had passed.

"Just coming into view on the port side," he reported, indicating the chimneys and turrets and towers of Welkinstead silhouetted against the stars. "Wind from the north. The house will be drifting in a southerly direction tonight."

Simon's home, Welkinstead, was considered one of the wonders of the world. Built by the wealthy Elsinor family, the house had started life as a villa located on the outskirts of the Freyan capital, Haever. Down through the years, the rich, eccentric Elsinors had done renovations to the house, adding on or tearing down as the mood seized them.

One day, so the story goes, the last and most eccentric living member of that family, the Duchess of Elsinor, had looked out her window and decided she was bored with the view. A noted scientist, globe trotter, inventor, and collector, the duchess had outfitted her house with lift tanks, imbued it with magical constructs, and hired engineers to dig it up out of the ground. Welkinstead rose gracefully into the sky.

The house did not really fly. The duchess had liked to say, "Welkinstead drifted with panache." The house now drifted above Haever, the wonder and admiration of all who observed it.

When Simon was shot during an attempt to save Godfrey, then Crown Prince of Freya, from assassination, he was left paralyzed from the waist down, and the duchess invited him to come live with her. The duchess felt a good deal of affection for the young man, who shared her interests in science and inventing. When she died, she bequeathed the house and her considerable wealth to him.

Arriving at the house, Albright reversed the airscrews and brought the carriage to a smooth landing on a platform at the front entrance. They were climbing out of the carriage when the front door flew open and Simon floated out in his chair to meet them.

"What kept you?" he demanded irritably.

Alan and Randolph stared at him in astonishment.

Simon had never before greeted them at the door. He was generally to be found in his office on the second floor, so absorbed in his work that he wouldn't hear them if they fired off pistols.

"Nothing kept us!" Randolph said, annoyed. "I didn't even get to finish my dinner!"

"We came as soon as we got your message," Alan added. "What is this emergency?"

"Come to my office," said Simon. "Albright, fetch Henry, but not now. Wait an hour. You should find him at home. I know that Lady Ann was planning to dine with friends, but Henry said he had work to do and he wasn't going with her."

Albright silently nodded. He placed his hand on the helm, and the carriage sailed into the night. Simon whipped his chair around and floated back into the house.

"Why are we meeting without Henry?" Alan asked as they followed Simon inside.

"Because what I am about to tell you involves him," Simon replied. He paused, turned his chair around to face them again. "I have never before been in the situation where my ability to think logically is compromised by my friendship, and I require your advice. Hang your coats and hats on the hydra. I'll meet you upstairs."

Simon swiftly steered his chair up the stairs.

"I'll be goddamned!" Randolph exclaimed, staring after him.

"Something is most definitely wrong," said Alan, as they divested themselves of their coats and hats.

Welkinstead was as much a museum as it was a house. The duchess had traveled the world in search of the grotesque and the beautiful, the outré and the absurd, and anything else that happened to catch her fancy, and brought them back to adorn her house. Alan and Randolph draped their greatcoats over a tallboy that stood in the entryway and contained a fine collection of glass eyeballs and hung their hats on the heads of a stuffed, imitation hydra acquired from a carnival.

Due to the fact that the floating house was constantly on the move, the items of the collection tended to move, as well, occasionally falling off the walls or surging out from dark corners to accost unsuspecting visitors.

The stairs to the second floor were a hazard, for they contained various objects that had either been placed on the steps or found their way there. Alan had to circle around an enormous jardinière on his way up. Randolph tumbled over a concrete frog meant to be used as a doorstop and swore loudly.

Simon's office occupied most of the second floor. The only other rooms were his bedchamber and a water closet. The office resembled a library. The walls were lined floor to ceiling with bookshelves containing books on every conceivable subject. Wooden filing cabinets stood in orderly rows on the floor with aisles in between wide enough to accommodate Simon's chair. The file cabinets had been bolted to the floor and did not move. Simon had the files organized by a system of numbers and letters that allowed him to lay his hands on any document, paper, letter, or journal in minutes.

His desk was six times the size of a normal desk. The room had windows that provided a stunning and ever-changing view of the city of Haever some five hundred feet below, or the countryside around Haever, depending on the wind.

Simon could be found at his desk most hours of the day and night. No one had ever seen the surface of the desk, for it was covered with stacks of documents, newspapers, letters, journals, books, and pamphlets, many of them tied up with ribbons of various colors that meant something to Simon, if no one else.

A large telescope stood at one of the windows, and a blackboard lurked off to one side. Alan glanced at the board with some trepidation. The last time they had visited their friend, Simon had spent an hour drawing diagrams of islands in the Aligoes, with arrows denoting wind speeds, direction, fluctuations in barometric pressure, temperatures, and so forth, all of which he used to advance his latest theory: that pools of liquid Breath could be found in the Aligoes.

He had, in fact, been badgering Alan to take his ship, the *Terrapin,* on an expedition to the Aligoes to find these pools. Alan had tried to explain to Simon that he was now a captain in the Royal Navy, no longer a privateer, and he could not simply sail off without orders. Since receiving his commission, Alan had not yet been given orders to sail to the Aligoes or anywhere else, and he was growing restless. He had been ashore long enough.

The *Terrapin* had recently been refitted to use the more powerful and efficient crystals of the Breath to achieve lift, instead of relying on the liquid form of the Breath. Alan was eager to test the crystals; his crew needed to be trained in their use. All the ships of the Expeditionary Fleet were currently undergoing refitting to use the crystals.

He had been looking forward to the test sail, and had tried to persuade Henry to travel with him, but Henry had refused. He had been in a dark mood for weeks and had brusquely told Alan that he could not under any circumstance leave the country at this time. Alan did not understand why, but apparently Simon did, for he had dropped the idea of Alan sailing to the Aligoes and ordered Albright to move the blackboard with the drawings to the back of the room.

Simon was generally so deeply engrossed in his reading that he would motion to them to sit down and make them wait quietly until he came to a stopping place.

This night, he did not read. He sat in his chair, doing nothing. He stared at nothing, his hands idle in his lap. His thin face, usually alight with enthusiasm over his current project, was drawn and haggard. He was forty-six, but his eager, boyish face tended to make him look twenty. Tonight, though, he looked older than his years.

Alan and Randolph exchanged uneasy glances, not certain what to do.

"We need to talk," Simon said at last. "Bring those chairs close to the desk."

Since the chairs tended to wander about the room, Alan and Randolph each grabbed one and carried them over to sit near their friend.

"Simon, you are scaring the hell out of us," said Alan.

"Good," said Simon grimly. He drew in a breath, then fired a volley of words at them. "I have uncovered a plot by members of the Faithful, that secret organization I told you about, to overthrow Queen Mary and proclaim Prince Thomas Stanford to be the true and rightful king of Freya. The instigator and leader of this conspiracy is a murderer by the name of Isaiah Crawford, who now calls himself Jonathan Smythe. If you will remember, I suspected him in the gruesome death of the dragon, Lady Odila."

Simon spoke rapidly, as he always did. His words went off like gunshots, stunning his friends.

"Eh?" said Randolph, blinking.

"Say that again, Simon," said Alan. "More slowly this time."

Simon repeated himself, adding, "The devil of it is that I do not know when Smythe is going to make his move. I put together the final pieces of his plot only a short time ago. He could strike tonight, or a week from tonight. I simply do not know."

"Wait a moment," said Alan, trying to catch up. "You talk as if Smythe or Crawford or whoever he claims to be is the one who is behind this plot. Don't you mean Prince Thomas and the Faithful? Smythe works for them."

Simon shook his head. "Smythe is clever. He managed to worm his way into the confidence of the Faithful by presenting himself as a loyal soldier dedicated to their cause. I am convinced that neither the members of the Faithful nor Prince Thomas know the truth about Smythe—that he is a cold-blooded killer. I have proof that he murdered three humans, as well as the dragon, Lady Odila. I suspect there are more victims. He will stop at nothing to achieve his goal."

"What is his goal?" Alan asked.

"I have my suspicions, but I do not know for certain. Suffice it to say, for now his goal is to overthrow our queen."

"Then what the devil are we doing sitting here?" Randolph demanded, jumping to his feet and knocking over his chair. "We have to stop him!"

"We can't, Randolph," said Simon. "Pick up the chair and sit back down."

"What do you mean 'we can't'?" Randolph grumbled, righting his chair.

"No one would believe me. I have no evidence," said Simon. "Smythe is devilishly clever. He has kept his secret well. What little we do know about his plans came from Mr. Sloan, who is now risking his life masquerading as one of Smythe's lieutenants. Think back to what Mr. Sloan told us: Smythe's soldiers wear Freyan uniforms, his ships fly Freyan flags. And why not? Prince Thomas is Freyan. He has a legitimate claim to the throne."

"Not if he takes it by force, by God!" Randolph growled.

Simon only shook his head.

Randolph flushed an angry red. "Then what the devil—"

Alan rested his hand on Randolph's arm. "Let Simon finish. There's more, isn't there? This has something to do with Henry."

Simon nodded. "One of the leaders of the Faithful is Sir Richard Wallace, Henry's brother."

"Balderdash!" Randolph roared. "I don't believe it."

"I didn't want to believe it myself," said Simon. "But it's true."

He picked up a folder and tossed the file in Randolph's lap. "I will not take the time to describe the tortuous and twisted trail of my investigations, but I now know for a fact that the 'Old Chap,' as Henry calls his brother, has been leading a double life. For forty years, he has been plotting with this group to restore an heir of James the First to the throne."

"Henry's own brother?" Randolph gaped. "A traitor?"

"In Sir Richard's defense, he and the Faithful have always maintained that Queen Mary's forebears were the ones who usurped the throne and that she has no right to it. The Faithful have a cogent argument. According to history—"

"Spare me!" said Alan hastily.

Simon smiled. "Suffice it to say, Smythe is using their sincere and earnest beliefs to manipulate them into doing his dirty work.

"Even now, as we speak, Prince Thomas is a secret guest in Richard's house. The prince traveled to Freya to meet with Queen Mary, at her behest. Her Majesty plans to name him her heir. The moment she does that, she is doomed. Smythe will not wait. He and the Faithful—including Henry's unwitting brother—will have the queen arrested and locked up in Offdom Tower. I suspect Smythe means to do worse. They will plunge the country into chaos, perhaps even civil war."

"Good God!" Alan murmured.

"We have to stop them!" Randolph stated. "Not just goddamn sit here!"

"And what would you do to stop them, Randolph?" Simon asked impatiently. "Smythe's army numbers in the thousands. His soldiers have infiltrated every army post in Freya and more troops are *en route* to Haever from Bheldem. He has armed his soldiers with the latest in weaponry, as I have good reason to know, for it was a stolen shipment of pistols with those new rotating barrels that led me to Richard."

"We have to do something!" Randolph insisted.

"We might be able to stop Smythe and the Faithful by exposing the plot," Simon said, as he regarded them both steadily. "But you know what that means."

"We would have to expose Henry's brother as a traitor," said Alan.

"Expose him, then!" Randolph said, glaring at both of them. "Arrest the bastard! Hang him!"

"Think what you are saying, Randolph," said Simon grimly. "Hang Richard and you hang Henry. Our friend has enemies in court who would be glad to see him brought low. They will claim he is involved in the plot."

"But Henry detests Prince Thomas!" Randolph argued. "He calls him the Pretender!"

Simon waved his hand. "Forget Prince Thomas. People will say Henry intended to seize the throne for his son. His wife is in the line of succession, after all. Even if Henry escaped the noose, he would still be ruined. He would have to endure the public humiliation of his brother's trial, see him go to prison, perhaps to the gallows. . . ."

"All right, all right. I understand. I don't like it, but I understand."

Randolph rose to his feet and marched up and down a few times, as though he was back on the quarterdeck. "You both realize that a bullet in Smythe's goddamn skull would bloody well stop all this."

"Randolph has a point," said Alan.

Simon raised his eyebrows. "Murder him?"

"I didn't mean that," Alan said. "But we could at least apprehend him. I could lock him up in the brig on board the *Terrapin*. Then we confront Richard with the truth about Smythe. He would realize he's been duped. That would put an end to the conspiracy."

Simon considered. "Much would depend on Prince Thomas. If he is, as I believe, innocent of all knowledge of what Smythe intends to do, His Highness could put a stop to it. The Faithful would listen to him."

"How do you know His Highness is so bloody innocent?" Randolph asked.

"I have made inquiries, and from the reports I have received, Thomas Stanford is an estimable young man who would never willingly participate in such a plot. His adviser is the Countess de Marjolaine."

"Rosian spymaster and our longtime enemy," Alan pointed out.

"True, but she serves a king and would never consent to the violent overthrow of a monarch. She read Mr. Sloan's report on Smythe and was so concerned, she has reportedly left Rosia and is on her way to Haever."

Simon drew out his pocket watch. "Albright is supposed to pick Henry up at eleven of the clock. What do we tell him? We need a plan."

Alan marshaled his thoughts. "What is the date?"

"The twenty-eighth," said Randolph.

"Richard is a member of the House of Nobles. They are not in session and so he will be at home, for he never goes anywhere except Parliament and the palace. Once we have informed Henry, we will travel to Richard's home. Henry will talk to Richard, tell him the truth about Smythe, and urge him to help. He will tell us where to find him and we will take him prisoner."

"What if Richard doesn't believe us?" asked Simon.

"The man has a wife, grown children and grandchildren," Alan said. "We will tell him to think of his family."

Simon was dubious. "Richard has had years to think about his wife and family and thus far such considerations have not deterred him from this dangerous course of action. Still, I believe that plan is as good as any. We should proceed with it."

"Now all we need to do is convince Henry that Richard is involved with the Faithful," said Alan, shaking his head. "He won't want to believe you."

"Thus, the file," said Simon. "The evidence I have amassed against his brother is damning. Richard foolishly put his signature to a great many compromising documents. I fear the Old Chap is not very adept at treason."

A clock on the lower level began to chime the hour, ringing eleven times. The friends looked at each other, all thinking the same thing.

"Albright will be arriving at Henry's house now," Simon observed. "Our friend should be here within the half hour."

"We might as well be prepared to deal with Smythe once we find him," said Alan, rising to his feet. He needed something to do, something to keep him occupied. "Where are those pistols Albright keeps for emergencies, Simon?"

"Bottom drawer of that file cabinet behind Randolph," Simon replied.

Alan located the pistols, powder, and shot and started to clean and load the weapons.

"I cannot bear the thought of facing Henry," he said as he worked. "Even if we manage to stop this terrible plot and hush up Richard's involvement, Henry will have to live with the knowledge that his brother is a traitor."

"I fear you are right," said Simon. "Henry has dedicated his life to the service of his queen and country. Richard's betrayal will cut deep, inflict wounds that can never heal. Every time he looks at us, he'll think 'My friends know my shame.' He will wonder if we secretly despise him."

"I wish to God we didn't have to be the ones to tell him!" said Randolph.

"Henry knows us," said Simon. "He knows we will stand by him. We've been through a lot together. I nearly died. Alan lost his hand."

"I lost my hair," said Randolph, running his hand over his balding head.

They laughed and felt better. Their friendship was strong. The bonds would survive.

"See if you can find that bottle of Aqua Vitae," said Simon. "Filed under 'V.'"

A clock in the entry hall rang the quarter hour. Alan finished loading the pistols and placed them on top of a file cabinet. He hunted down the bottle of Aqua Vitae and poured each of them a drink.

Simon shook his head. "None for me, thanks."

Alan drank his swiftly; the fiery, caraway-flavored liquid burned in his throat. He began reading through the contents of the file Simon had compiled and poured himself another drink.

Randolph joined him, standing behind him, reading over his shoulder.

The clock chimed the half hour.

"Henry and Albright should be here any moment," said Simon.

Alan gathered up the various papers and documents and placed them back in the file, then laid it on the desk.

"I'll go downstairs, to wait for him," said Randolph.

He clumped ponderously down the stairs. Alan walked over to the window to watch for the carriage. Welkinstead had drifted south of Haever, past the suburbs, into the open country. The lights of the city were visible to the north. Five hundred feet below the house, the land was dark, for they were gliding over forests and fields.

Alan and Simon were silent, waiting tensely. Neither felt like talking.

The clock chimed three quarters of the hour. They looked at each other worriedly.

"Albright should have been back by now," said Simon.

"Maybe Henry wasn't home," said Alan.

"Maybe," said Simon, but he didn't sound convinced.

The clock chimed midnight and still Albright had not returned, nor had Henry come.

Simon sighed and turned away from the window.

"This is bad. Very bad," he said. "I was too late."

TWO

Alan hurried around Simon's desk to the telescope that stood in the center of the window and trained it north on the city of Haever.

"I have no idea what you expect to see from here," said Simon.

"Something! Anything to tell me what the hell is happening!" said Alan, frustrated. "Albright has the carriage, which means we're trapped in this goddamned house."

Simon was silent. Alan realized what he had said and looked around.

"I am sorry, Simon. I didn't mean—"

"Never apologize for the truth," said Simon. "We *are* trapped here. If I had known . . . If I'd had some idea . . ."

"It's Henry!" Randolph bellowed from the entry hall, his shout booming throughout the house.

Alan grabbed two of the pistols and ran as fast as he dared down the cluttered stairs, reaching the front door just as Randolph flung it open. Henry dove inside. He was disheveled and dirty, covered in dust, with dried blood splattered on his face and his clothes. He wore no hat, his hair hung loose about his face, and his stockings were torn.

He had flown here by griffin, apparently, for Alan could see the beast bounding off the landing platform, spreading its wings and taking to the sky.

Henry shoved his way past Randolph. "Shut that door and douse the light!"

They did not waste time with questions. Alan slammed the door shut as Randolph touched the construct on the lamp and the magical light died, leaving them in darkness.

"Where is Simon?" Henry demanded.

"Upstairs, where he always is."

"Fetch Albright," said Henry. "I need him to bring the carriage round."

"Albright isn't here and neither is the carriage. He went to your house to fetch you!"

"Damn and blast!" Henry swore. "If he went to my house, he's probably either dead or under arrest! I barely escaped."

"Henry, what the—"

"I will explain later. We must first deal with a black ship armed with a green-beam gun."

Randolph demanded, amazed, "How is that possible? Those accursed weapons were destroyed in the goddamn war!"

"Apparently, they missed one," said Henry. "This same black ship attacked the palace. The queen . . ." He paused, swallowed. "The queen is dead."

"Dead!" Alan repeated, aghast. "What? Are you sure?"

Henry stared at him, grim-faced. Alan saw the blood on his clothes and his hands. "Oh, my God, Henry, I'm sorry—"

"Damn it, where is Simon?"

Henry shouldered past them and ran toward the stairs, shouting for his friend, only to be met by Simon coming out of his office. He halted his floating chair on the landing.

"Henry, I heard. I am so sorry—"

"The hell with that now!" Henry said, his voice rasping. "What matters is keeping you alive. This blasted house is built with magic. If that contramagic beam hits it, the whole damn house could disintegrate! You saw what it did to my house."

He bounded past Simon and into his office, shouting, "Kill the lights!"

Simon spoke a word and the lamps in the office went dark. Henry was trying to grope his way through the forest of filing cabinets until Simon came to his rescue, lighting a small lamp he had mounted on his chair.

"Why would the ship attack me?" Simon asked, following Henry. "It doesn't make sense. Only you and a few others know I secretly work for the government—"

"My brother, Richard, told him," said Henry.

Reaching the window, he stared out into the night.

"You know about Richard," said Simon.

"That he is a traitor? Yes, I know," Henry said bitterly. "Right now, we must protect you."

He pressed his face against the glass as Alan and Randolph joined him. "I can't see a damn thing! But then the black ship is moving slowly. Our pirate friend, Captain Kate, managed to damage one of the airscrews."

"There it is," said Alan, pointing.

The ship itself was difficult to see in the darkness, but they could see the running lights and the ominous green glow of the contramagic on the barrel of the gun.

Alan remarked, "The ship is in range of the house. I am surprised they have not opened fire."

"Smythe would have given them orders to take me alive," said Simon.

Henry angrily rounded on him.

"Smythe! Why the devil do you keep talking about Smythe? That black-guard, Prince Thomas, is the man responsible for assassinating the queen!"

"You are wrong, Henry, as I have tried to tell you before," said Simon sharply. "Now you must listen to me. I have evidence that this man, Smythe, used Prince Thomas to advance his own cause. Mr. Sloan's own evidence attests to the truth, if you will only pay heed. Prince Thomas is in danger. He is as much Smythe's victim as our beloved queen."

Henry stood rigid, his face pale and haggard.

"You know I'm right," said Simon. "I can see it in your face."

"The countess told me the same," said Henry. "Her Majesty met with the young man and named him her heir. She asked me to serve him as faithfully as I had served her. . . ."

He fell silent, pressed his lips together. His fist clenched.

"The prince needs you, Henry," said Simon.

"I will think about it," said Henry.

"How valuable is Simon?" Randolph asked. Seeing the others look at him, he added, flushing, "Goddamn it! You know what I mean! Simon is valuable to us, but I was wondering how valuable he would be to Smythe?"

"Very valuable," Simon answered. "I have key information on every government official of every government on Aeronne, not to mention the thousands of secrets locked in these file cabinets."

"Which means they won't blow up the house," said Alan matter-of-factly. "They will have orders to secure Simon first, then search it."

"That must be their plan, for they are about to launch a ship's boat," said

Randolph, peering through the telescope. "I cannot see how many soldiers are boarding, but a boat that size usually carries about six men."

"They don't expect resistance, or they would send more," said Alan. "I doubt they know Randolph and I are here. Henry, did they catch sight of you?"

Henry thought back. "I rode on griffinback and the ship was still some distance away. I don't think they could have seen me."

"Then they believe I am here alone or, at most, with a manservant," said Simon.

"We need weapons—" said Henry.

"Pistols are already loaded," said Randolph, pointing to the weapons on top of the nearest file cabinet.

"I don't suppose Albright keeps a rifle somewhere?" asked Henry.

"Just pistols," said Simon.

"You do realize that once they know we will not give up without a fight, they will open fire on the house," said Henry. "Even if Welkinstead crashed to the ground, they might be able to salvage something."

"Too bad this bloody house can't really fly," Randolph grumbled. "Is there anything you can do to move us out of range of that blasted gun?"

Simon snorted. "This house weighs several hundred tons. Welkinstead can go up, down, and sideways, moving at about eight thousand feet per hour. But don't worry, gentlemen. I have made arrangements to magically destroy the file cabinets and the documents they contain, should I ever be captured."

Henry glanced at the others. "He means igniting a magical conflagration that will consume the house and everything and everyone inside it."

Alan smiled. "I don't think much of that idea myself."

"To be used as a last resort," Simon said gravely. "The house has magical defenses similar to those found on board a ship. As you recall, I reinforced the magic several years ago, following the discovery of the Seventh Sigil."

"Will the magic withstand a green beam?" Henry asked.

"Perhaps for a short time," said Simon. "I must confess that I never anticipated coming under attack from one. I thought they had all been destroyed in the war."

"We need to find some way to sink that bloody ship," Henry said.

"We have a way," Simon cried triumphantly. "The duchess's rockets! You remember, Henry!"

"Good God!" Henry exclaimed. "The rockets on the roof! I had forgotten all about them."

"Not surprising," said Alan. "She installed them there over twenty years ago."

Following the attack that had paralyzed Simon, the duchess had declared that she would never again go unprepared. She had purchased rockets and launching tubes and mounted them on the roof.

"Do the rockets still work?" Alan asked doubtfully.

"They do," said Simon. "Albright fires them off every year on the queen's birthday."

"Then it will be fitting that we fire them tonight in Her Majesty's memory," said Henry.

THREE

Simon eyed the distance between Welkinstead and the ship's boat and estimated they had about thirty minutes to prepare for the visitors. Alan hastily formed a plan of attack.

"Henry, you are the doddering manservant who greets them at the door. Simon is the helpless cripple. Randolph and I will acquaint ourselves with the rockets."

The four friends shook hands, armed themselves with the pistols. Alan and Randolph put on their hats and coats, for they would be exposed to the wind on the roof and it was bitterly cold, then climbed up several flights of steep, narrow stairs to the attic and from there the roof. Henry could hear Randolph puffing and grumbling and swearing every step of the way.

Henry reloaded his own pistols, having emptied them at the soldiers that had chased him from his house, and thrust them in his belt.

"Do you want a pistol?" he asked Simon.

"Thank you, I prefer my 'crackers,'" Simon replied.

He opened a cabinet and carefully removed hollow glass tubes about a foot in length. He had named them "crackers" after the party favors that entertained children at Yule. When pulled at each end, they produced a cracking sound.

Yule crackers were harmless. Simon's were not. Once he activated a cracker, the magic at one end of the tube collided with the contramagic at the opposite end with explosive force.

Henry eyed the crackers, alarmed. "Are you certain you want to use those? They do considerable damage, as I recall. Randolph still maintains that you set fire to his ship."

"A very small fire that the crew put out with ease," Simon observed. "And you need not worry. Those first crackers I made were crude. I have lately refined the magic. I will greet our guests at the door. As the helpless cripple, I will require a lap robe. Albright keeps one in my bedroom. And since you are taking the role of Albright, you should change clothes."

"Good thought," said Henry, glancing at his ruined stockings and blood-stained jacket. "Albright's will not fit me."

"Some of my clothes should," said Simon. "We are a similar size."

He studied his friend, then said, "Henry, you have every right to be angry with me. I failed you. I failed our country."

"No time for that now," said Henry brusquely.

He entered Simon's bedroom. He did not light the lamp, for fear he would be seen, but relied on light from the office lamp on Simon's chair shining in the room. He rummaged through his friend's wardrobe, picking out a somber-colored jacket and trousers and a fresh pair of stockings.

As he dressed, he thought about what Simon had said. Henry was angry. He was angry at Simon, angry at himself, angry at the whole damn world that had blown up in his face, torn him apart, and left him in fragments. He felt barely able to hold together the tattered pieces of his being.

He was also suddenly very tired. The adrenaline that had kept him going through this terrible night was starting to ebb. Looking at Simon's neatly made bed, he wanted nothing more than to crawl beneath the blankets and pull the pillow over his head. He had to find the energy to stay strong for his friends, who were in peril and counting on him. He had to stay strong for what remained of his poor country.

Henry reached into the pocket of his bloodstained jacket and removed the queen's letter. He had no need to light the lamp to read it. He knew the contents by heart.

> To Be Opened On the Event of My Death.
> I, Queen Mary Elizabeth Ann Chessington, hereby appoint His Royal Highness Crown Prince Thomas James Stanford my heir to the throne in accordance with the Palace Law on Succession.

The letter was dated, signed, and sealed with the royal signet ring; the same ring Henry had removed from Mary's cold, still hand.

Henry was still not convinced that Prince Thomas was the paragon of virtue Simon claimed, but he was now willing to give the young man the benefit of the doubt. He trusted Mary's judgment, he trusted Simon's and, oddly enough, he trusted his Rosian counterpart, his avowed foe, the Countess de Marjolaine. He even gave credence to the opinion of his privateer, Captain Kate, although he could plainly see that she was in love with the prince.

Henry started to put the letter in his pocket, then realized that the soldiers might search him. He grabbed the book from Simon's nightstand, titled: *Fenyman's Lectures on Theoretical Magic with Emphasis on the Use of Coefficients in Building Constructs.*

"Simon's bedtime reading. It would certainly put me to sleep," Henry remarked, grimacing. He glanced out the window. The ship's boat had drawn alarmingly closer in the past few minutes. Opening the book, he thrust the letter between the pages and carried it and a lap robe to Simon's office.

He handed the lap robe to Simon, then went to hide the book in plain sight. Choosing the third bookcase from the bedroom door, he placed the book on the third shelf from the top, sliding it between the third and fourth book from the left.

"The soldiers are about five minutes away," he reported.

Simon did not answer. Henry glanced at his friend. He was seated in his chair, busily arranging the lap robe to conceal the crackers.

Henry walked over to Simon and rested his hand on his shoulder, silently letting him know their friendship remained intact.

Simon gave a faint smile. "I was going to warn you about Richard. I sent a message to the house, but Lady Ann told Albright that you had left the city and she did not know where you had gone. I had no way of contacting you."

"I was in Herringdon with the queen," said Henry. "Her Majesty had suffered a bad spell with her heart, and she wanted to keep her illness quiet for fear the news would cause further turmoil in the country."

Henry wondered what would have happened if he had received Simon's warning about Richard. Perhaps he could have prevented this tragedy.

"Bad luck. Stupid bad luck," he said, his mouth twisting.

"How are Lady Ann and the children?" Simon asked, as they continued to prepare for the arrival of their guests. "Did they escape? Have you heard from Mr. Sloan? Is he still spying on Smythe?"

"No, Richard betrayed him and Smythe shot him. He was badly wounded, but he will recover. He accompanied my wife and children, who are in the care of the Countess de Marjolaine. She is taking them to safety in Rosia," said Henry.

He glanced out the window. He could see the running lights of the black ship and the sails glimmering white in the starlight. The ship had reduced its speed to launch the boat and would likely circle the house until it returned with the captive.

The ship's boat was rounding the corner of the house. Henry wondered how Randolph and Alan were faring on the roof. Both of them were skilled at combat, cool and competent under fire. He could trust them to wait for the proper moment.

"Time to move into position," he told Simon.

"Light the lamps. Everything should appear perfectly normal. We have no idea anything is amiss."

They went down the stairs, Henry walking and Simon floating down in his chair, both moving quietly. Henry doubted if the soldiers would be able to hear his footfalls or the faint whirring sound of the small airscrew that propelled Simon's chair, but he did not want to take chances.

They reached the ground floor, or what would have been the ground floor if the house had been on the ground. Simon propelled his chair toward the kitchen in the rear and concealed himself. Henry waited by the front door. He did not light the lamps in the entry hall. The only lights that shone streamed down from the office on the second floor, which left the entry hall in partial shadow.

The ship's boat landed with a thud on the concrete platform in front of the house. Henry peeked out the window and saw two soldiers climb out of the boat and approach the house. Four others waited in the boat.

The soldiers were armed, but they carried their rifles slung over their shoulders. Clearly they did not expect trouble from a man confined to a wheelchair.

Henry hunched his shoulders and let his hair straggle over his face. He crept forward with a faltering gait, transforming himself into the aging man-servant who has spent his life waiting on a frail, sickly man.

The soldier gave a thundering knock on the door.

Henry waited an appropriate amount of time, then timorously opened the door a crack and peered out.

"How may I assist you, gentlemen?" he asked in a quavering voice.

"We have a warrant for the arrest of Master Simon Yates," said one of the soldiers.

"Warrant?" Henry screeched. He turned around to shout in panicked tones. "Master Yates! Soldiers are here to arrest you! They have a warrant!"

"Calm down, Albright," said Simon irritably, emerging from the kitchen in his chair.

He appeared very frail and fragile. The lap robe covered his legs, and he wore one of the duchess's silken shawls draped around his shoulders. He had shut off the chair's airscrews and was propelling it by hand.

He started to add something, but was seized by a racking cough that sounded as though he was on his deathbed. He barely managed to clear his throat enough to speak.

"I demand to know who has issued this warrant," he said weakly.

"Colonel Smythe of the Army of Royal Retribution," the soldier replied.

"I have never heard of this colonel or his army," said Simon, frowning. "I consider this warrant illegal and I refuse to go anywhere with you. Albright, shut the door."

"Oh, Master, please be reasonable," Henry begged. He turned to the soldier. "There must be some mistake, gentlemen. . . ."

"No mistake," said the soldier.

He roughly shoved open the door, letting it bang into the wall. His comrade thrust Henry aside and strode past him into the entry hall.

"I am a private citizen!" Simon screeched indignantly. "I will not be treated like this!"

Henry remained standing near the door. No one was paying any attention to the doddering old manservant. The two soldiers had their backs to him.

Simon began berating them. "What do you mean by barging into the home of a private citizen? I know my rights."

"We can wheel you out in the chair, Master Yates, or carry you out bodily," said the soldier coldly. "Either way, you are coming with us. If you come peaceably, sir, you will not be harmed."

Simon smiled. "On the contrary, if you gentlemen leave peacefully, *you* will not be harmed."

Henry slid his hand into his pocket.

"Well? Are you going?" Simon asked.

He rolled into position in the middle of the hall, about five feet away from the soldiers.

"Seize him," said the soldier.

Simon gave a shrug. "Remember that I warned you."

He reached beneath his lap robe, drew out a crystal tube, and hurled it at the two soldiers. The tube struck one of the men in the chest and exploded on contact, bursting into magical blue-green flame that set his clothes ablaze. His partner stared at him in shock until a second tube hit him in the leg, setting his pants on fire.

Both of them cried out and began to frantically beat at the flames with their hands. Henry grabbed hold of one by the coat collar, yanked him off his feet. Simon propelled his chair forward and rammed the other man in the knees, knocking him to the floor. Henry took hold of both men and dragged them out the door.

"I'd drop your rifles if I were you!" he advised the men. "If the contra-magic touches them, they'll explode!"

He slammed shut the door and bolted it, then hurried to look out the window in the entry hall. He smiled to observe the soldiers trying to divest themselves of their weapons as they flailed about on the landing platform, screaming in pain. Their four comrades jumped out of the boat, rifles drawn.

"Here they come," Henry reported.

"Out of my way!" Simon ordered.

Henry nimbly sidestepped and stumbled back against the tallboy to allow Simon to surge past him. He placed his hand, palm flat, on the door. Henry could not see the magical constructs that covered the door, for he was one of those benighted souls who were not born with the gift of magic. He could see the result, however. The door began to glow with a radiant blue light.

One of the soldiers struck the door with the butt of his rifle. The gun exploded in his hands and he stood staring in shock at mangled fingers, streaming blood.

The other soldiers raised their rifles and took aim.

"Watch out," Henry warned, crouching. "They're going to open fire."

"Ah, that's a mistake," said Simon gravely.

Gunshots rang out. The bullets struck the door and promptly ricocheted, hitting those who had fired. One of the men fell, clutching a bleeding leg. The other soldier remained stubbornly intent on pursuing the assault, and he started to kick at the door.

"Now would be a good time, Alan," said Henry.

A rocket shell burst above the ship's boat, showering it with flaming shrapnel. The soldiers stared up into the sky as another rocket soared above them. Realizing they were under attack from the roof, they grabbed their wounded comrades, carried them back into the boat, and set sail.

The captain of the black ship could now see that he was facing a formi-dable and well-armed foe and altered course, heading toward the roof and leaving the ship's boat to catch up as best it could.

Henry heard the sound of gunfire coming from the roof, and he opened the window and leaned out to see.

"Alan and Randolph are taking potshots at the black ship," he reported.

Simon joined him at the window. "Move over so I can see."

They watched two shells fly through the night, leaving a fiery trail behind. Both missed the ship. The first shell flew long and the second fell short.

"Still finding their aim," said Henry. "How many rockets do you have?"

"Albright would know," said Simon. "Not many. It never occurred to me to replace them."

"Ah! There's a hit! And another!"

The ship's brightly colored balloon burst into flame, and the next shell tore through a sail, shredding it, but doing little damage.

The black ship opened fire with a swivel gun, spraying the roof with bullets.

"Covering fire," said Henry.

"While they ready the green-beam gun," Simon agreed.

Green light mingled with blue glowed at the bow of the ship. The light was so bright, they could read the name, the *Naofa*. Simon drew out a telescope from his chair and looked through it.

"They are not using blood magic to power the weapon," he said. "They must have learned how to use the Seventh Sigil to combine the magicks to make the weapon operational. No more human sacrifices."

"I suppose that is an improvement," Henry muttered.

Alan and Randolph had seen the green-and-blue glow and realized that the green-beam gun was preparing to fire, for they were aiming their rockets at the ship's bow. Henry watched the fiery sparks of a shell's trajectory and he thought for a hopeful moment that it was going to make a direct hit on the gun. The shell fell short, however, and exploded on the deck.

The crew had mounted the green-beam gun on a rotating platform so that the gunner could fire at targets in any direction, and Henry watched the gun swing about to take aim at the house. The crew were still firing the swivel gun, but they had shifted the weapon and were aiming at the lower levels of the house.

"They are trying to hit the lift tanks and the airscrews," said Henry.

Alan and Randolph set off two more rockets. One shell scored a hit on an airscrew of the black ship. Another struck the hull near the bow beneath the gun platform, setting the hull on fire.

The green-beam gun remained undamaged, and it was aiming at the light in Simon's office. Henry had to give the gunner operating it grudging credit for remaining at his post as smoke from the flames enveloped him.

The green beam stabbed through the smoke and the darkness. Green light flared. A tremor shook the house, causing it to shudder as though in pain. Simon propelled his chair backward and Henry dove to the floor as the window shattered, showering him with shards of glass. The hydra slid across the floor and smashed into the tallboy, and he could hear thuds and bumps and clatters as bookcases toppled and paintings and books crashed to the floor. The jardinière tumbled down the stairs and smashed.

Henry picked himself up and glanced worriedly at Simon. He was reassured to see his friend sitting safely in his chair in the center of the room. Hearing a thundering racket on the stairs, Henry looked up to see Randolph running down.

"Are you both all right?" he asked.

"We are fine," said Henry. "Where's Alan?"

"We have one more rocket," said Randolph. "I left it for Alan to fire. He's the one with the devil's own luck."

"Let's hope the devil is paying attention," said Henry.

He looked out the hole in the wall where the window had been. The green beam fired again, this time aiming for the roof. Alan shot off the last rocket.

The shell struck the ship's helm, which was located in a wheelhouse on the upper deck, setting the wheelhouse on fire. The panicked crew of the *Naofa* scrambled to put out the flames before they destroyed the helm and cut off the flow of magic to the lift tanks and the airscrews.

The fire spread to one of the masts and flames began to crawl up the shrouds. The crew were now engaged in fighting for their lives. The black ship broke off the attack.

The *Naofa* started losing altitude. The black ship retrieved the ship's boat with her wounded and limped off into the darkness, trailing fire and smoke.

"Good old Alan," said Henry. "The black ship is sinking, hopefully in the deepest pit of hell."

Randolph gave a bellowing cheer.

"Be quiet!" Simon snapped. "Don't make a sound."

He cocked his head, listening. Randolph clamped his mouth shut. Henry strained his ears. The night was silent, except for the occasional thud as something else fell off a wall.

"I don't hear anything," Randolph whispered.

"That's the problem," said Simon grimly.

Henry suddenly realized what he meant. The night was quiet, too quiet. He meant they could no longer hear the whirring of the gigantic airscrews that kept the house afloat.

"That last shot must have hit the helm," said Henry. "Where was Alan?"

"Near the helm," said Randolph.

He began to ponderously climb back up the stairs. Henry took pity on his portly friend.

"Simon and I will see to Alan. Randolph, you go to the cellar, check the lift tanks. You need to make sure they weren't hit."

Randolph gave a him a grateful look and headed down the stairs. The duchess had installed six lift tanks in the foundation of the house, each of them braced and integrated into the structure. The lift tanks were huge. Only the Sunset Palace that had once floated in the air above Everux had tanks that were larger. The lift tanks were protected by stone walls, but a puncture by a lucky shot would cause the lift gas to leak out.

Henry climbed the stairs to the upper level two at a time. Simon passed him in his chair, heading for the attic and from there the roof.

Two broad staircases led to a narrow staircase that led to a door that opened onto the roof. They could see damage to the magic in the walls, the ceiling. All the building materials from bricks to wooden beams were made using magical constructs. The contramagic in the green beam had disrupted that magic and continued to eat away at it.

Surveying the damage, Simon shook his head. "I used the Seventh Sigil to strengthen the protective magical constructs on the walls. But I never planned on my house taking a direct hit from a green-beam gun."

Henry helped Simon navigate the narrow staircase in his chair, then opened the door and stepped out onto the roof. When the cold air hit Henry, he shivered, for he had forgotten to put on his coat. He stared around in dismay.

The Elsinors had been fond of experimenting with architecture, embellishing their home with towers and turrets, gable roofs, valley roofs, and mansard roofs. The largest roof was the flat roof that covered the main portion of the house. The duchess had enclosed this roof with a wrought-iron fence, decorated it with potted trees and flowers, and termed it her garden. The rocket launchers stood between the ornamental pine trees and the aloes in tubs.

She had placed the helm that steered the house and provided magic to the lift tanks and airscrews inside a square cupola surrounded by windows in the center.

The cupola was in shambles. The beam had taken out most of the cupola's north-facing wall, and now its roof sagged. Every window was shattered, as were the lamps. The floor around the cupola was littered with broken glass and cracked and splintered wood.

"Alan!" Henry called urgently.

"In here!" came a muffled voice.

Henry crunched across broken glass to what remained of the cupola and peered inside. He could see Alan crouched on his hands and knees, pawing frantically among the debris. He looked around as he heard Henry.

"The airscrews aren't working," Henry reported.

"I bloody well know that!" Alan said. "The helm is under here somewhere. I need light!"

"I have a lantern," Simon stated.

"Bring it to me, Henry," said Alan. "Watch your head when you come in and for God's sake, don't touch the beam by my right shoulder. I think it's the only thing holding up the roof."

Simon opened one of the compartments built into his chair and took out a small bull's-eye lantern. He activated its magic with a touch and handed it to Henry, who gingerly made his way through the wreckage to Alan.

"Shine the light here!" he instructed.

He had taken off his greatcoat. His shirt was torn and bloodied. He had lost his hand in a fight years ago and wore a mechanical hand fashioned by Simon in its place. His good hand was bleeding from several cuts. He was crouched near the brass helm that had once stood in front of the north-facing window. The helm had been mounted on a solid oak base that was now lying on its side. The helm itself was buried beneath the wreckage.

"Help me lift it," Alan said to Henry. "Watch out for that beam. And be careful of those cables! We don't want to sever any of them."

The brass helm was covered with magical constructs connected to cables that ran from the helm across the roof and down the walls and transmitted magical energy to the four enormous airscrews and the six lift tanks. If the helm had been hit, the contramagic might have erased the magical constructs on the helm, leaving them with no way to activate the lift tanks or the airscrews.

"Was the helm damaged?" Henry asked.

"I don't know yet," Alan answered. "I saw the beam strike the cupola, but I couldn't see if it hit the helm or not."

Henry hung the lantern from a nail sticking out of the wall near his head, then bent down beside the helm. He thrust his hands beneath the base on one side while Alan took the other. Alan counted to three and between them they slowly and carefully raised the base out of the debris.

The light gleamed off the brass and shone on the braided strands of cables attached to the underside of the brass plate. Henry stared at the cables, startled. "Those are not leather."

"They're copper," said Simon, peering in at them from beneath the sagging roof. "More efficient than leather for transmitting the magic. I had Albright switch to copper two years ago."

Alan studied the helm and ran his hands over the constructs. "Some of the constructs are broken, but at least the beam didn't completely erase the magic."

"I used the Seventh Sigil to protect it," said Simon. "But no magic is flowing to the airscrews. We need to see if we can get them started."

"Don't bother," said Randolph grimly as he joined them by what remained of the cupola. "Every goddamn lift tank on the port side of the house is riddled with bullet holes. You can hear the goddamn gas hissing as it leaks out."

"The house is sinking," said Henry.

"Crashing will be a more apt description unless we can find a way to activate the magic to the lift tanks," said Randolph.

"If Welkinstead falls on a populated area, the loss of life would be catastrophic," said Henry. "We need to steer the house as far from the city as possible, even if that means sinking it in the Breath."

"And we go down with the house," said Alan with a faint smile. "Not a bad way to die. The brutal cold will kill us long before we hit the bottom of the world."

He frowned, eyeing the helm. "I have an idea. When I was a midshipman on the *King Frederick,* I once saw a ship's crafter use his own magic as a bridge between broken constructs. The constructs were on a cannon, not a helm, but I wonder if Simon could do the same?"

"Is that possible?" Henry asked his friend.

"I believe it could work, but only if the cables are attached to the helm," said Simon. "You can see where some of them have fallen off."

"The damn things must be buried beneath the rubble. We need to dig them out," said Alan.

He and Henry began to search for the cables amid the debris and soon found most of them.

"Now what do we do?" Alan asked.

"Connect the cables to the constructs that operate the airscrews. The foundation of this house is made of stone and concrete that has been reinforced with strengthening magic. If we can slow our rate of descent by reversing the airscrews, we might be able to avoid crashing, and land the house safely."

"Henry, shine the light on the helm," Alan instructed. "I need Simon in here with me. Randolph, bring his chair. And watch out for that beam!"

Randolph helped Simon enter the damaged cupola and positioned his chair near the helm. Henry shone the lantern on the constructs while Alan, on his knees, tried to attach the copper cable to the screws. His wooden fingers fumbled at the wires and he began to swear.

"We need two good hands for this job," he said.

"I'll do it," Henry offered. "Just tell me what goes where."

Alan showed him how to twist the copper cable around the brass screws and then held the light so he could see. Henry got down on his knees and picked up a length of cable. He stopped, staring in dismay at the myriad screws that were dotted all over the underside of the helm.

"How do I know which of these cables connect the constructs to the airscrews?"

"I'll tell you," said Simon.

"We need to know where we are," said Henry, trying to untangle the cables. "In case this doesn't work."

"The house was traveling in a southerly direction when Randolph and I arrived after dinner," said Alan. He glanced at the shattered binnacle and shook his head. "I can't use that to determine our location. Randolph, go look over the edge of the roof and see what lies below us."

Henry twisted the wire around the screws as fast as he could, given that his fingers were stiff from the cold and the broken wires jabbed into his flesh.

"That's all of them," said Simon at last. "The airscrews should now be connected."

Henry crawled out from under the helm and staggered to his feet.

Randolph came back to report that the house was south of Haever.

"I can't see any lights below us, though I suppose there might be farm houses or small villages. Most people would be in their beds by now."

"How fast are we sinking?" Henry asked.

Randolph gave a helpless shrug. "How can I tell? I can't see the ground."

"If there are houses, we will have to use the airscrews to push us out into the Breath, not slow our fall," said Henry.

"Provided we have airscrews," said Simon.

Alan adjusted the brass helm so that Simon could reach it from his chair, careful not to detach any of the wires.

Henry watched tensely as Simon placed his hand on the brass helm, touching the magical constructs. Alan stood with his hand on Simon's chair, holding him steady. Randolph leaned over the wrought-iron fence, peering down.

"I think we're over a forest!" he shouted.

Henry looked out at the horizon and saw the distant lights of the city of Haever suddenly rise into view, as out of a sea of darkness. Now he could judge their rate of descent. They were falling rapidly.

"Did I hear something?" Alan asked suddenly. "Did one of the airscrews come on?"

The airscrews were located at the corners of the house several stories below them, and the men had to strain to listen. Henry thought he could detect a whirring sound, but he wanted to hear it so badly he did not trust his judgment.

"One is working!" Simon exclaimed. "I can feel the magic respond. And there is a second and now a third!"

Henry watched the lights of the city. They continued to rise as the house sank, but the movement seemed to have slowed.

"What about the fourth?" he asked.

"Nothing," Simon replied. He ran his fingers over the helm, then shook his head. "Still nothing. The fourth airscrew on the port side is not working. It must have been hit by gunfire."

Randolph waved his arms and pointed to the east.

"The house needs to shift direction or we'll crash into the trees," he yelled.

Simon made the adjustment. "Let me know when we're close. I'll reverse the airscrews to try to cushion the fall."

Randolph bent over the iron railings, trying to see.

"I have to remain at the helm to operate the airscrews," Simon continued. "That beam will give way once we hit. The rest of you should go into the attic—"

"Clear!" Randolph roared. He came lumbering across the roof, waving his arms. "Quick! Reverse the goddamn screws!"

Simon slammed his hand palm down on the helm. Henry could feel the vibration in the floor as the airscrews labored. The lights of the city suddenly vanished behind the treetops.

"We need to get off the roof!" Henry said. "Alan, help me with Simon. Randolph, open the door to the attic."

"Not yet!" Simon said, his hand on the helm.

"Now!" said Henry firmly.

He and Alan picked up Simon bodily—chair and all—and carried him out of the cupola just as its ceiling collapsed with a splintering of wood and breaking glass.

Randolph had reached the door to the attic and was holding it open. Henry and Alan carried Simon through the door, and Randolph slammed the door shut. They lowered Simon's chair to the floor and crouched down beside him in the darkness.

Henry could not see his friends, but he could sense them near him. He had no way of knowing how close the house was to crashing and he was glad he could not see it coming.

Alan's hand clasped his. Randolph put his strong arm around Henry's shoulder. Henry reached out to Simon, doing what he could to brace his friend.

Henry drew in a breath, closed his eyes.

The house struck the ground.

FOUR

Colonel Jonathan Smythe stood in the middle of a lavishly decorated room in the Freyan royal palace and took a moment to revel in the knowledge that his plot had succeeded. The queen—that spawn of the Evil One—was dead. Once he was coroneted, Prince Thomas Stanford would be king of Freya and Smythe was one step closer to achieving his goal: ruling Freya himself.

For now, he had to make certain Stanford knew who was in charge. Thomas would soon be king, but it was Smythe who held the crown. Thomas should feel gratitude to the man who had put him on the throne.

And if he refused the crown, if he was too squeamish to put it on his head just because it had a little blood on it, Smythe had made contingency plans, and he waited with some curiosity to see what Thomas would do. He did not know, because he did not know the young man well. Most of what he knew about Thomas came from his mother, Constanza, and she was a dot-ing fool.

Smythe was the commander of the prince's small army, whose mission was to serve as escort, taking the prince to Freya when he succeeded to the throne. He knew Thomas had been an officer in the Estaran army and that, according to his mother, he had served with distinction in the war against the Bottom Dwellers. Thomas himself rarely spoke of the war and evinced no interest in military matters. He left all decisions regarding his army to his colonel.

This arrangement had suited Smythe well. He had taken advantage of the prince's disinterest to plot the invasion of Freya.

He did have to give Thomas grudging credit for the fact that, while shocked and shaken by the terrible events of this night, Thomas maintained his composure, even though he had just discovered the commander of his army was in truth a violent revolutionary who had murdered the queen, while his best friend, Phillip Masterson, lay bloodied and beaten at his feet.

Yet Thomas had strength enough to rise from the side of his unconscious friend to confront Smythe.

"What do you want from me?"

"Ah, now we get to the nub of the matter, sir," Smythe replied. "When I undertook this command at the behest of your mother and the members of the Faithful, I believed I was doing God's work. Together we would remove the last surviving member of a profligate, corrupt family from the throne and restore Freya to her rightful position as a power in the world. I believed in you and in your cause. And then I came to know you."

Or perhaps Smythe had come to know himself.

He was an ambitious man, hungry for power, and frustrated to know that as the eldest son of a strict, God-fearing and impoverished Fundamentalist minister, he would be forced to live on scraps of power tossed to him by his "betters." He could not understand how Thomas, given the gift of royal birth by the hand of God, could so lightly toss it aside, as he might toss aside a soiled handkerchief.

God had placed Smythe in the position of being able to pick up that handkerchief and tuck it into his own pocket. God had brought him to the attention of Sir Richard Wallace, a member of the Faithful, a secret organization devoted to restoring the Stanford family to the throne.

Richard had recommended Smythe to Thomas's parents, who had hired him to raise and train the army that was to support and protect their son. God had seen fit to drop a mast on Queen Mary's son, the heir to the throne, and inflict diphtheria on his little child, thus clearing the way for Thomas. Admittedly, Smythe had helped God along a little by assassinating the queen, but he believed the Scriptures, which said the Lord helps those who help themselves.

"You are a man of honor and strong principle," Smythe told Thomas. "I have been told these are excellent qualities in a king. Sadly, you are also a fool who doesn't have the wit to know what to do with the power I was going to give you."

Smythe's plan had been for his armies to seize control of Freya with as little disruption as possible. The revolution would happen and few would be aware of it, and those who tried to resist would be silenced. When Freya was under Smythe's control, he would permit Thomas to enter and hand him the keys to the kingdom.

Unfortunately, Thomas, who had turned out to be more energetic and resourceful than Smythe had expected, had foiled this plan by traveling to Freya in secret to meet with the queen. Queen Mary, acting with confounding good sense, had been going to name him the heir to the throne and make her announcement public. Thomas would have been able to enter the kingdom in peace, without need for Smythe or his revolution.

Smythe had been forced to act swiftly to regain control of the situation.

"I do know what to do with power, Your Highness," Smythe informed him. "I have plans for Freya and her people. For years, I watched a feeble queen and her lackwit councilors, such as Sir Richard, beggar my country, groveling before godless infidels such as King Renaud. I could no longer stand idly by and watch my country sink into the stew of corruption.

"But then, I thought, who will pay heed to me and my ideas? Who am I? A man of low birth. A common soldier, as your lady mother delights in reminding me. The meanest beggar on the street would pay no heed to me. Your Highness speaks, and kings jump to do your bidding."

Thomas regarded him with contempt.

"I see what you are planning, Smythe, and I would sooner dance with the devil. You might as well put a bullet in my head now, for I will not be a party to this deranged scheme of yours."

"I will not harm you, sir," Smythe was careful to assure him. "You are the true and rightful king. I need you, and I hope you will eventually realize that you need me. We will make a good team. But in case you don't come to your senses, I am holding His Grace as surety for your good behavior, as well as your mother and father, who are now prisoners in Bheldem. They will remain safe so long as you do what you are bidden. Your first test will come with the dawn."

Smythe had rehearsed that speech many times during the long watches of the night in that wretched fortress in Bheldem. Thomas would see that he had no choice. The enemy had him surrounded on all sides. He would have to make an unconditional surrender.

He went on to tell Thomas a great deal more, explaining his plan to him, how he intended to blame the Rosians for the death of the queen and implicate Princess Sophia in the plot.

"You will start a war!" Thomas protested, horrified.

"Such is my intent," said Smythe.

All had gone according to plan thus far. His plot to kill the queen with a green-beam gun had succeeded. A few minor problems had arisen, but Smythe had dealt with those swiftly and effectively. He had been quick to take advantage of God-given opportunities. Learning that Princess Sophia of Rosia had been dining with the queen this night, he had sent his soldiers under command of Corporal Jennings to find the princess, place her under arrest.

Smythe's only regret was giving way to his temper and shooting Sir Richard Wallace, an influential member of the House of Nobles and a leader in the Faithful. That had been a mistake, but he had lost patience with the old fool. Too late, Smythe had remembered he would need the support of the Faithful and the House of Nobles in days to come and Richard could provide it. At least, he hadn't killed him; only winged him. Smythe was confident he could frighten Richard into keeping his mouth shut and doing what he was told.

Thomas cast a glance toward the door to the balcony that was standing wide open. The thought came to Smythe that the young man might be contemplating jumping off the balcony to his death.

"One of you, shut those doors," he ordered. "His Highness finds the sound of gunfire distressing."

As the soldiers did his bidding, Smythe walked over to Thomas and placed his hand on his shoulder. No man was supposed to touch the person of the king; Smythe not only touched him, he tightened his grip.

"Make up your mind to accept God's will and this trial will be easier for you. You will be king, Your Highness, for as long as I say you will be king."

Thomas regarded him with a look of contempt and struck his hand aside.

Smythe shrugged. "At least Your Highness has the wit to *act* like a king."

He turned to his soldiers and gestured to Phillip, who was starting to regain consciousness. "Take His Grace to Offdom Tower and lock him in a cell. Do not worry, Your Highness," he added as the guards picked up Phillip and hauled him away. "So long as you behave, His Grace will be well treated."

He fancied he could see Thomas sink beneath his words, crushed and humbled. Thomas disdained to answer him and Smythe again saw him glance toward the balcony door.

Why the devil does he keep looking that direction? Smythe wondered.

He recalled that Thomas had been standing outside on that balcony when he had entered the room. Thomas had left the balcony to confront him and the door remained open behind him. Smythe had been preoccupied with more important matters and had paid little heed. A chill wind was blowing into the room. Leaving the door standing wide open made no sense—unless Thomas had left it open for a reason.

Smythe walked outside to investigate. As he passed Thomas, he thought he noted a crack in the king's calm demeanor.

The balcony was not large, and Smythe was soon satisfied that no one was lurking in the darkness. He walked to the stone rail and peered down to the ground below.

The palace walls shone with faint white radiance that came from the magical constructs placed into the stone. The magical constructs lit the night with a pale glow, like moonlight. The only people he could see in the garden were his troops, wearing the uniforms of the palace guard.

He looked to either side. Every room on this level had its own balcony that overlooked the palace gardens. The adjacent balcony was not ten feet away. The balcony appeared deserted, its glass windows dark. He was about to go back inside when he heard the clock in the room behind him chime midnight and he could faintly hear a clock in the room next door chime the hour.

Someone standing on that balcony could have overheard his conversation with Thomas.

"Who was in that room?" Smythe asked one of the soldiers.

"His Highness was there with Sir Richard, sir," the soldier answered. "We brought them both to this room on your orders."

Smythe was struck by a sudden unwelcome thought. He had never before been inside the palace, but he had studied the layout extensively in order to deploy his men. He recalled that Sir Richard had brought Thomas to the Rose Room, which contained a secret passage. Sir Richard had chosen that room for that very reason, for he had smuggled Thomas through the secret passage into the palace to meet with the queen.

Smythe walked over to confront the wounded man.

"Sir Richard, is that room known as the Rose Room?"

Richard lay back in his chair, his hand pressed over the bullet hole in his arm. His face was white and haggard, but he rallied enough to glare at Smythe. "Go to the devil."

"You two, keep watch on His Highness," Smythe ordered. "He is not to leave this room."

Drawing his pistol, Smythe flung open the door and walked out into the hallway. His sudden appearance startled the guards.

"Where is Corporal Jennings?"

"I don't know, sir," said one. "We haven't seen him since he posted us here. He said he had orders to search for the princess."

"Did you see anyone come out of that room?" Smythe demanded, gesturing.

The guard blinked. "What room, sir?"

"That room!"

Smythe pointed at the door to the Rose Room, only no door was there, which meant no room was there. But the room that didn't exist had a balcony. He had not imagined that.

"Illusion magic," he stated. "There is a door. The magic tricks your mind into thinking there isn't. Concentrate your thoughts and you will see through the illusion."

The moment he spoke the words, he broke the spell and had the satisfaction of seeing the magic shimmer and ripple like the surface of a pond when a stone hits the water. The door to the Rose Room appeared. The soldier gave an audible gasp of astonishment.

"I know of only one person who is adept at casting illusion magic," Smythe said grimly. "I believe we have found the Princess Sophia."

He looked back and saw Thomas tending to Sir Richard's gunshot wound and pointedly ignoring Smythe. The prince could not fool him, however. Smythe fancied he saw Thomas smile and he guessed the reason why.

"The princess was hiding on the balcony of the Rose Room, wasn't she, sir? That was why you left the door open, so she could hear us."

"On the contrary, sir," Thomas returned coolly. "I left the door open to rid this room of the foul stench."

He looked pointedly at Smythe.

FIVE

Smythe had judged astutely when he realized that someone on the balcony of the Rose Room could have overheard his conversation with Thomas. Kate and Sophia had both been out on the balcony, hiding from his soldiers, and while they had not been able to hear everything, they had heard enough.

They had listened in horror to Smythe telling Thomas the queen was dead and boasting that he was responsible. They had then heard the sound of a pistol shot, and after that, they had heard Smythe ask a "Corporal Jennings" if he had found Sophia.

They had not been able to hear the man's reply, but they heard Smythe's order: "Search every room on this floor until you find her. Go room by room."

"Jennings mustn't find us here!" Kate said urgently, jumping to her feet. "He knows me. Smythe will know we were eavesdropping. We have to leave. Quickly, before the search gets organized!"

She opened the balcony doors and entered the Rose Room. Sophia picked up her dog, Bandit, and hurried after her. The room was dark, for they had not dared light a lamp. Their eyes had already adjusted to the darkness out on the balcony, and they swiftly made their way through the room, doing their best to avoid bumping into the furniture.

They had just reached the door when they heard voices out in the hall-way. They both froze in alarm, and Sophia clamped her hand over Bandit's muzzle to keep him from barking.

"But, Corporal Jennings," one of the soldiers was saying, "there's nothing here. This is a wall."

"We are meant to think this is a wall, Sergeant," said a voice Kate recog-nized as Jennings'. "But it isn't. It's an illusion spell. Remember, the princess is a witch."

"A witch?" Sophia gasped, shocked.

"No time! Hide!" Kate whispered back frantically.

Hiding places were few and time was short. Sophia crouched behind a sofa, holding Bandit in her arms. Kate ducked behind a curtain. She hoped Jennings would simply look inside, glance around, and then move on.

Parting the curtain slightly, Kate saw the door open. Jennings and his companion, the sergeant, were both carrying bull's-eye lanterns, which they sent flashing about the room. To Kate's dismay, they both walked into the room.

"Close the door, Sergeant," Jennings ordered. "We must conduct a thor-ough search."

Kate bit her lip. Smythe would catch both of them, and he would make short work of her, for when she had previously encountered him, he had re-alized by the horrified expression on her face that she recognized him as the man who had murdered Lady Odila. Needing a weapon, she looked around and saw the fireplace, directly opposite.

The sergeant turned to close the door.

Jennings drew his pistol and used it to savagely strike a blow to the back of the sergeant's skull, dropping the man to the floor. Jennings stepped over the body, locked the door, and then turned around, holding the lantern.

"I know you and a companion are in here, Your Highness. Only a savant could cast such a spell."

As Sophia slowly rose up from behind the couch, Bandit wriggled in her arms and started to growl. Kate stepped out from behind the curtain and hurried over to stand protectively near Sophia. She cast a surreptitious glance at the fireplace, noting that the tools used to clean it rested in a stand beside the grate.

"I am glad I found you, ma'am," Jennings was saying in a respectful tone. "We must hurry. We don't have much time."

Sophia gave Jennings a defiant stare. "I do not know what you mean. What are you going to do with us?"

"I am going to take you to a place of safety, ma'am. I am an agent for the Countess de Marjolaine."

Both women regarded him in astonishment. Bandit growled.

"I agree with the dog," said Kate, recovering from her shock. "Don't trust him, Sophia. He works for Smythe."

"You may trust me, Your Highness," said Jennings gravely. "I have a message from the countess. 'In the sky, I see a bee plucking its lute.'"

Sophia gasped in relief and extended a hand to him. "Thank God!" She turned to Kate to explain. "This man is telling the truth. He knows the code. The words are from a nursery rhyme the countess taught me as a child."

"We have no time to lose, Your Highness," Jennings urged. "The colonel is searching for you and for this young woman as well."

"We know. We heard. He thinks I'm a witch and he's going to use me to start a war with Rosia!" Sophia flushed, indignant. "But how can we escape? His soldiers are everywhere!"

"This room contains a secret passage," said Jennings. "The door is behind a painting that depicts a woman holding roses."

"I saw it," said Kate. "It's over there."

Jennings lit the bull's-eye lantern and shined the light in the direction she indicated. The woman in the painting seemed to step out of the darkness to greet them. Jennings hurried over to the painting, accompanied by Sophia, who was still carrying Bandit. Kate circled around past the fireplace, surreptitiously picked up the brass poker and hid it in the folds of her cloak, then joined them.

"How is Phillip—His Grace?" Sophia asked worriedly.

"He was beaten and drugged," said Jennings. "But don't worry, ma'am. His Grace is a strong young man. He will recover."

"And Thomas? What will happen to him?" Sophia asked. "We heard that horrible man claim to have him in his power."

Jennings shook his head. "I do not know His Highness well, but he appears to be courageous and resourceful. You must think of yourself now, ma'am. The colonel plans to implicate you in the queen's death. He could have you executed."

"I am a royal princess of Rosia! He would not dare!" Sophia exclaimed, shocked.

"You do not know the colonel," Jennings replied grimly. "He would dare a great deal."

They gathered around the painting, which was an immense, full-length portrait mounted in a gold-painted and elaborately carved heavy wooden frame.

Jennings flashed the lantern up and down the frame. "The magical latch is supposed to be concealed somewhere among the carvings. I know the magic still works, for Sir Richard brought His Highness through this passage only a few hours ago."

All three of them were crafters and they studied the frame. They could see the faint blue of magical constructs glowing amid the carved roses and lilies, grapes and pears and leafy vines and garlands. But the constructs were very old, many of them broken and starting to fade.

"I wish I knew what we were searching for," Sophia said, frustrated.

"Look at those roses in the center of the frame on the right!" Kate said, pointing.

"Did you find the construct?" Jennings asked.

"No, but I think it must be there. You can see where the dust has been cleaned off, as though a hand had recently touched it—"

"I see the construct!" Sophia exclaimed. "Kate is right. It is concealed beneath those roses. The magic is quite cunningly done."

"Can you unlock it?" Kate asked.

"Yes, I believe so," said Sophia. "Here, hold Bandit."

She handed the dog to Kate. Bandit squirmed, but he had stopped growling. The spaniel gave a whimper, then resignedly settled into Kate's arms. He was undoubtedly tired of being manhandled.

The clock in the Rose Room chimed midnight. Kate could hear the faint echo of the clock in the next room where Thomas was a prisoner. She hoped he knew she knew the truth. She hoped he knew she would do everything in her power to help him.

Sophia ran both hands over the carving on the frame.

"One, two," said Sophia, touching the constructs in turn, counting as she went. She drew a line between them with her finger. "Three."

The constructs connected with a bright blue flash, and they heard a click as the latch gave way. The painting moved slightly, then a crack appeared in the wall behind the frame, and the door slowly swung open.

They stared into darkness lit here and there by a faint glimmer of blue.

"The passage will take Your Highness to the back of the palace—" Jennings began.

"Hush!" Kate whispered. "Listen!"

Someone was outside the Rose Room, rattling the door handle, reporting that the door was locked.

"I know you are inside, Princess Sophia," Smythe called through the door. "Your Highness would do well to surrender."

"You must hurry, Your Highness!" said Jennings. "Into the passage! Quickly!"

"Smash down the door," Smythe ordered.

Sophia darted into the passage, accompanied by Kate, carrying Bandit and the poker. Jennings started to shut the door.

"You must come with us, sir!" Sophia said softly, reaching out to him. "Smythe will know you helped us escape!"

"I will tell him I was out on the balcony looking for you," Jennings replied. He drew one of his pistols and held it out to Kate. "I will trade this for the poker you are trying to conceal. I wish I could give you the lantern, but if the colonel saw it was missing, he would grow suspicious."

Kate wordlessly handed over the poker, took the pistol, and tucked it into the waistband of her slops. Jennings shut the door. The latch clicked and they heard him walking away. Then they heard a gunshot.

Sophia paled and put her hand to her mouth.

"Jennings! Oh, God!" she murmured.

"We must keep going," Kate said, urging her along.

She placed Bandit on the floor, turned around, started to take a step, and nearly pitched headfirst down the steep staircase.

She gasped and reached for the wall to steady herself, as Sophia caught hold of her and dragged her back.

Now that she took time to look, she could see that the landing was narrow, only a few feet wide. The staircase plunged straight down into darkness, its walls dimly lit by the faint blue glow of magical constructs which must be as old as those on the picture frame. The stairs were made of stone, rough and uneven.

Bandit pattered down the stairs, glad to be free and apparently determined to stay that way, for he ignored Sophia's whispered calls to come back. Kate could hear the sounds of the wooden door splintering and Smythe issuing orders.

"You go ahead with Bandit," said Kate, drawing the pistol. "I'll be right behind you. Be careful. Those stairs are treacherous."

Gathering up her skirts, Sophia placed one hand on the wall and began to descend. Kate slowly crept down the stairs after her. She could hear Smythe's voice coming from the Rose Room. She couldn't understand what he was saying, but she didn't have to. She quickened her steps as much as she dared.

Sophia reached the bottom of the stairs and came to a halt. The hall branched off in three directions.

"Which way?" she asked as Kate caught up with her.

Kate looked down all three and saw one glowing with faint blue light. She pointed to the constructs.

"We know Sir Richard brought Thomas to the Rose Room through this passage. He probably intended to take him back the same way and left the constructs as a guide so that they wouldn't get lost. If we follow the constructs, they should lead us to the ground floor."

They took the hall that branched off to the right. It led them to another set of stairs. Bandit ran on ahead of them, pausing every so often to look back to make certain they were coming. They descended the stairs and came to another passage and more stairs lighted by magic.

As they went down the staircase, which was wider and not as steep as those before, Kate listened fearfully for the sounds of pursuit. All she could hear was the patter of Bandit's feet and the rustling of Sophia's silk skirt.

When they reached the bottom of the stairs, they paused to rest.

"Jennings wouldn't tell Smythe where to find us," Sophia said with a catch in her throat. "And that horrible man shot him."

"We don't know what happened," Kate said, trying to reassure her. "What we do know is that Smythe knows *we* know the truth. He can't let us reveal what we heard. If Jennings is dead, he died so that we could escape and help our friends."

They descended more stairs and encountered more branching hallways. The constructs glowed so faintly they could barely see them and then they ended altogether. They had come to a door.

"I think this must be the way out," said Kate. "We should have reached the ground level by now."

She warily eyed the door.

"I don't see any warding magic. Do you?"

Sophia shook her head. "We wouldn't. If this door leads out of the passage, it must also lead into the passage. The warding spells that keep people from finding the door would be on the other side."

Kate had to think through that argument for a moment, then conceded Sophia was right. Her idea was confirmed by several lanterns that hung from hooks on the wall, undoubtedly placed there for the convenience of those entering the secret passage.

"The question is, where does the door lead?" Sophia asked.

"I'll be happy if leads us out of this passage," Kate said. She was feeling a little panicked, starting to wonder if she would ever see sunlight again.

She put her ear to the door and listened.

"Do you hear anything?" Sophia whispered.

Kate shook her head.

She saw no sign of a door handle, so she gave the door a shove. The door was heavy and barely moved. Pushing harder, Kate forced it open a crack and peeped through it.

Sophia made a deft catch as Bandit started to dart inside.

"I can't see anything. It's too dark," said Kate, disappointed. "But I don't hear anything either and that's good."

"I don't smell fresh air," said Sophia, sniffing. She added, startled, "I smell perfume! Wait here. I'll bring a light."

Sophia took down one of the lanterns from the hooks and touched the construct that caused the light to glow.

"Let me go first," said Kate, gripping the pistol.

"Don't be daft. We go together," said Sophia.

The two women crept through the door. Sophia raised the lantern, shone the light about.

"Nothing but clothes!" Kate said, disappointed. "This isn't the way out. It's someone's dressing room!"

"If this is a dressing room, the owner has eclectic taste in clothes," said Sophia, looking dubious.

The light shone on hats with large floppy brims and dangling plumed feathers for both men and women hanging from hooks on the walls, as well as a variety of cloaks: some made of homespun, others of silk and trimmed with fur. They saw velvet gowns smelling of stale perfume, lacy chemises and petticoats stuffed into armoires, while a trunk contained uniforms such as those worn by the palace servants: black dresses and white aprons for the women and long-tailed black jackets and white stockings for the men.

"This reminds me of backstage at the theater," said Sophia. "Oh, Kate, that explains it! These are costumes! Think about it. People who have to resort to using hidden passages are people who don't want to be recognized because they are having affairs. They come into this room and change clothes to disguise themselves. Once they are wearing the clothes of a maidservant or hiding beneath a floppy hat, they sneak into the palace through the secret passage. It's ingenious."

"It's disgusting," said Kate. "Fine lords and ladies with nothing to do except cheat on their spouses and jump into each other's beds. But . . . it's a godsend for us."

"What do you mean?" Sophia asked.

Kate glanced with a smile at Sophia's elegant silk and lace dress. "The soldiers are going to be looking for a princess. They won't be looking for a servant. First, though, we need to make certain this leads out of the palace. There must be another hidden door somewhere."

The two of them tried to search the walls, but they were covered with clothes and hats hanging from hooks. Kate soon realized they might search for hours and not find it.

"We might have to go back into the passage and look for another way out," suggested Sophia, growing discouraged.

"I'll be damned if I will," said Kate. "Wait! What's Bandit doing?"

He was sniffing at the bottom of one of the walls and then excitedly pawing it.

"I think he's found the door," said Sophia excitedly.

She gave the wall an experimental push.

"I felt something move! This must be the way out."

"Thank God! I will give you a tea cake!" Kate patted Bandit on the head. "We should change clothes before we leave."

"You're going to have to help me out of this dress," said Sophia. "It takes two servants to lace me into it."

Kate stripped off her slops and her shirt and put on one of the black dresses and tied a white apron around her waist. She stuffed the slops and the gingham shirt into the bottom of one of the trunks, but slipped her red kerchief into a pocket.

After she had changed, she went to assist Sophia. Removing her finery took some time. Kate had to untie the ribbons that laced up the bodice and held on the petticoats, then unfasten what seemed innumerable tiny hooks and eyes that closed the back of the dress.

Sophia put on her own black dress and apron and tucked her curls beneath a white frilly hat.

"Such a simple outfit," she said, smoothing the apron with her hands. "The dress is extremely comfortable. You're very clever, Kate. How do I look?"

"Like a scullery maid who has expensive taste in jewelry," said Kate.

She pointed to the ruby and diamond rings on Sophia's fingers, her diamond earrings and the ruby and diamond necklace.

Sophia flushed and pulled off the sparkling rings and earrings, as Kate unfastened the necklace.

"What do I do with them?" Sophia asked. "I don't mind leaving them. I have lots more."

Kate produced the red kerchief. "Since we're fugitives, we're going to need money. We can pawn these if need be."

She made a packet of the jewels inside the kerchief and thrust them into the pocket of her apron. She slipped the pistol into the other pocket, then selected two thick cloaks and handed one to Sophia.

"Fugitives . . ." Sophia repeated, as she draped the cloak around her shoulders. "I can't stop thinking about Corporal Jennings. If he is dead, he gave his life to save me, Kate. How can I ever be worth such a sacrifice?"

Kate squeezed her hand in sympathy. "By continuing his work. We have to warn someone about Smythe. We can't do that while we are inside the palace, which is crawling with his soldiers."

Kate was about to open the door Bandit had discovered, when Sophia stopped her.

"Wait a moment, Kate. We may escape the palace, but where will we go? Smythe will search the city for us. You said it yourself: We are fugitives. We will bring danger to anyone who shelters us."

Kate paused to consider. Her immediate concern was to get out of this palace and as far away from Smythe as she could manage. She had not thought beyond that. But now that Sophia had asked the question, Kate knew the answer.

"Dalgren," she said.

Sophia brightened. "Your dragon friend! Is he here?"

"His cave is nearby."

"We will be safe there," said Sophia, relieved. "That horrible man would not dare attack a dragon."

"Unfortunately, that horrible man has murdered two dragons," Kate said. "But if he does find us, Dalgren will be glad—extremely glad—to meet him."

She clasped her hand over the pistol. Sophia picked up Bandit and gave the door a gentle shove.

SIX

Sophia opened the door a crack. Fresh, cold air flowed inside, and they both breathed deeply and thankfully.

"We've found the way out!" Kate whispered. "Let's hope this leads to some deserted place behind the palace."

"I don't think it does," said Sophia.

The chill breeze carried sounds of panic and bustling activity: women were weeping or screeching in loud, shrill voices; men were shouting as carriage wheels crunched on gravel and horses' hooves clattered on the pavement.

Alarmed, Kate drew back from the door. "Douse that light before someone sees us! Do you know where we are?"

Sophia touched the lantern and the light vanished.

"We are near the carriageway at the east entrance," she replied. "This is the old part of the palace. The east entrance used to be the main entrance, but they haven't used it as such in years."

They stood together inside the doorway and peered into the night to get their bearings before venturing outside. The door was located in a recessed corner of the palace at ground level, hidden in the shadows of a wide staircase that flowed down from the first floor in waves of white marble.

The windows of the palace blazed with light. People milled about on the steps. They sounded angry, frightened, and distraught.

"Who are they?" Kate wondered.

"Those are the fine lords and ladies you disparage," said Sophia. "They were guests of the queen. Many have rooms in the palace."

"And now they are fleeing like rats," said Kate.

"I don't think they have a choice," said Sophia somberly. "They are being ordered to leave."

She pointed to the soldiers standing in the driveway, directing the flow of traffic. They stopped each carriage as it rolled up to the steps, and before they permitted the passengers to enter, they searched the carriage inside and out and even looked underneath. They questioned the drivers and the servants and the departing guests.

"They are looking for you!" Kate realized, alarmed. "Damn! This is the last place we should be!"

"They will be looking for us everywhere, Kate," said Sophia calmly. "We won't be safe anywhere around the palace."

More carriages rolled up and took their places in line. The carriages gave Kate an idea.

"Where are the Royal Stables from here?"

"On the other side of the Royal Garden," Sophia said.

Kate thought this over. "Could we reach the stables by cutting through the garden?"

"We can!" said Sophia, in growing excitement. "When Her Majesty and I would go to visit the griffin stables, we sometimes walked through the garden to reach them."

"Did the queen keep horses in the stables, as well as griffins?" Kate asked.

"The stables are filled with horses. Her guests keep their own horses there. The queen kept saddle horses for herself and her guests. She loved to hunt and she would always insist that her guests join her. You're thinking we could ride the horses! That's a splendid idea!"

Kate grimaced. Just the thought of being around horses made her gut shrivel, but she couldn't think of a faster or better way to reach Dalgren.

The carriage lane ran between the palace on one side and the garden on the other. The lights from the palace illuminated the lane, but did not reach beyond the garden walls.

"Give the lantern to me. You should put Bandit down on the ground. We'll have to run for it."

"If I put him down, he'll chase after the carriages," said Sophia. "Don't worry. I can carry him."

Kate sighed, but supposed, after all, Sophia was right to keep hold of

Bandit. Smythe would have probably given orders to search for the spaniel as well as the princess.

She and Sophia hurried out the door, and it slid shut silently behind them, vanishing into the wall, looking like just another slab of marble. Even though they kept to the shadows, Kate felt very exposed. Sophia was whispering to Bandit, promising him pudding if he would keep quiet.

They watched carriages drive past, one at a time. Each left with its passengers as soon as the soldiers completed their search and gave the driver permission. The moment one carriage had rolled away, the soldiers motioned for another to take its place.

They were questioning the guests before they left the palace. Each person was asked the same questions:

"Have you seen Her Highness, the Princess Sophia? Have you seen Sir Henry Wallace or the Countess de Marjolaine?"

Kate thrust the pistol into the sash of the apron and whispered to Sophia, "The best time to make a dash for it will be when the soldiers are occupied searching the carriages. After this next carriage passes us, we run."

Sophia drew in a deep breath. "Bandit and I are ready."

A large carriage drawn by four matching white horses pulled up to the stairs. The soldiers opened the doors and began their search. The nobleman who owned it stepped forward to loudly protest.

"What the devil do you mean by this outrage, sir? Searching my carriage as though I were some common criminal. Do you know who I am?"

"No, but God bless you!" said Kate gratefully. "Now!"

She started to run and promptly tripped over the hem of her skirt. Swearing under her breath, missing her slops, she hiked up her skirt and ran across the lawn.

The pistol dug into her stomach. The lantern bumped against her leg. Sophia had sensibly kilted her skirt so that she could carry the dog. She ran with both arms around Bandit, clutching him tightly. His head bounced against her shoulder, his ears flapped, and his tongue lolled. He appeared to be too shaken to bark.

They reached the carriageway without incident, but about halfway across the lane, Sophia began to falter, her strength failing. The nobleman was still yelling at the soldiers, but they were not paying the least attention, forcing him and his guests inside the carriage and slamming shut the doors.

Kate and Sophia reached the entrance to the garden as the horses galloped past. Kate could still hear the man complaining loudly as the carriage rolled by.

The garden was surrounded by a hedgerow of green beech that stood twelve feet tall and had been clipped to form an archway. Safe in the shadows, Kate and Sophia sank down on a bench to catch their breath.

Sophia set Bandit on the ground, where he immediately ran to a fountain and began to lap up water. Kate realized she herself was parched, and after she and Sophia were rested, they both knelt down at the side of the fountain, cupped their hands, and gratefully scooped up the brackish water.

Kate was also hungry, and couldn't remember the last time she had eaten. She told her stomach to make do with the water.

The garden had seemed impenetrably dark when they had first entered, and they wondered how they would find their way. As their eyes adjusted, however, they found that the lambent glow of the stars provided enough light for them to see a path that wound among flower beds covered with straw for the winter.

"This isn't a maze, is it?" Kate asked worriedly.

Sophia shook her head. "It used to be, during the time of King Godfrey. Queen Mary ordered the maze cut down and this garden planted. She didn't like mazes. 'I have no idea why grown people think it great fun to mislay themselves,' she always said."

Sophia was silent a moment, then added with a sigh, "Queen Mary was like that: practical, straightforward, forthright. If she was fond of you, she told you. If she detested you, she told you that, as well. I am glad she was fond of me. I will miss her very much."

As they walked along the path, Kate thought that the queen's garden seemed to mourn her, now preparing itself for death with winter's killing frosts. The perfume of lilies and roses had been replaced by the smell of damp loam and decaying leaves. Skeletal trees cast faint, ghostly shadows that shivered in the chill wind.

A light suddenly flashed in the darkness, alarming Kate. She started to draw the pistol. Sophia stopped her.

"It's only the sundial," she said. "It's magic. It serves as a functioning sundial during the day. At night a little silver orb mimics the phases of the moon. The moon is rising tonight."

Kate started to breathe again. The sounds coming from the palace were muffled. All she could hear were dead leaves rustling around the bases of cold marble statues, and the creaking of tree branches. She was exhausted, her weariness as much of spirit as in her body.

Only a few hours had passed since she had warned Sir Henry that the palace was going to come under attack. The hours might be few, but the time seemed to span centuries. She was glad Sophia was with her, to keep her going.

"Do you need to rest?" she asked her friend.

"Yes," said Sophia. "But we shouldn't stop."

They kept going. Bandit trailed after his mistress, head down, ears drooping. The garden was laid out in a practical manner, with straight paths and wide walkways. Apparently Queen Mary had scoffed at romantic little nooks or grottos, and barred any fanciful meanderings. They had walked about a mile without deviating from the path when Sophia indicated two rows of tall poplar trees that stood straight as soldiers on parade, forming two lines, one on either side of a broad walkway.

"The trees extend to the gate that leads to the Royal Stables," she said.

Kate shook off her weariness and peered ahead. "I can see lights."

"The stables will be in an uproar," said Sophia. "Soldiers will almost certainly have my carriage under guard."

"Where are the horse barns?" Kate asked.

"The buildings form a square around a main quadrangle," Sophia explained. "In the center is an open grassy area for riding and training. The coach houses are in a building to the west. The griffins are stabled in the Queen's Stables, which are to the north, and the horses and wyverns are in the Equestrian Stables, which are to the south. They keep the horses away from the griffins. Griffins are said to be quite fond of horse meat."

Kate dreaded the thought of having to ride a horse, and she was tempted to try to convince griffins to carry them, but she immediately rejected the idea. Griffins were proud beasts, very touchy and difficult to handle. They agreed to carry a rider as a favor, and then they had to be flattered and cajoled and paid for their services. And griffins wouldn't go anywhere near dragons.

Sophia seemed to know what Kate was thinking. "We should avoid the griffins. They adored the queen. The beasts will be shocked and upset to hear she has died. I doubt if anyone could ride them this night or maybe ever."

Kate and Sophia had come to the end of the garden and they could now see the Royal Stables, a sight that was astounding to Kate, who had expected just another horse barn, though perhaps larger than most. The red brick complex seemed at first glimpse to be as immense as the palace. The buildings were two stories high, with lead-paned windows, and topped with tall, ornamental spires, all surrounded by a brick wall. The entrance was a double wrought-iron gate between two marble posts surmounted by statues of griffins rampant. The gate stood open.

Soldiers guarded the entrance, stopping the carriages that were leaving for the palace, trying to question the drivers and servants. They seemed to be having a difficult time. People who worked and lived at the stables had formed a crowd around the soldiers, shouting at them, asking questions and demanding answers.

Noting Kate's concerned look, Sophia said, "Don't worry. We don't have to go through the gate. That building at the far end is the riding school. I took lessons there when I was a student at University after the war. The school has its own entrance and it's attached to the stables. No one will be there tonight, of course."

"Do you think the soldiers will be guarding it?" Kate asked.

Sophia considered, then shook her head. "I wouldn't think so. They appear to have work enough to do as it is."

They had to wake Bandit, who had fallen asleep. He whimpered in protest, but permitted Sophia to carry him. Leaving the garden, they kept to the shadows cast by the wall of poplar trees.

They gave a wide berth to the carriageway running in front of the entrance, where soldiers posted at the main gate were trying to placate the stable hands and search the carriages.

The riding school was a single-story building that stood to the south of the main gate. The windows were dark; the school's horse stalls were empty, and there was no sign of soldiers. Kate handed Sophia the lantern and carried Bandit, to give her a rest. They ran across the open carriageway and fetched up against one of the walls, keeping in the deep shadows. For the convenience of the stable hands none of the doors were locked, so they easily slipped inside, then stopped to listen.

All the noise and commotion was coming from the quadrangle, the coach house, and the main gate. The stables were quiet. Sophia knew her way around and she led Kate past the empty stalls across the darkened quadrangle toward the Queen's Stables.

The area was dark; only a few lights appeared at intervals and those probably belonged to the night watchmen, who were slowly and methodically checking on their charges.

Kate and Sophia slipped in the back and were immediately assailed by the smell of the horses. The smell brought unpleasant memories to Kate. She nervously kept clear of the stalls.

The horses had heard the unusual stir and commotion outside and they were wakeful and restless. As Kate and Sophia walked past the stalls, the horses thrust their heads over the partitions to see what was going on.

Sophia approached the animals, speaking to them soothingly. Some were merely curious and inquisitive, sniffing at her and growing calm at her touch. Others were nervous, though, rearing back their heads, flattening their ears, and shying away from her. Sophia did not approach them.

Kate was worried about Bandit and how he would react to horses, but Sophia said she took him with her when she went riding and he was used to them. Bandit was more at ease than Kate. The dog had perked up. Kate put him down. The dog trotted along at Sophia's heels, sniffing at the hay on the floor and occasionally sneezing.

Kate paused at a window, glanced outside, and was alarmed to see one of the night watchmen come out of one of the stables carrying a lantern. She watched him, thinking he must be making his rounds and wondering uneasily if he would head in this direction.

The man was walking away from the stables, however, not toward them. The lantern light crossed the quadrangle and headed toward the coach houses, and she sighed in relief.

"The watchmen are prowling about," she warned Sophia, who had stopped to stroke the nose of a large black horse with a white blaze. "What are you doing with that animal? We don't have time—"

"This is Charlie," Sophia explained. "I came to know him when I visited the queen. I will ride him. Now we must find a horse for you—"

"I can't," said Kate. She looked askance at the horse as Sophia led Charlie out of the stall, and backed away. "I don't like horses."

Sophia was perplexed. "Kate, you ride dragons that fly among the clouds! You said yourself we need to leave quickly. This was your idea, and it is a good one."

"I know." Kate swallowed. "It's just . . . When I was a little girl, the horse I was riding jumped a fence and I fell off. He stumbled and broke his leg. They had to shoot him. Right there in front of me."

Kate could still hear the horse screaming and see him thrashing about in pain. She remembered the stable master standing over the horse, pressing the gun against its head. He pulled the trigger, as tears streamed down his weathered face.

"Oh, Kate. I'm so sorry. Don't worry. Charlie can carry us both. You will ride pillion. Stay here with him while I fetch the saddle."

She handed Kate the reins and Kate took them, keeping as far from Charlie as she could. The horse apparently thought as little of Kate as she did of him, for he rolled his eyes and snorted at her. Finally, after what seemed like much longer than a few moments to Kate, Sophia returned, lugging a small, lightweight leather saddle.

Kate was impressed to see Sophia heave the saddle onto Charlie's back and strap it into place.

"Where did you learn to saddle your own horse?" she asked. "I would have thought you had an army of grooms to do that for you."

Sophia smiled. "The countess taught me. She says every woman should know how to do three things: saddle a horse, load a pistol, and bake a loaf of bread."

"You know two more than I do," said Kate. "What about Bandit?"

"He will ride in front . . ." Sophia began.

An eerie wailing sound—part ragged caw and part grief-filled roar—shattered the stillness. The wail began softly and slowly rose in intensity. Kate clutched at Sophia, who grasped her hand.

"The griffins are mourning their queen," Sophia said softly.

Their cries throbbed and pulsed. Kate could feel their grief in her bones.

The keening swelled, rending the night. The strange sound unsettled the horses. Already restless, they whinnied and kicked at the stalls.

Charlie lunged sideways, showing the whites of his eyes and yanking on the reins, almost dragging Sophia off her feet. Kate stumbled backward, away from the enormous hooves. Sophia knew how to handle him. She quickly seized hold of the bridle and swung Charlie's head around so he had to look at her, and talked to him soothingly.

Kate grabbed Bandit and ducked into a corner. Sophia steadied the horse and pulled herself up into the saddle. "The stable hands will be coming. We don't have much time. Give me Bandit."

Kate lifted Bandit up onto the saddle and he lay down across the front. Sophia reached out her hand to Kate. She hesitated a moment, a sick feeling in her gut.

The stables were in an uproar. Across the paddock, the wyverns began shrieking and biting and flinging themselves against the walls of their stalls. Grooms and stable hands ran from their quarters, converging on the horse and wyvern stables, while others were trying to calm the carriage horses. No one dared go near the griffins.

Kate grabbed hold of Sophia's hand and managed to awkwardly scramble onto Charlie's back. Sophia gave his flanks a little kick and he lurched forward, almost unseating Kate. She flung her arms around Sophia and held on tightly.

"I can't breathe!" Sophia protested.

"Sorry!" Kate muttered and eased up a little.

Charlie galloped out of the barn and into the carriageway. Someone shouted that a horse was loose, but everyone was too busy trying to control the other animals to chase after one.

Sophia guided Charlie onto a road that ran behind the stables. Judging by the wheel ruts, it was used by wagons transporting goods and supplies. Kate jounced up and down on the horse's rump, holding fast to Sophia in fear of being thrown off.

They rode about two miles and saw no signs of pursuit. Sophia slowed Charlie to a trot, so as not to tire him out. The road was dark, lined with oak trees that still retained some of their leaves. Even at this distance, though, they could still hear the griffins wailing.

Kate had assumed the road would be empty this time of night and she was dismayed to hear the sound of wagon wheels coming toward them. Sophia didn't seem worried, though, and she calmly guided Charlie into the shadows as the wagon rumbled by.

"Night deliveries," Sophia explained. "They're bringing supplies, especially perishables such as fresh vegetables and milk that are delivered daily."

Two more wagons rolled past them as they waited in the shadows. No more came after and Sophia guided Charlie back onto the road. They followed it through the palace grounds until they reached the outer boundary. One final obstacle remained: the wall that surrounded the palace and a gate with a guardhouse. A light shone in the guardhouse, revealing two soldiers inside. The gate stood open to admit the delivery wagons.

Sophia slowed the horse and turned around in the saddle to confer with Kate.

"Those guards are going to be suspicious the moment they see us—two lowly housemaids riding a fine horse."

"We've made it this far," said Kate. "Let me do the talking. Your Rosian accent will give you away. Follow my lead and be ready to ride like the Evil One is after us when I give the word."

Sophia nodded and they rode slowly toward the gate. Kate wondered if these were Smythe's soldiers, and if so, whether they had received orders to watch for the princess.

"Start crying," she whispered. "Hide your face."

Sophia obligingly put her hand over her face and began to sob.

A soldier carrying a lantern came out to stand in the road. Kate was relieved to see he wore his rifle slung over his shoulder, not expecting trouble. He lifted the lantern and stared at them in wonderment. He appeared puzzled at first and then disapproving.

"Here now, what do you two girls think you're doing? Out for a joy ride? And where did you get that horse?" He frowned at Sophia, who was sobbing uncontrollably. "What's the matter with her?"

Kate gave a gulp and wiped her eyes and spoke breathlessly, jumbling her words together. "Oh, sir, we are so frightened! We had to get away and we found this horse and it seemed like God Hisself sent it, so me and Ida took it, not meaning no harm, sir, but there was the explosion and we thought the ceiling was going to come down on top of us, and then William the footman, he says the queen was dead—"

"The queen dead?" the guard repeated, aghast. "Hey, Wilson, they say the queen is dead!"

His fellow left the guardhouse and came to join him. He was older and clearly did not believe them.

"What a load of crap! You two! Get down off that horse—"

"Now!" Kate cried.

Sophia kicked her heels into Charlie as Kate struck the horse on the rump with the flat of her palm. Charlie leaped forward, forcing the guards to dive to either side of the road to avoid being run down.

They clambered to their feet and shouted for them to stop, threatening to open fire. Looking back, Kate saw them fumbling with their rifles.

"Look out!" Sophia yelled at the driver of a wagon heading for the gate. He had to swerve to miss Charlie, and he shook his fist at them as they galloped past.

They kept to the road and finally arrived in the park outside the walls of the palace where the common folk could stroll about beneath the trees, peer through the wrought-iron palisade and gape at the splendor. Kate had jumped off the *Naofa* onto the roof of a building not far from here and she knew where she was.

The church clocks chimed the hour of one of the clock. The street was deserted, save for an occasional solitary cab or wagon. The taverns had closed, the drunkards would be in their beds or lying in alleys. Most of Haever slept in happy ignorance. The terrible news of the queen's death would flow out of the palace with the coming of daylight and spread through the city like raging flood waters, drowning peace in grief and sorrow, outrage and fear.

Sophia slowed Charlie, who was scarcely even breathing hard. She looked back at Kate.

"What do we do now?"

Throughout Freya, as news of their loss spread, a bereft nation would be asking the same question.

"We go home," said Kate. "To Dalgren."

SEVEN

Thomas watched the door slam shut as Smythe and two soldiers left to search the Rose Room. Two more soldiers stayed with Thomas and Sir Richard with orders to prevent them from leaving. The soldiers took up positions in front of the door, holding their rifles across their chests. Thomas was interested to note that when they answered Smythe, the soldiers spoke with thick Guundaran accents—members of Smythe's Army of Retribution, disguised as soldiers belonging to the Twelfth Westlands regiment.

An astute move, Thomas thought, giving Smythe grudging credit. The Twelfth Westlands regiment was made up of Guundaran mercenaries who served in the Freyan Royal Army and, indeed, most armies around the world. Guundarans were much admired for their heroism and tenacity in battle. No one would think to question their presence in the palace, especially when the palace was in the grip of tragedy and chaos.

Thomas had been a soldier himself. He had fought alongside Guundarans during the war against the Bottom Dwellers and he judged these men to be veterans of that war and perhaps others.

He went to speak to Sir Richard, who was slumped in his chair, his face drawn with pain, his eyes closed.

"How are you feeling, my lord?" he asked.

"Pay no heed to me, sir," said Richard. "We must think of how to free Your Majesty—"

A shot rang out nearby, and then another. The sharp cracks echoed through the hallway.

Sir Richard sat bolt upright. "What the devil was that? He would not be mad enough to kill the princess!"

"On the contrary, sir, he has already assassinated a queen," said Thomas.

He strode toward the door. The guards raised their rifles, barring his way.

"Let me pass!" Thomas commanded angrily.

"Keep back, sir," said one, respectful, but firm and cold. "You don't want to get hurt."

"We are responsible for Your Majesty's well-being, sir," said the other. They both spoke Freyan, though with a thick accent. "Stand away from the door."

He turned to his fellow, switching to Guundaran. "Find out what is going on, who fired those shots."

"Your Highness, he is right," said Richard. "You must stay here for your own safety!"

Thomas seemed to capitulate, but as the guard shifted the rifle in order to open the door, Thomas lunged at him, hoping to twist the rifle out of his hand.

He managed to seize hold of it, but before he could wrest it away, the other guard struck him expertly in the back with the butt of the rifle, near the kidney. Thomas collapsed, dropping to his hands and knees.

Sir Richard lurched to his feet. "How dare you strike your prince?"

"He is not *my* prince," returned the soldier in his thick accent.

The door opened and Colonel Smythe strode into the room. He came up short at the sight of Thomas, who was still on the floor, gasping in agony.

"He tried to escape, sir," the guard reported.

Smythe bent down to assist Thomas. "Allow me to help you, sir."

Thomas would have liked to have angrily refused the man's aid, but at this point he could scarcely breathe for the lancing pain. Smythe put his arm around Thomas and assisted him to hobble to a chair.

"These men are Guundaran mercenaries. They owe no allegiance to you, sir," Smythe cautioned. "They are loyal to those who pay them, and I pay them very well."

"What were those gunshots?" Thomas demanded, gritting his teeth against the pain. "Is the princess safe?"

"The matter does not concern you, sir—"

"The hell it doesn't!" Thomas cried angrily. "For better or worse, you made me ruler. Tell me what is going on!"

"If you insist, sir. Corporal Jennings discovered the princess and a friend in the Rose Room. Jennings recognized the friend as a female spy who works for Sir Henry Wallace, this man's treacherous brother. When Jennings attempted to apprehend the two, the woman shot him, wounding him. The two women managed to escape. We will find them soon enough, however."

Thomas could scarcely contain his relief. He thought he had heard Kate's voice and Bandit's bark and he was glad to know she and Sophia were together. At least for the moment, the two appeared to have been able to evade capture.

Smythe shifted his gaze to Richard, who was shakily standing with one bloodstained hand pressed over the wound in his shoulder, glowering at the colonel.

"Sit down, my lord, before you swoon," Smythe caustically advised him. "I have sent for my own surgeon to attend to you. We must keep you alive to speak before the House of Nobles."

"I look forward to publicly denouncing you," said Richard.

"Quite the contrary, my lord, you will endorse me according to the wishes of His Highness," said Smythe.

Thomas's pain was starting to recede and he was at last able to draw a ragged breath. "I will denounce you myself!"

Smythe poured a glass of water from the pitcher, lifted the glass to his lips, and slowly drank. He set down the glass with deliberation and reached for the pitcher.

Smythe poured another glass of water and offered it to Thomas. He ignored the offer and Smythe drank the water himself.

"Suppose you denounce me. Let us look at this through the eyes of the people of Freya, sir. They will soon learn that the Rosians assassinated our queen in order to put you on the throne. I can make a clear case against Rosia. The Countess de Marjolaine, who is an agent for Rosia, was in the palace last night. She knew in advance that the queen was going to die and she conspired with Sir Richard to smuggle you into the palace. You planned to claim the crown before Her Majesty's body was cool."

"I came to meet with the queen!" Thomas said angrily.

"I will testify to the truth!" Richard stated.

Smythe cast him a scathing glance. "And who will believe you, my lord, when I have correspondence in my possession between you and members of the Faithful advocating revolution, the violent overthrow of the queen.

"As for you, Your Highness, your own mother told me that Sir Richard traveled to Bheldem to meet with her to conspire to remove the queen. You yourself were present at the meeting."

"I told her I wanted no part of her scheme!" Thomas said.

Smythe shrugged. "Your mother will testify that you knew about the conspiracy in advance, sir. Everyone will believe you were complicit."

"You are a devil, Smythe," said Richard.

"I do what I do for God's glory, my lord," said Smythe in humble tones. "He wants me to return my nation to the path of righteousness from which it has strayed.

"I will make you a king, sir," he continued, turning to Thomas. "You will live a life of luxury. You will dance at royal balls, grace functions with your royal presence. I will relieve you of the onerous task of ruling the kingdom."

"I will renounce the throne sooner than let you rule!" said Thomas.

Smythe shook his head. "In that instance, dark rumors will start to circulate regarding Your Majesty's sanity." He drew his pistol and casually toyed with it, all the while looking pointedly at Thomas. "Sadly, you will make an attempt to try to take your own life. You may or may not succeed, depending on my mood. Either way, as Chancellor of War, I will take over governing the country."

"You could not seize control!" Thomas said.

"You are obviously not a student of Freyan history, sir," said Smythe. "I suggest you study the reign of King Charles and his war with Estara and Travia. He was known as the Mad King. His Chancellor of War took over ruling Freya during His Majesty's illness. He eventually became Lord Protector of the Realm and ruled until Charles's death."

Thomas sat stupefied, unable to think, and he wondered if he *was* losing his sanity. He had to find a way to stop Smythe, prevent him from carrying out this heinous plot, but he had no idea how.

"Give up, sir," Smythe suggested. "I have walled up every possible escape route. No one is coming to your rescue. Accept your fate. You will find life easier and far more pleasant."

Thomas shook his head. "I will never—"

They were interrupted by a knock on the door. The guards opened it to admit the surgeon and another officer.

"How is Corporal Jennings?" Smythe asked the surgeon, switching from Freyan to Guundaran, a language Thomas both spoke and understood. He wondered if Smythe knew he spoke the language and guessed that he didn't or he would not have been so free with his words.

Thomas remained seated, his head bowed, seemingly lost in his misery, watching and listening.

"Lucky, sir," said the surgeon in the same language. "The bullet struck the fleshy part of the arm. He will make a full recovery."

"Tend to that gentleman," Smythe ordered, indicating Sir Richard. "He stepped in front of a bullet."

The surgeon nodded and started unpacking his bag, laying out his instruments on a side table.

"Did you remove the queen's body?" Smythe asked the surgeon. "Has she been officially declared dead?"

"The woman is dead beyond doubt, sir," the surgeon grunted. "She was buried beneath a half ton of marble, as Captain Reinhart can confirm."

"We have completed the task of removing the remains, sir. What are your orders, Colonel?"

"When the surgeon is finished tending to His Lordship, he will return to take charge of the corpse. Place the remains in a coffin and seal it shut. The official report will state that she died of wounds suffered in a bomb blast. Were you able to clear the area, Captain?"

"Yes, sir," Reinhart answered. "When my men arrived on the scene, we found some of the servants attempting to dig through the rubble with their bare hands. We ordered them out, saying it was unsafe, warning that there might be more bombs."

"Did the servants see anything? Did the green-beam gun leave any traces?"

"I could see the residual green glow left by the contramagic on some of the debris, sir. But then, I am a crafter and I knew what to look for," Captain Reinhart replied. "The servants were in a state of shock. When I said the blast looked like a bomb, undoubtedly planted by the Rosians, the servants seemed to latch onto that."

Smythe smiled in satisfaction. "Once word spreads that the Rosians were responsible for killing the queen, I would not be a Rosian in this city for a thousand klinkerts. The people will tear them to shreds."

Thomas clenched his fists beneath the lace on his sleeve to keep from betraying his outrage. Smythe was going to deliberately start a war with Rosia. The bitter hatred between the two countries dated back centuries and the Freyans would find it easy to believe that Rosians had killed their queen. They would demand revenge, clamor for blood.

As Chancellor of War, with the country going to war, Smythe would wield immense power. All that made sense. But what didn't make sense to Thomas was the fact that this was a war Freya would most certainly lose.

Rosia was powerful, wealthy, whereas Freya teetered on the brink of bankruptcy. Rosia had more troops, more ships. Most important, they had the famed Dragon Brigade.

And so why, Thomas wondered, is Smythe starting a war he knows he can not win? A Chancellor of War who lost his war would be forced to resign, driven out in disgrace.

He was trying to puzzle this out when the surgeon looked about and spotted him. Pointing to the bottle containing brandy, the surgeon ordered in crude Freyan, "You there. Bring brandy."

Sir Richard was shocked beyond words. Thomas did not want to stop the flow of talk, for Smythe and the captain were now discussing the search for the princess and her companion. He did as he was told. Going to the table, he poured a glass of brandy and brought it to the surgeon, who handed it to Sir Richard.

"Drink. This is going to hurt."

Sir Richard drank the brandy, then stiffened in anticipation and closed his eyes.

The surgeon was a grim-looking, grizzled veteran, deft and skilled at his work. He first removed the heavy, bloodstained brocade jacket Sir Richard had worn to attend the audience with the queen. He tried to ease it off, but couldn't avoid causing his patient to cry out. Richard turned quite pale.

The surgeon exposed the bloody shirt, which had adhered to the wound. He cut through it, then yanked it free. He prodded and probed the wound, muttering to himself in Guundaran.

Sir Richard shuddered, and beads of sweat broke out on his forehead. He pressed his lips together to stifle a cry. The surgeon plucked out the bullet, then unwound a bandage roll and began to bind the wound.

Sir Richard lay back in the chair, breathing heavily.

The surgeon eyed him, took his pulse, and appeared grave. "This man's pulse is weak, Colonel. He has lost a quantity of blood. He should be immediately conveyed to his home to rest and recover."

"I will take your opinion under advisement, sir," said Smythe.

The surgeon shrugged, packed up his bag, and departed. Smythe turned back to the captain to finish their discussion.

"Gate guards stopped two women dressed as servants trying to flee the palace on horseback," the captain reported.

"Are you certain one of them was Her Highness?"

"Yes, Colonel. The description fits that of Princess Sophia *and* she was carrying a small dog. I regret to report, sir, that the guards were unable to apprehend them."

Smythe went livid. "Are you telling me the princess escaped the palace?"

"Yes, sir," said the captain.

Smythe controlled himself. "What of Henry Wallace and the Countess de Marjolaine? Were they captured?"

To judge by the captain's unhappy expression, he had more bad news. "Not yet, sir. Troops went to Wallace's house to place him and his family under arrest, but they fled before they could be apprehended. They were seen entering the carriage of the Countess de Marjolaine. We located her yacht, but it was gone before we could seize it. They have probably left Freya by now."

"Maybe not." Smythe was grim. "I will close the ports. Have every ship searched! Issue warrants for the arrest of Sir Henry Wallace, the countess, and the princess."

He cast a sardonic glance at Thomas. "On the orders of His Highness, of course. You return to the queen's office, Captain, make certain all is kept secure and no one enters until you have removed all traces left by the green-beam gun."

"I suggest you take these guards with you, sir," said Reinhart. "You might not be safe—"

"And whose fault is that, Captain?" Smythe said bitingly. "Who permitted these criminals to escape?"

Captain Reinhart could only salute and leave as quickly as possible. Smythe again departed, taking the guards with him.

"Do not think of trying to escape," Smythe warned before he left. "There are two guards on the balcony and two outside the door with orders to detain you by any means necessary."

The room was quiet, save for Sir Richard's ragged breathing. He sprawled in the chair, his eyes closed. The room was hot and stank of blood. Thomas thought of opening the door to the balcony to let in fresh air, but he feared the chill might not be good for the wounded man.

Richard opened his eyes and glanced about the room, as though to assure himself Smythe had gone. When he saw they were alone, he sat up and gestured to Thomas.

"Come closer, Your Majesty. I must talk to you."

"You should not tax yourself, my lord," said Thomas.

"Bah! I am well enough to talk," said Richard.

"What is it, my lord?" Thomas asked, rising to move a chair near him.

Sir Richard kept his voice low. "I have been thinking, sir. You need Henry!"

Thomas recoiled, repelled by the suggestion.

"May I remind you, my lord, that your brother has been one of my most implacable foes. You said yourself he refers to me as the 'Pretender.'"

"He was your foe, sir, I do not deny it. But for all his faults, Henry is a loyal Freyan. He was devoted to the queen. She would have asked him to serve you as he did her. I am certain of it."

Thomas was not so convinced. "You heard Smythe, my lord. Your brother has undoubtedly fled the country."

"Henry would not leave Freya in this time of crisis," said Richard emphatically. "He knows that I am a member of the Faithful, loyal to Your Highness. He will find a way to communicate with me, if for no other reason than to confront me with the fact that I betrayed Mr. Sloan to Smythe. I would like your permission to tell him what has happened and ask for his help. Henry has a vast network of agents he can use to come to your aid."

Thomas hesitated. He did not trust Henry Wallace, but he needed help and he had nowhere else to go to find it.

"Very well," he said curtly. "And now I need your counsel, my lord."

"Do not ask counsel of me, sir," said Richard bitterly. "I was the one who recommended that devil, Smythe, to your mother and father. He fooled me completely."

"If you are a fool, then I am another—or worse. I am now become his puppet," said Thomas, brooding. "What am I to do?"

The two sat in silence, then Sir Richard said softly, "I will tell you what my brother, Henry, would say if he sat here in my place."

Richard leaned close. His eyes burned, his pale face was fixed, intent.

"Henry would tell you to dance at the end of the puppet strings until the day comes when you wrap those strings around Smythe's neck and strangle him."

Thomas understood all too well what Richard was asking him to do. He rose to his feet and began to pace restlessly. Richard watched him with sympathy.

"I understand, sir. Your pride and honor will urge you to defy Smythe. If you do, you sacrifice your people. You made a promise to Her Majesty—a deathbed promise, as it turns out. You promised the queen you would do your duty. Buy time until we find a way to destroy him."

Thomas stopped pacing and turned to listen.

"Freya cannot go to war with Rosia unless you authorize it, Your Highness," Richard continued. "You hold power Smythe cannot take away. You do not need to openly defy him, but you can dither, prevaricate, tell him you want to study the matter, refer it to the Privy Council or committees in the House.

"You will be playing a dangerous charade, Thomas. Smythe is cunning and if he suspects for one moment that you are seeking to destroy him, he will destroy you first. You must pretend to be subservient, swallow your pride, choke down your rage, endure the shame and humiliation."

"The only way I win is by seeming to lose," said Thomas, mulling over the idea. "Smythe will believe my act. He already has a low opinion of me. He will be glad to know that I am as weak and pusillanimous as he thinks me."

"Know this, sir. You will not fight alone, though it may seem so, for Smythe will make you a prisoner in your own palace. He will intercept your correspondence and surround you with spies. He will insist on being present during all your meetings and prevent you from going anywhere alone. But always remember—you have friends on the outside who are fighting for you. I will see to that and so will Henry. I stake my life on it."

They both heard sounds of the guards at the door snapping to attention, which meant that Smythe had returned. Richard closed his eyes and pretended to sleep. Thomas walked over to the windows facing the balcony. He was gazing out into the night when Smythe flung open the door.

"You must come with me, Your Highness," the colonel said. "A crowd has gathered in the rotunda. You will take the opportunity to speak to them, lay claim to the throne before witnesses."

Thomas glanced at Sir Richard, and saw the old man's eyes flicker as he gave an almost imperceptible nod.

"I will do so, Smythe," said Thomas coolly, "but you must first agree to convey Sir Richard to his home."

"Out of the question, sir. He cannot be trusted."

"His Lordship has pledged his loyalty to me," said Thomas. "As you know, he has immense influence with the Faithful and the House of Nobles."

Thomas hesitated, swallowed, then said, "*We* need him."

Smythe heard the emphasis on the word "we." He smiled, pleased, yet disdainful.

"Very well, sir."

Smythe spoke to the guard and ordered him to convey Sir Richard to his house. He then turned back to Thomas.

"I have taken the liberty of writing down your speech to the people. You must say what I have written. If you think of defying me, speaking for yourself, consider the welfare of your friend in Offdom Tower."

Smythe bowed and indicated Thomas was to precede him out the door. Thomas had to clench his fists tight beneath the ornamental lace on his cuffs to keep from giving way to his most heartfelt desire, which was to throttle Smythe, slam him to the floor, and order the guards to arrest him and drag him to Offdom Tower.

Smythe leaned near to whisper, "The guards would not obey you, sir. You are not their king. In fact, you are not anyone's king. Keep walking."

Thomas felt the sharp edges of the black diamonds and sapphires that adorned the ring of his ancestor, King James, pierce his flesh. He remembered Mary's words when she gave it to him.

"This belonged to poor James, your unhappy ancestor," Mary had told him. "The man made a pig's breakfast of being king, damn near ruined the country. Still, he was the anointed king, and my own ancestors were wrong to plunge Freya into a bitter and bloody civil war to overthrow him."

Mary had placed the ring in his palm and closed Thomas's hand over it. She had then rested both her hands on his and looked into his eyes.

"You and I, between us, must do everything within our power to keep Freya strong and united, Thomas Stanford. I do my part by naming you heir to the throne. You do yours by doing your duty."

Thomas walked down the stairs that led to the rotunda. He could hear Smythe crowding close behind him, almost tripping on his heels. He could feel the man's eyes on him.

Thomas clasped his hand over the ring and renewed his vow. "I will do my duty, Your Majesty."

EIGHT

Dalgren was currently residing in a cavern located along the shoreline of Freya's Great Eastern Bay. The coast of Freya was rocky and remote, with only a single road that led to a mining village about twenty miles north. Winding among rocks, the road was little traveled these days, for the mine owners now shipped the ore by barges that sailed the Breath.

Those who did travel the road had no idea a dragon was living nearby, for the road was five miles from his cave. Dalgren rested well in his snug darkness, secure in the knowledge that only Kate knew where to find him.

Dragons living in Freya had to be careful. The Freyan people had no love for dragons. Their hatred dated back centuries to their ancestors, the ancient Imhrun, and was inflamed by the Battle of Daenar, when the Freyans had fought the Dragon Brigade in a short but brutal conflict both sides now wanted to forget.

Dalgren felt little threat from humans, but they could be as annoying as scale mites, sending armed hunting parties after him. Bullets couldn't kill him, for they bounced off his scaly hide, but they stung painfully. Humans were incredibly stupid. They did not appear to realize that if he wanted to defend himself from their attacks, he could simply breathe on them to roast them as they would roast a chicken.

What humans did not know was that Dalgren would never attack them, no matter what the provocation. On the day he had deserted the Dragon Brigade, he had made a personal vow never to take another human life. And thus he found it much easier to simply stay hidden from humankind.

He had spent the night hunting and he was resting in his cave after a big meal, stretched out to his full length to promote digestion, with his chin on the stone and his tail extending behind. He gazed out from the mouth of the cave at the stars and the moon that was just starting to rise and wondered irritably what had become of Kate.

They had parted some time ago on the western coast of Freya. Kate had stowed away on board a black ship after discovering the Freyan crew was smuggling young Bottom Dwellers from their homes Below to the world Above. Kate had planned to rescue the young people, only to find out they didn't want to be rescued.

"Typical of Kate," Dalgren grumbled aloud.

The black ship had been armed with a green-beam gun, which Kate had been forced to help make operational. The presence of that gun had been upsetting to Dalgren. Green-beam guns were one of the few human weapons that could do lethal damage to a dragon.

Kate had defended her actions. These men had claimed to be serving her friend, Prince Tom, and she knew that couldn't be true. She had promised Dalgren she would leave the black ship when it reached Haever, then find Thomas and warn him about the threat of the ship with its terrible weapon. After that she would meet Dalgren in his cave.

Dalgren wished she would come. He was all alone with his thoughts, which kept turning back to the path that brought him to this lonely cave. Months earlier, he had voluntarily given himself up to the members of the Dragon Brigade to go on trial for his desertion from the Brigade following the ill-fated Battle of the Royal Sail. As his punishment, he was to spend a year in service to Father Jacob Northrop and the Bottom Dwellers, doing menial labor, such as hauling lumber.

He dutifully made the perilous journey Below, but Kate had refused to let him go alone. She had traveled Below with two Trundler sisters, Father Jacob's friends, which is how Kate had come to be mixed up with a black ship.

She had traveled to Haever with the ship, leaving instructions for Dalgren to remain Below with Father Jacob so he could complete his year-long service. Dalgren, though, had been concerned about Kate and had chosen to follow her.

He did not regret that decision.

"I couldn't let her sail off on a black ship, bound on some sort of nefarious mission, without trying to talk some sense into her," Dalgren told the cave walls.

The walls must have been tired of hearing him; he said the same or variations on the same several times a day.

"And what am I to tell the Dragon Council?" Dalgren wondered despondently.

He considered it likely that he had forfeited his chance to redeem himself, and would be banished from dragonkind, forced to live out his long life nameless and alone.

When he was with Kate and she had embroiled him in one of her harebrained schemes, at least he could forget about the forbidding future awaiting him.

"But Kate is human, with a human's short life-span," Dalgren said with a sigh that filled the cave with smoke. "I will live hundreds of years after she is gone. Those years of lonely existence will be bleak and empty."

Dalgren shifted his chin on the stone to make himself more comfortable.

"With any luck, Kate will get us both killed, and then I won't have to worry," he muttered.

Dalgren closed his eyes. He was just dozing off when he was wakened by a noise outside his cave—a scrabbling sound that created a small rock slide.

"Kate? Is that you?" he called, lifting his head.

The noise stopped.

Dalgren continued to listen, but he did not hear the sound repeated. At length, he dozed off, only to wake moments later to the sound of a horse's hooves clattering over stones and the strong, delicious smell of fresh horseflesh.

"Dalgren!" Kate yelled. "Are you there? It's me!"

"I'm here!" Dalgren responded.

"Thank God!" Kate called back. "I'm so glad I've found you! I've brought company, the Princess Sophia."

"The princess!" Dalgren lurched to his feet, nearly hitting his head on the cavern ceiling, and lumbered to the front of the cave.

The sun was just starting to rise, its light banishing the shadows cast by the rocks. He could see Kate, wrapped in a cloak, riding pillion with Princess Sophia of Rosia. He recognized Sophia, who had attended his trial for desertion. How she had come to be here in Freya in company with Kate was a mystery.

"I am glad to see you under happier circumstances, Lord Dalgren," Sophia called to him.

"Your Highness," said Dalgren, gulping.

Kate slid off the horse and landed on the ground with what sounded like a heartfelt sigh of relief. She stood for a moment, grimacing and rubbing her backside, then she reached up her hands.

"I'll hold Bandit."

Sophia handed over the dog, who had been draped over the front of the pommel. She dismounted and stood stroking the horse's neck in an effort to soothe him. The beast was terrified in the presence of a dragon and stood shivering and trembling.

"We can't keep the horse, Kate," Sophia said. "Poor Charlie is terrified of your dragon friend. We need to let him loose. He'll probably run straight back to his stable."

"I suppose you are right," said Kate. "But that means we will be on foot."

"Since I plan to sleep for the next three days, I don't care," said Sophia, smiling.

She released the horse and gave him a slap on the rump. The beast bolted, bounding over the rocks. Kate put Bandit down on the ground. The spaniel barked threats at Dalgren and made little runs at him to show off his bravery, though he took care not to come too close.

"I am glad to finally have a chance to talk to you, Lord Dalgren," said Sophia. "At your trial, I wanted to tell you that I considered your punishment most unfair, but, of course, as an observer for Rosia, I couldn't interfere. I realize that dragons have very strict and rigid rules regarding proper protocol. Since I was present as a representative of the Rosian crown, I could not offend the court by violating those rules. I feared I would have made matters even worse for you."

"You spoke up for me at the trial, Your Highness," said Dalgren. "Your support meant a great deal. Please, come inside, ma'am. You look worn out."

Sophia picked up Bandit, who had barked himself into exhaustion.

"He's been around dragons before, my lord," she said by way of apology. "He just needs to get used to you."

Bandit may have been around dragons before, but he obviously didn't trust them. He growled menacingly at Dalgren as Sophia carried him inside the cave.

Dalgren stopped Kate as she was about to follow.

"What the hell is going on?" he hissed through his fangs. "What is the princess doing here?"

"I'll explain later," said Kate wearily. "I am half-frozen and far too tired to go into it now. Do you have some place where we can sleep? Where it's warm?"

Dalgren heaved an exasperated sigh. If Kate had been alone, he would have insisted that she tell him. She was with the princess, however, and Her Highness was his guest. He could not abandon his duties as host.

Apologizing for preceding them, Dalgren guided Kate and the princess to a snug room not far from the chamber where he slept. Their room was too small for him to enter, but he thrust his snout inside and gently breathed fire on the walls, heating the stone, which gave off a warm red glow.

"There's a stream a short distance from here, Your Highness, just past that outcrop, so that you can drink and bathe. I don't have any food and you will have to sleep on the stone floor," said Dalgren apologetically. "I regret I have so little in the way of comforts to offer you."

Sophia smiled at him. "I am so tired, my lord, that any bed, even one of stone, will seem to me as luxurious as one of the finest goose down."

"Please call me Dalgren, ma'am," said Dalgren. "I have lost the right to my title. I was found guilty."

"I did not agree with the verdict, but I accede to your wishes, Dalgren," said Sophia gravely. "Thank you for your help."

She and Kate walked to the stream to drink and perform their ablutions. On their return, Sophia wrapped herself in her cloak and lay down with Bandit curled up in her arms on the stone floor that had been pleasantly warmed by Dalgren's breath. Both were almost immediately asleep.

"Thank you for helping us, my friend," Kate said, yawning.

"I'll go hunting," Dalgren offered. "Find some small game."

"No," said Kate quickly. "I'll go hunting when I wake up. I need you to stay here."

Dalgren glowered. "I *knew* something was wrong! Who is after you this time?"

"The Freyan army," said Kate.

Dalgren stared, eyes widening. "An army?"

"The soldiers didn't follow us here," Kate assured him. "I think we lost them on the way. But, just to be safe, I'd feel better if you were around."

Dalgren eyed her. Kate was slumping from exhaustion, so tired she could barely stand.

"Get some rest," he told her. "I'll keep watch."

Kate gave his snout a grateful rub, then went back into the room. She removed the pistol from her sash and placed it on a boulder where she could reach it at need, then wrapped herself in her cloak.

Dalgren waited until Kate fell asleep. Remembering the odd sound he had heard earlier, he went outside to take a look around. He didn't see anything and he returned to his chamber to keep watch.

He entertained himself by trying to figure out how Kate could have managed to end up with a dog, a Rosian princess, and the Freyan army in pursuit.

Quite a feat, even for Kate.

Not far from where Dalgren had made his lair, Trubgek was sitting among the rocks, keeping the dragon's cave in sight. The arrival of the two women had upset his plans. He scratched his stubbled chin and wondered what to do.

He had come here to kill. Dalgren was to be his first victim, the test case.

Following the death of the dragon Coreg, Trubgek had gone to work for Coreg's killer, Jonathan Smythe, who had needed Trubgek. He was the only one who knew the details of the dragon's involved and lucrative business— buying and selling arms on the black market.

Few knew that Coreg was the brains behind the operation. He had used a human named Greenstreet to interact with other humans. Greenstreet handled bank transactions, bought and sold the weapons through various buyers around the world, made arrangements to transport the shipments, and so on. Trubgek had been Coreg's servant and he had generally been the one to deal with Greenstreet.

Smythe had killed Coreg using the same powerful magical spell he had used to kill the dragon Lady Odila. Smythe had asked Trubgek to continue to run the business, telling him he needed the profits to fund his Army of Retribution.

As part of Smythe's plan, he intended to foment war with Rosia.

"People foolishly imagine this is a war I cannot win because Rosia has the Dragon Brigade," Smythe had told Trubgek a long while ago, while they had yet been in Bhelden, training his army. "All things being equal, people would be right. The Dragon Brigade would make short work of our navy and our coastal defenses. I intend to make short work of the Dragon Brigade. I have the spell that paralyzes dragons, makes them helpless and easy to kill."

Trubgek had seen what the spell did to Coreg. He had watched the dragon die. And for the first time since he was a child, he had known a flicker of feeling. Another person would have called it joy.

"You cannot use this spell to kill the dragons in the Dragon Brigade," Trubgek had told Smythe. "This spell requires the dragon to be alone, solitary. You must catch it unawares. The Brigade dragons live and work together."

He had shaken his head. "Not practical."

"Bah! You do not need to kill a single dragon in the Brigade to make my plan work," Smythe had stated. "Go to the Dragon Duchies. Kill dragons there. One or two a month in different locations, but all by the same means. You will start a panic. The Brigade dragons will be forced to return home.

They will find out humans are responsible for the deaths and that will breed distrust and suspicion between them and their human riders. The Brigade will fall apart."

Trubgek had conceded that likely, but he didn't care one way or the other. "I will require the dragon-killing spell."

"I will give it to you on one condition," Smythe had said. "I want proof that you can use it. I am not convinced you are as skilled in magic as Greenstreet made you out to be. *I* have yet to see any evidence."

I can use it, Trubgek thought, and he felt again the stirring of emotion that was a faint light in the bleak, dark emptiness of his being.

"What would you have me do?" he had asked.

"Travian dragons have moved into northern Freya, somewhere in the mountains along the western coast. Kill one or two of them. You will prove to me you know what you are doing and the deaths will revive the fears caused by Lady Odila's death and disrupt their cozy relationship with the Freyan government.

"I may have other work for you in Freya, as well. Gaskell is causing trouble, refusing to work with me. You know him. I may need to send you to keep him in line, as well as to check on the Bottom Dwellers and the green-beam guns. A black ship called the *Naofa* will be bringing parts from Below. I want to make certain they work."

Trubgek had traveled to Freya, but he had not been able to locate any Travian dragons. Following the death of their leader, Lady Odila, the dragons had concealed their whereabouts using powerful dragon magic to create illusions and set traps and raise barriers. Trubgek knew better than any other human alive the power of dragon magic and he knew it would be a waste of time for him to try to track them down.

He had been carrying out his other orders in regard to Gaskell and checking on the green-beam guns, when he had discovered Kate was working on the *Naofa*.

Trubgek had been intrigued by Kate ever since he had hired her at Coreg's behest. She had picked up a smattering of dragon language from Dalgren and she was the only human Trubgek had ever encountered who knew that the name "Trubgek," given to him by Coreg, was a foul and insulting term. Kate was also the only human who had ever taken an interest in him. She had feared him, for she had seen the power of his magic, but she had also seen the emptiness inside him and she had viewed him with compassion.

Kate had unwittingly led him to Dalgren. Trubgek had heard the two talk about traveling to Haever. Dalgren would meet her in a cavern on the coast not far from the city.

Trubgek had traveled to Haever and patiently waited and kept watch on the skies at night, the time when Dalgren would feel safe enough to go out hunting. Trubgek's patience was rewarded. He saw Dalgren, and was able to track him to his lair.

The spell induced paralysis in the dragon, and once that happened, Trubgek could use his own powerful magic to collapse the ceiling of the cave and crush the paralyzed dragon.

If this trial succeeded, Trubgek would follow the orders Smythe had given him, travel to the Dragon Duchies in Rosia to summarily kill dragons, burying them beneath the rubble of their stately mansions.

One by one, he would murder them. Killing here, killing there. Miles apart. He would choose his victims at random, and as each fell, the terror would spread.

Word would reach the dragons of the Dragon Brigade, who would abandon their duty to return to their stricken homeland to try to stop the murders. And soon the famed Brigade would itself be destroyed, no longer a threat to Freya.

That was Smythe's plan for winning the war with Rosia. Trubgek didn't give a damn about Rosia or Freya or Smythe. His only interest was in killing dragons. Dalgren was to be the first to die.

Earlier this night Trubgek had just begun to sneak into the cave to cast the spell when an unlucky slip on a loose stone started a small rock slide. The noise woke the dragon.

Trubgek was patient. He settled down to wait for Dalgren to fall asleep again to cast his spell. But Kate and the princess appeared before he could act.

Trubgek regretted Kate's arrival. He would now have to kill her, as well. But she and the princess were minor complications. He cared only about killing dragons.

Trubgek would have to wait until he was certain the two women, the dog, and the dragon would be deep in slumber and never hear him coming. He would wait as long as it took. He was, as always, very patient.

NINE

Kate woke from dreamless slumber to the sound of muffled moaning. She was at first disoriented and wondering why her bed was hard and cold as stone and then remembered that her bed *was* stone. Groggy and still half-asleep, she closed her eyes and tried to ignore the sound. The moaning continued, and Kate woke up enough to realize something was wrong. Sophia was moaning in pain.

Kate sat up, sore and stiff and cold. The stone walls still gave off warmth and a faint warm light and she could see Sophia, lying next to her, clutching her head. Tears ran down her cheeks, and she had pressed her cloak over her mouth to stifle her cries. Bandit crouched by her side, whimpering and pawing at her hair.

"Sophia, what's wrong?" Kate asked softly, resting her hand on Sophia's shoulder.

"I am sorry I woke you," Sophia whispered. She sucked in a pain-filled breath and shuddered.

"Sophia, please, tell me!" Kate urged. "You're scaring me."

"Magic!" Sophia said in a choked voice. She half turned to peer up at Kate. Her forehead was covered in sweat. Her eyes glistened with tears and her words were disjointed. "Powerful magic. Splintered shards . . . inside my head. The contramagic . . . the drums of the Bottom Dwellers . . ."

She moaned again, closing her eyes.

"Bottom Dwellers . . ." Kate repeated, bewildered. "Drums?"

Sophia only nodded and moaned again.

Kate had only a vague idea what she was talking about. During the war, the Bottom Dwellers beat drums that sent waves of contramagic to destroy the magic in the world Above.

"But the drumming ended years ago, Sophia," Kate told her. "They can't hurt you now."

She brushed Sophia's hair back from her clammy forehead and tried to think what she could do to ease the pain.

"I will fetch a cold cloth," she offered. "Maybe that would help. I won't be gone long."

Sophia didn't answer, but she nodded.

Kate reached for her red kerchief, only to remember it was serving as a jewelry box. She was still wearing the ridiculous apron tied around her waist and she took that off, dumped the diamonds and rubies into the apron and bundled them up. She shook the wrinkles from her kerchief and crept out of the snug chamber where they had been sleeping, padding quietly so as not to disturb Sophia.

Kate came to a sudden stop, frozen, afraid to move.

The blue glow of magic lit the cavern, emanating from what appeared to be a linen scroll spread out on the stone floor. By the eerie light, she could see a man crouching over the glowing scroll, staring at it intently and muttering to himself. The distance from where Kate was standing to the man was about twenty feet, allowing her to see his face clearly in the blue light of the magic.

She was shocked to realize the man was Trubgek. Kate recognized the scroll because she had seen it once before and she would never forget it. The scroll was covered from top to bottom, corner to corner, with hundreds of sigils strung together to form a single magical construct that was designed to kill dragons.

A white mist tinged with a faint blue light began to flow from the scroll into the chamber where Dalgren lay sleeping.

Kate shrank from the light, afraid Trubgek would see her. She turned around to run and nearly fell over Bandit, who was glaring at Trubgek and growling softly, hackles raised.

Kate grabbed the dog, clamped her hand over his muzzle, and crept back to Sophia. She knelt down beside her and gripped her shoulder tightly.

"Hush!" Kate breathed. "Don't make a sound!"

Her fear and intensity penetrated Sophia's pain. She gulped and fell silent, staring up at her.

"What is it?" she whispered. "What is wrong?"

"The magic that is hurting you is right outside this room!" Kate said, not daring to speak above a whisper. "A man is casting a spell that will kill Dalgren! I know this man," she added, shivering. "His name is Trubgek and he is horrible and very powerful, and he knows dragon magic. The same spell killed Lady Odila. I warned the dragons about him, but they wouldn't listen."

Sophia sat up, wincing in pain. "Did he see you?"

"I don't think so," said Kate. "The spell is very complex. He has to concentrate on it."

"How did it kill Lady Odila?"

"The spell itself didn't kill her. The magic created fumes that paralyzed her, so she couldn't defend herself. Smythe used a sword to murder her, stabbing her over and over. Miss Amelia was there. She saw the body. I can't let him do that to Dalgren!"

Kate reached for the pistol she had rested on the boulder. "I have one shot. Only one. You have to help me, Sophia. Use your magic. I know it hurts, but we must stop him!"

Sophia pressed her lips together, closed her eyes a moment, then said in a trembling voice, "Yes, I'll try . . . Oh, God!"

She stuffed her cloak in her mouth and doubled over, rocking back and forth in agony. The magic was not only going to kill Dalgren. It was killing Sophia.

Bandit struggled in Kate's grasp and tried to bite her. As she set the dog on the floor, she saw wisps of fumes snaking into the chamber, crawling over the stone.

Kate had not heard a sound from Dalgren, not even so much as the rustle of a wing, and she feared the magic was already working on him. He was probably lying there, helpless, unable to move, knowing he was going to die as Lady Odila had died.

Kate jumped to her feet. She was angry, as angry as she had ever been in her life, and determined. She walked out of the room and down the passage. The fumes swirled around her skirts as she swept through them.

Trubgek knelt on the ground. Concentrating on his magic, muttering the words of the spell, he did not hear Kate coming until she was almost upon him. He raised his head and stared at her.

"Stop!" Kate ordered him.

She pulled back the hammer, cocked the pistol, and aimed it at his head. She felt no compunction about killing him, but she feared that if he was dead and she could not stop the magic, Sophia would die, Dalgren would remain paralyzed, and he would die a slow and terrible death.

"Stop the spell," Kate ordered. "Reverse it. End it. Do whatever you have to do to make the magic stop or I will put a bullet in your skull. You know me. You know I will."

Trubgek gazed up at her. His eyes reflected the blue glow of the magic radiating up from the linen scroll. He was no longer speaking the words, however, and the blue glow slowly started to fade.

Holding the gun on him, keeping her eyes on him, Kate reached down, grabbed the linen scroll, and thrust it behind her back.

"Now stop the magic," she said.

The glow faded from Trubgek's eyes, leaving them dark and empty. He slowly rose to his feet and reached out his hand for the scroll.

Kate crumpled the linen, clutched it tightly, and shook her head. "It's my fault you have this magic. I stole the scroll. I had no idea what it did, but now I do know and you won't get it back, Trubgek."

"My name is Petar," he said.

Kate blinked, confused. "What? Who is Petar?"

"Petar is my name. Not Trubgek. You know what 'trubgek' means. You are the only human who ever did, who ever understood. Trubgek is a foul word, the most insulting term a dragon can use for a human. Coreg gloated over me, the monster he had created, and he named me. Not human. Not dragon. Less than either."

He spoke in a monotone with no emotion, as though he were talking about someone else. Kate said nothing, letting him talk. She cast a swift, agonized glance into Dalgren's chamber. She could not see him or hear him.

"I was a child," Trubgek continued. "He forced me to learn dragon magic. 'It's in your blood,' Coreg would tell me. He should know. He spilled enough of mine."

Trubgek gazed into the darkness as into a mirror. "I was with Coreg when he died. He was paralyzed. He couldn't move. I could have saved him. He knew I could. He begged me to save him. I made him say my name. My real name when I was a little boy. Petar. I made him say 'Petar.' He said it. And then he died."

Trubgek stomped on the ground with his boot, and the stone shook beneath Kate's feet. Small chunks of rock cascaded down from the ceiling.

"See that? I can bring down this mountain if I choose." Trubgek gazed at her and, in that moment, the empty eyes were not empty. Kate saw a flicker in them that lit the darkness and hiding there was a small boy, alone and suffering and desperately afraid.

"I am sorry," Kate said. "Coreg is dead. He can't hurt you anymore. But if you kill and keep killing, you are still Trubgek, doing his bidding. You can be free of him. You can be Petar. *He* would never hurt anyone, would he?"

Trubgek seemed to consider. And then the flicker faded, the eyes were dark and empty.

"You keep the scroll," he said. "I know now that I don't need it. The magic Coreg made me learn is powerful enough."

He started to walk off.

"Please, help me!" Kate cried. "Don't leave! Don't let Dalgren die!"

Trubgek walked out of the cave, then stopped, turned back. "I think the magic will wear off in time." He shrugged. "But I don't know."

He walked away. The sky was a pale yellow-blue, but night's shadows clung to Trubgek. Kate soon lost sight of him. She could hear his boots crunching on the stone, however, and she stood at the entrance with the pistol until the sound faded away.

She drew in a shivering breath, released the hammer, and lowered the pistol. Then she began to shake in reaction to her anger and her fear. Sophia came to join her. She looked pale and haggard, and her movements seemed a little unsure, but her eyes were clear. Bandit followed her, still growling.

"Are you all right?" she asked Kate.

"I'm fine," said Kate. "What about you?"

"The pain has stopped," said Sophia. "Who was that man? How do you know him?"

Ignoring the questions, Kate said, "I have to check on Dalgren. I hate to ask, but could you keep watch? I don't think Trubgek will come back, but if he does . . ."

Sophia nodded. "Give me the pistol."

Kate handed the pistol to Sophia, who sat down on a boulder near the entrance. Kate gave Bandit a pat.

"Sorry," she said.

She had to find her way into Dalgren's chamber in the dark, for the light from the walls did not extend that deep into the cave. She called his name. He didn't answer, but she thought she heard a rasping, indrawn breath, which gave her hope.

She pressed close to the wall and groped her way along the passage until it came to an end. She could not see, but the air smelled of sulfur and she had the impression of a vast chamber opening up before her. She called Dalgren's name again, and again heard the rasping breath. She crept toward the sound, feeling her way with her hands outthrust until she bumped into him.

He lay sprawled on the floor. He was still breathing, but each breath was a shuddering struggle.

Frightened, Kate sank down beside his head and wrapped her arms around as much of his snout as she could reach.

"I am here, Dalgren! You are safe now. Trubgek is gone. He thinks the spell will wear off in time."

She heard his breath sigh out of him. And though she waited, he did not draw breath again.

"No! Don't stop breathing!" she cried. "Fight! You have to fight!"

Dalgren did not stir. Kate laid her cheek on his snout, on the cool, smooth scales.

"Breathe, Dalgren," she said softly. "I need you."

She waited and waited and knew he was dead, and then Dalgren shuddered and drew in a long, slow breath. He let it out and drew in another, each breath seeming to come a little more easily than the last.

Kate sighed in relief and smiled, tasting tears in her mouth.

"I'm getting you all wet," she said, wiping his snout with her kerchief.

Dalgren grunted and croaked feebly, "The spell . . ."

"I have it," said Kate. "Don't worry."

Dalgren grunted again. His front claws scraped against the floor. He thumped the stone with his tail.

"Put the scroll on the ground in front of me. Then go back to Sophia. It won't be safe for you in here."

"You're too weak to do any spell casting," Kate argued. "I'm not leaving—"

"Do as I say, Kate," said Dalgren harshly.

He had never used that tone with her before. She placed the linen scroll on the stone floor and smoothed it with her hands, then stood up and made her way out of the chamber. She didn't go back to Sophia, however. She stayed where she could keep watch on him.

Dalgren breathed a jet of fire on the scroll. The linen instantly burst into flame, but the constructs were more difficult to destroy. Etched in fire, they rose into the air, as though trying to flee destruction, and hung in front of Dalgren. He breathed on them again, not fire, but magic.

The constructs had been laid down in layers, overlapping one another. As his breath destroyed the outer sigils, they began to blaze and give off sparks. He breathed again and the magic ate away at the sigils, breaking the constructs. The fire burned hotter and brighter. The sigils glowed, white hot, searing Kate's eyes. She had to close them to avoid the intense heat.

When the blaze died, Kate opened her eyes and rubbed them to try to see again, then stole back into the room. Dalgren had collapsed onto the floor, his strength gone. He looked at Kate, a gleam of triumph in his eyes. In front of him lay a pile of smoldering ashes.

"This will never kill another dragon," he said.

Kate ground the ashes into the stone with the heel of her boot. "Trubgek said he didn't need the spell to kill dragons."

"He doesn't," Dalgren growled. "You should have shot him."

"Fine words, coming from a dragon who vowed never to take a human life," Kate scoffed.

She sat down by his side on the stone floor. Daylight was starting to filter into the cave, enough to allow her to see.

"Anyway, he's gone. The dragon-killing spell is gone and that's an end to it and to him," she said. "We have to decide what to do. We can't stay here. Sophia and I are starving. We need to eat and then we have to find a way for her to return to Rosia—"

"I'm not going to Rosia," said Sophia, walking into the chamber. "I won't leave while Thomas and Phillip are in danger."

"I thought you were standing guard," said Kate.

"I left Bandit to keep watch. He'll warn us," said Sophia.

She saw the startled look on Kate's face and laughed. "I was teasing. I don't think we need to worry. That man won't be back. We know Dalgren took a vow never to kill a human, but Trubgek doesn't know that."

"True enough," Kate conceded.

Sophia returned the pistol to Kate and then sat down beside her. She wrapped herself in her cloak and drew her knees up to her chin. "I wish you hadn't mentioned food. I wasn't hungry before. How is Dalgren?"

The dragon lay sprawled on the floor, legs splayed, his chin resting on the stone. He scraped his claws on the floor and twitched his tail.

"The spell is wearing off. It's going to take time. So if you won't leave Haever, where can you go that is safe? No one will recognize me, but you can't walk down a street without drawing a crowd."

Sophia smiled. "On the contrary, everyone in Haever knows the notorious Captain Kate."

"That's an idea," Kate said thoughtfully. "Captain Kate! We will go to Miss Amelia's house. She will know what to do. She might know where to find Sir Henry."

"And we can tell her what we found out about Smythe," Sophia added eagerly. "She can expose him in the newspaper, tell the world he assassinated Queen Mary—"

"The queen is dead?" Dalgren gasped, appalled. "How? What happened?"

"I forgot you've been living in a cave," Kate said, rubbing his snout with affection.

"You need to tell me what is going on," Dalgren said, glowering. "Why is the Freyan army chasing you? How did you meet up with the princess?"

"It's a long story, Dalgren," said Kate, sighing. "A long, long story."

"Apparently I'm not going anywhere until this spell wears off," said Dalgren, adding gruffly, "So you might as well start at the beginning."

TEN

Henry Wallace was annoyed. Someone was flicking water in his face and refused to stop. He kept shouting at the person to go away and leave him alone, but the person paid no heed to him. Finally Henry grew extremely angry and lashed out with his fist.

"Ah, good," said Alan. "He's coming around."

"About goddamn time," Randolph said.

Just as Simon flicked more water into his face, Henry opened his eyes.

"Stop that!" Henry shouted, or at least he thought he had shouted. His words came out a pitiable mumble.

He tried to sit up, only to feel what seemed to be rockets explode inside his skull. He groaned, and Alan gently pressed him back down.

"Steady, there. Take it easy. You've had a nasty knock on the head."

"For a time we feared we were going to goddamn lose you," said Randolph gruffly. He fished a handkerchief from his pocket and blew his nose.

"What is your name?" Simon asked him. "What year is it?"

"Why? Have you forgotten?" Henry demanded, annoyed.

"He's all right," said Alan, smiling.

Henry grunted. He was in Simon's bedroom, lying on the bed with his friends gathered around him. Alan sat next to him on the bed, Randolph stood at the foot, and Simon was beside the bed in his chair. They were all disheveled and dirty, bruised and bloodied. Randolph's left wrist was tied up in a sling, and Alan had a bandage wrapped around his arm.

"Seriously, how do you feel?" Simon asked Henry, taking his pulse. "I know your head must hurt like the devil, but are you experiencing pain anywhere else? Stomach? Liver? I'm checking for internal injuries."

"My liver is fine," Henry snapped. He shoved aside Simon's hand and tried again to sit up.

Pain sliced through his skull, seeming to crack it open and lay bare his brains for all the world to see. A wave of nausea swept over him.

"He's going to be sick," Simon predicted. "Hold his head, Alan. Randolph, fetch the wastebasket."

Henry threw up and then fell back with a groan. He closed his eyes, but that made him feel worse, so he opened them again. The room was bright with sunlight and he was puzzled. Last he remembered, it had been night.

Henry looked out the door of the bedroom into Simon's office. Books covered the floor. Most astonishingly, he could see trees through the window.

Henry frowned. He was in a floating house and he should not be seeing trees. He should be seeing blue sky and the mists of the Breath. Maybe he wasn't as fine as he thought he was.

He groaned and was sick again.

"What's the last thing you remember?" Simon asked.

Henry frowned, concentrating, grimacing at the pain in his head. "We were on the roof. I remember the black ship, and Randolph and Alan firing rockets at it. And . . ." Henry started to shake his head, winced, and thought better of it. "Nothing after that, I'm afraid."

"The black ship fired a green beam that struck the house, knocked out the airscrews, and punctured the lift tanks," said Simon. "The house began to sink. We chose a suitable site for a landing and then took refuge in the attic. The house came down in what I term a controlled landing—"

"More like a bloody awful smash-up," Randolph stated dourly.

"You insisted on running downstairs and saving a book: *Fenyman's Lectures on Theoretical Magic*," said Simon. "I think you must have been looking for the note we found inside. You were clutching it in your hand. Don't worry. I tucked it in your pocket."

Henry pressed his hand in silent thanks.

"We were knocked about a bit when the house hit the ground," Simon continued. "Randolph sprained his wrist. A beam hit you on the head and rendered you unconscious. When the house finally settled, we carried you downstairs and here you are with a bump on your head the size of a frigate."

"I don't remember any of that," Henry said.

He tried sitting up again, taking his time, moving slowly and deliberately so as not to jar his pounding head. Alan assisted him, placing pillows behind his back.

Henry reached gingerly to touch the back of his skull, and while the bump wasn't as big as a frigate, it was certainly large, and painful to the touch. He felt something greasy in his hair and wrinkled his nose.

"What is that smell?"

"Tea tree oil," Simon explained. "Prevents infection."

"What time is it?" Henry asked. "Where are we? How bad is the damage to the house?"

"He is definitely back to normal," Alan stated, grinning.

"The time is about six of the clock in the morning," Simon replied. "The house landed in an open field, and just missed crashing into the forest. We have been waiting for first light to assess the damage."

"You realize we can't stay here," said Henry.

"*Some* of us realize that," said Alan. He cast a grim look at Simon. "Some of us don't. You must see reason, Simon. Once your enemies look into the sky and notice Welkinstead is gone, they will begin the search for you."

"Nonsense. They won't bother. They will think the house sank into the Breath," Simon returned.

Alan tried again. "Anyone flying overhead—"

"—will look down and see the roof of a house," Simon said. "Nothing unusual in that."

"A house in the middle of a goddamn hay field with no goddamn road for miles," said Randolph.

"What will you do for food? Heat?" Henry asked. "The water tank may have been damaged. We should go back to Haever."

"I remind you that you and I are both wanted men," Simon said mildly. "Smythe's soldiers will be searching for us in Haever, and if we are in Haever, they will be much more likely to find us there than out here in the middle of a hay field."

"But in order to stop Smythe we need to be in Haever," Henry insisted. "I own a house in a secret location in the city that will suit our needs. I have everything we need to survive while we are in hiding: new identities, clothes, documents, money . . ."

Henry winced and put his hand to his head as though he would hold the pieces of his skull together. He had to struggle to think clearly.

"Unfortunately, you cannot hide the fact that I am in a wheelchair and Smythe will be looking for a man in a wheelchair," Simon stated. "I will put you in danger."

"You are not the only man in Haever in a wheeled chair, Simon," said Alan. "Henry's plan is a good one."

"I am not saying it isn't. I was merely pointing out possible problems in order that we do not go unprepared." Simon wheeled his chair around and headed for his office. "Give me some time to gather up the work I am doing on current projects."

"Randolph, you stay and help Simon," said Henry. "Alan and I will go into the city to make arrangements."

Alan protested. "You can't go, Henry! We will have to walk miles and you are in no fit state! You stay with Simon and let Randolph and me go. Just tell us where to find the house."

"I *have* to go," said Henry. "Mr. Sloan placed warding spells on the storage chests in the attic. He and I are the only ones who can safely release them."

"Ha!" Randolph snorted. "The real reason you're leaving is that you don't want to stay to help Simon sort through mounds of paperwork."

"Damn right," said Henry.

Welkinstead had landed about fifteen miles from Haever, which meant at least a three-hour walk for men in prime condition. Henry had only walked about three miles through forest and tromped over fields through the stubble left by harvest wheat, when he realized he could go no further. He could scarcely see for the pounding in his head.

Alan regarded him with concern. "You're not going to make it all the way to Haever."

"I know. I suggest we find the owner of this wheat field and ask to borrow a wagon."

The field ended in what passed for a road: two wheel ruts in the ground. The road led them to a prosperous-looking farmhouse with a barn, stable, and outbuildings in back. Chickens and ducks roamed about the yard and several goats came to the front of their pen to stare at the men as they walked past. Alan knocked on the door, which was answered by a brisk, plump older woman.

She was understandably startled to find two disheveled and battered—albeit well-dressed—gentlemen standing on her stoop.

Henry had done his best to scrub most of the blood from his face and hair. His greatcoat concealed his bloodstained shirt and he wore one of Simon's wide-brimmed hats to cover his wound. But neither he nor Alan could hide the bruises and cuts on their faces or hands.

"I am sorry to disturb you, ma'am," said Alan. "My friend and I have been involved in an accident. The wyvern pulling our carriage went berserk and dumped us out. We were walking back to Haever when my friend fell ill. We were hoping that we could rest a little, perhaps beg a sip of water. . . ."

"Walk to Haever!" The woman was dismayed. "You poor gentlemen will do no such mad thing. My good man and our boy are out with the wagon, but they'll be back before long and Nate will drive you to the city. Come inside, sit down, and I will put on the tea kettle."

She bustled about the neat kitchen, pouring the tea and serving them raisin cake and cheese that had come from the very goats who had taken such an interest in them.

"Lord, no, we don't hardly see any visitors out here," the woman said in answer to Alan's question. "Our nearest neighbor is eight miles to the north. Weeks go by without me seeing a soul other than my good man and my boy."

Alan and Henry exchanged relieved glances. No one was likely to stumble upon Welkinstead and wonder what a house was doing in the middle of a wheat field. And since the wheat was harvested, the farmer wasn't likely to be going back there for a time. If he did find the house, it would be empty.

The woman insisted on cleaning Henry's wound and treating it with a salve of her own making. She mixed a few drops of a potion into his tea.

"Relieves the pain and that sick feeling in your gut. My mother was a healer and she taught me the art."

The woman bound his head with bandages while Henry drank the tea.

By the time he had finished, the woman's husband and son had returned.

The young man was sixteen and more than happy to have a chance to drive into the city. He ran to wash up after his chores and put on a clean shirt in honor of the occasion.

The husband was interested in hearing details about the accident. He wanted to know what had happened, where the accident had occurred, was the wyvern injured, should they tend to the beast, and so forth.

"The wyvern flew off," said Alan. "The carriage is a total loss. Nothing much left of it, I'm afraid. As to where we came down, I cannot tell you. I am not familiar with this part of the country. That direction, I think."

He pointed to a location in the opposite direction of Welkinstead. Henry let Alan do the talking while he concentrated on remaining conscious and he was thankful when he saw the wagon roll down the lane.

Alan sat up front with the driver. Henry lay down in the wagon bed, which was cushioned with straw. Alan had cautioned him not to fall asleep, for fear he might never wake up. Henry was groggy, the noon sun was warm, the potion made him pleasantly drowsy, and he found it hard to obey that injunction. Alan was continually forced to reach back to seize him by the shoulder and shake him awake.

As they were nearing the outskirts of the city, they could see people milling about the streets in confusion and turmoil.

"Henry, wake up," said Alan. "You need to see this."

A man mounted on horseback galloped up to them. He was in a high state of excitement and he waved for them to stop.

"Have you heard the news, gents? The queen is dead! There's going to be war!"

He galloped off down the road to spread the news.

The young man driving their wagon was aghast.

"The queen dead!" He turned to look at Alan. "Do you think it's true, sirs? Are we going to war?"

"Let us off here, son," said Alan. "You should go back home. We will find a cab."

He took several silver coins and held them out to the young man, who shook his head.

"Ma wouldn't like that I took money for helping folks in need. Good luck to you, sirs!"

He turned the wagon around and drove off before Alan could insist.

"I'll hail a cab," said Henry. "You find a newspaper."

The news boy was not difficult to find. People had crowded around him, snatching up copies of the *Haever Gazette* as fast as he could take their money.

Some were openly sobbing. Others were angry, shouting, "Death to the Rosians!" Children were playing at war, picking up sticks to use as rifles to shoot the "Rosies."

Henry managed to snag a cab. The driver looked askance at their unsavory appearance and demanded his money up front. Alan paid him and Henry gave him an address near the docks, close to the Naval Yard.

The driver shouted at people to get out of his way and the cab drove off.

Alan opened the newspaper. The front page was bordered in black and featured an illustration of the queen and another of Thomas Stanford.

Henry tried to read, but the pain made him see double. "Read it aloud," he told Alan.

Alan read the official statement from the palace. That statement did not go into detail, but announced the death of the queen and said that before her death she had named Thomas Stanford her heir.

"'The Accession Council will meet as soon as is possible to assemble the members to make it official,'" said Alan. "Listen to this, Henry. The paper is quoting a spokesman, Colonel Jonathan Smythe. He reports hearing a horrific explosion that shook the walls and he notes the excellent work of the palace guards who took control of the terrifying situation."

"Palace guards, my ass!" said Henry angrily. "Smythe's soldiers."

"According to Smythe, the heir apparent, Thomas Stanford, took command of the situation. 'The prince appeared in public, wearing the ring of King James, that had been given to him by the queen only hours before she died.'"

Alan looked up. "I'm sorry, Henry. Do you want me to go on?"

"Yes," said Henry. "I need to know."

"'Colonel Smythe is quoted as saying that the queen was killed by a bomb placed in her office by a Rosian assassin. "We consider this an act of war," Smythe stated to journalists.'

"Well at least something good has come out of tragedy. War with Rosia!" Alan said exultantly, flinging aside the paper. "About damn time!"

"Are you mad, Alan?" Henry said in scathing tones. "We cannot go to war against Rosia! Our country is bankrupt, the fleet is in wretched shape. I doubt we can afford to buy gunpowder. Rosia will crush us."

Alan flushed in anger. "I make allowances for the fact that you are grieving and that your head hurts. But you are not thinking clearly, Henry, or you would have never made such an outrageous claim. The Freyan Royal Navy is the finest in the world. The Rosians are no match for us."

"I am sorry, Alan," said Henry wearily. "I did not mean to disparage you or the navy. But you and I both know the Rosians had nothing to do with the queen's death. Smythe killed her and now he is stoking the fires of a trumped-up war to rally the Freyan people to the side of their new young king."

The carriage wheel struck a rock, causing the pain to seem to shoot from one side of Henry's head to the other. He groaned and put his head in his hands.

"How do you feel?" Alan asked.

"Rotten," Henry replied.

They rode in silence, then Henry sighed and raised his head.

"So what is your plan?" Alan asked.

"I've been thinking about that," said Henry. "Did you or Randolph tell anyone at the Naval Club that you were going to Simon's house last night?"

Alan thought back. "I don't think we did. Albright sent Simon's note in to us by the waiter while we were in the middle of dinner. The note said it was urgent, so we grabbed our coats and hats and left. Albright was waiting for us in the Visitor's Room."

"Good," said Henry. "Then no one knows you two were in the house when it was attacked."

"I don't see how this helps," said Alan.

"Simon and I are both wanted men, but you and Randolph are not. You two can return to your rooms in the Naval Club with some story of being away on a hunting trip. You and Randolph have access to the Naval Yard, your ships, your fellow officers, the Admiralty. You can use your positions to uncover information, discover Smythe's plans."

"People know Randolph and I are your friends," Alan pointed out.

"Denounce me as a traitor," said Henry. "You heard me make disparaging remarks about the Royal Navy going down to defeat."

"I know you didn't mean that," said Alan.

Henry sighed. "Unfortunately, I did mean it, Alan. The *Terrapin* is the finest ship in any navy in the world with the finest captain at her helm. But how will she fare against the Dragon Brigade, my friend? Her steel-plated hulls were designed to withstand magical attacks, not a prolonged assault by dragon fire. As for the rest of the fleet, they will go up like so much kindling."

Alan flung himself back in the seat, angrily folded his arms across his chest, and glared in brooding silence out the window.

"But I could be wrong," said Henry with a faint smile.

"You are," said Alan. "I accept your apology."

The two shook hands.

"Don't return to the Naval Club until I have time to find out for certain that no warrants have been issued for you and Randolph," said Henry. "I would not want the two of you to walk into a trap."

"We can stay on board our ships," said Alan.

Looking out the window, Henry saw the Naval Yard and realized they were nearing his destination. He ordered the driver to stop. Alan gave the man something extra for his trouble and they left the cab. They drew their hats low over their faces and made their way through the crowds of sailors and dockworkers on the street. Anticipating war, many were already drunk. The talk was ugly, as was the mood.

A man who smelled of rum seized hold of Henry's arm.

"Here, now! You two aren't bloody Rosians, are you?" he demanded. "If you are, we're going to make you regret it."

Several of his mates gathered around them, fists clenched.

"Certainly not," said Henry. "Death to the Rosies."

Alan fished several coins out of his pocket. "To prove our loyalty, I give you good Freyan coin and invite you and your friends to drink to the health of our new king. God bless him."

Their Freyan accents and the sight of the money satisfied the men, who took the coins, touched their hats, and ran off to stop more people and demand to know if they were Rosians.

"There will be murder done before this day is out," Henry predicted.

He and Alan turned into a deserted street lined with shops and businesses whose windows were shuttered and boarded up. Henry went to a shop located at the end of the block. A shabby gilt sign hanging over the door proclaimed it to be Tom's Coffee and Tea shop.

Henry did not enter the shop, but walked down an alley to the back. He came to a small house that butted up against the tea shop. The house was obviously abandoned. The yard had been appropriated by the neighbors as a garbage dump, for it was filled with refuse: broken flower pots, discarded lumber, and a pile of bricks.

Henry looked over the pile of bricks and selected one that had a chip on the corner. He upended it and touched a hidden spring on the bottom. A small drawer shot out. Henry removed a key from the brick, released the spring, and the drawer slid back inside. Henry carefully placed the brick back onto the scrap heap.

He did not immediately enter the house, but first knelt down to make certain that the sliver of wood he had stuck beneath the door was still in place. He located it and stood up.

"No one has been inside," he reported.

"The chap, Tom, who owns the coffee shop," said Alan. "Do you know him? More to the point, does he know you?"

"Tom is one of my agents," said Henry. "Extremely trustworthy, especially as I am his landlord and I charge him no rent."

Henry put the key to the lock, opened the door, and entered the small house. Alan followed, looking about curiously as Henry shut the door behind them.

The house consisted of two floors that both smelled strongly of coffee. The first floor was sparsely furnished, containing a metal-framed bed and mattress, a couple of wooden chairs, an empty wardrobe, a nightstand, and an iron stove to provide heat. A single window covered in grime let in dismal light. The house was bitterly cold with the settled chill that comes from years of being uninhabited.

"What do you think?" asked Henry.

"I think this is the dirtiest, ugliest, most disreputable excuse for a dwelling that it has ever been my misfortune to visit," Alan stated.

Henry chuckled. "The very reasons I bought it."

The two climbed the rickety-looking staircase that led to the floor above. The only articles of furniture were another bed, a slop bucket, a lantern, and a ladder lying on the floor. This room had two grimy windows, however, one facing out on the alley and the other overlooking the backyard.

Henry started to pick up the ladder, then winced in pain. Alan took over. Acting under Henry's direction, he lifted the ladder, carried it to the back of the room, and stood it against the wall.

"There's a trapdoor in the ceiling," said Henry.

"You are *not* climbing ladders," Alan said sternly.

"No choice," said Henry. "Everything we need is in a trunk in the crawl space. I have to remove the magical warding constructs."

"At least let me go first, then," said Alan. "I can give you a hand."

Henry allowed his friend to precede him. Reaching the top of the ladder, Alan warily eyed the panel in the ceiling.

"If I touch this, will one of Mr. Sloan's spells fry my eyeballs?"

"No," said Henry. "The panel itself is quite harmless. Just don't touch the trunk."

Alan shoved the panel aside and thrust his head and shoulders into the crawl space. He promptly sneezed.

"It's dark as the bottom of the world," he reported.

"Thus the lantern," said Henry, holding it up to him.

Alan pulled himself up into the crawl space and then reached down to assist his friend. Henry handed up the lantern. Alan set it on the floor, and then hauled Henry up after him.

The crawl space was aptly named, for they could not stand upright, but were forced to crawl about on their hands and knees. The trunk was quite ordinary looking, the sort used by seamen during long voyages. It was made of wood with a rounded top, banded with leather and secured by a leather strap with an ornate metal lock. Alan took care to keep as far from it as possible.

"I hope you remember how to disarm the magic," he said.

"Actually quite simple," said Henry.

He placed his left palm flat on the left side of the front of the chest, then put his right palm on the right side of the chest. Faint blue light began to glow on both sides. The lock in the middle of the chest remained dark.

He then drew back his hands and rested his palm flat, with fingers splayed, over the lock. Blue light flared. Fearing an explosion, Alan cringed, squeezed his eyes shut, and averted his face. The lock clicked, the blue light faded away, and Alan relaxed and opened his eyes.

Henry lifted the lid and Alan helped him unpack the contents, including a leather billfold filled with banknotes and a wide variety of clothing.

"Disguises," said Henry. "I put on this shabby coat, vest, shirt, worn trousers, and hat and I am a humble clerk. The black cassock, white dog collar, and broad-brimmed hat transform me into a deacon. The aging footman of an aristocratic household wears this blue velvet coat, matching breeches, and waistcoat. I have documents swearing to all these identities, as well as suitable footwear."

"Let me guess," said Alan. "The deacon goes with this worn copy of the Scriptures, wire-rimmed spectacles, and a cane. The clerk owns this battered pocket watch. The aging footman wears this powdered wig and takes snuff. And they all go armed," he added, removing several pocket pistols, powder, and ammunition. "Who you will be?"

"Pastor Tobias Johnstone," said Henry, shaking out the black cassock. "I must pay a visit to my brother, and his servant, Henshaw, would not admit the down-and-out clerk, Todd Wells, or Arthur Porter, aging footman."

"Is meeting with Richard wise?" Alan asked, concerned. "You have informants inside the palace. Contact them."

"I do not trust any of them," said Henry, adding bitterly, "They did not inform me that Prince Thomas was meeting with Her Majesty."

"The queen kept her secret well," Alan suggested.

Henry made no comment. The queen *had* kept her secret well. She had not told even him.

He was bent almost double in the confined space, his knees up around his chin. He sank back against the wall. Alan regarded him with concern.

"You don't look well. I'm going to fetch a healer."

"My head is actually much better," said Henry. "Whatever was in that potion appears to have helped."

"Then what is wrong?"

"Can't you guess?" Henry returned. "I failed her, Alan. Every time the queen tried to talk to me about Stanford, I railed against him. I sent my agents to spy on him. I made it clear to Her Majesty that I despised him. And because of my obdurate stubbornness, Queen Mary did not trust me to meet with him. She met with him in secret and then she died—alone. If I had been with her . . ."

Henry clenched his fist in anger at himself. "If I had been there, I might have saved her. . . ."

Alan gripped him by the arm. "Henry, stop or you will go mad! You have no idea what would have happened. The most likely outcome is that you would have died with Queen Mary and Smythe would succeed in destroying our country."

"Perhaps," said Henry, not believing him, but too tired to argue.

"Queen Mary trusted you, Henry. She trusted you to such an extent that she placed the welfare of our new king in your hands. She knew you would not abandon him."

Henry sighed deeply. "We have to haul all this stuff downstairs."

"I'll handle that," said Alan. "You stay here and rest."

Henry leaned back against the wall. He needed rest and a stronger potion. He could not meet his brother in this condition. Hidden beneath the mattress of the bed on the second floor, Mr. Sloan kept several healing potions, aware that Henry would make use of this place only if he was in trouble.

He wondered if there was one labeled: "Cracked Skull."

Alan began tossing clothing and shoes and documents out of the crawl space to the floor below.

"You go on ahead," said Henry. "I'll lock up the trunk."

Alan descended the ladder.

When he was alone, Henry took out the letter the queen had given him, naming Thomas Stanford her heir. He placed the letter in the empty trunk and closed the top for safekeeping. The magic flashed blue, indicating that Mr. Sloan's magical warding constructs were back in place.

Henry descended the ladder, feeling as though he had locked away a part of his life in that dark and empty crawl space.

ELEVEN

Alan found the bottles of potions carefully packed beneath the mattress. He did not find one marked "Cracked Skull," but he did find a bottle that Mr. Sloan had labeled in his neat, precise handwriting: *Concussion, brain fever. Mix with hot tea and sip slowly.*

Alan repaired to the coffee shop to obtain the tea, leaving Henry to change clothes. When Alan returned with a pot of tea, he gave a start on opening the door to find a stooped-shouldered pastor benignly peering at him from behind spectacles, his squinting eyes almost hidden in the shadow cast by a broad-brimmed hat.

"Good God, Henry, don't do that to me!" Alan exclaimed irritably. "I almost dropped the teapot."

Henry grinned, straightened to his full height, and removed the hat.

"You must recognize Pastor Johnstone, Alan. The two of you were childhood friends."

"We were?" Alan raised an eyebrow.

"You were. He was a curate at the time. Remember that in case you should ever run into him should he have news for you."

"Ah, yes, of course," said Alan, smiling. "Tell me about him."

"Tobias Johnstone is a gentle soul," said Henry, holding the spectacles up to the dim light to see if he needed to clean them. "He is very short-sighted and thus walks happily through this world blind to all its ugliness. For him, daily life passes in a pleasant blur."

Alan dumped the potion into the tea. Henry laid aside the spectacles and sat down to drink it, taking care to sip slowly as Mr. Sloan had instructed.

"I hope it tastes better than it smells," said Alan, wrinkling his nose.

"It doesn't," said Henry, grimacing.

Between the farm woman's potion and Mr. Sloan's, Henry was feeling much better. The pain was starting to subside and the dizziness and nausea had eased.

"What do you need me to do?" Alan asked.

"Hire a wagon and return to pick up our friends," said Henry. "You will also need to purchase a wheelchair for Simon. Make it a cheap one, very ordinary. The struggling clerk, Todd Wells, cannot afford anything better on his meager salary."

"Simon will kick up the devil of a row over having to leave his flying chair behind," Alan predicted.

"Let us face it, my friend, Simon will be in a foul mood until Welkinstead is once more 'drifting with panache' above our heads. At least *you* won't have to live with him," Henry added.

"You must focus his energies on something more pleasant than losing his beloved Welkinstead. I have an idea. Encourage his latest theory about freezing pools of liquid Breath in the Aligoes," said Alan. "Appear interested. Ask questions."

"Such as how in God's name could there possibly be freezing pools of liquid Breath in the Aligoes?"

"I'm sure he will have a scientific explanation," said Alan.

"One which will last hours and require a blackboard." Henry returned to his instructions. "Once I know about the warrants, you and Randolph repair to your rooms in the Naval Club. Talk to your fellow officers, find out what you can about Smythe. You should also make inquiries about Mr. Albright, who was apparently on his way to my house that was crawling with Smythe's soldiers. Ask at the prisons, the hospitals and—I hate to say it—the morgue."

"Where are we to meet you and when?"

"The Weigh Anchor. No one there knows Pastor Johnstone. He will be extremely glad to see an old childhood friend."

"How do I send a message to you should I have anything to report?" Alan asked.

"The post office on High Street. Address the letter to 'Franklin Sloan, to be left until called for.' I will be checking daily, for that is where Mr. Sloan is sending reports on my family."

Henry fell silent, his thoughts on his wife and son and baby daughter who were so very far away. He felt guilty for sending them off without him, even though Lady Ann understood that he had his duty to his country. She had her own duty, as well, for she had calmly accepted the fact that she must care for their family while he cared for their nation.

"I am certain they are safe and well, Henry," said Alan, seeing his friend's shadowed expression.

"Ann is the queen's niece," said Henry. "Smythe will do his best to eliminate all those who might oppose him."

"Your wife and children are under the protection of Mr. Sloan and the Countess de Marjolaine," said Alan. "They could not be in better hands."

"I know," said Henry. He shook off his despondence. He could not worry about situations over which he had no control. He had to deal with those he could. "And now I must leave you. Pastor Tobias Johnstone has to pay a call on Sir Richard Wallace."

"What will you say to your brother?" Alan asked, as Henry hooked the wire-rimmed spectacles over his ears.

Henry picked up one of the pocket pistols and stood regarding it thoughtfully.

"Despite Simon's claims that my brother was duped by Smythe, I believe Richard to be complicit in the death of the queen. I know for a fact that he was responsible for exposing Mr. Sloan and nearly getting him killed. My inclination is to put a bullet in his head."

"He is your brother, Henry," said Alan.

Henry frowned at the weapon, then sighed and slipped the small pistol into a secret pocket sewn into the cassock.

"I won't kill Richard, Alan," said Henry. "He *is* my brother and, much as he might deserve to die, I require information that only he can provide."

"But if you don't trust him . . ."

"The fault is mine. I think back to the conversations I had with him over mutton and cabbage in his club," said Henry. "I deliberately shared information with him, hoping he would use his influence in the House of Nobles to further my own causes. I never dreamed that Richard would be using me to further his own. I did not know my staid and boring elder brother even *had* a cause."

Henry shook his head. "If I had been paying attention to him instead of thinking only of myself, I might have picked up on clues he let drop, information he inadvertently revealed. Before the queen's death, Simon suggested that Richard might be involved with the Faithful. I laughed at the notion, as I recall. I smugly thought I knew him. I was blinded by my own cleverness, and my queen and my country have paid the price."

Alan rested his hand on Henry's. "You told me that Queen Mary was very ill. Her Majesty was dying of the same disease that killed her father. His death was dreadful. He was pleading with the healers to end his suffering. I know this is not much comfort, but at least Queen Mary died swiftly, Henry. She did not suffer."

Henry adjusted the spectacles, pushed them back on his nose, and said, "Richard will not lie to me again."

With that declaration, he put on the broad-brimmed hat, adjusted his dog collar, and picked up the cane and his Scriptures. He was now ready to greet the world as the humble preacher.

"You know how it is with older brothers, my friend," Henry said, smiling. "You shot yours."

"Thank God, I missed!" said Alan. "Good luck, Henry. Randolph and I will wait to hear from you. Be careful in the streets."

"So long as nobody takes me for a Rosian, I will be fine," said Henry.

The two shook hands, and Pastor Tobias Johnstone walked out the door, smiling and peering as he made his way out of the house and down the crowded street in search of a cab.

A driver took pity on the pastor, who appeared quite confused and upset by the tumult in the street, and gave him a ride, guiding the horse down the side streets, which were less clogged than the main thoroughfares.

Henry saw the mobs at work throughout the city. The cab passed a group of people hurling paving stones through the window of a shop owned by a Rosian as several men dragged the owner from his store and began beating him. A frantic woman pleaded with them to stop.

His brother, Richard, lived in a staid and boring house located in a well-to-do, staid and boring residential neighborhood on the north side of the city. Henry was glad to note as they drove farther away from the inner city that the mobs were concentrating their wrath there. The unrest and tumult had not yet reached his brother's neighborhood. But fear had.

The usually quiet neighborhood was bustling with unusual activity, as those fortunate enough to own homes in the country were hurrying to flee the chaos in the city.

Richard owned his own country house, but he rarely visited it. His life was in the city, in the royal court, in the House of Nobles. His wife spent much of her time at the country house, for she disliked the city. Richard would have made certain she was there now.

As Henry's cab approached the house, he noticed another cab parked a short distance down the block. The cab had no markings and, judging by the horse droppings, it had been there for some time. He could not see who was inside, for the windows were covered.

Yet Henry knew surveillance when he saw it. Open surveillance. Whoever was watching the target wanted his target to know he was being watched.

Henry paid the cab fare, then stood gazing at Richard's house. The curtains were drawn, the wrought-iron gate shut. The house appeared deserted at first, but then he noted smoke rising from the chimney. Leaning on his cane, he pushed open the gate and hobbled down the path to the front door. He made use of the brass door knocker and then waited.

No one came to the door.

Henry tried the door knocker again, louder and more emphatically.

A voice came from the other side of the door. "Who is there? What do you want?"

"Pastor Tobias Johnstone," said Henry in a quavering voice. "The new pastor of Gatestown Parish. I come with an urgent message for Sir Richard Wallace."

The door opened a crack. Richard's valet, secretary, butler, and servant, Henshaw, peered out.

"What business do you have with Sir Richard?"

"Most distressing business, I fear, sir," said Henry, pushing his spectacles up on his nose. He fumbled at his cassock. "I regret I do not have a card. I am Tobias Johnstone, the new pastor of the Gatestown Parish. Sir Richard's estate is located in my parish—"

"I am aware of that, Pastor," said Henshaw, impatiently. "Come to the point."

"Yes, of course," said Henry, fumbling with his cane. "I fear it is my sad duty to inform His Lordship that his lady wife has been taken ill with a fever. The servants did not want to leave her alone in her condition and I offered to bring the message. Is Sir Richard at home?"

Henshaw listened gravely to this news, and opened the door.

"Come inside, Pastor. Sir Richard is at home, although he himself is poorly. I will let him know you are here. How is Lady Susan?"

"The physicians are with her and the servants tell me they are quite hopeful," said Henry, blinking and bumbling his way into the house. "I keep Her Ladyship in my prayers."

"I am glad to hear that," said Henshaw, as he shut and locked the door. "Allow me to take your hat—"

"Thank you," said Henry in his own voice.

Henshaw gasped and staggered backward a step, startled. He stared first at Henry and then at the pistol in his hand.

"Take me to Richard," said Henry, aiming the pistol at Henshaw's breast.

Henshaw swallowed, but he swiftly regained his composure. "As I said, His Lordship is poorly. He is resting and cannot be disturbed."

Henry frowned. "Which will my brother find more disturbing, Henshaw? Speaking to me or seeing your blood spattered across the wall?"

Henshaw regarded him with loathing. "His Lordship is in his study, sir. I will take you to him."

He led the way through the silent house with noiseless tread. Henry followed, keeping the pistol aimed at Henshaw's back.

"A visitor, my lord," Henshaw said, opening the door.

Richard was asleep in an overstuffed chair. He looked very gray and haggard. One arm was done up in a sling. He woke at the sound of Henshaw's voice.

"I told you, I am not seeing anyone," Richard said testily.

Henry shoved Henshaw aside and strode through the door, slamming it against the wall. "By God, you will see me, Richard!"

Henshaw made a swift movement, reaching for something in his pocket. Henry lashed out with his cane, striking Henshaw on the wrist.

Henshaw cried out in pain and clutched at his wounded wrist.

"Remove the pistol, Henshaw," said Henry, keeping his eyes on his brother. "Slowly. You would not want my pistol to go off accidentally. Good. Now place your weapon on the floor and then go stand by your perfidious master, where I can keep an eye on both of you."

"I am sorry, Sir Richard," said Henshaw, crossing the room to stand protectively at his master's side. "Your brother caught me unawares."

Richard saw the pistol and heard the anger, and looked into Henry's eyes. He faintly smiled. "As it happens, I have been expecting you, Henry. I am glad you have come. I need to speak to you—assuming you don't kill me first."

Henry was discomfited. Richard had always been fastidious about his appearance, as became a successful businessman and member of the House. He did not emerge from his bedchamber in the morning until he was shaved and his sparse hair neatly brushed, fully dressed in snow-white cravat and snuff-colored jacket with every button buttoned down to the last button on his vest.

Today, he was unshaven. His graying hair straggled about his face. He was still in his nightclothes and dressing gown, his bare feet thrust into slippers. His eyes were red and rheumy. He was only in his fifties, but he seemed suddenly ancient. Yet he regarded Henry quite calmly, facing death with the Wallace family courage.

"God knows I should kill you," said Henry gruffly. He lowered his pistol and reached down to pick up the pistol Henshaw had relinquished. "God knows you deserve killing. I was the one who found Her Majesty's body. She lay in a pool of her own blood. Would you like me to further elaborate? Describe the gruesome scene?"

Richard raised his hand to his face as though to deflect the terrible words.

"Stop tormenting him, my lord!" Henshaw said, his face flushed in anger. "Your brother is not well."

"He is no brother of mine," said Henry. He paused, then asked, "What is wrong with him?"

Henshaw cast a questioning glance at Richard, who nodded and waved his hand in acquiescence.

Henshaw faced Henry. "His Lordship is suffering from a bullet wound in his shoulder."

Henry was astonished. "Who the devil shot him?"

"Jonathan Smythe, my lord," Henshaw replied.

"Ah, the old adage. Thieves fall out. Smythe is not his true name, by the way," Henry added. "His real name is Crawford. Isaiah Crawford."

Richard looked at him in bewilderment. Henry, watching closely, realized his surprise was not feigned.

"But why would Colonel Smythe lie about his name?" Richard asked. "I don't understand."

Henry drew a chair near to that of his brother's.

"I will brew some tea," said Henshaw, starting to sidle out of the room.

"Stay where I can see you, Henshaw," Henry ordered. "I don't want you rushing out to summon a constable. Your master needs something stronger than tea. Make yourself useful and pour him a brandy. He is going to need it."

Henshaw walked noiselessly across the room to the sidebar. He poured the brandy and carried a snifter to his master. Richard drank a little and some color returned to his haggard face. Henshaw took his place behind his chair.

"Colonel Jonathan Smythe is in reality a retired marine named Isaiah Crawford," said Henry. "He is responsible for the murders of at least four people, including the queen, the noble dragon Lady Odila, and another dragon named Coreg, a criminal mastermind who was in league with Smythe. He attempted to murder Mr. Sloan; after you recognized him and informed on him, the colonel shot him."

"Oh, God! No!" Richard sank back with a groan. "I am sorry, Henry. When I recognized Mr. Sloan, I thought you were plotting to harm Prince Thomas and I warned Smythe. I had no idea he would try to kill him. Is he all right?"

"Mr. Sloan is recovering or I *would* have shot you. But never mind about that now. What did you know about the assassination of the queen?" Henry demanded. "Were you and Thomas Stanford aware of the plot? Answer truthfully, Richard, for I will know if you are lying."

"I did *not* know, Henry, and neither did Prince Thomas," Richard said earnestly. "I swear to you on the lives of my wife and children. Smythe assured me that Her Majesty would be confined to a cell in Offdom Tower on the palace grounds until I and other members of the Faithful could speak to her, convince her that it would be in her best interest to renounce the throne in favor of Thomas."

Richard sighed. "As it happened, our plot was unnecessary. Queen Mary came to meet the prince in the Rose Room the night of her death. She gave His Highness the ring of King James and named him her heir. I was present. I was a witness. I was pleased, though confused. I did not know why she chose to name her heir at that particular time. . . ."

Henry regarded his brother grimly. "The queen was dying. She had months, perhaps only weeks to live. She did not know how much time she had left. If you only would have waited, there was no need to kill her."

Richard flinched and sloshed brandy onto his dressing gown. Henshaw gently removed the snifter. Richard did not even seem to notice it was gone.

"I was going to inform the Faithful and that would have put an end to the plot. Again I swear to you, Henry, by all I hold dear, we had no knowledge Smythe intended to assassinate her. We would have been content to know that Her Majesty had named an heir. I need you to believe me. If not, you may as well kill me here and now."

"As it happens, I do believe you," said Henry. "Or rather, I believe Simon. Tell me what is going on in the palace. I can only assume Smythe has seized power."

Richard shook his head; his lips tightened. "The man is the Evil One incarnate! He has made Thomas a prisoner in his own palace. Smythe intends to be the true ruler of Freya. He must be stopped, Henry!"

"Is this Stanford so weak that he allows Smythe to pull his puppet strings?" Henry asked, his lip curling. "Why didn't he refuse him? Renounce the throne?"

"You do not know Thomas Stanford or you would not accuse him of being weak!" Richard stated, his cheeks flushed. "Smythe is forcing Thomas to do his will. He has imprisoned his dearest friend, Phillip Masterson, in Offdom Tower and threatens his torture and death. He has taken Thomas's parents hostage and threatens them, also.

"Even then, I think Thomas would have defied him for the sake of the country," Richard added proudly. "I advised him to appear to go along with Smythe. Or rather, *you* advised him."

"I did?" Henry demanded, taken aback.

Richard faintly smiled. "When His Majesty and I had a moment alone together, I told him I would give him the advice you would give him. 'My brother would tell you to dance at the end of the puppet master's strings until the day comes when you wrap those strings around his neck and strangle him.'"

Henry regarded his brother a moment in silence. "And here I always thought you never knew me, Richard. What will young Stanford do?"

"I believe he will take my advice," said Richard. "Rather, *your* advice. You must save Thomas and our country, Henry. I told His Highness you were the one person who could help him."

"Smythe sent his soldiers to my house. My wife and children were forced to flee in the night and his troops are searching for me as we speak," said Henry bitterly. "I will be lucky to save myself, Richard, much less an embattled king. How do you propose I rescue a man who is imprisoned in his own palace?"

"You will find a way. You loved our queen, Henry," Richard said. "She met with Thomas. As I said, I was present for the interview. The two became immediate friends. She gave him the ring of King James and told him she believed in him. Help Thomas for Her Majesty's sake."

Henry thought back to his last conversation with Her Majesty, the final words Queen Mary had ever spoken to him.

You have served us well and faithfully for many years, dear friend. We could not have asked for a more loyal and devoted servant. I ask you as a friend . . . Be the same devoted servant to your new monarch.

"Why did Smythe shoot you?" Henry asked abruptly.

"I spoke out against him. I tried to stop him." Richard spoke with quiet dignity. "I may have been a great fool, Henry, but I am not a coward."

Richard's eyes now glinted with the fierce Wallace spirit. He sat up straighter and impatiently threw off the blanket.

He risked everything to place Thomas on the throne, Henry reflected. Wealth, title, his very life.

Henry relented. "I will do what I can, but I will need your help, Richard. What is more important, Thomas Stanford needs your help. He needs someone he can trust by his side, not languishing about in a rocking chair. When you are well, you should return to the palace—"

"You cannot be serious, my lord!" Henshaw protested. "Sir Richard dare not go back! That man, Smythe, tried to kill him! He missed the first time, but he will not miss again."

"On the contrary, Smythe is a crack shot. If he had wanted to kill Richard, he would already be dead," said Henry coolly. "The bullet was a warning, intimidation. Richard is a leading force in Parliament and Smythe needs the backing of the members. He will be conciliatory toward you. You counseled His Highness to act a part. You must do the same. Fool Smythe, as you fooled me."

"I am sorry," said Richard. "I had no choice—"

Henry waved off the apology. "You must be obsequious, fawn and cringe in Smythe's presence. Do nothing overtly to cross him. Promise to accomplish whatever he asks of the House, but make certain his measures get bogged down in committee," said Henry dryly.

"I was already planning to do so, Henry," Richard said. "I suppose one could say that devious minds think alike."

He started to rise from the chair, but fell back with a gasp of pain, clasping his shoulder.

"I said 'when you are well,'" said Henry, smiling.

"You should leave now, my lord," Henshaw stated coldly.

Henry ignored him. He had more questions to ask, information he would need if he and Richard were going to try to help his new young monarch. Then he remembered that Smythe had planted spies outside the house and they would start to grow suspicious if Pastor Johnstone overstayed his welcome.

Henry rose to his feet. Walking over to his brother, he placed his hand on his shoulder. "Take care of yourself, Richard. I will provide Henshaw with information on where you can reach me."

"Be careful, Henry," said Richard. "God save our king."

"God save us all," said Henry.

As Henshaw escorted him to the door, he asked, "What do the physicians say?"

"His Lordship refused to allow me to call a physician or a healer," said Henshaw. "He fears they will talk."

"He is probably right," said Henry. "I will send a man I trust to treat him. His name is Wilkins. He has removed a bullet or two from me in my time. He knows how to keep his mouth shut."

"Thank you, my lord," said Henshaw.

He was still cold, still obviously disapproving. He fetched Henry's hat and cloak and cane. Henry paused in the entry hall to loop the wire-rimmed spectacles over his ears.

"I did not tell my brother, Henshaw, but you should know that the house is under surveillance. Smythe is having Richard watched."

Henshaw was shocked. "Sir Richard is a member of the House of Nobles! Smythe would not dare—"

"Smythe dared murder a queen," said Henry grimly. "Do you trust the household staff?"

"We keep only a cook and a housemaid at present, my lord. I can vouch for their loyalty. The remainder of the staff are with Lady Wallace in the country."

"Do not admit any stranger into the house. If anyone asks, tell them that Sir Richard is suffering from a heart condition. He is confined to the house, and may not receive visitors."

"Yes, my lord," said Henshaw. He handed Henry his broad-brimmed hat.

"Take care of my brother," said Henry.

"I will do so, my lord," Henshaw replied.

He opened the door and stood waiting impatiently for Henry to leave.

Henry picked up a card, scribbled down a name and address, and handed it to Henshaw. "If you need to reach me, you can find me at the Weigh Anchor." He put on his hat and departed.

Pastor Johnstone went tottering down the street, clutching his Scriptures and smiling beneficently on all he met.

Henshaw stood in the doorway, holding the card in his hand. After a moment's silent deliberation, he tucked the card in his pocket, shut the door, and returned to his master.

He found Richard sitting up in his chair. "I believe I will get dressed, Henshaw. Lay out my clothes."

"My lord, it is much too soon for you to be up and about!" Henshaw said worriedly. "I will fetch some warm milk."

"You will do no such thing!" said Richard. "I am not a child in need of a nursemaid. Bring me another brandy."

Henshaw poured the brandy and placed it at Richard's hand. "I was about to tell you, my lord, before the arrival of your brother, that we are running low on the '87 tawny port. I was planning to step around to the wine merchant's."

"We can't have that," said Richard, smiling. "Yes, go along, Henshaw. When you are back, you can help me dress. Hand me the book I was reading and place the brandy bottle near me."

"Yes, my lord," said Henshaw.

He put the brandy bottle within reach and gave Richard the book. He started to withdraw, then paused and turned to address his employer.

"My lord . . ."

"Yes, what is it, Henshaw?"

"I hope you know, my lord, that your welfare is my paramount concern." Henshaw spoke with some emotion.

"You have been with me a great many years, Henshaw. You and I have been through a lot together and you have always been most loyal," said

Richard. "I rely on you implicitly. What is this about? Are you angling for a raise in your salary?"

"No, my lord," said Henshaw, dutifully smiling at the jest. "I should not be away long."

Richard gave an absent nod and returned to his book and his brandy.

Henshaw put on his hat and coat and departed. Mindful of those watching the house, he left by the servants' entrance.

His path took him nowhere near the wine merchant's.

TWELVE

Amelia Nettleship, journalist for one of the leading newspapers in the world, the *Haever Gazette,* sat at the kitchen table, drinking tea, eating toasted cheese, and jotting down notes regarding the momentous events of the previous night, while they were still clear in her mind.

The hour was noon and she had only just awakened. She was accustomed to rising at dawn and would have generally considered such laziness a mortal sin, but she had been awake all night, pursuing what she believed to be the true story regarding the assassination of the queen.

The people of Haever had been told by officials from the palace that Her Majesty had been killed by a bomb planted by a Rosian assassin. Amelia knew that wasn't true. She had been in the carriage with Sir Henry when Kate had warned them that a black ship armed with a green-beam weapon was planning to attack the palace.

Henry had sent Amelia to alert Captain Northrop and Admiral Baker to the danger, hoping they might somehow be able to act to stop it. He had told her they might be dining with Simon at Welkinstead. If not, try the Naval Club.

Amelia had decided to start at Welkinstead, which meant she had to find a wyvern-drawn cab to take her to the floating house. Cabs being difficult to find at that hour of the night, she had been searching when she had heard a frightful explosion, and she realized that she was too late, the assassins had struck.

She had, of course, attempted to enter the palace grounds, but the soldiers— mindful of Henry's warning about assassins and not knowing what was going on—had threatened her at gunpoint and she had been forced to retreat.

She had eventually found a wyvern-drawn cab to take her to the floating house. As they drew near, she saw green flaring light and the fiery traces of rocket fire and realized that, once again, she was too late.

Amelia had promised to pay the driver any amount he named to take her to the house so that she could cover the attack firsthand. The driver had flatly refused and had basely fled.

"Coward!" Amelia muttered, still angry.

She had then ordered him to take her to the offices of the *Haever Gazette*. She found the office in a state of inky confusion trying to rush a special edition to press. The printing machines clanged and clattered, and a crowd had gathered out front, impatiently waiting for the latest news.

Amelia told her editor the story of the black ship and a green-beam weapon.

"I was with Sir Henry Wallace at the time I received the report of this ship," Amelia had stated. "His Lordship can corroborate my account."

"First you have to find His Lordship," said the editor. "I've sent reporters to his house and to the foreign office, but both places are crawling with soldiers. Find him, interview him, and I'll give you the front page for your story."

Amelia had no idea where to even start searching. Henry Wallace was adept at disappearing, and she was extremely tired after the upset and the rushing about. She decided to return home to snatch a few hours' sleep and let her brain consider her problem while her body was in repose. She had wakened at noon with a fully formed plan of action.

She finished the toasted cheese and was about to set out to try once more to talk to Sir Henry's friends, Captain Northrop and Admiral Baker. If anyone knew where he was, they would. She was putting on her pork-pie hat when a horse-drawn hansom cab rolled to a stop in front of her house. The driver dismounted from the box and walked up to her door.

Amelia kept no servant although, as a spinster woman of independent means, she could have afforded one. She believed in the dictum stated by Mrs. Ridgeway of Mrs. Ridgeway's Academy for Young Ladies, "One is never served so well as by oneself," and thus, Amelia answered the door herself.

The disgruntled driver jerked his thumb in the direction of the cab.

"Two serving girls hired me to bring 'em to this address. I bring 'em and now they tell me they got no money to pay me. They say you'll foot the bill. Will you, lady? I give you fair warning that if you don't, I'm leavin' 'em and their dog in the street."

Amelia was accustomed to receiving strange visitors at all hours, especially servants, who were valuable informants on their masters. She looked with interest at the cab. The young women seemed certain of their welcome, for they were already climbing out. One of them waved to her.

"It's me, Miss Amelia!" Kate called.

"Wait here," Amelia told the driver and ran to get her reticule.

She paid the man and held the door for Kate and her companion, who hurried inside with their dog trotting along at their heels.

Amelia had seen Kate only last night when she had warned them about the black ship. But last night Kate had been dressed in her slops and now she and her mysterious companion were disguised as palace servants. Their black dresses and white aprons were rumpled, as though they had slept in them. Both young women looked weary, footsore, and hungry.

"Come inside, quickly!" Amelia said.

"Thank you, ma'am," said Kate gratefully. "We didn't know where else to turn."

"Yes, thank you," said the mysterious young woman with her. She lifted her head, shook back her hair, and smiled. Amelia knew her at once. Princess Sophia had lived in Haever following the war with the Bottom Dwellers to further peaceful relations between Freya and Rosia. Relations may not have improved as a result, but the princess and her little dog had won the hearts of the Freyan people.

The *Haever Gazette* had been the first to report Sophia's engagement to Thomas Stanford, who was now the ruler of Freya. The princess was beloved by the gossip columnists, and her illustration was in the paper nearly every week.

Artists had captured her likeness well, Amelia thought, although they had missed the winsome sweetness of her expression.

Amelia dropped a curtsy. "Welcome to my home, Your Highness."

"Miss Amelia, we have to tell you—" Kate began.

"—a great many things, I have no doubt," said Amelia. "But first things first. You know your way around the house, Kate. Escort Her Highness and the little dog upstairs to wash up. You will find some of your clothes still in the wardrobe. After you both have changed, come to the kitchen and I will fix you something to eat. I'll keep watch, make certain you were not followed."

"I don't think we were, Miss Amelia," said Kate. "The streets are filled with angry people. No one paid any attention to two maidservants."

"Pish-tosh!" Amelia snorted. "I recognized Her Highness the moment I clapped eyes on her. And you both are running from some sort of serious trouble, aren't you."

"I am afraid so," said Kate, sighing. "We were both in the palace last night. We know the truth about the queen's death, and there are those who know that we know and will do anything to keep us from telling it. We managed to escape, but Smythe's soldiers were on our heels."

Amelia was highly gratified. She had been about to leave her house in search of a story, only to have the story walk right into her house.

"I am eager to hear your tale. Now go change. You will find your bedchamber just as you left it, Kate."

"I fear our presence places you in danger, Miss Amelia," said Sophia.

"I would not miss being part of your story if I were to be hanged for it, Your Highness," said Amelia.

Sophia looked rather startled, but Kate only laughed and shook her head. Amelia shooed them both upstairs, telling Kate to draw the window curtains. Bandit went with them, although he smelled the cheese and kept casting wistful glances in the direction of the kitchen.

When they were out of sight, Amelia opened the front door and looked outside. The cab had driven off. Her neighbors were flitting from house to house, eager to discuss the queen's death and share the latest rumors. Amelia trusted they would not come to pay her a visit. Her neighbors considered her "eccentric," a reputation she fostered, for she did not like to be interrupted while she was writing.

Since no one appeared to be taking an unusual interest in her house, she went back inside, shut and locked the door, and drew the curtains. She went to the kitchen, brewed more tea, toasted more cheese, and cut cold roast beef and bread for sandwiches.

Kate and Sophia came downstairs to do justice to the food. Amelia set down a plate of roast beef for Bandit, forever earning his regard. She was eager to hear their story, but Mrs. Ridgeway had often expounded on the duties of a hostess, and Amelia insisted that they finish their meal and drink their tea before they related their adventures.

When they finally pushed back their plates, Amelia took her place at the table, armed with paper, pen, and a full inkwell. Bandit fell asleep under the table, his head resting on Sophia's foot.

"The last I saw of you, Kate, you and Sir Henry were in the carriage on your way to the palace to warn Thomas about the black ship. Tell me what happened after that."

Kate marshaled her thoughts, then began her story, as Amelia took notes.

"When we arrived at the palace, Sir Henry insisted that I come inside with him. I don't think he trusted me. The Countess de Marjolaine was there and she accosted us, saying she had heard the queen was going to be assassinated. She and Sir Henry left to go find Her Majesty. He told me to stay in the entry hall, but a . . . uh . . . friend of mine was in the palace and I was worried about him—"

"Name of this friend," said Amelia, continuing to write.

When Kate didn't immediately answer, Amelia paused in her writing to look up.

"His name?" Amelia prompted.

"Thomas Stanford," said Kate, blushing.

Amelia stared, amazed. "Do you mean our new ruler, His Highness, Prince Thomas Stanford?"

"She does," said Sophia, glancing at her friend with a smile.

"I did not know you and His Highness were acquainted," said Amelia, writing furiously. "You must tell me sometime how the two of you met. I will write a special Captain Kate story all about it. But, go on. You went searching for the prince . . ."

Kate related how she searched the palace for Thomas, only to encounter Smythe.

"I knew him the moment I saw him," said Kate, shivering at the memory. "He was the man who attacked me and stole the dragon-killing spell, then used that spell to kill Lady Odila."

"And he is the man who is now governing Freya," said Sophia gravely.

Amelia glanced up. "How is that?"

Kate continued before Sophia could answer. "I was trying to get away from Smythe. He recognized me, and sent his men after me. I was running down a hall when suddenly Sophia grabbed me and pulled me inside a room."

"Bandit and I had been dining with the queen," said Sophia, picking up the tale. "I was leaving her chambers when Bandit got away from me and ran to the one of the doors. He began scratching at it and barking. His Grace, Phillip Masterson, was locked inside the room."

Amelia saw Sophia's cheeks redden when she mentioned the duke's name.

She's engaged to Prince Thomas and she's in love with this duke while Kate is in love with the prince. A tangled love story, as well as danger and intrigue! Amelia thought exultantly. She had never been happier.

"I tried to find help," Sophia continued, "but I realized then that the palace guards were imposters. I locked myself in the Rose Room and cast an illusion spell over the door. I was keeping watch out the door when I saw Kate running down the hall and I grabbed her."

"As it turns out," said Kate, "Thomas and that man, Smythe, were in the room next door to where we were hiding."

Kate and Sophia took turns describing the conversation they had over-heard between Thomas and Smythe and a man known only to them as "Sir Richard."

"Smythe confessed to having Her Majesty killed," said Sophia, her voice trembling. "He will make Thomas king, but Smythe is going to be the true ruler."

They related how Smythe had taken Phillip hostage, then beaten and drugged him. They had heard a pistol shot and had been terribly frightened, for they didn't know who had been shot. And then Smythe sent his soldiers to search the palace for the princess.

"We were saved by one of the countess's agents who showed us a secret passage, and that's how we managed to escape the palace," said Sophia. She grew very pale. "He may have given his life to protect us. And so you see, Miss Amelia, this horrible man knows that Kate and I were in that room and that we know the truth about what he is plotting."

"I was thinking you could write the story for the newspaper, Miss Amelia," said Kate. "Reveal the truth about him. Tell the world he is a monster."

"But that would put Miss Amelia in danger," Sophia protested.

"I don't mind that," said Amelia briskly. "This will be the story of a life-time! Our king and our country are in the clutches of this dreadful Smythe."

Someone knocked on the front door. Bandit jumped up and barked. Sophia grabbed him and clamped her hand over his mouth.

"Bloody hell!" Kate swore.

"I think you may relax, my dears," said Amelia. "Smythe's soldiers would not bother to knock. They would simply batter down the door. You wait here. I will go see who it is. I will leave you this, just in case."

Opening the reticule, she took out a pocket pistol made to her own specific design, featuring two barrels that could be fired independent of each other. She handed it to Kate, then went to the entry hall and peeped out a window.

A clergyman stood on the door stoop, leaning on a cane and peering about nearsightedly from behind a pair of spectacles. Amelia assumed he was collecting money and was about to fetch her reticule, when she heard him give a strangled gasp, and saw him clutch at his throat. He leaned weakly against the porch railing, and seemed on the verge of collapse.

Amelia flung open the door and hurried outside. The clergyman was breathing heavily.

"Water . . ." he whispered.

"Please, come inside," said Amelia.

She assisted him to enter. Once through the door, he made a gurgling sound and dropped his book of Scriptures. His eyes rolled back in his head and he fell to the floor and lay unmoving.

"Merciful goodness," said Amelia.

She stared at him a moment, then knelt by his side to put her hand on his wrist, searching for his pulse. As she did so, he opened his eyes, looked up at her, and said softly, "I would be obliged, Miss Amelia, if you would shut the front door."

THIRTEEN

Henry stood up, grimacing as he straightened. Walking stooped-shouldered for hours took its toll on his spine. He removed his spectacles and his hat, smoothed back his hair, and effectively shed Pastor Johnstone as easily as he shed his cloak.

"You are indeed a man of many talents, Sir Henry," said Amelia, shutting the front door. "You had me fooled completely."

"I apologize for my unorthodox method of obtaining entry, Miss Amelia. I need to speak—"

Henry heard a muffled sound coming from the back of the house, as of a dog starting to bark and being quickly silenced.

Henry eyed Amelia. "You are not alone." He picked up his hat. "I will take my leave."

Amelia placed her hand on his arm to detain him. "I am not given to prayer, my lord, for I believe that God does as He pleases and is not to be cajoled, threatened, or bribed. Yet I would say that you come in answer to a prayer."

"Who are your guests?" Henry asked, frowning, still inclined to make his escape.

"Two young women who seek to stop the assassin Smythe from seizing power," Amelia stated. "They know the truth about what happened in the palace last night for they were there. They also have other vital information you need to hear."

Henry trusted Amelia only as much as he trusted anyone, always mindful that her primary goal was to obtain a story. He believed her to be a patriot, however, loyal to Freya. That said, he kept his hand near the hidden pocket where the pistol was tucked snug against his ribs and followed Amelia into the kitchen.

"Sir Henry Wallace," Amelia announced, throwing open the kitchen door and performing the introduction with the aplomb of a royal herald. "Sir Henry, I have the honor to present Her Highness, Princess Sophia of Rosia, and her companion, Captain Kate."

Kate and Sophia both started up from the table in astonishment. Henry was equally astonished at the sight of the two women. Kate was aiming a pistol at him and Sophia held onto a dog with its head wrapped in a dish towel.

Amelia rubbed her hands in satisfaction.

"A council of war," she stated. "I will put the kettle on."

Henry swiftly regained his usual poise. He bowed low to the princess, who received his homage with cold, polite disdain. He could hardly blame her, considering how assiduously he had worked over the years to destroy her country.

"If you could put away the pistol, Captain," he said.

"Sorry, my lord," Kate muttered, flushing. She released the hammer and laid the pistol back on the table.

Sophia freed Bandit from the dish towel and set the dog on the floor, where he went immediately to sniff Henry's shoes.

"Please, everyone, be seated," said Amelia, bustling about the kitchen. "May I offer you something to eat, my lord? I have cold roast beef and mustard."

"Thank you, no, Miss Amelia," said Henry.

He had stopped at his neighbor's coffee shop to bolt down some food he hadn't really tasted and which he could not have said now what it was. He had come to Amelia's in search of information. He had certainly not expected to find Princess Sophia or Captain Kate in her company.

The last he had seen of Kate was the night the queen had died. She had been in the palace, searching for Thomas. Henry was not surprised Kate had managed to escape the palace, for he was well aware of her courage, resourcefulness, and determination. He did wonder how she had ended up in company with a princess who was by all accounts safely on her way back to Rosia by now.

Sophia remained standing. She seemed of two minds—whether to remain in the same room with him or to withdraw from his odious presence.

Henry understood her dilemma. Sophia's dearest friend and mentor was the Countess de Marjolaine, Rosia's spymaster and Henry's implacable foe. There was a time not long past when each would have rejoiced to hear news of the death of the other. All that had changed in a single night.

"My queen's death has made allies of enemies, Your Highness," said Henry quietly. "The Countess de Marjolaine and I were together when we found Her Majesty's body."

Sophia sat back down and leaned forward eagerly.

"Tell me about the countess, my lord. I did not know she was in Haever."

"The countess discovered the plot to assassinate Queen Mary and came to warn her. Hearing you had dined with the queen, she was worried for your safety. She was reassured by the servants, who said that you had left the palace prior to the attack. The countess believed you were safely on the way back to Rosia. She herself was in danger, and she left Haever that night. She took my wife and children with her."

The three stared at him, incredulous.

Henry gave a faint smile. "Sometimes old enemies make the best friends. The countess and I understand each other. I owe Her Ladyship a debt I can never hope to repay."

He concealed his emotion by reaching down to scratch Bandit behind his ears. The dog licked his hand and curled up at his feet.

Amelia said briskly, "If that is the case, Your Highness, the countess will be deeply distressed to learn that you did not arrive in Rosia."

"You are right," said Sophia, dismayed. "I must find a way to send a message to her."

"Don't send a message," said Kate. "Return to Rosia where you will be safe. Sir Henry, you must know someone who could smuggle Sophia out of the country."

"No one I would trust with such valuable cargo," said Henry gravely. "The ports are under heavy guard. According to my friend, Captain Northrop, the ships' passengers are being questioned, their belongings searched. Her Highness is known by sight in Haever, and while I might disguise her, I could not disguise her companion. These floppy ears give him away."

Henry petted Bandit, who rolled over onto his back with his paws in the air to have his belly rubbed.

"Her Highness will be safe here," said Amelia with a smile for the two young women.

"I agree," said Henry. "In fact, I would say that Her Highness is safer in your company, Miss Amelia, than she would be anywhere else in Freya."

"But I must send word to the countess," said Sophia worriedly. "I need a trusted messenger."

She pondered a moment, then said, "I know! Rodrigo! Oh, dear!" she added in sudden concern. "He is Rosian! I hope he has not been arrested!"

"I do not think you need fear for Monsieur de Villeneuve, ma'am," Henry said. "If ever there was a man adept at taking care of himself, that man is Rodrigo de Villeneuve. If Your Highness would write a brief note to him so that he knows he may trust me in this matter, I will deliver it. He and I are acquainted. We met during the war under . . . um . . . difficult circumstances."

"You held a pistol to his head," said Sophia, smiling. "Rigo told me about it." She reached across the table to press Henry's hand. "Thank you, my lord. As you say, sometimes enemies do make the best friends. I will go write the letter."

"You will find pen and paper in my office upstairs," said Amelia.

"I'll come with you," Kate offered. She slid the pistol in her pocket. "Just a precaution."

Henry politely stood as the women left with Bandit pattering at Sophia's heels. Once they were gone, Henry turned to Amelia.

"I came to ask you if Smythe has issued warrants for Captain Northrop or Admiral Baker."

Amelia thought back. "Arrest warrants have been issued for you, Master Yates, and the princess. I believe your friends—being naval officers—are safe, particularly since we are about to go to war with Rosia."

"I had hoped as much," said Henry.

Sophia and Kate returned. Sophia handed Henry an envelope and gave him Rodrigo's address. "You may read the letter, my lord. See if you think it will suit."

Henry opened the letter.

> *My dearest aunt,*
> *Please assure my mama when you see her that I am well and safe*
> *and in the care of friends, one of whom delivers this message. My*
> *love to her and to you.*

The note was signed with a simple drawing of a forget-me-not.

Henry tucked the note into his pocket. "I will see that it is delivered today, Your Highness."

"I was wondering, my lord. Is there some way you could smuggle a letter to Thomas?" Kate asked. "Let him know he and Phillip are not alone. Tell him that his friends know the truth and we are going to try to help them."

Henry shook his head. "I am afraid not, Captain. Smythe will screen the king's mail, and he will certainly never let him meet with anyone by himself. You would put both yourself and His Highness at great risk."

Kate sighed deeply. "I suppose you are right."

Henry bowed to both young women and made ready to depart. Kate's suggestion left Henry thinking. He wondered if there might be some way to communicate with the king. He turned the matter over in his mind as Amelia escorted him to the door.

"You must have some idea how we can rid ourselves of this villain, Smythe, my lord," Amelia said. "Kate suggested I expose him by publishing the true story in the newspaper."

"That would be *most* unwise, Miss Amelia," said Henry, alarmed. "There is talk in the streets that the palace has issued an edict placing Freya under martial law, which means that they will be censoring the newspapers. Not only would the palace never permit such a story to be published; Smythe would have you arrested you for sedition—"

He stopped talking in midsentence.

"By God! You are a genius, Miss Amelia!" Henry stated. "Kate was right. We need to communicate with Thomas and I know how!"

He looped his spectacles over his ears and picked up his cane. Amelia handed him his broad-brimmed hat.

"What is your idea, my lord?"

"Romance fiction, Miss Amelia," said Henry. "I must work out the details with Simon. I will be in touch."

Amelia's voice was grave. "A moment, my lord. In the past you have termed Thomas Stanford 'the Pretender,' and questioned his legitimacy as the heir to King James. I would even venture to suggest you had thoughts about assassinating him. Now you are seemingly prepared to risk your own life to place this young man on the throne. Why the change?"

"Her Majesty left me a letter naming Thomas her heir," said Henry. "She asked me to be his friend, to be as loyal to him as I was to her."

"You are fully committed to him, my lord?" Amelia persisted.

"I am, Miss Amelia," said Henry. "I hope you believe me."

"I do, my lord."

The two shook hands. Henry put on his hat.

Pastor Johnstone opened the door and took his leave.

FOURTEEN

Phillip Masterson, Duke of Upper and Lower Milton, close friend to His Majesty the King, languished in a cell at the very top of Offdom Tower.

He had a vague memory of Smythe's guards carrying him to the tower, dumping him onto the floor of the cell, and departing, locking the door behind them. Phillip had finally managed to fight his way out of his drug-induced nightmare, only to find himself in a waking nightmare.

According to Queen Mary, Offdom Tower had been constructed on the palace grounds during the reign of Queen Esther of Travia to protect the royal family from attack by Rosian dragons. The walls were built of stone blocks strengthened by magical constructs intended to defend against dragon magic and their fiery breath. The builders had added a reservoir containing water at the top of the tower to be used to put out fires. Should dragons attack the palace, the royal family would flee into the tower through an underground passage.

"Crawling with rats," Mary had told him. "Personally, I would prefer taking my chances with the dragons."

Offdom Tower had never been needed to escape dragons, and it occurred to someone that it would make an excellent prison. They had added locks and magical constructs, and its first prisoner—King Frederick—had spent years here, eventually dying in this very cell.

Phillip thought a great deal about King Frederick. The king had been well treated while he was in the tower, and so was Phillip. He had been here a week and he had received three meals a day, accompanied by wine, tea, or coffee. The guards lit a fire in the small grate to ward off the chill. The room was furnished with a bed, two comfortable chairs, and a desk with pen, ink, and paper. The guards brought him books to read and the daily newspaper, albeit late. He was permitted a sponge bath. He was not, however, allowed to shave because, they told him, they did not trust him with a razor. One of the Guundaran orderlies came in every morning to act as barber.

Phillip took little comfort in these amenities, which were similar to those provided to King Frederick.

"Since I am clearly intended for the same fate," Phillip remarked somberly.

He had taken to talking to himself, just to hear a voice. He had tried to talk to the guards, if only to discuss the weather, but they were apparently under orders to not talk to him, for they maintained a silence as stony as the walls.

Phillip was forced to rely on the *Haever Gazette* for information. He had only this morning read the news that the queen had been killed by a bomb planted by the Rosians. Phillip knew the truth. He recollected bits of conversation between Thomas and Smythe, and he knew the colonel was the person responsible for the queen's death.

Phillip read another story claiming the Princess Sophia was involved, for she had dined with the queen the night she was murdered, and that a warrant had been issued for her arrest. He would have laughed aloud at the absurdity of the notion, if he had not been consumed with worry over Sophia's fate.

He thought bitterly that only last week this same *Gazette* had praised Princess Sophia for her charity work among the poor and talked about how all of Freya was eager for the upcoming nuptials between the princess and His Highness, Thomas Stanford. Now the paper featured a lurid illustration portraying Sophia, wrapped in a Rosian flag, with snakes for hair, holding sizzling bombs in her hands.

He read that arrest warrants had also been issued for Sir Henry Wallace and the Countess de Marjolaine, who had been seen fleeing the palace shortly after the explosion.

Phillip could not fathom how anyone could believe such lies. Henry Wallace was a dangerous man, but only to his enemies. The Countess de Marjolaine was a popular villain with the Freyan public, for she was reputed to be the Rosian spymaster. But Phillip knew her to be a staunch monarchist, loyal to her own king. She would have never sanctioned the assassination of an anointed ruler.

The *Gazette* assured the terrified public that the police were searching for these dastardly miscreants. A later edition stated that the countess was presumed to have fled back to Rosia and she had taken the princess with her. They had no news on Wallace, who had apparently gone into hiding.

"At least Sophia is safe," Phillip said, relieved.

The rest of the news was devoted to talk of imminent war, with stories of thousands of loyal Freyan men rushing to join the military, while Rosians were being rounded up and imprisoned.

Phillip threw the paper to the floor in disgust and lay down on his bed to worry about his own predicament. He was surprised to hear the key rattle in the lock and the guards removing the magical constructs.

He jumped to his feet, thinking Smythe had sent his henchmen to beat him or drug him again, or finish him off. Instead, though, when the door slowly creaked open, he was amazed to see it was Thomas who entered.

Phillip sighed in relief and went to greet his friend. The two shook hands and then embraced. Neither could speak for several moments. Neither knew where to begin.

"How are you feeling?" Thomas asked, studying Phillip's bruised and battered face.

"I am quite recovered," said Phillip, trying to give a reassuring smile, though he was shocked by his friend's physical appearance.

Thomas was pale and unshaven. His eyes were red, and the lids red-rimmed. His hair was unkempt, and his coat unbuttoned despite the chill. Phillip had not known Thomas when he had been trapped in the Estaran fortress, but he guessed he must have looked very much then as he did now—under siege, surrounded by the enemy, dropping from fatigue, but afraid to fall asleep.

Thomas cast a bleak glance around the tower room.

"I am so sorry, Pip."

"My incarceration is not your fault," said Phillip, trying to be cheerful. "I have only myself to blame. If I had been working for Sir Henry when I was captured, he would have chastised me most severely. I let down my guard, you see. Smythe's bully boys took me unaware."

Thomas's gaze lingered on Phillip's face, on the bruises that had changed from purple to gruesome shades of green and yellow, and on the cuts on his eyebrow and lip. He clenched his fist, not to strike, but as though to hold fast to his sanity.

"They say every man has his breaking point. I have reached mine," Thomas said. "I cannot decide whether to kill him or myself."

Phillip was alarmed. "My friend, don't say such things, even in jest! And keep your voice down. The guards can hear."

"Let his lackeys hear me!" Thomas said recklessly. "I don't give a damn. *He* knows."

"Smythe?" Phillip asked as he drew Thomas away from the door and led him to the far end of the chamber. Phillip brought over two chairs and placed them in front of the grate.

Thomas turned to face his friend, his eyes fevered and a hectic flush on his cheeks. "These past few nights, I have been visited by a dread specter. The thing leers at me and holds out a skeletal hand to offer poison, knives, pistols. A drop for his drink, a bullet for his head . . . Or is the poison, the bullet for me?"

Thomas shuddered, sank down in a chair, and lowered his head in his hands. Phillip drew up his chair beside him, not knowing what to say and thinking it might be better that he should allow his friend to talk.

Thomas raised his head. "If we were enemies on the field of battle and Smythe was aiming his rifle at me, I would kill him without hesitation. He has beaten and imprisoned you. He threatens to torture and kill my family. He is a threat to my people, who look to me to protect them. He assassinated a queen and makes a puppet of me and yet I shrink from killing him."

Thomas laughed bitterly and restlessly jumped to his feet. He began to pace back and forth, his booted feet ringing on the stone floor with each step.

"Perhaps I am what he calls me—a weak, cowardly fool."

Phillip let his friend walk for a few moments, to work off his frustration and anger. When Thomas's steps started to slow, Phillip said quietly, "Tell me you are not serious about taking your own life."

Thomas stopped and stared at the walls. He glanced at Phillip and faintly smiled. "No, thank God. There was a moment that first night after he had told me what he plotted. . . ."

Thomas paused, then shook his head. "But only a moment. I came to my senses. I will not kill myself, but as to killing him, I am not so certain. My soul would be damned to hell, but I would sell my soul if I thought I could rid the world of this monster. Have you ever wondered why God sanctions the taking of a life in battle, yet harshly condemns murder?"

Phillip did not like his friend's dangerous and desperate mood. "Leave that argument for theologians and philosophers, Thomas. You know you cannot find it in your heart to murder this man or any man, no matter how richly he deserves it. Stealing a life is shameful, ignoble, and despicable. Murder is an act of cowardice, not of bravery."

Thomas flung himself back into the chair, and gradually the hectic flush faded. He regarded Phillip with something of his old spirit and the faint ghost of a smile. "I have missed you, Pip! Just when I most need your advice and counsel, you manage to get yourself locked up in a tower."

Thomas saw the newspaper bordered in black lying on the floor. His expression grew somber, reflective.

"Queen Mary came to visit me the night she died. She asked me why I wanted to be king. Sir Richard had told me to flatter her, to charm her, and I could almost hear my mother's voice advising the same. But when Her Majesty looked at me, she looked at *me*, Pip. I knew she would see through the banalities and the platitudes. I told her the truth: that I didn't want to be king. But if God saw fit to place me on the throne, I would strive my utmost to do my duty to my people. My answer pleased her, and she gave me this ring."

Thomas pulled back the lace that covered his hand to reveal a ring made of gold with black diamonds and blue sapphires set in intricate patterns, like a mosaic.

"The ring of King James," said Phillip. "Queen Mary would not bestow that ring on you if she did not esteem you and trust you."

"I know," said Thomas softly. He covered the ring with his hand. "I liked her honesty and bluntness, Pip. I wish I could have come to know her. I think we would have been good friends. There was much she could have taught me."

"That paper is a week old," said Phillip, glad to change the depressing subject. "What has happened in the interim?"

"The Accession Council met and named me king," said Thomas carelessly. "Smythe managed the proceedings. Sir Richard Wallace rose from his sick bed, where he was recovering from a bullet wound inflicted by Smythe, to provide a signed testimonial swearing that he was present the night the queen made me her heir. The Royal Physician gave his testimony to the effect that the queen had only months left to live, and her lawyers testified that she had made her wishes known in a document, though it seems no one can find it."

Thomas laughed bitterly again. "You should have seen Smythe's face when he heard the news that she was dying. If he had known, he needn't have gone to all the trouble of killing her."

"What about her half brother, Hugh Fitzroy, and her sister, Elinor? Did they contest your ascension to the throne? Both have claims, though not as strong as yours."

"Which is why Smythe sent armed guards to keep them locked up in their own homes," said Thomas. "He produced forged documents at the Accession Council stating that both swore their fealty to me."

"The man is thorough, I'll give him credit for that," said Phillip. "He has thought of everything. So the council agreed? We can now refer to Your Highness as, 'His Majesty'?"

"The vote was unanimous, as was the vote in the House of Nobles," said Thomas. "They could not very well dispute the queen's final wishes or disregard the fact that I am the legitimate heir to King James. After they made me king, the House's next order of business was to advocate that we go to war with Rosia. They named Smythe Chancellor of War."

Phillip stared at him, incredulous, and too sickened to speak.

"You can hardly blame them for wanting a loyal son of Freya to keep an eye on me," Thomas continued. "I am young and inexperienced. I am a foreigner, known to be a friend to Rosia, and I am engaged to a Rosian princess."

"Good God!" Phillip murmured.

"And now I am as much a prisoner in the palace as you are in this tower," Thomas concluded. "Smythe is present at all my meetings. He speaks for me, makes decisions for me, reads my correspondence, dictates what I am to write, screens my servants. He places guards outside my door at night, ostensibly for my own protection, of course. He finally permitted me to come visit you, but I believe he made that concession only to remind me of the extent of his power over me. You will not be surprised to hear that my time is limited and his toady, Corporal Jennings, is waiting for me outside the door."

"I do not think God would object if you *did* murder him," said Phillip. "Are we going to war?"

"Not at the moment," said Thomas, faintly smiling. "I was able to delay that decision, at least. I may be inexperienced, but I know that our nation cannot go to war without my sanction. I spoke before the House, talked affectingly of the loss of life, the expense which our country can ill afford, and the fact that we had no evidence that it was the Rosians who had killed the queen. I said I wanted time to consider the matter and I suggested that the House refer the matter to committee."

"Well done!" said Phillip, regarding Thomas with admiration. "How did Smythe take it?"

"He was furious. He blustered and threatened, but there wasn't much he could do. I am king, after all."

"Speaking of Your Majesty, I read in the newspaper that the engagement to Sophia has been broken."

"The one good thing Smythe did for all of us," said Thomas. "He is currently seeking another princess for me to marry."

"At least Sophia managed to escape Freya along with the countess—"

Phillip stopped talking, dismayed by Thomas's darkening expression. "What is wrong?"

"Sophia did not escape," said Thomas. "The countess left Rosia the night the queen was assassinated, but by some mischance, she did not take Sophia with her."

"Where is she?" Phillip asked, alarmed.

"I have no idea. I know she is safe only because Smythe is still hunting for her. I have reason to believe that Kate is with her. The two fled the palace together."

"Kate?" Phillip repeated, startled and not entirely pleased. "I am not certain whether that knowledge fills me with confidence or dread. How did Kate come to be in the palace?"

"You know as much as I do, my friend."

A fist hammered on the door.

Thomas rose to his feet. "That will be Corporal Jennings. I would gladly let him beat on the door until he breaks his hand, but I must leave. Dignitaries are due to arrive to attend Her Majesty's funeral, King Ullr of Guundar among them. Smythe has insisted I must be on hand to welcome him. The countess once warned me about King Ullr. She believes him to be intent on ruling the world. Do you know of this man?"

"The countess is right. King Ullr is not to be trusted," Phillip said promptly. "He is ruthless in his drive to increase Guundar's influence in the world. He will welcome a war between Freya and Rosia. As our troops march out the front door, Ullr will order his forces to march in through the back. You must be extremely wary of him, Thomas."

"I know the Countess de Marjolaine does not trust him either," said Thomas. "But Smythe seems to admire him. He tells me I should look upon King Ullr as an example of a strong ruler."

"Ullr is a clever, devious man, and he has spies in your court," said Phillip. "Beware especially of Baron Rupert Grimm. He is one of Ullr's best."

Phillip paused, looking thoughtful. "Ullr detested Sir Henry and he undoubtedly knows about his downfall. Note that he has taken the first opportunity to pay a visit just when Henry has disappeared. Which reminds me: Do you know what has become of him?"

"Smythe is hunting for him, as well. I believe Wallace is alive, simply because Smythe has not gloated over his death."

Phillip seemed relieved. "Henry will find a way to help you."

Thomas grimaced. "Sir Richard said the same thing. I am not so sure. Wallace has no love for me."

"Henry is a loyal Freyan and he loved Queen Mary," said Phillip. "He will find some way to contact you. When he does, accept his help. Meanwhile, there is one way you can find out what King Ullr is plotting."

Phillip detained Thomas, resting his hand on his arm. He said softly, "You speak Guundaran, don't you?"

Thomas nodded. "I served with Guundaran mercenaries during the war. I understand the language better than I speak it, but I do well enough."

"Invite Ullr to be your guest in the palace. Put him on the third level in the suite of rooms known as the Godfrey Suite for the famous painting of King Godfrey that hangs on the wall of the main chamber."

Thomas was puzzled. "Why those rooms in particular?"

Phillip lowered his voice. "The painting was commissioned by Sir Henry, and is very special. Behind the wall on which the painting hangs is a secret alcove. The painting covers holes concealed by magic in the wall. Anyone standing in that alcove can see and hear everything that is being said in that room."

Thomas drew back from him. "You are saying I should spy on King Ullr."

"Ullr will have his agents spying on *you*, Thomas," said Phillip. "This is war, my friend. The king comes here for one reason. He smells blood and the scent of weakness. You are alone, surrounded by enemies with no one you can trust. I know what it is to be a spy. I spied on you, after all. I know it is sordid and dishonorable—"

"Which is why you stopped being a spy and confessed to me what you had done," said Thomas. "Now you are asking me to do the same."

Phillip regarded his friend with sympathy. "I am sorry, my friend. But you need to know what is going on between Ullr and Smythe!"

The fist banged on the door again, this time harder.

"I will think about it," said Thomas in a tone which meant he never would even consider it.

Phillip understood his friend's disgust. Spying on another was shameful, dishonorable. Yet, as he said, this was war. "If you change your mind, go to the servants' closet near the Godfrey Suite where the servants store brooms and mops. One wall has three coat hooks on it. This wall is a secret door. The key to opening the door are three words, spoken aloud in this order, 'Albert, Godfrey, Mary.' The door leads to the alcove and the painting."

Thomas nodded, though he seemed to have been only half listening.

"I will free you from this prison, Pip. I don't yet know how, but I will do it. You have my word."

"I am not your first concern," said Phillip. "Concentrate on finding a way to free our people. God go with you, my friend."

The two shook hands. Thomas rapped on the door and it swung open. He walked out and the door closed after him. Phillip heard the keys rattle and a voice chanting magic, replacing the warding spells on the door.

Phillip paced the chamber around and around, worried, helpless, frustrated. He remembered as a little boy capturing a sparrow and putting it into a cage. The bird had repeatedly flung itself against the bars of the cage until his mother had told him it would bash itself to death if he did not set it free.

He walked until he wore himself out and then he lay down on the bed and stared at the stone walls.

FIFTEEN

Henry sat at the table in the small and wretched house behind the coffee shop, gazing out the window and seeing nothing.

Simon was with him, seated at a desk that he had complained was far too small, almost lost amid his maps and charts, old books that smelled of mold, new books that smelled of leather, and papers that had fallen off the desk and now formed drifts around the wheels of his chair. Absorbed in his work, Simon would not have noticed if a barrel of gunpowder had exploded underneath the window.

Henry had just completed a letter to the Countess de Marjolaine, the Rosian spymaster who had long plotted Freya's destruction. The fact that he had written such a letter would forever brand him a traitor in the eyes of his countrymen—and his friends—if they ever found out about it. He enclosed Sophia's note, sealed it, and thrust it into his pocket.

"You are in a dark mood," Simon observed.

"We are in hiding, both of us wanted men with bounties on our heads. Our country is in dire peril and I have sent my family into exile. I believe I am entitled to my dark mood," Henry returned.

"I have something that will cheer you," said Simon. "Come look at my work."

He rolled his chair away from the desk to give his friend room to see. Henry gazed down on a piece of paper covered with numbers in parentheses with other numbers trailing down the margins, as well as wavy lines, squiggles and blobs and, most mysterious, a crude face with puffed-out cheeks and pursed lips in the upper left-hand corner.

Simon regarded his work with pride. "What do you think?"

"If you will remember, my mathematics tutor at university gave me up as hopeless," Henry said dryly. "I recall very little, but I am fairly certain algebraic equations did not involve this chubby chap with the cheeks."

"The drawing represents the prevailing wind currents. These lines," Simon stated, pointing, "indicate the strange behavior of the magical riptides, while these others are the unusual fluctuations in temperature at this particular location. Add other factors such as proximity to the mountain and my theory is confirmed!"

Simon slammed his hand down on the paper in triumph. "What do you think of that?"

"I don't know what to think," Henry said, thoroughly confused. "Which theory?"

Simon gave him an exasperated look. "The theory that I have been talking about for months, Henry! A pool of liquid Breath exists in the Aligoes and I have found the location."

He tapped his finger on a map showing the Aligoes and a blob not far from a dot marked "Wellinsport"—Freya's prosperous port city and stronghold.

Henry gazed down at the black dot, the lines, squiggles, and the blob, then shifted his gaze to his friend. "You are serious, aren't you?"

"God's balls, Henry, of course, I'm serious!" Simon stated, glaring at him. "What the devil do you think I've been doing all this time? Tallying up Randolph's gambling losses?"

Henry stood frowning down at the equations.

"Think of it, Henry. If we could find this pool, we could refine the liquid Breath using my formula to develop it into the crystalline form," Simon explained. "Other nations, such as Rosia, would be forced to buy the crystals from us to power their ships. Freya could become one of the wealthiest countries in the world. I've been telling you that for a month."

"Forgive me if I sound skeptical—" Henry began.

"Since when are you ever anything else?" Simon muttered.

Henry pulled up a chair and sat down.

"If this pool is where you say it is, Simon, why hasn't someone discovered it before now? A vast quantity of liquid Breath would be hard to miss. I've seen the pool in Braffa—a dazzling white light shining in the mists of the Breath. Damn hard to miss!"

"I theorize the pool would be located in the *Deep* Breath, which is why it hasn't been discovered," said Simon. "What people *have* noticed down through the years are the strange effects produced by the pool. The famous explorer, Robert Trame, wrote about these in his journal in the year three eighty-one. He noted sudden inexplicable fluctuations in temperature and the presence of dangerous magical riptides. He considered these phenomena to be anomalies, nothing more. Others have noted the same through the years, but similarly dismissed them. No one ever asked why such anomalies existed. I asked and I found the answer: a pool of liquid Breath."

"You know where it is."

"I know within a radius of a few hundred miles or so," Simon replied. "I would like to be able to sail to the Aligoes to perform tests, narrow the field of search, but Alan says he can't sail without orders—"

"He's right, you know," said Henry. "Besides, neither you nor I can leave Freya now. The situation is too dire."

"I am aware of that and I have an idea. I spoke to Alan and Randolph. They know sailors who hail from the Aligoes and they are going to bring them to the Weigh Anchor tonight so that I may question them."

"Good . . . good," said Henry.

He should take the opportunity to tell his friends about the letter to the countess, but he rejected the idea. They would not understand that he was acting in his country's best interests and he could not think of a way to convince them.

Simon regarded him with a frown. "Henry, I know you have far more urgent and important matters that demand your attention, but this discovery could save our country."

"I appreciate your efforts, my friend, but we may not have a country to save," said Henry. "And now I must try to decide what disguise to wear to visit the licentious and ever entertaining man-about-town, Rodrigo de Villeneuve."

"I doubt Pastor Johnstone would be a welcome visitor," said Simon, grinning.

"I believe I will go as Arthur Porter, the aging footman attached to a well-to-do family," said Henry. "I will hire a suitable carriage so as to allay any suspicions."

He put on the powdered wig and the velvet livery, assumed a supercilious and stuffy expression, and ordered the coachman, who was one of his agents, to drive him to Rodrigo's house, which was located in a fashionable residential neighborhood near Clattermore Street.

Rodrigo made no secret of the fact that he was a Rosian, and Henry braced himself to face the wrath of an angry mob surrounding the house, hurling brickbats and insults. He was surprised and somewhat alarmed to find the street quiet.

He wondered uneasily if Rodrigo had been arrested.

When the coachman stopped in front of the house, Henry saw evidence that the mob had paid Rodrigo a visit: two of the windows were broken and the small yard was littered with garbage and shattered glass.

As Henry approached the door, he was further disheartened to see what appeared to be blood splashed on the front stoop, along with a large number of smashed slate roofing tiles, their jagged edges stained with blood.

He was wondering if he should summon the local constabulary, when he noticed a curtain in the front window twitch, as though a hand had slightly pushed it aside. Henry continued up the walk and was about to place his foot on the door stoop when the door opened a crack.

"I would keep back if I were you, my good man," warned a sepulchral voice. "Not safe."

Henry recalled that Rodrigo was an extremely talented, albeit considerably lazy, crafter, and he immediately surmised that he had placed some sort of magical trap on the door. He came to a dead stop and exhibited the note, saying in a haughty tone that matched his velvet jacket, "I am the bearer of an urgent message for Sir Rodrigo de Villeneuve."

"Never heard of him," Rodrigo said, and started to slam the door.

"The message is from my mistress, sir," stated Henry.

The door remained open a crack.

"I don't recognize the coach," said Rodrigo. "Did Lady Rosalinda send you? No, wait. She was just married. I have it! The Countess of Hereford! Can't be her, though. She's gone to her estate in the country. The Baroness of Rathmore?"

Henry stiffened. "I will not bandy about my lady's good name in public, sir."

"No, no, of course not," said Rodrigo. He thrust his arm out the door. "Just hand the note to me. Be careful. Don't put your foot on the stoop. Wouldn't want something nasty to tumble down on your head."

Henry glanced down at the bloodstained slate tiles, looked up at the roof, and understood. Taking care not to touch the stoop, he reached across it as far as he could to hand Rodrigo the letter. Rodrigo took it, shut the door, and almost immediately opened it again.

He cast Henry a shrewd look. "Do I know you?"

"We have met at Her Ladyship's house, sir," said Henry.

"I thought so," said Rodrigo. He shot a wary glance up and down the street. "Any signs of the rabble?"

"No one is visible at present, sir," Henry replied.

"You had better come inside," said Rodrigo, opening the door. "I don't want to remove the spell. Beastly hard. Took me an hour to craft it. How are you at jumping?"

Henry managed to vault over the stoop. Rodrigo caught hold of him by his arm and pulled him inside the house. He promptly shut the door after him and stood regarding him with a smile.

"Unless I am mistaken, I believe I see Sir Henry Wallace beneath that frightful wig."

Henry inclined his head.

Rodrigo gestured to the note. "I gather this is from the Princess Sophia. What is the meaning of this enigmatic message? Is she safe?"

"Her Highness is safe and in excellent care," Henry replied. "Given the unfortunate circumstances surrounding some of our previous meetings, I asked her to write this note to let you know you can trust me."

"Considering that the unfortunate circumstance to which you allude involved a pistol to my head, you will forgive me if I am somewhat hesitant to regard you as a boon companion," said Rodrigo. "Why are you here, my lord?"

"The princess was supposed to accompany the countess to Rosia the night of the queen's assassination, but Her Highness became trapped in the palace. She escaped and she is safe. She requires a bold and daring friend to convey that message to the Countess de Marjolaine and her brother, the king."

"A bold and daring friend," Rodrigo repeated. "Not finding that sort of person, you had recourse to me."

"You underestimate yourself, sir," said Henry. "The blood on the door stoop attests to the fact. I propose to smuggle you out of the country and put you on a boat bound for Rosia this night."

Rodrigo frowned. "If you can help me escape Haever, why can't you find a way to smuggle the princess out, as well?"

"Far too dangerous for Her Highness, sir," said Henry. "All outbound ships are being searched. Princess Sophia is well known and even if I could disguise her, I could not disguise her little dog. She will not leave him behind."

Rodrigo nodded in understanding.

"I am not convinced she would go if I could find a way," Henry continued. "Her Highness is most reluctant to depart Haever. She is concerned over the welfare of a friend of hers—"

"His Grace, the Duke, Phillip Masterson," Rodrigo said, nodding sagely. "Is he in some sort of danger?"

"I believe he is," said Henry. "And so is our young king, Thomas Stanford. I would like you to convey this information to the countess."

"You may rely upon me, my lord," said Rodrigo.

"I was certain I could," said Henry. "Tell Her Ladyship that Jonathan Smythe was responsible for assassinating the queen. He has made the king a prisoner and is planning to rule Freya in his stead."

"You amaze me, my lord!" said Rodrigo, appalled. "Does the countess know this villain, Smythe?"

"Given that I know him, I would be much surprised if Her Ladyship did not," said Henry dryly.

"Yes, of course," said Rodrigo. "Peas in a pod, you two. Whose watching who's watching who's watching whom and all that."

"To insure the king's compliance, Smythe has taken Phillip Masterson hostage, as well as His Majesty's parents, the Marchioness and the Marquis of Cavanaugh. Assure the countess that friends of the king, including myself, are working to save His Majesty and put an end to Smythe. I suggest her agents make certain the king's parents are safe.

"Finally and most important, give this to Her Ladyship," said Henry. He withdrew the letter from his pocket. "Deliver it directly into her hands. Do not trust it to a servant or anyone else."

"I promise, my lord," said Rodrigo.

"Read the letter and memorize the contents so that if you are forced to destroy it, you can still convey the message to Her Ladyship."

"I understand," said Rodrigo with unusual gravity. "I assure you, my lord, I am far more trustworthy than I appear. How am I to reach Rosia?"

"A man of my acquaintance operates what appears to be an ordinary fishing trawler on the River Woldrith. By making some adjustments, he can transform the trawler into a ship that can sail the Breath. He is quite reliable. He has done business for me in the past."

"Fishing!" Rodrigo repeated, shuddering. He sank down in a chair. "Cod and flounder! I am to sail with cod and flounder."

"There will be no fishing done while you are on board, sir," said Henry in soothing tones. "You will be sailing the Breath."

"But the stench!" Rodrigo cringed. "The smell of fish creeps into the wood, you know. Still, I am willing to make the sacrifice. I don't suppose I could speak to the princess before I leave?"

Henry shook his head. "Best for all parties if you do not know her location. In case you are captured."

"Torture and all that," said Rodrigo with a sorrowful nod. "I am certain I should succumb at the mere sight of thumbscrews and reveal all I know and most of what I don't. Where am I to be and when?"

Henry wrote down an address on a card. "Wait until dark to leave. I will send a conveyance to pick you up. Once you have arrived at the docks, look for the *Lucy Lou*. Captain Anderson will be expecting you. Will you be safe in this house until evening? I could convey you away in my coach now."

"I must pack and that could take hours. Besides, I doubt those lads will be back," said Rodrigo. "They were considerably disheartened when they saw their mates lying on the stoop with their skulls cracked open. Although," he added in thoughtful tones, "I rather believe from the threats they issued that they do plan to return tonight to set fire to the place."

"I will send an armed guard with the driver," said Henry. "Thank you for undertaking this mission."

"For king and country. The enemy of my something is my something. Can't recall the quote, precisely, but if I could, I believe it would sum up the situation between you and me. Along with that other quote regarding strange bedfellows."

Rodrigo opened the door. Henry cast a distrustful glance up at the tiles on the roof before stepping out.

"If you don't mind my asking, how did you manage to topple those onto your unsuspecting guests?" Henry asked.

"Magical constructs to loosen them," Rodrigo explained. "Magic to make them fly. Magic on the stoop. When I arm the magic on the stoop, a single footfall activates the sympathetic magic on the tiles on the roof. Up they go and down they come—smash."

"Ingenious," said Henry.

Rodrigo was pleased. "I originally designed them to deter those annoying do-gooders who come round to preach to one that I should repent my sins. The truth is, I enjoy my sins."

Henry was thankful he had decided to leave Pastor Tobias Johnstone at home. "The carriage will be here at eight of the clock."

"I will be dressed for the voyage in oilskins and a sou'wester—whatever that is," said Rodrigo. He grew more serious. "Assure Her Highness she may rely on me. Please convey my love."

The two men shook hands. Henry made an awkward leap across the stoop and managed to land on the sidewalk without breaking an ankle.

"The letter is delivered. What is done is done and, as Rodrigo would say, cannot be something something," Henry reflected. "And now that I have betrayed my country, I can make amends by trying to save her."

SIXTEEN

The queen's body lay in state before the altar of the Royal Chapel in the great cathedral where her husband, her son, and her grandson were interred in the family vault. The coffin was covered by a Freyan flag trimmed with golden fringe, mounted on a catafalque draped in purple. The queen's crown lay on a purple pillow atop the casket.

The people of Freya stood in a long line in the chill, gray autumn weather to file past the casket and pay their last respects to their monarch. The queen's griffins held their own vigil by perching atop the steep roof of the cathedral. Many felt their presence to be disconcerting, finding it difficult to withstand the fierce gaze of the beasts' eyes as they glared down on all who entered.

The funeral was held a fortnight after the queen's death to permit time for representatives of all the nations of the world to attend. These included King Ullr, who arrived on his royal yacht. He had intended to stay on his yacht, but the *Gazette* reported that His Royal Majesty, King Thomas, had invited his fellow monarch to stay in guest quarters in the palace.

The newspaper also reported that King Ullr was greeted upon his arrival at the palace by the newly named Chancellor of War, Jonathan Smythe, who belonged to the Fundamentalist religion which had its roots in the Guundaran religion. Both sects tended to view God as a strict general commanding his forces rather than a benevolent deity. Royal observers who were in attendance reported that the two men warmly shook hands before going off to hold private talks.

The Rosians had not sent a representative. They had most strenuously denied any involvement in the queen's death, but no one believed them.

The king and queen of Estara came to pay their respects to the queen and to warmly support Thomas, who was well known to both of them. They were immensely surprised to learn that his parents would not be in attendance. They knew his mother, Constanza, and were aware that she had worked and schemed her entire life to place her son upon the Freyan throne. Thomas informed them that his mother had unfortunately fallen ill and could not travel.

The two also thought it strange that Chancellor Smythe was always present during their meetings with the king. They said nothing to Thomas, though a great deal to each other. When the queen of Estara sought a private audience with Thomas, the chancellor informed her that His Majesty was indisposed.

The dragons of the Dragon Duchies did not attend either. They were outraged over suspicion falling on the princess and the Countess de Marjolaine—two humans held in high esteem by the dragons—and sent only a stiff and formal letter of condolence.

The Braffan oligarchs all attended, including Henry's nemesis, Frau Aalder, and prominent members of the Travian cartels.

The nobility of Freya traveled from all parts of the country, their yachts filling the harbor. The general populace of Freya came to pay their respects as well, riding in wagons or carts or walking on foot to say good-bye to their queen and to catch a glimpse of their new king, who would be making his first public appearance since ascending to the throne.

Haever was thronged with visitors. Innkeepers tripled their prices and still sold out. The streets were clogged with traffic and gawkers. Shopkeepers draped their storefronts with black bunting, and clothiers could not keep black crepe in stock.

The crowds suited Henry, for he could lose himself among them. He did not join those paying their respects to the queen, for he knew that Smythe would have his guards watching for him. Henry had bid farewell to the dead on that terrible night he had found his queen's body. His regard was now for the living, as Mary would have wanted.

Henry had arranged to meet his friends at the Weigh Anchor, along with Simon and his manservant, Mr. Albright, who had been missing since the night of the attack on Welkinstead. Alan and Randolph had been agreeably surprised one night to find Mr. Albright loitering on the street outside the Naval Club.

"He went to your house that night as you suspected, Henry," Alan reported. "He found it overrun with soldiers and escaped before they saw him. He was returning to Welkinstead when he was horrified to see the house come under attack and then disappear. He realized that searching for the house and Simon would be futile, and that his best of hope of discovering what had become of his master was to look for us at the Naval Club."

Henry arrived to find Simon, Alan, and Randolph already seated at a table. Henry paused in the doorway and sent a questioning look at Alan. He nodded his head, indicating that it was safe for Henry to enter.

"Where is Albright?" Henry asked Simon as he sat down.

"He is in Welkinstead, starting work on the house. I will have to restore the magic myself, but Albright can repair the damage done to the structure and the lift tanks, as well as the damage Alan and Randolph did to the roof."

"We didn't damage your roof!" Randolph said, offended. "It was that goddamn green-beam gun!"

"He was jesting, Randolph," Alan said.

"Well, it's not funny," Randolph muttered.

"In the interim, I have devised that cipher for you, Henry," said Simon. "Since you will be relying on it to convey urgent messages to the king, I have made it difficult to detect, as well as easy to use."

Simon handed over a folded piece of paper. Henry read through it, smiled, and secreted it in an inner pocket.

"I plan to spend my time continuing to search for the pool of liquid Breath," Simon continued. "Alan, I was thinking. You are friends with the owner of a tavern in Freeport. He had something to do with that female pirate with the dragon. . . ."

"Olaf," said Alan. "What about him?"

"I need you to carry a message to him," said Simon. "I have determined what I believe to be the approximate longitude and latitude for the location of the pool of liquid Breath. This Olaf is a sailor, as I recall, and he could search for it."

"I'll send him the message," said Alan. He added somberly, with a wink at Henry, "But you should know that Olaf is eighty years old if he's a day. I'm not sure he will be eager to go sailing about the Breath searching for a pool that exists only in mathematical equations."

Henry saw Simon about to launch into an explanation and hurriedly rose to his feet.

"I must deliver the cipher to Miss Amelia. What have you and Randolph been doing these days, Alan?"

"Preparing our ships to salute Her Majesty on the day of the funeral. After that, we will be awaiting orders and training our gun crews for war with Rosia," said Alan.

"If a shot should 'accidentally' sink King Ullr's yacht, I will stand you a round of drinks," Henry said.

Leaving the tavern, Henry went to pay Miss Amelia another visit disguised as Pastor Johnstone.

"My neighbors are going to start to talk," said Amelia with a chuckle as she ushered the pastor inside.

"I am here for the good of your soul, Miss Amelia," said Henry.

"If ever the devil wore a pleasing countenance, it is you, my lord," said Amelia.

She led him to the kitchen, where he found Kate and Sophia and Bandit waiting for him. The dog wagged his tail with such enthusiasm that the spaniel tipped himself over sideways.

Henry reached down to pet Bandit and declined Amelia's offer of tea.

"My friend, Simon Yates, and I have devised a way to communicate with His Majesty."

Kate flushed with pleasure. Sophia clapped her hands.

"We are going to send him messages in cipher through the *Haever Gazette*. The messages will be embedded in Captain Kate stories. Of course, Smythe could be preventing His Majesty from reading the newspaper, though I rather think not. I see no reason why he should. If that is the case, His Majesty should be able to find access to one."

"How does this cipher work?" Amelia asked.

Henry placed a newspaper on the table. "Here is a Captain Kate story. His Majesty needs to know only a single key word. Let us say that key word is 'dragon.'"

Henry underlined the word.

"Wherever that key word appears in the story, the next line conveys information. For example: 'Captain Kate flew to Haever on her dragon.' The next line reads, 'Once in Haever, Kate sent word to Prince Tom to meet the first night of the full moon.' The next time the word dragon appears, the sentence following states, 'She planned to meet Prince Tom beneath the large willow tree in All Saints cemetery.'"

"I don't see why we need to involve Prince Tom in the story," Kate protested.

"Or that Captain Kate falls in love with him," said Sophia slyly.

"Because Smythe has to approve everything the paper publishes and he will be certain to approve this," said Henry. "He wants to increase Thomas's popularity among the people since that will strengthen his own hold on power."

"But how do we provide His Majesty with the key to the cipher?"

Henry had been wondering that himself. He had devised several plans, but he didn't particularly like any of them.

"I have an idea!" said Sophia. "Thomas will be part of the royal procession to the cathedral. The route will be thronged with thousands of people hoping to catch a glimpse of him. Since Thomas is not married, all the young women in Haever will be particularly eager to try to catch his eye. Kate will be among them and she will find a way to give Thomas the message."

"An excellent plan! I have been longing for something to do," Kate said. "If I stay cooped up in this house a moment longer, I will go mad."

"You need to think this through carefully, Kate," Henry warned. "Smythe knows you. He will be keeping close to the king and he will not hesitate to kill you if he sees you. I can have my people nearby, but you will be on your own. If anything goes wrong, they won't be able to come to your aid."

Kate gave him a smile. "You know better than most that I can take care of myself, my lord. I managed to save your life."

Henry had to admit that what she said was true. On the other hand, he could have added that it was her reckless meddling that had placed his life in danger. He kept that to himself, however, though he privately determined he would form his own backup plan, just in case.

"Then we are decided. I will make the arrangements."

Leaving Amelia's, Pastor Johnstone traveled to a small church located on the banks of the River Woldrith that ran through Haever. The church was old and weathered, looking very much as if it had washed downstream and fetched up on the bank. The congregation consisted of those who plied the river and earned their living from it: fisher folk, ferry operators, bargemen. The church door was always open, day or night.

Pastor Johnstone tottered inside, leaning on his cane, and sank down on one of the wooden benches that served as pews, choosing the second from the back. He was not alone. Three older women were arranging flowers on the altar and gossiping about their neighbors. A man wearing a shabby pea coat and a stocking knit hat knelt in a pew near the front. The priest was talking to a young couple who were going to have their new baby blessed.

Henry removed his hat and clasped his hands to pray, leaning his cane against the pew. Unfortunately, he accidentally hit the cane with his foot and knocked it over and had to reach down to pick it up. He quickly felt beneath the bench. Finding no letter attached to the underside of the bench, he grimaced in disappointment.

The hushed stillness inside the small church lulled Henry into lingering longer than he had intended. He was not a believer. Henry viewed with scorn the notion that some all-knowing deity wielded cosmic control over his daily existence. But here, in the restful silence, he took a moment to think tender thoughts of his beloved Mouse and Master Henry and baby Mary.

He was putting on his hat, intending to depart, when he became aware of the man in the shabby coat sitting at the end of the pew. Something about him seemed familiar. Henry looked at him intently. The man turned to face Henry, who recognized him and nearly gave himself away with an exclamation of joy.

Henry managed to contain his happiness long enough to make his way out of the church. He went to the quiet cemetery behind the building and, ascertaining that it was deserted, he turned to grasp the hand of the man in the shabby coat who had followed him.

"Mr. Sloan! Franklin! I am so glad to see you! How are you? You look exhausted," said Henry. He noticed that Mr. Sloan had pressed his hand to his side and added worriedly, "You are not fully recovered from your wound. Here, come and sit down."

He guided his secretary to a stone bench placed among the tombstones for the benefit of mourners.

"I was not expecting you! Is something wrong?" Henry continued, a prey to fear. "My family—"

"Lady Ann and the children are well, my lord," Mr. Sloan hastened to reassure him. "They are in good spirits, though they miss you, of course."

Henry sighed in relief. "Thank you, Mr. Sloan." He had to take a moment to compose himself before he could speak again. "You must have flown here on the wings of angels to be back so soon."

Mr. Sloan faintly smiled. "Wings of a griffin, my lord. The countess is beside herself with fear for the princess, who has not returned to Rosia and appears to have vanished. The countess's agents cannot find her, and the countess was going to come herself, despite the danger. I offered to come in her stead."

"The countess may rest easy," said Henry. "I have already dispatched a messenger to assure her that the princess is safe and in good hands."

"Excellent news, my lord," said Mr. Sloan. "The countess will be most relieved. She also asked me to convey information to you. She thought it better if I delivered the message in person, rather than trusting to the mail."

Henry braced himself. "This must be serious."

"Have you heard from your agents in Guundar recently?"

"I have not, Mr. Sloan," said Henry. "My communications have been disrupted. I dare not return to the Foreign Office. I assume from your question that the countess has heard from *her* agents in Guundar. King Ullr is in Freya to attend the queen's funeral. What is that bastard plotting now?"

"The Guundaran fleets are on the move, my lord," said Mr. Sloan, keeping his voice low, despite the fact that they were completely alone in the quiet cemetery. "Her Ladyship's agent in Braffa reports that the Guundaran ships 'protecting' that country have departed. The fleet that was guarding the contested island of Morsteget has also left. The Coastal Fleet that was in Guundar set sail a fortnight ago."

"Where are they bound?" Henry asked.

"The agents do not know, my lord," Mr. Sloan replied. "But the countess fears it likely that King Ullr will seek to take advantage of a new young king's inexperience to strike a blow at Freya. Speaking of that, the countess asked me to once again assure you that the Rosians had nothing to do with the queen's assassination."

"I am aware of that, Mr. Sloan," said Henry. "I know who ordered the assassination."

Mr. Sloan hesitated. "I trust Sir Richard was not involved—"

"No, no," said Henry. "Richard knew nothing about it. The man responsible is now ruling Freya. Your old comrade-in-arms Isaiah Crawford, alias Jonathan Smythe."

"God forfend, my lord!" Mr. Sloan exclaimed, horrified. "But what of the king, young Thomas Stanford? I know you never trusted him. Was he involved?"

"It seems I was wrong about the young man, Mr. Sloan. He, too, was duped by Smythe, who has persuaded the Accession Council to name him Chancellor of War. We both of us recall the last time Freya was under the control of a Chancellor of War."

"The time of Mad King Charles," said Mr. Sloan. "The chancellor named himself Lord Protector and ruled the country."

"Our king is sane, thank God, but little better than a prisoner himself."

"Terrible news, my lord," said Mr. Sloan.

"And now, with King Ullr's arrival, the news can only get worse," said Henry grimly. "Smythe is a cold-blooded killer who will stop at nothing to obtain his goal, but I will wager he is as naïve as any country bumpkin when it comes to royal intrigue. Whereas King Ullr is a master."

"What of His Majesty?"

"Thomas might be young, but he was raised in the Estaran royal court," said Henry. "His mother, the Marchioness, was always embroiled in innumberable palace intrigues, and where she left off, the Countess de Marjolaine took over. The countess will have warned Thomas not to trust King Ullr, but we must convey our suspicions to His Majesty and urge him to discover

Ullr's true motives in visiting Freya. We may be certain he does not come to wish our new king well."

"That brings me to another piece of information from the countess, my lord," said Mr. Sloan. "She has a trusted agent inside the palace, close to Smythe."

"Of course, she does," said Henry bitterly. He himself had once had trusted agents in the palace. He had no idea what had become of them. Some had gone to ground following the queen's death. Others he dared no longer trust.

"Her Ladyship provided me with his name—Corporal Ernest Jennings."

"Do you know him from your time with Smythe?"

"No, my lord. The corporal was serving in Freya when I was in Bheldem. We should inform His Majesty of the man's name, but only if we can find a way to do so without endangering his life. Jennings' situation—being so close to Smythe—is precarious."

"As you have good reason to know, Mr. Sloan," said Henry. "Smythe shot you the moment he found you had betrayed him."

"Indeed, my lord," said Mr. Sloan. "The king should make use of Jennings only as a last resort."

"I will keep that in mind," said Henry. "Still, I am glad to know the young man has at least one friend inside the palace."

Henry consulted his pocket watch. "I have to leave. I have been reestablishing the lines of communication with my various agents around the world and I must send a message to my agent in Guundar, see what he can discover."

"Do you require my assistance, my lord?"

"Your help would be invaluable, as always, Mr. Sloan. But the authorities know you work for me and they will be searching for you, as well."

"I will take precautions, my lord. I should like to do my part for my country."

"I knew I could count upon you, Mr. Sloan," said Henry. "We have remained in this cemetery too long. I will hail a cab. I doubt one would stop for such a disreputable-looking fare as you, Mr. Sloan."

Henry hailed a cab, supplied the address, and he and Mr. Sloan climbed inside.

"I need a dozen or so good-sized men to do a job the day of the funeral," said Henry after the cab had started moving. "They risk being knocked about a bit, but assure them that they will be well compensated for their pains."

"Yes, my lord," said Mr. Sloan. "Anything else?"

"I require a fragrant nosegay, such as might be exchanged between lovers."

Mr. Sloan made his expression carefully blank. "Very good, my lord."

Henry smiled. "The flowers are not for a mistress, Mr. Sloan, although I appreciate how tactfully you managed to conceal your disapproval. The nosegay is to be given to His Majesty by a love-struck young woman."

Mr. Sloan considered this idea a moment, then nodded. "I understand, my lord. Violets would be most appropriate."

"I leave the choice to you, Mr. Sloan. And now," said Henry, leaning back in the carriage, "tell me all the news of my family."

"Lady Ann conveys her love and I am to remind you to wear your flannel waistcoat now that the weather is turning cool. Master Henry has learned his times tables and can say them up to seven times seven. Mistress Mary spoke her first word, which was 'da.' I would not know from personal experience, but according to Lady Ann, 'da' means 'father' in the language of babies."

Henry listened to all these small details, which were unimportant when compared with world-shattering intrigues, but vitally important to him. He thought of his son reciting his times tables without him, of his small daughter saying "Da" perhaps because she missed him.

He was glad for the shadows in the cab that concealed his emotions.

SEVENTEEN

Kate was up and out of bed early the morning of the queen's funeral. Too nervous to sleep, she told herself she was simply keyed-up about the mission, which would involve considerable risk. The truth was that she was worried about encountering Thomas.

He had been declared Freya's king. Perhaps he had grown cold, haughty and aloof. Perhaps he would regard her with disdain or, worse, pretend not to know her.

Kate knew in her heart she was being ridiculous. Thomas had risked his life to help her escape prison and save her from execution. A small ornament like a jeweled crown would not change him. But her head was ignoring her heart and doing the worrying.

As she tried to dress for the funeral, she could not make her trembling fingers grasp the small buttons and slide them into the equally small buttonholes.

"I quit!" Kate flung up her hands in frustration. "I will wear my slops."

"You will do no such thing. I will play lady's maid," said Sophia, taking over the task. "You have to stand still, Kate. I can't fasten these buttons while you are fidgeting."

Kate forced herself to stand perfectly still while Sophia quickly completed buttoning the blouse. Amelia had found a blouse and skirt for Kate to wear and dyed both of them black. The house still reeked of the fumes. She did not own a black cloak, but she was able to borrow one from a neighbor.

Sophia tied black crepe around the brim of a "boater" hat Amelia had scrounged up from the back of a closet. Kate tried it on and turned to the mirror.

The hat, wrapped with crepe, suited Kate's face and its cluster of short blond curls. A long tail of black crepe extended down her back.

"You look lovely," said Sophia, eyeing her with admiration.

"I look ridiculous," Kate said, and Bandit apparently agreed, for he did not know her and frantically barked at her from behind the door.

The barking was interrupted by the sound of the bell.

"Let us hope that is the messenger from Sir Henry," said Kate. "You go to the kitchen. I'll answer the door."

Sophia picked up Bandit, clapped her hand over his muzzle, and carried him downstairs to the kitchen.

The two young women were alone in the house. Amelia had left before dawn in order to make certain she had a seat in the cathedral to observe the funeral.

Kate ran down the stairs, looked out a window, then hastened to open the door.

"Mr. Sloan!" she said, relief evident in her voice. "We had no idea what had become of you! Please come in."

"Captain Kate," said Mr. Sloan, touching his hat. "I trust you are well. Sir Henry asked me to deliver this."

He held out a small bouquet of white and blue violets tucked inside a silver cone known as a posy holder.

"Where is the note?" Kate asked.

"I secreted the cipher with instructions for its use inside the posy holder," Mr. Sloan replied. "His Lordship asked me to make certain you know where you're supposed to go in order to meet His Majesty."

"The corner of Harley and Market across the street from the statue of King James in the park," said Kate glibly. "I will be there at one of the clock this afternoon. I walked the route yesterday. Twice."

"Our people will be in place," said Mr. Sloan. "You will not know them, but they will know you."

"I understand," said Kate. "Thank you, Mr. Sloan."

Mr. Sloan touched his hat. "Good luck, Captain."

Kate carried the nosegay into the kitchen to show Sophia.

"Beautiful," said Sophia. She held it to Bandit's nose so he could smell it.

The dog sniffed and sneezed. "You know what blue and white violets mean in the language of flowers."

"I didn't even know there was a language of flowers," said Kate.

"Very popular in the royal court. Men and women who are involved in secret affairs give flowers to say what they dare not speak aloud. If a woman gives a man blue violets, that means she is devoted to him. If a man gives a woman white violets, he extends an invitation to her to gamble on love."

Kate looked uneasily at the nosegay. "What does this say?"

"That you are in love and you ask him to love you," said Sophia.

Kate stared at her, appalled. "You are not serious!"

"I am very serious," said Sophia, helping Kate on with her black cloak.

Kate saw her lips twitch. "You are not! You are teasing me!"

"Maybe just a little," said Sophia, grinning.

She adjusted Kate's hat, which was all askew, and walked with her to the door. "I wish I could go with you. I feel very useless."

"Amelia says the risk of someone recognizing you would be too great."

"Please be careful," Sophia said, opening the door. "Smythe knows you by sight."

"Not in this hat," Kate muttered, glancing at herself in the mirror with a shake of her head. "Wish me luck!"

"Good luck," said Sophia, embracing her.

She closed the door behind her and locked it.

Kate walked down the street, admiring the flowers, inhaling their fragrance, and wondering if Thomas knew the language of flowers.

She decided that if he did, she didn't really mind.

Thomas dressed himself with care for the queen's funeral. He was assisted by his *valet de chambre,* a man employed by Smythe, who had dismissed most of the queen's household staff and installed his own.

Queen Mary had retained a staff of over two hundred, from footmen to maids to the Royal Griffin Handler. Smythe had reduced that number considerably.

"You may be certain, Your Majesty, that most of them were foreign spies," Smythe had said.

Thomas was certain that Smythe had replaced those spies with his own spies. Thomas trusted none of them. He dismissed the valet as soon as possible and studied his reflection in the mirror.

Tailors had been working for days on Thomas's mourning clothes. He wore a black velvet single-breasted coat lined with black silk and trimmed with white lace at the cuffs, a black waistcoat embroidered in black, a white shirt with black cravat, black breeches and stockings, and black shoes with black buckles. His hat was black with a white feather. He bound his black curls with a black ribbon at the nape of his neck.

He could finally approve of the face that looked back at him, for it was no longer drawn and haggard. He had slept well the night after his meeting with Phillip, no longer plagued by the dreadful dreams of pistols and poisons.

Thomas had taken his friend's advice and would no longer allow himself to be consumed by rage, self-pity, and despair. He was resolved to fight to regain his crown, make it his own. He did not dare confront Smythe, knowing Phillip would suffer for his defiance. But he could circumvent Smythe, wage a secret war.

Thomas had not refused to declare war against Rosia. He had vacillated, been unable to commit to a decision, and at last stated the matter required further study and sent it to the House of Nobles.

Smythe had fumed and sneered at him, but he was working hard to shore up his influence with the members of the House and he could not very well anger them by trying to go around them.

Thomas's next opponent was going to be Guundar's king, Ullr Ragnar Amaranphson.

King Ullr was in his fifties, tall and imposing. He was in excellent physical condition, for he exercised daily. He kept his gray hair cut short and was clean shaven. He did not dress in satin and silk, but wore the uniform of the Guundaran military, decorated with gold braid and rows of gleaming medals on his chest. He had not earned his medals in battle, for he had never served, but he had participated in any number of duels. Apparently dueling was considered Guundar's national pastime.

Thomas had met King Ullr for the first time yesterday, shortly after the king's arrival. Ullr had expressed a desire to see Thomas's horses. Thomas had offered to escort the king to the stables and Smythe had invited himself to come along with them.

Thomas had not needed Phillip's warning to distrust the man. Thomas had met men and women like Ullr in the Estaran court, those skilled in the art of manipulation.

He was well aware that Ullr was here to loot his kingdom as his distant ancestors had done when the Guundarans had raided up and down the coastline. He thought again of the painting of King Godfrey and the hidden alcove. He had invited Ullr to stay in the palace and given him rooms in the Godfrey Suite, yet could not bring himself to do something as dishonorable as spy on the man. Still, Thomas found himself thinking of the painting more and more.

Ullr first tried to intimidate Thomas by clasping his hand in a strong grip that would have choked a bear. Thomas clasped Ullr's hand in a bone-crushing grip of his own and deliberately retained the king's hand when he would have released him.

The two men eyed each other. Ullr raised an eyebrow and a corner of his thin lips twitched, as though amused, yet conceding the contest a draw. Thomas broke off the handshake and Ullr withdrew his hand. Thomas could see the indentations of his fingers white on the man's skin.

Thomas next watched Ullr take Smythe's measure as they walked to the stables. Thomas had hoped Smythe would be proof against Ullr's attempts to charm him. But while Smythe might be a cold-blooded killer with a professed hatred for those who considered themselves "his betters," he clearly admired strong and powerful men such as King Ullr.

Smythe obviously hoped to pattern himself after Ullr, and Thomas noted that he actually walked straighter, keeping his shoulders rigid, in emulation of the king. The two walked together, engaging in companionable conversation, as Thomas followed behind, observing them.

Ullr was discussing the war with Rosia with Smythe and noted Thomas's silence on the subject.

"You oppose this war, Your Majesty?" Ullr asked, pausing to turn around. "How is that possible? These Rosian fiends slaughtered your queen!"

"I oppose rushing into war when we do not have all the facts," said Thomas coolly. "The House of Nobles is looking into the matter."

"His Majesty is far too young to understand the devious Rosian mind," Ullr said to Smythe.

"As I have tried to make His Majesty understand," said Smythe, glowering at Thomas.

King Ullr paused to admire a stallion a groom was riding out to exercise, and turned to Smythe. "You and I, sir. We two military men are old enough to have seen the worst of mankind. We understand these Rosian scum and how to deal with them."

"Indeed we do, sir," Smythe replied, flattered.

"And yet, His Majesty is engaged to be married to the Princess Sophia of Rosia."

Smythe hastened to reassure his new friend. "You have not heard, sir. I terminated the engagement upon hearing that Her Highness is suspected of complicity in the death of the queen. I am searching for someone more suitable."

"I am surprised His Majesty approved. I have heard he and the princess are friends," said Ullr.

"His Majesty is guided by my decision," said Smythe, regarding Thomas with pride of ownership.

Ullr looked to Thomas to angrily refute such a claim, protest, or argue. Thomas remained silent, aloof and detached.

He stopped to rub the nose of a curious bay that had thrust her head out of the stall to view the visitors. He could see Ullr studying him, as a whist player might study an opponent, trying to guess what cards he was holding.

Smythe clearly took Thomas's reticence for a sign that he had been cowed into submission, but Ullr did not appear so certain. Accustomed to deceiving, he was convinced that everyone around him was deceitful. He rubbed his hand, as though he still felt the pressure of Thomas's handshake.

Ullr had no trouble understanding Smythe, who gulped down honeyed flattery like bonbons. The Guundaran king must be wondering if Thomas was truly a meek lamb being led to slaughter or a wolf in sheep's clothing.

As they left the stables to return to the palace, Smythe dismissed Thomas, saying he and King Ullr had business to discuss.

"I believe Your Majesty has a fitting with the tailor for a new suit of clothes," said Smythe, and added in a loud and snide aside to King Ullr, "You know these young men, sir. Concerned with nothing but their own looks."

Ullr watched Thomas walk off, and then continued on with Smythe. Ullr must be confused now, wondering which Thomas was which. Was he the Thomas of the strong and defiant handshake or the Thomas who meekly swallowed insults from his chancellor?

Thomas thought of advice the Countess de Marjolaine had once given him. "Be open to your friends and a puzzle to your foes."

Thomas completed his dressing and left to join the royal dignitaries and members of the nobility who were planning to walk from the palace to the cathedral in a solemn procession to mark their respect for the late queen.

Thomas saw Sir Richard among them, his arm still in a sling. He glanced at Thomas. Thomas glanced at him and Sir Richard walked on. He was the person in charge of the committee dealing with the matter of war with Rosia. Nothing more needed to be said.

Smythe accosted Thomas on his way out the door.

"There has been a change in plans, sir," Smythe said. "I was planning to accompany you back to the palace in the royal carriage. King Ullr has most graciously asked me to accompany him in his own carriage to continue our conversations. His Majesty might be offended if I refuse."

"We certainly would not want to offend King Ullr," said Thomas.

He was grateful to Ullr for relieving him of Smythe's odious presence and confounded the king by being exceedingly cordial to him when they took their places in the forefront of the line of mourners.

Kate left Amelia's house early, for her friend had warned her that the streets would be clogged with people and she needed to make certain she arrived in time. She walked to the intersection of Market and Harley streets without much difficulty and located the statue of King James in the park.

She had been instructed to stand on the corner of the street opposite the statue, but the crowds were already five and six deep. Kate could not get near the street and realized in dismay she would be fortunate to even catch a glimpse of the carriage as it rolled by, much less carry out her important task.

She was preparing to try to push her way to the front when a large, burly man tapped her on the shoulder. He had the look of a pugilist, for his nose had been broken numerous times and was spread over much of his face. He wore no jacket, even in the cool weather, but he was wearing a hat, which he politely doffed.

"Allow me, mum," he said, and before Kate could say a word, he took hold of her elbow and led her through the crowd.

He walked ahead of Kate, towing her behind him like a dinghy. People receded before him and then flowed in behind her, all seemingly by accident, for no one even glanced at her. The man deposited her at the curbside, near the gutter.

"Here you are, mum. Don't you stir. You'll have a grand view from this spot. His Majesty's carriage will pass only a few feet away. I won't be far if you have need."

He posted himself behind her, his muscular arms folded across his broad chest.

Kate had arrived an hour early and the waiting seemed interminable. She fidgeted, stamped her feet to keep warm, and tucked the nosegay beneath her cloak to protect the violets from the chill. At last the church bells in the cathedral began to toll, marking the moment of the interment, when the queen's coffin was laid to rest next to those of her husband, son, and little grandson.

The crowd fell silent and bowed their heads. The man standing behind Kate solemnly removed his hat and leaned forward to whisper, "The king and members of the royal court will leave the cathedral shortly, mum. That's when you will see His Majesty. He will be riding in an open carriage with guards mounted behind, so you must be quick."

Kate clutched the flowers, her heart beating fast, and waited.

EIGHTEEN

The funeral service in the grand cathedral was beautiful, melancholy, and solemn. The day was raw and chill and gloomy, as befitted a funeral. The cathedral was crowded and those unable to find places inside thronged the streets. Standing at the front, Thomas looked out over a sea of black that rustled, stirred, coughed, and wept. He spoke the queen's eulogy, then knelt beside the casket to bid a silent farewell to Queen Mary, remembering the look in her shrewd eyes the day she had asked him why he wanted to be king.

She was interred in the family vault, the last of the family of Chessington. Thomas reflected on his own mortality, as one does at funerals, and he was in a sober, contemplative mood as he entered the carriage for the procession back to the palace, where he would be hosting royal and noble guests at a reception.

He rode in an open carriage, black trimmed with gold, drawn by two black horses. A coachman in a gold-trimmed black uniform sat at the front with two footmen in matching uniforms at the rear behind Thomas. People lining the route to the palace shouted well wishes as he passed. Now that the funeral was over, they could in good conscience take pleasure in cheering their new king.

The female population of Freya was particularly interested in him, for he was handsome and he was unmarried and he was king. Every shopgirl, barmaid, and farmer's daughter could indulge in the harmless fantasy that he might see her in the crowd, fall in love at first sight, and make her his queen. Young women lined the route, waving handkerchiefs, calling out to him and throwing flowers.

Thomas looked at the people counting on him to rule over them and he was overwhelmed and daunted by the responsibility. He held the lives of these people in his hands: the shopgirl and the shop owner, the laborer and farmer, the boys who ran alongside the carriage, the elderly men and women who had once stood on these streets to cheer the late queen's grandfather. His people, in his care. He had promised Queen Mary.

The procession wound slowly through the streets. The royal guards riding in front kept the carriage moving, at one point breaking ranks and guiding their horses into the crowd, as the driver brought the carriage to a halt.

Thomas tried to see what was happening. "What is going on, Barkley?"

"An altercation has broken out, Your Majesty. Do not be concerned. The guards are dealing with it."

But the crowd lining the sidewalk overwhelmed the guards and surged toward Thomas, calling his name and shouting. The guards riding behind his carriage attempted to reach his side, but the people blocked their way.

The coachman had all he could do to manage the excited horses. The footmen mounted on the rear of the carriage were more ornamental than useful, for they could only sit and gape as one smitten young woman rushed toward the open carriage.

She sprang onto the step and leaned inside to thrust a nosegay into Thomas's face.

He drew back, startled, then realized something about her was familiar. He looked more closely and recognized her hazel eyes with the golden flecks and the cluster of "dishwater blond" curls beneath a crepe-covered hat.

"Kate!" Thomas gasped in disbelief.

"You have friends!" Kate told him breathlessly. "The code is in the flowers! You will hear from us!"

Thomas took the flowers, hardly knowing what he was doing. Despite what Sir Richard had promised, he had believed himself friendless and alone, and then suddenly here was Kate, clinging to the side of his carriage, giving him violets and hope.

Their fingers touched. He tried to hold onto her, but she jumped off the carriage and landed in the street where a large, burly man grabbed hold of her and whisked her away just as the guards arrived. A wave of black crepe washed over them and swallowed them up.

Thomas heard Smythe shouting about assassins and turned to see him jump out of Ullr's carriage, ordering the guards to find the young woman. They rode their horses into the crowd, using the flat of their swords to beat people back, which only served to increase the pandemonium.

Thomas watched all this in a daze. Kate had been with him one moment and gone the next. He wondered if she had been real and looked down at the violets she had given him. They were real enough.

"Your Majesty!" Smythe appeared at the side of the carriage and tried to yank open the door.

Thomas hurriedly thrust the nosegay inside his jacket.

"Drive on!" he shouted to the coachman.

The man plied the whip, and the carriage lurched forward. Smythe tried to cling to the side of the moving vehicle, but he was forced to let go or risk tumbling off. Thomas glanced back to see him swept away by the crowd.

The sun broke through the clouds. Thomas could smell the scent of the violets and feel the nosegay pressed against his heart. He longed to search for the note hidden among the flowers, but he did not dare, not while he was the object of so much attention. He waved at the crowd and the people cheered him and his spirits rose.

When the carriage arrived at the palace, Thomas had to exert all his self-restraint to receive the bows and congratulations of the staff who had lined the drive to greet him. He had to endure the fawning of courtiers whom he heartily wished were at the bottom of the Breath. Finally, after what seemed eons, he was able to make good his escape and reach his room.

He dismissed the servants, locked the door, and took out the nosegay of violets tucked inside an ornate silver posy holder. Thomas removed the flowers, inhaled their fragrance, and searched for the note.

He found it wrapped around the green stems. Opening the small note, he eagerly read the words.

> *You and P.M. are not alone. Tom and Kate stories Gazette. Code word: dragon. Read sentence that follows for important information. H.W.*

Thomas was disappointed. He had been hoping the note was from Kate, but he knew her handwriting and this was not her large, untidy scrawl. The writing was firm, neat and precise. The initials: H.W. Henry Wallace.

"Pip was right. He told me to be vigilant, that Wallace would find a way to get in touch," Thomas reflected.

He knew Smythe frequently had his room searched. Thomas memorized the note, then burned the paper and stirred the ashes, mixed them with water, and threw them in the slop jar. Going to the study attached to his bed-chamber, he selected a book from the shelf—a thick tome on the history of the ancient Imhruns—and pressed the violets between the pages. This done, he replaced the book and wondered what to do with the posy holder.

He remembered a gift his mother had given him when he attended board-ing school. Constanza always suspected the servants of spying on her, and she had warned Thomas not to trust them. To that end, she had given him a wooden valet with a false bottom.

Thomas had been seven at the time. He had been quite taken with the trick box. He had shown all his friends and they had once hidden a beetle in the false bottom to spring on the unsuspecting headmaster.

Now that he was older, he could appreciate the fine handiwork. The box was lovely, made of small blocks of wood arranged in an intricate geometric pattern. When Thomas touched three of the blocks in a certain order, a tray would slide out of the bottom.

He had not used it in years and he had difficulty remembering which three to touch and in what order. After several hits and misses, he found the right combination. The tray popped out. He placed the silver posy holder in-side and then had to try to remember how to close it. This done, he replaced the box on his nightstand and rang the bell for the servants.

As his valet was assisting him with his jacket, Thomas said coolly, "I failed to receive my copy of the *Haever Gazette* this morning. I left clear orders for the paper to be delivered daily with my breakfast tray."

The valet looked startled, as well he might, for Thomas had given no such orders. The valet could not very well contradict the king, however. He stam-mered his apologies and promised he would attend to the matter. He would deliver this morning's paper at once.

Thomas smiled inwardly, completed his dressing, and went downstairs to prepare to receive his guests and sit through an interminable dinner. He was immediately accosted by Smythe in company with King Ullr.

"I have been extremely worried about your safety, Your Majesty," said Smythe. "The guards tell me a woman tried to attack you. I attempted to enter the carriage to be at your side in case of another attack, but before I could do so, you ordered the coachman to drive off."

"I regret I did not see you in the confusion, sir," said Thomas. "I also feared assassins and I ordered the coachman to leave the scene immediately."

"Did you get a good look at this woman, sir?" Smythe demanded. "Can you provide me with a description."

"She was dressed all in black," said Thomas helpfully.

King Ullr laughed.

Smythe cast him a sour glance. "As you are aware, Your Majesty, every woman in Haever is dressed in black this day."

"Then I wish you luck finding her, sir," said Thomas.

"You make too much of nothing, Chancellor," said King Ullr. "A handsome young man such as His Majesty draws young women as a flame draws moths. I have experienced similar incidents myself. A young woman once threw herself into my arms while I was reviewing my troops. A pity the guards could not detain the wench for questioning, but so be it."

Smythe wanted to continue to talk about the episode, but King Ullr apparently felt enough had been said and he changed the subject. "Your Majesty, may I present the new Guundaran ambassador to Freya, Baron Rupert Grimm."

Rupert Grimm. Thomas heard Phillip's voice warning him. "Rupert Grimm is a Guundaran spy."

Thomas greeted the baron, who wore a great many medals and sported a magnificent red beard.

Immediately after the dinner had ended and the guests had departed, Thomas pleaded fatigue and retired to his room. He feared Smythe would insist on accompanying him, but again he was grateful to King Ullr, who insisted on conversing with Smythe in private.

Thomas found a copy of the *Gazette* lying folded on the nightstand. Informing the servants he had no further need of them, he picked up the paper and hurriedly searched for the story.

He located it toward the middle, identifiable by the title, "The Adventures of Captain Kate and Prince Tom" by Miss Amelia Nettleship. The story was accompanied by a woodblock illustration of Prince Tom and Captain Kate. The two were standing back to back, apparently about to fight some dastardly foe.

Thomas swiftly scanned the page for the word "dragon." When he found the first instance of the word, he read the sentence that followed.

The Marchioness had been confined to the house due to illness. The countess assured Prince Tom that his mother had recovered, though she was still under confinement to insure she did not plot mischief.

Thomas understood and he sighed in relief. Smythe had been threatening to kill his mother if Thomas did not cooperate. The countess had found out, perhaps from Sir Henry, and acted to set them free, although she was still keeping an eye on Constanza. Thomas could imagine his mother's fury.

He continued reading until he found the next "dragon," and read the sentence. It seemed to make little sense.

The baron's fleet was on the move.

"What baron?" Thomas asked aloud, perplexed. "What fleet?"

He decided that he needed to read the sentence in context and went back to read the entire story, smiling at Amelia's florid style, which landed Prince Tom, Captain Kate, and her dragon, Dalgren, in one improbable peril after another.

The baron, the dastardly Baron Osterhoff, was the villain of the piece. The description of the baron was quite detailed down to the dueling scar on his chin. Thomas stopped smiling. The baron was King Ullr.

Thomas read on and again came to the word dragon. *Kate knew that if she was ever in desperate straits, she could trust Jennings.*

"Jennings . . ." Thomas repeated to himself, mystified.

The only Jennings he knew was a corporal who served under Smythe. Thomas couldn't believe at first it was the same man, and then he thought back. Jennings had gone to the Rose Room to find Sophia and Kate and they had both escaped.

Thomas was dubious about trusting anyone, however, and he determined that he would have to be very desperate indeed before he trusted Corporal Jennings.

As Thomas strung together the sentences, they began to make chilling sense.

The "baron's" fleet was on the move.

King Ullr had been building up his fleet for years, taking advantage of the fact that his country had not been directly threatened by the Bottom Dwellers and had, for the most part, remained out of the war. He might be plotting to strike a blow either in Freya or at Freyan interests abroad such as Wellinsport, one of the most prosperous cities in the Aligoes.

The serialized tale concluded with a sentence clearly intended to entice the reader into picking up next week's edition of the paper.

Prince Tom resolved to find a way to uncover the baron's nefarious plot.

Thomas laid down the newspaper. He knew a way to find out what Ullr was planning: he could use the painting of King Godfrey. But the idea of spying on the man was still repugnant to him. He decided he would try to learn what he could by being around him, watching him, listening.

Two nights later, Thomas was in his office, working late, reading through a report from one of his ministers regarding the Estaran situation in the Aligoes. Estara had one major port in the Aligoes, San Artejo. The Estarans were interested in acquiring more territory and had been squabbling with the Rosians over a contested group of islands about halfway between the Rosian port of Maribeau and San Artejo. The agent reported that the Estarans were sending more ships to the area, which meant the Rosians would be doing the same.

Having recently served with the Freyan navy in that part of the world, Thomas was familiar with both Maribeau and San Artejo and read the report with interest. By the time he had finished, the clock had struck ten times. He rubbed his eyes and was thinking of his bed, when a servant arrived to announce that Smythe requested an audience.

Thomas would have liked to refuse, blaming the lateness of the hour, but he knew that nothing would have given Smythe more satisfaction than to be confirmed in his belief that the young king was indolent, lazy, and self-indulgent. Thomas ordered that he be admitted.

Smythe bowed and advanced to the desk.

"I have documents that require Your Majesty's signature."

Thomas took up the first of the five documents Smythe laid before him and began to read.

"Your Majesty needs only to sign them," said Smythe.

Thomas did not look up, but gestured to a chair.

"You have our permission to be seated, sir."

Smythe had no choice. He sat rigidly still, too disciplined to fidget. Only the soft tapping of his boot on the carpet betrayed his impatience.

Thomas was pleased with his small victory, then sneered at himself, realizing how pathetic that made him look.

He finished the first document and signed it and started on the second. The servant entered again.

"King Ullr requests an immediate audience on a matter of importance, Your Majesty."

Smythe hurriedly rose to his feet and turned to glower at the servant. "His Majesty is not to be disturbed. Advise King Ullr that I will attend him—"

Thomas coolly interrupted. "Tell His Majesty I am at liberty to receive him."

King Ullr entered without ceremony, dressed as though he were an old and valued friend of the family, for he was wearing a velvet lounging jacket with a shawl collar of contrasting silk over his breeches and stockings. Thomas was surprised. He had always rather imagined Ullr slept in his uniform.

"Forgive me for disturbing you at such a late hour, Your Majesty." Ullr cast a glance at Smythe. "I was seeking you, as well, Chancellor. I am glad to find you with the king. I have just received disturbing news out of the Aligoes."

"His Majesty was about to retire—" Smythe began.

"His Majesty would like to hear the news from the Aligoes," Thomas said, flashing a look at Smythe.

"I received a report from my agent in Rosia that King Renaud is planning to take advantage of Your Majesty's youth and, forgive me, inexperience to order the Rosian Rum Fleet along with the Dragon Brigade to attack and seize Wellinsport."

He's lying, Thomas realized. King Renaud had no reason to attack Wellinsport, a move which would be an act of war. As proof, he could have pointed to the report he had just been reading about the Rosians attempting to limit Estara's growing influence. With the Estarans threatening Rosian interests in the Aligoes, Renaud would not do anything so mad as try to seize the well-defended port city of Wellinsport.

Thomas was about to confront Ullr with the truth, only to realize he might be better served to see if he could lure Ullr into inadvertently revealing why he felt the need to fabricate such a tale.

"This news is indeed shocking, sir," said Thomas. "As I have no experience in such matters, I would be interested in hearing your advice on how to handle this situation."

"All the world acknowledges the supremacy of the Freyan navy, sir," Ullr said. "In particular, the amazing vessel with the magical steel plates known as the *Turtle*—"

"*Terrapin*," Thomas corrected.

"Indeed, yes, thank you, sir. My apologies," said Ullr. "I would immediately dispatch the *Terrapin* to Wellinsport. The Rosian fleet has nothing to match it. I have heard that the metal plates can withstand even the destructive magical fire of the dragons of the Dragon Brigade. The Rosians would certainly think twice about attacking if the *Turtle*—forgive me, *Terrapin*—was in Wellinsport to guard the harbor."

"But, after all, this report might not be accurate," Thomas suggested.

"My agent is most reliable, sir," said Ullr. "If he says this, you may believe it. However, let us suppose he is wrong. By acting boldly, with dispatch, you will be telling the Rosians that they cannot trifle with you."

Smythe had been waiting impatiently to speak and he barged into the conversation.

"As for the Dragon Brigade, I do not believe we need concern ourselves with them. They are not a factor. Their time has come and gone."

If Smythe had been hoping to shift Ullr's attention from Thomas to himself, he had succeeded. Ullr turned to him with keen interest.

"What do you mean by that, sir?"

Thomas was wondering, as well.

"I meant only that the Brigade is a relic of the past," said Smythe. "God be praised, the Seventh Sigil has given us the means to deal with them. Dragons are no longer a threat."

He turned to Thomas. "As your Chancellor of War, sir, I will issue orders at once for the *Terrapin* to be dispatched to defend Wellinsport."

"I appreciate your offer, sir," said Thomas, "but I would like more time to consider such an important move."

Smythe was angry. He opened his mouth to excoriate Thomas, only to recall they were not alone. He clamped his mouth shut, breathing hard through his nose.

Thomas ignored Smythe. He was more concerned with watching King Ullr, who observed the interaction without seeming to observe, understood without appearing to understand.

"Your Majesty will want to consult with your chancellor in private. I will withdraw," the king stated.

Thomas said what was polite and rang for the servants. Smythe barely waited for the door to close behind the king before he rounded on Thomas.

"We must act with dispatch, sir. This is not the time for your dithering and dallying. You imagine that the Countess de Marjolaine is your friend, but she is only using you."

"What did you mean about the Dragon Brigade and the Seventh Sigil?" Thomas asked. "Why would you say they are not a factor? The dragons of the Brigade are formidable and would appear to me to be a major factor in a war with Rosia."

"Your people demand war, sir," said Smythe, evading the question. "The Rosians assassinated the queen."

"You and I both know that they did not," said Thomas.

Smythe regarded him with unblinking enmity. "Since you have no stomach to order men into battle, sir, I will do so."

He stood up. "I will draw up the orders for the *Terrapin* myself."

"You may do so, but such orders require my signature," said Thomas.

Smythe leaned near him to say softly, "Remember that Phillip Masterson is my prisoner. I have only to say a word and he will be tied to a grate and flogged until the flesh is stripped from his bones."

He did not wait for Thomas to dismiss him, but turned on his heel and stalked out of the office.

Thomas sat unmoving for long moments after Smythe had gone. He had to think carefully about his next move.

He remembered the proud dragons of the Brigade. He remembered the time he had flown with Kate on Dalgren and he recalled her telling him stories about the Brigade when the two of them had been together in the Aligoes.

Those days he had spent with Kate and Phillip had been the happiest of his life. And he owed his life to Dalgren, who had once served in the Brigade.

Rosia was not Freya's foe. Thomas was hoping to avert this bitter conflict between the two nations and bring about lasting peace.

Ullr was plotting something with his lies about Wellinsport, that much was certain. And what had Smythe meant about the Dragon Brigade and the Seventh Sigil?

Thomas picked up the copy of the *Haever Gazette* lying on his desk and thrust it in a drawer. He told himself he was keeping the paper in case he needed to refer to it again. But he was also keeping it because, in a way, it was a connection to Kate.

He thought over the final instruction.

It is left to me to find out.

NINETEEN

Three days following the queen's funeral, Henry received a message at the post office on High Street, addressed to *Franklin Sloan, to be left until called for*.

He knew Alan's handwriting and he opened it hurriedly. Alan wrote that he had news and he had also dredged up several sailors from the Aligoes who had agreed to talk with Simon. He asked Henry to meet him and Randolph at the Weigh Anchor the following evening at six of the clock, and to bring Simon.

"I will be in our usual booth in the back," Alan concluded.

Henry was intrigued, and glad he'd be talking with his friends; he had news of his own to share. He had formed a plan that, if it succeeded, would free his country and his king, and he could start to seriously consider his future. After a life of tumult and adventure, he found himself longing for peace. He could bring his family home and know they would be safe. He would no longer have to skulk about in disguises. And he would forever rid the world of Jonathan Smythe.

The Weigh Anchor was a tavern owned by a retired naval officer, a friend of Alan's, who had earned enough prize money to purchase it. The tavern was perfect for Henry's purposes. With a rear exit, wooden booths that were high-backed, and dim lighting, it offered a certain amount of privacy for confidential conversations. The ale was drinkable and the patrons were loud enough to allow Henry and his friends to talk freely.

When Henry walked in, he was pleased to find the tavern crowded and noisy. Many of those frequenting the Weigh Anchor were naval officers, but the tavern also catered to the local gentry who had business dealings with the navy. Everyone from naval officers to rope manufacturers was talking war with Rosia. For the officers, war meant battles with "a worthy foe" as described by the traditional naval toast, a chance for faster promotion, and prize money.

Some of these men had been languishing on half pay since peace had left them without a ship or employment. Others were impatiently waiting for their ships to be refitted to use the crystalline form of the Breath. Those lucky enough to have a ship were eagerly awaiting orders to set sail.

For the businessmen, war meant sales of rope and sailcloth, powder and shot, and salt pork. Henry listened to everyone talk of profits, boast of their future heroics and how they would spend the fortunes they would earn. If his plan succeeded, he would put an end to all talk of war. Alan and Randolph would grouse and mope for weeks.

Henry came in the guise of Pastor Johnstone, here to reunite with a childhood friend. He pushed Simon in his rickety wheeled chair, acting the part of a retired ship's crafter who had been wounded in battle and was living off his pension.

Henry wheeled Simon inside the tavern and headed for their usual booth, located in a shadowy corner near the entrance to the back room, which was occupied mostly by whist players.

Henry slid into the booth and sat facing the front door. He placed Simon at the end of the table and gestured to Alan, who was seated at a table with friends enjoying a mug of ale. Alan excused himself to his companions and came to join them.

"Where are the sailors I am supposed to interview?" Simon demanded.

"They are waiting for you at that table," Alan said. "I'll take you to meet them."

He assisted Simon to a small table near their booth where three men dressed in slops were seated. The sailors jumped to their feet as Alan came over and knuckled their foreheads.

Alan introduced Simon, who took out a leather-bound notebook and pencil, as well as a hand-drawn map of the Aligoes, and placed them all on the table. The sailors pulled up chairs and sat down, looking abashed and extremely uncomfortable being around so many officers. Their own tavern was down the street and they were undoubtedly looking forward to returning to their mates and more congenial surroundings.

Alan left Simon to his liquid pools and went back to Henry. Alan was too restless to sit sedately in a booth. Turning a chair around, he straddled it and rested his arms on the back.

"I have news," said Alan.

"I hope it is good news," said Henry. "I could use some now."

Alan glanced over his shoulder. Simon was busy taking notes and no one else was paying any attention to them. He leaned forward and said quietly, "You always say I have the devil's own luck. I have received orders. The *Terrapin* sets sail tomorrow. Fortunately, my ship is ready, since I had been planning to set sail to test the crystals, and I have a crew, otherwise my press gangs would be sweeping the streets this night."

"You must let me know the results of the tests," said Henry.

Alan shook his head and further lowered his voice. "I will not be testing lift tanks, Henry. My mission is secret. The orders are sealed and I am not to open them until the ship has rounded Upton Point."

Henry frowned. "What does Randolph say about this secret mission?"

"He knows nothing about it. The orders did not come from the Admiralty. They came directly from the palace. They bear the king's signature."

"From the palace . . ." Henry repeated, startled and displeased. "That means from Smythe."

He eyed his friend. He knew what he was about to ask was hopeless, but he had to try.

"You need to unseal those orders, Alan. I must know what is going on."

Alan regarded him gravely. "You know I cannot do that, Henry. I would be breaking my word of honor, not to mention disobeying a direct order."

Henry sighed. He recalled a time when he would have known where the *Terrapin* was bound before her captain knew. Now he was reduced to begging a friend to disobey orders.

"I am sorry, Alan," Henry said despondently. "I had no right to ask that of you."

"You are fighting for our country, Henry, as am I," said Alan, sympathizing. "Just in different ways. I am glad you understand."

Henry gave a bleak smile. He had ordered food, but when the meat pie arrived he had no appetite. He shoved it to one side.

"Where is Randolph?" he asked.

"Playing whist in the private room in the back with some of his junior officers," Alan replied, adding with grinning commiseration, "I pity his poor partner."

Randolph Baker was passionate about the game of whist, despite the lamentable fact that he bore the distinction of being the world's worst player. He constantly forgot which suit was trumps and if there was a card in his hand that was certain to lose the game for him and his partner, Randolph invariably led with it.

"How in the name of heaven did he convince anyone to play whist with him?" Henry asked.

"He ordered them," said Alan. "If you are a captain and your admiral asks you to be his partner in whist, you jolly well play whist with him. I told him you were coming. Should I go fetch him?"

"No hurry," said Henry. "Let him keep losing."

Alan ate the pie, since Henry could not. Henry glanced over at the table where Simon was sitting with the sailors, scribbling notes.

"What did you tell these men about Simon?" Henry asked Alan.

"I told them to answer any questions he asks, no matter how strange, and I promised to pay them each a half eagle for their trouble. Do you suppose there's anything to this theory about liquid Breath in the Aligoes?"

"Whether there is or there isn't, I thank God for it," Henry replied. "This theory has kept him occupied and stops him from fretting about Welkinstead."

"He seems thinner. Is he well?"

"He is living in a run-down, land-bound house, bereft of his books and his newspapers, his files, his letters, and Mr. Albright," said Henry. "No, he is not well. I brought him here hoping to get a good meal inside him; you know he often forgets to eat."

"If we put food in front of him, he'll eat it," said Alan. He called to the barmaid and instructed her to deliver meat pies to Simon and the sailors.

"I have news of my own," said Henry when they were again alone. "I have formed a plan. I am going to kill Smythe."

"About damn time," Alan said coolly. "I was wondering what was taking you so long."

"The fact that my likeness is nailed to the wall in every constabulary considerably hampers my movements," said Henry dryly. "Nor am I a welcome guest in the palace these days."

Alan smiled. "That has never stopped you before."

"Well, it has stopped me up until now," said Henry. "Then I learned from our friend, Captain Kate, that her dragon is living near Haever. She and I have formed a plan."

"Involving Kate?" Alan asked, raising an eyebrow. "Do not misunderstand me. I admire Kate immensely. But she can be a bit . . . reckless."

"Thus speaketh the pot about the kettle," Henry remarked with a smile.

Alan grinned. "I have mellowed in my old age. Caution is now my watchword."

Henry snorted. "As it happens, for reasons of her own, Kate is wholeheartedly committed to helping the king. The truth is that I need her dragon

more than I do her, and Dalgren would not stir without Kate. My biggest obstacle will be obtaining access to the palace grounds. Smythe has increased
the numbers of the palace guard, not merely to keep unwanted visitors out,
but to keep His Majesty in. Most of these soldiers are Guundaran mercenaries, loyal to Smythe.

"I spent a day observing them and their movements. They stop all vehicles
entering and leaving the palace and search them. In addition, Smythe has
reinstated the air defenses Queen Mary deemed a waste of money. A naval
patrol boat now guards the skies above the palace day and night."

"I always said grounding the patrol boats was a mistake," Alan observed.
"If the navy had been in the air, they might well have stopped the black ship
and saved Queen Mary's life."

"I do not think even the presence of the navy would have helped," said
Henry somberly. "The black ship's green beam would have knocked a patrol
boat out of the sky before they knew what hit them."

"We would at least have given them a fight," said Alan, feeling called
upon to defend the honor of the navy. "But I begin to see where you are
going with your plan. Kate and Dalgren can evade the patrol boat, carry you
safely over the castle walls, and land you on the palace grounds."

"That is the idea," said Henry. "Once I am inside, I will gain access to
Smythe's bedchamber through the secret passages, put a pistol to his head
and blow out his brains. I will make it look like suicide, of course. A pity I
cannot leave a note from him confessing his crimes, but I have no sample of
his handwriting for Mr. Sloan to copy."

"Did you tell Kate you are involving her in an assassination plot?" Alan
asked, frowning.

"She and Dalgren will not be involved," said Henry. "They will drop me
off and then leave. No one will see the two of them. If my plan goes awry
and I am captured or killed, they will not be implicated. Kate assures me
that she and Dalgren are experienced in a maneuver called a 'slam down' in
which Dalgren plummets down from the sky, touches the ground, drops off
a rider, then immediately departs."

"I have heard of dragons performing such maneuvers," said Alan. "That's
how the Brigade dropped their riders onto ships during battle. I'll wager
Kate didn't want to leave you by yourself. She won't be pleased to be missing
out on the action."

"She argued to come with me," Henry admitted. "As I said, she has her
own reasons for wanting to help Thomas Stanford. I was adamant, though,
and she finally relented and agreed to do what I asked of her."

"I still think you should tell Kate the truth, that you are going to kill Smythe."

"I prefer not to risk it," said Henry. "The fewer who know the better. She is staying with Miss Amelia who is, after all, a journalist."

"Always the cautious Henry," said Alan with a smile.

"I would not be alive today if I were not," Henry replied. "Here comes Simon, brimming over with good news, by the looks of him."

Their friend rolled his chair up to the table. Simon was in an excellent humor.

"The men told me an old sailor's tale about the *Manuel Gomez*," stated Simon. He cast Alan an accusatory glance. "Why did you never tell me that story? It confirms my theory."

"Because not even old sailors believe the tale of the *Manuel Gomez*," said Alan, laughing.

Simon was annoyed. "And no one believed tales of ships being attacked by giant bats until the Bottom Dwellers attacked ships with their giant bats."

"Tell Henry your tale then," said Alan, rising from his chair and going to pay the sailors.

Simon rolled his chair closer to the table and expanded upon the tale.

"The *Manuel Gomez* was an Estaran merchant vessel during the Blackfire War. It crashed on Whitefalls Island."

Henry shrugged. "I suppose many ships have crashed on Whitefalls."

"Ah, but what makes this unusual is that searchers found the ship well inland, far from the Breath, long after it would have run out of lift gas, which would be tantamount to finding an ocean-going galleon perched on top of a mountain. When the searchers boarded the *Gomez*, they discovered all the crew members were dead. Henry, are you listening to me?"

"Yes," said Henry, who had in truth been watching a stir among the crowd clustered near the entrance. People were turning their heads and curiously looking toward the door. "Everyone was dead."

"Henry, the bodies were frozen stiff!" Simon exclaimed exultantly. "The sailors who found them were terrified and attributed their deaths to the freezing touch of some roaming specter, but that's nonsense. The tale confirms my theory. The *Manuel Gomez* was able to sail inland due to the fumes of magic being given off by the pool of liquid Breath. The sailors perished of the cold."

"Brilliant, Simon," said Henry absently.

Alan returned to his seat to find Henry staring fixedly at the door.

"What is it? What are you looking at?" Alan asked.

"Three soldiers just entered the tavern," said Henry.

Simon glanced at their uniforms. "Two Guundaran mercenaries in service to the Freyan army and a Freyan officer."

Alan shook his head. "The army has made a sad mistake to do their drinking in a navy tavern, as they will soon discover."

"Those soldiers are not here for pleasure, Alan," Simon observed. "They are carrying rifles and they appear to be searching the crowd. We should leave, Henry."

"Too late," said Henry. "We would only draw attention to ourselves. We do not know that the soldiers are here for us and they have no way to penetrate our disguises."

"Even a man in a wheeled chair?" Simon asked.

"You are not the only man in this tavern to be missing the use of his limbs," Henry pointed out, which was quite true.

By this time, everyone in the tavern had stopped what they were doing to make rude comments regarding the troops, jeering at the "Spuds"—a derogatory name for the foreign mercenaries due to the well-known fondness of Guundarans for a potent liquor made from potatoes.

"What's that other chap doing with them, that civilian all bundled up in a scarf?" Alan wondered.

"An informant," said Simon.

A man wearing a greatcoat and tricorn with his face covered by a wool scarf had entered with the soldiers. He was looking about the room, as though searching for someone, but was so bundled up he was having difficulty seeing. He pulled down his scarf to gain a better view.

Henry sucked in his breath and let it out in a hiss. "Henshaw!"

"Your brother's servant?" Alan asked.

"The same," said Henry in grim tones. "I told him where he could find me in case something happened to Richard."

"Your brother would not betray you, but Henshaw would," Alan said. "I have never trusted that obsequious bastard."

Henshaw raised his hand and pointed straight at Henry.

The Freyan officer nodded and gave an order in Guundaran. Henshaw ducked out the door.

Alan shoved back his chair. "I'll handle this."

"Alan! Keep out of it!" Henry told him. "You can't be seen to be involved with me!"

"Stay seated and wait for my signal. When I give it, wheel Simon into the whist room. The back door leads into the alley," said Alan. "Tell Randolph what's going on and send him to me."

Henry did not argue. Alan might be reckless and hotheaded on occasion, but there was no one Henry trusted more in times of crisis. The two Guundarans walked into the crowd, their sights fixed on the booth where Henry and his friends were seated.

Their commanding officer raised his voice. "Gentlemen, we are here to arrest a traitor to Freya. We ask that you, as loyal Freyans, assist us in our duty!"

He was greeted with angry jeers and taunts as a group of younger officers began pounding their mugs on the table to a rhythmic chant of "Spuds, spuds, spuds."

Alan lurched unsteadily to his feet.

"A toast!" he shouted, raising his mug. "The king! God bless him!"

In the time-honored tradition of the navy, every officer in the tavern shoved back his chair, pushed back from a table, and rose to drink to the king. A veritable forest of naval officers now stood between the soldiers and their prey.

Henry slid out of the booth, grabbed hold of Simon's chair, and began wheeling him toward the back room. Glancing over his shoulder, he saw the soldiers looking at each other in frustration, wondering what to do. They undoubtedly understood that the toast had been a ploy to assist their prisoners to escape, but they had no desire to fight their way through a crowd of intoxicated naval officers thirsting for a brawl.

Simon shoved open the door to the whist room and Henry propelled him through it and inside the small room. The door shut behind them. After the tumult outside, the room was a haven of peace.

Whist players studied their hands, quietly bidding and laying down cards, while kibitzers lounged about, observing the play. Hardly anyone looked up as the door opened, despite the commotion taking place in the main room where angry shouts of "Spuds, spuds" had now become general.

Randolph didn't even glance at Henry as he pushed Simon past him, heading for the back door. Henry had to bump the wheeled chair into Randolph's leg in order to draw his attention.

"Here now! Watch where you're going!" Randolph stated in ire, rubbing his knee.

"Sorry, sir," Henry said.

"Eh?" Randolph blinked at Pastor Johnstone a moment, then recognized him and Simon. He was instantly on alert. "What the devil is going on in there, my good man?"

"I am sure I couldn't say, sir," said Henry meekly. "You should ask Captain Northrop."

Randolph laid down his cards.

"If you will excuse me, gentlemen. Sounds like a goddamn fight has broken out."

He hurried toward the door to the main room. Many of the other players were now aware of the commotion and were also leaving the games, fearing they were missing out on the action. None of them paid attention to Henry and Simon, seeing only a caring friend helping his wheelchair-bound companion escape injury in a barroom brawl. The card players at one table did not look up at all, but remained intent on their game, oblivious to the tumult.

Henry reached the exit.

"I'm going out first. Wait here."

He parked Simon by the door and then thrust it open and walked outside, leaving the door slightly ajar. He couldn't see well, for his eyes hadn't adjusted to the darkness, but he could hear quite clearly the sound of someone cocking a pistol.

"Stop right there!" a voice ordered.

Simon yelled his name.

The soldier fired.

The bullet slammed into Henry's chest. He staggered and fell backward through the open door, lost his balance, and fell into Simon's lap. Henry stared at the ceiling as pain tore through his body. Each breath he drew was agony; he could hear broken bones creaking and feel the warm blood soak his clothing.

Simon shut the door and swiftly activated the warding constructs placed there to deter thieves, adding a few touches of his own magic. Satisfied that no one would come through the door, he grasped hold of Henry's shirt with one hand and propelled his chair backward with the other.

"Sorry, Henry," Simon said. "I know I'm causing you a great deal of pain, but it's only going to get worse. The best thing you could do now would be to lose consciousness."

Pain seemed to consume him. Henry decided to take his friend's advice, and passed out.

TWENTY

Having set chaos in motion in the main room, Alan was heading for the back when he heard the sound of the gunshot. He broke into a run and almost collided with Randolph, who was coming out of the whist room just as Alan was running in.

Randolph pulled Alan through the door into the whist room and slammed it shut. "Henry's been shot!"

"Who shot him?"

"Some soldiers. They were in back waiting to ambush him," said Randolph. "They shot Henry when he went out the door."

"What about Simon?"

"He's safe. He used his magic to block the door. You can hear the bastards trying to break it down."

Alan could hear the blows hitting the door. Simon was shouting for a physician and officers were grabbing weapons, yelling that the tavern was under assault.

Alan had to shout to be heard. "Take Henry and Simon out the back. I'll fetch a cab and meet you in the alley."

"What about the soldiers?"

"Leave them to me."

As Randolph started to return to his friends, Alan caught hold of his arm. "How is Henry?"

Randolph gave a grim shake of his head. "Not good."

Alan returned to the main room where he was confronted by several officers. "Northrop! What the devil is going on back there?"

"Some damn drunken Guundaran lout has just shot one of my friends!" Alan roared angrily, making certain as many people as possible heard him.

He was thinking coolly and swiftly, as he would on the deck of his ship with battle raging around him. The confusion and turmoil worked to his advantage. He fanned the flames and stoked the fire by pointing to the Guundaran soldiers who had entered the front in pursuit of Henry.

"The cowards shot him in the back!"

Men began shouting and shaking their fists, hurling mugs and insults. Some drew their swords, and there was a general call to take the soldiers prisoner. The tavern owner was attempting to intervene, fearing a brawl that would wreck his establishment.

"Please leave, sirs. I have sent a boy to fetch the constable. These gentlemen are extremely angry and I cannot vouch for your safety!"

"We are here to serve a lawful warrant!" the army officer insisted stubbornly. "Our informant pointed out the guilty man."

"Blood money!" Alan shouted.

The crowd surged toward the soldiers, swords raised, as the barmaids either ducked behind the bar or armed themselves with pewter mugs and plates.

The Guundaran soldiers were already backing out the door. Their officer remained, scowling. His long mustaches quivered and he had his hand on his sidearm. Alan had been disturbed to hear that the owner had summoned the constable. He needed to find a cab and he couldn't do that with this stubborn bastard blocking the door. He shoved his way toward the front to speak to the officer.

"We do not want more bloodshed, sir," Alan told him. "Please see reason. Your troops shot an innocent man—a pastor, at that. The constable will be here any moment. You could be the one facing arrest."

The army officer considered a moment, then slammed out the door. Once outside, he placed a whistle to his lips and blew three times. The soldiers posted around back came running. He swore at them in ire as he led them down the street.

The patrons gave a cheer of triumph at the sight of their enemy retreating, and rushed out of the tavern onto the pavement to jeer at the soldiers as they were departing. Two constables arrived at about this time. The owner seized hold of them and began to air his grievances. The patrons returned to celebrate their victory.

Several cab drivers always stationed themselves in front of the Weigh Anchor, knowing that they could generally find well-paying and inebriated customers. Alan took advantage of the confusion to mount the box of one of the cabs.

"Here now, sir!" The driver glared at him. "What do you think you're doin'?"

Alan flourished a banknote in the light of a street lamp. "I am going to borrow your cab. Don't worry. I will return cab and horse in good condition. Here is money for the inconvenience."

The driver glowered until he saw the denomination of the banknote. His eyes widened. He plucked it out of Alan's fingers, handed over the reins, and swung himself down from the box.

"Where should I leave the cab so that you will find it?" Alan called.

"Don't worry, sir!" the driver returned, heading for the tavern to celebrate his luck. "Miss Mab'll find her own way home."

Alan drove the cab around to the alley, where he found Randolph and Simon placing Henry on a makeshift litter, assisted by a naval officer Alan did not recognize.

Alan jumped down from the box. They had wrapped Henry in a greatcoat. He was ghastly white. His eyes were closed, his head lolled.

"Is he . . ." Alan couldn't go on.

"He's alive, Captain Northrop," said the strange officer. He touched his hat and introduced himself. "William Perry, ship's surgeon. Where do you propose taking him?"

Alan hesitated to tell him, wanting to keep Henry's whereabouts secret. The surgeon guessed his dilemma.

"The gentleman requires immediate medical treatment or he will die, sir. My preliminary examination leads me to believe the bullet broke his left clavicle and is still embedded in the shoulder. He faces a high risk of infection and he has lost a great deal of blood. I would like to remain with him. Rest assured, sir, that my first duty is to my patient, not to the authorities."

"Very well, thank you, sir," said Alan, relieved.

The surgeon issued orders and, acting under his supervision, Alan and Randolph picked up Henry and conveyed him to the cab, handling him as gently as possible. Once he was settled on the seat, the surgeon climbed in with him.

Alan turned to his friends. Randolph was standing protectively alongside Simon, whose clothes and hands were covered in Henry's blood. Alan eyed the crimson stains and had to take a moment to compose himself before he could speak.

"There are two constables out front," he said. "I'm taking Henry to the *Terrapin*. He'll be safe there. We set sail tomorrow. Simon, you should sail with us. I'll take you to the ship. Randolph, fetch Mr. Sloan—"

"Randolph, take me home," Simon interrupted, countermanding the order. "After that, you can fetch Mr. Sloan and bring him to my house. He'll need to go through Henry's papers."

"Simon, it's not safe for you in Haever—" Alan argued.

"I don't plan to remain in Haever," Simon stated. "I am going back to Welkinstead."

"Simon, listen to me—"

"Don't waste your breath," Randolph advised. "You know you won't goddamn budge him."

"Indeed, you won't," said Simon. "Mr. Sloan can help me gather up Henry's papers and destroy the rest. When we are finished, I will send him to join you and Henry on board the *Terrapin*. When do you set sail?"

"Tomorrow. Do you know this surgeon, Randolph?"

"Perry? He's a damn fine sawbones," Randolph stated. "I hear he's looking for a posting if you need a surgeon."

Alan already had a surgeon, but the man was probably dead drunk by this time of night. The mere fact that Perry was sober at this hour was recommendation enough. Alan went to the door of the cab to check on Henry.

"The gentleman is holding his own," Perry reported. "I advise you to drive slowly, Captain. He should not be jostled lest the bullet do more damage."

Alan climbed onto the box and gave a reassuring wave to Randolph, who was wheeling Simon down the street. Picking up the reins, Alan looked searchingly up and down the alley, fearing the soldiers might be lying in wait, hoping to still lay hands on their prey. They were apparently not that dedicated to their duty, however, for he saw no sign of them.

Alan gently slapped the reins on the horse's back and told Miss Mab to take it easy. The cab rolled off at a pace that would have suited a funeral procession. Alan immediately regretted thinking of funerals and he leaned over the box to spit three times to take away the bad luck.

TWENTY-ONE

Kate was wakened by the sound of someone knocking on Amelia's door. She peered out from beneath the blanket to see that the room was still dark. The sun had not yet risen. She could hear Amelia leaving her bedchamber and going down the stairs to answer it.

Kate pulled the pillow over her head as the clock chimed five times. Far too early to be wakened on a cold morning.

This week alone three people had arrived in the middle of the night to alert Amelia to the latest disaster. A warehouse had gone up in flames, a building in the slums had collapsed, and a wyvern-drawn carriage had fallen out of the sky and landed on an orphanage.

Whatever the news, Amelia would swiftly dress in the clothes she had laid out before going to bed and rush off to visit the scene, leaving her guests to try to go back to sleep.

Kate was burrowing down into the blankets when she heard Amelia call.

"Kate! Come quickly!"

Kate could tell by the urgent tone that something was wrong and she was immediately awake and alert, her first thought that someone had discovered Sophia.

Kate wrapped a shawl over her nightdress and emerged from her room to find Sophia peering into the dark hallway. She had hold of Bandit, who was whining to be let out.

"Stay in your room," Kate whispered. "Shut the door and keep Bandit quiet!"

Sophia closed her door and Bandit's whining ceased.

Kate hurried down the stairs and found Amelia waiting for her at the foot. She was wearing a man's flannel dressing gown with a shawl around her shoulders and a mob cap covering her hair.

"Mr. Sloan is here," she told Kate. "He asked to see you."

"Mr. Sloan!" Kate repeated, startled. "What is he doing here at this ungodly hour?"

"I have no idea. He said only that he needed to speak to you on a matter of the utmost urgency. I invited him in for a cup of tea, but he said he didn't have time."

Amelia ushered Kate into the front entry hall where Mr. Sloan stood waiting near the door. He held his hat in his hand, as though prepared to immediately dash out. He looked extremely grave.

"Captain Kate, I am sorry to have to wake you," he said. "I fear I have bad news."

"What has happened, Mr. Sloan?" Kate asked, exchanging worried glances with Amelia.

"Sir Henry has met with an accident," Mr. Sloan replied. "His Lordship apprised me of your intention and that of your dragon to fly him to the palace in order to try to assist the king. I regret to say that this plan must now be abandoned. I bid you good day, ladies."

Mr. Sloan put on his hat and started out the door.

"Wait, Mr. Sloan, please!" Kate cried, seizing hold of his coat sleeve. "We can't call off the plan! Sir Henry promised to help Thomas! I must talk to him. I can be dressed in five minutes!"

"I fear that will be quite impossible, Captain," said Mr. Sloan gravely, pulling away from her. "Sir Henry is seeing no one."

He walked out and shut the door behind him. Kate grabbed a coat, intending to pursue him. Amelia stopped her.

"Leave him be, Kate. Did you see his face? I have written that a man was 'pale beneath his tan,' but until now I have never actually seen such a thing. Mr. Sloan looked worse than the time I saw him in hospital after he had been shot."

"What do you think is wrong?" Kate asked.

Amelia shook her head. "Sir Henry moves in dangerous circles. I fear something terrible has happened to him."

Sophia crept down the stairs wearing one of Amelia's flannel dressing gowns. Her hair hung in a long braid over her shoulder.

"I heard the door slam," she said. "Is everything all right?"

"No, it isn't," said Kate dispiritedly.

Bandit dashed to the front door and pawed it, needing to go out. Kate held the door open while he took care of business. Bandit dashed back into the house and began to bark, letting them know it was time for his breakfast.

Kate shut the door. "Mr. Sloan came to say we must abandon our plan to smuggle Sir Henry onto the palace grounds. He has met with some sort of accident."

"I hope Sir Henry is all right," Sophia said, concerned. "Did he say what had happened?"

"Mr. Sloan rushed off without telling us anything except that we must give up our plan to help Pip and Thomas," said Kate, frustrated. "It was a good plan."

"He never did tell us what his plan was," Sophia pointed out.

"He did, just not in so many words," said Kate. "He was going to kill Smythe."

Sophia's eyes widened in shock.

"We should discuss this over a cup of tea," said Amelia. "I will light the fire. Kate, you put on the kettle. Sophia, for mercy's sake, feed that dog so he will stop barking."

A short time later, they sat around the kitchen table, drinking tea and discussing the morning's events. Bandit lay at Sophia's feet, gnawing on a beef bone.

"You don't know Sir Henry intended to kill that man, Kate," Amelia stated, adding more hot water to the teapot.

"So maybe he wasn't," Kate said. "We know Sir Henry told Thomas in code to spy on King Ullr. Perhaps he was going to talk to Thomas, see what he had learned."

"Or perhaps he had found some way to free Phillip from prison," said Sophia.

Amelia briskly rose to her feet. "It's no good wasting time speculating. I must write a Captain Kate story to let His Majesty know we have been forced to call off the plan."

"Please wait a day or two, Miss Amelia," Kate begged. "We may yet hear from Sir Henry. I don't want Thomas to think we failed him."

Amelia regarded her with sympathetic understanding. "I know how you feel, my dear, but Thomas might put himself in jeopardy for nothing. It is only fair that we let him know."

Kate sighed, frustrated and feeling helpless. "You didn't see Thomas in the procession, Miss Amelia. He was surrounded by people cheering him and shouting his name, and he was alone. So alone."

Kate had to stop talking for a moment to clear her throat. "When I handed him the violets, I gave him more than flowers. I gave him hope. I told him that he wasn't alone. That he had friends who are working to help him and Pip. Now we must snatch hope away."

The three sat in despondent silence. The only sound was Bandit gnawing at the bone.

"I won't let that happen," Kate said determinedly. "We will form our own plan to help Thomas and free Pip. We don't know what Sir Henry meant to do, but that doesn't matter. We can do this ourselves."

"Oh, Kate, that's a splendid idea!" Sophia said.

"Dalgren can fly us over the wall," said Kate. "Sir Henry told me to observe the movement of the patrol boats. I know their schedule and the route they take. Dalgren can easily evade them."

"And once we are inside the palace grounds, we know how to sneak into the palace through the concealed door. We know where to find the secret passages," said Sophia.

"Ladies!" Amelia rapped sharply on the table with her teaspoon. "I must ask you both to be reasonable. Consider what you are proposing! Think of the difficulty and danger! Once you are on the palace grounds, do you know your way around? Do you even know where Offdom Tower is located?"

"It's a bloody great tower. How hard can it be to find," Kate said. She sighed again. "I know you are right, Miss Amelia, but please wait another day before you tell Thomas."

"Yes, Miss Amelia, please," Sophia added her entreaty.

"Very well," said Amelia. "I will wait. Meanwhile, I will go to the office of the *Gazette,* see if I can learn what happened to Sir Henry."

"Kate and I will do the washing up," Sophia offered.

After Amelia had departed, Sophia began gathering up the tea cups. Kate dumped the remnants of the tea in the slop bucket.

"I suppose Miss Amelia is right," said Sophia. "We are being foolish to imagine we could sneak into the palace. We must hope to hear from Sir Henry."

"I don't think there is much chance of that," said Kate.

Sophia smiled, their thoughts in accord. "So we form our own plan?"

"We form a plan," said Kate, resolute.

Once they reached the *Terrapin,* Alan led a group of sailors with a litter to the cab. Under Perry's supervision, they conveyed Henry on board the *Ter-*

rapin and carried him to the sick bay. The lieutenant on duty was startled to see a man bundled in coats arrive on a litter, but he had served with Alan during their privateer days and knew better than to ask questions.

Alan ordered the ship to be made ready to sail with as little noise as possible. The crew of the *Terrapin* were all seasoned sailors fiercely loyal to their captain, and they crept about the deck soft-footed, passing along orders in whispers, and cringing when winches squeaked or some poor soul dropped a handspike on the deck.

As Alan had expected, he found his own surgeon passed out on his bunk, an empty rum bottle lying nearby. Alan ordered several men to haul him off the ship and dump him and his belongings on the dock. He then offered to take Perry on as ship's surgeon.

Perry readily agreed. "It would be an honor, Captain Northrop."

The surgeon wrote a brief note to his wife, and Alan sent a midshipman to his home to deliver the message and fetch his belongings. The surgeon's mate, a healer who had probably done more than the drunken surgeon to treat his fellow crew members, worked along with Perry to try to save Henry's life.

He lay in the sick bay, unconscious, covered in blood and pale as a corpse. Alan had resolved to remain with him, but when he saw the surgeon's blade flash in the light, his gut twisted and he had to leave. He hurried to his cabin to take a drink of brandy and try to imagine what life would be like without his best friend.

"I will have to be the one to tell Lady Ann," Alan said to himself.

He couldn't bear the thought. He poured himself another drink and went up on deck to wait for Randolph and Mr. Sloan. The ship was ready to sail, but he did not want to leave before talking with his friends. The sun had been up an hour by the time they arrived.

"Come down to my cabin," said Alan. "We can talk in private."

"How is Henry?" Randolph asked.

"How is His Lordship, sir?" Mr. Sloan asked at the same time.

Alan shook his head. "I haven't received the report from the surgeon. I was with him, but I couldn't stay. Not with him lying there—" He couldn't go on.

Mr. Sloan handed over a leather pouch. "This contains papers His Lordship deems important. Master Yates and I destroyed the rest. I have also brought clothes for His Lordship, as well as information Master Yates wanted him to have regarding the liquid Breath pool he terms the White Well. Master Yates says that if we are anywhere near the Aligoes, he expects us to search for it."

Alan smiled, shook his head, and took the pouch. He opened the iron safe and placed it inside along with his sealed orders. He closed the safe and locked it.

"I don't suppose you managed to talk Simon into coming?"

"Stubborn as a goddamn wyvern," Randolph stated. "Mr. Sloan and I both tried to persuade him to leave, but he is determined to go back to Welkinstead."

"Since the house landed in an open field, and just missed crashing into the forest, Simon will probably be safe enough there," Alan said thoughtfully. "And he has Albright."

Mr. Sloan appeared preoccupied. "If I might ask a question, Captain?"

"Certainly, Mr. Sloan," said Alan. He exchanged glances with Randolph. They both knew what he was about to ask.

"I understand that Sir Richard's manservant, Mr. Henshaw, betrayed His Lordship. Is that true?"

"It is, Mr. Sloan," said Alan. "I saw him."

"Do you suspect Sir Richard of taking part in this betrayal, sir?" Mr. Sloan asked.

Randolph shook his head. "Not the Old Chap."

"I agree with Randolph, Mr. Sloan," said Alan. "I would guess that Henshaw took it upon himself to betray Henry, probably with some misguided idea of keeping his master safe."

"Knowing what I know of Sir Richard, I concur, sir," said Mr. Sloan. "Regarding Mr. Henshaw—"

"We will find a way to deal with Henshaw, Mr. Sloan," Alan said quietly.

"It would be my distinct pleasure to assist you in that endeavor, sir," said Mr. Sloan. "And now, if I am not needed, I would like to be with Sir Henry."

"I was about to suggest that, Mr. Sloan," said Alan. He tried to sound positive. "When he regains consciousness, assure him that all is well. He must concentrate on healing."

"You're sailing this morning," Randolph said to Alan after Mr. Sloan had departed.

"I have my orders," said Alan. "Which is fortunate, for I need to smuggle Henry out of Freya before the soldiers think to look for him on board the ship."

They were interrupted by the surgeon. Alan and Randolph faced him in tense, strained silence, neither of them able to ask the terrible question.

Perry gave a weary smile. "Sir Henry is alive and he has regained consciousness."

"Thank God!" Alan breathed.

Randolph muttered something and removed his handkerchief from his sleeve. He loudly blew his nose.

"The trick will be keeping him alive," Perry added.

"Infection?" Alan asked anxiously.

"Well, yes, that, of course," said Perry. "But I was thinking more about the fact that His Lordship is quite determined to leave the ship."

"Don't worry," said Alan. "That won't happen."

He summoned his lieutenant and gave the orders to take the *Terrapin* out of the harbor. "No need for tiptoeing about anymore. Tell the crew to make all the noise they want."

As the lieutenant departed, they could hear him shouting orders, those orders being repeated, and then the drumming of feet on the deck.

"I believe this news calls for a drink," said Alan, offering them each a glass of Calvados. "How did the surgery go?"

"I must admit I was doubtful about His Lordship's chances," Perry said, refusing the offer. "The bullet broke the clavicle and did considerable damage. His Lordship came near bleeding to death, but your surgeon's mate is a deft hand at healing magic. I set the clavicle and contrived a sling to prevent His Lordship from moving his arm.

"His Lordship was mercifully unconscious during the procedure, but now that he is awake, he is in a great deal of pain made worse by his attempts to leave his bed. I have offered to give him laudanum, but he refuses to take anything. He demands to speak with you, Captain."

"I will join you in a moment," said Alan.

Perry returned to his patient. Randolph gulped his Calvados and Alan walked him to the gangplank, which the sailors were just about to raise.

"I saw your orders still in the safe," said Randolph. "You haven't read them."

"I am ordered not to read them until the ship reaches Upton Point."

"I'll find out about this secret mission of yours if I have to go to the king himself," said Randolph grimly.

"By God, that's a good idea, Randolph!" said Alan, struck by the notion. "If anyone could gain access to the king, it would be one of His Majesty's admirals. Find out what you can. But be subtle. Remember that the king is surrounded by spies."

"I'm always goddamn subtle," Randolph said, offended. "I am known for my subtlety."

"Subtle as a brickbat," said Alan, grinning. "Stay in touch with Simon."

"Good luck to you and Henry," said Randolph. "Let me know how he mends."

The two men shook hands, Randolph left, and Alan gave orders to raise the gangplank. He went below and found Mr. Sloan seated at Henry's bedside, moistening his master's lips with water.

"Do not stay long, Captain," Perry cautioned. "His Lordship requires

rest. Summon me if you have need. And try to persuade him to take the laudanum. Pain interferes with healing."

"So does bull-headed stubbornness, but I will do my best," said Alan.

He walked over to the bed, looked down at his friend.

Henry was pale and feverish, his eyes sunken, his skin gray from blood
loss. But he was awake and alert, and glaring at Alan.

"What the devil are you doing? Mr. Sloan tells me that the ship is preparing to set sail!"

"I have my orders," Alan said.

Mr. Sloan started to place a cooling cloth on Henry's forehead.

"Get that damn rag off me!" Henry snarled. "I'm not staying on board.
I'm going ashore—"

He tried to move, but cried out in pain and fell back onto the bed. He
sucked in his breath and groaned in agony. Beads of sweat broke out on his
forehead. He lay in the bed, breathing heavily, until he found the energy to
speak.

"I cannot . . . leave now!" he gasped. "My country . . . Smythe . . ."

He groaned again and clamped his lips together.

Alan rested his hand gently on the limp hand of his friend.

"Henry, if you remained in Haever, there is nothing you could do for your
country except die."

Henry gazed at him, silently pleading with him, not so much to change his
mind, but to change fate.

Alan understood and pressed his hand.

Henry closed his eyes in bitter resignation. Tears of frustration and an-
guish mingled with the sweat on his cheeks.

"Give him the laudanum, Mr. Sloan," said Alan.

He sat with Henry until he had fallen asleep, then went back up on deck.
Sails billowed, and magic flowed to the lift tanks that contained the crystals
known as the Tears of God. Crew members stood by and, at his command,
cast off the lines that tethered the *Terrapin* to the dock.

Alan drew in the fresh air as the *Terrapin* caught the wind and rose into
the Breath. She was a magnificent sight with her sails spread and the sunlight
of a new day shining on the metal plates that gave the ship her name.

Alan ordered the helmsman to set a course that would take the ship
around Upton Point and went back to his cabin. He removed the sealed
orders from the safe and laid them on his desk, then kept impatient watch
for the sight of the familiar landmark.

An hour later, the promontory came into view. Alan sliced through the
wax with his knife, opened the packet, and read.

"I am ordered to sail to Wellinsport to engage the Rosians and prevent them from capturing the city. I'll be damned," Alan remarked. "So we are going to war with Rosia."

He poured himself a drink, then replaced the orders in the packet, which was lined with lead, and prepared to toss it overboard into the Breath.

Thinking of his friend, Alan shook his head. "This will be a blow to Henry. Just as well he's unconscious."

TWENTY-TWO

After long wrestling with his conscience, Thomas finally made up his mind to spy on King Ullr. Now that he had decided, he was impatient to proceed. He had the means to do so through the portrait of King Godfrey, but what he lacked was opportunity. He needed to find a time when the king was meeting with Baron Grimm in order to discover what the two were plotting.

The baron was not a guest at the palace, but he was a frequent visitor. He came almost daily, arriving at various hours. And though Thomas watched him closely, he never saw him enter King Ullr's private chambers. They seemed only to exchange pleasantries or speak of inconsequential matters. Yet Grimm was Ullr's agent. They must be meeting in Ullr's chambers in secret. Thomas needed to know when and he decided this could be an opportunity to see if he could rely upon Corporal Jennings.

Thomas had deliberately developed a habit of roaming about the palace. He took long walks both inside and outside, letting it be known he was trying to learn his way around. He once blundered into a servants' closet on the third floor near the Godfrey Suite, completely by accident, or so he said, much to the delight of the maids.

Smythe had reluctantly agreed that Thomas could ride his horse daily, even though that meant venturing outside the palace. He was always attended by members of the palace guard, either mounted on horseback or accompanying him on griffinback. The guards were there to keep him safe, but Smythe had also informed Thomas they had orders to see to it that he did not leave the palace grounds.

As he had hoped, the servants and the palace guard became accustomed to his ramblings, his showing up in odd places at odd times. He happened to overhear one of the maids say to another in pitying tones, "Poor lad. Restless as a caged bear, he is."

Every day, at about noon, Jennings made his rounds of the palace, checking that all was secure and receiving the reports from the guards. Thomas decided that a "chance" meeting with the corporal in the hallway would not look suspicious. This day, as he walked the long gallery at noon, he paused to admire some of the paintings that lined the walls.

Thomas observed Jennings coming down the hall just as the clock was chiming twelve. The corporal was still wearing a sling on his arm from the wound he had suffered in the Rose Room.

Thomas feigned to take no notice of him, but stopped to gaze at a display of weaponry dating back to the Sunlit Empire that was mounted on the wall. Hearing footfalls, he glanced around.

"Ah, Corporal Jennings," Thomas called, summoning him with a gesture. "You are just the man. I have a question. I have heard that you are familiar with weaponry of this ancient period."

"Warfare of that period happens to be an interest of mine, Your Majesty," Jennings replied.

Thomas gestured to one of the weapons on the wall. "I have made a bet with one of my ministers. I say that this is a pike. His Lordship maintains that it is a spear."

"I fear you will lose your bet, sir," said Jennings. "The pike is similar to a spear, but much longer. A soldier requires two hands to wield a pike, whereas he needs only one hand to throw a spear."

Thomas took down the pike from the wall and hefted it. "How is it carried?"

"Place one hand here, sir," said Jennings, moving close to Thomas to demonstrate. "And the other hand there. Thus, you see, you may now use the pike to thrust at the enemy."

Thomas did as he was told and said in a low voice, "I need to know the next time King Ullr meets privately with Baron Grimm."

Jennings' eyes flickered, but he said only, "Do not hold your hands so close together, sir. There, that is better. That is the proper grip."

"Thank you, Corporal," said Thomas. "I will let you return to your duties."

"Allow me, sir."

Jennings took the pike from him and replaced it on the wall. Thomas was cautiously pleased with the encounter. Jennings had been quick-thinking and prompt to act, agreeing to undertake the assignment without wasting time asking questions.

Thomas waited to see the outcome.

Later that day, he was taking a fencing lesson when he saw Jennings walk over to stand by a window and gaze out, as though admiring the view. As he was leaving, one of the leather gloves that he had tucked into his belt fell to the floor. He walked off without noticing he had lost it.

Thomas ended the lesson, removed his mask, and handed his foil to the instructor. Mopping his face with a towel, he walked over to the window and bent down to pick up the glove.

He discovered a note tucked inside.

Tonight. Eleven. Office.

Thomas handed the glove to a servant to return to Jennings and destroyed the note.

He dined with several members of the Travian cartel that evening. He had expected Smythe to join them, but he did not appear.

Thomas thought his absence odd, for Smythe rarely let him meet with anyone on his own. After his guests had departed, Thomas went to Smythe's office, hoping to learn more. He was pleased to find Corporal Jennings alone, loitering about, almost as though waiting for him.

"I have been searching for Chancellor Smythe, Corporal," said Thomas. "No one seems to know where he has gone or why."

"He was called away last night, sir. He said the matter was urgent, but he wouldn't say what. As far as I know, he has not returned," Jennings said.

Thomas retired to his private quarters, puzzling over what urgent matter could be keeping Smythe away and thinking that whatever it was, he was undoubtedly up to no good.

He left orders that he was not to be disturbed. He had carefully laid his plans, but whenever he thought about the disagreeable and shameful task he was about to undertake, his heart failed him.

He opened the book in which he'd placed Kate's violets for reassurance. The faint, lingering fragrance brought a vivid memory of Kate bounding onto his carriage and thrusting the flowers into his hand. She seemed bathed in sunlight, her hazel and golden eyes laughing for the thrill of the adventure and probably at the astonished look on his face. He could feel the warmth of her touch as their hands met.

"She is counting on me, expecting me to do my part. They are risking their lives to save the country they love," Thomas murmured. "How can I face them and tell them I failed them—failed my country—because of some code of conduct from the *Gentleman's Book of Etiquette and Manual of Politeness?*"

He returned the flowers to the book and was replacing it on the shelf when a servant knocked, requesting admittance.

"I left orders not to be disturbed," said Thomas, irritated.

"I have the tea Your Majesty requested," the servant replied.

Thomas was about to say he had not requested tea, then realized that if he had not, someone else had, and there must be a reason.

The servant entered carrying a silver tray with a silver tea service and placed the tray on a table. He poured the tea, then departed, shutting the door behind him. Thomas picked up the tea cup and looked beneath the saucer, then lifted the teapot and found nothing. As he was unfolding the linen, a note slid out and fell to the floor.

He opened it and read:

> *Smythe returned to the palace early this morning and would not say where he had been. I spoke to his carriage driver, who said he had driven Smythe to a tavern known as the Weigh Anchor where Smythe expected some well-known criminal to be arrested. Smythe planned to have the man conveyed to Offdom Tower. As it happened, however, a riot broke out at the tavern and the criminal escaped. Smythe exited the carriage and was gone for some time. When he returned, he was in a black mood and ordered the driver to return to the palace.*

The note was not signed, but Thomas had no doubt it was from Jennings. He held the note in his hand and considered telling Jennings about the Godfrey portrait and sending him to spy on King Ullr. Jennings had offered convincing proof of his loyalty.

Thomas was mindful of the teachings of his instructors at the Estaran military academy, who had impressed upon him that if there was something of vital importance to be done, he should trust no one to do it but himself.

He burned the note and summoned his valet.

TWENTY-THREE

The clock in Thomas's bedchamber struck half past the hour of ten. He had changed out of his evening attire into more comfortable clothing and told the valet he would have no more need of his services.

"You may retire for the night," Thomas said.

The man gave Thomas a knowing look and said, with an insinuating smirk, "I trust Your Majesty has a pleasant evening."

Thomas smiled and winked. "I have been told it is my duty to help entertain our foreign visitors."

The valet dutifully laughed. Thomas dismissed the man, knowing he would rush to immediately report to Smythe that Thomas was involved in some sort of illicit romantic liaison.

He hung a bull's-eye lantern beneath his jacket and buttoned it over the lantern, then left his chambers through what the Lord Chamberlain referred to as the "family door."

The first night Thomas had spent in the royal chambers, the Lord Chamberlain had escorted him around the multitude of rooms and had shown him the "family door," a private entrance and exit that had been installed during the time of King Alfred.

"The king liked to sneak out of the palace to go carousing with low friends," said the Lord Chamberlain. "Since his time, all our monarchs have made use of it. King Godfrey smuggled his mistress, Lady Honoria, into his bedchamber. Queen Mary, God save her, used the door to sneak down to the kitchen to raid the pantry."

The Chamberlain shook his head in fond amusement. "I always told Her Majesty that she could ring for the servants to bring her anything she wanted to eat at any hour. Queen Mary would tell me in that sharp manner of hers, 'But how the devil do I know what I want to eat until I have had a good rummage through the larder?'"

The Lord Chamberlain went on to further state that since Thomas was a young man with a young man's "appetites," he would undoubtedly find the door extremely useful.

"The door leads into the servants' passages. You will find those rather confusing at first, sir, but you will soon learn your way around."

Thomas had learned his way around on his rambles and had memorized the route to the third floor and the servants' closet where he had startled the maids by bursting in on them.

Fortunately, the palace would be deserted at this time of night, since Smythe had closed up most of the guest rooms, complaining that the upkeep was a waste of money. The only guests staying in the palace at this time were King Ullr and his retinue. Among these were several ladies from Guundar, who had made it known to the handsome young king that they would be open to receiving late night visits.

Accustomed to the Estaran court, Thomas was familiar with how such amorous games were played, and he flirted with them and indicated he was open to all possibilities. If Smythe heard of his flirtations, he would probably be glad his profligate king was pleasantly occupied, for then he could do as he wanted without interference.

When Thomas reached the third floor, he concealed himself in a shadowy alcove to keep watch on the entrance to the Godfrey Suite. As the clocks throughout the palace chimed eleven times, the punctual baron arrived to keep his appointment with Ullr and was immediately admitted into the Guundaran king's presence.

Thomas entered the servants' closet and shut the door behind him. The door did not lock, but he was not worried that someone would find him. The servants would not return to work until just before dawn. He lit the bull's-eye lantern by pressing on a magical construct and flashed the light about the closet, finally locating the wall with the three coat hooks.

Thomas stood in front of the wall and, feeling rather foolish, spoke the three words in order: "Albert, Godfrey, Mary."

He was not certain what to expect—if anything—and he was startled by a bright flash of blue light and the loud "snick" as of a lock clicking. A door in the wall swung slightly ajar, just wide enough for him to squeeze through it.

The passage was dark as the Deep Breath and almost as cold. The ceiling, walls, and floor were made of stone and thick with dust. Thomas flashed the beam of light around and saw that the hall was narrow and straight, with no curves or turns. He padded soft-footed along it until he reached the end—an alcove shrouded by a velvet curtain.

Thomas shut off the lantern and stood in the impenetrable darkness, listening. He could hear voices, as clearly as if he was standing in the room. He recognized both of them: Ullr's deep, smooth voice and Grimm's husky gruffness.

They were speaking in Guundaran. Thomas's mastery of that language had improved from being around his Guundaran guards, who found it amusing to indulge Thomas in his desire to learn their native tongue.

Thomas stealthily drew aside the curtain and saw two holes that must, he knew, correspond with Godfrey's eyes. He put his own eyes to the holes and gazed through the portrait. He could see King Ullr and the baron sitting at their ease before the fire, enjoying the potent liquor made from potatoes, for which Guundar was justifiably famous.

"—working out far better than we had anticipated," Ullr was saying.

"Your 'dear friend' has no suspicions you are using him?" the baron asked with a smile.

"None whatsoever," said Ullr with satisfaction. "Smythe is as susceptible to flattery as a young girl attending her first ball. I tell him God wants him to save Freya from this heathen young king. I blather on about how Stanford plans to hand the country back to the corrupt priests of Rosia, and Smythe eagerly gulps down the lies."

"Your Majesty speaks to him as an equal," said Grimm, slightly frowning.

"All part of the plan. I even told him that he and I must be distantly related. 'It is obvious, sir,' I said to him, 'that the royal blood of Guundar flows in your veins.'"

Baron Grimm laughed uproariously at this notion.

"Meanwhile, he serves my purpose," Ullr continued. "I have promised him my full support for his war against Rosia. I warned him of a Rosian plot to seize Wellinsport and attack Sornhagen."

"Sornhagen?" Grimm was alarmed and Thomas knew why. Sornhagen was a Travian stronghold in the Aligoes, and the Travians were allied with Guundar, which was the only major nation in the world that did not have a port in the Aligoes. If the Travians lost Sornhagen to Rosia, Guundar would be cut out of the lucrative trade in the Aligoes. "Is this true, sir?"

"No, of course not, Baron," said Ullr, slightly frowning at his agent's gullibility. "The Rosians are already squabbling with Estara, plus they know better than to offend the Travians, who could play havoc with Rosian finances by refusing to do business with them.

"I devised this ruse as a means to remove the threat of that iron-plated ship, the *Terrapin*. Smythe reacted as I hoped, and he dispatched the *Terrapin* to Wellinsport to confront the Rosians."

"Is Your Majesty certain this *Terrapin* will not interfere with our plans to seize Wellinsport?" Grimm asked.

"She will be vastly outnumbered. I have given orders for our ships to capture her, for I would give a great deal to possess the only operational iron-plated ship in the world. If that is not possible, however, they are ordered to sink her."

Thomas was chilled. At Smythe's behest he had signed those orders, that were now sending the *Terrapin* and her crew into an ambush. And what did Ullr mean about seizing Wellinsport? He hoped the king would expand on that subject, but Baron Grimm was still talking of iron-plated ships.

"What of the other two ships with the magical steel plating, sir?"

"They are languishing in the Royal Naval Yard for lack of funding," said Ullr. "But I look forward to the day when they, too, will be flying the Guundaran flag."

"Smythe is eager for war with the Rosians," Grimm stated. "I cannot understand why, except perhaps to prop up his puppet-king. The Rosian Dragon Brigade will tear the Freyan fleet to pieces and scatter them about the Breath."

"Smythe believes he can defeat the Rosians," said Ullr, sipping his drink.

"The man has the brains of a goose." Grimm gave a dismissive snort.

"On the contrary, Baron, he is right," said Ullr.

Grimm stared, incredulous. "You cannot be serious, sir."

Ullr appeared to enjoy astonishing his agent. "Smythe salvaged one of those black ships used by the Bottom Dwellers and outfitted it with a green-beam gun—one that has been modified and does not require blood magic."

"Modified?" Grimm frowned. "How can such a fiendish device be modified?"

Ullr shrugged. "He went on about the Seventh Sigil. Not being a crafter myself, I cannot explain. But we will know soon enough if his modifications will work. Smythe is sending the black ship, the *Naofa,* to attack the Dragon Brigade headquarters in Maribeau in the Aligoes. I have alerted our agents and ordered them to observe this weapon in action and report back to me.

"I hope it does work," Ullr added coolly. "For I have acquired five of them."

Baron Grimm gaped at the king. "How is that possible, sir? They were all destroyed!"

Ullr permitted himself a rare smile. "So I thought. But it occurred to me that if Smythe had one, he might have more. I asked him, but he was uncharacteristically tight-lipped on the subject. His aide, one Corporal Plackton, keeps a mistress with expensive tastes. The man is deeply in debt and was happy to provide me with all the information I wanted, including the location of the guns. Smythe kept them hidden away in a cave in northern Freya. I sent our troops to seize them and I am now refitting five of our ships to make use of them."

"Armed with such weapons, our ships will be invincible," said Grimm, regarding the king with unbounded admiration.

"Let us hope so. What do you have to report?" Ullr asked with an air of nonchalance.

"Our own forces, which Smythe so obligingly hires as mercenaries, are now established in Fort Upton, Port Fahey, Glenham Castle, Kerrington, and the naval base at Whithaven, as well as the palace. They await only your signal to attack their Freyan comrades and officers and take control."

"Excellent," said Ullr. "In this pouch you will find your orders in regard to Wellinsport."

"The Freyans paying for their own destruction, an ingenious plan, sir, as I have said before." Grimm took the pouch and tucked it into his coat. "I commend you."

Ullr smiled again, appreciative of the compliment. "You will, of course, destroy these documents once you have read them. And now, if there is nothing more—"

"There is something more, sir," said Grimm. "Smythe has arrested His Grace, Phillip Masterson, and locked him in Offdom Tower. Is Your Majesty aware that this duke works as an agent for Sir Henry Wallace?"

"What of it?" Ullr asked contemptuously. "The duke is, as you say, locked up in Offdom Tower and Wallace is dead."

"His death cannot be confirmed, sir," Grimm warned.

"He has vanished. You yourself said you could not find him," said Ullr.

"The very fact that I cannot find him concerns me, sir," Grimm said insistently. "And if Wallace is dead, his agent is very much alive. The duke is said to be close to King Thomas, who heeds his advice. Even behind bars, Masterson remains a threat."

Ullr shrugged. "Then remove him. The prison guards are loyal Guundarans. They will assist you. How do you plan to go about it?"

The baron reflected. "Masterson once foiled a delicate plot of mine and very nearly got me killed. I know of a remarkable poison that can be slipped into his wine. Masterson will linger in agony for days and die a most excruciatingly painful death. I owe him that."

"As you will," said Ullr. "But do not kill him until after you have returned from the Aligoes. The king might become suspicious, and I want nothing to interfere with our plans to invade Freya."

Thomas gave an audible gasp.

Baron Grimm glanced around, frowning. "Did you hear something, sir?"

Thomas froze, afraid to breathe.

"A log broke apart in the fireplace," said Ullr. "You are unaccountably jumpy these days, Baron."

"One does not plot an invasion every day, sir," said the baron. "Have you decided on a date, sir?"

"Hallen Day, which celebrates a notable Freyan naval victory over the Rosians. All Freya will be observing the holiday, most notably the navy. I hear the young king plans a grand naval review. Crowds will gather at the docks, the navy's ships will be on display. . . ."

Baron Grimm chuckled. "What is it the Freyans say? Something about sitting ducks in a barrel?"

King Ullr smiled and downed his drink.

Thomas could not stand to hear any more. He was enraged and appalled by what he had heard already and he did not trust himself to stand by quietly and listen to them plot to invade his country and murder his friend. He switched on the dark lantern, but the light did little good, for he was half-blind with fury. He stumbled and groped his way down the hall until he fetched up against the door to the closet.

Tasting blood in his mouth, he realized he had bitten through his lip, and he pressed his forehead against the cold stone, drew in deep breaths until he felt calmer. He shuddered with dread when he considered how close he had come to refusing to spy on Ullr out of some misguided sense of honor.

Thomas remained in the darkness of the passage until he had stopped shaking with rage. He returned to his chamber and, once inside, poured a brandy with a trembling hand and drank it in a gulp.

He had two immediate concerns: saving his country and saving Phillip. He could not rid himself of the terrible image of his friend drinking poison, falling horribly ill, and dying in agony.

He couldn't allow Phillip to remain there another moment, and he made up his mind to go immediately to the tower to order the guards to free his friend, when he finally listened to the voice of reason shouting in his head.

The guards were loyal Guundarans—that is, they were loyal to Guundar, not to him. They would probably refuse to obey him and then hasten to report to King Ullr or Smythe or both. Ullr would wonder how Thomas had found out about the plot to kill Phillip and he would have his suite of rooms searched and discover the holes in the eyes of the portrait. Thomas's ability to spy on him would come to an end, and he needed to know more about Ullr's plans to invade Freya and seize Wellinsport.

"Pip warned me about him. The countess warned me," said Thomas. "Ullr hardly speaks of me, and when he does it is to dismiss me as nothing but a callow, feckless youth. Which is precisely what I am!"

He drank another brandy and turned his thoughts to the other alarming information he had gathered: a black ship armed with a green-beam gun was going to attack the Dragon Brigade. And Ullr was refitting five of his ships with more green-beam guns.

"I should tell someone, warn someone. I should send someone to do something!" Thomas said, frustrated.

You need Henry, Sir Richard had once told him. Phillip had told him the same thing.

"Wallace is no friend to me, but I don't need a friend," Thomas reflected. "I need someone who has the knowledge, the means, and the ability to help me save Phillip and our country."

The question was, how to reach Henry Wallace? According to the baron, the spymaster had vanished.

Thomas retrieved the newspaper with the Captain Kate story from its hiding place in the desk and reread the sentence that spoke about Jennings.

"'Captain Kate can use Jennings to send a message to her friends.'"

Her friends had to include Wallace.

Thomas had no choice. He would now have to trust Jennings—trust him with his life and the lives of his people.

TWENTY-FOUR

Kate had never been one to sit idle. As a little girl, she had sailed the world on board her father's ship, calling no one place home. Each new day had brought her a fresh adventure.

After her father's death, Kate's life as a wrecker in the Aligoes had been difficult and dangerous, but it had suited her restless nature. When she was not salvaging wrecked cargo, she was flying with Dalgren or refitting her ship, serving drinks at the Perky Parrot or dodging Greenstreet's henchmen.

During rare moments of peace and quiet, she had dreamed of joining the Dragon Brigade or making her fortune as a privateer and restoring her child-hood home, Barwich Manor, to its former glory. She had eagerly risen from her bed every morning with myriad dreams and schemes in her head.

This morning she rose from her bed in Amelia's house with her head filled with plans and schemes to free Phillip and rescue Thomas. Or rather, she was filled with hopes of freeing Phillip and rescuing Thomas. As yet, she and Sophia had not formed a viable plan.

Amelia had tried without success to find out what had become of Sir Henry. She had contacted her underworld sources, made the rounds of the hospitals, and even been so bold as to inquire at his house.

He had apparently vanished.

"We have no choice," Amelia said to Kate and Sophia. "We must let His Majesty know that we have abandoned the plan to sneak into the palace."

Kate and Sophia exchanged glances.

"You promised us to wait until tomorrow morning, Miss Amelia," said Kate.

Amelia eyed the two of them. "You young ladies are up to something. Very well. A promise is words engraved upon the soul, as Mrs. Ridgeway often taught us."

That morning, when Amelia shut herself up in her office to write, Kate and Sophia sat down at the kitchen table to work on their plan, disappointing Bandit, who had thought they were going to eat.

"We know how to sneak into the palace," said Kate. "We know the secret door to the secret passage."

"But I am not sure we could find our way around once we are inside the passages," said Sophia. "We took an awful lot of twists and turns."

"I have been thinking. Perhaps we won't need to use the passages," said Kate. "We still have the maids' uniforms. The palace employs hundreds of maids. Odds are no one would notice us. Once we are inside, you know where to find the Rose Room."

Sophia was dubious. "I'm not certain—"

Kate ignored her protest. "You know. So here's my plan. I came up with it last night. We will send a message in Amelia's next story to Thomas, telling him we will meet him in the Rose Room. He will take us to Offdom Tower where we will set Pip free. We will meet Dalgren on the palace grounds and he will fly all four of us to Barwich Manor. We will be safe there until we can find a way to leave Freya."

"Oh, Kate," said Sophia, regarding her unhappily.

Kate sighed and ran her hand through her curls. "You think I am being silly and impractical, although you are too polite to tell me. None of this will work. It's nothing but a dream."

"Fight for your dreams," said Sophia unexpectedly.

Kate looked at her, startled.

"You told me that Stephano de Guichen said that to you when you were a little girl," Sophia explained. "Maybe we should fight, find a way to *make* this work—"

They were interrupted by Bandit, who let out a yelp, leaped to his feet, and raced out of the kitchen. They could hear him in the entry hall, barking wildly. The next moment, a knock sounded on the door.

"Sir Henry!" Kate exclaimed.

She jumped up so fast, her skirt caught in the chair and swept it over. Sophia hurried out into the hall, calling for Amelia, who had also heard Bandit and was running out of her office.

The person was still knocking. Bandit was jumping at the door, scratching at it with his paws. Kate was about to yank it open, when she remembered that they were housing a fugitive.

"Sophia! Bandit! Kitchen!" Kate ordered.

Sophia caught hold of the dog and ran back to the kitchen.

"Look out the window first," said Amelia, arriving breathlessly.

Kate went to one of the two narrow windows that stood on either side of the door. She parted the curtain to peep outside.

"Oh, my God. It's a Freyan army officer! Warn Sophia—" Kate stopped, looked more closely, then gave a relieved sigh. "No! Wait! I know this man. It's Corporal Jennings!"

She flung open the door.

"Corporal! Thank God, you are alive! Please, come inside."

"I am very much alive," said Jennings, mystified. "Did you think I was dead?"

"We heard a pistol shot after you helped us escape and we feared the worst," Kate explained.

Jennings smiled. "Fortunately, I managed to survive my encounter with the notorious Captain Kate, though I fear I did make the false claim that you shot me, Captain."

Kate laughed and introduced Amelia, who advanced to shake hands.

"Welcome, sir," said Amelia. "I want to add my thanks for saving Kate and Sophia. They are both very dear to me. Come into the kitchen, have some tea."

"Thank you, no, ma'am," said the corporal. "This is not a social call. My time is limited. His Majesty sent me with a message for Sir Henry Wallace. Can you tell me where to find him? The matter is of extreme urgency."

Kate and Amelia looked at each other in concern.

"We would be glad to, sir, but we ourselves do not know where to find Sir Henry," Amelia replied. "The day before yesterday, his secretary, Mr. Sloan, came to tell us that His Lordship had met with an accident."

Jennings was dismayed. "You have no idea how to reach Sir Henry?"

"I have no idea if Sir Henry is even still alive," said Amelia gravely. "What message do you carry from the king?"

Jennings appeared uncertain about delivering it, but he didn't seem to know what else to do. "His Majesty has discovered that an agent of King Ullr's, Baron Rupert Grimm, is planning to murder King Thomas's friend, Phillip Masterson. King Ullr also intends—"

Sophia gasped. "Phillip! Oh, dear God! No!" She had heard Kate say Jennings' name and come out to see what was going on. Hearing the news, she paled and dropped Bandit, who landed on the floor with an indignant yelp. Jennings was distressed.

"Forgive me, Your Highness," he said, bowing. "I did not mean for you to overhear."

"Do not worry, my dear," said Amelia, giving Sophia a reassuring pat on her shoulder. "I know you and Kate have been plotting. I am sure you will think of something. And now, carry on, sir. What else do you know?"

"His Majesty has acquired the information Sir Henry requested regarding King Ullr and his designs upon our country. His Majesty needs to speak to His Lordship urgently."

Amelia sighed and shook her head.

"We cannot let them murder Phillip!" Sophia said, recovering from her momentary weakness. "Corporal Jennings, you saved our lives. Can't you do something to free Phillip from prison?"

"I am sorry, I cannot, ma'am," said Jennings. "His Majesty has ordered me to travel to Rosia to report what he has learned to the countess. She must speak to King Renaud, do all she can to try to prevent this disastrous war."

"And we must do all we can," said Kate decisively. "How was Sir Henry going to communicate with the king?"

"An advertisement in the Agony column, Captain," Jennings replied. "A single word: 'Yes.' Sir Henry was to convey his instructions to His Majesty in one of Miss Nettleship's stories."

Kate and Sophia exchanged glances. Kate picked up Bandit, who had been sniffing the corporal's boots. Sophia gave Jennings her hand.

"Thank you for coming, Corporal," she said. "I hope you have a safe journey. Please give the countess my love."

Amelia opened the door. "Good-bye, Corporal."

"Godspeed," said Kate.

Jennings understood perfectly well what they contemplated, and he was appalled. "Your Highness, Captain Kate, I beg of you! Please do not consider taking any action yourselves. Smythe is searching for you! If you return to the palace, you will be in great danger!"

"You need have no fear for me, sir," said Sophia. "I was raised by the Countess de Marjolaine."

Jennings looked to Amelia for help, but she only shook her head. "You had best be on your way, young man. The journey to Rosia is a long one."

Jennings still hesitated, unwilling to leave.

"You are dismissed, Corporal," said Sophia with a smile.

Jennings was forced to retreat. He bowed and Amelia shut the door on him.

"I will place the ad in the *Gazette,*" she said. "You two make a fresh pot of tea. We're going to need it."

By that afternoon, they had devised a plan.

Kate rose early the next morning and went to visit the palace, armed with a sketchbook and a box of pencils. The palace was a popular subject for artists, and no one paid attention to her.

She approached one of the gardeners, who was wrapping the ornamental fir trees in burlap to stop the deer from eating them.

"Which of these buildings is Offdom Tower?" Kate asked. "My art teacher has assigned us to do studies of the architecture."

The gardener pointed out a building in the interior of the palace compound that stood some distance from the palace itself and looked very dark and forbidding.

"I am afraid you can't see much of it from this side of the palace walls, miss," said the gardener.

"Is there any way I can get closer?" Kate asked.

"By getting yourself arrested, miss," said the gardener with a smirk.

Kate looked up into the sky. "What a delightful little boat. Is that used for sightseeing?"

"No, miss," said the gardener, rolling his eyes. "That there is a patrol boat, keeping watch for Rosian scum."

"Rosians!" Kate gasped. "Oh, dear! I hope His Majesty is safe from those fiends! How does the boat protect the king when it's so far away from him?"

The gardener was pleased to show off his knowledge and happy to take a break from his work. Kate heard all she wanted about the patrol boats, most of which she already knew, for she had investigated them when she had thought she and Dalgren might encounter them.

She thanked the gardener and left him to go back to his work, then walked about the grounds until she found a vantage point that provided her with a view of the top of the tower. She made a few drawings of the exterior. Noting several windows at the very top, she wondered if those belonged to Phillip's cell.

Having seen all she could of Offdom Tower, she noted the numbers of guards placed at the various entrances to the palace and again observed the rounds made by the patrol boats, to make sure nothing in their routine had changed. Kate closed her sketchbook and returned to Amelia's house to report.

"There are two boats that take turns guarding the palace. The boat on duty sails in a figure eight formation above the palace grounds. It takes about an hour to make a full sweep of the grounds. Each boat is armed with two eighteen-pound carronades and six swivel guns. The only time the boat lands is when the crew changes shifts, and that is every twelve hours. The boat lands on the roof of the palace."

"I feel sorry for those poor sailors," said Sophia. "I cannot imagine anything more boring, doing the same thing over and over, day and night."

"Which means they will be lax in their duties," said Amelia.

"Especially at night when they can't see much," Kate added. "The lookouts will be half-asleep. We will wait until the boat is at the opposite end of the palace grounds, then Dalgren will fly us over the wall as Sir Henry had planned. If for some reason the patrol boat does see us, they'll only see a dragon."

"Freyans are terrified of dragons. What if they fire at him?" Amelia asked.

"A little ball like an eighteen pounder won't hurt him," said Kate.

Sophia raised an eyebrow, as if she wondered what Dalgren would say to that. She knew better than to argue, though. She had drawn a map of the palace interior as best she could remember, and she and Kate tried to re-create the route they had taken through the secret passages. They soon gave up.

"Maybe Bandit remembers," said Kate, throwing down her pencil in frustration.

The spaniel wagged his tail, indicating he would be helpful if he could. Sophia rewarded him with a tea cake.

"What did you find out about Offdom Tower, Miss Amelia?" Kate asked.

Amelia had spent the day at the library, doing research. She referred to her notes.

"No prisoner has ever successfully escaped from the tower, which is reputed to be the most secure fortress in the world."

Kate and Sophia regarded her in dismay. Amelia shook her head and continued.

"The tower is four stories tall with cellblocks on three levels. A staircase tower attached to the main building provides access to these levels. The warden and his staff live in rooms on the ground floor. The cellblocks on levels two and three are no longer in use, since the construction of the prison at Hampstead. The upper level contains only four cells, which historically have housed prisoners of noble blood, such as King Frederick. He was the most famous prisoner at Offdom Tower, though there have been others. I will not bore you with their names."

She flipped a page. "The staircase tower provides the only access to the cellblocks. Each cellblock is secured by a door leading off the staircase. Soldiers guard the entrance to the tower, as well as the doors to each cellblock. The staircase has no windows and is protected by warding magicks, although these were allowed to lapse when the cellblocks were closed down. If a prisoner does manage to escape his cell, he can make his way to freedom only by means of the staircase, and it can be sealed off from the rest of the prison, so that the prisoner is trapped inside."

"Bloody hell!" Kate said.

"I fear I must relate worse," said Amelia. "The magical warding constructs on the cell door are notorious for being extremely complex, requiring a magical key to open them. If a crafter attempts to dismantle them without the key and makes even a single miscalculation, the magic resets and locks the door for twenty-four hours, during which time no one can enter, not even with the key.

"I endeavored to find more information on the constructs. I searched for a diagram or even the name of the original crafter, thinking that I could study his or her workmanship. I found nothing."

"Oh, dear," said Sophia.

"Sophia, you are a savant," said Kate. "You're the best crafter I've ever seen."

Sophia shook her head. "I am familiar with warding constructs like these on the door to the Jewel Tower in the palace at Everux. Picture this table covered with a myriad of magical sigils that make up myriad constructs. In order to work, each construct is dependent on the constructs before it as well as those that come after it. Not only that, they are designed to work in a certain order. Hidden within the constructs is a magical 'keyhole'—a single construct that causes a cascade of magic when it is activated with the key. Only then will the door open.

"As a savant, I could see the magical constructs. Given enough time, I might be able to solve the puzzle. But that could take days. And if I were to guess and make a mistake—"

"The door would lock for twenty-four hours," said Kate. "There must be a way! We are so close! We can't let Pip die!"

"I will continue my research tomorrow," Amelia offered. "We should not yet relinquish hope."

But she didn't sound hopeful. Sophia picked up Bandit and buried her face in his fur.

"Don't give up, Sophia," said Kate. "If I have to, I'll force the guards at gunpoint to open the damn door!"

Sophia raised her head. "Not even that will work. All the guard has to do is touch the wrong construct and the door will lock."

"And once that happens not even the guard could open it," said Amelia.

"No matter how many guns you have aimed at his head. There's a reason no one has ever escaped."

———————

The next day, Amelia left for the library to continue her research. Sophia tried to recall as much as she could about the warding constructs on the door to the Jewel Tower. Kate left to go talk to Dalgren.

The dragon had moved to a different cave after the incident with Trubgek and he had laid magical traps around the cave to alert him if anyone was trying to sneak up on him.

He had told Kate how to find the cave and she had to remember where he had placed the traps in order to avoid them. That wasn't easy, for dragons have the ability to manipulate their surroundings with their magic. Dalgren had left marks on the stones to warn her when she was nearing a trap and she had to keep careful watch as she climbed among the rocks. What appeared to her to be solid ground could be an illusion concealing a deep pit, while touching the wrong boulder to steady herself could trigger a rock slide.

She navigated her way safely through the traps and found Dalgren resting on sun-warmed rocks, napping after his midday meal. She tickled his snout with a weed until he snorted and woke up.

Several days ago she had explained their predicament to him, how they could not find Sir Henry and were thus forced to scrap their original plan. She had told him she and Sophia were devising a new plan, which caused him to gloomily shake his head. He had too much experience with Kate's plans.

The first thing he said when he saw her glum face was, "I knew something would go wrong."

Kate explained the intricacies of the warding magic as Sophia had described them. As Dalgren listened, Kate saw his nostrils twitch and his eyes crinkle in a grin that caused smoke to puff out from between his fangs.

Kate stopped her explanation to glare at him. "This is not funny, Dalgren! They're going to kill Phillip unless we can free him!"

"It is funny," said Dalgren smugly. "All your talk about sneaking into towers and secret passages and silencing guards and magical keys. You don't need any of that."

He lifted his head, preening himself, and said loftily, "You have me."

Kate didn't know what he meant at first and then she understood.

"I do have you!" she said, affectionately rubbing his snout. "And what would I ever do without you."

TWENTY-FIVE

When Thomas read the single word "Yes" in the Agony column of the *Haever Gazette*, he was elated. He eagerly looked forward to hearing about the plans, but he had to contain his impatience to read the next installment of the escapades of Captain Kate. During that time, he kept close watch on King Ullr and, more importantly, Baron Grimm.

Ullr continued his friendship with Smythe. Thomas had been trying to make up his mind whether or not to tell Smythe that Ullr was using him as a cat's-paw. Thomas doubted if Smythe would believe him, but he felt he must at least try to warn him.

He brought up the subject when Smythe entered his office to bring him the usual round of reports and documents that required his signature. Smythe indicated which ones Thomas needed to sign and waited with ill-concealed impatience as he read through them.

They were almost finished when a servant arrived bearing a calling card on a salver. "Admiral Randolph Baker requests an audience, Your Majesty."

Smythe picked up the calling card, glanced at it. "Did this admiral say what he wanted with His Majesty?"

"No, sir," the servant responded.

Smythe tossed the card back onto the salver. "His Majesty cannot meet privately with every admiral in the navy. We would be besieged. Send him away."

Thomas could have countermanded Smythe's order and requested that the admiral be shown into his office. He had never heard of the man, however, and he needed to talk to Smythe about Ullr.

Thomas gestured and the servant departed.

"You met with King Ullr this morning," Thomas said, signing the last document. "What did the two of you discuss?"

"Nothing that need concern Your Majesty," said Smythe.

He gathered up the pile of documents and prepared to leave.

"I do not trust that man," Thomas said, detaining him. "King Ullr seeks to extend his power, as we see when he maintained he was Braffa's friend and declared Braffa a 'protectorate.' Now he comes here claiming to be our friend. Mark my words, he is intent only upon furthering Guundaran interests to the detriment of our own."

Smythe listened with an unpleasant smile, then said coldly, "May I remind Your Majesty that King Ullr warned us of a Rosian plot to invade Wellinsport, which we have countered by dispatching the *Terrapin*."

Thomas had to bite his lip to keep from telling Smythe that the "Rosian plot" was nothing more than a ruse to lure the *Terrapin* into an ambush. Smythe would scoff at him and he had no proof. He dared not reveal how he had found out.

"King Ullr is a *king*," Smythe was saying, his lip curling in a sneer. "You could take lessons from him. As for our meetings, I am negotiating your marriage with a wealthy Guundaran princess."

Smythe leaned over the desk. "If you wonder why I do not include you in my meetings with King Ullr, let me make it plain. *You* are the one I do not trust, Thomas Stanford. You do the bidding of the Rosians. You served in their navy. You engaged yourself to their witch of a princess. You are the lover of the Countess de Marjolaine—"

"That is a lie!" Thomas cried angrily, slamming his hands on the desk.

Smythe regarded him with disdain. "The Rosians are heretics. Their profligate nobles wallow in sin and gluttony and leave the poor to starve. Their priests are abominations. They are in league with the dragons, the spawn of the Evil One, who intend to destroy us."

Smythe drew himself up. "With the help of King Ullr, I will destroy the dragons and crush Rosia into the dust. After my victory, I will have no more use for you. I will denounce you for the traitor you are and I will give glory to God when you mount the executioner's block and the axe falls and your severed head rolls about in the muck. I will rule Freya, then. As God has long intended."

Thomas stared at him in shock so great he was robbed of speech. He had never imagined this man could be consumed by such hatred for him.

"Have I your leave to go, sire?" Smythe asked with contempt.

He made a sardonic bow, turned on his heel, and left the room before Thomas answered.

Two days later, Thomas retired to his chambers, leaving orders he was not to be disturbed, and eagerly read the latest Captain Kate story in the *Haever Gazette*. He read the story carefully and found his instructions couched amid the captain's heroic escapades following the word "dragon."

Kate and Prince Tom were to meet in the garden beside the sundial on the first night of the month at the stroke of one. After that came the words: *Kate and her dragon carried Prince Tom and his friend to freedom.*

Thomas wished that happy ending could come true. He thought longingly of escaping the palace, escaping Smythe. He sighed and read on.

They wore evening attire. And the last, *They came armed.*

No hours in the history of mankind had ever passed so slowly as did the hours of those next two days. Thomas went through the motions of his daily routine as though he was one of those mechanical figures that popped out of the famous Travian clock every hour on the hour to strike a gong.

Sleep was difficult, for his restless mind was intent on keeping him awake. He would need his strength and his wits, however, and he fatigued himself as much as possible during the day, so that sleep would finally overtake him at night.

The day dawned at last, as days will do, no matter how distant they seem. Thomas was awake to watch the sun rise. He was filled with nervous energy and anticipation and he hoped to be able to avoid Smythe, for fear he could not conceal his emotions.

Unfortunately, Smythe and King Ullr chose this morning to apprise Thomas of the fact that he was now engaged to be married to Princess Wilhelmina Rostoff of Guundar.

"Your Majesty is fortunate," said Ullr. He handed Thomas a miniature portrait of the woman in question. "The princess is considered to be the most beautiful woman in Guundar, as well as one of the richest."

Thomas glanced at the portrait. "I have met the princess. The painting does not do Her Highness justice."

"Indeed?" King Ullr seemed surprised. "I was not aware."

"We met in the Estaran court," Thomas said, adding dryly, "I was four years old at the time. Her Highness was twenty."

Ullr shrugged. "Her Highness is some years older than Your Majesty, that is true. But she is a woman of vast experience in the realm of international politics and foreign affairs. She will be a true helpmate, able to advise and provide wise counsel."

"Indeed, sir, I have heard of the princess's vast experience *and* of her affairs," said Thomas. "The latter are notorious."

"Spiteful rumors, I assure you, sir. I make allowances for your youth and inexperience," said Ullr. "I suppose you would prefer marrying a female pirate."

Thomas managed to keep the smile on his lips, but only because his facial muscles were paralyzed. He remembered Phillip warning him that Ullr would have spies watching him, but he could not believe they could uncover the secrets of his heart.

He recovered himself enough to try to turn the conversation back to the engagement. Smythe had been quick to notice Thomas's change of countenance and he frowned and turned to Ullr.

"I fail to take your meaning, sir," he said. "What is this about a female pirate?"

"I was merely making a jest," said Ullr. "I refer to the romance stories of the clever Miss Nettleship in your newspaper, the *Gazette*. Don't you enjoy those, Chancellor?"

"I do not, sir," said Smythe harshly. "The Reverend Blackthorn teaches that fiction is a sin in the eyes of God, for it is filled with lies and serves no virtuous purpose."

Ullr seemed amused. Thomas said something about looking forward to meeting the princess and rose to his feet, indicating the audience was at an end.

After they were gone, Thomas sank back in his chair.

Night could not come fast enough.

TWENTY-SIX

The morning of the mission, Kate and Sophia dressed as servants, putting on the black twill dresses and white aprons they had "borrowed" during their escape from the palace. Amelia insisted that they be accurate down to the last detail, so they put on black stockings.

Amelia was a proponent of serviceable shoes and managed to obtain lace-up black boots with low heels that were a relatively good fit. Kate and Sophia arranged their hair beneath frilly caps and wrapped up for warmth in plain ankle-length black cloaks Amelia had purchased from a pawn shop.

Kate had sewn secret pockets inside the bodices of the black dresses, for she planned to carry Amelia's watch to keep track of time, as well as the journalist's most prized possession, her pocket pistol with the two barrels.

"Please remember: do *not* stand anywhere close to me with a pistol when I am casting the spell," Sophia warned. "I'm going to be using contramagic."

"Trust me, I'll keep my distance," said Kate.

"Why such precautions?" Amelia asked, ever curious.

"As you know, Miss Amelia, pistols like yours are manufactured with magical constructs that light the gunpowder," Kate explained. "Contramagic plays merry hell with the magic and can set off the gunpowder, essentially turning your pistol into a small bomb in my hand."

"Interesting," said Amelia as she jotted down details in her brown note-book. "Now that the church has removed the ban on contramagic, I should write a series of articles on the subject."

"Most people still believe contramagic is evil," Sophia pointed out.

"Then it's time they learned differently," said Amelia with a sniff.

Sophia did not carry a pistol, preferring to trust to her magic. She tucked several small net bags resembling scented sachets into her pockets. The bags did not smell of lavender and rose hips. Kate sniffed at them and sneezed.

"What is in these?"

"Flour and pepper," said Sophia. "I learned this spell from Rodrigo. He used a variation of it to save Phillip when assassins broke into the house while we were at the dinner table. Rigo had to act quickly, and the only ingredient he had available was salt, which happened to be handy. I have since made refinements. All I have to do is add magic, contramagic, and the Seventh Sigil to the mix and these should work extremely well."

Kate sneezed again and agreed.

"Now all we have left to do is pack your picnic basket," said Amelia.

The pawn shop again provided a large straw basket with a lid. They packed two dark lanterns; a jug of the potent Trundler liquor, Calvados; two balls of tightly wound wool coated with paraffin; a coil of rope; a black silk mask such as those worn by revelers; and two griffin-rider helms. Amelia frowned over the liquor.

"Kings do not drink Calvados," she said.

"This king does," Kate said, smiling at fond memories of her time together with Thomas in the Aligoes. "And we need a liquor with a strong odor."

The afternoon sun was bright, the day clear and cold. The clock on the mantelpiece chimed twice as the cab Amelia had ordered arrived.

Sophia bid good-bye to Bandit, kissed him on his head, and promised him tea cakes if he was good while she was gone. She attached a lead to his collar and left him in the care of Amelia.

"If something were to happen to me, you will take care of him, won't you, Miss Amelia?" Sophia asked.

"Nothing is going to happen to you," said Amelia. "And if it does, you will have Dalgren to deal with it."

"The theory being that if we can't escape it, he can set fire to it," Kate said, laughing.

"Not exactly what I had in mind, but that would do in a pinch," said Amelia. "My one worry is that His Majesty will be expecting Sir Henry, not two servants."

"Trust me, Miss Amelia, Thomas won't be at all disappointed to find Kate instead," said Sophia.

Kate picked up the basket, and the two women hurried out to the cab. They were early, for they did not plan to meet Thomas until after one of the clock, but they needed to reach Dalgren's cave while they still had daylight, in order to avoid his traps.

Amelia waved good-bye from her door. The last sounds Kate and Sophia heard as their cab drove away were Bandit's dismal howls.

"He does not like being left behind," said Sophia. "I hope he will not misbehave and do something naughty. The last time I left him alone he ate one of my shoes. Do you think we remembered to pack everything?"

"If we didn't, it's too late now," Kate said, adding somberly, "We have told Thomas we are coming. He has faith in us."

"I wish Phillip knew we were coming," said Sophia, sighing. "He must feel so hopeless and despairing."

"He will be filled with hope soon," said Kate.

Sophia smiled, but her smile turned into a sigh. She clasped her hands together to stop them from shaking, and huddled into her cloak. "I know I shouldn't say this, but I'm a little frightened. I am glad you are with me, Kate. You are so bold and not afraid of anything."

Kate shook her head. "I'm more than a little frightened. I'm a *lot* frightened. If we are caught sneaking into the palace, Sophia, they will think we are assassins and they will hang us. Not even Thomas would be able to save us."

"Nothing will go wrong," said Sophia. "Our plan is a good one. It will work."

"It has to," said Kate.

The cab driver dropped them off on the outskirts of the city not far from the harbor, close to the coastline. From there, they walked to Dalgren's cave. They managed to avoid the traps and arrived just as the sun was setting. Dalgren was waiting for them, and he greeted Sophia with respect and courtly courtesy.

"I have been telling Sophia that riding a dragon is much like riding a horse," Kate told him.

"It is not!" Dalgren objected, indignant. "I am nothing like a horse."

"Yes, you are," said Kate, giving a meaningful glance at Sophia. "Especially for someone *who has never ridden a dragon*!"

Dalgren coughed. "I was about to say, Your Highness, before Kate interrupted me, that riding a dragon is much safer and easier than riding horseback."

"I am certain you will take good care of me, Dalgren," said Sophia.

"You and I will sit on his back in this area, just in front of his shoulders between where the spines on his neck end and those on his back start," Kate told Sophia. "I would ordinarily put my dragon saddle there and we would be securely strapped in. But I don't have a saddle, which means we're going to have to ride bareback. I've done it before and, while it isn't very comfortable, it's safe, so long as Dalgren doesn't do any barrel rolls."

"He's not likely to, is he?" Sophia asked, alarmed.

"Of course not, Your Highness," Dalgren said, snorting smoke at Kate.

"I'll sit in front and you'll ride pillion," Kate continued. "I'll hold onto his mane and you'll hold onto me."

"Will there be room on Dalgren's back for Thomas and Phillip?" Sophia asked.

"We will be snug," Kate admitted. "But Dalgren says he can manage."

"This will be an adventure for me," said Sophia, trying to sound brave. "Not even the countess has ridden a dragon."

Kate consulted the watch. "It's only six of the clock. Now I know what we forgot to pack—food."

"I don't think I could eat anything," said Sophia.

Kate didn't think she could either, but she didn't want to say so. They sat down to wait.

Time passed so slowly that several times Kate thought the watch had stopped. Finally she had the satisfaction of shining the dark lantern on the watch and seeing the hands at eleven.

Kate stood up. "We should leave. It's early yet, but we need to watch for the patrol boat and I'm not sure where it will be. Dalgren can't land until it has reached the end of its run and starts sailing back toward the palace."

She put on the griffin-rider helm and helped Sophia put on hers. Kate drew in a deep breath to calm her nerves. "Is everyone ready?"

"Ready," said Sophia, stoutly determined.

"Ready," said Dalgren.

Kate rubbed his snout, climbed up on his foreclaw, and pulled herself up onto his back by grasping the lowest spine of his mane. She then reached down for Sophia, who scrambled up awkwardly onto Dalgren's foreclaw and handed Kate the basket. She then gave Kate her hand and Kate hauled her up onto Dalgren's back.

Sophia took her seat a little breathlessly and put her arms around Kate's waist. When she was settled, Kate wedged the basket between Dalgren's shoulder blades and his spine.

Kate cast a questioning glance over her shoulder.

"Are you all right?"

Sophia gave a tremulous nod and her grip on Kate tightened.

"Here we go."

Kate patted Dalgren on his neck, giving him the signal that he could take off.

Dalgren would have ordinarily made a long, loping run along the cliff, spreading his wings wide to catch the wind and then glide on the air currents. He did not have room to run, however. He had to spread his wings and leap off the side of the cliff.

Kate felt her own stomach drop and she couldn't imagine what Sophia must be feeling. She was clutching Kate so tightly Kate had a hard time drawing breath.

Dalgren caught an updraft, and soared effortlessly into the Breath.

"That was the worst part!" Kate shouted to Sophia.

She didn't know if Sophia heard her or not. Between the helmet and the rushing wind, she doubted it. But Sophia must be feeling more at ease, for she slightly loosened her grip.

Dalgren silently glided over the slumbering city of Haever. He had flown out the night before to view the landing site, watch the patrol boat, and observe the movements of the palace guards. Dragons could see well at night, for they preferred to do their hunting after dark.

The day had been clear, but the mists of the Breath rolled in with the setting sun. Sky and ground seemed to Kate to have switched places, for the sky above her was black, while the street lamps below glittered like orderly rows of stars.

When the palace came into view, its magic-encrusted walls glimmering silvery white, Dalgren turned south, flying toward the stables. He flew low, watching for the broad boulevard known as King's Way that ran in front of the palace and would let him know when he was near the wall.

Kate glanced back at Sophia. She no longer sat rigid with fear, but was relaxed, gazing down at the breathtaking sight of a city at nighttime.

Kate understood her fascination. One could see the same view from the windows of a yacht or a wyvern-drawn cab. But the experience of seeing the world unfolding beneath the wings of a dragon was different, more exhilarating and awe-inspiring, perhaps because riding on the back of a dragon was the closest humans would ever get to flying themselves. Kate could feel the ripple of Dalgren's muscles, hear the creak of his wings. She was one with the dragon, as though when he spread his wings, she spread hers.

As the boulevard came into sight, Kate gave Dalgren a pat on the neck and he nodded to indicate he had seen it. He soared over the wall about a mile south of the entrance. The grounds below appeared dark and deserted. Even if someone had been around, Kate doubted if they would have seen or heard the dragon silently gliding above the treetops.

Dalgren grunted and shifted his head to the right, his signal for Kate to look that direction. She could see the lights of the patrol boat coming into view. The boat had reached the southernmost point of the figure eight and would be turning back, probably sailing now over the field where Dalgren intended to land.

The dragon rose slightly and flew farther south, allowing the patrol boat time to leave the area and sail northward until it reached the end of its route; then it would turn and head back to the south.

Once the boat had flown past the field and was headed back toward the palace, Dalgren began his descent.

Kate shouted, "Hold on!" and Sophia did as she was told, clasping her arms tightly around Kate.

Dalgren raised his wings and plunged straight down toward the ground. As many times as he and Kate had performed such landings, she could still not find the courage to look down. She concentrated on watching the patrol boat to see any change in its routine that might denote the lookout had spotted them.

Dalgren landed on his back legs first to absorb as much of the shock as possible before dropping down on his front legs. Kate hardly felt a jolt; she knew Dalgren had taken extra care because of Sophia.

Safely on the ground, Dalgren lowered his head, folded his wings at his sides, and wrapped his tail round his legs to make himself as small as possible.

Kate took off her helmet and turned to help Sophia remove hers. Sophia had to gulp in several deep breaths before she could speak.

"Are you all right?" Kate asked worriedly.

"Oh, Kate!" Sophia gasped. Her eyes shone. "I don't know what to say. That was wonderful, marvelous, terrifying, awful, and exhilarating—all at the same time."

Kate smiled. "We will make a dragon rider of you yet. But now we have to hurry."

She nimbly climbed off Dalgren's back and dropped down onto his leg, then grabbed the basket and helped Sophia dismount. Once they reached the ground, Kate took a moment to get her bearings and give Sophia a chance to catch her breath.

Dalgren nudged Kate with a claw. "How did you like that landing? Gentle as a baby bird. I hope the princess wasn't too shaken."

"She didn't even know we were on the ground," said Kate. "She thought she was still floating among the clouds."

"Truly?" Dalgren asked.

"No." Kate scoffed. "And why can't you land like that when I'm on your back instead of smashing nose-first into the ground and rattling every tooth in my head? We're setting out now. Watch for my signal."

Dalgren grinned at her. Small flames flickered from his jaws. "You watch for mine!"

TWENTY-SEVEN

The afternoon of the mission to free Phillip, Thomas made the uncharacteristic move of seeking out Smythe instead of actively avoiding him. He found the chancellor in his office with his aide-de-camp, studying a large map of the Aligoes. He had stuck a pin in the city of Wellinsport and surrounded the island with other pins, presumably representing the Rosian navy.

"According to King Ullr—" Smythe was saying as Thomas entered.

The aide caught sight of him and said in a loud whisper to Smythe, "Sir! The king!"

Smythe turned from his task with an impatient scowl.

"How may I serve Your Majesty?" he asked.

"You may serve me by attending a dinner engagement tonight," said Thomas. He indicated two letters he was holding. "I have invited the Reverend Jeddah Blackthorn and the Reverend Elijah Byrd. We need the support of the Reformed Church and I understand that these two reverend gentlemen hold great influence with their flock. Since you are a follower of that religion, it seems logical that you should be the one to entertain them."

Smythe stared at him in slack-jawed disbelief. The man seemed utterly confounded to the point of being rendered speechless.

Thomas held out the two letters. "I am sorry I did not consult you sooner, but the gentlemen only just sent word that they would be available tonight, after services. I have made arrangements for dinner to be served at ten of the clock. The hour is late, but I wanted to accommodate you, as well as the reverend gentlemen, for I know they hold services until nine and that you are generally in attendance. I have informed them that you will be hosting them."

He handed over the two letters of acceptance. Smythe took them and gazed at them in awe.

"I have studied the words of these gentlemen since I was a child," he said, sounding dazed. "My father taught me to read using the writings of Reverend Byrd."

Smythe was red in the face, his hand trembling. He swallowed and replied in a voice husky with emotion, "I . . . I do not know what to say, Your Majesty."

Thomas was surprised to see Smythe so genuinely touched and deeply affected. He wondered, not for the first time, how Smythe managed to reconcile his seemingly deeply held spiritual beliefs with the ability to brutally murder those who threatened his ambition.

"Dinner will be served in the Small Dining Room, a more intimate setting than the Grand Dining Room that will allow you and your guests to talk without interruption. I have invited both gentlemen to spend the night in guest rooms in the palace. I trust you will see to their accommodations."

"Certainly, Your Majesty," said Smythe. He swallowed, then added, "Thank you, sir."

Thomas walked away, pleased with his success. Smythe would be busy the remainder of the day arranging for the servants to open guest chambers and air them out, wash the linens, clean and dust, consult with the cook and the steward and insist that they serve ale, not wine. With dinner served late, Thomas felt confident that the theological discussions would last into the morning hours.

Bolstered by Smythe's emotional reaction to the prospect of meeting his spiritual idols, Thomas was reasonably certain that he had disposed of the chancellor for the night.

Thomas changed into his evening attire. He had arranged to dine with his finance minister and the chancellor of the exchequer in order to keep up appearances, though when he returned from his dinner at the hour of eleven of the clock he realized he had no recollection of a word they had spoken. He trusted he had not agreed to anything too outrageous.

The instructions in the *Gazette* had told him to wear evening attire as though attending a late-night party, so he did not change for the mission.

Since he was going out, he added his tricorn, a silk-lined cloak, and silken scarf to his attire.

To conceal his absence, he took several bolsters and arranged them in the shape of his slumbering form, then covered them with the sheets. He placed his nightcap over the end and drew a heavy down-stuffed satin duvet over his "head" until only the tip of the nightcap remained visible, and closed the bed curtains.

As he finished this operation, he heard the clock strike thirty minutes past the hour of midnight. Anxious to be prompt for his meeting, Thomas quickly secreted a dark lantern beneath his cloak, slid two small pistols into his pockets, and left the palace by the "family" door, heading for the garden and the sundial where he was to meet Sir Henry.

Thomas was early, but he preferred walking outdoors to restlessly pacing his room watching the hands of the clock slowly crawl toward the hour of one.

He located the sundial and sat down on a cold stone bench. Gazing about, he reflected that a garden in winter was as somber and mournful as a graveyard.

The palace was some distance away, the magical walls shimmering with an eerie white light. People thought it beautiful and perhaps it was, but tonight Thomas thought it looked spectral, ominous. Near the frozen fish ponds, the shrubs and fir trees, wrapped in burlap, were ghostly shapes in the night. The ornamental wrought-iron fence against the glowing backdrop of the palace walls resembled prison bars. The thought made him shudder.

Thomas could not sit still. He took out his watch, noted the time, shook his watch in irritation and held it to his ear to make certain it was ticking. He occupied his mind by studying Offdom Tower, or at least what he could see of it from the garden.

The square, squat tower stood by itself, detached and dark and foreboding. Thomas could see a single light shining in a window in the guardroom at the top. The guards kept a light burning all night. No light burned in the window in Phillip's cell.

He was probably trying to sleep, for only in sleep could he forget for a few hours that he was a prisoner. And even then, only if he did not dream of being locked inside four walls.

"Not long, my friend," Thomas promised softly. "Not long."

He again looked at his watch. The hands had actually moved, nearing the hour of one. He should start watching for Dalgren.

Thomas did not know where the dragon was going to land, but he could guess it would be in the open field near the stables. He searched the sky, staring into the mist-shrouded darkness. He listened intently, hoping to hear him if he could not see him.

What he heard was the faint whirring of airscrews. The patrol boat was sailing almost directly overhead. Thomas did not think those in the boat could see him through the mists, but he took no chances and hid among the shrubs. The boat continued on its way, reached the end of its run, and turned back toward the palace.

Thomas looked up to catch a fleeting glimpse of a dark winged shape drop down through the mists and disappear behind the garden wall. He quickly walked back to the sundial, trying to calculate how long it would take for Sir Henry to dismount from the dragon, enter the gate at the far end of the garden, and make his way toward the sundial.

Thomas waited what he considered a reasonable time, but when Wallace did not come, he began to wonder uneasily if something had gone wrong. He rose to his feet, hoping to locate Dalgren, but the dragon had utterly disappeared in the thick darkness.

Thomas grew increasingly worried, and then he heard movement in the darkness and saw the quick flash of a beam of light shine from a dark lantern. He could tell by the sounds that more than one person was out there. Fearing the plot had been discovered, he slipped back into the shrubbery and saw two figures, hooded and cloaked, approaching the sundial. Oddly, one was carrying what appeared to be a picnic basket. The two stopped near the sundial and took off the helms they were wearing.

Thomas recognized both of them in shocked dismay. He heard Kate ask softly, "Where is he? Do you see anyone?"

"No," Sophia replied, sounding worried. "I hope nothing has happened. What should we do?"

"We will wait," Kate said. "He will be here. He's been delayed, that's all."

Thomas didn't know what to do. He did not want Kate and Sophia involved in such a dangerous plot. If he remained hidden, they would both give up and go away.

But . . . this was Kate. Thomas knew her, knew she would never "give up and go away." Far from it. She could take it into her head to march into the palace in search of him and put herself and Sophia into even greater jeopardy.

"I have to make Kate see reason," Thomas said to himself as he went out to meet them. "Convince her to leave."

He took care to rustle through the leaves so that he did not appear to be creeping up on them. Even so, the sound of his footfalls startled them both.

"Stop where I can see you!" Kate warned. "I have a pistol!"

"It's me, Kate!" Thomas called softly, as he emerged from the shadows. Kate sighed in relief and lowered her pistol.

"Is everything all right?" Sophia asked worriedly. "Is Phillip safe?"

"As far as I know," Thomas replied. "Where is Sir Henry?"

"We have no idea," said Kate. "He might be dead. We came to free Phillip instead."

"Then you have both acted foolishly," Thomas said sternly. "Especially you, Sophia! It is far too dangerous. Smythe's men are searching everywhere for you."

"Then this is likely the last place they will look," said Sophia calmly.

"And we are not being foolish," Kate said irately. "We need her magic—"

"No, we don't, because I'm calling this off," said Thomas. "You two go home."

Kate confronted him, her eyes glinting. "So we let Pip die?"

"He would not want you to risk your lives for his sake," said Thomas.

"Bloody hell!" Kate cried, losing patience. "We are going to save Pip and you can help us or not, as you choose!"

"We have a plan," Sophia added.

Thomas regarded them helplessly.

"Besides, it's too late to call off Dalgren," said Kate. "He'll be getting into position. Are you coming with us? Or are you going back to your nice warm bed?"

"I'm coming," said Thomas grimly. At least if he was with them, he might be able to protect them. "What is your plan?"

"You are a drunken libertine taking advantage of two serving maids. Stand still."

Kate placed the basket on the ground, took out the Calvados, uncorked the jug and splashed some onto Thomas's clothing.

"What was that for?" Thomas gasped and shivered as the cold air hit his wet clothes.

"So we can get past the guards," said Kate. She handed him the jug. "Take a drink, swish it around in your mouth, and spit it out."

Thomas obediently took a swig of the fiery liquid, coughed, and spit it on the ground. Kate took the jug back and poured Calvados over her own clothes and Sophia's. Then she took a drink, and handed the jug to Sophia, who drank as well, choking and grimacing in disgust.

"We're ready," Kate said. She gave Thomas the black silk mask. "Put that over your face."

"Take off the royal sash and those rings you're wearing," Sophia ordered.

Thomas obediently put on the mask, removed the sash, and took off the rings.

"I will not take off this one," he said, referring to the ring of King James. "Her Majesty gave it to me."

"Then turn it around so that the diamonds are not visible," said Kate. "You take the lead. You know where you are going and we don't."

"Where are we going?" Thomas asked.

"Offdom Tower, of course," said Kate. "I'll carry the basket."

Thomas was starting to understand at least part of their plan. He led them across a deserted lane, taking care to keep to the shadows and avoid the entrance to the palace, where the guards would be yawning their way through their shift.

They rounded the west wing of the palace, now under repair, the hole in the wall covered by scaffolding.

"Smythe was the one who gave the orders to kill Queen Mary," said Thomas. "He boasted to me of the murder."

"We know," said Kate. "Sophia and I heard him. We were in the Rose Room next door."

"That *was* you," said Thomas. "I thought I heard your voice. And Bandit's bark."

They entered the courtyard at the rear of the palace, avoiding the glow of the walls for fear the patrol boat would see them. The square edifice of the tower stood apart from the palace, but the two were inextricably linked in Thomas's mind—the dark half of a bright moon.

"What are those lights?" Kate asked, stopping.

"The guard box at the entrance to the tower staircase," Thomas replied.

"How many guards?" Kate asked.

"Two inside the box, Guundaran mercenaries. They work for Smythe," Thomas warned, remembering clearly the Guundaran soldier telling him, *You're not my king.*

"Have you been inside the tower?" Sophia asked. "Do you know your way around?"

"Yes. Once we are past the guards at the gate, we enter the staircase tower. Pip's cell is at the top level, up six flights of stairs."

"Any other prisoners?" Kate asked.

"The other cells are empty, the floors sealed off. There are two guards posted outside Pip's cell door, which is guarded by powerful magical warding spells, impossible to break."

"We know," said Sophia complacently.

"You have the key?" Thomas asked.

"Better," said Kate. "We have Dalgren."

She set the basket on the ground, handed him the jug of Calvados, and took out a ball of yarn. Thomas watched in amazement as she traced constructs on the ball with her fingers, then held it poised in her palm. Sophia drew out what appeared to be a sachet from her pocket.

"I'm going to signal Dalgren," said Kate. "When he sees the flare, he will give us time to enter the tower."

Thomas frowned. "Give us time before he does what?"

"Attacks the tower," said Kate.

"Attack!" Thomas repeated, shocked. "But what about Phillip? He'll be trapped inside!"

"Do you trust me?" Kate demanded.

"You know I do," said Thomas. He added hesitantly, "But this is Pip. . . ."

"He is my friend, too," said Kate. "Dalgren and I won't let anything happen to him."

She spoke a word of magic and the ball of yarn began to glow with a soft blue light. With another word of magic, she tossed the glowing ball of yarn high into the air, letting the magic carry it like a balloon filled with lift gas. The ball soared past the palace walls, higher and higher.

"The paraffin causes it to burn really brightly," said Kate, observing her work with pride.

The ball burst into bright blue-white flame, trailing blazing sparks like a comet.

"Quickly, Thomas!" Sophia ordered. "Put one arm around my waist and one arm around Kate."

"I'll take the jug," said Kate. "I'm going to offer the guards a drink and Sophia will work her magic. Just be sure to avert your head, look away from the guards when she does."

Thomas glanced up at the solitary light burning in the darkness.

Kate knew what he was thinking. "I admit, our plan involves some risk, but if we don't save him, Pip will die. He would want to make the gamble."

"You are right," said Thomas. "I will play my part."

He tugged on his cravat to loosen it, and tossed away his tricorn. Shaking hair over his face, he adjusted the mask. "Cue the dissolute noble."

Stealthily, the three drew nearer the guardhouse, keeping to the shadows as long as possible in order to watch what the guards were doing. They had no difficulty seeing, for the guard box blazed with light. Lanterns hung over the door and other lanterns shone inside. The guards were talking loudly, Thomas could hear every word.

The two were pitching coins against a wall and he realized with a start that they were discussing plans for the invasion. He raised his hand, warning Kate and Sophia to stop.

"What is it?" Kate whispered.

"I need to hear what they are saying," Thomas whispered back.

"Your throw," said one. "So when are we to seize control of the palace?"

"Tonight, tomorrow night, a year from now. What does it matter? We do what we are told."

"We are the first to risk our lives and the last to know anything," the other grumbled.

"Loose tongues wag," said his friend.

He threw the coin. His friend tossed his and won, for his coin came closer to the wall.

"King Ullr knows that none of us would talk," the other argued. "We have spilled our blood for other nations. Now is the time for Guundar to rise."

"Damn! I keep missing!" said the other. "I have no luck tonight."

Thomas had heard all he needed.

"Now," he said softly.

He slid one arm around Sophia's waist and the other arm around Kate's, and the three lurched forward into the light, giggling and talking.

The guards dropped their coins, picked up their rifles, and came to investigate.

Kate and Sophia and Thomas wobbled and slipped on the frosty cobblestones. The three reeked of Calvados.

"Trundler swill," one guard remarked in disgust. "How anyone can drink that stuff is beyond me."

His fellow raised his rifle and aimed at them.

"Halt!" he said, speaking broken Freyan. "Stand and be recognized."

The three stumbled to a stop, leaning against one another and staring at the guards in inebriated confusion.

"*You* stand and be recognized, my good man," Thomas said good-naturedly. He released his hold on Kate and Sophia and sauntered forward.

"That's far enough, my lord," said the guard.

"I am Count Reginald Fortheringale, friend of the king's, and I go where I please. It pleases me to take a look around this damn tower."

Thomas leaned forward to add in a wheedling tone, "I promised the young ladies! You wouldn't want to disappoint them, would you?"

"Gives you the horrors, don't it, Reggie," called out one of the women.

The guards glanced at each other, grinning. They lowered their rifles.

"I cannot permit you or the young ladies to enter, my lord," said one.

Thomas shrugged. "Well, well. You are doing your duty, I dare say. Damn cold, isn't it," he added conversationally. "I don't know how you chaps stand it. Will you have a drink with us? Come, girls. Offer the lads here a swig."

Kate and Sophia laughingly ran up to the guards.

"It's good stuff, sir!" Kate said, holding out the jug.

The guard grimaced. "We are not permitted—"

Sophia spoke a word of magic and flung the sachet in his face.

The sachet glowed blue and exploded. The guard happened to have his mouth open at the time and the flour and pepper combination flew down his throat. The flour caught the other guard in the eyes and drifted down on both of them, coating their uniforms.

The guards began to sneeze uncontrollably. One dropped his rifle to rub his burning eyes. The other coughed and retched between sneezes. He was still holding onto his rifle, however. Sophia spoke another word and the flour began to glow green.

"Contramagic," she warned. "If you have seen what happens when contramagic and magic mix, you know you should drop your weapon before it explodes."

The green glow of the contramagic grew steadily brighter, and the guard flung his rifle to the ground. Thomas kicked both of the weapons well out of reach.

Sophia ended the spell and the green glow started to fade.

Thomas took hold of one guard and Kate grabbed the other and they shoved them into the small guardhouse.

"On the floor," Thomas ordered.

Kate had brought rope to bind them, but when she saw several sets of shackles hanging from hooks, she clamped these over their wrists.

As she was working, one of the guards gave her a shove that knocked her backward and jumped to his feet. He got as far as the door. Sophia stood there, blocking his way.

She pointed to his flour-coated sleeve; the flour shone blue and burst into flame.

The guard cried out. Thomas punched him in the face and the man tumbled backward and collapsed by his friend. Kate removed a ring of keys from the hook on the wall.

Sophia continued to block the doorway.

"Your coat is still covered with my magical potion," she told the Guundarans. "The potion is in your hair and your eyes. If you make a sound, I will turn you both into living torches."

As the guards shrank away from her, Thomas slammed the door on them and Kate locked it.

"Now what?" Thomas asked.

"We rescue Pip," Kate answered.

TWENTY-EIGHT

Kate delved into the basket again and took out the second ball of paraffin-soaked yarn. She started to head toward the tower entrance, then realized Thomas wasn't with her. He had torn off the silk mask and was still standing by the guardhouse, staring at the guards, his expression dark. Kate handed the ball to Sophia and went back to yank Thomas by the sleeve. He joined her and they walked past the guardhouse to the staircase tower.

"What's the matter?" Kate asked Thomas. "We've made it past the guards. The hardest part is done."

"Not that," said Thomas. "Something the guards were saying."

"What was it?"

"Merely confirming what I already knew," said Thomas.

Kate would have liked to question him further, but they had reached the door to the tower and she had to keep her mind on the mission.

"Any magic on the door?" she asked Sophia.

"I see constructs, but they don't appear to be working," Sophia reported.

"That's common practice," said Thomas. "Otherwise the guards have to remove the spells every time they go in and out. When I was here, the guards left the door unlocked, as well. Pip's the only prisoner and they know he isn't going to escape."

Kate regarded him in concern. He was downcast, dispirited. She reached out to him in the darkness, squeezed his hand tightly.

"We are going to save Pip, then Dalgren will fly the four of us to safety and freedom. Tomorrow we will watch the sun rise far away from this dismal place."

Thomas clasped her hand and held fast, as though holding onto a lifeline.

Kate pushed on the door and it creaked open to reveal a spiral staircase, lighted by magical torches that burned with a bright blue light.

"Simple magic," Sophia said, examining one. "I can easily handle it."

Thomas went first, leading the way. Sophia followed and Kate brought up the rear, keeping an eye out for pursuit, though she wasn't truly expecting any. The Guundarans had been so terrified of Sophia, she doubted if they would move for a week.

The three climbed the stone stairs, moving as swiftly as they dared, while trying not to make any noise that would alert Phillip's guards. They came to the door on the first level. Thomas pushed on it and found it locked, which was what they had expected. When they came to the second level, they stopped to confer.

"What is the plan from here?" Thomas asked softly. He motioned to the upper levels. "The door on the third floor is always locked, for it leads to the guardroom outside Phillip's cell. You have the guard's key, but the moment we open that door, the guards will hear us."

"We are not going to open it," Kate told him. "The guards are going to open it for us."

She drew Amelia's double-barreled pocket pistol.

"Keep close to me. Did you bring a pistol?"

"I brought two." Thomas drew one of the pocket pistols.

"Sophia, the torches!" Kate said softly.

Sophia reached up to touch the iron sconce that held one of the torches, and traced a construct. Green flared and the torch went out. Sophia doused two other torches. The only light now shone from a torch on the staircase above them, shining on the door that led to Phillip's cell.

"Now what?" Thomas asked.

"We wait for Dalgren," said Kate.

Minutes passed and all was quiet.

Kate fidgeted. The waiting was the worst part, for she imagined everything that could go wrong had gone wrong. Most of all, she worried about failure. This plan might go awry, like any number of her plans. She thought of so many things now that she should have thought of before, and she shivered in the cold.

Just when she had decided that something terrible must have happened to Dalgren, she heard him launch his attack. Dragons in the Brigade were trained to batter down fortress walls. Dalgren struck the crenellations on top of the tower with his tail. Kate had warned him not to hit them as hard as he would have if he had been attacking in earnest, for she did not want him to accidentally bring down the tower on top of Phillip.

The walls shook from the blow and Kate could hear stone from the broken battlements crash onto the cobblestones in the courtyard below. The guards must have looked out the window to see what was going on, for they started shouting in alarm. Kate didn't speak Guundaran, but she knew enough to recognize the word "Drachen."

She heard the sounds of glass shattering. Dalgren must have knocked out the window. She could not see him from here, but she could visualize him thrusting his snout into the small aperture, gnashing his fangs at the guards and snorting flame.

A rifle went off. One of the guards must have fired. She wasn't worried. A single bullet would have little effect on Dalgren, as the guard must have realized, for the next moment the door at the top of the staircase flew open, and the guards came dashing down the stairs in such panic they did not see the three pressed against the wall in the darkness.

Sophia waited until the two Guundarans were almost level with her, then flung the ball of yarn into the air and caused it to burst into flame as bright and hot and red as a dragon's fiery breath.

The guards shrieked and stumbled and missed their footing. One tripped the other, and both of them tumbled down the stairs.

Kate caught hold of Thomas by the sleeve and pointed to them.

"Make certain they don't come after us!" she told him.

Thomas nodded and ran down to see what had become of the guards. Kate and Sophia climbed to the top of the stairs and hurried through the door into the cellblock.

The walls were charred and starting to fill with smoke. Kate saw Dalgren peering in through the window and she waved at him.

Phillip was beating on the door of his cell, demanding to be let out. Sophia ran to the door and pressed herself against it.

"Phillip! It's me, Sophia!"

"Sophia?" Phillip repeated, astounded. "But how—"

"No time, Pip!" Kate yelled. "Move as far away from your door as you can, and take cover."

"Right!" Phillip said, and Kate heard him running to the back of the cell.

Thomas returned, thrusting his pistol into his pocket. "One of the guards is unconscious. The other has a broken leg. He's a stubborn bastard. He was trying to stand on it. I clouted him on the head, and he's going to be quiet now."

Kate nodded and shouted at Phillip, "Are you somewhere safe?"

"I hope so!" Phillip called. "Did I hear Thomas?"

"You did!" Thomas yelled. "We're going to get you out. Though I'm damned if I know how," he added, turning to Kate. "That cell door is bristling with magic."

"Amazing work," said Sophia, gazing at it in awe. She touched it and the brass door glowed bright blue, the magic coming to life. "See how this construct appears to be the end, but it is really the beginning of this other construct that folds in on itself, then wraps around this third construct. And that leads to another."

Sophia shook her head. "Unraveling this is impossible without the key."

"You don't have the key?" Phillip called, alarmed.

"Keep your head down!" Kate told him. "Thomas, you and Sophia take cover on the staircase."

"What about you?" Thomas asked.

"I'll join you in a moment. I have to talk to Dalgren. Go with Sophia."

Thomas and Sophia left, but they went only as far as the landing.

The window was covered by iron bars that were now glowing red hot from Dalgren's breath. Kate came as near as possible. Dalgren had his wings spread, floating on the air currents. He grinned at Kate through the window.

"Has anyone raised the alarm?" Kate shouted.

Dalgren puffed smoke from his nostrils. "All quiet."

Kate was pleased, though not surprised. Offdom Tower was a considerable distance from the palace. Everyone inside would be asleep at this late hour except the palace guards. If they had even heard the sound of stones and cement crashing to the ground, they would assume the noise came from the section of the palace under repair.

"What about the patrol boat?"

"It's still sailing northward, moving away from us."

"Good. Then we can proceed. Pip is at the back of his cell," Kate told Dalgren. "Please try not to roast him. I'll be in the staircase tower. Once we have Pip out of here, we will meet you at the field."

Dalgren gnashed his teeth. Flame flickered between his fangs.

"Remember, a *concentrated* jet of fire," said Kate.

"I know what I'm doing," Dalgren snapped.

Kate ran out the door to join Thomas and Sophia on the staircase. She was going to shut the door, but Thomas intervened. "Please leave it open a crack. I want to see this."

"So do I," said Sophia.

"Only a crack," Kate cautioned. "The heat will be intense."

"Will Phillip be safe?" Sophia asked worriedly.

"Of course," said Kate. "Dalgren knows what he's doing."

The three crowded in the doorway, their heads together. The chamber glowed bright blue, lit by the shimmering magic and the gleaming brass of the door.

Dalgren flicked away the red-glowing iron bars with a claw, then knocked a hole in the stone wall with his forefoot that was large enough for him to thrust his head inside the room.

He sucked in a deep breath and shot a jet of flame at the brass door. The flame struck the door in the center and a wave of fire rolled across the brass, accompanied by a strong smell of sulfur.

The blue constructs on the door went dark and the three could hear the iron bolts drop down and slam into the floor.

"The cell is bolted shut," said Thomas.

Sophia gave a cry and put her hands over her mouth.

"Wait!" Kate breathed.

The magical fire spread, devouring the constructs on the door. The brass gleamed red hot. The heat seared their skin and the light dazzled their eyes. Dalgren was about to blast the door again when the hinges gave way. The brass buckled, and the door crashed to the floor with a resounding clang.

The door to the cell was gone, but the flames had also set the furniture in the room on fire, as well as the wooden beams in the ceiling. The chamber was rapidly filling with noxious fumes and smoke.

"I have to save Pip before the whole place goes up in flame," said Thomas.

"Not so fast!" Kate stopped him. "Dalgren will handle it."

The dragon drew in another breath and then breathed it out in a powerful gust that swept through the chamber like the fierce winds of a wizard storm, extinguishing the flames. The fire was out, but the room was still smoky.

Kate sighed in relief. "Thomas, you fetch Pip."

Thomas took off his scarf, tied it over his nose and mouth, and plunged into the cell. Kate and Sophia waited, coughing in the smoke and fumes and rubbing their eyes.

"I hope Phillip is all right!" Sophia said, blinking her streaming eyes, trying to see in the darkness.

"He will be," said Kate.

She could hear Thomas call out his name and, after a stomach-wrenching moment of silence, she heard Phillip answer him.

The next moment both men emerged from the smoke. Sophia flung herself at Phillip with a glad cry, and he embraced her, as well as a fit of coughing would allow him.

Dalgren called through the window. "The patrol boat is coming."

"Did they see the fire?" Kate asked worriedly.

"I don't think so," Dalgren replied. "They haven't sounded the alarm. But they will see the smoke."

"We need to get out of here," said Kate.

"You'll never make it as far as the field before the boat raises the alarm," said Dalgren. "So where do I meet you?"

"I'll find someplace. Watch for my signal."

Dalgren shook his head in exasperation and made a deep rumbling sound, then flew off.

Kate eyed Phillip. "You look wobbly. Can you walk on your own?"

"I can manage," Phillip said. He held out his hand to Sophia. "With help."

Sophia took hold of his hand and they ran down the stairs.

"Well done, Kate," said Thomas, regarding her with admiration.

"We're not out of this yet," she said, but she was pleased by his praise.

They dashed down the stairs, passing the injured guards, who were both still unconscious. Phillip and Sophia waited for them at the bottom, near the open door.

"See or hear anything?" Kate asked.

Phillip shook his head. "All quiet now, but it won't be for long. I looked outside. The mists have cleared. Dalgren shows up nicely against the stars, as does the smoke, and the patrol boat is sailing this way."

As they left the tower, Thomas closed and locked the door behind them and threw the ring of keys into the darkness. Dalgren flew overhead, his bulk visible against the stars.

"We were supposed to meet him in the field near the stables," said Kate. "Is there someplace closer where he can land?"

"Over there," said Phillip, pointing. "Across the courtyard, that direction, we will come to lawn tennis courts with plenty of open ground."

"You lead the way. I'll let Dalgren know to follow us."

She opened the dark lantern, aimed it into the air, and flashed the light three times. Dalgren dipped his wings in acknowledgment.

Sophia handed Phillip her dark lantern and he started off. Kate was thankful he knew where he was going; she was soon completely lost. Every so often Phillip stopped to open the lantern and briefly flash the light around, making certain they were still heading the right direction.

The night remained quiet. Kate glanced up at the patrol boat. She could see its sails black against the stars, as well as its lights. She looked back at the tower.

Smoke drifted out of the broken window, but Kate had to look hard to see it, and she realized that the sailors on board the patrol boat might miss it completely.

She looked back and saw Dalgren start to descend.

Pip was free and no one had noticed he was gone. No one had raised the alarm. All they had to do now was meet up with Dalgren and he would fly them safely away.

Kate suddenly realized that for once in her life, her plan had worked.

TWENTY-NINE

Kate and her friends arrived at the lawn tennis courts to find Dalgren already settled on the ground, waiting for them. They watched the patrol boat sail harmlessly overhead, never noticing anything amiss.

Once it was out of sight, Sophia began explaining to Phillip how to pull himself up onto the dragon's back by climbing onto Dalgren's forepaw and then grabbing hold of one of the spikes of his mane. She sounded as experienced as a member of the Dragon Brigade.

Kate smiled and came to tell Thomas the rest of the plan. "Dalgren is going to take us to Barwich Manor, my family's ancestral home. The house has been abandoned for years. I've done what I could to make it comfortable."

Thomas took hold of her hand. "I am truly grateful to you, Kate. . . . But I'm not coming with you."

Kate pulled away from him.

"You saved Pip and you have given me hope. But I must stay here," Thomas continued. "I am king and you were the one who taught me about my duty to my people."

Kate glared at him. "You can't stay here with that horrible Smythe. Pip, come talk sense into your friend!"

"Kate is right, Tom," said Phillip. "You can't stay here. You're not safe. Smythe murdered the queen and he would not hesitate to kill you."

Thomas shook his head. "If I leave Freya, Smythe will denounce me, declare that I am in league with Rosia. My absence would give him a perfect excuse to name himself Lord Protector."

"But you would be king," Kate argued.

"A king in exile," said Thomas.

"Have Smythe arrested and hanged," said Phillip. "He can't use threats against me anymore."

"The Freyan people are already nervous about me. They distrust my youth, my foreign accent, my ties to Rosia. I must work to gain their regard, and I can't do that by hanging a man who is a native son, and seen as an honorable soldier serving his country."

"We all know he's a murderer," said Kate.

"But I can't prove that," said Thomas. He raised a hand, forestalling any further attempts to persuade him. "My mind is made up. We do not have much time before the patrol comes back and I must pass on what I have discovered, for it is of vital importance.

"King Ullr is plotting to invade Freya. He is positioning his fleets for the attack from the air, while his mercenaries in our army attack from within. I heard the two guards talking about it this very night."

The others stared at him in shock.

"I knew Ullr was power-hungry, but I never thought he would be either so bold or so reckless as to do this," said Phillip.

"Do you know when?" Kate asked.

"He mentioned the national holiday, Hallen Day. All of Freya will be celebrating—including the Royal Navy. Ullr and the baron referred to our ships as 'sitting ducks.'"

"Good God!" Phillip murmured.

"My news gets worse," said Thomas grimly. "Ullr suggested to Smythe that he order the *Terrapin* to the Aligoes to defend against a Rosian invasion of Wellinsport—"

"That is a lie!" Sophia cried indignantly. "My brother has no intention of attacking."

"I know, and so does King Ullr," said Thomas. "He has arranged for the *Terrapin* to be ambushed. Ullr fears the *Terrapin* and he wants the ship far from Haever when he invades. I signed the orders myself," he added bitterly. "I had no idea. And Smythe is sending a black ship called the *Naofa* armed with a green-beam weapon to attack the Dragon Brigade headquarters at Maribeau."

Dalgren overheard. He snarled and bared his fangs. Flames flickered between his teeth. "I will roast him."

"You vowed to never take a human life, remember?" Kate told him.

"I'll make an exception," Dalgren growled.

"That is bad, but not the worst," Thomas continued. "Ullr boasted that he had acquired five more green-beam guns that do not require blood magic sacrifices. He plans to mount them on his ships. I saw the terrible destruction caused by those guns during the war. They can sink ships, knock down buildings."

Kate looked stricken. "I think I know where he got those weapons. It's my fault."

"What?" Thomas asked, startled.

"Never mind that now," said Sophia, squeezing Kate's hand. "We have to stop King Ullr."

"I am friends with Admiral Baker," said Phillip. "I can alert him—"

"Baker," said Thomas suddenly. "Admiral Randolph Baker? He requested an audience with me. I did not know him, and I was preoccupied, so I refused. You say he is a friend?"

"He is one of Henry's best friends," Phillip answered. "He likely came to you at Henry's behest. You can trust him, Thomas. Randolph is a bit rough around the edges, but you won't find anyone more courageous or loyal."

"I will alert the admiral. We must keep this information secret, tell only those who absolutely must know," Thomas warned. "If Ullr realizes his plans have leaked out, he could launch his invasion tomorrow. We are not prepared to defend ourselves."

Dalgren had been watching the sky. "The patrol boat has turned. It's heading back this direction."

"You must leave before they see you," said Thomas. "And I must return to the palace before I am missed."

He reached into the inner pocket of his jacket and drew out a letter. "I'm giving this to you for Sir Henry. I've written down everything I learned from King Ullr. The letter states that the bearer is acting in my name and it has my signature and royal seal. Sir Henry might not trust me otherwise. That reminds me. Ullr did say something else I thought strange in regard to Wellinsport. He said, 'The Freyans will pay for their own destruction.' Do you know what that might mean?"

"No idea," said Phillip, taking the letter and tucking it into an inner pocket. "Henry might know—if I can find him. I'll leave at dawn."

"What are you planning to do?" Thomas asked.

"Travel to the Aligoes by griffin to warn Alan about the ambush of the *Terrapin*. I think it likely Henry might be with him."

"I'll talk to Admiral Baker," said Thomas. "Perhaps he can get word to the Dragon Brigade."

The four stood looking at one another, knowing the moment of parting was at hand.

Thomas spoke what they all felt. "I am reluctant to let you go, for I do not know when I will see you again."

Sophia gave him a loving kiss on the cheek. "God be with you, Thomas."

He kissed her hand. "Tell the countess she must make up her mind to the fact that you will marry Phillip and no other."

"I believe she knows that already," said Sophia.

Phillip gripped his hand. "Thank you, Tom. I will not let you down."

"I know you won't," said Thomas. "Go be with Sophia. I need a moment alone with Kate."

Phillip nodded in understanding. He walked off with Sophia and the two held fast to each other, knowing their time together this night would be brief.

Kate had been standing off to one side, observing Thomas with a grave expression. He held out his hand.

"Thank you, Kate. And thank Dalgren for me."

Kate ignored his outstretched hand and twined her arms around him. Drawing close, she looked up into his face.

"When you and I were together in the Aligoes, you told me that so long as you were alive, I would always have a friend," Kate said. "I am telling you the same thing. So long as I am alive, you are not alone, Thomas. Never alone."

Dalgren growled and impatiently thumped his tail on the ground.

"I'm coming!" Kate said over her shoulder.

She kissed Thomas, sweetly and softly, and before he could recover from his shock, catch his breath, or keep hold of her, she pushed away and ran to help Phillip and Sophia climb onto Dalgren's back.

When they were settled, Kate waved good-bye. Dalgren dipped his head in salute, then lifted his wings and sprang into the air with all the force of his powerful back legs. He rose into the starlit sky and flew off.

Thomas watched until the dragon and his friends were safely out of sight, then began the long, solitary walk back to the palace.

Thomas slipped back into his chambers through the private door, more than half expecting to find that his absence had been discovered, the palace in an uproar.

All was quiet, however. He took off his clothes that were covered with soot and smelled of smoke, made a bundle of them along with his muddy shoes and stockings, and thrust them under the mattress.

Changing into his nightclothes, he removed the bolsters, put them back on the couch, and climbed into bed. He closed the bed curtains and lay propped among the pillows, gazing into the darkness, reliving those last few precious moments with Kate. Her kiss was still warm on his lips.

He tried to temper his joy by counseling himself that Phillip's escape had not lessened his danger. Smythe would be furious, and he would know to blame Thomas. But he could not stop smiling. Phillip was safe and Kate loved him. . . .

The palace clocks chimed six times, jolting Thomas out of sleep.

The guards would be changing shifts, the night guards leaving and the new guards coming on duty now. Thomas pictured them arriving at the guard-house to discover their comrades lying bound and gagged inside. Someone would run to report to the senior officer, while others dashed to the top of the tower. They would find the wounded guards, the empty cell, the broken window and the charred walls, the burnt furniture. The senior officer would run to the palace.

He would have to awaken Smythe and report that the prisoner had escaped. Smythe would hear the news in astonishment and rage. He would dress, summon the guard, and storm through the halls to the royal chambers. . . .

Thomas heard the commotion in the corridor outside his chambers roll toward him in a tidal wave of outrage. He burrowed down beneath the covers and pulled the blankets over his head.

Smythe shouted to the servants to open the doors, barged inside, and yanked open the bed curtains without ceremony. Thomas groaned as the sunlight struck him and he swore and flung up his arm to cover his eyes.

"What the hell! You half-blinded me. Shut those curtains and get out!"

The sergeant was Freyan and extremely uncomfortable in the angry king's presence. He would have left immediately, but Smythe ordered him to stay and search the room.

The sergeant glanced uneasily and apologetically at Thomas. "Begging your pardon, sir, but what are we searching for?"

"Evidence," said Smythe.

The guard opened his mouth again, but catching Smythe's baleful eye, he shut it and began to halfheartedly open drawers and look beneath chairs.

Thomas flung off the bedcovers and climbed out of bed. He covered himself with his dressing gown.

"What the devil is going on?"

"You know perfectly well what is going on, sir! Your friend, the duke, has escaped."

Thomas glanced at the sergeant, who was peering inside a wardrobe. "I doubt you will find him there. Perhaps you should look under the bed."

"Do not play the fool, sir!" Smythe said angrily. "He could not have escaped without your help!"

"And, yet, I have been in my bed all night," said Thomas. "As I am certain those you send to spy on me will testify."

Smythe regarded him with seething fury, and Thomas guessed he had probably asked his spies, only to hear that they had looked in on Thomas at various times during the night and found him asleep.

Smythe vented his ill temper on the officer. "Well, Sergeant? Have you found anything?"

"No, sir," said the sergeant.

"You are useless! Get out!"

The sergeant was only too happy to depart.

Thomas turned his back on Smythe and went over to his dressing table. He poured water into a bowl and splashed it over his face. He deliberately ignored Smythe, hoping he would leave. Smythe remained, however, glaring about the room. As Thomas dried his face with a towel, he heard a newspaper rustle and was filled with foreboding.

He looked into the mirror to see Smythe holding a copy of the *Haever Gazette* that Thomas had left lying on his nightstand. Smythe held up the newspaper and smiled, a cold, humorless smile of vindication.

"It took me some time to figure out this cipher, after King Ullr drew my attention to it. I managed to crack the code just last night, following the dinner you so kindly arranged to keep me occupied. I was too late to prevent Masterson's escape. But I will not be late in arresting the author and co-conspirator, Amelia Nettleship. Once I have her and she implicates you, I will have all the proof I need to denounce you as a traitor."

Thomas rose to confront him. "You can no longer use Phillip or my parents as hostages to my good behavior, Smythe. I could have you arrested, proclaim *you* a murderer and a traitor."

"You won't," said Smythe with a disdainful smile. "Try arresting me. My guards are loyal to me and they would merely laugh at you. Face the truth, Your Majesty. I hold the executioner's axe poised above your neck. I have only to make this information public to see it fall."

"You are bluffing. The people will never accept you as Lord Protector. You are not strong enough. The late queen's half brother, Hugh Fitzroy, would oppose you. Sir Richard warned me that Hugh would attempt to challenge *my* claim and I am the heir of King James. What do you think Hugh would do if you tried to seize the throne? You don't dare kill him. He has powerful friends among the nobility. He would assert his claim and the Accession Council would choose him long before they would think of choosing you."

Smythe swallowed; his jaw worked. A vein throbbed in his neck. He regarded Thomas with such enmity that Thomas was glad Smythe wasn't armed or else he might have shot him dead.

Smythe regained control with a visible effort. "You may have the nobility siding with you, sir, but I have the people, as the reverend gentlemen assured me last night. They are eager for war with the heathen Rosians, and when we achieve our first momentous victory, I will be the one to claim credit. I will be the people's champion, not their young and feckless king."

Meaning your black ship attacking the Dragon Brigade, which, God willing, we will thwart, Thomas thought. And what will you do when you find out your friend, King Ullr, has been using you and means to betray you?

Thomas had to clamp shut his lips to keep from speaking the words aloud.

He was afraid to say anything, for fear he would say too much, and he could only regard Smythe in grim silence, which Smythe took as weakness.

"Be warned, sir," Smythe said, pointing at him. "I will turn the city upside-down and inside out to find Masterson. When I do, he will hang, along with Amelia Nettleship and anyone else involved in this conspiracy. Do not think of leaving the palace again. And there will be no more reading this trash!"

He flung the newspaper on the floor at Thomas's feet, then opened the door and summoned the guards.

"I have uncovered an assassination plot against His Majesty. Remain with the king wherever he goes. He will not be leaving the palace until we have captured the escaped prisoner and those working with him."

The guards took up positions by the door. Smythe walked out and slammed the door shut behind him.

Thomas sat down on the bed and tried desperately to think of some way to warn Amelia and Kate and Sophia of their danger. But he could not leave the palace and his only friend here, Jennings, was gone.

Whoever thinks kings are omnipotent should see me now, Thomas reflected bitterly.

He had never felt so helpless in his life.

THIRTY

Smythe was starting to think God had abandoned him.

After leaving the king, he went to his office to prepare orders to dispatch every soldier and every constable in the city of Haever to find the escaped prisoner, His Grace, Phillip Masterson. He provided a description of the man and ordered that it be copied and circulated. No ship would leave until it had been searched. He would close down all hostelries that hired griffins or wyverns and order that all horseback riders and those occupying horse-drawn conveyances leaving Haever were to be stopped and questioned.

This done, he dispatched a troop of soldiers to the offices of the *Haever Gazette* with instructions to arrest the journalist, Amelia Nettleship.

He next had to write a letter to the queen's half brother, Hugh Fitzroy. Thomas had brought up a valid point. Hugh had a legitimate claim to the throne, though not as long as Thomas Stanford was alive. Having placed Hugh under house arrest to make certain he did not create mischief and interfere with Smythe's plans, Smythe had forgotten about him.

But it occurred to Smythe that he might be wasting a valuable asset in Hugh Fitzroy, since Thomas was not proving to be a very satisfactory puppet. The young king had turned out to be far more courageous and clever than Smythe had anticipated. He was not yet a danger, but Smythe could no longer rest easy, smugly secure in the knowledge that his puppet would dance when he pulled the strings.

He was writing a humbly apologetic letter to Hugh Fitzroy when he felt the flesh on the back of his neck crawl. Smythe gave an involuntary shudder. His old granny would have said a goose had walked across his grave. He lifted his gaze from his work.

Trubgek stood in front of him. Despite the cold, he was wearing only a leather vest over his shirt, breeches, stockings, and boots, and he carried a rucksack.

Smythe had not seen or heard from Trubgek in weeks, ever since he had dispatched him to Freya with the dragon-killing spell and the order to test it on Travian dragons. Smythe had fondly believed Trubgek was hundreds of miles away in northern Freya killing dragons or in Estara or Guundar making deals for black market weapons. What he did not expect was to find the man standing on his carpet.

"What the devil are you doing in my office, Trubgek? I told you never to come to the palace! If you need to report to me, you send word to me and I will come to you."

Smythe had no idea how Trubgek had managed to enter the palace or walk the halls unchallenged. Smythe had never completely trusted the man and he had regretted the necessity of keeping him alive to deal with Coreg's contacts in the black market. While he was talking, he stealthily opened a drawer where he kept a loaded pistol and slid his hand inside.

Trubgek made a slight gesture and the desk drawer slammed shut on Smythe's hand with bruising force.

Smythe withdrew his hand and looked grimly at his bleeding knuckles.

"Don't worry," said Trubgek. "No one saw me."

He sat down, uninvited, and dropped the rucksack on the floor.

"Did you test the spell?" Smythe asked irritably. "I have heard nothing about dead Travian dragons."

"You won't," said Trubgek.

Smythe sucked in an irate breath. "What happened? Why not? What of the dragon-killing spell?"

"Destroyed," said Trubgek.

"Destroyed!" Smythe repeated, stunned. "That's impossible!"

"Not for a dragon," said Trubgek.

"In other words, a dragon caught you in the act," said Smythe. "You were supposed to go to the Dragon Duchies and start killing dragons there, but you bungled that. Fortunately I made alternative plans to deal with the Dragon Brigade. I don't need to rely on you. If all you came here to do is tell me you failed, you may go."

"I did not succeed, but I did not fail. The spell casting took too long," Trubgek added with a dismissive shrug. "I do not need a human spell to kill dragons. I can kill dragons when and where I choose."

"Then go to the Dragon Duchies and start killing," said Smythe.

"I need money," said Trubgek. "I cannot live on air."

"I am not going to pay you for a job you did not do," said Smythe sourly.

"I took care of Gaskell, as you wanted. He will never question your authority, or anyone's for that matter. I have spoken to my contacts on the black market to inquire about the additional rifles. I have information. Important information."

"Very well. What is it?" Smythe asked.

"I need money," Trubgek repeated.

Smythe glanced at the clock. The morning was early yet, only seven of the clock. But his aide would soon be coming to work and he did not want to have to explain Trubgek's presence.

Smythe walked to his safe, opened it, drew out a sheaf of banknotes, and handed them to Trubgek. He did not bother to count them, but stuffed them into a pocket of his shabby vest.

"King Ullr is making plans to invade Freya," said Trubgek.

He spoke without emotion, calm and uncaring. Smythe stared, momentarily taken aback. Then he came to his senses.

"Don't be ridiculous," he snapped. "Get out and take that filthy sack with you. And do not come to the palace again. If I need you, I will send for you."

Trubgek shrugged and stood up. Picking up the rucksack, he started to leave.

"Wait," Smythe said. "Tell me what you think you know. After all, I have paid for it."

Trubgek sat down. "I spoke to Alonzo about acquiring more rifles. He does not have access to those particular rifles, but he can buy others from a different supplier."

"For the same amount of money," said Smythe.

Trubgek shrugged. "Alonzo added that he had heard Freya will soon be embroiled in war against Guundar and he offered to sell us powder, shot, ammunition, artillery pieces, cannons, whatever we need. A good price."

"Your Alonzo has heard wrong. I am preparing for war against Rosia and King Ullr is my ally."

"Then King Ullr has made a fool of you," said Trubgek.

He shoved at the rucksack with his boot. "See for yourself. Bills of lading, letters, confirmation of deliveries, secret stockpiles, weapons caches . . ."

"Hand that to me," said Smythe.

Trubgek did not move. "I need more money. Somewhere to live, passage to the Dragon Duchies."

Smythe clamped his jaw tight. He went to the safe and drew out more banknotes. This time he did not hand them over. He held onto them.

"Show me."

Trubgek opened the rucksack and rummaged about among his clothes. He drew out several documents and gave them to Smythe.

As he reviewed them, his expression grew grimmer and darker. He would have to go over them carefully, but initial examination indicated that Guundar was spending vast sums on weapons and having them shipped to Freya.

"Secret stockpiles," Trubgek repeated. "Under your very nose."

Smythe handed over the money. Trubgek stuffed the notes into his pocket and picked up the rucksack.

"Remain in Haever," said Smythe. "I may have need of you."

Trubgek nodded and walked out of the office, startling Smythe's aide, who had just arrived for work. The aide stared at him in astonishment, then hurried into the room.

"I am sorry, Chancellor! I did not see him! I would have never let him pass. I thought we were well rid of that fellow, sir."

"Close the door," Smythe said. "I am not to be disturbed."

He carefully read the papers Trubgek had provided and matched these with recent intelligence reports he had received regarding Guundaran fleet and troop movements, and he swore, viciously and bitterly.

He had succeeded beyond even his ambitious designs in gaining power and he seen God's hand at work in his success. Now he felt betrayed, as though God had spread a bountiful feast before him, laying the cloth, smoothing out wrinkles. And just as he was sitting down to eat his fill, he saw rats swarm the table and devour the food.

Smythe labored to catch his breath. His heart thudded; red mist covered his eyes. He grew dizzy and there was a foul taste in his mouth.

Smythe recalled how friendly Ullr had been to him and he was nauseated to the point where he feared he might vomit. . . . The monarch had flattered him, treated him as his equal.

"The royal blood of Guundar runs in your veins. . . ." Ullr had told him.

Smythe gave a low, inarticulate, feral moan.

He had been born to poverty, shame, and ignominy. People of wealth in positions of power had used him, mocked him, demeaned him. Smythe had suffered every blow with a smile, swallowed every insult with humility. And he had connived, plotted, and schemed to either remove those in his way or to grind them beneath his heel.

And King Ullr was like all the others, laughing at him.

The blood pounded in Smythe's head; he feared he would burst a blood vessel and collapse in an apoplectic fit. He gripped the desk with both hands and slammed his forehead against it.

He reeled from the pain, but it restored his sanity. Placing his elbows on the desk, he rested his throbbing head in his hands and tried to think what to do.

Ullr was plotting to invade Freya!

Smythe believed Trubgek at last. He searched through the documents, trying to find some clue as to when Ullr planned to invade, but he came up with nothing. Not that a date mattered.

Smythe was under no illusions as to the outcome of such a war. He was a military man and he knew his nation could not hope to survive. Freya would go down to defeat and, as Chancellor of War, he would go down with her, for he was the one who had nurtured the viper in his bosom.

People would recall the sight of him riding in Ullr's carriage during the funeral, their numerous private meetings together, their close friendship. Smythe had privately let it be known that he had been the one to send the *Terrapin* to the Aligoes. Thomas had signed the orders, but it was Smythe who had persuaded him.

He would be destroyed, his career ended, perhaps even lose his life. Most galling, Thomas Stanford would survive. Ullr would make Thomas his puppet-king, leave him on the throne to placate the Freyan people. Ullr had done the same in Braffa. He had permitted the oligarchs to continue in office, but lacking any real power. Ullr, not Smythe, would be pulling Thomas's strings.

Smythe pictured the Guundarans dragging him to a field, shooting him in the head, then kicking his body into a hastily dug grave. They would laugh at the thought of how he had trusted them.

He feared he would go mad. And then, he heard a voice. He raised his head.

"If Thomas is dead and you are Lord Protector," the voice said to him, "King Ullr would have to deal with you. He might not dare proceed with his plans for war, for he knows you are not some weak, sniveling youth."

God had not abandoned him, after all. Smythe rose to his feet to pace the floor, consider his options. He had planned all along that Thomas should not outlive his usefulness. He would suffer some sort of fatal accident, as had several of Smythe's former enemies: a tumble over a balcony or a tragic carriage mishap. Such things could be arranged.

Smythe had been going to wait until he had fully established his base of power, extended his influence. It seemed events were going to force his hand.

An idea had been in the back of his mind for some time. He had liked it, but he could not figure out how it would all come together. At last, he knew the answer.

He consulted his calendar and noted that Hallen Day was fast approaching. On that holiday, Thomas and his retinue would board his royal yacht in order to perform the annual tradition of His Majesty reviewing the fleet. Thousands of people attended every year to view the magnificent spectacle of the ships of the Royal Navy lined up in the Breath.

Smythe went over his idea in his mind, searching for flaws, and could not find one. Arriving at a decision, he summoned his aide.

The man entered and came to a dead stop, staring at Smythe's forehead in shock.

Wondering what was wrong, Smythe put his hand to his head and felt blood. He had completely forgotten.

"Sir, you're hurt!" his aide gasped.

"I tripped on that loose rug," Smythe replied.

"I will fetch a healer—"

"Never mind that now," said Smythe irritably. "That man, Trubgek, who just left. Send someone to fetch him and bring him back. Then arrange a meeting for me with King Ullr. Inform His Majesty that the matter is urgent and I prefer that we meet in private."

King Ullr received Smythe's message and sent word that he was at liberty to meet with him at noon in his guest rooms.

"Do you have any idea what he wants?" Ullr asked his agent, Baron Grimm.

The baron shook his head. "I have been gone for a week on that other matter and have only just arrived in the palace. I have no idea."

"Smythe wants to meet in private," said Ullr. "You know what to do."

Grimm left to conceal himself behind the door to the sitting room. Once Ullr was certain his agent was in place, he told his secretary he was at liberty. Smythe entered the room and Ullr rose to his feet to greet him, noting that he was flushed and he had suffered an ugly gash on his forehead. Ullr wondered idly what had happened, but was not interested enough to ask.

"Forgive me for making you wait, Chancellor," Ullr said. "Affairs of state. You of all people will understand."

"Spare me the flattery, sir," said Smythe. "I know the truth. I have been made aware of your plans."

"You must tell me to what plans you refer, sir," Ullr said affably. "Will you be seated?"

"I prefer to stand, sir," said Smythe, stiff and rigid as though on parade.

"As you will, Chancellor."

Ullr remained standing. He cast a swift glance toward the sitting room. The door was closed, but the baron would have his ear pressed to it.

"I trust you will explain yourself."

"I know Your Majesty has secret plans to invade Freya. Do not waste my time with denials. I have proof."

Ullr regarded him with a faintly derisive smile. "That blow to your head has addled your brains, sir."

Smythe flushed. He had to stop to swallow his outrage. A muscle in his jaw twitched. A vein in his neck throbbed.

"I am a military man, Your Majesty. A pragmatist. I know the strength of your forces. I know Freya must go down to defeat. We cannot withstand Guundar's might." Smythe drew himself up. "But we Freyans are not afraid of war. We will fight. You will win, but your victory will cost Guundar dearly."

"You have an active imagination, sir. Have you spoken of these wild notions to anyone else? His Majesty, perhaps?"

"I have not and I will not," said Smythe. "This concerns the two of us. We understand each other, as you are fond of telling me."

Ullr made a deprecating gesture. "I fear you do not understand me, sir. I am a man of peace."

"I came to talk peace, sir," said Smythe, advancing a step. "I am now Chancellor of War. But if I ruled Freya, if I were Lord Protector, I could negotiate a peace treaty between our two great nations. Naturally, I would be willing to provide certain concessions, such as allowing Guundar to establish a base in the Aligoes near Wellinsport. Guundar would at last be able to share in the riches of the Aligoes."

"Magnanimous terms, Chancellor," said Ullr. "Unfortunately, you have a problem. You are *not* Lord Protector and so long as King Thomas lives you never will be. Your king being a young and healthy man, I find this discussion entertaining, but pointless. I am quite busy. If there is nothing more—"

"Hallen Day is approaching, sir," said Smythe abruptly.

King Ullr had found Smythe amusing up to this point. His amusement died with this mention of Hallen Day. Ullr was suddenly wary. He planned to launch his assault on Haever on Hallen Day and he wondered if Smythe knew something, after all.

"Hallen Day. I believe I have heard something of this date," said Ullr, treading carefully. "A national holiday celebrating a great Freyan naval victory. Although, as I recall, Freya won the battle, but she ended up losing the war."

Smythe scarcely seemed to hear him. He was intent on his speech, as though he had memorized and practiced it before delivery.

"On Hallen Day, tradition holds that the king reviews the fleet. His Majesty boards the royal yacht. The ships are decorated, sailors line the yardarms, cannons fire salutes as the king sails past. The event draws large numbers of spectators."

King Ullr was aware of this. He had chosen Hallen Day for precisely this reason. While the Freyan navy was celebrating, his ships would be preparing to bring the Hallen Day party to a swift and bloody conclusion.

"The Crown Prince Jonathan died of injuries he suffered during an accident on board a naval warship," Smythe continued. "As a man of faith, I should not be superstitious, but I have a premonition King Thomas might suffer the same fate. If a tragic accident were to occur to His Majesty on Hallen Day, for example, I would be in a position to swiftly declare myself Lord Protector and take over control of the government so that Freya would avoid the civil unrest and chaos that followed the untimely death of Queen Mary."

"You act with considerable foresight, sir," said Ullr. "I am certain we all pray to God that His Majesty, King Thomas, remains in good health on Hallen Day and every day."

"God be praised for His mercies great and small," said Smythe unctuously. "As the Scriptures remind us, 'Watch, for ye know neither the day nor the hour.'"

With that enigmatic phrase, he appeared to come to the end of his speech, for he bowed his way out of the room. The door had barely closed behind him when Baron Grimm left his hiding place and returned to speak to the king.

"You heard?" Ullr asked grimly.

"Everything," said the baron. "I could scarcely contain my laughter when he mentioned a peace treaty. As if we would negotiate peace with Freya when we can demand her unconditional surrender! But then he spoke of Hallen Day and I found that less funny. Perhaps he has in truth discovered our plans."

"The fool knows nothing," said Ullr dismissively. "He made his lack of knowledge abundantly apparent when he brought up Hallen Day and then went blathering on about the king suffering an 'accident.'"

"What will you do, sir? The chancellor obviously plots to kill the king. He as much as admitted it. Should we warn His Majesty?"

"We will proceed with our plans for the invasion," Ullr said. "The sudden and tragic death of the young king would throw Freya into chaos and that would suit me well."

"It was kind of Smythe to offer us Wellinsport," said Grimm, smiling hugely.

"Kind but unnecessary," said King Ullr.

He began to laugh. Since he rarely smiled, much less indulged in laughter, his astonished secretary opened the door a crack to see what was amiss.

THIRTY-ONE

Amelia Nettleship was wakened in the night by a rattling sound. She sat up in bed, frowning, wondering why her house should be rattling, when she heard the sound again and realized someone was throwing gravel at the bedroom window that faced the back of the house. Bandit had been sleeping on the floor by her bed, waiting for Sophia to return, and he jumped to his feet with a warning growl.

Amelia went to the window, raised the sash, and peered curiously down into the backyard. Three figures, wrapped in cloaks, were preparing to throw more gravel.

"Here, now, what is your business?" Amelia said sternly.

"Miss Amelia! It's us!" Kate called in a loud whisper. "Let us in!"

"Merciful goodness," Amelia exclaimed.

She put on her flannel dressing gown, slid her feet into slippers, and hurried down the stairs, nearly tripping over Bandit, who was underfoot. Lighting a lamp, she glanced at the clock on the mantel. The time was thirty minutes past three of the clock in the dead of night.

Amelia went through the kitchen and the pantry to the back door.

"Come in! Come in! You must be half frozen!"

Kate and Sophia and Phillip hurried inside. Bandit recognized Sophia and began barking wildly and jumping at her.

"Keep him quiet!" Kate whispered.

Sophia caught hold of Bandit and he quit barking and began to lick her face.

"We have brought a friend, Miss Amelia," said Kate softly. "You remember Pip?"

"Indeed, I do," said Amelia. "You are welcome, Your Grace."

Before shutting the door, she looked up and down the back alley to see if they had been followed. The alley was empty. Amelia shut the door and locked it, then turned to fuss over her guests.

"Come into the kitchen where it is warm," she said. Sophia guided Phillip to the kitchen and Bandit followed, now jumping on Phillip.

Amelia drew Kate into the pantry. "What went wrong? I thought you were going to Barwich Manor."

"Plans changed," said Kate. "Thomas refused to leave the palace. He said he has a duty to his people."

"Good for him," said Amelia.

"I suppose," Kate said, sighing, clearly not happy. "But he is in so much danger."

"Thomas Stanford is an intelligent and resourceful young man," said Amelia. "He knows what he's about. Now come have something to eat. You are in low spirits because your brain requires nourishment. We can discuss all this after you're warm and fed."

She ushered her guests into the kitchen, built up the fire, and served them her specialty, toasted cheese. As an added treat, to warm their blood, she mixed hot rum punch.

The three drank the steaming punch and ate toasted cheese. When they were finished, they described their adventures, how they had managed to free Phillip and escape the prison with no one the wiser.

"One of my plans actually worked," said Kate. "Dalgren was astonished."

Phillip passed on the information Thomas had gathered from spying on King Ullr.

"Secretly plotting to invade Freya! This is wonderful," Amelia stated, taking out her notebook and writing furiously.

"Miss Amelia!" Sophia said, shocked.

"Oh, I don't mean the invasion," Amelia said. "That is quite appalling. I mean the fact that this will be the story of the century. The *Gazette* will put out a special edition—"

Kate seized hold of the notebook. "You cannot write about this, Miss

Amelia. We cannot make what we have learned public knowledge. Thomas warned us that if Ullr thinks his plans have been discovered, he could launch his invasion before we are ready."

Amelia laid down her pen with a sigh. "You are right, of course. I take it you three have formed a plan. What is it? How can I help?"

"I know a man who will provide me with a griffin," said Phillip. "I will fly to the Aligoes to warn Alan that the *Terrapin* is sailing into an ambush. If Henry is on board, as I think possible, I can warn him about King Ullr."

"Sir Henry thinks you betrayed him, Your Grace," said Amelia sharply. "He might well shoot you on sight!"

Phillip gave a cheerful smile. "Henry is actually quite reasonable. He will allow me to explain first and *then* shoot me."

Sophia sighed and shook her head and fed Bandit most of her toasted cheese to keep him quiet.

"I would still feel better if we could find a way to smuggle Sophia out of the country," Phillip added.

"Far too dangerous," said Amelia. "Smythe will lock down the city in an effort to find Your Grace and that includes the ports."

"I wouldn't leave anyway," said Sophia. "I will stay in Haever with Miss Amelia."

"The question is: what are we going to do about warning the Dragon Brigade about the black ship?" Phillip wondered. "I could fly to Maribeau after I talk to Alan, but I might arrive too late."

"Dalgren plans to warn the Brigade," said Kate.

"Did he say so?" Amelia asked.

"He didn't have to," Kate said. "I know him."

"He will have to fly through the storms of the Winter Witch," said Amelia doubtfully. "If he reaches the Brigade alive, he is a deserter who fled before he finished serving his sentence. The Brigade will take him into custody again."

"I know the risks and so does Dalgren," said Kate calmly. "What he doesn't know is that I am going with him."

"To Maribeau?" Phillip said, startled. "That's the last place in the world you should go!"

Kate shot him a glance, pleading with him to keep quiet.

Phillip didn't heed it. "They were going to hang you in Maribeau, Kate. They would have hanged you if Thomas and I hadn't rescued you! You're an escaped prisoner. A fugitive from justice. If they catch you—"

"They won't," said Kate. "I'm certain the authorities have forgotten all about me by now. And besides, we're not going to Maribeau. We're going to Brigade headquarters."

Phillip shook his head, unconvinced. Sophia looked at her worriedly.

"We're only going to stay long enough to warn the dragons about the black ship and then we'll leave," Kate assured her. "I won't have time to get into trouble. And I won't let Dalgren go alone." She folded her arms across her chest. "So that is settled."

Amelia regarded the three of them with affection and pride.

"I think you young people are daft, reckless, and foolhardy, but I love you for it." She paused to dab at her eyes with a handkerchief from the reticule. That done, she briskly resumed. "We can do nothing at this time of night. We must try to get some rest. I will go to the *Gazette* first thing in the morning to see what I can find out."

"I will likely be gone by the time you return, Miss Amelia," said Phillip. "Thank you for your help."

Kate and Sophia and Bandit went up to their rooms. Amelia made up a bed for Phillip on the sofa in the parlor, then went to her bed. She prided herself on being able to fall asleep instantly, but this morning she lay awake, fretting and thinking of everything that could go wrong.

Hearing Phillip slip out of the house near dawn, Amelia went to her window and watched him set out, and silently wished him Godspeed. She heard Bandit bark in the next room and saw Phillip look up at Sophia's window and put his hand to his lips. He hurried off down the street and disappeared around the corner.

Amelia dressed and went to her office and wrote down notes on the story of the century. As the clock struck eight, she prepared to set off for the *Gazette*. She checked on Kate and Sophia before she left. Kate and Sophia were asleep. Bandit lay protectively across Sophia's feet.

Amelia walked to the offices of the *Gazette* every day, no matter the weather. Mrs. Ridgeway of Mrs. Ridgeway's Academy for Young Ladies taught that "daily exercise prevents dyspepsia, assists the actions of the liver, and causes the blood to flow more freely through the vessels to the brain, thus improving the thought process."

Amelia could attest to the truth of this statement for she never suffered from liver complaints and she considered her brain to be more than usually active.

She enjoyed the brisk walk in the cold. She deeply inhaled the crisp air that sparkled with a few drifting snowflakes and felt the blood surge to her brain, clearing away any fuzziness caused by lack of sleep. She was laying out her story in her mind when she turned onto the block where the *Gazette*'s offices were located and came to a sudden halt.

Soldiers, armed with rifles, were standing guard in front of the office, where a crowd had gathered, waiting eagerly to see if there might be bloodshed. Amelia knew at once that Smythe had cracked the code. He had discovered the messages she had been sending to Thomas in the Captain Kate stories and he was going to have her arrested.

He did not know where she lived, however, and had sent his soldiers to the office to either arrest her there or force the editor to provide her address. Her editor would be reluctant to dispense such information, but if the soldiers threatened to smash up the office, he would have little choice. And if the soldiers went to her house, they would find Kate and Sophia.

Amelia looked around and saw a gentleman entering a wyvern-drawn carriage only steps away. The driver was holding the door open. Before he could shut it, Amelia nimbly hopped into the cab. She gave the driver the address and said, "Drive with all haste."

"I don't know," the driver began reluctantly.

Amelia reached into her reticule, drew out a banknote, and thrust it into his hands.

"Here, now, Madame, this cab is taken!" said the gentleman already inside the cab. He was highly irate. "You must find your own."

"For king and country, sir," said Amelia, settling herself on the seat beside him.

The driver stuffed the banknote into his hat and scrambled up onto the box. He sent the magic flowing to the lift tank and gave the wyvern a magical shock with the whip. The beast leaped into the air with a startled snarl and flew off.

Amelia straightened her hat.

"You are performing a great service for Freya, sir," Amelia told the gentleman, who was glaring at her. She gave him an approving tap on the leg with her umbrella. "Your country salutes you."

The gentleman did not appear to appreciate the sentiment. He crammed himself in a corner as far from her as he could manage and made rude comments regarding "hysterical females."

As the cab drew near her house, Amelia flung open the door and sprang out while the cab was still a foot or two off the ground.

She ran into the house, shouting for Kate and Sophia and banging the dinner gong to rouse them. The young women stumbled down the stairs in their nightclothes. Bandit howled. The gong hurt his ears.

"Dress and pack your things, ladies. We must leave immediately," Amelia stated. "We have been discovered. Soldiers are now raiding the offices of the *Gazette*. They will soon be headed for my house."

"Fortunately, we have very little to pack," said Sophia.

She and Kate hurried to their rooms. Amelia rummaged through some of the trunks in the attic for warm clothes and delivered them to Kate.

"You will need these, my dear, since you will be braving the Winter Witch."

She handed Kate a pair of trousers made of the warm and serviceable cloth known as fustian. "Those belonged to my uncle, a stevedore by trade. They will be big on you, but you can keep them up with these suspenders. I also have several pair of woolen stockings, two flannel shirts, and a thick wool sweater. I'll pack a valise. You'll need food, as well."

Amelia did not pack for herself. She needed only her portable writing desk, the clothes on her back, her reticule, umbrella, and double-barreled pistol and she could travel the world. She met Kate and Sophia at the bottom of the stairs.

Sophia was disguised in some of Amelia's clothes and she had Bandit on his leash. Kate had changed into the fustian trousers, flannel shirt, and sweater, with her red kerchief around her neck. Both young women wore hooded cloaks and, Amelia was glad to see, sensible shoes.

They left by the back door, which opened onto the alley. Servants were out sweeping snow from the stoops or emptying slop buckets. They glanced curiously at the three, but otherwise showed little interest.

"I have to reach Dalgren before he leaves for Maribeau on his own," said Kate. "I don't like to leave you and Sophia."

"Sophia and I will be fine," said Amelia.

She shook hands with Kate and gave her the valise, cab fare, and money for the journey. "My best to Dalgren, and have a safe trip."

Sophia embraced Kate and gave her a kiss. "Godspeed! Please be careful. And do not worry about me. I am in good hands."

"I know you are," said Kate. "Take care of your mistress, sir," she ordered Bandit.

The dog gave a menacing growl to indicate he was prepared to battle all comers and then plopped down in the alley to scratch his ear.

Kate left in search of a cab, as Sophia and Amelia continued down the alley.

Amelia sighed a little to think of the soldiers breaking down her door and invading her house, smashing up the furniture and rummaging through her papers. She then reflected that this exciting incident would be the talk of the neighborhood for years to come. Her neighbors would never trust her again. The thought cheered her considerably.

"Where are we going, Miss Amelia?" Sophia asked.

"Welkinstead," said Amelia.

Kate knew her way around Dalgren's traps by now. Her only worry was that he would have already left for Maribeau. Although he had deserted the Brigade, Dalgren remained loyal to his comrades, both dragons and humans.

She was relieved to find him still asleep after the rigors of last night's adventure. She tried to be quiet, to let him rest, but he heard her. He reared up his head to glare at her.

"You are *not* coming to Maribeau with me. You will only slow me down."

Kate had expected this. She sat down on his forepaw.

"May I remind you that you are a deserter, not once, but twice. You left Glasearrach before you could serve out your sentence to spend a year helping Father Jacob."

Dalgren scowled. His eyes narrowed and he shot puffs of smoke from his nostrils.

"I am well aware of my crimes," he grumbled.

Kate continued, relentless. "The dragons will carry out their threat to exile you and take away your name, and this time no one will be able to save you."

"I know that!" Dalgren snapped his jaws. "The members of the Brigade may arrest me, but first they will have to listen to me."

"They will listen to *me*," Kate stated. "Captain Thorgrimson knows me."

"He knows you, but the dragons don't," Dalgren countered.

Kate had no answer to that. Dragons were friendly toward humans, but they considered humans changeable and capricious, and therefore untrustworthy. A dragon might change his mind about some decision he had made, but only after years of deliberation, whereas humans changed their minds in an eyeblink.

Kate recalled the reception the dragons had given her when she had tried to warn them about Trubgek and his knowledge of dragon magic. They had been polite and grateful for the information, but they had not believed her.

"Then I will talk to Captain Thorgrimson and you can talk to the dragons," said Kate. "I'll be able to speak on your behalf, explain to the captain why you left Below, that you left because of me."

Kate stood up. "We should be leaving. The moment the guards see that brass door lying in a puddle on the floor they will know a dragon attacked the tower and they'll be out searching for you."

Dalgren made no move to stand up. "It's too dangerous. You don't have a dragon saddle. The flight will take days. You will freeze to death crossing the Breath."

"I won't freeze. I'm wearing Miss Amelia's uncle's trousers," said Kate, laughing. She rubbed his snout. "I brought a leather braid I found at the dockyards. I'll tie it to your mane and secure it around my waist. I'm not letting you go alone. You know better than to argue with me, and we're wasting time. Now hold still while I wrap this around your neck."

Dalgren gave a sigh that filled the cave with smoke, and grumpily submitted.

THIRTY-TWO

Simon Yates was a man with a disciplined and highly organized mind, an analytical thinker devoted to logic. He did not believe in such sentimental nonsense as being homesick, for that implied an emotional attachment to what was, after all, nothing more than a collection of stone, wood, metal, and magic he used for shelter.

Simon was therefore surprised to feel a rush of warmth when Albright wheeled his rickety wooden chair through the field where Welkinstead had landed. At the sight of his home, Simon was forced to pull out his handkerchief and blow his nose.

Mr. Albright had transported Simon and his wheeled chair from Haever to Welkinstead's current location in a horse-drawn wagon in the belief that the wagon would draw far less attention in the rural farming community than a carriage. Simon had lain at his ease among the straw in the back and questioned Albright regarding the house and repairs, wanting to know all the details.

The eccentric old duchess would have been proud of her house; Welkinstead had survived the attack and the subsequent crash landing with only a modest amount of damage: the smashed cupola, broken window panes, and a crack in one of the towers. One of the chimneys had collapsed in a heap of bricks, all the paintings had fallen off the walls, and the duchess's collection of curios were strewn about the house.

"What is that clutter on the roof, Albright?" Simon demanded as the house came into view.

"Tree branches and tarpaulins, sir," Albright replied in his laconic fashion.

"I can see for myself that it is tree branches and tarpaulins," said Simon testily. "I mean, what are tree branches and tarpaulins doing cluttering up the roof?"

"Camouflage, sir," said Albright.

"Camouflage!" Simon repeated. "You camouflaged the roof? Why? You have my permission to speak as much as necessary in order to explain."

"I observed the house from the air in a carriage, sir. The greenish gray color of the slate tiles of the roof blends nicely with woodland, but the house was still visible from the air."

"Because you knew what you were looking for, Albright. The casual traveler, flying about in a carriage, would never notice it."

"Perhaps not, sir. But I deemed it best not to take a chance. I happened to see a dragon flying around the vicinity the other day."

"Undoubtedly one of the Travian dragons looking for deer, not my house," said Simon, irritated.

"One never knows, sir. I covered those parts of the roof that were visible with tree branches and the tarpaulins."

"And you will be responsible for removing the tree branches and tarpaulins when we return to the air. Did you repair the heating system?"

"First thing, sir," Mr. Albright replied. He wheeled his master up a ramp he had built on the front porch and into the entry hall.

Simon looked around his home with intense and heartfelt satisfaction and greeted his own specially designed floating chair as a long-lost friend.

"I will be thankful to be out of this contraption," he said, referring to the wooden, wheeled chair he had been forced to use in the city.

Albright lifted him and placed him in the floating chair.

Simon settled into his chair, checked the various pockets and pouches attached to the chair to see that his books and papers were still tucked neatly in their places, and gave a deep and satisfied sigh.

"It is good to be home, Albright."

"What shall I do with the old chair, sir?"

"I would tell you to burn it, but someone would see the smoke."

"I will remove it to the cellar," said Mr. Albright.

Simon floated outdoors to study the house's exterior and inspect the repairs.

"Looks very good, Albright," Simon told him. "And now I would like to see the lift tanks. I want to have Welkinstead floating again as soon as possible."

Mr. Albright looked grave.

"What is wrong, Albright?" Simon asked, frowning. "Whenever I mention lift tanks you get a pained expression on your face."

"As you know, sir, the lift tanks are enclosed and protected by thick walls. When the house crashed, the walls sank deep into the soft ground. The lift tanks are now below ground level."

Simon shrugged. "Is that all?"

"I fear not, sir. If you will come with me."

Mr. Albright retrieved a lantern and descended the stairs that led to the lift tanks, while Simon followed in his chair.

"These lift tanks on the port side suffered the most damage, sir."

Albright shined the light on an area of the wall near the floor and pointed.

"I see bullet holes," said Simon.

"I patched those, sir. Look down near the bottom."

Simon looked closely and saw the telltale green glow of contramagic. "You should have told me when you first found this, Albright."

"I did not want to upset you, sir."

"How far has the contramagic spread?"

"The three tanks on the port side are all affected, sir," Mr. Albright answered. "Those closest to the wall where the green beam struck are the worst."

Simon could almost see the contramagic crawling across the tank, devouring the magical constructs.

"I would have thought the Seventh Sigil would have protected them. Perhaps the constructs could not withstand a concentrated blast. I must remember to conduct a study on the effects of concentrated green beams on the Seventh Sigil. Make a note of that, Albright."

Mr. Albright silently nodded.

"I suppose there is nothing we can do now. It will be dark soon and I want to straighten up my office while the daylight lasts."

He sent his chair floating up the stairs to the second floor and entered his office. He stopped in the doorway to survey the damage. Bookcases had toppled over, spilling their contents. File cabinets lay on their sides, disgorging their contents. The floor was covered with books and papers.

"I thought Randolph was going to help you clean this mess," said Simon, irritated.

"Admiral Baker and I made some attempt to restore order, sir. The admiral became frustrated, however, and after damning my eyes, he began heaving books out the window. I deemed he was doing more harm than good and I thanked him for his help and told him I could manage."

Simon chuckled at the thought. "I will sort through the papers and you pick up the books, although I have no idea what to do with them. It will be a waste of time to put them back on the shelves, because they will only fall off when we raise the house."

"I was thinking we could pack them in the wooden crates I have been using to haul supplies," said Mr. Albright.

"An inspired thought, Albright," said Simon.

He and Mr. Albright sorted through the mess as long as they had light to see. The work progressed slowly due to the fact that Simon would often become so interested in what he was reading that he would forget he was supposed to be sorting.

He was tempted to risk lighting the magical lamps in the office in order to continue working into the night, but reluctantly abandoned the idea. The house was far from the well-traveled routes. Still, there was a risk someone would see the lights, and Simon decided not to chance it.

He was glad to be able to sleep in his own bed. Lying in the darkness, he thought about Henry and wondered how he was doing. Simon was not given to prayer, for he did not believe in God, but he decided that a word of encouragement, even unheard, would not go amiss.

"Keep fighting, Henry," Simon told him. "We can't do without you."

The next day, he and Albright returned to what Simon had begun to call the root cellar to rig up lights in order to work on the lift tanks. Albright collected the lamps that had not been broken and suspended them from the ceiling. Simon attached the lights to braided leather cables. This done, he could operate all the lanterns with a touch of his hand.

Simon inspected the damage the contramagic had done to the lift tanks.

"This is a bloody mess, Albright. Look at the constructs on this lift tank. Or rather, look at where the constructs are supposed to be, but aren't."

Albright gave an unhappy nod.

"The contramagic has penetrated so deeply in some places that it has attacked the magic on the metal itself. See where it is starting to disintegrate. Looks as though someone spilled acid on it, like the hole I burned in the carpet in the entry hall which you covered with the umbrella stand.

"Three of these lift tanks will have to be replaced," Simon added, glumly. "Picture it, Albright. Workmen clomping about the house, ripping out lift tanks, installing new ones that will have to be specially constructed. Our house will be crawling with strangers, banging and clanging and disrupting my studies."

"Do you propose bringing strangers here, sir?" Albright asked, alarmed.

"I don't plan on being stuck in the middle of nowhere for years," said

Simon. "But, no, I believe I can jury-rig the magic on the tanks enough to get us airborne in the next fortnight."

Mr. Albright coughed.

Simon glared at him. "Speak, Albright."

"I respectfully submit, sir, that you and the house are far safer in that field than floating in the sky above the city."

"Events are happening in the world, Albright—"

"Ahoy, the house!" a woman's voice shouted from outside. "Is anyone at home?"

Mr. Albright drew his pistol.

"Do not shoot anyone, Albright," Simon said. "This woman is undoubtedly some innocent person who has lost her way."

Mr. Albright returned the pistol to his pocket and mounted the stairs. Simon reached into one of the chair's compartments to retrieve the magical weapons he termed "crackers" and followed. He found Mr. Albright crouched in front of one of the windows that were now on the ground level, peering outside.

Mr. Albright glanced around. "Please return to the cellar where it is safe, sir."

"Bosh!" said Simon.

He joined Mr. Albright at the window and looked out to see two women approaching the house. They had apparently walked some distance through the woods, for their skirts and the hems of their cloaks were stained with mud and covered with twigs and dead leaves. They were accompanied by a small dog with muddy paws and dead leaves clinging to his fur.

"Relax, Albright," said Simon, sighing. "Our visitor is Miss Amelia Nettleship, intrepid journalist and a veritable bloodhound. Trust her to track me down."

"Who is the young woman with her, sir?" Albright asked.

"We are honored, Albright. She is Princess Sophia of Rosia, sister to King Renaud. She was once affianced to His Majesty, King Thomas Stanford. Their engagement has since been broken off. The spaniel is her dog, Bandit. She never goes anywhere without him."

"But . . . what is a Rosian princess doing *here,* sir?" Albright asked, bewildered.

"A good question," said Simon. "You are most astute today, Albright. I suggest we ask her."

Simon propelled his chair to the front door and flung it open. "Your Highness, Miss Amelia! Enter. Welcome to Welkinstead."

Sophia picked up Bandit and she and Amelia walked up the ramp and into the house. Amelia deposited her umbrella in the hall. The umbrella was in sad shape, for she had apparently used it to slash at weeds and branches.

"You may hang your cloaks on the hydra," Simon added, waving. "I would invite you both to my office, but it is a mess. Albright, fetch chairs for our guests and place them here in the hall. Now, Miss Amelia, I see by your expression you are the bearer of bad news. How can I help?"

"As you deduced, sir, soldiers are searching for Her Highness. Sophia has been staying with me, but my house has been compromised. It occurred to me that she would be safe here. Unfortunately, we ran into a troop of soldiers on the highway who stopped us to ask if we had seen Welkinstead."

"How far away were these soldiers, Miss Amelia?" Simon asked sharply.

"Several miles. They are stopping all travelers and asking questions at the farmhouses."

Albright returned with the chairs. Amelia sat down gratefully. Sophia took a seat and released Bandit from his leash. The dog pattered over to sniff Simon's chair. Bandit didn't like the looks of it, apparently, for he began to bark at the chair and make little runs at it.

"Bandit, do be good," Sophia pleaded.

The dog paid no attention to her, but continued to dash at Simon's chair and bark frantically.

Simon bent down, looked the dog in the eye, and said sternly, "Stop!"

Bandit froze in mid-bark, flopped down onto the floor with a whimper, and laid his head between his paws.

"Albright, the dog is hungry," said Simon. "Take him to the kitchen and feed him. He might enjoy some of your stewed chicken from last night. Possibly more than I did."

Sophia attached Bandit's leash and handed it to Albright. He departed with the dog, who willingly trotted along with him, keeping a wary eye on Simon until he was out of the room.

Simon bowed from his chair. "Welcome to my home, Your Highness. I am Simon Yates. Forgive me if I dispense with further formalities, but we must decide what to do regarding this situation."

"I am pleased to meet you, Master Yates," said Sophia. "I have read with interest many of your articles on the scientific principles of magic."

Simon was pleased. "I have heard that you are an extremely talented savant. I look forward to discussing my theories with you. But now, Miss Amelia, I need details. First, how did you locate my house? Albright assures me it is difficult to see from the air."

"Not for a dragon, sir," Amelia said. "I asked Kate to ask her friend, Dalgren, to do some investigating for me."

"Ah, of course." Simon nodded. "I should have guessed. Albright mentioned seeing a dragon, but I thought he had been nipping the Aqua Vitae. How did you know where to tell Dalgren to look?"

"Like many people in Haever, I watched Welkinstead come under attack that terrible night. Most people speculated the house had fallen into the Breath, but I did not think so. I made calculations based on wind speed and the prevailing currents of the Breath and I determined the house might have come down over land in this area. You have done a very good job of hiding it, I must say."

"Albright deserves the credit for that," said Simon magnanimously.

"When Sophia and I entered the woods, we searched for signs of a trail and saw tracks of wagon wheels. We followed those."

Simon nodded. "Diligent investigating, Miss Amelia."

"Thank you, sir. Coming from you, that is high praise."

"Tell me about your encounter with the soldiers," Simon instructed.

"I had hired a pony cart and Sophia and I were driving along the toll road when we were stopped by a troop of Guundaran mercenaries. The commander asked where we were going and if we had seen your famous house. He had been given information that it had crashed somewhere in the area. I told him we had not seen any house that was not where it was supposed to be. He looked quite put out. He said he and his men had been tramping about the fields for days, no one had seen the house, and he was starting to think he had been sent on a wild goose chase."

"He did not recognize Her Highness?" Simon asked.

"He was looking for a house, not a princess," Amelia said with a smile. "Sophia kept the hood of her cloak pulled low over her face and he did not evince interest in her. He asked what we were doing in this part of the country. I said we were visiting my mother in Carlin, a town not far from here. He appeared satisfied with my answer and allowed us to depart."

Simon nodded. "Well done, Miss Amelia. I would venture to say we do not need to worry about being discovered, at least not for a while. The longer the house is on the ground, though, the greater the risk. But this is not your only bad news."

"We need to show you what Thomas discovered, sir," said Amelia.

She drew her notebook from her reticule and handed it to Simon. "The king has been doing some investigating of his own. I have written down all the pertinent details of what he uncovered."

Simon flipped rapidly through the notebook, seeming to devour whole pages with his eyes in seconds and muttering to himself. "Invading Freya. Yes, I had surmised that. Black ship, green-beam gun, Dragon Brigade. Nothing to be done there."

"Kate is going—" Amelia began.

Simon raised his hand. "Do not interrupt. King Ullr. Five green-beam guns . . . Seventh Sigil . . . replace blood magic. Remarkable."

He tapped the notebook on the page with the note about the green-beam guns. "These guns Ullr has acquired are the greatest threat to our people, the threat we must find a way to counter. I wonder . . . If I designed my own gun . . ."

He sat in silence, thinking. Amelia and Sophia exchanged glances and kept quiet. Albright returned from the kitchen with Bandit, who was now his new best friend. The dog gave Simon a wide berth and took refuge beneath Sophia's chair.

"You know you are not are safe in Freya, Your Highness," said Simon. "You should sail back to Rosia. I am acquainted with the owner of a ship who could smuggle you out of the country."

"Everyone seems intent on getting rid of me," said Sophia, smiling. "My friends are risking their lives to fight for Freya, and while I am not Freyan, I have close ties to this country."

Simon nodded his head. "I thought you might say that. Judging by the heightened color in your cheeks you are in love—an emotion that is responsible for nine-tenths of the irrational decisions made by otherwise rational human beings.

"You are in a precarious position, ma'am. These soldiers may not be inclined to tromp about the woods, searching for a house. That said, these Guundarans work for Smythe. He must have reason to believe I am in the vicinity and he will not stop looking. I cannot promise you will be safe here."

Sophia reached down to stroke Bandit's silky ears. "As you say, sir, they are searching for you, yet you do not flee."

She clasped her hands and regarded him earnestly. "I cannot compel you to allow me to remain as your guest, Master Yates, but I would be deeply grateful if you would. I can earn my keep."

She glanced about the entry hall. "I noticed when I came in that some of the magical constructs on the walls have been damaged. I could assist you in repairing them—"

"You are a savant!" Simon struck himself on the forehead. "Where are my brains? Are you familiar with the workings of contramagic and the Seventh Sigil?"

"I am," said Sophia. "My friend, Kate, taught me."

"Excellent. Albright, arrange for rooms for Her Highness and Miss Amelia."

Mr. Albright gave a cough and appeared highly distressed.

"What is it, Albright?" Simon demanded impatiently. "You have leave to speak."

"Her Highness is a not a crafter-for-hire, sir," Mr. Albright said in a rebuking undertone.

"I will enjoy helping, truly, Mr. Albright," said Sophia. "I want to be of use!"

"You heard her, Albright. Soldiers are searching for Welkinstead. We are not safe on the ground. King Ullr has five green-beam guns. We will be needed to assist in the battle. Now, while you are dredging up clean linen and airing out the guest rooms, I will escort Her Highness to the lift tanks—"

Mr. Albright took a stand on the side of chivalry. "Her Highness and Miss Nettleship have walked on foot through the wilderness, sir. The ladies require rest and refreshment."

Simon regarded him with a frown. "You imply, Albright, that a vigorous walk requires women to imbibe cucumber sandwiches and then lie down with cold compresses over their eyes. Errant nonsense. My studies indicate that whereas men are physically stronger, women are hardier. Observe Her Highness and Miss Amelia. Aside from a few mud stains and a generally dirty and disheveled appearance, neither of them appears to be on the verge of collapse. As for you, Albright, you have been talking a great deal too much."

Albright did not wither beneath this barrage. "I beg your pardon, sir. I will prepare the guest rooms, provide water and clean towels, and then I will make tea." He fixed Simon with a cold look. "We are out of cucumbers, but I will fix sandwiches with the remainder of the chicken."

He departed in high dudgeon. Simon regarded him with interest.

"I believe you have turned Albright's head, Your Highness. He has not spoken that many words together in a year. And now, ladies, I should think ten minutes would be sufficient for washing up, drinking tea, and eating a sandwich or two. If Your Highness has no objection, I will call you 'Sophia.' Saves time. What did you do with your pony cart, Miss Amelia?"

"I left it at a farmhouse. I told the farmer I was visiting my mother and she had no place to house the horse. I paid him to give the animal room and board for a fortnight."

"Well done," said Simon. "I'll be in the cellar working on the lift tanks. I expect you to join me shortly, Sophia. Albright will show you where to go. Ten minutes."

Simon whipped his chair around and floated down the steps. Bandit dashed after him, barking all the way.

THIRTY-THREE

Hugh Fitzroy, Earl of Montford, second in line for the throne after Thomas, sent back a cold response to Smythe's humble request for a meeting. Hugh had deigned to see him, but he made it clear he was conferring upon Smythe a vast favor that he did not deserve, given that Smythe had kept him a prisoner in his own manor ever since the death of the queen.

Smythe was pleased. A man of principle would have told him to go to hell. The fact that Hugh had readily agreed to meet meant that everything Smythe had heard about the man was true. Hugh Fitzroy was much like his father, King Godfrey. He was venal, ignorant, and cunning. Such men were generally easy to manipulate.

Hugh and his younger brother, Jeffrey, now Bishop of Freya, were Godfrey's illegitimate sons, the products of a scandalous affair with a married woman. Godfrey had acknowledged his bastards, provided them with fortunes and titles. He would have named Hugh his heir over his legitimate daughter, Mary, if Henry Wallace had not convinced him that such a move would have resulted in the downfall of the monarchy.

Hugh's brother, Jeffrey, was a gentle, self-effacing man who had found refuge from humiliation and scandal in the church. The Reformed Church of the Breath allowed its ministers to wed, and Jeffrey had married young. He and his wife had one daughter, Ann. He had made peace with his half sister, Queen Mary, by sending his daughter to be raised at court. Ann had become a favorite of the queen's and was now the wife of Sir Henry Wallace.

Smythe would have had Jeffrey placed under arrest, as well as Hugh, but the church was a powerful force in Freyan politics and Smythe was not yet prepared to open a war on that front. Smythe had investigated, and deemed Jeffrey harmless. The bishop did not live in Haever, nor did he have much to do with his daughter or her family. According to reports, Jeffrey kept his eyes fixed on heaven and left worldly matters to his underlings. Smythe contented himself with placing the bishop under surveillance, having him watched day and night.

Not surprisingly, Hugh had been Godfrey's favorite son. He had made his fortune in iron. He controlled all aspects of iron production from mining to milling. He had made no secret of the fact that he despised his half sister, Mary, and believed that by rights he should have been king. Hugh had been confounded to discover that Thomas Stanford had a better claim to the throne than he did. He had tried to drum up support among the nobility to oppose Stanford, but he could not fight the powerful men and women who belonged to the Faithful, and he had sullenly given up.

Smythe traveled to Hugh's estate in Chadwick to meet with him. Upon his arrival, he spoke briefly to the captain of the guard of the troops deployed outside Hugh's mansion, which was as large as a palace and furnished with all the taste and elegance of a high-class brothel.

Hugh kept Smythe waiting, of course. He sat without moving in an uncomfortable chair in the antechamber for an hour, patient as a sniper, until a servant came to fetch him.

Smythe entered the room behind the servant and wondered if he had walked into a museum by mistake. The study might have been labeled: THE HISTORY OF IRON THROUGH THE AGES. The vast room was a monument to iron, featuring all the products produced by Hugh's ironworks, from carriage wheels, barrel hoops, pistols and rifles to a replica of a bridge and a full-size twenty-four-pound cannon.

Hugh stood at one of the windows with his back to Smythe to let him know he was affronted. When the servant announced him, Hugh glanced over his shoulder, glowered at him, and greeted him with a grunt.

Smythe meekly swallowed the insult and walked over to join him.

"Damn fine view," Hugh remarked.

Smythe looked out on the chimneys of a smelting plant belching forth smoke. Hugh inhaled a lungful of air.

"Smell that. Know what that is, Smithee? No, of course you don't. It's success."

Smythe set his jaw. He had been introduced to Hugh at the queen's funeral. The earl knew perfectly well how to properly pronounce his name. By
calling him Smithee, Hugh was being deliberately antagonistic, hoping to
make Smythe angry, put him at a disadvantage.

Smythe had learned self-control from his reverend father, who had quoted
the Scriptures while beating his son with a stick. He was proof against such
tactics.

"You are to be congratulated upon your success, my lord," Smythe said,
bowing.

Hugh was clearly determined to be offensive. "Why the devil are you here,
Smithee? Come to gloat over your prisoner? Or maybe you're going to lock
me up in Offdom Tower. Oh, sorry, I forgot." Hugh grinned unpleasantly.
"You don't have a tower. A dragon knocked the damn thing down."

Smythe gritted his teeth and reminded himself of his objective.

"I have come to apologize, my lord," Smythe said humbly. "My officers
must have given you the wrong impression. I did not place Your Lordship
under arrest. I placed the soldiers here for your protection."

Hugh sneered. "Protection! From what?"

"Your Lordship knows of Sir Henry Wallace. I believe he is married to the
daughter of your brother."

"Wallace?" Hugh said, his demeanor changing. He seemed uneasy. "What
has he been saying about me?"

Hugh was a tall man, heavyset, with a red face and red-veined nose, who
was said to like his port. He was accustomed to using his bulk and height
to intimidate, and he crowded Smythe into a corner. "Wallace told you I
wanted him to assassinate Elinor, didn't he? That's a damn lie! I asked him
to do me one small favor, to see to it the woman didn't press her claim to
the throne. I meant only that he was to offer her money, that sort of thing.
Instead Wallace twisted my words, made it sound like I wanted him to break
her neck. I had to chuck him out."

Hugh stared at Smythe, unblinking. Smythe had learned over the years
that when someone holds your eyes with his gaze, he is trying to keep you
from seeing the truth. Smythe smiled inwardly. So Hugh had wanted Wallace
to assassinate his half-sister. Good to know.

"How did Wallace react, my lord?" Smythe asked.

"He was damn offensive," said Hugh. His puffy eyes crinkled with cunning. "So you are telling me that the soldiers are here to protect me from
Wallace. He wouldn't dare harm me. The man is a coward. He spent his life
hiding behind Mary's skirts."

"But if King Thomas had ordered him—"

Smythe abruptly stopped talking, as though he had inadvertently said too much. He tried to cover his mistake. "I have taken up too much of Your Lordship's valuable time. The troops are here to protect you and your family, my lord. I am sorry for any misunderstanding. I admire you immensely and I want to be on terms of trust and friendship with Your Lordship."

"Wait a damn minute," said Hugh. "What was that you said about King Thomas ordering Wallace? Ordered him to do what?"

"I did not mean that the way it sounded, my lord—"

"You're a damn liar, Smithee!" Hugh glowered at him. "Tell me the truth. What the devil is going on?"

Smythe cast a glance at the door. "The servants, my lord . . ."

Hugh walked across the room, flung open the door, and yelled, "Get out! The lot of you!"

He slammed the door shut. "There. Now we can talk."

He sat down in a chair near the fire and pointed to a chair for Smythe. Once he was settled, Hugh reached for the decanter that was always close to hand. "A glass of port?"

"Thank you, no, my lord," said Smythe. "My faith prohibits me—"

"Your misfortune, not mine." Hugh drained the glass in a gulp. "Now talk."

"His Majesty heard a report that Your Lordship planned to challenge his right to rule in court."

Hugh thrust his chin out. "What if I did? Now that Mary's dead, I should be king. The only reason I'm not is because the Rosians conspired to put this Stanford puppy on the throne."

"I must say I admire your courage, my lord," said Smythe. "The truth is, our young king fears that if the matter does go to court, he will lose. His Majesty was alarmed to hear of your challenge. He has spoken openly of sending you into exile or . . ."

Smythe hesitated.

"Or what?" Hugh growled. "You think he means to have me killed."

"I cannot believe His Majesty capable of such a heinous act, my lord. Still, given the king's close connections with the Rosians and secret meetings he held with Wallace, I deemed it better to be on the safe side. I sent troops to protect you and I issued a warrant for Sir Henry's arrest. He was apprehended in a low drinking establishment. I was hoping to force the truth from him, but he was shot while attempting to escape."

"Good." Hugh grunted, nodding in approval. "About damn time someone shot him."

"Unfortunately, I have reason to believe Wallace survived, my lord," Smythe said. "The king still considers you a threat. . . ."

Smythe did not finish his thought, leaving the rest to Hugh's imagination.

Hugh may not have been overly imaginative, but he was clearly worried. His face was flabby and he paled beneath the flush of the strong drink. He poured himself another glass of port and again gulped it down.

"Wait a damn moment, Smithee. Now that I think of it, these soldiers of yours arrested me the day *after* Mary died. Was this damn Stanford plotting against me even then?"

"Thomas Stanford has long feared you, my lord."

"Ah! He has good reason to," Hugh stated, pleased. "Wait until I tell my lawyer!"

"On the contrary, I would advise that you drop the challenge, my lord," said Smythe gravely. "A pending court case would look bad, particularly if something were to happen to His Majesty."

Hugh fixed him with an intense look, his puffy eyes glinting. "Do you think that's likely, Smithee?"

"I'm sure we all hope and pray for His Majesty's well-being," said Smythe.

Hugh winked at him. "I guess we understand each other, then. I like you, Smithee."

He slammed Smythe on the shoulder, nearly knocking him out of his chair, then poured himself another glass. He raised it in a salute.

"God save the king."

Hugh laughed and gulped.

Smythe left soon after, satisfied with the meeting, for he now knew that Hugh was a dunderhead who could be cozened and blackmailed and would not hinder Smythe's plans. And if worse came to worst, Smythe could always poison his port.

THIRTY-FOUR

The weather had turned ugly during the early part of the *Terrapin*'s voyage to Wellinsport.

Fog and the thickening mists of the Breath and the incessant damp left Henry chilled to the bone. Water dripped off the sails and the ropes; the damp pervaded everything.

After two days of thick mists, the wind rose and shredded the fog. This morning he had wakened to clear skies and sunshine. The wind died, the sails hung limp, and the *Terrapin* was forced to rely on her airscrews to keep sailing.

The lubbers cheered the sight of the sun. The old hands shook their heads and muttered, "The Winter Witch is going to come to call."

Henry's bullet wound was mending well, thanks to the excellent services of the ship's surgeon, Mr. Perry; the surgeon's mate, who was skilled at healing magic; and the attentiveness and patience of Mr. Sloan.

Henry no longer needed to take laudanum, which he despised, for the pain, but his fever had left him weak as watered wine. When he first insisted on leaving his bed, he could walk only with assistance from Mr. Sloan. Henry was pleased to find that he regained his strength quickly. Only a few days later, he was able to walk on his own and to go out on deck and bask in the sunshine.

The surgeon's mate was also the ship's chaplain, and he told Henry he must have lived an exemplary life for God to have blessed him. Once, Henry would have laughed with Alan over that comment. Unfortunately, he and Alan had not spoken since they had left Haever. Henry could not forgive his friend for having abducted him, as he put it.

"Captain Northrop did not abduct you, my lord," said Mr. Sloan, gently remonstrating. He was assisting the surgeon, Perry, to change Henry's bandage. "He saved your life by removing you from the danger in Haever."

Henry stirred impatiently.

"Please hold still, sir," Perry admonished. "The more you fidget, the longer this procedure will take."

"Perhaps I didn't want to be saved," said Henry petulantly. "What the devil good to me is my life if I return to find that Smythe has named himself Lord Protector?"

Henry winced and stifled a groan as Perry peeled off the bloodstained bandage that had adhered to the wound. "The countess warned me that King Ullr is plotting something. There is a reason Smythe dispatched the most formidable ship in our navy to Wellinsport to protect against some ridiculous threat from the Rosians. They have no intention of attacking Wellinsport. Ullr made this up because wants to be rid of the *Terrapin* so that he can attack with impunity."

"You do not know that for certain, my lord."

"Which is why I should be in Freya!" Henry bellowed. "Alan must take me back."

He gasped from the pain and swore beneath his breath. He glared at Perry. "Where the devil did you train, sir? The Royal Slaughterhouse?"

"I must ask you to calm down, my lord," Perry said. "You will bring on a return of the fever."

"Damn the fever! Fetch Alan, Mr. Sloan! I want to talk to him," Henry ordered.

"I will do so, my lord, if you will rest quietly while you wait," said Mr. Sloan.

Henry grumbled, but he lay down in his bed and gazed grimly out the porthole at the darkening clouds that presaged the arrival of the Winter Witch, the name the sailors gave to the unusually fierce wizard storms that plagued the Breath during the winter.

Perry accompanied Mr. Sloan as he went up on deck. The wind was rising. Lightning flashed, and thunder rumbled in the distance. The surgeon and the secretary conferred in low voices.

"How is His Lordship, sir?" Mr. Sloan asked.

"Physically, he is healing well," said Perry. "Mentally, he is extremely agitated, and that is not good for him. This talk of King Ullr invading Freya. Is there any truth to this? I do not ask out of idle curiosity. If His Lordship is delusional . . ."

Mr. Sloan did not respond, and Perry was quick to add, "Only if you can tell me without betraying state secrets, Mr. Sloan."

"You are His Lordship's physician and you should know what is needful to protect his health, sir," said Mr. Sloan. "The Countess de Marjolaine did warn Sir Henry that Guundaran fleets were on the move. She believes that Ullr may try to take advantage of the king's youth and inexperience to further Guundaran interests."

"The countess is a Rosian, Mr. Sloan," said Perry, frowning. "Is she to be trusted?"

"His Lordship would have said no to that question at one time. Since then, he has changed his opinion and believes the countess to be telling him the truth about Ullr. Captain Northrop maintains that the countess is duplicitous in professing her friendship for His Lordship, hoping to convince Sir Henry that Ullr is about to attack Haever, when the countess's true goal is to seize Wellinsport in the name of Rosia."

"To hear you speak of such tangles makes me thankful I am nothing but a simple sawbones, Mr. Sloan," said Perry. "What is your opinion?"

"I believe the danger to Freya is very real, sir," said Mr. Sloan. "My primary concern, however, is the danger to Sir Henry. Captain Northrop is right. If His Lordship returns to Haever, his life is forfeit."

He and Perry found Alan on deck, keeping grim watch on the approaching storms. Mr. Sloan deferentially approached him and relayed Henry's request.

"I cannot come now, Mr. Sloan," said Alan curtly. "You have only to look at those clouds massing to the east to know why. Mr. Perry, you should return to your surgery. Your skills will soon be needed. Mr. Sloan, tell Henry I will speak to him once the danger to my ship is past."

He walked away, shouting orders. Perry and Mr. Sloan exchanged glances, both knowing how Henry would react to this answer. Perry went below to prepare for broken bones, cracked skulls, and other injuries the crew would be likely to suffer when the Witch began to bat the *Terrapin* about like a shuttlecock.

The *Terrapin* had been a massive Deep Breath cargo ship before she was transformed by the installation of crafter Pietro Alcazar's magical steel plates that covered her hull and gave the ship her name. Alcazar had found a way to reinforce the steel with magical constructs that made the plates able to withstand not only cannonballs and gunfire, but also a dragon's fiery breath.

Since the heavy cargo ship had to be capable of sailing the Deep Breath, she came already equipped with large lift tanks. The refitters used the cargo space to add more lift tanks to accommodate the increased weight of the metal plates, as well as larger airscrews. Like her namesake, the *Terrapin* was well protected from predators, but she was also ungainly and slow.

Mr. Sloan returned to tell Henry that Alan could not leave the deck due to his concern for the safety of the ship and crew. Henry was furious, and jumped to his feet, saying he would speak to Alan himself. At that moment, a gust of wind buffeted the ship. Lightning half blinded them and the thunder struck with a violent boom. Henry staggered, and would have fallen if Mr. Sloan had not been there to catch him.

"I suggest you return to your bed, sir," said Mr. Sloan. "Perry warns that if you reinjure your clavicle, you might lose the use of your arm."

"What does he know—the quack!" Henry muttered, but he did take Mr. Sloan's advice and returned to his bed.

The storms lasted for days. The rain changed to sleet, pelting the crew with stinging pellets of ice, coating the deck and riming the rigging. Men slipped and slid and fell. Perry and the healer had all the work they could manage mending lacerations and broken bones.

The Witch proved deadly. A cannon broke loose from its moorings and went careening about the gun deck, crushing a man. Another died of a broken neck when he tumbled down the stairs, and a third was blown overboard and lost.

The Witch howled and moaned and screeched; the ship lurched and rocked, threatening every moment to turn turtle. Alan found it nearly impossible to take navigational readings. He and his officers could only hazard a guess as to where the Witch was taking them.

At last the Witch relented and released them from her grip. The winds calmed and the sun shone, melting the ice and raising their spirits. They committed their dead to the Breath and set about trying to claw their way back on course.

Alan went down to Henry's cabin to check on his friend. With his ship in peril, he had slept little the past few days and he was gray from fatigue. Henry was too preoccupied with his own concerns to notice.

"How are you feeling, Henry?" Alan asked. "The healer and Mr. Perry both tell me you are on the mend."

"I am fine," Henry snapped. "Or rather, I would be fine if I were not being held prisoner in a ship far from where I need to be! Alan, you must sail back to Haever!"

"You know I cannot, Henry," said Alan wearily. "My orders are to sail to Wellinsport."

"You are being duped, Alan!" Henry said impatiently. "The Rosians have no intention of invading Wellinsport. They would be fools to do so, for they would have to contend with the Estarans—"

"Damn the Estarans!" Alan flared, losing patience. "Did it ever occur to you, Henry, that for once in your life you might be wrong?"

"I am not wrong about this!" Henry said through gritted teeth.

He started to add something about being wrong in his choice of friends, but he closed his mouth on the biting words that would have resulted in an irreparable rupture between him and Alan.

Henry massaged his shoulder, which ached abominably.

"Alan, I understand what I am asking you to do is difficult—"

"Difficult!" Alan repeated in outraged disbelief. "By asking me to refuse to obey an order to engage the Rosians in Wellinsport, turn my ship around and sail back to Haever, it will be said that I am fleeing battle with the enemy. Shall I quote the naval regulation: 'Any Captain or other officer, mariner or others, who shall basely desert their duty or station in the ship and run away while the enemy is in fight, or in time of action, or entice others to do so, shall suffer death or such other punishment as a court-martial shall inflict.'"

"But you are not fleeing a battle in Wellinsport, Alan," Henry argued. "There *is* no battle in Wellinsport because the Rosians aren't going to attack Wellinsport. King Ullr is going to attack Haever!"

Henry clenched his fist and slammed it on the table, jarring the broken bone. He groaned in pain and clutched his arm.

"I am sorry I spoke harshly, Henry," Alan said wearily. "The storm blew the ship off course. I have had four hours' sleep in two days."

He paused, then added, "I know your family is in Rosia. Even if we are at war, I am certain that no matter what happens, the countess will keep them safe."

"This has nothing to do with my family!" Henry said, his jaw tight.

A midshipman appeared at the door. "Begging your pardon, Captain, but you are wanted on deck."

Alan looked at Henry. Henry glared at him. The silence became unendurable. Alan shook his head and left.

Henry, thinking of his family, put his hands to his eyes.

Mr. Sloan poured a snifter of brandy and placed it at his elbow. Henry sighed deeply and raised his head.

"I know I was being unreasonable to demand that Alan defy his orders and return to Freya." He took a sip, then pushed it aside. "But I also know with more certainty than I have ever been certain of anything in my life that

I am right. Our beloved country is in peril and we are sailing away and leaving her."

The *Terrapin* reached the Trame Channel after a seven-day voyage that should have taken three. Henry's health continued to improve. He was able to walk about the deck in the sunshine, enjoying the warmth and fair weather of the Aligoes.

The *Terrapin* was slated to arrive in Wellinsport the next day. Henry would prove to Alan that the city wasn't under siege by the Rosians. This knowledge should have lightened his mood, but his spirits did not mend. He barked at Perry and snapped at Mr. Sloan. He and Alan had not spoken since their last meeting. The two men avoided each other as much as was possible given the confined area of a ship. Each drank his after-dinner brandy alone.

Mr. Sloan had been hoping to find a way to reconcile the two friends, but before he could do so, Henry dispatched him to Freeport to talk to Olaf and Akiel.

"You will need to hire one of the island hoppers to take you there. I promised Simon I would contact Olaf, find out if he'd had any success with the search for his White Well," said Henry. "I don't expect it, Mr. Sloan, but I can at least assure him we made every effort to find the damn thing."

The morning the *Terrapin* entered the Trame Channel, the ship was besieged by a flotilla of the small boats known as island hoppers that traveled among the islands of the Aligoes, offering to ferry people to port or trying to sell their wares to the sailors.

Wellinsport was famous for its whorehouses, and women in gaudy clothes shouted invitations to the men to visit their various establishments. Trundlers offered to sell bottles of Calvados or the famous Aligoes rum. Alan posted marines to stand guard to try to keep the sailors from smuggling liquor on board.

Mr. Sloan located a small inter-island hopper whose skipper would take him to Freeport, and negotiated a price.

"The man says we are within a half-day's journey from here to Freeport, my lord," Mr. Sloan reported to Henry, who had come up on deck.

"That means you will be gone two days," said Henry. "I will remain on board ship, so report to me here. Unless, of course, I am battling Rosians," he added caustically.

Mr. Sloan pretended he had not heard that last.

The Trame Channel was not much traveled this time of year due to the Winter Witch. Only a few intrepid merchant ships would venture to cross the Witch, and these were generally owned by the Travian cartels, who dealt in everything from cotton to gunpowder and who could afford to risk a ship and her crew for the sake of profit.

Henry put his spyglass to his eye and swept the channel. Only a few ships had docked along the shoreline of the Trame Channel where they waited to obtain permission to enter Wellinsport Harbor and obtain the services of a harbor pilot that would guide them.

No ship was permitted to sail into the harbor without permission from the governor. Every ship needed a harbor pilot to advise the captain of the best route to take to navigate the narrow entrance to the harbor and show him where to dock once the ship had arrived. The only ships Henry saw were merchant vessels: two Travians, an Estaran, and one from Bheldem.

Alan was on deck awaiting the arrival of the harbor pilot. He was studiously ignoring Henry. For his part, Henry was about to make a caustic remark regarding the absence of a Rosian invasion fleet, when he saw something that caused him to forget the Rosians. He trained his spyglass on three Guundaran warships docked along the shore of the channel, presumably seeking permission to enter Wellinsport Harbor.

Henry turned to say something to Alan, but he was welcoming the harbor pilot on board the ship. The pilot took his place beside the captain and the helmsman, and the island hoppers scattered as the ship sailed toward the entrance to the Deep Breath harbor for which Wellinsport was renowned.

Located on the island of Whitefalls, the city of Wellinsport stretched out in a crescent along the western shore of the harbor. The naval dockyards were located on the southern end of the crescent, guarded by a series of gun emplacements built into the hillsides. Commercial and private docks dominated the rest of the shoreline. Smaller vessels, such as the island hoppers and a floating colony of Trundler houseboats, docked to the north. Low hills rose to rugged cliffs in the east, ending in a narrow passage that led to the Trame Channel.

The harbor pilot stood by the *Terrapin*'s helmsman, giving him directions. Alan oversaw the proceedings, issuing orders to reduce sail as the ship crept through the Neck, as the entrance to the harbor was known, so called because on a map, the harbor resembled a person's head.

Alan was dressed in his finest. After the ship docked, he would go ashore to pay his respects to the governor. He had given orders to ready his pinnace, and stood surveying the ships in the harbor while he was waiting.

Henry continued to watch the Guundarans through his spyglass and said suddenly, in an altered tone, "Alan, where are the ships of the Aligoes Fleet? They are not at their usual station."

The Aligoes Fleet consisted of two warships and a large number of frigates and brigs. The smaller ships were more practical for sailing the narrow passages between the islands while two ships of the line could still command the Trame Channel. It was not unusual for half of the fleet to be away hunting pirates and smugglers, but it was rare for the entire fleet to have left the harbor unguarded.

At Henry's question about the fleet, Alan jerked his head around and looked immediately to the south, where he should have seen Admiral Tower's flagship, *Indomitable*. The only ship in sight was a Trundler vessel with its bright-colored balloon and sails, "trundling" along the channel.

"You were asking about the fleet, sir?" said the pilot, glancing at Henry. "They sailed away three days ago. No one knows where. Secret orders, or so I heard."

Henry shifted his spyglass to scan the Trame Channel that was now behind them as the *Terrapin* emerged from the Neck and sailed into the harbor. He looked once again at the three Guundaran warships.

He slammed shut the telescoping spyglass, thrust it into his pocket, and raised his voice to shout for Mr. Sloan, only to remember that he had sent him away.

The sailors were readying the pinnace for the captain's use, checking to make certain its lift tank was filled and the small brass helm was working. The pinnace's crew, dressed in elegant matching uniforms, stood ready to take their places in the small boat.

"Alan, don't leave yet!" Henry called. "I'm coming with you. I must speak to the governor."

Alan started to say something, but Henry didn't wait to hear. He dashed below to his cabin and began to rummage through his clothes.

Alan appeared at the door. "Henry, what the devil are you doing?"

"Trying to find a jacket!" Henry said impatiently. "The one I was wearing the night I was shot is soaked in blood and Perry cut off one of the sleeves. I know Mr. Sloan brought some of my clothes. Where did he put it?"

"I mean why are you going to see the governor?"

Henry rounded on him. "Do you have to ask? The Aligoes Fleet is nowhere to be found. We have not seen a single Rosian ship, but there are three Guundaran warships in the Trame Channel!"

Alan was grim. "True, the Rosians are not attacking Wellinsport this moment. But the entire Rosian navy could be hidden among the thousand or so islands of the Aligoes and we would be none the wiser. Their Dragon Brigade is headquartered in Maribeau, within a day's flight of Wellinsport. For all we know, Admiral Tower's secret orders could have been to intercept and engage the Rosian invasion fleet!"

Henry snorted, but he had to admit Alan was right about the Rosians, though he knew he was right about Guundar. The sight of three Guundaran warships here was disconcerting. What the devil were they doing in Wellinsport when they should be in Haever?

He had no answer and he continued to search for the jacket and found it where he should have realized it would be if he'd been thinking clearly: Mr. Sloan had neatly folded it and packed it in a sea chest.

"As for the Guundarans," Alan continued, "what would you have me do, Henry? We are not at war with Guundar, though God knows we would be if I attacked their ships without provocation. They have every right to sail the Trame Channel. Besides, according to you, they should be preparing to attack Haever."

"Unless they are preparing to attack Wellinsport," said Henry, suddenly struck by the idea.

"In which case King Ullr very kindly arranged for the *Terrapin* to be in Wellinsport to stop himself," Alan said caustically.

Henry had no answer to that. Holding up the jacket, he glared at the sling covering his left arm and transferred his glare to the jacket.

"I need help putting this on," he said, struggling to thrust his arm into the sleeve.

Alan was silent a moment, watching, then he said coldly, "I will send my steward to assist you. If you will excuse me, I must return to my duties."

He departed, leaving Henry to gaze at his retreating form with a keen sense of loss. He tried to think what he could say to end the quarrel. He was not going to apologize, for he was in the right, but he could certainly understand that Alan would not want to risk ruining his career and face possible court-martial and death.

The steward arrived to assist Henry, draping the shoulder of the jacket over the sling and buttoning it closed. He then pinned the empty sleeve across the front so that it would not dangle and helped Henry put on clean breeches and change his stockings, and handed him his hat.

When Henry went back up on deck, he saw that the *Terrapin* had come to a stop. The sailing master ordered all the airscrews to a slow spin to maintain a zero position, holding the ship at rest. The crew cast out mooring lines to secure the ship to the anchor buoys.

Once the *Terrapin* was tied down, Alan entered the pinnace and Henry took his place alongside him. Alan gave the order and the pinnace set sail for the landing on the south side of the harbor.

Henry studied the shore batteries that had been destroyed three years ago during the Bottom Dwellers war. He was pleased to see the progress that had been made in repairing them. The new forty-eight-pound cannons were in place, and workers were dismantling some of the scaffolding, indicating the work had been completed and the guns were ready for action.

"I am pleased to see Governor Crichton has made good use of the money I sent him," Henry remarked. "Unlike that fool viscount Queen Mary named as governor, who spent the funds intended to replace the guns on decorating the governor's mansion."

Alan glanced at the guns as they sailed past but said nothing.

"Finchley, that was his name," Henry recalled. "He won the queen's favor by giving her a monkey. Do you remember, Alan? His name was Jo-jo. God, I hated that monkey!"

Alan sat in silence.

"Alan," said Henry, trying to make amends, "I want you to know that I do understand—"

"No, you don't, Henry," said Alan, facing him. "That is the point."

He rose to his feet and made his way forward.

Henry gazed unseeing at the shops and the people along the wharf and thought about the monkey and how he had found little Jo-jo dead, lying in a pool of the queen's blood.

THIRTY-FIVE

The office of the governor in Wellinsport maintained its own official private docking facility. Governor Crichton kept his personal yacht here. Boats carrying supplies or those who had business at the governor's mansion were permitted to dock here. On those evenings when the governor entertained, the dock was host to a glittering armada of private vessels.

Henry and Alan arrived at the governor's dock in the late morning. They disembarked, walked the short distance to the mansion, and gave their cards to a servant, requesting an audience with the governor.

The servant invited them to wait in the garden, then went off, presumably to deliver the message. Alan declined to sit with Henry, and walked into the garden, saying he needed to stretch his legs. He spent his time pacing beneath the shade trees.

Henry chose to find a bench. He was already fatigued by the trip in the pinnace and he began to think he should not have come. His shoulder throbbed, the bandages itched, the sling was hot and uncomfortable. He fanned himself with his hat and watched Alan make a point of ignoring him.

Alan had been known as a hothead in his youth. He was quick to act, quick to anger, reckless, daring, and bold. As captain of a ship, responsible for the lives of his crew and the successes of his missions, he had learned to temper his impulsiveness and give careful consideration to his actions. He could still be reckless, but he was now "mindfully reckless," as he always said with a laugh. Quick to take offense, he was also quick to forgive offenders. He had never been one to harbor a grudge, nurse his anger.

But he could not forgive what he considered to be an insult.

Henry could concede that Alan had every reason to refuse to listen to him. Henry had urged him to risk his career—which was his very life—on what he considered to be a mad whim. Henry had no evidence to back up his claim that Freya was in danger from King Ullr. Alan was correct. The Countess de Marjolaine was a Rosian who had actively worked for Freya's downfall for most of her life; Henry could see why Alan would not be willing to accept her as a reliable source of information.

But Henry knew from his own experience that there were times when one had to take risks, throw caution—even wisdom—to the four winds. Henry believed with every fiber of his being that this was one of those times. Their country was in dire peril. And the *Terrapin*, the most formidable ship in the Royal Navy, was far from Haever, hoodwinked into confronting a Rosian threat that he was certain did not exist.

Henry found the inexplicable absence of the Aligoes Fleet and the simultaneous presence of three Guundaran warships in the Trame Channel extremely troubling.

"In which case, Alan will be in the right place at the right time for the wrong reason," Henry muttered grimly. "Just like his goddamned luck!"

The servant returned to say that Governor Crichton would be pleased to see them—as indeed he should be, for he owed his governorship appointment to Henry. The servant escorted them into the governor's office. The hallway was cool and dark, shaded from the blazing sun by the thick stands of trees in the gardens outside the house.

As Henry paused to admire the beauty of the exotic flowers, he noticed three gentlemen walking the garden path—and came up short at the sight of them.

The three men were Guundaran naval officers, two captains and a commander. They were leaving by a private entrance. Henry was intimately familiar with the mansion, and he knew that a door from Crichton's office opened onto a veranda and a pathway into the garden.

"Alan," said Henry, calling his friend's attention to the visitors.

Alan paused, brought up short by the warning tone in Henry's voice. He looked outside, saw the officers, glanced at Henry, and continued walking.

Crichton was in his office, waiting for them. He rose to his feet and advanced to shake hands.

Born and raised in the Aligoes, Crichton had the brown, weathered complexion of one who spends much of his time in the sun. He still oversaw the work on the family sugar cane plantations, and because he was one of them, he was well-liked among the populace.

He was friends with Henry and knew Alan from the latter's Rose Hawk privateering days. He had been Henry's choice to succeed the profligate and corrupt Governor Finchley. The three men spent a few moments reminiscing and catching up on family news and tidings of old friends before turning to business. Crichton was concerned to see Henry's heavily bandaged arm in a sling.

Henry made light of his injury. "I was leaving work, slipped on the ice, and took a tumble down the steps of the Foreign Office. Broke my collarbone. Tell me, Your Excellency," he added, his tone sharpening, "I saw three Guundaran naval officers in the garden. I assume they belong to those three Guundaran warships in the Trame Channel."

"You don't miss much, do you, my lord," said Crichton with a smile. He was a tall man with a shaved head in deference to the heat, and sported a golden earring. "Yes, those were three of their officers. They've had a rough time of it. They were bound for Bheldem when the Winter Witch caught them and blew their ships off course. The storm winds did considerable damage to masts and rigging. They have requested permission to enter the harbor to make repairs and to take on water and provisions."

"Those ships did not appear to me to be badly damaged, Your Excellency," said Henry.

"I wouldn't know, my lord," said Crichton. "Being a landlubber, I can't tell a bowsprit from a keel. Captain Northrop, I would very much like a chance to tour the *Terrapin,* if that is possible given your duties here. I have read a great deal about your wonderful ship."

Alan was about to reply, when Henry interrupted him.

"What duties, Your Excellency?"

"I assumed Captain Northrop and the *Terrapin* are here to guard the channel in the absence of the Aligoes Fleet," Crichton replied.

"We noticed the fleet was not in the usual station," said Henry. "Where did they go?"

Crichton appeared bewildered at the question. "I thought you must have known, my lord. Admiral Tower received orders a fortnight ago to sail immediately to Sornhagen."

Alan had been sitting in his chair, staring out the window, absently clenching and unclenching his fist. His gaze suddenly snapped to the governor.

"Sornhagen!" he repeated, startled.

"Yes, Captain," said Crichton. "Are you telling me you didn't know?"

Alan sat back in his chair, his expression darkening.

"What were Admiral Tower's orders, Excellency?" he asked.

"The orders were secret, of course, but he had permission to tell me since the safety of Wellinsport was involved. Our new Chancellor of War—I think his name is Smythe—ordered the fleet to Sornhagen to protect Freyan interests in the region from an attack by the Dragon Brigade. As you know, gentlemen, we do a great deal of business with the Travian cartels. Admiral Tower did not want to leave until another ship had arrived to take over, but since he had to be in Sornhagen by this date, he had no choice but to depart."

"We were delayed," said Alan. "We ran into the same foul weather as the Guundarans. But no matter. The *Terrapin* is here now. We will take over the fleet's duties."

"Admiral Tower was duped, as were you, Governor," said Henry. "The Dragon Brigade is not about to attack Sornhagen, or Freya either, for that matter."

"But we are at war with Rosia, or we soon will be, my lord," Crichton protested. "They assassinated our queen!"

Henry was grim. "The Rosians are no more responsible for assassinating our queen than you are, Excellency."

Crichton blinked at him, shocked.

Alan attempted to draw him away. "Henry, you do not look well. I think we should leave."

Henry ignored his friend and faced Crichton. "I know for a fact, sir, that our queen was killed by this Smythe, an evil man who has seized control of our kingdom. He had himself named Chancellor of War and is trying to lure Rosia into war with us. Thank God, our king has refused to rush into battle and the Rosians have more sense than to take the bait. All the while, Guundar lies coiled like a snake in the grass, preparing to strike. And now I find three Guundaran warships in the channel about to be invited to sail into the harbor. You must refuse the Guundaran ships permission to dock here, sir. Send them on their way."

Crichton was astonished by Henry's vehemence. Despite his piratical appearance, the governor was a mild-mannered man who disliked unpleasantness and confrontation.

"My lord, the captain of the *Sunsvall* tells me that they have been forced to ration food and water for a week and their crewmen are suffering," Crichton said. "The *Godswald* was struck by wizard lightning that disrupted the magic on their lift tanks. They barely made it this far without sinking."

"As I have said before, we are not at war with Guundar, Henry," Alan added tersely. "Governor Crichton cannot in good conscience deny aid."

Henry leaned forward to fix the governor with a gaze meant to intimidate. A wide expanse of mahogany desk separated Henry from the governor, but he had the satisfaction of seeing Crichton nervously shrink back.

"Yet we are presumably at war with Rosia with not a single Rosian ship in sight," said Henry in biting tones. "I arrive in Wellinsport, which I remind you, sir, is our country's most valuable asset in the Aligoes, to find three Guundaran ships in the harbor and our fleet in Sornhagen! You must deny the ships entry, Excellency!"

Crichton drew himself up, finally prepared to assert his authority. "I have made my decision, Sir Henry. I have already granted the Guundaran ships permission to enter the harbor. They have ordered new rigging, new masts, and victualing, bringing much needed revenue to our city."

Henry glared at the man in impotent fury. Afraid of what he might say, he jumped from his chair and stalked out of the room. As he flung open the door to the office, he heard Crichton say in troubled tones to Alan, "Did His Lordship hit his head when he fell?"

Henry slammed out of the office, catching the servants by surprise. He snarled at them. "Leave me alone! I know the way!"

Once outdoors, he had time to cool his anger while he waited for Alan, who was undoubtedly spending a few moments apologizing for Henry's outburst.

Henry walked rapidly about halfway through the garden before pain and fatigue got the better of him. He stopped beneath a lime tree to rest and think what he should do.

Alan found him a few moments later.

"Henry, we have to talk," Alan said, his voice grating.

"Not here," said Henry, indicating the thick growth of trees and flowering bushes in which an army of spies could be lurking.

Alan took his meaning and managed to contain his fury until they had reached the docks, which were out in the open. The pinnace had not yet returned to pick them up. The afternoon sun was hot, and the docks were deserted, save for the two of them. Henry sat down on a bench. Alan sat down beside him.

"Ullr again!" Alan said, exasperated. "Frankly, Henry, you are obsessed with this man. You are making him into some sort of diabolical monster!"

"Think of it, Alan. Ullr takes us by surprise while our ships are scattered all over the world and the *Terrapin* is hundreds of miles away. Our king is young and inexperienced. Ullr defeats Freya and then what? He has the

Freyan navy as well as the Guundaran navy under his control. He attacks Rosia. Guundar could well rule the world!"

"And what about the Dragon Brigade?" Alan asked.

"I am certain Smythe has found some way to deal with them," Henry muttered.

"That is nothing but wild speculation!" Alan said in exasperation.

Henry gave a faint smile. "On the contrary, it is a careful calculation based on twenty years of knowledge of our adversaries."

Alan regarded him grimly. "What have you done, Henry?"

"What I had to do," said Henry with a shrug of his shoulders, which he immediately regretted. He grimaced at the pain. "I sent a letter to the Countess de Marjolaine warning her of Smythe's scheming, asking her to keep Rosia from declaring war."

Alan was livid. He abruptly stood up, walked to the end of the dock, and stood staring down into the Breath, breathing hard until he had mastered his anger. He turned around and walked back to confront his friend.

"You are a traitor, Henry. I should clap you in irons, lock you in the brig, and carry you back to Freya."

Henry was tired and in pain. "All the years of our friendship you have trusted me, Alan."

"All these years, you have never betrayed our friendship!" Alan retorted. "For the sake of your wife and children, I will not expose them to the shame of seeing you stand trial. But from this moment, our friendship is at an end. I denounce you. I no longer know you."

Alan waited a moment to give Henry a chance to say something, perhaps apologize or plead for forgiveness. The wind rustled the leaves. A bird sang nearby. Henry sat unmoving, his head bowed.

"Since you will not be returning to the ship, I will send a sailor with your things," said Alan. "I assume you will be in your usual lodgings."

Henry raised his head. "Tell Mr. Sloan—"

But Alan was gone.

Henry Wallace kept hired lodgings in every major city and many minor ones throughout the world under one or another of his aliases. He generally chose nondescript boarding houses for single gentlemen and in each he kept a locked chest containing clothing, papers to prove false identities, funds in the local currency, pistols, powder, and ammunition. He paid well for the privilege of being left undisturbed.

The boarding house in Wellinsport overlooked the harbor. His single room was sparsely furnished, stuffy, hot and cheerless, and smelled of boiled cabbage. He opened the window to air it out and stood watching the ships. The first of the Guundaran warships was just entering the harbor when there was a knock on his door.

"Who is there?" Henry called, hoping without much hope it would be Alan.

"Perry," was the answer.

Henry opened the door to find the surgeon with his black bag, accompanied by a burly sailor lugging Henry's sea chest.

"Put it there," said Henry, pointing.

The sailor deposited the chest on the floor. Henry paid him for his trouble and the sailor left.

Perry looked about the small room in some surprise. "Quite cozy, my lord."

"Indeed, sir," said Henry, smiling. Perry was nothing if not diplomatic. "How can I help you, sir?"

"Captain Northrop said you had decided to stay in the city. I came to check your wound and change the bandages."

Henry offered Perry the only chair and sat down on the end of the bed. Perry removed the sling, studied the wound, sniffed at it for signs of putrefaction, and smiled.

"Healing nicely," he said. "The bones are knitting well. Still in pain?"

"Not that I notice," Henry lied.

"I can give you something for it," said Perry, having learned not to believe his patients.

"Thank you, no," said Henry.

Perry began to rummage about in his bag. "Captain Northrop says you have business in Wellinsport and will not be returning to the ship. I will leave clean bandages and a jar of this healing ointment. Spread it liberally over the wound three times a day. And keep your arm in the sling," he added, noting that Henry had removed it and flung it on the bed.

Henry grimaced, but he obediently slipped the sling over his head and gingerly slid his arm inside. He eyed the Guundaran ship, the *Godswald,* as it glided past. He noted some signs of damage, but most of it was superficial, nothing that couldn't have been done deliberately and easily repaired.

"Anything else you require, my lord?" Perry asked.

"Thank you, sir, no," said Henry.

Perry packed up his bag. Henry accompanied the surgeon to the door and opened it for him.

Perry wrinkled his nose in disgust. "Judging by the smell from the kitchen, I recommend for the sake of your health that you take your meals elsewhere."

Henry laughed and agreed to do so. But his laughter must have sounded hollow, for Perry regarded him intently.

"Is everything all right, my lord?"

Alan would not have said anything to reveal that he and Henry had parted in anger, but Alan was easy to read, and Perry was both astute and observant.

Henry held out his hand. "Good-bye, sir. Thank you for coming."

"Good luck, sir," Perry said, shaking hands. "Send word to me if you need anything."

Henry promised that he would. Perry departed and Henry went back to watching out the window, just as the second Guundaran warship was starting to sail into the harbor.

THIRTY-SIX

The Winter Witch, having blown the *Terrapin* off course, was not content with that. She caught Kate and Dalgren in her grasp on the second day of their journey to the Aligoes. The Witch tore at them with bitter cold, buffeted them with fierce winds and stinging sleet, and tried her best to kill them with lethal bolts of magical purple lightning.

Kate wore a griffin-rider's helm to protect her from the elements, but the rain and sleet coated the helm's visor, and she had to remove it, for she couldn't see. She spent most of the journey pressing her head against Dalgren's neck.

The cold was biting, seeming to sink through her clothes, her flesh, bone, and muscle, into her very soul. They flew all day the first day and when darkness fell, Kate was tempted to tell Dalgren to find someplace to land for the night, for she was shivering uncontrollably.

But she knew Commander Franklin of the *Naofa,* having served as his crafter when she made her short and disastrous journey Below. Franklin was dedicated to his mission. He was the one who had fired the green-beam gun that struck the palace and killed the queen. He would not stop for any reason on his way to Maribeau to kill dragons. Kate gritted her teeth to keep them from chattering, and she and Dalgren pressed on long after dark.

She had no idea where they were. Every time she tried to look for the lighthouses that marked the safest route through the Breath, she was blinded by sleet and rain. Dragons have excellent night vision and possess an unerring sense of direction; she trusted Dalgren to find the way.

They flew through the storm until Dalgren's indefatigable strength began to flag and he had to rest. He landed on a what passed for an island, but which was really nothing more than a large chunk of floating rock. At least the boulders provided shelter from the Witch's fury.

Kate tried to climb down from Dalgren's back, but she was so stiff from the cold that her hands lost their grip and she collapsed onto the ground. She could not move, but lay there, shivering. Dalgren heated the stones around her, breathing on them with his fiery breath until they radiated warmth. Then he lay down beside her and draped one wing over her, to protect her from the wind.

Kate gradually warmed enough to move. She had to dry her wet clothes or she would "catch her death" as her mother had always said. She opened the valise where Amelia had packed a change of clothes, as well as food. Kate put on the dry clothes and spread her coat and stocking hat and other rain-soaked clothing over the heated rocks.

She slept on the ground, pressing against Dalgren's rib cage beneath his wing, and woke in the morning to clear skies and warm sunshine. She ate some of her rations, then began packing her things.

"You must be starving," she said to Dalgren.

"I can hold out until we reach the Aligoes," he replied. "We are not far from Maribeau. About a day's journey."

"And no storms in sight," said Kate. "I wonder where the black ship is. They had a head start on us, but the storm would have slowed them or maybe even blown them off course."

"Maybe it sent them to the bottom," Dalgren growled.

"From your mouth to the Witch's ear! I still feel guilty about repairing that green-beam gun," said Kate. "I was the one who brought it back to life."

"You had no choice," Dalgren pointed out. "You were their prisoner. They would have killed you."

Kate knew it was more complicated than that, but she wasn't going to try to explain. She changed the subject.

"As you say, we'll reach Maribeau today. I've been to Ile de Feuroi, but I don't recall ever seeing Fort Vaila, the brigade headquarters. Is it close to the city?"

"No, and for good reason," said Dalgren. "City dwellers would not want their skies filled with dragons. Fort Vaila is a half day's journey, located on the north side of the island at its highest point."

Kate was thoughtful. "I suppose the dragons post lookouts at the fort."

"Day and night," said Dalgren.

"What will they do when they see us?" Kate asked, as she put on her coat and her helm.

"The dragons will fly out to challenge me," said Dalgren. "Once they know who I am, they will take me into custody."

He sounded matter-of-fact, almost nonchalant.

"Then we won't fly that close," said Kate, fastening the chin strap of the helm. "Is there someplace near the fort where you can hide?"

"I'm not going to hide, Kate," Dalgren said sternly. "I don't plan to spend the rest of my life hiding. I've given a lot of thought to what Father Jacob said to me about accepting the fact that I deserved my punishment. He was right. I may have admitted my guilt at my trial, but I didn't really mean it."

"You had good reason to do what you did at the Battle of the Royal Sail and so I will tell Captain Thorgrimson," said Kate, indignant on his behalf. "Your own navy fired on you and the other members of the brigade."

She climbed up on his foreleg and began to tie herself securely to his back.

"True, but that didn't justify my response," Dalgren said. "I should have stayed in the brigade like Captain de Guichen and denounced those who committed that vile act. The truth was that I was sick of the killing. As I've told you before, Kate, it was easier to fly away and put the blood and death behind me. So I've made up my mind. I will accept the Banishment. I've been thinking I could return to Below and spend my life helping the Bottom Dwellers and Father Jacob. That will be my penance."

Kate remembered Below, the island at the bottom of the world. She remembered the loneliness, the isolation, the bleak and desolate landscape, the scarcity of food, the hostility of the people. Admittedly they had reason to be hostile, for the world had tried to kill them. She couldn't imagine spending her life among them.

"I don't think I could go back there, Dalgren," she said. "Why can't you find people up here who need your help?"

"I'm going, Kate," said Dalgren. "I've made up my mind. I don't expect you to come with me."

"But, you can't go off and leave me! You're my dearest friend. I need you!"

Dalgren gently shook his head. "I will always be your friend, Kate. But you have a life here now, with humans who are dear to you. My life is down there, where I can make reparation for my crime by being of service to those in need."

Kate was upset and angry. Dalgren had known she wouldn't approve and he had deliberately waited to tell her his decision when she didn't have time to talk him out of it.

"We'll discuss this later," Kate said, and slammed down the visor of the helm.

Now that the weather had cleared, she watched for the black ship as she and Dalgren flew toward Maribeau, traveling the well-marked shipping lane that ran between Freya and the Aligoes. Much the way ships of the sea followed the same routes crossing the inland oceans, ships of the air traveled shipping routes.

The Breath was like the sea, having its own currents, waves, eddies, and winds, as well as magical tides that ebbed and flowed. Mariners down through the ages had determined the fastest and safest routes for crossing the Breath and charted them on maps.

Following the Blackfire War, when the world was finally at peace, the powerful Church of the Breath began a vigorous campaign of establishing churches to convert the benighted throughout the world. Their missionaries required safe, swift passage through the Breath and the Church undertook an ambitious program to mark major shipping lanes with lighthouses that relied on magic and liquid Breath to remain in place.

The lighthouses were ships much like those that sailed the Breath, but instead of being designed to sail, these were designed to remain in stationary locations amid the tides and currents within the Breath.

The hulls had to be strong enough to withstand the currents of magic in the Breath and also to support a thirty-foot tower topped by a magical white light that flashed every twenty seconds, with red and green lights that remained constantly lit.

Six airscrews located around the middle of the vessel allowed for easy maneuverability. Four large lift tanks built into the upper part of the hull provided steady lift and stability, while each lighthouse had an additional pair of lift tanks to provide ballast. The lowest section of the vessel housed water barrels that were refilled by rainwater channeled off the hull.

Each lighthouse operated with a crew of two or three people who were stationed on the vessel for one month, then rotated to one of the resupply ships that traveled from lighthouse to lighthouse for two months.

Kate and Dalgren flew low over the shipping lanes in order to view the ships sailing beneath them. She was hoping to catch the *Naofa* out in the open Breath in the daylight, so that the ship would not have a chance to run for cover along the coastline. Dalgren could swoop down on it from the air, catch the crew by surprise, and use his fiery breath, claws, and tail to destroy the gun, before they could turn the green beam on him.

They covered a vast area of the Breath, but morning passed into late afternoon and still they saw no sign of a black ship. Kate's eyes ached from the strain of watching and she eventually gave up.

The sun was starting to set as they reached the first of the islands known by mariners as the Channel Islands, which bordered the Imperial Channel. Maribeau was about a two-day journey from Wellinsport, which was off the Trame Channel. Kate had traveled to Wellinsport often, to sell her salvage at auction. She had only ever visited Maribeau with her father, and wasn't nearly as familiar with it.

Kate looked for Mount Eridous, one of the Six Old Men, the six mountains that had their roots in the bottom of the world. Their peaks thrusting up out of the Breath formed landmarks used by sailors to navigate their way among the islands.

Dalgren flew southeast of the Channel Islands until Mount Eridous came into view. From there he turned due east. Kate gave Dalgren a pat to indicate he had done a good job of navigating. They followed the Imperial Channel until they reached Ile de Feuroi, home of the Rosian city of Maribeau and Fort Vaila.

By the time they reached the fort, night had fallen. The stars were bright in a cloudless sky, and they could see an immense cliff rising up from the mists of the Breath.

Kate had worried the entire journey that the *Naofa* might have reached the fort ahead of them and destroyed it. With relief, she caught sight of a building blazing with light. Raising her visor, she shouted to Dalgren, "Is that the fort? Is everything all right?"

Dalgren also gave a relieved sigh that sent clouds of smoke puffing from his nostrils.

"The fort is safe! We arrived in time!"

Kate was about to cheer, when Dalgren shook his head. The scales between his eyes wrinkled. "That's odd."

"What's odd?" Kate asked, alarmed.

"The fact that the fort is lit up like a Yule tree," said Dalgren.

"Maybe they're hosting a party," said Kate. "That's what it looks like."

"The Brigade does not encourage visitors," said Dalgren. "Still, I think you might be right. I can see two large yachts and several smaller ones docked nearby."

"Can you see the names on the yachts? What flags are they flying?"

Dalgren shook his head. "Even my eyes aren't that good. We'll have to fly closer."

"If we do, the lookouts will see us," said Kate.

"They already have," said Dalgren calmly.

As he spoke, two dragons rose into the air and flew toward them. Dalgren slowed almost to a stop, hovering in the air, to show them he was not a threat. "Something is wrong. Ordinarily the dragons would have questioned me on their own. These dragons have riders."

Kate shifted uneasily on Dalgren's back.

"I've . . . uh . . . been meaning to tell you," she said. "I'm wanted by the Rosian authorities. The brigade members could arrest me."

"Arrest?" Dalgren whipped his head around to glare at her. "What did you do? And why didn't you say anything before now?"

"I'm a fugitive from justice. I escaped from a Rosian prison on Maribeau the night before I was supposed to be hanged for piracy," Kate explained. "And I did say something. I told you about that."

"You told me Thomas obtained pardons!" Dalgren roared.

"He did," said Kate. "He obtained pardons for my crew, but he couldn't get one for me."

"And you're just now telling me this?" Dalgren demanded.

"I knew you wouldn't let me come with you," said Kate.

"Damn right I wouldn't!"

"If I'm lucky, the officers won't recognize me," said Kate. "They don't know what I look like. I won't tell them my real name and you shouldn't tell them yours."

"If any of the dragons or the officers were present at my trial, they will recognize you," Dalgren growled.

"The dragons from the Aligoes didn't attend your trial," Kate said triumphantly. "Captain Thorgrimson wasn't even there. He and the brigade were helping the Rosian navy clear out the pirates. I have a plan. . . ."

Dalgren snorted fire from his nostrils. The Brigade dragons and their riders were drawing closer, flying slowly and warily, not certain what to expect from a strange dragon.

"My last plan worked," Kate told him, annoyed. "All you have to do is keep your mouth shut. I will warn these riders about the black ship and then you and I will leave—"

"Forget it, Kate," said Dalgren grimly. He had been watching the dragons. "I know the lead dragon and so do you. It's the judge from my trial. Countess Anasi."

"Bloody hell," said Kate with a sigh.

THIRTY-SEVEN

Kate had no difficulty recognizing Countess Anasi, who had the short, thick neck of a common dragon, not the long elegant neck of nobility. She had not allowed her low birth to prove an impediment and she had risen through the ranks of the Brigade to become one of its leaders. She had served as the judge at Dalgren's trial for desertion and she had been strict and stern, though also fair.

Still, if there was one dragon on Aeronne Kate would not want to encounter now, that dragon was Anasi.

"Let me do the talking," said Dalgren.

As Anasi and her fellow dragon drew close enough to see Dalgren, Anasi viewed him with astonishment. Small wonder, she had supposed he was at the bottom of the world, serving out his punishment for desertion.

Anasi's surprise changed quickly to anger. She twisted her head to say something to her rider, who raised his helm and shouted to his partner. He placed his hand on his sidearm, but did not draw it. His partner did the same.

Dalgren was practically motionless in the air, stiff and rigid. Kate sat straight and tall on his back, keeping her hands where the riders could see them. She reminded herself that for once in her life, she was on the side of the angels. She was going to give them news that would save their lives, perhaps save the Brigade.

Anasi didn't spare her a glance. She focused her anger on Dalgren, refusing to even use his name.

"We granted you a reprieve on your sentence, Nameless Dragon. The judgment of the court was given that you would be permitted to go Below, serve out your sentence with Father Jacob Northrop, rather than suffer banishment from dragonkind. You have flouted our attempts at mercy and are seemingly bold enough to openly defy us!"

Kate was angry at the countess's imperious tone and accusations. Dalgren opened his mouth, but before he could say a word, Kate interrupted.

"I am Katherine Fitzmaurice-Gascoyne and I am a friend of Lord *Dalgren's*," she said, emphasizing his name. She raised her voice so that both dragons and their riders could hear her. "Lord *Dalgren* came to the brigade knowing he faced arrest, to warn you that a black ship, armed with a green-beam gun, is planning to attack Fort Vaila. The ship left Haever two days ago. It could arrive at any time. You need to be prepared."

Anasi gave a smoke-laced snort of derision. "Those guns were destroyed in the war."

"I know for a fact that some survived," said Kate. "I don't have time to bandy words with you! Take me to Captain Thorgrimson. I will explain everything to him."

Anasi regarded Kate with narrowed eyes, then shifted her head to cast a questioning glance over her shoulder at the man who was riding her.

Kate had been keeping her eye on the rider. He had removed his helm and she could see his face. He was a big man with dark eyes and a dark beard and he was wearing the traditional leather coat trimmed with dragons.

Kate knew who he was before he said it.

"I am Captain Thorgrimson."

Kate felt Dalgren quiver, saw his jaw clamp together tightly. She gave him a reassuring pat. He gave her a grim glance.

"I am telling the truth about the threat to the Brigade, sir," Kate said. "Dalgren and I have flown day and night to reach you with this news."

Thorgrimson regarded her gravely, then turned to his comrade who was mounted on the second dragon and issued orders. "Double the patrols, Lieutenant, and evacuate the fort. Inform His Majesty, King Renaud, and Her Ladyship and assist them to make preparations to immediately depart."

Kate gasped at this, then groaned and swore beneath her breath. Of all the damnable luck! The King of Rosia must be making a royal visit to the fort. His presence explained the yachts and the fact that the fortress had

been ablaze with lights. Also why two dragons and their riders had swiftly
flown out to confront the strangers.

The lieutenant saluted and spoke to his dragon. They made a banking
turn and flew swiftly back to the fort.

"If this is Lord Dalgren," Captain Thorgrimson continued, "you must be
his partner, the notorious Captain Kate."

Kate sighed. She hadn't really expected that using her full name would
fool anyone, but it had been worth a try.

"I swear to you, Captain, those stories you've read about me in the newspaper aren't true!" Kate said, talking so fast her words fell all over each
other. "I don't thirst for the blood of Rosians. Dalgren and I didn't know
King Renaud was here! We don't mean His Majesty any harm. It is true that
I was sentenced to hang for piracy, but I was a privateer—"

Captain Thorgrimson raised his hand to stop the torrent. "Please, Captain. I believe you. I read the reports and gave orders for your sentence to be
commuted. Didn't you know?"

Kate sighed, weak with relief. "Thank you, sir! No, sir, I didn't know. I
have been living in Freya and I heard no news of it."

Dag regarded both her and Dalgren thoughtfully. "So Dalgren came to
Maribeau knowing he would be placed under arrest and you came knowing
you would face a death sentence."

"I don't see why you should sound so surprised, sir!" Kate said, bristling.
"Whatever you might think of us, Lord Dalgren is a former member of the
Brigade and I—"

"I meant that as a compliment, Captain," Dag said with a glimmer of
amusement in his dark eyes. "I admire your courage and Lord Dalgren's."

"Oh," said Kate, feeling stupid. "Sorry, sir. Thank you, sir."

Captain Thorgrimson gave her a grave look. "You said you traveled from
Freya, Captain. Rosia is at war with Freya, or at least Freya is at war with
us. Did His Majesty, King Thomas, send this black ship?"

"No, sir," said Kate emphatically. "Thomas—I mean, His Majesty, King
Thomas—was the one who sent me to warn you."

Thorgrimson raised his eyebrows at this news, then leaned down to confer with Anasi. She seemed reluctant, but she grudgingly agreed. "I have no
objections, sir, so long as he is kept under guard."

Captain Thorgrimson straightened in the saddle. "We have a great deal to
discuss, it seems, Captain, and I don't want to have to keep shouting. I must
deal with the immediate danger first, of course, but if you will accompany us
to the fort, we can speak at length."

"What about Lord Dalgren, sir?" Kate asked boldly. "If the dragons are
going to take him into custody again, we'll be on our way. Dalgren came

here of his own free will to save his fellows and I want your surety that he will be able to freely leave."

"Lord Dalgren's fate falls within the purview of the dragons," said Thorgrimson. "What do you say, Countess?"

"We need to hear more about this black ship," said Anasi. She did not look at Dalgren, nor refer to him directly. "This dragon came to warn us knowing the peril he faced, and that is to his credit. He may come to the fort, but since he is under the sentence of Banishing, he should remember that no dragon will speak to him or acknowledge his presence."

Kate stirred angrily and had to bite her tongue to keep silent. The decision was Dalgren's, as he reminded her with a stern look.

"Let the countess be assured that I will not attempt to make contact with any of my fellows."

Countess Anasi still did not look at or otherwise acknowledge him, but she gave a cold nod.

"Lord Dalgren is granted safe passage. For seventy-two hours, he may come and go as he pleases."

"If you will accompany us, Captain, Lord Dalgren," said Thorgrimson.

Kate understood that wasn't a request. It was a command.

Anasi made a steep, banking turn and she and the captain led the way back to the fort. Kate and Dalgren followed more slowly. Kate leaned over his neck so they could talk.

"We nearly killed ourselves to save their lives!" Kate said angrily. "She treats you like a criminal!"

"I *am* a criminal," Dalgren pointed out.

"But they don't need to treat you like one. I don't care what they say. We are not staying where we are not wanted. I will tell Captain Thorgrimson what we know about the black ship and then we'll leave. You have Anasi's permission to move about freely, so don't do anything noble and stupid like offering to surrender."

Dalgren didn't answer. Instead, he changed the subject. "I have always wanted to see Fort Vaila. I am glad to have the chance."

"I don't want to talk about a fort," Kate said.

"And I don't want to argue. Do you want to hear about the fort?"

"Not really," Kate said. "I suppose this fort is like every other fort."

"No, it is not," said Dalgren. "And that is why I have looked forward to seeing it. Fort Vaila is the only human structure in the world designed by a dragon. You can see it from here." He indicated the building perched at the top of the cliff.

Kate knew he was wrestling inwardly with his decision and that he would talk about it when he felt like it and not before. And so she talked about the fort.

"Is that it?" she asked. "That oddly shaped building? Why is it shaped like that?"

"The fort has ten sides, allowing for accommodations for ten dragons," said Dalgren. "Vaila was a common dragon who worked for the Brigade. Since common dragons aren't permitted to take part in battle, she hauled supplies, foraged for food, ran errands. When the Brigade was talking about building their headquarters, Vaila went to a human architect and asked him to draw up the plans for her idea for a fort. She knew, you see, that the Brigade would never accept her design if they knew it was created by a common dragon, so the architect presented it as his own.

"The Brigade was impressed with his design and hired him to build the structure. After it was completed, he told them the truth, and the Brigade named the headquarters in the designer's honor: Fort Vaila."

"What makes her design so special?" Kate asked, now intrigued.

"The structure is made of granite, five stories tall, with ten sides constructed around an inner courtyard that is open to the air. The fort is designed solely for the use of the dragons, who like to sleep in dark, cavernous spaces.

"The fort can house ten dragons, two wings of four battle dragons and a command dragon. Each has his or her own chamber that opens onto the courtyard. The dragons descend into the fort from above, land in the courtyard, then go from there into their sleeping chambers."

"What about the human riders?" asked Kate. "Where do they live?"

"They have their own quarters nearby, but the Brigade holds meetings in the fort. The humans enter from a door that is on the ground level. It is an excellent arrangement. Too bad I won't get to spend much time here," Dalgren added wistfully. "I should like to see inside."

"Better we leave before Anasi changes her mind," said Kate. "My plan is to talk to the captain. Once I've done that, we can return to Freya. You *are* coming home with me, aren't you?"

"Don't badger me," Dalgren growled.

The bells on the fort chimed twelve times. A huge silvery moon was rising, lighting the edge of the cliff where the dragons would land to allow their riders to dismount and to visit with each other before going to their rest.

The fort was some distance away from the landing site, giving the dragons plenty of room to maneuver. The only impediment they faced was a low stone safety wall built by the dragons along the edge of the cliff.

Kate and Dalgren waited deferentially for Thorgrimson and Anasi to land.

The moment Anasi touched down, Thorgrimson vaulted from the saddle and hurried off in the direction of one of the yachts, which was the largest and most elegant Kate had ever seen. She guessed it must belong to King Renaud. She could see that the yacht's captain had heeded the warning and was already preparing to depart. Sailors swarmed the decks, hastily raising sails and fully inflating the balloons.

Anasi and Thorgrimson both appeared to have forgotten Kate and Dalgren. Thorgrimson was swarmed by several other officers, who had heard the news from the lieutenant and were eager to find out what was going on. Countess Anasi lumbered off toward the fort, where dragons were waiting to talk to her.

"I guess we have permission to land," said Kate. She added, teasing, "Don't do a belly flop."

Dalgren was clearly nervous, fearing that every dragon in the fort would be watching and judging his performance as they had when he was only a raw recruit. He circled the cliff, testing the air currents.

He was always a little awkward, because he had to put his weight on his bad leg, and to make certain his wings didn't clip the wall. The air was calm, the mists hardly stirring, and he came down, rear legs first, then settled onto his forelegs.

"Light as thistledown," Kate told him.

Dalgren grunted.

Once he had settled, Kate started to slide off his back, then saw a woman watching them from a safe distance. The woman wore an elegant silk cape with the hood pulled over her head to protect her from the night air. Seeing Kate notice her, the woman drew back her hood and Kate saw her face in the moonlight.

Kate groaned. "My luck just keeps getting worse and worse!"

"Why? What's wrong? Who is that woman?" Dalgren asked.

"The Countess de Marjolaine."

"I thought you liked her."

"I do, but she will want to hear about Sophia and she will insist that we stay the night. Don't worry, I will make some excuse."

"I'm not worried," Dalgren said. "You're the one who's worried. As for me, I would like to spend the night. I'm bone tired, and I haven't eaten in days."

"Get something to eat and then we'll leave," said Kate firmly, jumping to the ground.

She was preparing to formally curtsy and was startled when Cecile swept forward, embraced her, and greeted her with a warm kiss. Kate was astonished by this effusive display of emotion from a woman who had survived decades in the royal court by keeping her emotions locked in some secret recess in her heart.

"I have been worried to distraction about Sophia. Then Rodrigo brought me the message from Sir Henry that you helped her escape the palace and she is safe," said Cecile, clinging to her. "Thank you, Kate! How is she?"

"Sophia is safe and well, my lady," said Kate, managing to talk even as she was half-smothered in rustling folds of silk and velvet. "We tried to persuade her to leave Freya, but she refused to go."

The countess recollected herself and returned her emotions to the lockbox. She released Kate from her embrace and took a moment to arrange her mussed hair. "I think I can guess why she is staying. I will not ask you where she is, for I would not endanger her."

"Miss Amelia made the arrangements," said Kate.

"Miss Amelia? Not Sir Henry?" Cecile asked, slightly frowning.

Kate didn't want to talk about Sir Henry. "My lady, didn't you hear the warning about the black ship? You should leave the fort immediately. You are not safe."

"I was present when the lieutenant informed the king. His Majesty is leaving. You can see Captain Thorgrimson speaking with His Majesty."

Cecile indicated the king's yacht. Two dragon riders from the Brigade circled above the yacht, waiting to act as escort. Kate saw Thorgrimson bow and take his leave. The sailors raised the gangplank, others released the mooring lines, and the royal yacht, accompanied by a Brigade escort, sailed into the Breath.

Cecile turned back to Kate. "When I told His Majesty you were Sophia's friend and that you had helped her escape the palace the night the queen was assassinated, he asked me to give you a message. I am to convey His Majesty's heartfelt gratitude."

"Sophia helped me as much as I helped her," said Kate, embarrassed. "Your Ladyship should be leaving, as well."

Cecile gave Kate a look that reminded her she was speaking to a countess and one of the most powerful women in the world.

"I appreciate your concern, Captain," said Cecile and walked over to speak to Dalgren.

"I am pleased to see you again, Lord Dalgren. The other dragons in the fort are making preparations to evacuate. They plan to travel to caves farther inland. Countess Anasi has given you leave to spend the night, so long as you do not speak to any of them."

"Thank you—" Dalgren began.

Kate interrupted him. "Dalgren and I will *not* be staying. I came only because Captain Thorgrimson asked me to tell him what I know about the black ship. After that, we will be going."

Kate looked toward the courtyard around the fort, hoping to see Thorgrimson. The news of the black ship had spread and riders and brigade staff were making arrangements to evacuate and she could not find him in the crowd.

"Do you know where he is?" Kate asked.

"Captain Thorgrimson will not be free to talk to you for some time," said Cecile. "He has a great deal to do as I am certain you can imagine."

She turned back to Dalgren. "You appear to be exhausted, my lord. I suggest you go with the other dragons to the caves. They will provide food for you and a place to sleep. I will take care of Kate. She can spend the night on board my yacht and speak to Captain Thorgrimson in the morning."

Dalgren looked to Kate, who gave a helpless shrug. "You should go," she said, relenting. "You do look tired and hungry. I'll be fine."

Dalgren was relieved. He thanked the countess and gave Kate a pleading glance, begging her not to cause trouble. He shifted his bulk around to head for the fort, taking care with his tail to keep from accidentally knocking down either Kate or the countess.

Kate started to follow, but Cecile detained her.

"Please wait a moment, Kate. I need to speak to you in private."

Cecile led her over to the wall and stood near it, gazing out into the mists of the Breath that drifted past them, calm and placid this night.

"How is Thomas?" Cecile asked abruptly.

Kate had been expecting more questions about Sophia, but she was not prepared to talk about Thomas. She could already feel the blood rising from her heart to her cheeks. She wondered uneasily how much Cecile knew or guessed about her feelings for Thomas and his feelings for her.

Afraid Cecile would notice her cheeks burning even in the moonlight, Kate ducked her head to avoid her scrutiny.

"His Majesty . . . uh . . . is fine . . . I suppose," said Kate. She started to sidle away. "I should really catch up with Dalgren—"

"Did Thomas send the black ship to attack the Brigade, Kate?" Cecile asked. Her face was pale, her voice cold. "Is he declaring war on Rosia?"

Kate whirled to face her, indignant and angry. "No, my lady! Of course not! How could you think such a thing? He sent me here to warn the Brigade. Thomas has been doing what he could to stop this madness. King Ullr and that evil man, Smythe, are behind all of this. Thomas spied on the king and discovered Ullr is planning to invade Freya on Hallen Day."

"So Sir Henry feared," said Cecile. "He did not know the date, but he feared it would be soon, and I agree. The Rosian navy has been tracking the movements of the Guundaran fleets. They are massing near Freya."

She was silent, thinking. She walked back over to the wall and suddenly stiffened. Leaning over the wall, she stared intently down into the Breath.

"What is that out there?" Cecile asked, pointing off shore.

Kate ran to the wall and looked down. The mists were boiling, frothing and bubbling in the moonlight as something darker than the darkness rose up out of the Deep Breath.

"The black ship!" Kate gasped.

She cast a desperate glance back at the fort, at the dragons and humans.

Cecile continued to watch. "The ship is rising fast, Kate. I can see the tops of the masts."

Kate looked out into the Breath. The ship was wreathed with mists and she could not see what was happening on deck. But she had served aboard that ship, and she didn't need to see. Commander Franklin would be standing at the green-beam gun, prepared to open fire the moment he had a target in sight. Kate had a vivid memory of the green beam blasting a hole in the side of the cliff.

"Get down, my lady! Take cover behind the wall! Dalgren, to me!" Kate shouted. "You have to warn them!"

The dragon whipped his head around. He looked first at her, then looked past her. He went rigid, his tail thudded on the ground in anger, his eyes glittered in the moonlight, and flames flickered between his clenched jaws.

Dalgren threw back his head and trumpeted the warning. His furious roar echoed off the mountains and rebounded down the side of the cliff. He emphasized his call by belching forth a blazing ball of fire.

Kate cast a fearful glance back at the *Naofa*. The fog stirred up by the ship began to flow over the wall in silver-gray waves. She could now see Commander Franklin, illuminated by the faint glow of magic cast by the green-beam gun, crouching behind it, preparing it to fire. The green glow of the gun strengthened as she watched, growing brighter until it was almost blinding.

Cecile remained standing at the wall, gazing at the ship. Kate grabbed hold of her and dragged her to the ground, using the wall as cover. She looked back at Dalgren, back at the fort.

Dalgren's call had alerted humans and dragons to the danger. They might not be able to see the black ship, but they could certainly see the green glow of contramagic. Several dragons leaped into the air, the moonlight flashing on their wings. Brigade officers summoned their mounts. Dalgren was still bellowing the alarm.

"Look out!" Kate shouted at him, though she knew he couldn't hear her and he wouldn't have listened anyhow.

The *Naofa* fired.

The green beam lanced high above Kate and Cecile, bathing them in bright, piercing green light. The light hurt her eyes and Kate shut them against the glare. Even then, she could still see the light blaze through her eyelids.

Dalgren suddenly ceased to bellow. Frightened, Kate scrambled to her feet, terrified to see what had become of him.

Dalgren had taken flight, soaring into the sky before the green beam hit. Silver moonlight flashed on his scales and shone through the thin membrane of his wings. Kate shouted and waved her arms to draw his attention as he flew overhead.

"Strike quickly before Franklin has a chance to fire again!"

Dalgren dipped his head in a nod and sped on.

THIRTY-EIGHT

"Oh, my God!" Cecile breathed.

She had pushed herself to a sitting position. Her hood had fallen from her head, her beautifully coiffed hair straggled over her face and into her eyes. Staring at the fort, she impatiently pushed her hair aside and Kate saw a look of horror on her face.

"What is it, my lady?" Kate asked, frightened. "Are you hurt?"

"I am not hurt, but I fear others are," said Cecile. She rose unsteadily to her feet.

Kate looked back at the fort. The beam had struck about midway between the ground level and the top of the north wall, and the green glow of contramagic was spreading from there, devouring the magical constructs. The builders had mixed magic into the mortar and used magic to strengthen walls and ceilings, and to fortify the wooden support beams.

But the fort was old, and so were the magical constructs. Gigantic cracks opened in the walls. Huge chunks of stone broke off and smashed to the ground. And then the walls suddenly gave way and the fort broke apart and collapsed in on itself with a dull roaring groan.

Most of the dragons inside the fort had heard Dalgren's warning and had taken flight. Judging by the terrible screams, at least one dragon was trapped inside. Humans and the other dragons ran to the rescue, heedless of their own danger.

"I must go," said Cecile. "They will need my help."

"Warn them that the ship will fire again as soon as they recharge the weapon," Kate told her. "I would tell them myself, but I cannot leave Dalgren."

"God be with him," said Cecile.

She glanced at the black ship and Dalgren flying rapidly to the attack. The green glow of contramagic had faded to almost nothing now, but it would strengthen as Franklin used his magic to recharge the weapon.

Cecile gathered up her skirts and ran toward the ruin of the fort. Kate watched Dalgren.

She wished desperately she was out there with him, but he had to take on this battle alone. At least she could let him know she was with him in spirit. She waited by the wall, her fists clenched, watching as he swooped down on the black ship.

"Hit the masts! The balloons!" Kate yelled, beating her fists on the wall, shouting directions he couldn't possibly hear.

The crew had caught sight of the dragon by now and opened fire with the swivel guns mounted on the rails. Dalgren was a moving target, however, and dragons are difficult to hit under the best of circumstances. The spray of bullets from a swivel gun were far more dangerous to a dragon than cannon fire. The bullets could not penetrate his scaly hide, but they could rip holes in his wings, strike him in the eyes or shatter his legs.

But the sailors manning the swivel guns had never fought a dragon, as Kate knew, and they were making the common mistake of aiming for Dalgren's massive body instead of trying to hit him in the head or wings. Dalgren, though, was trained in battling an enemy ship.

He sucked in a huge breath, dove down on the ship and breathed out a sheet of flame. Fire enveloped the tops of the masts, the rigging, the sails and the balloons.

Most ships had protective spells that would shield against flame and cannon attack. Kate had offered to place such constructs on the ship, but Franklin had been far more concerned with her work on the green-beam gun.

Kate watched the silk balloons disappear in a whoosh of fire and howled in glee and clapped her hands.

Dalgren circled back around to strike again.

Flaming rigging snaked down around the crew and burning spars crashed onto the deck. The crew had to abandon the swivel guns to deal with the fires. Sailors ran to man the water pumps and grab buckets and axes.

Two Brigade dragons who had been in the fort flew out to join in the attack, roaring defiance and fury as they came. At the sight of two more dragons, the crew gave up trying to save the ship and ran to the lifeboats to save themselves.

Franklin alone was still on board, remaining with the green-beam gun, waiting with terrible calm to fire again. Kate could tell by the green glow that the gun was fully operational by now. Franklin shifted the gun on its swiveling platform and Kate saw that he was not aiming at the fort. He was aiming at Dalgren.

The dragon was planning to rake the foredeck with flame and destroy the gun and he was in the direct line of fire. Kate shouted, attempting to warn him.

Dalgren saw his danger, but he continued flying straight toward the gun. Franklin stood behind it, holding his nerve, waiting to take his shot. The beam would strike Dalgren full in the breast.

Kate held her breath, watching in terror.

Dalgren snaked his body around, twisting out of range as Franklin fired. The beam lanced harmlessly into the mists. Dalgren struck the gun with his tail, lashing the weapon with a blow that pulverized the gun and smashed Franklin into a bloody ruin. The mangled gun toppled over into the Breath, along with whatever was left of Commander Franklin.

The brigade dragons and their riders arrived in time to see the *Naofa* sink into the Breath in a ball of fire. Dalgren gave a proud roar and turned a somersault in midair. The brigade dragons and their riders saluted him, then flew off in pursuit of the crew, who were desperately trying to flee in lifeboats.

Dalgren landed on the cliff near Kate and she could see bloody trails along his flanks. One of his foreclaws oozed blood, and he had an ugly gash across his snout. She shuddered, realizing how perilously close the bullets had come to blinding him.

Dalgren didn't see her. He was breathing heavily and staring, stricken, at the ruins of the fort where humans and dragons were working desperately to try to free the dragon trapped in the rubble.

"I have to go help."

"Take me with you!" said Kate.

She climbed onto his back, clinging to his mane, and he took to the air again. Kate could now see the extent of the destruction. The fort was nothing but a heap of shattered stone and broken beams, dust still rising from it. The dragon was trapped alive somewhere inside the ruins, screaming in agony. She had likely been asleep when the beam hit and now lay in the ruin, her body crushed beneath tons of stone.

Kate pointed to a building near the fort.

"Set me down on that rooftop!"

Dalgren flew as low to the roof as he could manage. Kate slid off Dalgren's back and managed an awkward landing, coming down on her hands and knees. She was wearing enough heavy clothing to protect her from scrapes and, blessing Amelia, she dashed down the stairs and out into the street.

She came to a stop, arrested by a tragic sight. A Brigade officer was attempting to shift a block of stone as big as he was with his bare hands, all the while shouting encouragement to the trapped dragon. He was able to move the stone a fraction, but the movement caused one of the wooden beams to collapse, launching an avalanche of rock that struck him on the shoulder and a glancing blow to the head.

Captain Thorgrimson shouted a warning.

"Keep clear, Reynard! It's not safe!"

"She's my partner, damn it!" the officer returned, and despite the fact that he could scarcely see for the blood pouring down his face, he continued his frantic efforts to free the trapped dragon.

Kate judged by the horrible screams that the dragon was mortally wounded, and her heart ached for them both. Thorgrimson went over to try to persuade the man to leave.

"I will not abandon her!" the officer cried, and aimed a savage blow at him.

Thorgrimson calmly ducked the wild swing, then put his arm around the man's shoulders.

"Let the dragons do their work," said the captain. "You're only in the way."

The officer seemed to realize the truth of this, for he backed off, though he did not go far.

Dalgren had joined a party of dragons who were shouting back and forth, devising a plan. Working together, they began to carefully lift the huge chunks of stone and mangled beams. They had to work with agonizing slowness, figuring out which blocks were safe to move, stopping if it appeared the rubble would shift and do even more damage.

Kate felt helpless, standing around watching. Humans, too, had been injured, and she joined Cecile, who was organizing parties of litter bearers to carry people to the infirmary.

"What can I do?" Kate asked.

"The surgeon needs help," said Cecile.

She pointed toward the infirmary.

Kate climbed through the rubble to reach it and offered her assistance to the Brigade surgeon. He was too busy to wonder who she was or how she got there, but set her to work. Under his direction, she splinted broken bones and bandaged lacerations.

Cecile appeared in the doorway, the hem of her silk velvet dress filthy and soaked in blood. She had tied her hair back to be out of her way, and her face was streaked with dirt.

"Sir, you are needed," she said to the surgeon.

He was wrapping a bandage around the chest of a man who had broken several ribs. He cast her a questioning glance and everyone in the infirmary stopped talking to hear her answer.

"The dragons have managed to reach Lady Rowan," Cecile said. "There is nothing they can do for her. Her partner is with her. He is injured, but he refuses to leave her."

"I will come," said the surgeon.

He left with Cecile.

"Poor Reynard," said someone. "He will take this loss hard. He and Lady Rowan have been riding together since the Brigade was re-formed after the war."

Kate thought about how she would feel if she lost Dalgren and she went outside to see how he was faring. He would take the death hard.

The dying dragon lay on the stone amid the rubble, her breath coming in shuddering, pain-filled gasps. Her partner was on his knees at her side, kneeling in her blood. He rested his hand on her head, gently stroking her and talking to her in a low voice, his words for her alone.

As he kept talking, eventually the painful gasps eased. The dragon gazed up at him, her breathing slowed.

"Fly free, Rowan," he said to her.

Her breathing stopped.

The officer reached out to gently close her eyes. Those gathered around them allowed him a quiet moment to be alone with the dead, then Cecile glided forward and put her hand on his arm and whispered something to him. The surgeon approached, saying he needed to tend to his injury. The officer shook his head.

Covered in blood, he pushed away both the surgeon and Cecile and walked off by himself.

Countess Anasi raised her voice in a keening wail. Dalgren and the other dragons formed a ring around the body of their dead comrade and joined Anasi, singing in their own language, lifting Lady Rowan's spirit skyward so that she might forever fly free.

The song was beautiful and haunting. Many in the crowd bowed their heads, some began to pray, and others joined in. Kate wiped her eyes.

After the song ended, the dragons set to work building a pyre. They would spend the night keeping watch over the dead, then, with the coming of dawn, consign the body to flames. Dalgren was about to join them, to fly to the forests to gather firewood.

"Do not go with them, Nameless Dragon!" Countess Anasi shouted.

"Bloody hell!" Kate swore and started to intervene, only to find Captain Thorgrimson and the Countess de Marjolaine blocking her way.

"Leave them be, Kate," the countess advised. "This is between dragons."

"Not if that old biddy is going to keep tormenting him! I'll . . . I'll rip out her scales!" Kate cried fiercely.

Thorgrimson gave a faint smile. His face was pale beneath his dark beard. He had a long night's work ahead of him and undoubtedly many more sleepless nights after that.

"The dragons are not going to torment him, Captain," he said.

Dalgren stood stiffly at attention. He was wounded and weary, but he faced them with dignity, his head held high.

"They are going to thank him and lift the Banishing," said Cecile.

"Lord Dalgren is a hero this night, and so are you, Captain," said Thorgrimson. "If you had not warned us, the attack could have killed a great many more dragons and humans and might well have meant the end of the Brigade."

Kate didn't know where to look or how to respond. In the newspaper, Captain Kate and her Dragon Corsairs were heroes in every issue, capturing Rosian treasure ships and outwitting evil barons. Her fictional self always made some gallant and witty remark before boldly flying off to fight again in the next installment.

Kate did not feel gallant or bold or proud. She was sick to her stomach, shaking with fatigue, and emotionally drained. She could still see the deadly green glow of contramagic and hear Lady Rowan's screams. Kate wanted only to find somewhere dark and safe where she could sleep until the screaming in her head stopped.

She guessed that Dalgren was feeling the same, only worse.

"Thank you, sir, but I need to be with my friend," Kate said.

"I understand how you feel, Captain, but first *I* need to know who sent this black ship and why," Thorgrimson stated. "Lives are at stake. Was this attack a Freyan declaration of war against Rosia? How did you know about it? Are more black ships coming?"

"You don't have to worry about any more black ships," said Kate. "The *Naofa* was the last one. Now I need to be with my friend."

"Captain, this is important—" Cecile said.

"So is Dalgren," Kate said.

She walked away before they could stop her.

Anasi was speaking in the dragons' language as Kate took her place at Dalgren's side. Anasi acknowledged her presence with a look and a nod. Kate rested her hand on Dalgren's foreclaw to let him know she was with him, and stood in silent support.

Anasi concluded her speech by speaking Dalgren's dragon name. Kate could not pronounce his name in his own language, but she recognized the sounds and understood their import.

Anasi had called Dalgren by his name. He was no longer Nameless Dragon.

Dalgren replied in Freyan in deference to Kate, so she could understand.

"I thank you for your commendation, Countess Anasi, but I do not feel I have done anything that would warrant lifting the Banishing. I was only doing my duty. I deserve my punishment and when time permits I will return to Glasearrach to work with Father Jacob."

Anasi and her fellow dragons seemed surprised by this response.

"I don't understand, Lord Dalgren," Anasi said, condescending to also speak Freyan for Kate's benefit. "You have fulfilled the terms the court set down for you to earn your name back."

"I did not, Countess," said Dalgren with dignity. "I deserted the Brigade because I had vowed to never again kill another human. I broke that vow tonight."

"You had good cause, Dalgren," said Anasi. "You saved lives by destroying the black ship."

"My vow did not come with conditions," said Dalgren. "Of all vows we take, I believe that those we make to ourselves are the most sacred."

"I cannot argue," said Anasi. "As the judge at your trial, I was witness to your valor and I rule that you have met the conditions that lift the sentence of Banishing. If you want to work for Father Jacob to help ease the suffering of those humans who live Below and to make reparation for breaking your oath, that is your choice and I laud you for it. But it is not necessary. Your name is now restored."

Anasi again pronounced his dragon name, speaking with warmth and admiration. One by one, the other dragons in the Brigade spoke his name and congratulated him. Dalgren accepted their well-wishes, looking dazed. Finally Captain Thorgrimson and Cecile both offered their congratulations.

"Her Ladyship and I would like to speak to you, Lord Dalgren, and to your partner," Thorgrimson added.

Before Dalgren could reply, Kate intervened.

"What more do you want from us, sir?" she demanded impatiently. "Dalgren needs to eat and heal his wounds and I need some sleep. We've told you all we know."

"We have come to ask for your help, Kate," said Cecile. "Rosia cannot allow the attack on the Brigade to go unpunished nor can we permit the Guundarans to conquer and seize Freya. That would make King Ullr far too powerful. I propose an alliance between Freya and Rosia to stop Guundar."

"The Dragon Brigade will offer our service to His Majesty, King Thomas. We will fly to Haever to join the battle against Guundar," Thorgrimson added.

"That's wonderful," said Kate. "I am sure Thomas—His Majesty will welcome this news. How soon can you leave? And what does this have to do with me and Dalgren?"

"We hope to be ready in forty-eight hours," Thorgrimson replied.

"Two days!" Kate gasped. "Why so long?"

Dalgren gave a warning cough and nudged her with a claw. Kate ignored him.

"I don't understand," she persisted.

"The Brigade cannot leave for Freya without obtaining orders from King Renaud and, given the fact that the Freyans falsely accused our king of ordering the assassination of their queen, the countess may have a difficult time persuading His Majesty," Thorgrimson said with a glance at Cecile.

"As for the Brigade itself, we were not prepared to go to war. We must consider matters of logistics, supplying our forces, both human and dragons, and that will take time. We are a miltiary force, Captain, not corsairs," he added wryly.

"No, sir," said Kate. She wondered why Thorgrimson was bothering to explain when he could have just dismissed her. "Sorry, sir."

"And that is where you and Dalgren come in. We need to dispatch a swift messenger to bring word to King Thomas," said Thorgrimson.

"Someone Thomas knows and trusts," Cecile added with a smile. "Someone who knows ways to gain access to the palace."

"Dalgren and I will go!" Kate said eagerly.

Thorgrimson smiled. "I was hoping you would. I cannot reinstate Lord Dalgren to the Brigade, but I could accept you both as volunteers." He glanced askance at Kate's jury-rigged harness and added, "We will provide you with a saddle. Also whatever else you need: a uniform, gear, weapons."

"Rest here tonight," said Cecile. "The dragons have expressed their desire that you and Lord Dalgren attend the funeral. If it were not for your courage, we would be grieving many more dead."

"We can discuss the details of our proposal after you have rested," said Thorgrimson. "You will need to leave at first light tomorrow."

"Yes, sir," said Kate. All her life she had fought for her dreams and now the dream of being part of the Dragon Brigade was real.

But it still felt like a dream.

THIRTY-NINE

Henry Wallace spent his time in Wellinsport shut up in his cheerless room, observing the two Guundaran warships that had entered the harbor.

He sat at his window with a spyglass trained on the vessels, hoping to find proof for Alan and the governor that the Guundarans were secretly preparing to attack.

He searched for signs that the Guundarans were hiding troops on board the ships, keeping them stashed belowdecks. He watched to see if they were actually making repairs to the ships or if the damage had been a ruse to allow them to enter the harbor. He woke at midnight to take advantage of the full moon to note unusual activity on board the ships during the night.

Henry watched the Guundarans until his eyes ached and his vision blurred, and he saw no sign that the Guundarans were plotting anything nefarious . . . with one exception. They did not grant their sailors shore leave.

Generally, when ships were in port, their captains permitted the sailors to go ashore to take advantage of the pleasures Wellinsport had to offer. Governor Crichton had talked about how the tavern owners and madams would be counting on filling their coffers with Guundaran coins, but thus far they must be disappointed. The Guundaran sailors had not been allowed to leave the ships. Henry found that circumstance suspicious, though he knew Alan would not.

He could almost hear Alan's voice.

"Oh, for God's sake, Henry, they have urgent repairs to make to keep their ships from sinking. Of course, they're not going to let their crews go ashore to get stinking drunk."

As Henry sat at the window keeping watch, he also worried that he had not heard back from Mr. Sloan. He had allowed a day for Mr. Sloan to travel to Freeport and talk to Olaf, then a day to return, which meant Mr. Sloan should have been back by now. But as yet, Henry had heard nothing from his secretary.

That morning, Henry rubbed the stubble on his chin and decided he would have to leave his post long enough to visit the barber for a shave. He had kept the sling on his right arm in deference to Perry's advice, and attempted to shave himself using his left hand, with near disastrous results. He was starting out when he heard a knock on the door and opened it to find Mr. Sloan.

"You do not know how glad I am to see you!" Henry said, welcoming him inside. "I expected you days ago, and when you did not arrive I began to be concerned. Come in, come in."

"I am sorry, my lord. I was delayed by unforeseen circumstances. I trust my news will make up for any inconvenience you suffered."

Mr. Sloan was a highly disciplined man who prided himself on keeping his emotions in check. He was not given to transports of joy, nor did he permit himself to wallow in despair. Henry had once known Mr. Sloan, in a moment of great excitement, to raise an eyebrow. Henry detected a thrill in his voice, however, and he tingled with anticipation.

"I am afraid I have only one chair."

"You take the chair, my lord. I will sit on the bed." Mr. Sloan glanced out the window. "An excellent observation post. I assume you have been observing the Guundaran warships."

"Indeed I have, Mr. Sloan. But we can discuss them later. I can tell by the twinkle in your eye that you have momentous news."

"I was not aware that I 'twinkle,' my lord," said Mr. Sloan, looking shocked. "I will endeavor to correct such a lapse."

Henry smiled. "Just tell me the news, Mr. Sloan."

"Yes, my lord. I traveled to Freeport and spoke to Olaf and Akiel. I found what they had to say so interesting that I deemed you needed to hear them for yourself and I have brought them with me. We sailed on Olaf's small vessel, the *Barwich Rose*. Since I believed I would find you on board the *Terrapin*, the *Rose* docked alongside her in the Neck near the harbor entrance.

Not finding you there, I left Olaf and Akiel in the care of Captain Northrop and came to search for you."

"I suppose Alan told you he and I had a falling out," said Henry, grimacing.

"He said nothing, but I did notice a distinct coolness in his tone when he spoke of you, my lord. I am sorry to hear that. Perhaps my news will have a cheering effect."

"Go on with your tale," said Henry.

"I met Olaf in the Perky Parrot and asked if he had heard the story of the *Manuel Gomez*. He replied that he had heard it and, what's more, he knew the story to be true. It seems Olaf was in Wellinsport serving under Captain Fitzmaurice at the time and he saw the *Manuel Gomez* being towed into port. The ship's arrival occasioned great interest, for they had heard rumors that the crew had perished of the cold."

"You have thus far confirmed Simon's ghost story," said Henry. "I don't see, though, how that advances his claim."

"I have more to relate, my lord," said Mr. Sloan. "While Olaf was relating the tale to me, one of his customers—a gentleman known as 'Old Benito'— spoke up to say that it was common knowledge that the *Manuel Gomez* had ventured too near a place known somewhat romantically as the 'Wall of Frozen Fog.'

"Olaf scoffed at the notion, saying the Wall of Frozen Fog was an old wives' tale. Old Benito demanded to know with some heat if Olaf was calling him an old wife. Olaf stated that if the shoe fit Old Benito should wear it, at which point I feared the two elderly gentlemen were going to come to blows.

"Akiel settled the argument by saying that he had seen the Wall of Frozen Fog for himself, albeit from a distance. He said it was located south of a former pirate haunt known as Nydrian's Cove on the northern end of Whitefalls Island. I purchased several rounds of drinks and peace ensued."

"So you believe this Wall of Frozen Fog could be liquid Breath and Simon's crackpot theory could be true," Henry said, musing.

"We will not know for certain until we see for ourselves, my lord. Akiel swears to the veracity of his statement and I believe he saw *something* strange, though I cannot say what. He has offered to serve as our guide and Olaf has agreed to transport us to Nydrian's Cove in the *Barwich Rose*."

"I'll be damned. I certainly did not expect this. What do you think, Mr. Sloan? How did Akiel come across this wall?"

"According to him, he was traveling on board a ship that was in Nydrian's Cove searching for the treasure that was said to have been buried there by the Pirate King. The ship encountered a wall of thick white fog and experienced a severe drop in temperature, such that frost began to form on the masts.

"The sailors had all heard about the tragic fate of the *Manuel Gomez* and insisted that the captain leave the area. When he refused, the crew mutinied, took over the ship, and fled."

Henry remained irresolute, still unconvinced. "Did Akiel show you this location on a chart? Is it near where Simon claims we should find his White Well?"

"A chart was not available in the Parrot," said Mr. Sloan. "If the Wall of Frozen Fog is located inland, south of Nydrian's Cove, as he says, that would approximately correspond with Master Yates's readings. Olaf estimates the journey to this area should take about a half a day."

"Simon would never forgive us if we didn't investigate. The truth is that I don't like leaving Wellinsport right now. You saw the Guundaran warships?"

"I observed them as we entered the harbor, my lord," said Mr. Sloan. "Two docked and one in the channel."

"The Guundarans told Governor Crichton some cock-and-bull story about needing to make repairs and the fool gave them permission to enter. Our fleet is in Sornhagen chasing Rosians. Alan refused to support me and now Crichton is happily supplying the Guundarans with everything they require to invade his city! Bah!"

"Most unfortunate, my lord," said Mr. Sloan.

"Crichton will rue the day, Mr. Sloan," Henry predicted grimly.

He paused, staring at the ships out the window, then added with some bitterness, "On second thought, Mr. Sloan, I have no reason to stay in Wellinsport. I might as well sail off to fairyland and search for Simon's well."

"Very good, my lord. Nydrian's Cove is known to serve as a refuge to pirates who prey on shipping in the area. The *Rose* is a small vessel with no cannons, and I have only a brace of pistols. If we could obtain rifles, pistols, shot, and powder from Captain Northrop . . ."

Henry was grim. "I will ask nothing of Alan. We can purchase the weapons."

Mr. Sloan gave a deferential cough. "Such a large purchase would occasion considerable comment among the locals, my lord. I trust we would prefer to keep the nature of our journey secret."

"Oh, very well," Henry said crossly. "But you must talk to Alan. I will not!"

The *Barwich Rose* had belonged to Kate when she was engaged in the wrecking business, sailing to sites of shipwrecks in order to recover objects she could sell at auction.

The *Rose* was about forty years old and in her best days was charitably described as "serviceable." Kate had given the ship to Olaf when she left for Freya, and although his sailing days were past him, he liked keeping the *Rose* in working condition.

"In case Katydid should ever need her," Olaf told Henry as he boarded.

The *Rose* looked very small and shabby as she floated beside the mighty *Terrapin*. Her crew consisted of Olaf's patrons, some of the local Freeport "lads," the youngest of whom was about fifty.

Henry paced the small deck and kept an eye on the *Terrapin*. He had sent Mr. Sloan to deal with Alan and he could see the two of them talking together on the *Terrapin*'s foredeck. He knew Alan could see him, but his friend did not once acknowledge his presence.

Alan readily agreed to provide rifles and pistols, powder and ammunition, and ordered the crew of the *Terrapin* to transfer the supplies to the *Rose*. He waved to Olaf and bid him have a safe journey, then remained to watch the *Rose* cast off and head out into the Trame Channel.

Henry saw him, but pretended not to notice.

Once in the Trame Channel, the *Rose* left Wellinsport and sailed in a northwesterly direction that would take them up the coast of Whitefalls Island to Nydrian's Cove.

According to the legend, the infamous Pirate King would hide his ships in the cove, then swoop out into the channel to nab a prize. Alan had himself made use of the cove during his Rose Hawks days when he was a privateer, lying in wait for rich Rosian and Estaran merchant ships.

"Captain Northrop said he never encountered any frozen fog, my lord," said Mr. Sloan. "He wished us luck on our expedition."

"Humpf," said Henry.

The *Rose* did not provide the most luxurious mode of transportation, nor did it appear that safe. Olaf and the crewmen were all experienced sailors, and they swore that the *Rose* was air-worthy and reliable at least for the short distance she would have to travel.

The weather was typical of the Aligoes, which meant that one moment the sun was shining and the next dark clouds were dumping down rain. As the *Rose* chugged along the coastline of Whitefalls Island, Henry further questioned Akiel about the Wall of Frozen Fog.

"The captain of our ship was searching for the treasure of the Pirate King," said Akiel. "He had a map that he claimed came from the captain of the *Manuel Gomez*."

"The same *Manuel Gomez* whose crew froze to death," said Henry, intrigued.

"That is right, sir," said Akiel. "Some of the crew believed that the map was cursed and was going to lure us to our deaths. They tried to warn the captain, but he was a bad man who was very greedy. He said he did not believe in curses. We sailed inland and had not gone far before the air began to grow colder and colder and a wall of white blocked our way. The deck was coated with ice and it was so cold our teeth were chattering in our heads. The captain would have pushed on, but the crew was having none of it. They fell upon him and tied him to a mast and turned the ship around.

"I tried to stop them," Akiel added. "I told them I could speak to the spirits who were guarding the treasure, but the sailors said that the spirits were welcome to it."

Henry pondered the story as the ship sailed the Breath north along the rugged emerald-green coastline.

"Consider this possibility, Mr. Sloan. Suppose the treasure map was real?"

"I doubt if that is possible, my lord. According to historians, the Pirate King did not bury his treasure. He spent the vast majority—"

"Devil take historians, Mr. Sloan," Henry interrupted irritably.

"Very good, my lord."

"Suppose the treasure to which the map referred had nothing to do with the Pirate King," said Henry. "What if the treasure marked on the map was not gold. Instead it was the pool of liquid Breath."

"An interesting theory, my lord."

"Let us say Simon was not the first man with a scientific mind to note the odd natural occurrences in this area. Someone investigated, then set out on the *Manuel Gomez* to search for the pool. The ship found it, but something went wrong and they froze to death. No one was alive to tell the tale. Searchers found a map with references to wealth and fortune. Everyone would immediately leap to the conclusion that the map referred to pirate treasure."

"Highly plausible, my lord. A pool of liquid Breath would be worth far more than a hundred chests filled with gold and jewels," said Mr. Sloan.

"Such a discovery could make Freya one of the wealthiest nations in the world," said Henry wistfully. "But seeing is believing, as they say, Mr. Sloan, and until I have seen this pool, I refuse to allow myself to believe in it."

FORTY

The *Barwich Rose* reached Nydrian's Cove shortly after midday. Olaf did not remain in the cove long. Under Akiel's guidance, the ship sailed inland, flying over the blackened ruins of a once prosperous town.

Nydrian's Cove had been founded by wealthy plantation owners who grew indigo, logwood, and sugar cane. They had originally transported their cargo south to Wellinsport by ship, but after losing much of their cargo to pirates, the plantation owners had invested their money in building a road that ran from Nydrian's Cove to Wellinsport and began to send their goods overland.

The road became known as the Indigo Road, named for one of White-falls' most valuable crops.

During the Third Travian Trade War, the Indigo Road proved the salvation of Wellinsport when the city came under siege by the Travian cartels. The Indigo Road remained open, despite Travian efforts to cut it, and goods kept flowing, bringing relief to the city.

Following the war, Wellinsport realized the value of the overland route and built two forts at the northern entrance to the city, both to guard the road and to collect tolls used to maintain the forts.

Several years later, pirates formed an alliance with one of a long line of corrupt governors of Wellinsport and took over Nydrian's Cove. The governor agreed to turn a blind eye to their occupation of the town in return for a share of their spoils.

The good relations between the governor and the pirates ended during the war with the Bottom Dwellers, when the pirates formed an alliance with the Bottom Dwellers, seizing ships, taking slaves and transporting them Below to serve as sacrifices in their heinous blood magic rituals. The Freyan navy attacked the cove, drove out the pirates and the Bottom Dwellers, and in order to prevent their return, reduced the town to cinders.

Following the war, a few of the surviving rogues hoped to once again establish the cove as a base of operations. They repaired the dock and made a start at rebuilding the town, but that was as far as they got. The Freyan navy did not permit them to remain. Only a few pirates still lurked about the cove these days, hoping to catch a merchant ship unawares, but they rarely stayed long, avoiding naval patrols.

The plantation owners continued to rely on the overland routes to transport their goods and Nydrian's Cove remained abandoned. Nature was gradually reclaiming the land on which the town had been built. Vegetation thrust up through the blackened floorboards, and wooden buildings rotted away.

As Henry gazed down over the rail of the *Rose,* the thought came to him that if he discovered a pool of liquid Breath, Nydrian's Cove would be an ideal location for a mining town. He could picture the town prosperous and thriving once more with transport ships coming and going.

He banished the happy thought from his mind, refused to let himself think about it, figuring this way he would merely be confirmed in his belief that Simon had allowed his scientific theories to run amuck, rather than face bitter disappointment.

The *Rose* left the town behind and headed inland, traveling westward into an uninhabited part of the island. Henry worried that once they left the Breath, the ship would lose the benefit of the buoyancy that kept the *Rose* afloat, for the magic of the Breath did not extend far beyond the coast. Even though she had lift tanks, the *Rose* would eventually sink to the ground without the magic to keep her flying.

Akiel had assured him that the Wall of Frozen Fog was not far from the cove. Henry hoped he was right. He did not want to have to walk to find it, although he would if he must.

The air grew distinctly colder as the ship sailed farther west. Olaf's crew put on their pea coats and knit caps. Mr. Sloan brought Henry his greatcoat and assisted him in draping it over his shoulders.

"Not far now," Akiel stated.

Henry permitted himself a modicum of hope.

He was so interested in the search for Simon's well that he did not dwell on his injury, with the result that his shoulder did not pain him as much as when it was constantly on his mind. He disliked the sling, which discommoded him and hampered his movements. Since the pain had receded, he was strongly tempted to take it off, but he knew Mr. Sloan would look disapproving, quote Mr. Perry and his injunctions to wear it, and remind him that if anything happened, he could lose his arm. Henry deemed it easier to leave the sling in place.

As the *Rose* continued her journey westward, the air grew colder and wisps of chill fog materialized, trailing about the boat and wreathing the sails. Olaf's "lads" had all heard the story of the *Manuel Gomez:* Henry, remembering that her crew had frozen to death, asked Olaf if the "lads" were growing nervous and might be inclined to turn back.

Olaf reassured him. "I've known these men for years. Each put his mark to the contract they signed to work for me and they are true to their word. I did take the liberty of telling them you would give them a reward if we found Akiel's Wall of Frozen Fog. Fifty eagles per man. I asked Mr. Sloan and he did not think you would mind."

"If we find this well, I will give every man on this boat one hundred eagles," said Henry.

"Very generous, Sir Henry," said Olaf, nodding. "To be honest, the lads are more worried about the ghosts than the cold. Akiel promised them he would use his spirit magic to persuade them to leave us alone."

He cast a glance at the big man who was standing by the rail, gazing into the mists, his head cocked as though listening.

"Let us hope there are no spirits and we won't have to resort to any sort of magic," said Henry, hiding his smile.

"I agree with you there, my lord. Spirits are a cantankerous lot," said Olaf. "A damned nuisance. I remember that time Kate salvaged a helm when she was out wrecking. The ship's captain had died at the helm and his spirit wouldn't let her take it. He kept knocking her hand away. Akiel claimed he talked to the dead and the spirit relented and gave Kate the helm. But I had my doubts."

"Any sane person would," Henry remarked.

"I don't think that damn spirit left," said Olaf grumpily. "Blasted helm never did work properly."

The *Rose* sailed on, the air grew colder, and the fog grew thicker. They were far inland, traveling away from the Breath, and the ship should be starting to lose altitude. Henry was surprised that it wasn't.

"Perhaps you should not be surprised, my lord," said Mr. Sloan. "The fact that we are not sinking could prove that Master Yates is right. We are near a pool of liquid Breath."

Henry considered this possibility with mounting excitement. "Simon theorized that such a pool would emit 'fumes' of magic. Perhaps those could be keeping the *Rose* afloat."

"We are close, very close, my lord," said Akiel. "I can hear voices."

"Voices?" Henry repeated, alarmed. "Are they speaking Guundaran? Rosian?"

"The voices belong to the dead, my lord, and they warn us to keep our distance," Akiel replied. "The dead have no allegiance to any nation."

Olaf looked at Henry. "Do we sail on, my lord?"

"Of course, we sail on!" said Henry, exasperated. "Did you ever hear such foolishness?" he added in an undertone to Mr. Sloan.

"Indeed not, my lord," said Mr. Sloan. "Dead or not, I will still be a Freyan."

Olaf spoke to the helmsman and the *Rose* sailed ahead, though he did slow her speed. The fog grew thicker. Henry could feel the moisture on his skin. Frost formed on the deck and coated the rigging. Those on board stamped their feet and blew on their fingers to try to keep warm.

"I do hear something, my lord," said Mr. Sloan, cocking his head. "A wailing moan. It has a very human-like quality."

"Nonsense," Henry said, trying to ignore the fact that he could hear the eerie sound, as well.

The members of the crew began casting glances at each other and muttering among themselves.

"My lord! Look at that!" Mr. Sloan exclaimed.

"The Wall of Frozen Fog," said Akiel solemnly. "Thus do I remember it."

A barrier of white, radiating cold, materialized in front of the *Rose*. At that moment, Henry became aware of a sudden, ominous silence.

"The airscrews have stopped working," he said grimly.

Olaf started swearing and hobbled over to the helm. Shoving the helmsman aside, Olaf ran his hand over the brass helm. He waited a moment; nothing happened. Muttering something, he tried again. No comforting whirring sound came from the airscrews. He sent the crew to check to make certain the leather braids connecting the helm to the airscrews were still attached, nothing frayed or broken. They reported that all was well.

"What is wrong?" Henry asked.

"Magic is no longer flowing from the helm, my lord. The airscrews have stopped working and so have the lift tanks. I have no idea why."

"The spirits are in control," Akiel stated. "We are not wanted."

Henry was shivering uncontrollably. "Spirits in control! Utter nonsense! There must be a logical explanation!"

"The loss of power *would* solve the mystery of the *Manuel Gomez,* my lord," said Mr. Sloan. "The crew was not able to escape and thus froze to death."

"Small comfort if we solve the mystery by dying the same way," Henry retorted. "I refuse to accept the idea of ghosts taking over a ship!"

Mr. Sloan looked down over the rail. "The ship is starting to sink, my lord."

"Damnation!" Henry swore. Although he was not a sailor, knew nothing about seafaring magic, and had no idea what he was looking at, he stomped over to the helm to see for himself. "There must be something you can do," he said to Olaf.

"There is," said Olaf grimly. "Akiel, tell those dratted spirits of yours to stop mucking about with my ship!"

"I will confer with them," said Akiel.

Mr. Sloan raised an eyebrow and cast a glance at Henry.

"I'll try anything," he muttered.

Akiel descended belowdecks and returned carrying a candle. Standing at the ship's prow, he faced the wall of white, and raised the candle, but did not light it. Placing his thumb and forefinger on the candle's wick, he began whispering. He removed his finger and thumb and the wick burst into flame. The wailing moan increased in intensity.

"I can hear them clearly. The spirits are the crew of the *Manuel Gomez,*" Akiel stated. "They warn us to turn back. They do not want to harm us. They are trying to save us."

"Then they have a funny way of going about it," Olaf stated angrily. "The *Rose* is sinking! Tell them to take their dead hands off my helm!"

"They say we have been warned," said Akiel, shrugging. "If we continue on, we will share their sad fate."

"Without a helm, how are we supposed to do anything else!" Olaf demanded.

The *Rose,* carried forward by momentum, drifted closer to the wall of fog. Henry peered over the rail. The mists flowing from the white wall writhed beneath the keel, which was about thirty feet above the ground and sinking fast.

He watched the mists in a kind of strange fascination, as the ship floated through the fog, and saw an enormous fissure in the ground filled with gray, undulating liquid like thick gravy that had grown cold and congealed. He remembered thinking the same when he had been in the refinery at Braffa, observing the pools of liquid Breath. Simon was right.

They say that when facing death, atheists become believers. In that moment, acting out of desperation and having found what he sought, Henry became a believer.

"Akiel, tell the spirits that we will honor their sacrifice. We will name the well the *Manuel Gomez*."

He turned around, only to find that Akiel had disappeared. "Where is Akiel?"

"Down here, my lord," said Olaf, pointing underneath the helm.

Henry saw Akiel lying flat on the deck, his head and shoulders underneath the helm, holding the candle to the underside. Within a few moments, Henry heard the welcome sound of airscrews whirring to life. The lift tanks began to glow blue as the magic flowed into them.

Akiel emerged from beneath the helm.

"No one checked the lines attached to the brass. Turns out they were coated with ice. I thawed them out."

He winked at Henry. "And by the way, my lord, the spirits say to thank you. They will let us depart now."

The *Rose* anchored near the pool long enough for Mr. Sloan to take readings and do what he could to determine their location. While he worked, Henry went belowdecks to the captain's cabin to attempt to try to warm up. Mr. Sloan joined him to note the longitude and latitude on a chart and the *Rose* set sail.

Henry gazed at the map. "Simon will revel in his triumph over us, Mr. Sloan. If we ever again dare to doubt him, he will answer with only two words: 'White Well.'"

"An acceptable price to pay for the sake of our country, my lord," said Mr. Sloan.

"It will be, Mr. Sloan," said Henry. He thought of the Guundaran ships in the harbor. "Providing we still have a country."

FORTY-ONE

Alan Northrop had been spending his time in Wellinsport supervising the repairs to the *Terrapin,* keeping watch on ship movements in the Trame Channel, and struggling to write a report to the Admiralty. He had to find a way to inform Their Lordships that thus far Wellinsport was not under attack and despite what he had told Henry about the Rosian navy hiding among the islands, he did not truly believe the Rosians had ever harbored any notion of attacking Wellinsport.

Alan was angry at being sent on this fool's errand and he was forced to tear up two brutally honest versions of his report that would have probably ended his career in the navy. He was laboring over a third when a midshipman came to tell him that a passenger on board a shore boat was hailing the *Terrapin,* requesting permission to come aboard.

"Henry is here to apologize," Alan said to himself as he went up on deck. "Though I admit he was right about the Rosians, he was wrong in demanding that I disobey orders. He must see that by now."

He was prepared to welcome him aboard, but the passenger seated in the bow of the shore boat was not Henry. He was a griffin-messenger by the looks of it, for he was wearing a helm and a long leather coat such as those worn by griffin riders.

Alan guessed the messenger was from the Admiralty, bringing new orders. Fortunately, the repairs to the *Terrapin* were nearly completed. The ship could be ready to set sail within the hour. He would be glad to leave. He didn't care where.

The shore boat did not bother to tie up alongside the *Terrapin,* but landed directly on the aft part of the deck.

"I need to speak to Captain Northrop!" the messenger stated. "The matter is urgent."

A crew member directed the messenger to the quarterdeck and he came on the run. Alan advanced to meet him. He was about to introduce himself when the messenger took off his helm.

"Alan! It's me. Pip!"

Alan stared, amazed. Phillip Masterson, Duke of Upper and Lower Milton, had been a member of Alan's infamous crew of privateers known as the Rose Hawks, and had gone on to become one of Henry's most trusted agents. He had sent Phillip to spy on Thomas Stanford when Henry had been convinced Thomas was attempting to usurp the Freyan throne. Phillip had shifted his allegiance to Thomas, with the result that a furious Henry had declared him a traitor.

Alan didn't know whose side Phillip was on now, but he wasn't taking chances.

He turned to the captain of the marines. "Take this man into custody. Search him for weapons."

Phillip raised his hands in the air.

"I'm not armed, Alan. I have an urgent message for Sir Henry."

He kept his hands raised as two marines roughly took hold of him and did a thorough search, turning out his pockets and patting him down, even to his boots.

"His Majesty, King Thomas, sent me. Alan," Phillip persisted, "I need to speak to Henry! Where is he? I have to warn him about the Guundarans!"

Alan looked at the third Guundaran ship that was just now starting to enter the harbor.

"Damn it all to hell!" Alan muttered.

"His Majesty's letter is inside my coat, Alan," Phillip said. "Let me show it to you."

"Move slowly," said Alan.

Phillip opened his coat and gingerly reached into a hidden pocket sewn inside the lining. He drew out Thomas's letter and handed it to one of the marines, who took it and gave it to Alan. The letter was sealed with the royal seal of His Majesty, the King of Freya.

Alan recognized the seal, but he did not immediately open the letter.

"Release him," he ordered. "I will speak to you in my cabin, Your Grace."

"I must talk to Sir Henry," Phillip insisted.

"He is not on board," said Alan. "He is staying at that disreputable boarding house where he always lodges when he's in Wellinsport."

"No, he isn't," said Phillip, as he accompanied Alan down the stairs. "I tried that place first. I arrived last night and went to see him. His landlady said he had packed his things and left. I assumed he had returned to the ship. I was going to come immediately, but the shore boats do not run after dark and I was dead tired. I had a chance to eat and snatch a few hours of sleep and came as soon as the boats were running this morning. Where has Henry gone?"

"Out of his mind," said Alan.

Phillip blinked, startled. Alan closed the door and gestured to him to take a seat.

"You mentioned the Guundarans. Tell me what is going on."

Phillip wearily dropped into a chair. "Read the letter. It is meant for Sir Henry, but Thomas would want you to know, especially as he sent me with a message to you. King Ullr has sent the *Terrapin* into an ambush. Those three Guundaran warships are here to attack Wellinsport. I saw two more in the Trame Channel, heading this way. Ullr has sent this fleet to make a surprise attack on the city and to either capture or sink the *Terrapin*."

Alan broke the seal and read the letter. He then folded it up and sat with it in his hand, tapping it on the desk. "Henry suspected King Ullr was up to no good. He warned the governor not to allow the Guundaran ships to enter the harbor."

"I take it the governor refused to listen, since I saw the Guundaran ships tied up at the dock," said Phillip.

"Damn it, Henry had no proof!" Alan said angrily. "How could I start an international incident over Henry having a bad feeling in his gut?"

He flung the king's letter onto the desk. Phillip retrieved it and slid it back into his pocket.

"What did the Guundarans tell the governor?"

"That they had suffered damage in a wizard storm. I have kept a watch on them since and I believe Henry was right. The damage was superficial, designed for show. Although . . ." Alan frowned and fell silent, thinking.

"What is it?" Phillip asked.

"Something doesn't make sense. The warships in the harbor are directly under the guns of the shore batteries. Our cannons will pound them to kindling the moment they open fire. The Guundarans would first have to silence the batteries. They must be planning to send a raiding party."

Phillip sat forward in his chair. "They don't have to go to all that bother. What forces are manning the batteries? Freyan army? Mercenaries . . . ?"

Alan stared at Phillip in sudden, awful understanding. "Mercenaries," he said grimly. "Guundaran mercenaries."

"They attack at midnight, catch everyone in their beds, slit their throats and the shore batteries are theirs," said Phillip. "Where is the Aligoes Fleet?"

"Sornhagen," said Alan.

"Good God!" Phillip was shocked. "What are they doing in Sornhagen?"

"Chasing their own tails, apparently," said Alan bitterly.

He gave a brief thought to what might have happened if he had done as Henry had asked, disobeyed his orders and returned to Haever. Wellinsport would have fallen without a shot fired. If he survived, which seemed unlikely given the odds, he would remind Henry of that. He might have come for the wrong reason, but he was in the right place.

"How long ago did the fleet leave?" Phillip was asking. "I have my griffin stabled nearby. I can carry a message to Admiral Tower."

"I will send one of my midshipmen," said Alan. "You need to find Henry, give him the king's letter."

"His Lordship will undoubtedly shoot me before I get a word out," Phillip predicted.

"Henry won't shoot. His arm is in a sling," said Alan, adding with a grin, "Mr. Sloan will be happy to oblige, however. Henry must have sailed to Nydrian's Cove. You remember that place. We used to hide out there in the Rose Hawks days."

"I remember a burned-out ghost town," said Phillip, sounding dubious. "What is Henry doing in that godforsaken part of the island?"

"Looking for a Wall of Frozen Fog," said Alan. "It's a long story. I'll send you in the *Terrapin*'s pinnace. Henry is traveling in Kate's old ship, the *Barwich Rose,* which you know, so you shouldn't have trouble finding it. Mr. Sloan said the plan was to spend the day searching for this wall, then return to the cove. You can meet up with him there. I'll dispatch messengers to the governor and the forts. We might be too late, but we have to try. You should leave now if you want to reach the cove by afternoon."

"Captain, sir," said a midshipman, opening the door. "Lookout reports two Guundaran warships sailing this way."

Alan and Phillip hurried up onto the deck. Alan ordered the crew to have his pinnace ready to sail. He first trained his spyglass on the batteries. He could not see anything amiss, but he probably wouldn't until the Guundarans lowered the Freyan flag and triumphantly raised their own.

He next trained the glass on the two approaching vessels.

"The *King of Guundar* and the *Hoffnagle*. Sixty-eight guns in each," said Alan. He snapped the glass shut. "Henry always said I had the devil's own luck. Looks like the devil has come to collect his due."

FORTY-TWO

The *Rose* left the pool of liquid Breath at around noon to sail back to Nydrian's Cove. Henry remained in the captain's cabin, working with Mr. Sloan to estimate the worth of the pool, which they both judged was far larger than the pool in Braffa.

Henry had long dreamed of this day, without truly believing his dream would ever come to pass. Simon's discovery would save Freya from financial ruin, transform his nation from a pauper to a prince among nations, place her upon an equal footing with her rivals, Rosia and Estara. Henry should have been jubilant. Instead he had never felt so downhearted.

"I fear we have gone to all this trouble only to enrich that bastard, Ullr, Mr. Sloan. Guundar will seize the well and claim it for their own."

He would have proceeded with his gloomy predictions, but a knock on the door interrupted him. Akiel thrust his head inside.

"Olaf says to tell you that we are within sight of Nydrian's Cove, sir, and that another boat has anchored there."

"Guundaran?" Henry asked, alarmed.

Akiel shook his head. "Olaf thinks it's a ship's boat from the *Terrapin*."

"I'm not taking any chances. I will hide this chart," said Henry. "Go with

Akiel, Mr. Sloan. Remind the crew that they are not to breathe a word of our discovery to anyone."

Mr. Sloan accompanied Akiel above deck, leaving Henry to swiftly roll up the chart and look for a place to hide it. He stashed it in a cubby hole already filled with other charts, and strolled up on the deck.

"What is going on, Mr. Sloan?"

"Olaf was right: the pinnace is from the *Terrapin,* my lord," Mr. Sloan reported. "Captain Northrop's own."

"Alan would not send his pinnace unless the matter was urgent," said Henry. "I fear this bodes ill, Mr. Sloan."

Dusk was falling, but he could see the pinnace tied up at the dock. The crew had remained on board the boat, while a man on the dock paced back and forth. Henry could only see him in silhouette against the backdrop of a flaming red sky.

"I don't recognize him," said Henry. "Although something about the way the fellow walks does seem familiar, Mr. Sloan."

"It should, my lord," said Mr. Sloan, whose eyesight was better than that of his employer. "Unless I am much mistaken, that is His Grace, Phillip Masterson, the Duke of Upper and Lower Milton."

"By God, you are right, Mr. Sloan." Henry scowled and started to reach for his pistol, only to be painfully reminded that his arm was in a sling. "What the devil is he doing here?"

"I would say we are about to find out, my lord."

A crewman aboard the pinnace alerted Phillip to the *Rose*'s approach. He turned to face them and, sighting Henry, gave him a tentative smile and a wave, while the *Terrapin*'s crew stood ready to catch the lines that would tether the *Rose* to the pier.

"Once we dock, Mr. Sloan, please be so good as to take His Grace into custody."

"I would be glad to do so, my lord, but I would be remiss in my duties if I did not remind Your Lordship that His Grace is the king's best friend. He is in a ship's boat belonging to the *Terrapin* and he knew where to find us. It is logical to assume that Captain Northrop sent him."

Henry glowered. "Logic be damned. He betrayed me. Hold him at gunpoint until I learn his business."

"With pleasure, my lord," said Mr. Sloan.

The crew of the *Rose* lowered the gangplank. Once it was down, Mr. Sloan and Henry left the *Rose* and advanced to meet Phillip, who remained on the wharf. Mr. Sloan had drawn his pistol and was holding it in plain view. Phillip glanced at the pistol and gave a faint smile.

"I promise you will not need your weapon, Mr. Sloan. I am not armed. I come with one message from His Majesty, the king, and another from Alan. He sent me to inform you that two more Guundaran warships have entered the channel."

"Five warships! What the devil is Ullr plotting?" Henry muttered.

"I have the answer, my lord," said Phillip. "To put it succinctly, King Ullr is planning to seize Wellinsport, ambush the *Terrapin,* and invade Freya during the Hallen Day celebration."

The shadow of the mountain engulfed the boat, flowing over the dock as the sun set and casting a dark pall over Henry.

"I have a letter from His Majesty," Phillip continued. "If I may—"

He reached into the inner pocket of his coat. Mr. Sloan raised his pistol.

"Careful, Your Grace," said Mr. Sloan.

Phillip slowly drew out the letter and handed it to Mr. Sloan, who conveyed it to Henry. He recognized the royal insignia.

"The seal is broken," he observed.

"I allowed Alan to read the letter, my lord," said Phillip. "He needed to know."

"Come on board the *Rose,*" said Henry. "We can talk there. I believe you know Olaf?"

"Indeed, I do," said Phillip, boarding the *Rose* and shaking hands with Olaf.

"I don't suppose you've seen our Katydid, have you, Master Pip?" Olaf asked.

"I left her in Haever only a few days ago, Olaf," said Phillip. "She and Dalgren are well. She knew I was coming to the Aligoes and said that if I saw you, I was to give you her love and tell you that she would write soon."

Olaf shook his head. "Donkeys will fly before Katydid writes anyone a letter. But thank you, Master Pip."

Mr. Sloan lighted a lantern and Henry read the letter in the cabin of the *Rose.* He read it through twice to make certain he understood. The missive was brief and to the point.

"How did His Majesty uncover this plot?" Henry asked.

Phillip smiled. "You remember the portrait of King Godfrey, my lord."

Henry did indeed remember the portrait. King Godfrey had ordered Henry to devise a means for him to spy on his guests in the palace and Henry had conceived the idea of the painting.

He had made use of it himself on numerous occasions in the service of both Godfrey and, later, Queen Mary. He smiled, remembering how she had not permitted him to spy on her guests and insisted that the portrait be removed.

Then came the day the griffins belonging to a Travian count had defeated hers in a race. The queen's trainer had suspected the count was mixing a magical potion into the food and Mary had ordered Henry to find out if that was true. He had made use of the painting to discover that she was right and Mary had banished the count and his griffins. After that, she had reluctantly agreed that the portrait could stay, though she had often grumbled about it.

"Put away the pistol, Mr. Sloan," said Henry. "My apologies for not trusting you, Your Grace, although I believe you would agree that you gave me just cause."

"Indeed, my lord, my one regret in aligning myself with Thomas was the knowledge that you and Queen Mary would believe me to be a traitor."

"If it is any comfort, Your Grace, Queen Mary never lost faith in you," said Henry. "She made Thomas her heir based primarily on your highly favorable recommendation."

"Thank you, my lord," said Phillip. "That means a great deal to me. What is the plan?"

Henry wondered that himself. His primary concern was the safety of the chart marking the location of the pool. He had to make certain that Simon received it in case something happened to him. Henry considered sending Phillip to Simon, but he abandoned that as being too dangerous. Smythe would have his soldiers searching the country for Phillip and he did not dare risk having the chart fall into the wrong hands. For the same reason, he could not send Mr. Sloan or go himself.

Phillip's mention of Kate gave Henry an idea. He went up on deck to speak to Akiel and Olaf. Night had fallen. Olaf had invited the pinnace's crew on board the *Rose* to share a bottle of Calvados and the latest news. The sailors scrambled to their feet when Henry appeared on deck. He motioned them to be seated.

"I have a great favor to ask of you, Olaf," said Henry, motioning him to the stern, where they could speak in private. "Mr. Sloan has recorded the location of the pool of liquid Breath on this chart. I need you to take it to the Parrot and keep it safe. I will send Mr. Sloan to retrieve it once I am convinced all is well in Freya."

"Rest assured I will take good care of the map, my lord," Olaf stated, accepting the chart.

"Thank you, Olaf. Mr. Sloan, transfer the rifles and pistols from the *Rose* to the pinnace."

Mr. Sloan transferred the rifles and pistols to the *Rose,* along with several bull's-eye lanterns and other supplies he thought might be necessary. He and

Phillip assisted Olaf and Akiel to cast off the lines, and the *Rose* sailed out into the Breath.

Henry watched the ship until her lights were lost to sight in the darkness and hoped that his dreams for his country were not disappearing along with it.

He turned to Phillip. "How did you travel, Your Grace?"

"Griffin-back, my lord," Phillip said. "I left the beast at a hostelry in Wellinsport to await my return."

"Excellent. I would like you to go to Rosia. I would rather swallow poison than to beg King Renaud for help, but we need troops, ships, whatever he can provide to repel this invasion. He and the Countess de Marjolaine put Thomas on the throne. The least they can do is help him hold onto it."

"The countess has no love for me, but she does love Thomas," said Phillip. "I will do as you ask, my lord."

"Thank you, Your Grace," said Henry. "We will transport you to Wellinsport in the pinnace. Mr. Sloan and I will proceed from there to the *Terrapin*."

"You could find yourself in the midst of a heated battle, my lord," Phillip warned. "Alan has no intention of allowing the Guundarans to succeed in their plan to take Wellinsport or the *Terrapin*."

Henry smiled. "I've been in heated battles before. Besides, Alan owes me an apology. It will be worth risking my life to hear it."

Henry was not about to admit it, but the truth was, he didn't want words of anger to perhaps be the last words he spoke to his friend. The *Terrapin* was, in a way, as much his ship as it was Alan's; a ship protected by magically enhanced metal plates had been Henry's idea. He would not allow that bastard Ullr to get his hands on it.

"Mr. Sloan and I will join you in the pinnace, Your Grace. What is the fastest route back to Wellinsport?"

"On the advice of the helmsman, we traveled overland, following the Indigo Road," said Phillip. "Since the pinnace does not require the amount of lift a large ship such as the *Terrapin* requires, we did not need to rely on the Breath."

"Tell the helmsman to convey us back the same way," said Henry.

Phillip relayed the message to the helmsman, then he and Henry and Mr. Sloan found seats.

Intended to be used to ferry men and supplies to shore, the pinnace was twenty-eight feet long with a six-foot beam and a single mast with one sail and two balloons. Three small lift tanks provided lift. A ballast tank insured stability. The small boat was equipped with two airscrews, making it fast and maneuverable.

The pinnace set sail, gliding over land in the dark, heading south. The moon would not rise until after midnight, which was about six hours away. The sky was cloudless, for a change. When the moon did rise, it would be a winter moon: full and bright.

The pinnace made good time, assisted by a tail wind that helped push them along. Phillip fell asleep sitting up, his head slumped on his chest. Mr. Sloan checked the weapons with the aid of a dark lantern to make certain none had suffered damage from the magical fumes of the pool.

Henry sat in gloomy contemplation of a future that looked to him very bleak and hopeless. He started thinking about his broken shoulder again, with the result that the pain returned and he wished he had thought to ask Mr. Sloan to bring along one of Olaf's bottles of Calvados. He eventually dozed off, waking when Mr. Sloan touched his arm.

"The lights of Wellinsport are in sight, my lord."

At this point in their journey, the Indigo Road ran almost straight down the side of the mountain. From their higher elevation, Henry could see the lights of the city shining far below, forming a bright crescent around the Deep Breath harbor, which was pitch black by contrast.

Phillip woke up at the news, grimaced, and stood to work out the kinks in his back. He yawned and ran his hand through his hair, then started to sit back down. He suddenly snapped to alertness.

"That sounded like cannon fire," he said.

Henry had also heard the dull, flat boom, which was followed by another and yet another.

"The Guundaran warships must have opened fire on the batteries," said Henry.

"I don't think so, my lord," said Phillip gravely. "That's not cannon fire. Those are rockets."

Three fiery trails soared into the sky, reached their zenith and then plunged straight down.

"The warships are not attacking the batteries, my lord," said Mr. Sloan. "They are shelling the city."

They heard more booms and watched as a great many more fiery trails blazed into the sky.

"I cannot believe even Ullr would commit such an atrocity," Henry said, appalled. "No civilized nation makes war on innocent civilians!"

People in Wellinsport would be home with their families, putting children to bed, writing letters, reading books. Or they would be out on the town, enjoying performances in the theaters and opera houses, losing money in the gambling dens, sharing drinks with comrades in the taverns. They would be doing the things they did every night and suddenly their lives would change—or come to a sudden and brutal end.

He waited for the shore batteries in Fort Godfrey and Fort Alfred to open fire on the enemy ships, hoping against hope that he'd been wrong about the Guundaran mercenaries seizing control. Nothing happened. The guns remained silent.

"As I feared," said Henry grimly. "The forts have fallen without a shot being fired. Damn it, we must do something to stop this outrage!"

"Captain Northrop will deal with them, my lord," said Mr. Sloan.

"Not even Alan can take on five warships!" Henry retorted, despairing as he watched more fiery trails soar into the heavens.

"Never underestimate Alan, my lord," said Phillip. "As you always say, he has the devil's own luck."

"Begging your pardon, my lord," Mr. Sloan interrupted. "The helmsman wants to know if we still want to sail to the *Terrapin*—"

"Yes, certainly—"

Henry was suddenly half-blinded by the dazzling light of a signal flare that soared into the air and burst directly over their heads, momentarily bathing the surroundings in a bright red glow. By its light, Henry saw what appeared to be several large barges filled with soldiers almost dead ahead of them. Some of the barges were in the air, while others had already landed.

"Hush! Not a sound!" Phillip called in a loud whisper. "No one move!"

The bright glow faded. Henry could no longer see the barges, but he could hear the whirring of large airscrews only a short distance ahead.

"Stop the boat," Phillip ordered urgently. "We're practically on top of them!"

The helmsman reacted immediately to reduce the flow of magic to the lift tanks and the airscrews. They whirred to a stop, and the blue glow of the lift tank faded away. The pinnace hung motionless in the air for a moment, then began to drift down toward the ground.

"Land there," Phillip whispered, pointing.

The helmsman brought the boat down in a sugar cane field near a grove of trees. They were within sight of the two tollhouses manned by the local militia, whose primary duty was to collect the tolls used by the city to maintain the Indigo Road. Their secondary duty was to prevent an invading army from entering the city by way of the road, though such a thing had never happened in the city's history.

The tollhouses were small, squat fortifications built on either side of the road. A fence with a gate in the middle stretched between the two, blocking entry. The toll takers stopped everyone to collect the toll and ask their business. After travelers had paid, the toll takers would open the gate.

Lights shone in the windows of the tollhouses. Travelers arrived at all hours and the toll takers had to be awake to open the gate. Henry had no doubt that every man inside would have been wakened by the sounds of the shelling.

Those in the pinnace waited in tense silence for the warning shout that would mean someone on one of those barges had seen them. Minutes passed and no one raised the alarm. Everyone started to breathe again.

Phillip crawled over the benches to speak to Henry and Mr. Sloan.

"Those are Guundaran troop transport barges, my lord."

"What the devil are the Guundaran soldiers doing in the middle of a sugar cane field?" Henry demanded, baffled.

"Good question," said Phillip. "I will find out, my lord."

Before Henry could say a word, Phillip jumped nimbly over the side and landed in the sugar cane field, which had recently been harvested, to judge by the stubble left behind. He disappeared into the night, his boots crunching on what remained of the stalks.

Mr. Sloan cast a worried, questioning glance at Henry. "How will His Grace find out, my lord?"

"Phillip speaks Guundaran like a native," Henry answered.

Mr. Sloan nodded, satisfied.

Henry kept watch, staring into the darkness at the barges until his eyes ached. He could see almost nothing except now and then the flash of a dark lantern. He could hear a great deal, however: men giving orders, boots shuffling, rifle butts thumping on wood, muffled swearing.

Henry removed the sling and tossed it onto the deck.

"Hand me a pistol, Mr. Sloan," he said. "Distribute weapons to the rest of the crew."

Mr. Sloan pressed a pistol into Henry's hand and stealthily and silently placed a rifle on the bench beside him, then handed out rifles and pistols to the crew. They sat unmoving, waiting for Phillip's return.

The moon rose, spreading pale light over the field. Phillip had chosen the landing site well. The pinnace had come down in the shadow of a grove of trees. Henry could now clearly see the large transport barges on the road ahead of them. The soldiers were lining up on the road, forming into ranks.

After what seemed an interminable amount of time, he heard someone hurriedly crunching through the field, approaching the pinnace. The man came into view. He was wearing a Guundaran uniform.

Mr. Sloan and Henry and half the crew raised their weapons.

"It's me! Pip! Don't shoot!" Phillip called in a piercing whisper.

He climbed into the pinnace. His hands were covered in blood, and he grimaced as he wiped them on a handkerchief, then tossed it aside. Seeing the blood, Henry had no need to ask Phillip how he had come by the coat.

Phillip motioned for Henry and Mr. Sloan to come close so they could hear.

"The Guundarans are here to rob the Bank of Wellinsport," he said softly.

Henry stared, speechless with astonishment.

"I know, my lord. I didn't believe it either," said Phillip. "I put on this coat, then approached a commander to ask in my best Guundaran for him to clarify his orders. He told me that I was a dunderhead who had no business being an officer in the Guundaran army, and then confirmed that we were here to rob a bank.

"They are using the shelling of the city as a diversion. Part of this force will attack the two forts that guard the toll bridge and hold them to protect their rear flank. The remainder of this force will enter the city under the cover of the confusion and chaos of the shelling to seize the bank. The main Guundaran force is on board the two warships in the harbor. They will land once the shelling has softened up the city."

"The Bank of Wellinsport . . ." Henry repeated, puzzled. "Why would the Guundarans want to rob it?"

Mr. Sloan suddenly sat bolt upright. "The Bank of Wellinsport, my lord! The gold reserves . . ."

Henry jumped to his feet. "We have to stop them. Tell the helmsman."

"My lord, hush, they will hear you!" Phillip warned, trying to urge Henry to sit down.

"That cannot be helped," said Henry grimly. "If the Guundarans succeed in robbing the bank, King Ullr will have no need to invade Freya. He can declare victory this very night. Freya will have no choice but to surrender."

FORTY-THREE

Henry gave a hurried explanation. "When Her Majesty was first diagnosed with a fatal illness and the matter of the succession was undecided, the Privy Council feared civil war. They deemed it would be prudent to transfer the gold and silver reserves of the nation from the Freyan Royal Treasury to the Bank of Wellinsport as a hedge against political and currency risks. We carried out the transfer successfully, with the utmost secrecy. Or so we thought," he added grimly. "The Guundarans must have found out."

"Queen Mary used to say there were more spies than vermin in the palace, my lord," said Phillip. "Thomas told me he overheard King Ullr laughing with Baron Grimm about Freya 'paying for her own destruction.' Neither of us knew what he meant at the time."

"He must have meant this," said Henry. "When our people become aware that the gold and silver reserves are in the hands of the Guundarans, they will flock to the banks to demand money that won't be there. The entire Freyan financial system will collapse. Freya will be plunged into ruin."

"How many men are in the barges, Your Grace?" Mr. Sloan asked.

"I estimate a force of three hundred or more. Elite troops. How many men in the tollhouses?"

"Twenty-five, at the most," said Henry. "Local militia."

"They will observe the shelling, my lord, and they will be worried about the fate of their families in Wellinsport," said Mr. Sloan. "We must assume that some or all may have abandoned their posts to go to their families."

"I cannot say I would blame them," said Henry.

"We must alert the tollhouses, if anyone is there," said Phillip. "I'll tell the helmsman."

"The Guundarans will be aware of our presence, my lord," Mr. Sloan observed.

"Then we should prepare for a fight," said Henry. "Tell the helmsman to crank up those airscrews as fast as they will go."

The helmsman sent magic to the lift tanks and the airscrews. The lift tanks glowed blue, and the airscrews hummed to life. The helmsman increased the flow of magic. The airscrews whirred loudly and the pinnace surged forward.

The Guundarans immediately caught sight of the pinnace and realized they had been discovered. They raised the alarm, pointing and shouting and grabbing their rifles.

Everyone ducked except the helmsman, who valiantly remained at his post. The Guundaran elite troops were well-trained and excellent shots. The first volley struck the helmsman, and he collapsed onto the deck, his face covered in blood. Phillip jumped up to take his place at the helm, crouching as low as he could while keeping his hands on the brass panel.

The second volley hit one of the airscrews. Henry heard the ominous sound of metal striking metal and the airscrew ground to a halt. The pinnace slowed.

Henry risked lifting his head to see how close they were to the tollhouses. A bullet slammed into the bulwark, nearly taking off his ear, and he ducked back down.

"Half a mile," he reported. "At least now the militia will be warned."

Another Guundaran shot hit the second airscrew and it crunched to a halt.

"We are going down, gentlemen," Phillip shouted. "Hold tight! The landing will be a rough one!"

Henry grabbed hold of the hull as the keel plowed into the sugar cane field, cutting a wide swath through the mud and the stubble until the pinnace finally lurched to a stop.

"Are you all right, my lord?" Mr. Sloan asked.

"I am, Mr. Sloan," Henry stated, picking himself up off the deck. He looked to see how everyone else had fared.

The crew members had gathered around their fallen comrade. Phillip gave Henry a wave to let him know he was well, and knelt down to tend to the wounded man.

Henry glanced back at the Guundarans. Having achieved their objective in bringing down the pinnace, their officers gave orders to cease fire and return to their task of unloading the barges. If the Guundarans had been counting on the element of surprise, that was gone, for both tollhouses now blazed with light.

"Mr. Sloan, run to the tollhouse and warn them they are about to come under attack."

Mr. Sloan hesitated. "I don't like leaving you and His Grace, my lord."

"We will be right behind you," said Henry. "Phillip and I will meet you at the tollhouse."

Mr. Sloan started off through the field, running and stumbling over the rough terrain in the darkness.

Henry went to check on the helmsman and was pleased to see he had regained consciousness and was on his feet.

"Bullet grazed his head," Phillip reported. "Lots of blood, but nothing broken. He was damn lucky."

"We'll take care of him, my lord," the coxswain offered. "The lads and I have talked it over and unless you have need of us, my lord, we're going to try to find a way to return to our ship. The captain will want all hands."

"I am certain Captain Northrop will be glad to have you back on board," said Henry. "Good luck to you."

The crew set out across the sugar cane fields, heading toward Wellinsport. Henry and Phillip slogged through the muck and stubble. Henry tried to catch a glimpse of Mr. Sloan, but he had ranged far ahead of them and was no longer visible.

The shelling of the city continued, and now that they were closer, they could see flames from burning buildings. He could smell the smoke, the foul odor of war.

Henry was soon exhausted, and his shoulder ached abominably. He longed to stop to catch his breath, but a glance over his shoulder showed him the lead ranks of the Guundaran army were on the move, marching down the Indigo Road.

"You should take off the Guundaran uniform, Your Grace," Henry advised. "The militia men are liable to shoot you."

"Good God, you're right, my lord!" Phillip exclaimed and hurriedly divested himself of the coat. "I had forgotten I was wearing it."

They finally reached the first tollhouse and learned that Mr. Sloan must have arrived and given the warning because they were immediately challenged by a panic-stricken young sentry, waving a rifle at them.

"Stand and be recognized!" he called in a quavering voice.

Henry and Phillip both raised their hands.

"I am Sir Henry Wallace. Mr. Sloan told you we were coming. Lower your weapon and let us pass."

"I dunno," said the sentry. "You might be spies."

Henry saw the rifle waver in his hand. His finger was perilously near pulling the trigger.

"Mr. Sloan!" Henry shouted.

"Here, my lord," said Mr. Sloan, hurrying to their rescue.

He reassured the sentry and escorted Henry and Phillip to the entrance of the tollhouse.

"A prime example of the local militia," Henry said. "Pimple-faced boys against Guundaran elite troops. They will be wiped out in the first volley. Who is the commander, Mr. Sloan? Where can I find him?"

"Captain Rader, my lord," said Mr. Sloan. "Veteran of the Bottom Dweller War. He seems a solid, steady old soldier."

"Thank God for that."

Captain Rader arrived to greet them. He was calm and unruffled and notable for a long white beard, of which he was quite proud, for he constantly stroked it.

"We heard the gunfire, and our lookouts spotted the army marching down the road," said Rader. "Hard to tell by moonlight, but there seems to be a fair number of them."

"We estimate three hundred, sir," said Henry.

Rader cast a glance back at his small force, who had lined up along the fence. "We could hold them off for a time. Not sure how long."

"I applaud your courage, sir, but you do not need to make such a sacrifice for your country. Your small force will be of more use to me alive," said Henry. "I require you and your men to guard the bank."

Captain Rader was surprised, as evinced by the fact that he stopped stroking his beard. "The bank, my lord?"

"The Guundaran forces are planning to seize the bank. I propose that you and your men leave the tollhouses to the Guundarans and take up positions around the bank."

Captain Rader gave a slow, resigned smile. "Some of the lads have already left the tollhouse, my lord. They were worried about their families, you see, sir. What with the shelling. I told them they could go."

"You did well, Captain," said Henry.

"The militia has a stockpile of weapons in the arsenal at headquarters if those would be of use, my lord," Captain Rader stated. "It's only a few blocks from the bank."

"Excellent," said Henry. "Mr. Sloan is a retired marine, sir. He can assist you and your men."

The captain was grateful. "We can use all the help we can get, my lord."

He left to prepare his men to march out.

Henry drew Mr. Sloan to one side. "The bank building is six stories tall, solid, constructed of brick reinforced with magic. It has iron bars on the windows, which is one reason I chose it to house the gold reserves. If we could get inside the building, I believe we could hold it for some time. You go to the arsenal with the captain. I will meet you at the bank."

"Very good, my lord," said Mr. Sloan.

Captain Rader and his small force left the tollhouse with alacrity, obviously glad they were not going to be called upon to die defending a tollgate. Henry saw the pimple-faced sentry fumble his rifle and almost trip himself.

"What now, my lord?" Phillip asked cheerfully. He was eager, excited, filled with energy, and seemed ready for anything. Henry felt his spirits revive just looking at him.

"You know the bank's owner, Sir Reginald Dawson."

"I do, my lord, from the time I spent here as your agent. Sir Reginald was an acquaintance of the viscount and in Pip's capacity as the viscount's clerk, I found occasion to invite myself to his parties. Pip gleaned a great deal of valuable information from his guests."

"And so you know where he lives!" Henry said, relieved. "That's excellent."

The two set out for the city, following in the wake of the militia. The shelling was now almost continual. The rockets had first hit the residential districts, but were concentrating on destroying the harbor, the naval dockyard, and the warehouses and businesses that surrounded the docks.

Henry could not count the number of columns of smoke he could see rising from the destruction. The streets were clogged with people either running toward the fires to help put them out, or fleeing them, while others were simply running, crazed with fear. Fires raged out of control, lighting the night sky with lurid orange flame.

"Sir Reginald lives near the harbor, my lord," said Phillip worriedly. "Let me go on my own. I'll meet you at the bank. The Guundarans will take care not to shell it."

Henry shook his head. "I know Sir Reginald. You will need me to help convince him."

Phillip grinned. "Probably so. He never did much care for poor Pip."

They were drawing closer to the harbor and the shelling. The rockets made shrill, high-pitched whistling shrieks as they fell from the sky, then came the boom of explosions that shook the ground. Smoke roiled, thick and black, and flames, fanned by the wind, crawled up the sides of tall buildings, devouring them until they collapsed into blazing piles of rubble.

People wandered about the streets dazed, wounded and bloodied. Wagons careened past at breakneck speed, carrying limp bodies to hospitals that were already filled to overflowing. People frantically dug through the rubble of fallen buildings trying to reach those trapped underneath. The local constabulary was doing their best, but they were overwhelmed, their help needed everywhere at once.

Choked by the smoke, Henry and Phillip stopped at a water pump to ease their thirst. Henry had visited Wellinsport many times, but he had no idea where he was, for nothing looked the same amid the destruction, covered by a pall of smoky haze. Phillip had lived in Wellinsport for years, however, and he knew every side street, every alley.

"Sir Reginald's house is not far now, my lord," he said. "I hope it is still standing."

Hearing the sound of another rocket, they both ducked into a doorway. The blast came only a few blocks away.

This area had thus far escaped the worst of the shelling. Buildings were still standing. The street lamps were still shining, their glow surrounded by halos of drifting smoke. Phillip pointed out Sir Reginald's house.

The windows in the upper stories were dark and shuttered. Lights shone in the lower level, probably the servants' quarters. Henry and Phillip both pounded on the front door and yelled Sir Reginald's name.

Light flared in a window on the third floor. A large and imposing man wearing a nightcap flung open the sash and aimed a fowling piece at them.

"Fair warning!" he bellowed. "I am a crack shot."

Henry stepped back so he could be seen. "Sir Reginald! I have come to warn you about your bank! The Guundarans—"

Sir Reginald slammed shut the window and they heard his voice booming through the house. A frightened-looking servant opened the door, and Sir Reginald came thundering down the stairs in his nightdress, still armed with the fowling piece.

"That you, Wallace? I thought so. Even under all that grime, I recognized that hawk's beak of yours. What's this about my bank?"

"The Guundarans have landed a force of three hundred elite troops on the Indigo Road. They intend to rob your bank, my lord. I believe they know about the gold. I have sent the militia to guard it. If you could open it and allow us inside . . ."

Sir Reginald didn't wait to hear more. "First the damn Guundarans lob shells at us and now they're robbing my bank. Wait here. I'll put on some clothes and fetch the keys."

He returned a few moments later, armed with the fowling piece and carrying a set of large brass keys on a ring. "Tell Lady Dawson I'm going out," he informed the servant in the same tone he might have used to say he was dining at his club.

"My wife and the rest of the family have taken refuge in the wine cellar," he remarked, as they set off down the street. "Damn Guundarans and their rockets! Shaking the ground and disturbing the sediment. Wine won't be fit to drink for a year."

He frowned at Phillip. "You look familiar, sir. Do I know you?"

"Name is Pip, my lord," said Phillip. "I used to clerk for the viscount."

"Rum bastard, that viscount," said Sir Reginald. "Never trusted him."

He eyed Pip with suspicion, then scowled in anger as a rocket screamed overhead and crashed down not far away. "Damn Guundarans."

Sir Reginald was an imposing figure, tall and broad, bluff and self-assured. He had arrived in Wellinsport forty years ago at age twenty, with nothing except the determination to make his fortune. Upon discovering that the island had no bank, he had decided to start one. The Bank of Wellinsport had begun life in a single dreary office with a safe the size of a hatbox and was now one of the largest and most respected banks in the world.

Sir Reginald set off at a brisk pace, holding the fowling piece in the crook of his arm and walking vigorously. Rockets screamed overhead or crashed down around them. Henry and Phillip cringed and ducked. Sir Reginald glared into the sky and shook his fist at the Guundarans.

They entered the business district, which was usually deserted this time of night; the law offices, money lenders, and real estate agencies generally closed and shuttered and guarded by the constables walking their beat. This night, however, the constables were battling fires and assisting the wounded. Several of the braver owners had taken it upon themselves to risk the rockets to secure money and valuable paperwork.

Sir Reginald turned down the street where his bank was located. Someone had shot out the street lamps, and between the night and the smoke they could see very little. Their boots crunched on broken glass. They came to a halt, their way impeded by crowds of enraged citizens erecting barricades and blocking the street with an overturned carriage and piles of refuse.

Some of the men and women were armed with clubs and broom handles, while others were amassing bricks and stones to be used as projectiles. Henry noticed groups of young men manning the barricades all dressed the same, wearing slouch hats, open-necked shirts, and shabby suit coats. They were armed with pistols, knives, and clubs, and gave every appearance of knowing how to use them.

"They are the unsavory side of Wellinsport," Phillip observed. "Members of the street gangs. They have long plagued Wellinsport, operating protection rackets and engaging in petty thievery, purse snatching, and fighting."

"What is that rum lot doing here?" Sir Reginald grumbled. "They don't care about this city or its people."

"But they do enjoy a good brawl," said Phillip.

Several people manning the barricades recognized Sir Reginald and gave him a cheer as they opened up the barricade for him and his companions. A soldier directed them down the dark street where they could see flashes of lantern light and hear sounds of activity coming from the bank. They arrived to find Mr. Sloan and several constables assisting soldiers to unload weapons from a large wagon.

"We are here with Sir Reginald, Mr. Sloan," Henry called. "Where are Captain Rader and his troops?"

"Manning a barricade on the main road, my lord," said Mr. Sloan. "He suggested that they engage the enemy to slow their progress and then fall back. I concurred. We shot out the street lights and blocked all the streets surrounding the bank. You will require light, Sir Reginald. Allow me."

Mr. Sloan handed his dark lantern to Sir Reginald. Henry prodded the banker, who had stopped to stare at the soldiers hauling swivel guns and canisters, rifles, cases of ammunition and powder, and other supplies out of the wagon and stacking them in the street.

"We need to gain entry into the bank, my lord," Henry reminded him.

Sir Reginald grimly nodded his head and unlocked the heavy door, which was made of oak, banded and studded with iron, and covered with magical constructs.

"This door was designed by a master locksmith, a fellow named Louie. Has a business in Maribeau."

"'Locks magical and mechanical,'" Phillip quoted with a smile.

"You know him? Figures," Sir Reginald said, snorting. "Louis is a damned Rosian, but a good locksmith. He designed this lock especially for me. It's both a manual and a wizard lock. The key controls the magic that controls the key. Can't have one without the other. Genius."

He started to fit the key into the lock, then glared at Henry and Phillip.

"I'll thank you gentlemen to avert your eyes! Especially you, Pip, or whatever fool name you call yourself."

Phillip grinned and winked at Henry. The two of them left Sir Reginald to open his magical and mechanical lock, and went to assist Mr. Sloan, who was directing the distribution of the weapons and supplies.

"You and Captain Rader have accomplished a great deal in a short amount of time," said Henry.

"We had help, my lord," said Mr. Sloan. "When we arrived at the militia headquarters, we found a large number of irate Wellinsport citizens attempting to break inside. We feared at first they planned to loot the armory, but we soon discovered they wanted to take up arms to fight the Guundarans."

Henry examined the collection of weapons. "Swivel guns! Excellent. Where would you suggest we mount them, Mr. Sloan?"

He craned his neck, peering up at the top of the building. "The roof, my lord."

Sir Reginald bellowed out that he had unlocked the door. He opened the bank and Henry and Phillip and Mr. Sloan trooped inside.

"The vault is below ground," said Sir Reginald. He indicated stairs that led to a subterranean level. "I had to blast a hole in the bedrock to build it. Locked and wizard-locked. Damn Guundarans won't break into my vault!"

"No, they'll just blow it open with a couple of barrels of gunpowder," Phillip offered helpfully.

Sir Reginald regarded him in horror. Before he could splutter in outrage, Mr. Sloan shouldered past him, carrying a swivel gun. The pimple-faced young soldier trailed after him, lugging bags filled with canisters.

"I see you have an aide-de-camp, Mr. Sloan," said Henry.

"I asked Captain Rader if the lad could serve in that capacity, my lord. Given that he almost shot himself with his rifle on the way here, I deemed he will be safer with me than manning the barricades."

"Kindly done, Mr. Sloan," said Henry.

Sir Reginald pointed toward the stairs and told them how to access the roof. Some of the citizens who had been manning the barricades offered to help protect the bank. Highly gratified, Sir Reginald distributed weapons, handing rifles to those who could shoot and telling others to assist by reloading. He drove out several of the "toughs" who had tried to enter the bank, jeeringly offering to help keep the money safe.

"Does the roof provide a view of the harbor, my lord?" Henry asked.

"Best view in the city," Sir Reginald boasted. "You can see the harbor *and* the channel."

"I need to see what's become of Alan," said Henry as he assisted Phillip in carrying rifles and ammunition up the stairs. They emerged onto the roof where Mr. Sloan was directing the placement of the swivel guns on the parapet.

Seeing that his secretary had the defense of the bank well in hand, Henry looked in the direction of the harbor.

"Any sign of the *Terrapin*?" Phillip asked, joining him. "I thought I could hear cannon fire."

Henry shook his head. "Too damn dark, and I left my spyglass on board the *Rose*. I can see flashes from cannon muzzles, but whether the cannons are theirs or ours, I have no idea."

He turned away in frustration to speak to Mr. Sloan.

"What do you think of our chances of saving the gold?"

"We can hold our position for some time, my lord, but not indefinitely," Mr. Sloan replied. "Not against three hundred well-armed troops."

"Wellinsport will not give up without a fight," Phillip predicted, taking up a rifle. "The battle will be a bloody one."

Henry looked out over the city. Fires were burning, and by the light of the city's own destruction, he could see the people of Wellinsport preparing for battle, taking to rooftops, manning barricades, arming themselves with whatever came to hand.

"I am proud of our people," said Henry. "Proud to be a Freyan."

"Me, too, sir," said the pimple-faced young soldier in a quavering voice.

Henry clapped the lad on the shoulder and took up a rifle. He looked back out into the harbor, trying to see what was going on.

Somewhere out in the firelit night, Alan and the *Terrapin* were all that stood between this city and disaster.

FORTY-FOUR

Alan stood on the deck of the *Terrapin* observing through his spyglass the two newly arrived Guundaran warships that had now taken up positions to block the Neck. The three other Guundaran ships were already in the harbor at the governor's invitation. If Henry was right—and Alan was chagrined to admit Henry had been right—the sheep had invited the wolves into the fold.

Those ships were too far away for him to see, but he had to assume the worst.

Speaking of the worst, he shifted his attention to the two forts guarding the harbor.

The gun batteries of Forts Godfrey and Alfred were always manned. Although Freya was not at war with Guundar, the arrival of three Guundaran warships should have raised alarm. The forts would have run out the guns just to remind the Guundarans to mind their manners.

A few lights burned in the windows of both forts, but otherwise they were dark and silent. Alan could see no signs of life and that, for him, was the most telling sign of all. The Guundarans were now in control of both forts.

"If I were the Spuds, I would have at least run out the guns to keep up the pretense," Alan remarked to his second-in-command, who also had his glass trained on the forts.

"No imagination, sir," said the lieutenant dismissively.

The two Guundaran warships loitering about the harbor were the sixty-eight-gun *Hoffnagle* and the sixty-eight-gun *King of Guundar,* the flagship.

According to Phillip's information, those two warships had orders to sink, capture, or burn the *Terrapin.* With one hundred and thirty-six guns to his twenty-four, the Guundarans must expect to accomplish their mission without breaking into a sweat.

The hour was approaching midnight and all was well. The citizens of Wellinsport slumbered, unaware of their danger. The moon rose, full and bright, silvering the mists of the Breath. Alan had been waiting for moonrise. He snapped shut the glass.

"If you were the commanders on board those two warships and you had no imagination, Mr. Hobbs, what would you expect the *Terrapin* to do?"

"I would undoubtedly expect us to maintain our position, sir. We are not at war with Guundar."

"And if we were at war?" Alan pursued.

Hobbs smiled. "As captain of a Guundaran warship, I would be aware of your exploits as a Rose Hawk and know you to be devious and dangerous, sir. I would not trust you. Meaning no offense, sir."

"Indeed, I take that as a compliment, Mr. Hobbs," said Alan, grinning. "Set a course for the *King of Guundar.*"

The lieutenant relayed the orders to the helmsman. The wind was favorable. The *Terrapin* carried all the sail she could manage and flew toward the flagship. Alan ordered the ship to be cleared for action and for a boarding party to stand by. He had the crew hurriedly paint the ship's boats, sails, and balloon black.

"I will take command of the boarding party, Mr. Hobbs. You will remain with the ship."

The lieutenant looked disappointed.

"Do not fret, Mr. Hobbs. You will have your share of the fighting," Alan assured him. "I will wager any amount you like that those three ships in the harbor are packed with troops preparing to invade the city."

The lieutenant smiled, restored to good humor.

The *Terrapin* continued on course, flying straight toward the Guundaran warship.

"It is my duty to remind you, sir, that the Guundarans have not committed any overtly hostile acts," said Lieutenant Hobbs. "If we attack them first, they will be able to claim we are the aggressor—"

The lookout bellowed, his cry taken up by many others on board the *Terrapin.*

"The Spuds are launching rockets, sir!"

Alan at first thought they were firing on his ship, but as he and everyone on board the *Terrapin* watched the fiery trails soar upward and then arc downward, he realized they were shelling the city. They could hear the sounds of explosions echoing across the Breath.

Some of the crew began shouting in outrage. The officers immediately silenced the outburst.

"I believe that counts as a hostile act, Mr. Hobbs," Alan remarked.

"Indeed it does, sir," said Hobbs grimly. "Do we alter course?"

"No, Mr. Hobbs," said Alan. "Straight for the *King of Guundar*." And God knows I wish that bastard, Ullr, was on board! Open the gun ports on the starboard side and run out the guns as though we intend to rake them with a broadside. Do not load the guns, however. I want the crews prepared to run the guns in again immediately on my command."

Hobbs issued the orders. The crews opened the gun ports and the guns rumbled out. Alan lifted his spyglass to survey the activity on the *King of Guundar*. He thanked the Guundarans for choosing a night with a full moon for their assault.

"Can't have their soldiers bumbling about in the dark as they slaughter women and children," he muttered.

"We will turn the moon to our advantage, sir," said Hobbs. "I imagine that our ship shows up quite well, bathed in moonlight."

The lookouts on board the *King of Guundar* would be able to see the *Terrapin*'s gun ports opening, the starboard side bristling with cannons. Alan hoped to lure the captain of the *King of Guundar* into tacking his ship and running out his guns, preparing to counter their broadside with one of their own.

Those on board the *Terrapin* who had no immediate duties were intently watching the *King of Guundar*.

"She swallowed the bait, sir," said Hobbs.

Alan waited until he was certain the ship was committed to the action and opened her gun ports. He did not change course, but continued sailing straight toward them. The Guundaran captain would not find this unusual. He would expect him to alter course at the last possible moment, though perhaps he would be starting to grow a trifle worried.

The moon rose higher into the sky. The warships in the harbor continued to rain rockets down onto the city. Alan gave a brief thought to Henry and Phillip and Mr. Sloan. He hoped they had sense enough to stay far away from Wellinsport, hunker down some place safe until the shelling stopped. Knowing those three, however, Alan could guess that they would be in the thick of the battle. He could do nothing except wish them well and try to put an end to the bombardment.

He kept an eye on the *Hoffnagle,* which was having a conversation with the *King,* signal flares from both ships bursting in the air. Alan could not read the signals, but he could guess that the two were planning to sandwich the *Terrapin,* catching her between them and attacking from both sides. The warships had come to Wellinsport with orders to ambush the *Terrapin,* and they were eager to either take her as their prize or watch her sink into the Breath.

"You are in charge while I am gone, Mr. Hobbs," said Alan. "You know what you need to do."

"I do, sir," said the lieutenant. "Good luck to you."

"Good luck to us all," said Alan. "The devil's own luck," he added to himself. He looked around to locate the best of the ship's crafters. "Mr. Henderson, you are with me."

Lieutenant Hobbs gave the order and the gun crews leaped into action, straining to heave in the guns and slam shut the gun ports. Alan joined the men in the boarding parties in three of the ship's boats.

Alan now had reason to curse the bright moonlight. They had oiled the airscrews to insure they would operate as quietly as possible. Still, he feared a sharp-eyed lookout on board the *Hoffnagle* might spot them.

The three boats lifted off the deck of the *Terrapin,* sailed into the mists, and glided toward the *Hoffnagle.* The *Terrapin* continued straight on course toward the *King of Guundar.*

"And now, gentlemen," Alan said to the crew of his boat, "you will see a wondrous sight."

The metal plates that covered the *Terrapin*'s hull, giving the ship her name, began to glow with a green and blue radiance. The gleam of the constructs was faint, at first, then strengthened as the helmsman sent the magic flowing into the steel plates.

Alcazar had revised his original formula, combining magic with contra-magic held together by the Seventh Sigil, to strengthen the steel and turn the plates themselves into a weapon. Alan had asked that the magic be enhanced to give off an eerie glow. The effect was even more spectacular than Alan had envisioned.

I owe this to you, Jacob, Alan thought, reflecting on his older brother, the priest, who had discovered the Seventh Sigil. Though I doubt you'd be overly pleased to see the use I'm making of it.

The *Terrapin* glittered, as dazzling as a blue and green star. She held her course and now the *King of Guundar* saw her deadly peril. Alan could hear Hobbs bellow, "All hands, brace for ramming!"

The *King* fired at the rapidly approaching *Terrapin,* but the Guundaran gunners must have been shaken by the sight of the gleaming ship bearing down on them for the guns fired sporadically and did little damage. The gun crews never had a chance to fire again.

The beakhead of the *Terrapin* plowed into the *King of Guundar*, catching her amidships, smashing into her with a horrendous crash that very nearly sliced the ship in two. The masts and rigging of the two ships were inextricably tangled, binding both ships to each other. Hobbs would have part of his crew already at work with axes to free the *Terrapin*, while others were racing to board and attack the Guundarans.

Alan could not take time to see if his ship had sustained critical damage. He had to concentrate on his own mission. The boats slipped through the Breath, hidden in the mists and the smoke that was drifting out into the harbor.

The boats crept near the *Hoffnagle*. Alan could see her ship's crew intent on watching the battle between the brightly shining *Terrapin* and the critically wounded *King of Guundar* and he could hear the *Hoffnagle*'s captain shouting orders, probably planning to attack the *Terrapin* before she could free herself from the tangle of wreckage.

The *Hoffnagle*'s lookouts never saw them. The first her crew knew their ship was being boarded was hearing the thunk made by the grappling hooks as they latched onto the ship's side. Alan and his men leaped from the boats to the attack, shouting and yelling like fiends, firing pistols and slicing through flesh and bone with their cutlasses. They tossed grenades down the hatches into the decks below, the blasts tearing apart those who had been rushing up on deck to defend the ship. Alan sent his men down the stairs to fight any who had survived.

The battle was short and brutal and over in moments.

The deck was slippery with blood. The wounded screamed or groaned or simply quietly died. Alan sent a man to take the helm and ordered his crew to round up prisoners. He sought out the *Hoffnagle*'s captain to demand his surrender.

"A valiant effort, sir," said Alan politely. "But the day is ours. I request your immediate surrender."

The captain swore at him in Guundaran and refused to relinquish his sword.

Alan did not have time to bandy words. He drew his pistol, cocked it and aimed it at the man's head. The captain continued to swear at him, but he did hurl his sword onto the deck. Alan picked up the sword and used it to point to the *Hoffnagle*'s boats.

"You and your men, sir. In there."

The captain stared at him blankly, either not understanding or feigning not to understand. Alan guessed the latter, since most Guundarans spoke Freyan from having served with Freyan troops.

"I'm giving you and your crew a chance to live, sir," said Alan. "I suggest you take it, otherwise we will throw you into the Breath. You may take your wounded with you. And I'll thank you to give me your uniform coat and your hat. Order your officers to hand over theirs, as well."

The captain glared at Alan in fury and swore at him again. Alan raised his pistol and the captain began stripping off his coat. He tossed it and his bicorn hat contemptuously on the deck, then ordered his crew to do the same with their uniforms. Alan's men harried them at gunpoint as they sullenly picked up their wounded and retreated to the boats.

"I would not sail into Wellinsport if I were you, sir!" Alan called to the captain as the Guundaran lifeboats sailed off. "You might receive an overly warm welcome!"

Once the Guundarans were gone and the ship was his, Alan took stock of the situation, which was better than he had expected. The unexpected attack had so completely overwhelmed the Guundarans that hardly any of his boarding party had been wounded and none of his men had been killed. The sailor with the most serious injury was a man who had sprained his ankle slipping in a pool of blood.

Alan took advantage of the moment's respite to study the *Terrapin*. She had freed herself from the tangled wreckage of the *King of Guundar,* which was good, for the *King* was sinking. Her crew had abandoned ship, taking to the lifeboats.

Regrettably the *Terrapin* had not escaped the collision unscathed. One of the masts and both balloons were gone. The crew had been forced to cut their own rigging to free the ship, which meant some of the sails were lost as well. Still the *Terrapin* remained afloat. Her airscrews all appeared to be in good working order and Hobbs would have the crew at work making repairs.

Alan signaled with his dark lantern, asking if the *Terrapin* could continue with the mission. The answer came back in the affirmative. The *Terrapin* doused her lights, including the blue-green glow of the iron plates, and Alan lost sight of his ship in the smoke and the darkness.

He donned the Guundaran captain's coat and hat, while his men changed into Guundaran uniforms. He glanced up at the Guundaran flag, which was still proudly flying, and gave it a mocking salute.

"Helmsman, sail into Wellinsport as though we owned the place," said Alan.

The helmsman grinned as he ran his hands over the brass helm. The *Hoff-*

nagle left the channel and sailed into the harbor, where the three Guundaran warships were still firing rockets into the city.

The smoke grew denser the nearer they sailed to the burning city. Alan was grim as he watched the flames flare red among the thick, black smoke. He had always loved Wellinsport from its happy association with the Rose Hawks days. If he ever retired from the navy, he planned to move to Wellinsport to live out his days in sunshine and fair winds.

Seeing the city in flames and thinking of the helpless civilians who had died in the fires, Alan felt no compunction about giving the next orders, though by doing so he was breaking every one of the so-called civilized Rules of Warfare.

He gathered his small crew together. "Those of you dressed as Guundaran officers join me on the quarterdeck. Remember, we must give the appearance that nothing is amiss. The rest of you pile anything that will burn on the deck: bedding, linens, blankets, the lot. Coat the bottom of the masts with pine tar and douse the rigging with spirits. Make absolutely certain you've thrown all barrels of gunpowder overboard. I want to start a conflagration, not blow us to kingdom come."

He turned to the crafter. "Mr. Henderson, you know what you are supposed to do. Stand ready for my order."

The *Hoffnagle* sailed confidently toward the three warships and Alan knew the moment he saw signal flares rise from the ship nearest him that the Guundaran lookouts had caught sight of the *Hoffnagle*. The captain was probably asking what was going on, why the *Hoffnagle* had entered the harbor.

Alan ignored the signals. The wrong response would be worse than no response.

He tied his handkerchief around his nose and mouth and kept his glass to his eye, keeping watch on the warships, pausing now and then to impatiently wipe away the tears caused by the smoke. The moon was visible, but only through a smoky haze, and he could not see much. So far, the Guundarans did not appear to be suspicious.

His crew had completed their work. They had thrown the gunpowder overboard, then piled up everything that would burn from straw mattresses to sailcloth and soaked it with the potent "Spud" spirits, pine tar, and bottles of wine from the captain's private store. They stood on deck, eagerly waiting to jump into action. The *Hoffnagle* drew closer to her victim, and Alan took his place beside the helmsman.

Two of the Guundaran ships rode at anchor, lobbing their rockets into the city with impunity, secure in the knowledge that no one could stop them. They knew the shore batteries that would have pounded them to bits were in friendly hands and the Freyan fleet was miles away in Sornhagen. The *Hoff-nagle* was able to sail so close to the third ship that the captain didn't bother with signal flares. He called to them across the expanse of the Breath, asking a question in Guundaran.

Alan cheerily waved his bicorn in answer. He had no idea what the man had said, but it didn't much matter.

"Mr. Henderson, give the Guundarans our answer."

The ship's crafter spoke a word and snapped his fingers. Blue sparks leaped from his hand, soared through the air, and landed on the piles of spirit-soaked refuse. He hurried about the ship, starting fires.

The magical flames spread quickly, running up masts doused with pine tar, licking at the sails.

"Hold your course," Alan told the helmsman, and shouted to his crew, "Stand by to grapple."

Fire was every ship's captain's worst nightmare. Crafters protected the hulls and masts and rigging, sails and balloons from flame by placing magical constructs on them during the ship's construction. But in a contest between fire—a force of nature—and magic, magic generally lost.

The crew of the enemy ship nearest the *Hoffnagle* saw her burst into flame. In the lurid light, they could see the sailors standing by with grappling hooks, ready to grapple and board. The Guundaran captain realized he had been tricked and his ship was in dire trouble. He shouted frantic orders for his marines to fire on the blazing *Hoffnagle*.

Bullets rattled around him, but Alan ignored them. The marines would have difficulty finding targets in the smoke. Most of the shots went over his head or smashed into the hull.

The helmsman guided the *Hoffnagle* close to the enemy ship and, at Alan's command, the sailors flung their grappling hooks over the side, then heaved on the lines, dragging the ships close together. Masts tangled, snaring the rigging. The flames quickly spread from the *Hoffnagle* to the Guundaran ship, even as her crew fought desperately to cut their ship free.

Aboard the *Hoffnagle,* the heat was growing intense. Pieces of blazing silk rained down from the burning balloons. A spar fell and landed, burning, on the deck in front of Alan, narrowly missing the helmsman.

"Into the boats and shove off before that ship blows up," Alan ordered his crew. "We tossed our gunpowder, but the Guundarans didn't toss theirs. I'll take the helm."

"What about you, sir?" the helmsman asked.

"I'll be right behind you," Alan promised.

The helmsman hesitated.

"That was an order!" Alan said sternly.

The helmsman reluctantly departed. He and the rest of crew piled into the *Hoffnagle*'s boats and released the ropes that held them. They did not sail away, however. Orders or no orders, they clearly intended to wait for their captain.

"Shove off, you fools!" Alan shouted angrily.

"Can't hear a word you're sayin', sir," an old sailor bawled in response. "Must be the smoke cloggin' my ears."

Alan remained at the helm, doing his best to steer the blazing *Hoffnagle* toward the other two enemy ships. That proved difficult, for the two ships were now inextricably tangled.

The remaining two Guundaran ships had ceased firing rockets. Their crews had more urgent matters as they tried to flee the *Hoffnagle,* which was now engulfed in flame. Alan wished them luck. The Guundaran ships might manage to escape him, but if they made it as far as the harbor's entrance, they would find the *Terrapin* lying in wait.

The heat was intense, the air hard to breathe, making his lungs ache. More spars fell, and one of the masts sagged. The sails had caught fire. Blazing cinders landed on Alan's sleeve, setting it on fire. He batted out the flames with his hat. Fire erupted on the deck at his feet, threatening to cut off his retreat.

His crewmen shouted at him, urging him to run. They were in danger, as well, for if the enemy ship attached to theirs exploded, they would all go down.

Alan ran. He leaped through a wall of fire and reached the boat with his coat in flames. The crew seized hold of him and dragged him into the boat, dumping him unceremoniously into the bottom and beating out the flames with their bare hands.

They sailed off as fast as they could go, heading back to the *Terrapin.* The crew assisted Alan to a seat. He could not feel the pain of his burns yet, but that was only a matter of time.

He started to give an order, but he was seized with a fit of coughing that doubled him over. The old sailor drew his attention, pointed back to the harbor.

"Look there, sir! You did it!"

Alan managed to stop coughing long enough to see a massive explosion rip through the Guundaran ship grappled to the *Hoffnagle.* Both ships burst into a gigantic ball of fire. The concussive force of the blast struck the boat, causing it to rock violently.

Alan shielded his eyes from the brilliant light, trying to see the outcome.

The fireball had vanished and with it the last of the *Hoffnagle*. The other two Guundaran ships were still afloat, although one appeared to be sailing erratically.

"Knocked out the helm," said the old sailor with a cackle.

The Guundaran ship veered wildly off course and collided with her sister ship. The two smashed into each other with such force Alan could hear the wood splintering.

"Sunk 'em both, by God," stated the old sailor.

He gazed at his captain in awe, as did everyone on board the boat. No one said a word.

Alan barely heard him. He was starting to feel the pain of his burns. His coat sleeve was charred and in tatters; his arm was red and starting to blister. He had burns on his legs, and his face radiated heat. He put his hand to his cheek and felt blood where a bullet must have grazed him. The excitement of battle began to ebb away, leaving him drained.

He turned back to his crew and saw them gazing at him, slack-jawed, open-mouthed.

"Five to one, sir," said the old sailor in solemn tones.

"What are you yammering about, Sikes?" Alan demanded irritably.

"Five to one, sir," the old sailor repeated, awed. "You took on five ships and scuppered 'em. Every one. I'll wager no other captain in the history of captains has ever done the like."

Alan blinked and looked around the harbor. Four of the Guundaran ships had disappeared beneath the mists of the Breath and the fifth was on her way to join them. Only the tops of her masts showed. The Guundaran flag fluttered pitifully and then the mists and smoke swallowed it.

Survivors in lifeboats were all that was left of the Guundaran warships. Some of the men were sailing for the shore batteries, hoping to join up with Guundaran troops. They would not stay there long, for when Admiral Tower and the Aligoes Fleet returned, the forts would soon be back under Freyan control. Others were hoping to escape into the Trame Channel. None of the Guundarans sailed toward Wellinsport, undoubtedly fearing, as Alan had warned, the warmth of the welcome.

Alan regarded his men with pride. "I'll wager no other captain in the history of captains has ever had a crew like mine. I could not have done it without you men."

He felt close to tears and he had to pause to clear his throat. Fortunately, he could blame his emotion on the smoke.

When he was recovered, he said sternly, "Did I see a jug of spirits at the bottom of this boat?"

The crew looked sheepish, and the old sailor shoved aside a tangle of rope with his foot to reveal the jug hidden beneath.

"Dunno how it got there, sir," he said and passed the jug to Alan.

He pulled out the cork and inhaled the reek of the strong Guundaran Spud liquor.

Alan raised the jug in the traditional naval toast. "The King. God bless him."

The sailors cheered as he lifted the jug to his lips and swallowed. The fiery liquid bit into his throat and he gagged and retched. "God! That stuff's awful!"

He passed the jug to the sailor nearest him in the boat, who solemnly drank the toast. The crew passed the jug between both boats until everyone had taken a pull and handed it back to Alan.

He held the jug high. "I give you King Ullr. May God rot his black soul and damn him to hell."

The crew roared with laughter that stopped abruptly when they saw Alan upend the jug, dump out the liquor, and then toss the jug into the Breath.

The crew watched the jug sink in sorrowful disappointment.

FORTY-FIVE

The citizens of Wellinsport were prepared to meet the enemy. They had thrown up barricades all over the city, blocking the roads with overturned wagons and carriages, furniture, barrels, and anything else they could find to toss on the pile.

Elderly veterans took down their blunderbusses from the walls and manned the barricades, standing side-by-side with razor-wielding street toughs and children armed with bricks and paving stones. Women stood on rooftops, armed with coal scuttles filled with red-hot coals.

Henry admired their spirit, but not only were troops marching over the Indigo Road into the north of the city, troops stashed on board the warships would soon be entering the city from the harborside. His people could soon face a thousand disciplined well-armed Guundaran soldiers that would crush all resistance like an avalanche thundering down the side of a mountain.

He could tell the moment the first ranks of the Guundaran soldiers encountered the barricades by the crackle of gunfire and cries of outrage and defiance. He shook his head in grim foreboding.

"I fear the worst, Mr. Sloan," he said, and added with a disapproving glower, "Why are you smiling?"

"It had occurred to me, my lord, that Guundaran soldiers are accustomed to fighting what we might term 'civilized' battles in which opposing forces line up across from each other in orderly rows on the field of conquest. The orders are given: Fire, reload, fire. Advance. Retreat."

"And what is your point, Mr. Sloan?"

"Street fighting is far more vicious and brutal, as the Guundarans will soon discover, my lord. They do not face the enemy across a field of battle. Instead the enemy lunges out of a doorway wielding a meat cleaver or throws hot grease on their heads."

Mr. Sloan was proven right. The gunfire became more sporadic and people began to cheer. Assailed from all directions, the Guundarans who had marched along the Indigo Road to seize the bank had been forced to retreat to reconsider their position.

"I fear the celebration is premature," said Henry. "The Guundarans will not give up that easily."

"Indeed, my lord," Mr. Sloan agreed. "In their place, I would make use of the transport barges to sail over the barricades and attack the bank from the air."

"For God's sake, do not give them ideas, Mr. Sloan!" Phillip protested. "We would not want your thoughts winging their way to some Guundaran commander."

"I will endeavor to control myself, Your Grace," said Mr. Sloan.

Henry took advantage of the lull in the fighting in the city to shift his attention to the battle taking place in the harbor.

He was puzzled by an eerie blue-green glow lighting the Breath near the entrance of the Trame Channel, until the glow strengthened and he realized it came from the magical steel plates of the *Terrapin*. He could tell by following the bright glow that the ship was on the move, but without a spyglass he could not see well enough to know where she was bound or why.

"Alan must be planning to take on the *King of Guundar* and the *Hoffnagle*," said Phillip. "Sixty-eight guns each."

"And the *Terrapin* has twenty-four," said Henry gloomily.

"And the devil's own luck," Phillip reminded him.

Henry sighed.

The lull in the fighting in the city continued. The Guundaran forces that had attacked the barricade had not returned, and the people began to celebrate in earnest in the belief that the fight was over. Henry was starting to think he'd been wrong and that the Guundarans had given up. His hopes were dashed by the arrival of one of Captain Rader's men, who came running upstairs to report.

"The captain says to tell you that the Spuds took to their barges and are preparing to attack our position from the air."

Henry glared at his secretary. "I blame you, Mr. Sloan."

"I am profoundly sorry, my lord," said Mr. Sloan. "I would suggest that Captain Rader and his men fall back to assist in guarding the bank."

"I agree, Mr. Sloan," said Henry.

The man ran down the stairs with his orders for his captain. He must have said something to Sir Reginald on his way out the door, for the bank owner came up to join them on the roof.

"Brought my glass so I could see the damn Guundarans for myself," he said, flourishing a spyglass. "I hear they are going to attack from the air."

"They are on their way, my lord," said Henry. "Right now, however, you can see the battle raging in the harbor."

Sir Reginald put the spyglass to his eye and trained it on the harbor. "So you can," he said.

Henry longed to see for himself and had to fight the temptation to snatch the spyglass out of Sir Reginald's hand.

"Damned if I can tell one ship from another," said Sir Reginald.

"If you would allow me, sir," said Henry, reaching for the spyglass. He started to look, then handed it to Phillip. "On second thought, Your Grace has the best eyesight."

"Your Grace!" Sir Reginald frowned at Phillip. "But he's a clerk!"

Henry did not choose to enlighten him. "What do you see, Your Grace?"

"The *Terrapin* is headed straight for the *King of Guundar,*" Phillip reported. "Wait! Damn it. Too much smoke. I can't make out . . . By God! The *Terrapin* rammed her! The two ships are locked together."

He paused at this critical moment.

"Well?" Henry demanded impatiently.

"The *King* is sinking, my lord. Looks like the *Terrapin* managed to free herself. But the *Hoffnagle* escaped," Phillip added in grim tones. "She's joining the three warships in the harbor."

"What is Alan doing? Is he just letting her get away?" Henry demanded.

"That would appear to be the case, my lord," said Phillip. "The *Terrapin* is not giving chase."

"It is not like Alan to give up!" Henry said.

"Perhaps the *Terrapin* was damaged in the collision, my lord," Mr. Sloan suggested.

"The *Terrapin* must be sinking then, because Alan would not let that stop him," said Henry.

Phillip kept watching and suddenly gave a whoop. "The *Hoffnagle*'s on fire!"

"What? Where? Let me see!"

Phillip handed Henry the spyglass and he trained it on an orange glow lighting the inky blackness of the harbor. The *Hoffnagle* was ablaze, and the burning hulk was sailing toward her three sister ships.

"Good old Alan! He must have captured it and turned it into a fire ship, my lord!" Phillip cried, practically dancing up and down with excitement.

Henry could not see the deck of the burning *Hoffnagle,* but he knew with certainty that Alan would be standing at the helm in the midst of an inferno, guiding the blazing wreck toward the other ships.

The Guundaran ships saw their danger and stopped firing rockets into the city to try to save themselves. An enormous ball of flame suddenly erupted in the harbor. The sound of an explosion followed, rolling across the city.

Everyone else on the roof cheered as the *Hoffnagle* went down in flames. Henry did not cheer. He wondered if Alan had been caught in the blast. He lowered the spyglass in silence and returned it to Phillip.

"The Guundaran ships are both on fire," Phillip reported. "Looks like one has lost control of the helm because it's veering toward the other. Good God! They've smashed into each other!" He waited a moment, then said, awed, "They're gone, my lord. Both of them sunk."

"Sir, sir!" The pimple-faced youth was stammering, pointing and frantically clutching at Mr. Sloan. "Mr. Sloan, sir! They're c-c-coming!"

Henry had forgotten their own peril in his worry for Alan. He turned his attention from the harbor to see the hulking shapes of Guundaran landing barges slowly sail over the barricades. People on the rooftops began firing at them and hurling bricks, slate tiles, or whatever else came to hand. The barges were forced to travel slowly, for the smoke obscured their view and they did not want to crash into a chimney or the side of a building.

Captain Rader and his men arrived at the bank on the run, and Sir Reginald went below to meet them. Phillip pocketed the spyglass and went to join Mr. Sloan manning the swivel guns.

Henry raised his rifle. He could hear Captain Rader shouting orders to his men and Sir Reginald booming defiance from inside the bank. He sighted in on the lead barge and waited for it to come within range.

"Hold your fire!" Phillip called urgently.

Henry lifted his head. The lead barge had slowed almost to a crawl to allow the other two to catch up. The officers were shouting back and forth.

"What are they saying, Your Grace?" Henry asked.

Phillip had the spyglass trained on the nearest barge. The Guundarans made no attempt to lower their voices. Judging by their tone, they were obviously shaken.

Phillip began to laugh. "They also saw the battle in the harbor and they have just realized that they are now stranded here in Wellinsport. Those three warships that just sank were supposed to pick them up and carry them back to Guundar."

"They might still attack," Henry said, not inclined to cheer yet. "You served with the Guundarans, Mr. Sloan. Will they die for a lost cause or retreat and live to fight another day?"

"I have found the Guundaran people to have a great deal of common sense, my lord," said Mr. Sloan. "They abhor waste."

The Guundaran officers were still shouting at each other and Phillip was listening.

"They intend to retreat. They have enough lift gas to make it as far as the Travian city of Sornhagen. They are going back to the tollhouses to pick up the remainder of their force."

"I hope they make it," said Henry, watching the barges until they had vanished into the smoke and darkness. "There has been enough death this day."

Phillip gave a sigh and slumped down, exhausted. "'All's well that ends well,' as the poet says."

"All's well that ends," said Henry.

FORTY-SIX

News that the Guundarans had been driven off swiftly spread throughout the city of Wellinsport. Church bells rang out in jubilant triumph. People flowed into the streets to sing and dance. Those manning the barricades threw down their weapons and raised bottles and jugs. Tomorrow the people of Wellinsport would bury their dead. Tonight they could rejoice in the fact that they had fought valiantly and saved their city.

Henry and Phillip left the roof to see how Sir Reginald and his forces had fared inside the bank, leaving Mr. Sloan and his pimple-faced young friend, whose name was Charlie, to secure the weapons on the roof and make certain they did not fall into the hands of the street gangs. Henry found Sir Reginald promising loans on generous terms to anyone interested in helping to rebuild the city.

He greeted Henry and insisted on opening the vault to prove that the gold and silver reserves were safe.

"I'll do my job, Wallace," said Sir Reginald. "You do yours. Stop that bastard Ullr."

Sir Reginald eyed Phillip askance, then drew him off to one side.

"You were Pip, a clerk for the viscount, when you were living here. Right? I didn't mistake that?"

"That is correct, my lord," said Phillip.

"But now you're a duke?" Sir Reginald asked, perplexed.

"I was a duke at the time I was a clerk, my lord. The Duke of Upper and Lower Milton," said Phillip.

"I'll be damned," said Sir Reginald.

Henry had one abiding, all-consuming thought, and that was to find out what had become of Alan. He was haunted by the sight of the *Hoffnagle* perishing in a ball of fire.

"Even the devil must set a limit on luck, Mr. Sloan. I'm going to find a cab."

"I fear that might be difficult, my lord," said Mr. Sloan.

He proved to be right. Henry left the bank and was immediately caught up in the celebration. He stared at the crowds in dismay.

"Even if we could find a cab, we wouldn't get far," said Phillip, joining him. "The streets will be jammed. Wait inside the bank for me, my lord, where it is quiet. I suggest you try Sir Reginald's excellent brandy."

Henry returned to the bank and sank down in a cozy chair in Sir Reginald's office. He was dazed from fatigue. His head buzzed, his skin twitched, and he felt as though he was standing off to one side, watching himself. He was seized by a fit of coughing and could not stop. Someone brought him a glass of water and he drank it without knowing what he was doing. He closed his eyes.

Henry started awake at the gentle touch of a hand on his shoulder.

"I have secured an island hopper, my lord," Phillip said. "We can sail out to the *Terrapin*. I left it in back under the care of Mr. Sloan."

"How did you manage to find an island hopper?" Henry asked, still half asleep.

"A costermonger of my acquaintance," Phillip replied. "Jenny earns her living selling her produce to the cooks in Fort Gregory and Fort Alfred. She was not home—I assume she is manning the barricades—but she will not mind if I borrow her hopper. I left her some money to recompense her, and a note saying that it was in my possession so that she would not think it was stolen."

Henry felt better after his short nap. He found Mr. Sloan in the alley behind the bank, standing guard over the small, single-masted boat. Captain Rader and his men were in the alley, as well, loading the weapons they had obtained from the armory into a wagon.

Mr. Sloan motioned Henry over to speak to him privately. "If I might make a suggestion, my lord. I was thinking you could dispatch Captain

Rader and his men to Nydrian's Cove with a view to keeping watch on the White Well."

"An excellent idea, Mr. Sloan. I will need the governor's sanction, but considering that this attack might have been prevented if he had listened to me, I believe Crichton will be amenable."

"Very good, my lord. I was also thinking that if you have no pressing need for my services, I could accompany Captain Rader. Master Yates will be eager to obtain information on the well and I could conduct scientific studies for him."

"I will miss you, Mr. Sloan, but I know Simon would appreciate your endeavors," said Henry.

"Any word of Captain Northrop, my lord?"

Henry shook his head. "No, none."

"I am certain he is safe, my lord."

Henry did not answer. He paused to watch Charlie lugging bags of swivel gun canisters into the wagon.

"You will make a soldier of the lad yet, Mr. Sloan," said Henry.

"Master Charlie has decided the rigorous life of a soldier is not for him, my lord," said Mr. Sloan. "He states that he intends to become a private secretary."

"He has a worthy model in you, Mr. Sloan," said Henry.

"Thank you, my lord. I did mention to him that he must first learn to read and write," said Mr. Sloan.

Henry boarded the island hopper. Phillip took the helm, and as the small boat rose into the air, Henry was surprised to see the eastern sky starting to lighten with the coming of dawn. Night had seemed unending.

He and Phillip sailed over what was left of the harbor district. They stared at the destruction in shocked silence, too appalled for words. A few buildings had escaped the shelling and remained standing, but most of this part of the city had been reduced to charred, smoldering rubble. Fires were still burning, but since the fire brigades had run out of water they could only stand by and watch helplessly until the flames burned themselves out. With the coming of dawn, people went to work among the ruins, trying to save the living and recover the dead.

Phillip suddenly pointed to a large mansion that had been burned to the ground. All that remained were blackened timbers sticking up at odd angles, and a chimney.

"The Governor's House," he said.

"Are you certain?" Henry was horrified. He could see nothing recognizable.

"I am, unfortunately," said Phillip. "Pip used to work there."

Henry wondered if the governor was dead or alive. If Crichton was alive, he probably wished he was dead. His political career was over. The citizens of Wellinsport would never forgive him for his foolhardy decision to give the Guundarans permission to enter the harbor.

"You tried to warn him, my lord," said Phillip, seeing Henry's dark expression.

"I should have reasoned with him instead of bullying him," said Henry. "Small wonder he took umbrage. The same is true for Alan. If anything has happened to him . . ."

He could not go on.

They sailed toward the *Terrapin,* taking care to avoid the guns of Fort Godfrey and Fort Alfred, fearing they might still be in the hands of the Guundarans.

"Not for long," Henry predicted.

Admiral Tower and the Freyan fleet would arrive with the dawn and dispatch troops to reclaim the forts. Having seen five of their warships sink into the Breath, the demoralized Guundarans would soon surrender.

The *Terrapin* had taken up station in the Neck. Her lookouts were still on duty, for the ship fired a warning shot, telling the hopper to keep her distance. Phillip waved his handkerchief as a white flag and they were allowed to approach within hailing distance.

"State your business," an officer shouted.

"Sir Henry Wallace to speak to the captain," Phillip shouted.

Henry glanced around at him. "Aren't you coming with me, Your Grace?"

"I would like to return to Freya, if you have no need of me, my lord. I am worried about Sophia."

"I am certain you have no cause to fear," said Henry, smiling. "She is with Miss Amelia and King Ullr himself would not dare to tangle with Miss Amelia."

He held out his hand. Phillip took it and they shook hands warmly.

"Thank you for your help, Your Grace," said Henry. "I am truly glad I did not shoot you."

Phillip laughed and guided the island hopper to a landing on the deck of the *Terrapin.* "I'll wait to hear about Alan, my lord."

Henry found the crew already hard at work repairing the damage. Lieutenant Hobbs recognized him and came over to greet him.

"Where is Captain Northrop?" Henry asked anxiously.

"In his cabin, my lord," Hobbs replied. "The surgeon is with him."

Henry tried to speak, but he could not ask the question.

"The captain was injured, but he will be fine, my lord," Hobbs assured him. "I will have someone take you—"

"I know the way," said Henry. "Go tell His Grace the good news. He's waiting in the island hopper."

Henry hurried down the stairs to Alan's cabin. He heard Alan before he saw him and he entered to find his friend sitting on a chair swearing roundly at Perry, who was smearing a foul-smelling, blue ointment onto his burned arm.

"What is that stuff?" Alan demanded, gagging. "It smells worse than a barrel of rotting fish!"

"A concoction of my own, sir," Perry replied. "Allow it to do its work. The balm will ease the pain, as well as heal the flesh. The smell dissipates after a time."

He began to pack up his instruments and glanced around when he saw Alan's gaze shift. Henry had entered and was standing awkwardly just inside the door.

Perry looked from one man to the other and acted to ease the tension.

"How is the shoulder, Sir Henry?" he asked. "I see you removed the sling."

"My arm is a little weak, but otherwise fine, sir," said Henry.

"Nevertheless, I would like a chance to examine the break. At your convenience, my lord."

"Certainly, Mr. Perry," said Henry.

The surgeon departed and Henry shut the door behind him. He turned to face Alan, who rose to greet him.

Neither spoke and then both spoke at once.

"I was wrong—"

"I am sorry—"

They stopped, discomfited, then Alan laughed and reached out. Henry grasped his hand and shook it heartily. He looked anxiously at the burns.

"That looks painful. What does Perry say?"

"That I was a damn fool," said Alan, grinning.

"A damn fool who sank five enemy warships!" Henry regarded his friend with pride. "You will be knighted, honored throughout Freya. And you deserve it, my friend. You saved Wellinsport."

"The least I could do since I was responsible for nearly losing it," said Alan ruefully. "You were right about the Guundaran warships."

"And you were right to remind me Freya and Guundar were not at war," said Henry. "A situation that has now changed."

They sat down at the table. Alan produced a bottle of Calvados.

"King Ullr thought to snap up two easy prizes: Wellinsport and my ship," said Alan, pouring them each a glass. "He failed in both, but that does not mean he will fail in his main objective, which is to rule Freya. Pip told me Ullr plans to invade on Hallen Day, which is not that far off. He caught us with our britches down around our ankles, our fleets scattered to the four winds. I fear our country may fall, Henry."

"I would have agreed with you yesterday, but not today," said Henry. "This day I have witnessed the courage and the spirit of our people, Alan. King Ullr will try to frighten us with his warships and his rockets and his high-stepping troops with their rows of gleaming bayonets. I saw our women fight those swords and rifles with broom handles. Our children pelted his soldiers with rocks. Our elderly rolled their wheeled chairs into the fray with the vigor of youth and our youth were prepared to give up their young lives for our country."

Alan regarded his friend intently. "I have never heard you speak with such emotion. You give me hope. You went searching for Simon's Wall of Frozen Fog. Did you find it?"

"You will be astonished to hear that I did," said Henry. "Almost right where he said it would be."

"Good God!" Alan exclaimed. "Are you serious?"

"I am. A vast pool of liquid Breath not far from Nydrian's Cove. If Freya survives, our country will be wealthy beyond the dreams of avarice."

"Well, I'll be damned," said Alan, marveling. "Simon was right."

"And you may be certain he will remind us of that daily," said Henry. "How soon can the *Terrapin* be ready to sail? I grudge every moment that passes. Can we be in Freya by Hallen Day?"

Alan mentally calculated and looked somber. "We will do our damnedest, Henry, but we must have fair winds and clear skies and that's rare this time of year. I will give the orders to set sail now. I was waiting only to hear word of you."

He rose to his feet, then stopped to rest his hand on Henry's shoulder. "I am glad you are safe, my friend. Our country needs you."

Henry gave a faint smile and shook his head. "No longer, Alan. If our nation survives, I am planning to hand His Majesty my resignation."

"Bah! You have said that before and you never mean it," Alan reminded him with a smile. "You are in low spirits, that's all. You will feel better after a hot meal and a good night's sleep."

Alan hurried up on deck and in a few moments Henry heard the *Terrapin*'s airscrews whir to life. He could hear the sailors running to their stations and feel the quiver of anticipation that ran through the ship at the prospect of setting out on the next voyage.

He felt the same quiver of anticipation run through him.

"This time, I mean it," he said.

FORTY-SEVEN

Thomas had been eager to meet with Randolph Baker after learning he was a particular friend of Sir Henry's. He hoped the admiral would have news of his friends for him. Since Smythe had made certain Thomas was no longer receiving messages through the *Haever Gazette,* he had not been able to find out if Phillip had managed to escape the country, nor did he know if Sophia and Miss Amelia were safe, or if Kate and Dalgren had arrived in time to warn the Dragon Brigade about the black ship.

He lived in dread every day that Smythe would come to gleefully report that he had captured the princess or that Phillip had been shot while attempting to evade arrest. Thomas guessed that he hadn't done either, because Smythe walked about the palace with a sour expression and a bandaged forehead.

Thomas kept watch for the admiral, and when he heard a booming voice outside his office announcing that Admiral Randolph Baker requested an audience, Thomas rose with alacrity and went to personally invite him to enter.

He was favorably impressed with the bluff, florid-faced, and outspoken man.

"Your servant, Your Majesty," said Randolph with a portly bow.

"A pleasure to meet you, Admiral," said Thomas formally. "I am interested to hear how the refitting of the ships of the Expeditionary Fleet progresses."

Thomas escorted the admiral into his office and shut the door.

"Be careful what you say, sir," Thomas added in an undertone. "My secretary acts as a spy for Smythe."

Randolph grunted. "I thought the bastard had a slimy look about him. I was tempted to punch his head."

Thomas smiled and invited the admiral to be seated.

Randolph reached inside his coat and took out a letter, which he handed to Thomas. "Miss Amelia asks that you destroy it once you have read it, sir."

Thomas took the letter. He glanced at the closed door, aware that his secretary would have his ear pressed to it. "Keep talking, sir. Tell me about the refitting."

As he read, Randolph went into a loud, grumbling, and profanity-laced account of the refitting of the ships of the fleet, professing his certainty that the ships were going to sink the moment they left the dock. Thomas would have been concerned to receive such a report, but he discounted much of it. He knew from reading his own reports on the subject that the refitting was almost complete and initial results were most satisfactory. He had also learned that the admiral's nickname among the sailors was "Old Doom and Gloom."

Thomas concentrated on his letter. Amelia reported that she and her "friend" were residing with a mutual friend, "Y," and that all were safe and they were both well. Their other friend, "K," had safely embarked upon her travels.

Thomas smiled, a burden lifted from his spirits. He walked over to the fireplace, tossed the letter into the flames, and watched it burn. He stirred the ashes with the poker, then returned to his desk, sat down, and motioned Randolph to draw his chair closer.

"Who is the 'Y' mentioned in the letter, sir?" Thomas asked quietly.

"That would be our friend, Simon Yates, sir."

"I don't know him," said Thomas. "Though the name is familiar."

"I'll wager you know his house, sir. Welkinstead. The house that once floated over Haever. The one the black ship shot down."

"Yes, of course. I assume, then, that the house landed safely on the ground somewhere and that Sophia is staying there."

"Correct, sir."

"I won't ask where," said Thomas. "So long as Her Highness is safe. Have you heard anything of His Grace, Phillip Masterson? Is he safe? Did he escape the country?"

"Last I heard, His Grace was on his way to the Aligoes to warn Henry of King Ullr's planned invasion of Freya—presuming Henry is still alive, which I doubt," Randolph added gloomily. "He looked like a goddamn corpse the last time I saw him. Surgeon was with him, but I don't trust those butchers. Goddamn drunks, the lot of 'em."

Randolph eyed the door, then leaned close to speak to Thomas in a low voice. "Miss Amelia told me what you discovered, sir. That King Ullr plans to invade Freya. I've been doing some investigating."

"What have you found out?"

"It's what I *haven't* found out that worries me, sir."

"Very well, Admiral," said Thomas. "What *haven't* you found out?"

"The whereabouts of the goddamn Guundaran navy, sir," said Randolph.

"I do not understand."

"They've goddamn vanished!" Randolph stated loudly, slamming his hand on the desk.

Thomas cast a warning glance toward the door.

Randolph muttered something and again sat forward in his chair, his heavy shoulders hunched. He spoke quietly and grimly. "No one knows the location of any of the Guundaran fleets, sir. As I said, they've up and vanished."

"But how is that possible?" Thomas demanded.

"It's a helluva big world, Your Majesty," said Randolph.

Thomas did not find this information particularly helpful. "I need details, sir."

"Yes, sir." Randolph drew out a notebook and referred to it. "The largest fleet in the Guundaran navy is the Braffan Fleet. It is divided into two squadrons with the northern squadron stationed in Braffa itself, while the southern guards the liquid Breath refineries. The northern squadron set sail from Braffa a month ago and no one's seen them since.

"The second largest Guundaran fleet is the Home Fleet. As the name implies, it guards the homeland. Ullr has been increasing the size of that fleet in the past year. He now has thirty warships, fourteen heavy frigates, twelve two-deckers, and four with three full gun decks each. Our agents heard they were planning to conduct naval exercises in the Breath, but the Home Fleet has also disappeared.

"To make matters worse, we have since received reports of a previously unknown fleet of twenty Guundaran ships with twelve ships of the line operating between Guundar and Travia. That fleet has also disappeared."

Randolph closed the notebook. "I have no need to tell Your Majesty that it is my opinion that these Guundaran fleets are now in a position to attack Freya. They could strike us any time from any direction."

Thomas sighed. "I have worse news. I have reason to believe Ullr is now in possession of five green-beam guns that can work without blood magic. We have to expect that at least some of his ships will be armed with them."

"Green-beam guns!" Randolph repeated, stunned. "Are you certain, sir?"

"I heard him boast about them myself," said Thomas.

"May God and all the goddamn saints in heaven preserve us," Randolph muttered.

"Where are our fleets located?" Thomas asked. "Will they be able to reach Haever in time?"

Randolph handed over the notebook. "I've written everything down for you, sir."

Thomas read over the information:

> *Expeditionary Fleet, Admiral Baker. Ships undergoing refitting. Only two, HMS* Terrapin *and HMS* Valor, *ready for service.*

"And the *Terrapin* is in the Aligoes, sir," said Randolph.

"She's there on my orders, sailing into an ambush. Let us hope Pip reaches Captain Northrop in time to warn him."

> *The Aligoes Fleet, Admiral Tower. Sailing the Trame Channel, maintaining its neutrality, as well as guarding the valuable Deep Breath port in Wellinsport.*

"At least Admiral Tower and his fleet are in Wellinsport," said Thomas.

"Begging your pardon, but he's not, sir," said Randolph. "The Aligoes Fleet is in Sornhagen."

"On whose orders?" Thomas asked.

"The Chancellor of War, sir. Smythe informed the Admiralty that the Rosians threatened Sornhagen."

"So the *Terrapin* is the lone ship guarding Wellinsport and the Guundarans are waiting for her," said Thomas. He sighed and read on.

> *The Channel Fleet, Admiral Dorchester. Patrolling the Strait de Domcado between Rosia and Estara.*

"I've dispatched urgent messages to Admiral Dorchester to set sail for home, but I doubt he can reach Freya in time," said Randolph. "He will have to cross the Breath in the teeth of the Winter Witch. Undoubtedly why goddamn Ullr chose this time of year to launch his attack."

Thomas shook his head and continued reading.

Vanguard Fleet. Ships were decommissioned due to lack of funding. Parliament determined they were not needed during peacetime.

"I gave orders for the fleet to come back into service, sir," said Randolph. "Their commanders are assembling their crews now and working to have their ships ready for action. We couldn't do that in secret, of course, sir, so Ullr probably knows all about it."

"He doesn't appear particularly worried," said Thomas dryly.

Western Fleet, Rear Admiral Green, patrols the Breath around Upper and Lower Milton.

"The smallest fleet, meant to deter pirates along the southern coast," Randolph explained. "The largest ship is twenty-four guns. Ullr has pleasure yachts that could blow that fleet out of the Breath."

"What about the Guundaran mercenaries serving in Fort Upton?"

"I warned the commander, sir. He is keeping watch on them," said Randolph. "If they try to seize the fort, they'll be in for a nasty surprise. The question now is, where will Ullr strike first? The only person who might be able to figure it out is Simon."

"Miss Amelia knows where to find him," said Thomas. "You said yourself he must be 'Y.' "

"If anyone can discover what Ullr is up to, it will be Simon. I'll get a message to Miss Amelia."

"Take care, sir. Smythe undoubtedly has agents watching you."

Randolph winked. "I know he goddamn does. I led them on a merry chase yesterday, sir. I walked round and round Wately Circle twenty times, then gave 'em the slip. Henry taught me how."

"I will continue to keep watch on King Ullr and Smythe," said Thomas. "How do we communicate?"

"I have given the matter some thought, sir," said Randolph.

He reached into a small pocket on his breeches, encountering some difficulty due to the tightness of the waistband around his expansive middle, and fished out a coin, which he handed to Thomas. The coin bore an insignia of a griffin with a crown around its neck on one side and a frigate in full sail on the other.

"How does this help?" Thomas asked, gazing at it. "This is not a Freyan coin, is it?"

"It's known as a challenge coin," said Randolph. "The tradition dates back to the days of the Sunlit Empire. Officers had coins struck with the insignia of their legions and awarded them to soldiers who fought well in battle. During the Blackfire War, an admiral in the Freyan navy heard that story and had his own coins struck in order to reward his crew for deeds of valor.

"These days," Randolph continued, "it's the tradition for a sailor to slam down his coin on a bar and challenge his fellows to do the same. Anyone without his coin on him must buy the ale."

Randolph pointed to the coin in Thomas's hand. "If Your Majesty needs to contact me, day or night, send that coin to the Naval Club with instructions to give it to me. I'll know the meaning of it and I'll come straightaway to the palace."

"An excellent idea, sir. Thank you," said Thomas.

He tucked the coin into his own watch pocket, then gratefully shook hands with the admiral and rang a bell, summoning the servants.

The admiral had not been gone five minutes, by Thomas's estimation, when Smythe entered the room. Thomas guessed he must have been waiting outside the office, fuming that Thomas was meeting with someone on his own and trying to overhear the conversation.

Thomas braced himself for an unpleasant encounter, but instead of issuing threats or berating him, Smythe placed papers in front of him, saying only that he needed his signature.

As Thomas was signing, Smythe mildly inquired, "How was Your Majesty's meeting with the admiral?"

Thomas was wary. He trusted Smythe even less when he was trying to be pleasant, if that was possible. "We discussed the refitting of the Expeditionary Fleet to utilize the crystals of the Breath."

"A pity I could not be present to speak with the admiral, sir," said Smythe. "An idea occurred to me. I suggest that we put on a particularly splendid Hallen Day celebration in honor of the Royal Navy and I was hoping to ask his advice."

Hallen Day . . .

Thomas was reading through the document and he was glad Smythe could not see his face, for he was having difficulty controlling his expression.

"Why choose that holiday to celebrate the navy?" he asked, feigning ignorance.

Smythe was an adept liar and dissembler, but he had not been expecting the question. Thomas saw a faint flush redden his neck. His pupils dilated, and his jaw tightened. Smythe mastered himself in an instant and resumed his usual expression of disdain and thinly veiled contempt.

"As Your Majesty *should* know, Hallen Day celebrates the Battle of Hallen, the first time cannons were used in action, with catastrophic results for the Rosian navy. It is the custom for the reigning monarch to review the fleet from on board the royal yacht. I will make the arrangements."

Smythe had kept his voice bland and mild. His eyes met Thomas's eyes and held them.

"Thank you, Chancellor," said Thomas.

Smythe bowed and took his leave.

Thomas tried to return to his work, but he was restless and could not concentrate. He decided to go riding, exercise his horse. He informed his secretary where he was going, knowing that the secretary would inform Smythe and that those tasked with keeping watch on him would be scrambling to reach their horses in time.

Thomas changed clothes and walked to the stables. The air was clear and cold. He could see steaming puffs of breath rising from the horses in their stalls. He was talking with a groom about one of his favorite horses, who had developed a slight limp, when he heard a commotion outside in the stable yard.

Thomas looked out the door to see King Ullr and members of his staff on horseback, apparently returning from a gallop. Ullr was in a good mood, chatting and laughing as grooms and servants came running to assist them.

Thomas stepped back into the shadows of the horse barn. He had come to be alone with his thoughts, at least as alone as a king could ever be, and the last person he wanted to see was the man making secret plans to invade his country.

Ullr and his companions walked past the barn without noticing Thomas. Ullr was swinging his riding crop and observing his surroundings with a self-satisfied smile, probably thinking to himself that after Hallen Day, the palace and grounds would be his.

Thomas started to turn away in disgust when a shout drew his attention back to the king. He looked out the door to see Baron Grimm, mounted on horseback, galloping up to the king. The baron's horse was lathered and breathing heavily. Grimm had ridden in haste.

His news must be urgent, for he slid from the saddle before his horse had come to a halt and ran toward Ullr. The king abruptly ordered his companions to leave him.

Grimm moved close to talk to Ullr. Thomas could not hear what Grimm was saying, but he could clearly see the impact of his words.

Ullr grew livid; his expression darkened. He clenched his fist over the riding crop so that his knuckles turned white.

"This cannot be true!" he shouted in Guundaran.

He started to walk off. The baron said something and reached out to halt him, as though to impress upon his king that he was telling the truth.

Ullr snarled and rounded on Grimm, raising the riding crop so that Thomas thought he might actually strike the baron. Grimm stood his ground, seemingly prepared to take the blow.

Ullr flung the crop into the muck. He glared down at it in silence, breathing heavily, his breath steaming in the cold air. When one of the grooms ventured to approach to take the baron's horse, Grimm ordered him to leave them. The groom obeyed with alacrity.

Ullr stood for long moments, clenching and unclenching his fist, as though trying to decide what to do. He had been red-faced with fury, but now he was pale, his rage cooled on the surface, though it still burned in his eyes.

"Carry a message to Admiral Schmidt," he said to the baron.

He lowered his voice. Thomas tried his best, but he could not hear the message. It must have been a short one, for Grimm almost immediately remounted his horse and galloped off.

Ullr continued walking toward the palace, his strides swift and angry.

Thomas changed his mind about his ride. He gave Ullr a good head start, then hurried back to the palace, hoping to discover what had happened that had so upset the Guundaran monarch.

"Is Chancellor Smythe about?" Thomas asked his secretary.

"No, sir. He left word that he is dining out this evening," said the secretary. "I could send a messenger for him—"

"No, that will not be necessary," Thomas said.

He dismissed the secretary, giving him permission to leave for the day, then went into his office. He sat down at his desk, picked up a report. He didn't read it, however. His mind kept going back to the meeting between Ullr and the baron. Thomas was more and more convinced that something important had happened. He needed to know what.

He fished the admiral's coin out of his pocket.

FORTY-EIGHT

Randolph Baker could see the bright moon shining through the window of the Naval Club as he sat playing whist, and he glared at it.

"Goddamn moon," he grumbled. "Full moons hold luck."

"They do, sir," said his opponent, saying with a wink at his partner, "for some of us."

He added casually, apropos of nothing, "The moon will be waning gibbous on Hallen Day, sir. Also said to be lucky."

The officers exchanged conscious glances and knowing smiles. Their ships belonged to the Expeditionary Fleet, secretly preparing to help thwart the expected Guundaran invasion. These officers would have been on board their ships, but Randolph had ordered them to follow their usual routine, which meant that they would be spending their evenings in the Naval Club.

Randolph paid his losses and made his way to the common room. He asked the club steward if anyone had left a letter for him. He should have heard news of Henry by now and he was worried that he had not. No news was not necessarily good news. If Henry had died, Alan would be loath to tell him.

The steward replied that he had not received any letters. Randolph sighed, and took a seat at a table and ordered a brandy. He was about to pick up the *Haever Gazette* when someone dropped a coin on the table.

Randolph looked up to see a gentleman bundled up in a greatcoat with a scarf around his face. The gentleman very slightly lowered the scarf, revealing bright blue eyes. Randolph gave a start.

"Your Maj—"

Thomas shook his head and covered his face.

"We need someplace where we can talk in private," he said in a low voice, muffled by the scarf.

"My rooms upstairs," said Randolph.

They ascended the stairs in silence. Randolph opened the door, ushered his guest inside his quarters, and closed the door. Thomas shed his scarf and coat and shook his head at the offer of a brandy.

"The Naval Club is quiet tonight," he observed.

"Work on the ships proceeds apace, sir," said Randolph. "A few of the officers are here to keep up appearances. We've let it be known that we're readying the fleet for the Hallen Day review."

"Good," said Thomas. "But that wasn't what I meant. King Ullr received some very disturbing news today."

He explained the mysterious meeting he had witnessed between King Ullr and Baron Grimm.

"I have no idea what Grimm told him, but whatever it was, Ullr was furious," said Thomas. "I came to see if you might know what happened."

Randolph shook his head. "I have no idea."

"Have you heard of an Admiral Schmidt, sir?"

Randolph set down his brandy snifter and sat bolt upright. "Schmidt is the Lord of the Guundaran Admiralty, sir. Why?"

"Ullr mentioned him—"

Their conversation was interrupted by the sounds of a commotion coming from downstairs: cheering and raucous laughter and jubilant shouts.

Randolph and Thomas exchanged glances.

"You are right, sir. Something *has* happened. I'll find out what. You should wait in the bedroom."

Thomas rose and retreated to the bedchamber as Randolph headed for the door. Before he could reach it, however, he heard the steward engaged in an altercation.

"Females are not permitted in the club as I have tried to tell you, Miss Nettleship. I must insist that you leave."

"Females not permitted! I never heard such rubbish!" Amelia returned. She leaned down to shout through the keyhole. "Admiral Baker! I must speak to you!"

"Miss Nettleship, you must leave!" the steward persisted. "The admiral is not to be disturbed."

"Admiral Baker!" Amelia struck the door with what sounded like the handle of her umbrella. "I have a message from Master Yates. Take your hands off me, you rogue!"

Randolph flung open the door in time to find Amelia clouting the steward with the umbrella. The admiral managed to disarm her.

"I will vouch for this lady, Rankin," Randolph said.

The steward straightened his rumpled vest and smoothed his hair. He cast Amelia a baleful look and started to leave.

"Wait a moment, Rankin. What the devil is going on downstairs?" Randolph asked.

"The gentlemen have just received word of a great naval victory, sir. The Guundarans launched a sneak attack on Wellinsport. The *Terrapin* was the only Freyan ship in the vicinity. Captain Northrop attacked the Guundarans against overwhelming odds and was victorious. The *Terrapin* sank five of their warships."

"Five! God bless my soul!" Randolph exclaimed. He cast an oblique glance toward the bedchamber. "Good old Alan! When did this battle take place, Rankin?"

"Four nights ago, sir. The news just arrived at the Admiralty. If you will excuse me, sir, I must return to my duties." The steward cast a last furious glance at Amelia. "Females are *not* allowed. If you will take responsibility—"

"Yes, of course," said Randolph.

Amelia stalked into the room. Her hat was askew, her bobby pins falling out, her skirt and coat splattered with mud. She wore a muffler wrapped around her hat and tied under her chin, thick gloves, and carried the ever-present reticule on her wrist.

"Greetings, Admiral." Amelia shook hands. "Is that brandy? I'll have a snifter. I'm cold through to my knickers."

She sent her sharp glance around the room.

"Who is your guest, sir?"

Thomas emerged from the bedchamber.

"Did you hear the good news, Your Majesty?" Amelia asked, inclining her head in what, for her, passed as a curtsy.

"I did, Miss Amelia," said Thomas, smiling. "Phillip must have reached the *Terrapin* in time."

Randolph helped Amelia untangle herself from the muffler, then poured her a brandy. Thomas drew up a chair near the fire and invited her to be seated.

Amelia downed the brandy in an unladylike gulp, then held out the snifter for a refill. "I must say I find it most advantageous that you are here, sir. Wonderful news."

"I trust the news is true and not some wild rumor," said Randolph. "Can't goddamn believe anyone these days."

"King Ullr believes it is true," said Thomas. "That must be why he nearly struck poor Baron Grimm. Never be the bearer of bad tidings."

He raised a glass. "I give you the *Terrapin,* her captain and crew."

They drank the toast. Amelia began tucking in the bobby pins that had come loose during her tussle with the steward.

"I know my men call me 'Old Doom and Gloom,'" said Randolph. "And I hate to say this, sir, especially now, but you realize that this news is not necessarily good news."

"What do you mean, sir?" Thomas asked.

"Ullr knows word of his defeat will spread fast. Every soul in Freya will hear that Guundar attacked Wellinsport and will be clamoring for war."

Even as he spoke, church bells all over Haever started to ring in celebration of the victory.

"King Ullr has lost the element of surprise. He dare not wait for Hallen Day," Randolph continued.

"He will launch his invasion as soon as he can make ready," said Thomas, agreeing. "And we still have no idea where he will strike."

"Yes, sir, we do," Amelia stated. "That is what I came to tell the admiral. As I said, I have just arrived from speaking to Master Yates. He received your message, Admiral Baker, and he found your missing fleets."

She took her leather notebook from her reticule and carried it over to stand in front of a large framed map of Freya that adorned one of the admiral's walls. Amelia placed her finger on a dot on the coastline in the north of Freya.

"According to Simon, Ullr's fleets are assembling here, not far from the city of Glenham. Master Yates calculates that the Guundarans have"— Amelia consulted the notebook—"thirty-two ships of the line. The smallest have sixty-eight guns; the largest, one hundred guns. And approximately sixteen heavy frigates."

Her listeners absorbed this information. Randolph marched over to glare at the dot.

"Glenham's in northern Freya. Why the devil would Ullr land an invasion force there? Why not Haever?"

Amelia was grave. "Because the ships do not intend to land, sir. Master Yates believes the Guundaran ships plan to sail south from Glenham"— Amelia drew a line with her finger—"to strike Haever from the north. Thus, they evade the city's defenses."

"But that means Ullr's ship would have to sail over land! Tommyrot!" Randolph gave a violent snort. "Without the Breath to keep them afloat, those big, hulking Guundaran men-of-war wouldn't get twenty miles! They'd sink like goddamn anvils."

"Master Yates insisted upon that fact, sir. He said—and I quote: 'Randolph will refuse to believe me, but you must convince him. The Braffans have supplied King Ullr with the crystalline form of the Breath. The Guundarans refitted their warships to use the crystals long before our navy. The Guundaran ships do not need to rely solely on the magic of the Breath.'"

Amelia turned away from the map, her expression grim. "Master Yates has more bad news, gentlemen. Your Majesty warned us that King Ullr acquired five green-beam guns. Five of the Guundaran ships are armed with these formidable weapons."

"The Navy will deal with them," said Randolph.

"The Guundarans do not plan to use them against our navy, Admiral," said Amelia. "Master Yates has information that these five ships intend to attack Haever with green-beam guns. Ullr means to wage war on the civilian population. The green beams will rain death down from the heavens. Master Yates asks you to remember that a green beam leveled Sir Henry's house with a single blast. Picture these heinous weapons striking tenements, boarding houses, the university, hospitals . . ."

Thomas was shaken. "I cannot believe even King Ullr could be so depraved as to attack civilians. Do you trust this information, Admiral?"

"He did so in Wellinsport, sir," said Miss Amelia.

"I would trust Simon with my life, sir," Randolph added. "In this instance, I *will* be trusting him with my life. The *Valor* will be in the thick of the fighting."

Thomas was impressed by this argument, but still not entirely convinced. "I would like to know how Master Yates found these Guundaran ships while sitting in his parlor, when our own navy could not locate them."

"Simon has agents all over the world, sir," Randolph stated. "He reads every goddamn newspaper, magazine, communiqué, letter, and document that he can lay his hands on, foraging for clues. He puts together this and that to arrive at what and where and when."

"In this instance, sir," Amelia added, "I can tell you that he based his deductions on a variety of information, including a message in an agony column in the Guundaran newspaper the *Morgenpost*, a 'to let' notice in the same paper and a description of a dress worn to a party by a Freifrau von Puttkamer, whose husband is an admiral in the Guundaran navy."

"You can't be serious!" Thomas was incredulous.

"Henry termed Simon 'Freya's secret weapon,' sir," Randolph said gravely. "If Simon says the Guundaran ships are north of Glenham, the Guundaran ships are north of Glenham. If he says green-beam guns are going to attack Haever, they're going to attack."

"Very well," said Thomas. "I do not know Master Yates, but I know you, Admiral. And I was present when King Ullr received word of the defeat in Wellinsport from Baron Grimm. He ordered the baron to take a message to this Admiral Schmidt. I do not know what the message was, but the baron rode off in great haste."

"I can tell you what the message was, sir," said Randolph. "Attack now. Hallen Day be damned."

"I believe you are right, sir," said Thomas. "How soon could the Guundaran ships be ready to sail?"

"If the ships are near Glenham, griffin riders could reach Admiral Schmidt's flagship within hours, sir," said Randolph. "The fleet commanders probably already have their orders to prepare for war. They could be ready to set sail as early as dawn tomorrow and arrive in Haever by late tomorrow afternoon."

"Can we stop them?" Thomas asked.

Randolph shook his head. "No, sir. If the *Valor* sailed for Glenham this moment, we would have to travel round the eastern part of the continent. With a fair wind, we could be there in two days."

"And that would leave Haever undefended, sir," Ameila stated. "Easy prey for the green-beam guns."

"We should make our stand at Haever, Your Majesty," Randolph urged. "We can take advantage of the shore batteries, as well as the patrol boats. I propose we intercept the enemy north of the city."

"That means *our* ships will have to sail over land," said Thomas. "The *Valor* is the only ship already refitted to use the crystals. The others have only lift gas. Once they deplete their stores of lift gas, they will start to sink."

Randolph gave a grim smile. "Don't fret about that, sir. The battle will likely be over long before our lift tanks run dry."

Thomas considered what he should do. Randolph regarded his king with sympathy. Ordering men to their deaths was an enormous burden to place upon such young shoulders.

"We must prepare our people for war," Thomas said at last.

He walked over to Randolph's desk, sat, and took up pen and paper and began to write. Randolph and Amelia discreetly withdrew to allow him to work in private.

"How is Simon?" Randolph asked.

"He is preparing to raise Welkinstead off the ground and return to Haever," Amelia answered. "He has invented some sort of weapon he plans to use to fight the Guundaran ships."

Randolph was alarmed. "I hope it's not like those goddamn crackers of his. He nearly sank *my* goddamn ship!"

Thomas rose from the desk. "Miss Amelia, ask the editor of the *Haever Gazette* to put out a special edition informing our people that we are at war with Guundar and that the enemy intends to attack Haever. I have written a personal message to our people, instructing them to seek shelter below ground, assemble the fire brigades, and turn out the local militia."

"Aren't you afraid this news will start a panic, sir?" Amelia asked.

"The people of Haever do not frighten easily," said Thomas, smiling. He handed the sheet of paper to Amelia, who read it aloud.

> *Citizens of Freya*
> *We face a foe who is threatening to destroy our city. I have faith in your courage and bravery. Know your king will be fighting alongside you.*

"I will join you on board the *Valor*, Admiral, if you will have me," said Thomas.

Randolph hesitated. "Are you certain, sir? As I said, the *Valor* will be in the thick of the fighting."

"I would expect nothing less," said Thomas. He added with a frown, "You would not have me cower in the palace while my people are at war, would you, Admiral?"

"Of course, not Your Majesty. We will be honored to have you on board," said Randolph, bowing.

Amelia continued to read.

> *In the event of my death, I name His Grace, Phillip Masterson, Duke of Upper and Lower Milton, heir to the Freyan throne. I have previously made my choice known to the Ascension Committee of the House of Nobles and since His Grace descends from Blanche Hunsmen, daughter of King Lionel, they have given their approval.*

"An excellent choice, my lord," said Amelia with a tremor in her voice. "We must pray it does not come to pass."

She dabbed her eyes with a handkerchief from the reticule and loudly blew her nose. She then tucked the king's message into her reticule, collected her coat and hat, and shouldered her umbrella.

"In case I meet that steward," she said darkly. "Females not allowed!"

She held out her hand. "God save you, sir."

"God save us all," said Thomas gravely, shaking hands.

Randolph accompanied her to the door and closed it behind her.

"How many ships can the navy provide at such short notice for the city's defense?" Thomas asked.

Randolph did some calculating. "Eight seventy-four-gun ships of the line, four sixty-four gun, and a single one-hundred-gun warship. Add to that a dozen gunboats and another dozen frigates. And the *Terrapin*."

"The *Terrapin*?" Thomas repeated. "She must have sustained extensive damage in the battle, sir, and she is in the Aligoes. We cannot count upon her, more's the pity."

"Alan would not miss this fight if his goddamn ship was sinking underneath him," Randolph predicted. "And even if it was at the bottom of the world, he'd still find a way."

He sighed and shook his head. "I readily admit, I don't like our odds, sir."

Thomas rested his hand on Randolph's shoulder. "Do not look so glum, Admiral. As Captain Northrop has proven, one Freyan ship is equal to five Guundarans."

Randolph grunted, but he did smile.

"I have one more request, Admiral," said Thomas before he departed. "I would like you to arrange for marines to replace the palace guard. I assume that King Ullr and his mercenaries will have packed their bags and departed, but we must not take chances."

"If he hasn't, we will pack their goddamn bags for them," Randolph stated. "I'll dispatch a force right away, sir."

"Have the officer report directly to me," said Thomas. "I will have additional orders for them."

Randolph said nothing, though he thought he could guess as to the nature of those orders. He and Thomas shook hands. Thomas put on his hat, wound his scarf about his face, and left the Naval Club. The celebration had died down somewhat, as most of the officers had gone to their ships in anticipation that they would soon be called to action.

Randolph stood at the window to watch the young man make his solitary way down the street.

"I wish you were here to see our king, Henry," Randolph said. "You would be proud of him."

He clasped his hands behind his back and added with a gloomy shake of his head, "I applaud His Majesty's courage, but, goddamn it, I wish he *would* hide himself in the palace. Cannonballs have no respect for crowned heads."

FORTY-NINE

Jonathan Smythe was dining with Hugh Fitzroy, the Earl of Montford, at his country estate in Chadwick. Hugh had invited Smythe to dine because he was still angling to become the ruler of Freya. Smythe had accepted for the same reason—he wanted to be ruler of Freya. Hugh was merely a means to that end.

Smythe enjoyed the fine meal, although he knew he was going to be expected to pay for it. The reckoning came when Hugh's wife rose from the table to leave the gentlemen to their port. Hugh sent the servants away and immediately poured two full glasses.

Smythe declined the port with some asperity. Hugh was well aware that as a strict Fundamentalist, Smythe did not imbibe strong liquor. Smythe knew that Hugh sought to embarrass him.

Hugh grinned and drank both glasses, then advanced his latest idea on how to claim the throne.

"Thomas Stanford is not a descendant of King Frederick, as he claims," said Hugh. "He is the son of a scullery maid."

This theory was so bizarre that even Smythe was caught by surprise. He floundered a moment, not knowing what to say. Fortunately Hugh was so eager to explain he didn't notice.

"I have it on good authority that the maid and Thomas's mother gave birth at the same time. The maid bore a son and Constanza bore a daughter. Constanza switched the babies. The Marquis paid the maid to disappear, and he and Constanza passed off the boy as their own.

"Eh? What do you think of that, Smithee?" Hugh asked, his face flushed both from the port and pride in his theory. "I have a midwife who will swear to it."

Smythe had no doubt that this midwife would swear the moon was made of plum pudding if Hugh paid her enough. But Hugh had given him time to think and he saw how this crackpot scheme might work to his advantage. Smythe appeared to give the matter serious consideration.

"Your claim would take some time to prove to the Accession Council and the House of Nobles, sir," said Smythe. "That said, if I were to become Lord Protector of the Realm, I could advance your cause."

"Eh? What? Lord Protector?" Hugh regarded Smythe with sudden suspicion. "That means you would be some sort of king, wouldn't it?"

"Not at all, sir," said Smythe, soothingly. "The title of Lord Protector is held by a person tasked by the House of Nobles to safeguard the realm in the unhappy event that the throne should fall vacant and there is no heir apparent. The position is not permanent."

Hugh drank another glass of port and thought this over. "You're saying that once I proved my claim before the House, you would step down and I would take the throne."

"Indeed, sir," said Smythe. "Gladly."

Hugh eyed him. "Do you think some unhappy event is likely to occur that will leave the throne vacant, Smithee?"

Smythe was suddenly wary. Hugh might be a boor, but he was a shrewd businessman who had used a number of unscrupulous means to crush his competition. He had also cultivated powerful adherents who would be glad to put him on the throne in order to promote their own causes and he was not above blackmail. But if he was hoping to hear Smythe implicate himself in removing the king, he was going to be disappointed.

"God forbid anything should happen to His Majesty, sir," said Smythe earnestly.

Hugh grunted and poured another glass of port. He was about to expand on the scullery maid notion, but at that moment the clock chimed ten. Smythe noted the lateness of the hour, recalled that he had pressing business in the palace, and rose to take his leave.

He had traveled to the estate in his own wyvern-drawn carriage. He reveled in the luxury of cushioned leather and settled himself comfortably to finalize his plans. The journey back to the palace should take about an hour, but they had only been traveling about half that time when Smythe felt the carriage start to make a rapid descent.

Smythe lowered the curtain and looked out the window. The moon was full, shining brightly. By its light, he could see an empty highway surrounded by farm fields.

"What is the matter, Bennings?" he shouted to his driver in irritation. "Why are we landing?"

"Trouble with either the helm or the lines to the lift tank, sir," the driver shouted back. "We can't keep afloat."

Smythe fumed, but there was not much he could do. The carriage made a rough landing, coming down in a field near the highway.

Bennings inspected and came to report. "One of the braided leather lines that carries the magic from the helm to the small lift tank on the back is broken, sir."

"What caused it to break?" Smythe demanded.

"Hard to say, sir," said Bennings. "The wyverns got into a rip-snorting fight while I was hitching them up. I suspect one of them bit through it."

"Can't you just patch it?"

The driver shook his head. "Won't work, sir. I have to replace the line. I have another, but it will take me some time to remove the old one and replace it with the new. There's an inn not far from here, sir. You should be able to get a room for the night."

Smythe went to see the line for himself. He could tell at a glance that it was broken past repair. He considered this accident a punishment for the sin of pride. He had originally planned to travel by griffin, but had decided at the last moment that arriving in his own wyvern-drawn carriage would look more impressive.

He could see the lights of the inn from where he stood, and it occurred to him that instead of asking for a room, he could hire a horse and continue his journey.

He left Bennings with the carriage and the wyverns and walked to the inn. The innkeeper was able to supply him with a horse, although he said it would take some time to wake the grooms and get them moving.

After about an hour's wait, Smythe finally mounted the horse and took the road to Haever. The night was cold, but he did not feel it. He was in a good mood, despite having to wait. He was now a wealthy man with money to spend on wyvern-drawn carriages and greatcoats protected by magical constructs. The magic on his new coat not only guarded him from knife attack and bullets, but kept him warm, as well. He was pleased with his meeting with Hugh and looked forward to Hallen Day, which would bring an end to Thomas Stanford and make Smythe Lord Protector of the Realm.

Smythe considered himself strong-minded, disciplined, above the weak-nesses of the flesh. He considered strong emotion of any kind a weakness. Yet while he considered hatred a weakness, he could not help himself. He hated the pup, King Thomas, with a passion that consumed his soul.

He rejoiced to think of the upstart's destruction, and was particularly pleased with the idea that Thomas would be struck down by the hand of a wrathful God. Or at least, that's how his death would appear.

Smythe had already written and practiced giving his speech at Thomas's funeral. He recited some of it now, relishing how his words sounded in the frosty air.

"As Lord Protector, I exhort the people of Freya to change your hedonis-tic ways!" he thundered, startling the horse. "To that end, I will close down the theaters and shutter the ale houses and taverns. Henceforth, we must devote ourselves to pious living, or God will not spare His wrath! We will meet the same dread fate as our profligate king!"

He topped a hill, and the lights of the city came into view. Smythe slowed the horse. Was it his imagination or were there more lights than usual for this time of night? Now that he was paying attention, he could hear church bells ringing; wildly clamoring—another oddity. Smythe checked his watch by the moonlight and saw the time was some minutes past three of the clock in the morning. Church bells rang only if there was some sort of emergency, such as fire or flood. He urged his horse to a gallop.

Arriving on the outskirts of Haever, he saw that he had been right, some-thing had happened, though it did not appear to be a disaster. Lights shone in the windows of every house. The occupants were not huddled inside in terror, but were milling about the streets, lighting celebratory bonfires, laughing and singing.

Smythe stopped his horse and leaned down from the saddle to ask what was going on.

"You must be the only person in Freya who hasn't heard the news, sir!" the man replied with a laugh. "There's been a great battle. The Guundarans attacked Wellinsport. Our Captain Northrop in the *Terrapin* sank 'em, every one. Five Spud ships gone to hell."

"Are you certain this news is true?" Smythe demanded.

"It's in the *Gazette,* sir. His Majesty—God love him—knew the Spuds were going to attack Wellinsport and sent Captain Northrop to stop them."

He was about to add more, but Smythe kicked his horse and the beast surged forward, forcing the man to jump out of the way. He had to reach the palace. Already, it seemed, Thomas was taking credit for sending the *Ter-rapin* to the Aligoes, when that had been Smythe's idea.

But he had not gone far when he realized reaching the palace was not going to be easy. The streets were choked with revelers, and more people were joining the party all the time.

The side streets were less congested, but the going was still slow, for they were a tangled maze of streets and alleys. Smythe had not lived in Haever long, and he was soon lost. He continued riding in the general direction of the palace and at last its towers came into view.

Smythe impatiently pushed his way through the crowds who had gathered in front of the palace gates, singing the Freyan national anthem and joyfully shouting, "God save the King!"

He avoided the main gate and rode around to enter a side gate. He jumped down from the horse and was about to order one of his Guundaran guards to take the beast to the stable, only to discover that the Guundarans had been replaced by Royal Navy marines.

Thomas had acted swiftly to see to it that the palace was guarded, which Smythe had to concede had been necessary, although he would have preferred it if Thomas had waited to consult him. But he wondered, why had Thomas replaced the entire palace guard with marines—even the Freyan guards? Of course, Thomas could feel that he could no longer trust anyone who had served with the Guundarans. But Smythe didn't like it. He had always mistrusted the Lords of the Admiralty, starting with Admiral Baker. They did not show him the proper amount of respect.

Smythe approached the marines with some trepidation, but they saluted him and readily admitted him. He had expected the palace to be crawling with ministers, courtiers, members of the House, all clamoring to see the king. He found instead a haven of peace.

The halls were quiet and deserted, save for the servants, and Smythe paid little heed to them. He was not well liked among the staff. They considered him cold and brusque, and spoke disparagingly of him as a person of low birth who "gave himself airs." He considered the servants idle laze-abouts and looked forward to the day he could sack the lot of them.

Smythe went first to his office, hoping to find his aide. The clocks were chiming the hour of six. Early yet, but in view of the news, he could reasonably expect Corporal Plackton to be at his post. Smythe planned to question him, find out if he knew the truth of what had happened in Wellinsport before he saw the king.

Plackton was not there, however, and none of the servants had seen him.

Smythe next went to the royal chambers, the part of the palace reserved for the king and his family. Here, too, the palace guards had been replaced by marines, who saluted him and admitted him into the royal chambers without question.

As they closed the doors after him, he was enveloped in quiet, although the corridors were brightly lighted. He paused to consider where he might find the king and determined he would be in his office, writing the speech he would deliver to the mob.

Thomas would undoubtedly take credit for the victory himself. Smythe would soon put an end to that. He would make it clear that he had been the one to uncover Ullr's plot. He would remind Thomas that he had insisted on sending the *Terrapin* to Wellinsport, never mind that he had done so at King Ullr's suggestion.

Smythe proceeded down a hall, rounded a corner, and came to a halt. The corridor in front of the king's office was lined with soldiers wearing the distinctive scarlet coats of the Royal Marines.

Smythe felt a twinge of unease, but he ignored it. Admiral Baker was certainly working hard to curry royal favor. Smythe would deal with him later.

He reached the king's office to find the secretary hurriedly shoving papers into a satchel.

"I heard the news about Guundar. Is His Majesty safe, Braxton?" Smythe demanded.

The secretary lifted his head. His face was ghastly white, his hair unkempt. He cast Smythe a harried look and kept grabbing papers.

"I have no idea, sir. The king is not in his office. His Majesty is in the new Queen Mary Room," said the secretary. He added in grim tones, "Your aide, Corporal Plackton, is with him."

"My aide?" Smythe felt the unease change to a chill of apprehension. "What is Plackton doing with the king?"

"What do you think he's doing, sir?" the secretary asked bitterly. "He's spilling his guts!"

He snatched up the bulging satchel and was about to leave when the door to the king's office opened. Sir Richard Wallace walked out, accompanied by several marines.

The secretary saw him and blanched.

"I will relieve you of the satchel, sir," said Sir Richard. "Arrest him."

He took the satchel from the secretary and handed it to an officer. Two marines took Braxton into custody, clamping manacles on his wrists.

The secretary cast a beseeching look at Smythe as the marines marched him away.

"You know I am innocent, Chancellor!" he cried over his shoulder. "Tell them the truth! I was working for you, Chancellor!"

Smythe pointedly ignored the man's pleas.

"I have no idea what that fool is talking about. I am glad you are here, Sir Richard. I have important business with His Majesty. Where is the king?"

"King Thomas is in the Queen Mary Room, sir," said Sir Richard.

"What do you mean, the Queen Mary Room, my lord?" Smythe demanded, annoyed. "I have never heard of it."

"I believe you knew it by another name, sir," said Sir Richard. "You knew it as the Rose Room. His Majesty ordered the room renovated to honor the late queen, for that is where she met him and bestowed on him the ring of King James. He thought meeting with you in the that room instead of his office would be particularly fitting given the circumstances."

Smythe remained outwardly cool and impassive. Inwardly, his apprehension deepened. He lowered his voice and drew near.

"Don't forget that you were a member of the Faithful who plotted to assassinate the queen, Sir Richard," Smythe said, softly lethal. "*I* certainly haven't forgotten, and others might be interested to know about your role."

"You know we never had any intent of assassinating our queen," said Sir Richard. "I have readily admitted I was a part of your foul scheme. I trust God will forgive me, for I can never forgive myself."

Smythe was sorry he had not killed this old fool when he'd had the chance. He saw the marines standing at attention, waiting, and decided it was time to make a strategic retreat.

"Our nation is at war and I cannot wait upon the king's pleasure. Inform His Majesty I will be in my office."

Smythe turned on his heel to find his nose planted against the brass buttons of a scarlet coat worn by an extremely tall marine.

"His Majesty will see you now, sir," said Sir Richard.

"I am far too busy—" Smythe began.

The marine clamped his hand on his shoulder.

Smythe was now truly afraid. He dropped all pretense. "Tell that sniveling puppy that he should think twice before he tangles with me! I will ruin him!"

"Search him for weapons," said Sir Richard.

Smythe stood rigid as the marines made a thorough search of his person. They removed a pocket pistol from the inside of his jacket and a knife from his boot.

Sir Richard led the way to the Queen Mary Room, formerly the Rose Room. Marines guarded the door. This time they did not salute Smythe, and he realized the other marines he had encountered had gulled him, lured him into this trap. He entered to see his aide, Plackton, slumped in a chair, his head in his hands.

Thomas was standing in front of the fire, gazing up at a portrait of Queen Mary.

Smythe knew that a bold front could sometimes take the enemy by surprise, disarm them. He stalked into the room as though he owned it, which in his mind he still did. Thomas Stanford would rue the day he crossed him.

"Why is my aide, Corporal Plackton, with you, Your Majesty?" Smythe demanded. "Is he being accused of some crime? If so, he is my officer, under my command. I should have been informed."

Thomas turned his head. His blue eyes were incandescent, like the blue at the heart of the hottest flame.

"Corporal Plackton came to me of his own accord, Chancellor, when he received word of the Guundaran defeat at Wellinsport. He came to plead for mercy. It seems he was the one who told King Ullr where to find your secret stockpile of green-beam guns, such as the one you sent to Maribeau on board a black ship to attack the Dragon Brigade and start a war with Rosia. The corporal has provided me with additional evidence which proves you are a traitor to your country."

Smythe gave a derisive smile.

"I remind Your Majesty that *I* was the one who sent the *Terrapin* to the Aligoes. If I had listened to you, Wellinsport would now be in Guundaran hands."

"The fact that Wellinsport is *not* in Guundaran hands is due entirely to the bravery of Captain Northrop and his crew, Smythe. You acted to send away the *Terrapin* at the behest of King Ullr."

"I have no idea what Your Majesty means," said Smythe stiffly. "Whatever Corporal Plackton has said is a lie."

"He said nothing about the *Terrapin*," said Thomas. "He didn't have to. I have been aware of King Ullr's plot to invade Freya for some time. Plackton did tell me that you also knew of King Ullr's plans, yet instead of coming to tell me in order to save your country, you went to King Ullr to save your own skin."

Smythe saw the enemy closing in, about to overrun his position. But he did not fall back. His nerve still held. He carried the fight into the enemy's camp.

"Very well, sir. I *did* meet with King Ullr," said Smythe, regarding Thomas with hatred. "I met with the king of Guundar in order to prevent you from plunging us into a ruinous war!"

Smythe pointed an accusing finger at Thomas. "I was doing you a favor, sir! Endeavoring to save you from your own folly, as I have so often done. I warn you, sir. If you dare bring charges against me, I will make public the truth about you. I will tell the Freyan people that you conspired with the Rosians and the traitor Henry Wallace to kill the queen and seize the throne. They will believe me. I have supporters in positions of power, members of the nobility who will back me."

Thomas gave a grave smile. "You may do your damnedest, Isaiah Crawford. For that, I believe, is your real name."

Smythe could not speak. He could not breathe. His true name had landed at his feet like a bomb with a lighted fuse. He was dimly aware that Sir Richard was droning on in sonorous tones like a judge, charging him with multiple counts of murder. Smythe could hear only the hissing of the fuse, see only the sputtering sparks as the flame crawled closer and closer to the gunpowder.

He had lost this battle, but he was not about to lose the war. He still had his ambition. He still had his plans.

He still had his hatred.

He saw without seeming to see that no one was guarding the double glass-paned doors which led to the balcony overlooking the palace grounds.

Smythe opened his mouth, as though to say something, then lunged for the doors. Flinging them open, he ran out onto the balcony before anyone could stop him. He slammed shut the doors and shoved the marble bench against them, effectively blocking them.

From inside the room, he could hear Sir Richard shouting and men beating on the doors, trying to force them open.

Smythe walked to the balustrade and coolly looked down to see the ground several stories below. Behind him, the marines were smashing the glass with the butts of their rifles.

Smythe placed his hand on the balustrade and vaulted over it.

Thomas had watched in shock as Smythe apparently ended his life in a fatal plunge off the balcony. When the marines were at last able to break down the double doors and shove the bench aside, Thomas ran out onto the balcony and looked over the edge, expecting to see a crumpled body on the ground below.

Smythe lay on the ground at first unmoving, and then he groaned and slowly leveraged himself to his feet and started to try to run off. He did not get far before his left leg crumpled and he fell to the ground. Aware that the marines were coming after him, he struggled to rise again.

"Surrender, Smythe!" Sir Richard called. "You cannot escape!"

Smythe cast a grim look of defiance at those gathered on the balcony and picked himself up, only to fall again. He picked himself up again and this time he managed to keep going, limping on his injured leg. He reached the shadows of the trees and they lost sight of him.

"He won't get far, Your Majesty," said Sir Richard. "The marines will search every speck of ground."

"They won't find him," Thomas predicted. "The Evil One takes care of his own."

The Evil One did indeed take care of his own.

The marines spent all that day and far into the night searching. They found no trace of Jonathan Smythe.

Or Isaiah Crawford.

FIFTY

Kate and Dalgren had departed Maribeau the day after Lady Rowan's funeral, tasked with flying to Haever as swiftly as possible to tell Thomas that
Freya was not alone in her fight against Guundar. Cecile had written an
urgent letter to King Renaud explaining the dire situation and he had given
orders for the Dragon Brigade to travel to Freya, to assist Freyan forces.

Brigade quartermasters began the task of assembling saddles and har-
nesses and other gear and equipment, taking them out of storage and distrib-
uting them among the riders. The dragons went out hunting for what would
be perhaps their only chance to eat before arriving in Freya.

Watching the dragons massing together, flying over the mountains, Kate
tried to imagine the reaction of the Freyan people when they saw their feared
and hated foes descend from Freyan skies.

"Some would undoubtedly prefer the Guundarans," Kate said to Dalgren
as they readied themselves for the journey.

Grooms from the Brigade were on hand to assist Kate with the saddle and
harness, a luxury previously unknown to her. She and Dalgren had always
wrestled with their old saddle themselves.

"Is that strap too tight around your belly?" Kate asked anxiously, watching the grooms work.

"I can scarcely feel it's there," said Dalgren.

Kate eyed him to see if he was telling the truth. Dalgren was so proud of being a part of the Brigade, even if only as a volunteer, that he might be lying so as not to offend anyone. She checked the saddle and harness herself, as every rider should, and found nothing wrong. The grooms knew their business.

The new saddle was crafted of leather with a high back, equipped with an intricate set of straps that would hold the rider securely during even the most dangerous maneuvers, such as rolling to evade gunfire or swooping down on a target at high speed.

The saddle came with built-in storage for four new pistols, each with the latest magical enhancements; a new rifle; and a cutlass with a dragon motif etched on the blade. Their equipment also included a knife, a braided leather rope, a chain ladder for use in boarding ships, and coils of rope, rations, and water.

Kate especially gloried in her Dragon Brigade uniform: a leather overcoat, a helm and boots, breeches, shirt, and gloves, all bearing the symbol of the Brigade. Military crafters had covered the clothes in magical constructs that protected against all manner of hazards, including flames, bullets, dragon-fire, and the elements.

Dragon appliqués wound up the wide lapels of the leather coat. As Kate tied the nonregulation red kerchief around her neck, hiding it beneath the shirt collar, she remembered the little girl who had told Stephano, all those years ago, she wanted to be a member of the Dragon Brigade.

The sun was rising red on the horizon when the grooms reported to her that Dalgren was saddled and ready. Kate climbed into the saddle. The grooms assisted her as she strapped herself in, then wished her luck and departed.

"We fought for our dreams," Kate said to him, patting him on the neck to indicate she was ready to fly.

Dalgren blew a triumphal gout of flame and sprang into the air.

The flight through the Breath to Haever was far easier and more comfortable than the exhausting trip she and Dalgren had made to Maribeau. The Winter Witch had seemingly grown weary of flinging lightning bolts and pelting travelers with sleet, for they flew through clear skies, and the sun, though it brought little warmth, at least was shining.

The full moon was starting to wane, but provided enough light for them to keep flying until both were too exhausted to continue. They made plans at night when they were resting on one of the floating islands in the Breath.

"When we reach Haever, we will fly to your cave," said Kate. "You can hunt and rest, regain your strength, while I go to the palace to talk to Thomas."

She carried with her two letters. One was from Captain Thorgrimson to

Thomas, giving him details about the Brigade and approximately when they might be expected to arrive. The other letter was from the countess and it was addressed to Sophia, marked personal.

"Give Sophia my dearest love," Cecile had said, handing the letter to Kate. "Tell her she has my blessing."

Kate hoped this meant that Cecile was going to give Sophia her blessing to marry Phillip. Kate was pleased for them and pleased for herself, too, although she tempered her joy with the reminder that just because Thomas was free to marry didn't mean he was free to marry her.

Thomas Stanford was the descendant of kings. Katherine Gascoyne-Fitzmaurice was the granddaughter of a viscount who had plunged his family into financial ruin, while her father had been a disgraced naval officer who had taken to smuggling, only to be killed by a gang he'd tried to cheat.

But Kate now felt free to acknowledge to herself that she loved Thomas, even if she could never tell the world. She had loved him from the moment they first met, when she had held him at gunpoint and looked into his striking blue eyes.

She and Dalgren reached Haever at around five of the clock the following afternoon. They kept hidden among the clouds, hoping to reach Dalgren's cave on the coastline without being seen. As they flew over the city, Dalgren drew Kate's attention to the harbor.

"The navy is preparing for war," he said.

Kate lifted the visor of her helm and looked down to see Freyan warships lining up in battle formation in the Breath. A large crowd had assembled at the dock.

"They can't be!" Kate said in dismay. "It's too early. The invasion is set for Hallen Day and that's still days away! What is going on?"

Dalgren twisted his head to speak to her. "More to the point, where do we go now? My cave overlooks the harbor. If we land there, half the Royal Navy will see us!"

Kate was wondering the same thing. They could fly to the caves near Barwich Manor, but that was a long way from Haever and she needed to be close to reach Thomas. She was trying to come up with a better solution when she saw Welkinstead wreathed in clouds not far from them. The house had returned and was once again triumphantly "drifting with panache" in the skies above Haever.

"We will talk to the man who lives in that house," Kate told Dalgren. "He's a friend of Sir Henry's!"

Kate had never met Simon, but Amelia had told her about him. He had a marvelous vantage point from his position directly above the city. If anyone would know what was happening in Haever, it would be Simon. And from what she had heard of him, he would not be frightened by a dragon arriving at his front door.

She patted Dalgren on the neck and pointed at the floating house. Dalgren disapproved, which he showed by blowing smoke from his nostrils. He didn't know this human and therefore didn't trust him. Kate repeated her gesture and thumped him on the neck by way of emphasis. Dalgren snorted flame in protest and reluctantly flew toward the house.

As they drew closer, Kate could see a wyvern-drawn cab parked in front of the entrance. Dalgren hissed at her and jerked his head. Kate followed his line of sight to the roof, where Sophia and Amelia were trying to draw her attention. Sophia waved her hand. Amelia waved her umbrella.

Dalgren hovered in the air just above the roof, keeping the motion of his wings to a minimum. Kate lowered the chain ladder, climbed down from the saddle, and hurried to greet her friends.

Sophia embraced her, then held her at arm's length to admire her. "You are wearing the Brigade uniform! Does this mean you and Dalgren are members of the Dragon Brigade?"

"Unofficially," Kate replied. "It's a long story, and I don't have time to tell it right now. Where's Bandit?"

"Locked in the pantry," said Sophia. "He has developed a very bad habit of chasing Master Yates in his chair." She touched the red kerchief that was around Kate's neck and laughed. "Is this now part of the uniform?"

Kate tugged at it. "I try to keep it hidden beneath the shirt collar. I am so glad I found you! What is going on in Haever? Dalgren and I saw the ships in the harbor—"

"We are preparing for war," Amelia stated. "King Ullr has launched his invasion early. His fleets are sailing toward Haever, and five of his ships are armed with green-beam guns."

"Simon and I have been developing a magical weapon of our own to stop them," Sophia added. "What about the Dragon Brigade? Did you reach them?"

"Yes, and they are coming to fight the Guundarans," said Kate. "But they won't be here in time. They don't know the date for the invasion has been advanced."

"I will fly to tell them," Dalgren offered. "You let the king know the Brigade is coming."

"A good idea," said Amelia. "I'll take you to Thomas. My cab is parked in front."

Kate climbed back up the ladder so she could retrieve the two letters from the saddle and arm herself with two of the pistols, powder and shot, and the cutlass, which she attached to her belt.

"Where should I meet you when you return?" she asked Dalgren.

"I'll find you," said Dalgren.

"But you won't know where to look," Kate objected.

"Wherever there's trouble, I know you'll be in the middle," Dalgren said, grinning at her, showing his fangs and puffing smoke.

Kate thumped him on the neck. "I'll meet you in your cave. By that time, the navy will know you're on our side and hopefully they won't shoot at you. Don't you dare fly into battle without me!"

Kate climbed back down the ladder onto the roof, then touched a magical construct at the bottom, releasing the ladder from the saddle so that it would not impede Dalgren's flight. The ladder landed in a tangle at her feet. She gathered it up and tucked it under her arm.

She waved at Dalgren and he took flight, dipping his wings to them as he passed overhead.

"Where can I find Thomas?" Kate asked. "Is he in the palace?"

"He is probably there now, although he won't be for long," said Sophia. "He said he would not hide in the palace when his country was going to war. He plans to sail to battle on board the *Valor*."

Amelia eyed Kate's uniform with the dragons emblazoned on the lapels. "You won't be allowed anywhere near the king wearing a Rosian uniform. The Dragon Brigade may be coming to fight for Freya, but the Freyans don't know that. You should take it off."

"No, Kate must leave it on for her own safety," Sophia corrected. She touched the coat, tracing her finger over the leather. "This coat is covered with some of the strongest protective magic I have ever seen. Layer upon layer of constructs that link together like chain mail."

Kate smiled and smoothed the soft, supple leather with her hands. "Wearing this uniform has been my dream since I was little. I will leave it on. In fact, I may never take it off."

"Then I suggest we meet Thomas at the harbor, or on board the *Valor*, Admiral Baker's flagship," said Amelia. "The admiral is a friend of Sir Henry's and he'll recognize you."

She added, frowning, "At least hide the dragon emblems. I am serious, Kate. That uniform could put you in danger. People are clamoring for Rosian blood. Countless Rosians have been attacked on the street, their homes and businesses burned. Here, you can borrow my muffler."

Kate conceded that Amelia was probably right. She draped the red wool muffler around her neck so that it concealed the dragons on her coat, then the three left the roof and descended the stairs.

"You didn't run into Phillip when you were in the Aligoes, did you?" Sophia asked anxiously. "I have heard nothing from him."

"No, but that reminds me," Kate exclaimed. "I have something for you. I almost forgot."

She reached into the pocket of her coat, pulled out the letter from the countess, and handed it to Sophia.

"I have not read the letter, of course. But from what the countess told me, I believe she is giving you and Pip her blessing to marry," Kate said with a smile.

Sophia flushed with pleasure and clasped the letter close to her heart. When they reached the second-floor landing, Sophia stopped to open the letter, only to be accosted by Mr. Albright. He looked very stern.

"I regret to inform you, ma'am, that your dog has absconded with a leg of lamb. When I attempted to take it away, he showed his teeth and seemed prepared to bite me."

"Oh, dear," said Sophia. "I must go scold Bandit and take the lamb away or he will be sick all night."

She embraced Kate. "God go with you! Thank you for my letter!"

She hurried down the stairs, and Kate was about to follow, but the moment she set foot in the house, she stopped to stare about in wonder. She had never before been in Welkinstead and everywhere she looked she saw some object that was either strange, beautiful, horrible, or curious. Oddities dangled from the ceiling; hung on the walls; perched on desks, cabinets, and side tables; lay on the floor—or were scattered about the stairs, where they proved a hazard to life and limb.

A man seated in a wheeled chair waited at the bottom of the stairs.

"I am Simon Yates. Forgive the mess," he called. "Everything has been in disarray since the house crashed. Albright and I haven't had time to clean up yet. Don't trip over the newts."

He gestured to a cage on the third stair that housed several of the lizards. Kate just managed to squeeze her way past.

"Miss Amelia, I am glad to see you," Simon continued. "Albright informed me of your arrival and said you had picked up my mail. Did you have any difficulty at the post office?"

"I did not, sir," said Amelia. "The postmistress had several large bags to deliver. She was extremely happy to hear you are well. She had been worried about you."

Simon shifted his gaze to Kate, regarding her with interest. He held out his hand.

"You must be Captain Kate."

"You have the advantage of me, Master Yates," Kate said. "I don't recall that we have ever met."

Simon chuckled. "We haven't. I observed you and your dragon friend fly-

ing toward the house. I knew from Miss Amelia that you two had traveled
to the Aligoes to warn the Brigade of the black ship and the green-beam gun.
Did you manage to reach the Brigade in time?"

"We did, sir," said Kate. "I would tell you the story, but I have to take an
urgent message to His Majesty—"

"—that the Dragon Brigade is coming," Simon finished her sentence.

Kate gaped at him. "How did you know, sir?"

"Isn't it obvious?" Simon returned. "I am glad you are here. You can deliver a message to the king from me. I have invented a new weapon which
we will be using against the Guundarans in the battle to defend Haever. Miss
Amelia, your notebook. Take down the following information. The captain
can give it to the king."

"Sir, I would love to hear," Kate protested, "but I must find the king. The
matter is urgent!"

Simon regarded her gravely. "You are right, Captain Kate. The matter *is*
urgent. The 'Eye' is the only weapon capable of destroying the green-beam
guns. I remind you that these heinous guns can be as deadly to dragons as
they are to people. Thus you understand why His Majesty needs this information."

"Yes, sir," said Kate, not knowing what else to say. She hoped Simon was
right, though she had her doubts.

Simon offered her a seat, but she remained standing, hoping that would
hasten the proceedings.

"Sophia named the weapon 'God's Eye,'" Simon stated. "A most ridiculous name, by the way, since it has no eyes and I am the inventor, not God.
The weapon makes use of the Seventh Sigil to combine magic and contramagic into a concentrated burst of white, 'pure' magic, and is thus more cor-
rectly termed a refocused energy emitter and generator. That name being
rather too long and cumbersome, she and I have compromised and refer to
it as the 'Eye.'

"I designed the Eye based on another of my inventions that I call
'crackers'—glass rods that are inscribed with contramagic on one end and
magic on the other. When I combine the two, the cracker explodes, doing
considerable damage.

"The Eye will have far greater destructive power than the crackers. My
most immediate problem was that I had no time to spend on development.
I would have normally taken a year producing it. Instead, Sophia and I had
to cobble together the device from whatever we could scrounge up about the
house."

"Which would have been a problem in any other house except Welkinstead," Amelia observed in an undertone to Kate.

"What does the Eye do to stop the green-beam guns, sir?" Kate asked, trying to hurry him along.

"I can't predict," said Simon. "I have several theories, but since we have yet to fire it, I cannot be certain of the outcome."

Kate stared at him, perplexed. "But, sir, if you don't know—"

She was interrupted by Welkinstead, which gave a lurch and then made a sudden, stomach-churning descent that startled the occupants and knocked objects off the walls or sent them bumping down the stairs.

The house fell only a few feet before it stabilized, but the effect on those inside was nerve-racking. Kate grabbed hold of the banister to keep from falling. Amelia was so shaken she dropped her umbrella.

"Albright!" Simon bellowed. "What the devil was that?"

"The flow of the magic to the lift tanks is proving to be unstable, sir," Albright shouted back.

"I had better handle this myself," said Simon, annoyed. "Albright maintains we should have never left the ground. I refuse to give him the satisfaction of crashing."

He started off, then paused to glance out the window. Kate was astonished to see two naval tugboats chug into view.

"Ah, excellent," said Simon. "The Admiralty received my message. The tugboats have arrived. I must give the commanders their instructions. Goodbye and good luck, Captain."

He whipped his chair around and sped off.

Kate looked at the tugboats and felt the house still quivering. "Is Sophia safe here?"

Amelia was grave. "No one in Haever is safe, Kate. Besides, Sophia would not leave. She enjoys working with Master Yates. As she says, she is finally able to put her skills as a savant to good use. Now we had best go before the cab driver leaves without us. He appears to be considerably unnerved by the gyrations of the house."

The white-faced driver hustled them into the cab and settled the wyvern with a few touches of his whip. Amelia told him to take them to the harbor, and he left with all speed.

Kate looked back at Welkinstead—ponderous, enormous, slow-moving.

"Why does Master Yates need the tugboats?"

"To maneuver the house into position during the battle," Amelia replied. "We will be targeting the ships armed with the green-beam guns. Master Yates is not certain of the Eye's range and one cannot 'drift with panache' when engaging the enemy."

"But, Miss Amelia, those ships will be firing back at you!" Kate protested.

"Tugboats can't push Welkinstead out of the way of cannonballs or green beams!"

"Oh, yes, we are, all of us, well aware of the danger," said Amelia complacently. "The house was sunk once before by a green-beam gun."

She added with frowning asperity, "Now, Kate, did any of us try to talk *you* out of flying into battle with the Brigade because of a little danger?"

Kate was about to argue that they wouldn't be facing a "little" danger, they would be facing Guundaran men-of-war. She could see by Amelia's stern expression she wasn't going to succeed.

"No, ma'am," Kate said, sighing.

Amelia gave a brisk nod.

Kate looked back at Welkinstead to see the tugboats taking up their positions, nuzzling the house's foundation, preparing to shove Welkinstead into battle.

FIFTY-ONE

Kate had worried that the *Valor* might already have set sail and she was relieved to see the ship was still tethered to the moorings. The rest of the fleet rode on the mists of the Breath, shining red gold in the light of the setting sun.

Despite the fact that their city was preparing for war, hundreds of people had gathered at the dock to watch their king board the *Valor,* preparing like kings of old to lead his forces into battle.

"Do we know for certain the Guundarans plan to attack Haever?" Kate asked Amelia.

"The admiralty received reports from Glenham that an armada of enemy ships sailed over that city at dawn, heading this direction," Amelia replied. "Just as Simon predicted they would."

The cab arrived at the harbor and Kate saw marines lining the dock, keeping the crowd under control. The navy docks were separate from the civilian docks, protected by a ten-foot-tall iron fence. Beyond that, another iron fence lined the edge of the cliff to prevent people from tumbling into the Breath.

"Can you fly over that barricade?" Kate asked the driver.

He glared at her. "Would that be before or after the marines shoot me, Miss?"

He pointed with the whip to an alley a short distance from the wharf. "I can set you down there. That's as close as I dare go."

After the cab had landed in the alley, Kate climbed out and waited for Amelia, only to see her settle back into the seat.

"Aren't you coming with me?" Kate asked.

"No, my dear. I've arranged with Master Yates to observe the battle from the air. This will be the story of a lifetime! And he will need my help constructing the weapon."

"He hasn't built it yet?" Kate asked, astonished.

"The Eye is currently in the design phase," said Amelia. She prodded the driver in the back with her umbrella.

"Make haste, my man!"

He turned to glare at her, but she must have been paying him well, for he only muttered something, put his hand on the helm, and snapped his whip. The wyverns took off and the carriage returned to the air.

Kate was starting down the alley, heading for the docks, when she heard pounding feet coming up behind her. She remembered Amelia's warning about her uniform, and she glanced over her shoulder to see a man in a stocking cap and sailor's pea coat dashing down the alley heading straight for her. The man's face and clothes were covered in mud, and he looked like a footpad. Kate reached for her pistol.

The man yanked off his cap to reveal a shock of unruly blond hair.

"Kate! It's me! Pip! Thank God I've found you! Saw you and Dalgren . . . lost track . . . Miss Amelia . . . I need to know. . . ."

Phillip had to stop talking to gasp for breath.

"Pip! You shouldn't be in Haever!" Kate told him. "Smythe is hunting for you! It's not safe!"

"Never mind that. Is Sophia safe?" Phillip demanded. "Where is she?"

"She's with Master Yates at Welkinstead. I just left her. She's fine, but—"

"Bless you!" Phillip cried fervently.

He looked up in the air at the floating house as though to get his bearings, grasped Kate's hand and shook it in gratitude, then ran off down the alley.

"Pip, wait!" Kate called after him. "Sophia is in danger! You have to convince—"

Phillip didn't hear her, and the next moment, he was gone.

Kate sighed. Continuing on down the alley, she plunged into the crowd, reminded of the time only days ago when she had been forced to fight her way through a similar throng of spectators to deliver the nosegay to Thomas.

The mood of the crowd was different this time. Then they had mourned their queen and cheered their new king. Today, people were not cheering. They were quiet, fiercely resolved. If they talked at all, they spoke in low tones. Children clutched small Freyan flags in their hands, but they could sense the tension in their parents and looked confused and afraid.

The Freyan people had come to the docks to support their king, to honor his courage, even as they understood the peril to themselves and their country. Thomas and their military were fighting to save them. If they went down to defeat, the Guundaran ships armed with green-beam guns would lay waste to their city and their nation would fall.

Kate had no difficulty making her way through the crowd. Men and women let her pass without question. Children gazed at her with frightened eyes. Kate longed to tell them that help was coming, but she knew they wouldn't understand. They would look up to see a sky filled with dragons and they would despair. She had to talk to Thomas, make *him* understand, and she realized reaching him was going to be a challenge.

She viewed in dismay the ten-foot iron palisade that prevented unauthorized people from entering the Royal Naval Dockyard and also kept them from tumbling off the edge of the continent into the Breath. A gate permitted entry and it was guarded by the Royal Marines.

In preparation for the king, who had stated he would address his people before he boarded the ship, workmen had hastily erected a small stage decorated with bunting in front of the palisade. Constables guarded the route the king would take to reach the stage and stood in a line in front of it.

The *Valor*'s three masts towered above the barricades. The sails were furled while the ship was at anchor, the balloons only partially filled. Officers waited on the quarterdeck to welcome the king. Sailors lined the yardarms. The *Valor*'s captain had even managed, on short notice, to scrounge up a small band consisting of two fiddles, a fife, and a drum.

Someone called out that the king was coming, and the crowd stirred in anticipation as the royal carriage, drawn by a pair of matching black horses, came into view. The band on board the *Valor* struck up a screechy rendition of the Freyan national anthem.

The carriage rolled to a halt, and one of the footmen jumped down from his seat at the rear of the carriage to open the door. Thomas emerged, wearing a Freyan naval uniform, bicorn, and gloves. His marine escort assembled around him.

The crowd cheered. Men took off their hats, and women fluttered handkerchiefs and told children to brandish their flags.

Thomas acknowledged his people with a smile and a wave and the cheering grew louder. The crowd surged forward, trying to see him. The constables planted their feet, pushing them back. Thomas walked toward the speaking platform along the path made through the crowd by the constables. The marines followed behind.

Kate was as close as she was going to get. She sucked in a deep breath and filled her lungs with air, using the bellow that shouted orders to her crew over the boom of cannons.

"Thomas! Tom! It's me—Kate!"

Thomas appeared to hear her, even over the din of the cheers and the music, for he stopped walking and turned his head to search the crowd.

Kate waved her arms and drew in another breath to call to him. *"Thomas, I'm here—"*

Her shout ended in a strangled gasp. "Trubgek!"

He was standing only a few feet from her. He had not seen her, he did not hear her. He was staring fixedly at Thomas, and Kate knew with sickening, unbearable certainty Trubgek was here to kill. She had no idea how he meant to use his powerful dragon magic, but she had seen the results and she was terrified. He had nearly brought down her family's manor house by simply placing the palm of his hand against a wall.

As Kate drew in another breath to shout a warning, she felt the barrel of a pistol jam into her rib cage.

"One word to Trubgek, Captain," said Smythe, "and you die."

Trubgek heard his name and turned his head, looking questioningly at Smythe.

"Keep your mind on your work!" Smythe told him angrily. "I will deal with this."

Trubgek nodded and started to turn away, and then he saw Kate and knew her. She could see the flicker of recognition in his empty eyes.

Smythe caught hold of her arm and dragged her closer.

He jabbed her with the pistol. "You know me, don't you?"

Kate glanced at him and gave a brief nod.

Smythe spoke softly, his breath on her cheek. "You know I will not hesitate to kill you. Face forward. Keep your hands where I can see them."

Kate nodded stiffly and turned away. She had seen in that brief glance that Smythe was favoring his left leg, unable to put his full weight on it. His fine clothes were muddy and disheveled, his torn breeches stained with mud and blood.

Kate's mouth was dry. Her breath came fast, her heart thudded against her ribs. She kept both hands in plain sight.

Smythe grasped her arm more tightly, causing her to flinch in pain. He signaled Trubgek and told him, "Wait until he boards the ship."

Trubgek gazed at Kate with eyes devoid of pity, emotion, fear . . . or life. He shifted his empty eyes back to Thomas and began to flex his hands.

Thomas cast another searching glance through the crowd. Kate didn't dare speak, and he gave a slight shrug and turned away. He climbed the stairs to the stage, where he was welcomed by the Lord Mayor of Haever and other dignitaries. The crowd hushed to hear their king. Thomas began to speak, but Kate had no idea what he was saying. Her entire being was concentrated on Trubgek, waiting in terror for him to attack.

Thomas ended his speech and the crowd gave him a rousing cheer. He waved again and then left the stage and entered the gate, which the guards shut behind him. He walked up the gangplank to board the *Valor*. The band played, pipes twittered, officers saluted.

Trubgek slowly raised his hands into the air and black storm clouds boiled up out of the Deep Breath in response, as if he had plunged his hands into the bottom of the world, seized the darkness, and dragged it to the surface.

A blast of icy wind swept over the wharf. The black clouds churned and bubbled and blotted out the setting sun. Day turned to night in a moment. A blast of howling wind whipped the flags on the *Valor* and caused the sails to flap. Sailors on the yardarms scrambled down for their lives.

Trubgek made a slight gesture and bolts of purple lightning streaked through the black, boiling clouds. Thunder boomed and the ground shook. A lightning bolt struck the *Valor*'s main mast. The ship's protective magic flared blue.

The wind blew even more fiercely, picking up debris and tossing it about. People on the docks panicked and tried to flee, seeking shelter. Trubgek gestured again and the raging wind struck at the *Valor*, tearing at the rigging and snapping the lines tethering the ship to the iron bollards on the dock.

The wind was aiming at Thomas, buffeting him, and hit him a blow that sent him staggering. The wind pummeled him, seemingly intent on hurling him overboard. Admiral Baker seized hold of him, and dragged him back away from the rail.

Trubgek spread his hands wide, and the wind howled like a living creature. Jagged streaks of lightning flared around the *Valor*'s masts.

Smythe raised his voice, almost deafening Kate.

"Behold the wrath of God!" he thundered. "He will destroy the wicked among you! Cast down the heathen king who seeks to betray you to the Rosians!"

Kate shuddered, wondering if Smythe had gone mad. She glanced at him again and saw the glint in his eyes wasn't madness—it was cunning. Kate understood his plan. Smythe was going to frame God, make Him appear responsible for Thomas's death. Already some among the crowd were falling to their knees, weeping and exhorting God to spare them.

"Thomas Stanford! Spawn of the Evil One!" Smythe roared. "God in His wrath will destroy you!"

Thomas heard him and knew his voice. He turned to look at Smythe, saw Kate and realized she was in danger. He ran down the gangplank toward her, shouting for the guards and pointing at Smythe.

Trubgek shifted his hand and the wind hit Thomas a savage blow that felled him. Guards surrounded him, trying to protect him even as they had to fight to remain standing.

Kate felt the pistol press against her rib cage. She looked down at the coat she had worn with such pride, the coat of a member of the Dragon Brigade, the men and women and dragons who fought to defend the innocent. The coat—covered with protective magical constructs—magic and contramagic connected by the Seventh Sigil.

Kate had no idea if the magic would stop a bullet, but she had to trust it, trust her dream. She clenched her fists.

"Petar!" she shouted. "Petar! Look at me!"

Trubgek started at the sound of his name—his true name. He stopped his spell casting and turned his empty eyes on her.

"Shut up!" Smythe snarled, squeezing her arm with bruising force.

Kate ignored him. "Petar, he is using you!"

She spoke rapidly, for she had no idea how much time she had. "Smythe is no different from Coreg. He calls you Trubgek. He doesn't know your true name. Only the insult . . . You are Petar! You can be free—"

Smythe fired. The magical constructs that covered the coat flared blue-green, half blinding Kate and knocking the gun from Smythe's hand. He cursed and hurled Kate to the ground.

She landed on her stomach and rolled over onto her back in agony, fighting to breathe and sobbing in pain with every breath. The magic had saved her life, but had been unable to stop the impact of the bullet that had smashed into her ribs like a blow from a blacksmith's hammer.

People screamed at the sound of the pistol shot and tried to flee. Kate heard Thomas cry out in fear and anger. He must have heard the shot and seen her fall. She could not see him. All she could see was Smythe standing over her and people milling about her and storm clouds swirling above her. But she knew Thomas as well as she knew herself, and as she had fought to save him, he would fight God Himself to try to reach her.

And Smythe knew Thomas as well. He coolly and calmly drew another pistol, ready to kill him when he drew close.

Kate lashed out with her foot and struck Smythe in his left kneecap. Smythe cried out in agony and staggered, trying to keep his balance. Seeing Thomas running toward him, he raised his pistol. Thomas slammed into him with bruising force and carried him to the dock.

The pistol went off. Smythe struggled to rise and Thomas drove his fist into the man's jaw, smashing his head into the wooden planks. Smythe lay, unmoving, with his eyes closed. Marines and constables converged on him, taking rough hold of him.

"We've got him, Your Majesty," said one.

Thomas worriedly turned to Kate, who lay on the dock, her hand pressed against her side. Guards surrounded them both, holding back the crowd of onlookers. Thomas knelt by Kate's side and took hold of her hand.

"Where are you hurt?" he asked anxiously.

"I'm all right," said Kate. "No, truly! The magic on my coat stopped the bullet. But what about you? The pistol went off. . . ."

"He missed," said Thomas. "And you are *not* all right. I can see you are in pain. I'll send for the healer—"

"No, wait! I came to give you a message!" Kate grabbed hold of him and then sucked in a pain-filled breath as the movement jarred her ribs. "The Dragon Brigade . . . They are coming to fight with us. . . ."

"The Dragon Brigade!" Thomas repeated, regarding her in wonder. "Can this be true? You give me hope, Kate! When will they arrive?"

"They were at least a day's journey behind me," said Kate.

Thomas's expression was grave, shadowed.

"Then they will be too late," he said. "King Ullr's ships are even now sailing toward Haever. . . ."

"Dalgren flew to warn the Brigade," said Kate. "He's coming back soon. I have to meet him."

She struggled to rise and, seeing that she was determined, Thomas put his arm around her and helped her to a sitting position.

Kate clamped her lips shut on a groan and smiled, trying to pretend she was fine.

She couldn't fool Thomas, who regarded her in concern. "I'm fetching a healer."

"No, please don't. Just give me a moment to catch my breath," said Kate. "And I think that young man standing behind you is trying to get your attention."

Thomas looked around at an abashed-looking midshipman who had been hovering near him, shuffling his feet and loudly clearing his throat in an attempt to attract the king's attention.

"Yes, lad, what do you want?" Thomas asked impatiently.

The midshipman flushed red with embarrassment. "Begging your pardon, Your Majesty, sir. Captain Mayfield says we must set sail now or we will lose the wind."

"The wind!" Kate gasped, stricken. "Oh, God! Trubgek!"

She pressed her hand against her ribs in an ineffectual attempt to stop the pain and staggered to her feet. She looked for Trubgek, searching the crowd, but he was gone.

The storm was receding. The wind was tearing the black clouds to rags. Lightning flared sullenly, but harmlessly.

"Who is Trubgek?" Thomas asked.

"He works for Smythe. He was right here!" Kate questioned the guards and those standing around her. "The man in the leather vest. Did any of you see what happened to him? Where he went?"

"I didn't see a man in a vest," said Thomas. "Smythe was alone. The constables are taking him to prison now."

They had slapped Smythe in the face until he had regained consciousness, then yanked him to his feet and clamped manacles to his wrists and chains to his ankles. He was able to walk, though just barely, hobbling on his injured leg. His face and head were bruised and bloodied.

Thomas went to confront him. "You had an accomplice, Smythe. A man called Trubgek. Where is he?"

Smythe answered with vile words and lunged for Thomas, manacled hands reaching for his throat. Smythe's attack caught the constables by surprise, but they quickly managed to wrestle him away from the king. Smythe's face contorted in fury and he continued to fight, grinding his teeth as though he could grind Thomas's bones. He raved at Thomas as the guards hauled him off, even twisting his head to keep him in sight and spewing invective.

Kate shuddered. "That man hates you with all his being, Thomas. He ordered Trubgek to kill you. We have to find him!"

"What does this man, Trubgek, look like, Kate?" Thomas asked. "I'll have the constables search for him."

"A strange man with empty eyes," said Kate. "They can search, but they won't find him. You should leave, Thomas. Now."

The midshipman agreed, for he coughed loudly and gave Thomas a pleading look. If the *Valor* missed the wind, the captain would vent his anger on his midshipman, not the king.

"You must join your ship and I must find Dalgren," said Kate. "He and I are flying with the Brigade."

Thomas pulled her close to him. "Do I have permission to kiss you now?"

In answer, Kate cradled his face in her hands and pressed her lips to his.

Thomas kissed her again and embraced her gently, mindful of her ribs. Kate looked into his blue eyes and, for a moment, the cheering crowd on the dock disappeared. The two of them were the only two people in the world.

"Take care of yourself, Thomas Stanford," Kate said. "Don't let our story end here."

"I won't," said Thomas, smiling. "You still owe me that dance."

He tore himself away and walked to the ship. The marine guard fell in around him. The guards opened the gate for him and closed it after him. The people gathered close to the palisade, peering through the bars, calling out well wishes.

Thomas arrived on deck and turned to wave to his people, who gave him a rousing cheer. The sailors quickly hauled in the gangplank. Dockworkers cast off the lines. The damage done to the ship by Trubgek's attack had been minimal, for it had mostly been aimed at Thomas. Sails spread, balloons inflated, and the *Valor* rose into the air.

The cheers of the crowd died away, and people gathered up children and headed home. They were not going back to put on the tea kettle and sit by the fire to talk over the events of the day. They were going home to prepare for war.

Kate stood on the dock, watching until the sunlit mists of the Breath closed around the ship and Thomas was lost to sight. She could feel the pain in her side more acutely now and she realized she was going to have to find a healer or she would never be able to ride Dalgren.

She started to turn away when she was arrested by the unusual sight of a man scaling the iron bars of the palisade.

The man was not wearing a coat, only a leather vest. Recognizing Trubgek, she feared he was planning to finish what he had started, perhaps summon another storm, and she looked frantically about for a constable. None were nearby and she realized that even if she found someone, they could not stop him. She could only watch, helpless.

Trubgek climbed rapidly and with ease, not an easy feat, for the barricade was ten feet tall and topped by iron finials. He attained the top of the palisade, grasped the finials, and climbed over them. He paused a moment at the top, then dropped to the ground the last few feet and stood looking around the docks.

The dockworkers had departed, their job finished for the day. No one was watching him. No one had seen him.

No one except Kate.

As if he felt her presence, Trubgek turned and looked at her. She could not see his eyes. He was too far from her. But she had the feeling that they would not be empty. The flicker of light would reveal that tormented little boy, Petar.

He was too far from her. She could not stop him and she was not sure she would have if he'd given her the chance. She could only let him know she understood.

"Be free," she told him.

Trubgek turned away. He walked out to the very edge of the precipice and paused a moment to gaze down into the mists that curled around his feet. As calmly as though he was stepping off a curb, he stepped off the edge of the cliff.

Kate stared at the place where he had been standing, hoping she would see him crawl back up over the edge, though she knew he wouldn't. The emptiness was always and forever empty. Shivering, she drew her coat more closely around her. She had to find a healer and, after that, she had a long walk to Dalgren's cave, and the sun was setting, darkness closing in.

Kate left the dock and walked into the city, pressing her hand against her side and wincing in pain with every breath.

As she made her way through the streets, she saw people hurrying to stock underground cellars with food and blankets and filling every container they owned with water. Apothecary shops were doing a brisk business in ointments, healing potions, bandages, and splints.

Hoping she might be able to purchase a salve for her injured ribs from an apothecary, she stopped in front of a shop that featured a mortar and pestle on its sign. Before she entered, she took off her Dragon Brigade coat and inspected it in the waning light. The coat had a large burned spot on the back and smelled strongly of gunpowder. She bundled it up and tucked it underneath her arm.

The shop was empty, except for the proprietor, who was removing glass bottles from the shelves and storing them away beneath the counter for safe-keeping. Hearing the door open, the woman called, "We're closed!"

"I just need something for bruised ribs," said Kate.

The woman straightened up from behind the counter. She glanced curiously at Kate's leather breeches and tall riding boots.

"I fell off my horse," Kate explained.

The apothecary nodded as though she believed her.

"I'm sold out of a lot, dearie. But I believe a mixture of arnica, comfrey, and a bit of magic will help, and I can make that up myself. Shut the door, will you, and turn the sign around to say I'm closed."

Kate did as she was asked. The apothecary eyed her, noted her grimacing with pain.

"I was a nurse before I opened my own shop. Let me check to see if anything's broken."

She took Kate to the back room and poked and prodded her. Then she sniffed at her and said with a sly smile, "Are you sure your horse didn't shoot you, dearie?"

Kate flushed. The woman shook her head.

"I don't think you broke any bones. The salve will ease the pain and reduce the bruising."

She smeared the salve over Kate's tender ribs and bound her midriff with bandages. She refused to accept any money, and invited Kate to stay with her if she had no place to spend the night.

Kate assured her she was going to stay with a friend, thanked her, and departed. She was still in pain, and every breath hurt, but after a time she noticed that the salve, bandages, and magic were helping, and she could breathe almost normally.

Leaving the city, she took the path that led to Dalgren's cave in the cliffs overlooking the Breath. The long walk did her good. She kept thinking about Trubgek. Part of her was glad he was gone and part of her felt guilty for being glad. She reminded herself that he had tried to kill Dalgren, tried to kill Thomas. Kate absolved herself from guilt. Trubgek was gone and, she trusted, out of her life forever.

She reached Dalgren's cave hoping to find the dragon had returned, but not really expecting it. She didn't think he would be back much before dawn. She bundled up in her coat for warmth, made herself as comfortable as she could, and waited for morning.

FIFTY-TWO

Henry Wallace was rapidly recovering from his wound. Unfortunately, the better he felt, the more he chafed at inaction. His country was in crisis and he was far from home, forced to rely on a ship that in his mind was the very epitome of the name, *Terrapin*. It seemed to him to crawl through the Breath.

In point of fact, the *Terrapin* was making good time. The devil did not fail Alan. His luck held. The repairs to the ship had gone better than he had expected, and the storms of the Winter Witch had abated. They sailed through cloudless skies, pushed along by a favorable wind, with the sun by day and the moon to light their way at night.

That was small comfort to Henry. Unable to sit still, he roamed restlessly about the ship, fretting and getting in everyone's way. The sailors were constantly bumping into him, the helmsman complained that Henry was continually peering over his shoulder and hinting that he did not know how to do his job. Henry drove Alan to the point of distraction by barging into his cabin several times a day to ask if he didn't want to take another navigational reading.

The third time Henry interrupted him, Alan sent for Mr. Sloan.

"I know Henry is worried about the Guundaran invasion, but I swear to

God, Mr. Sloan, if he interrupts my work one more time, I will throw him overboard."

Mr. Sloan sought out his master and found Henry standing on the quarterdeck, wrapped in gloom, frowning at the buoys that bobbed about in the Breath, marking the route.

When Henry saw Mr. Sloan approach, he knew by his secretary's deferential demeanor and apologetic cough that he had come to remonstrate with him.

"I know, I know," Henry said tersely, before Mr. Sloan could speak. "Alan sent you to tell me I am making a nuisance of myself."

"He did mention something about throwing you overboard, my lord," said Mr. Sloan.

Henry scowled.

"Alan doesn't understand! We could arrive in Haever to find King Ullr victorious, our king dead or in prison, and the flag of Guundar flying over the palace!"

"If you are right and the worst occurs, my lord, we will carry on the fight," said Mr. Sloan imperturbably. "You and I alone, if need be."

Henry gave a grudging smile. "I know you are trying to cheer me, Mr. Sloan, but—"

"Look there, my lord! We are nearing home!"

Mr. Sloan pointed to one of the buoys just then drifting into view. This buoy was different from the others they had passed, for it flashed with a red magical light warning ships that they were approaching land.

"By God, we are not far now!" Henry exclaimed.

The lookout had also spotted the buoy and was shouting the news. The officer on duty sent a messenger to inform the captain, and Alan hurried up on deck, buttoning his coat as he came. He studied the charts, glanced at the buoy and sky, then ordered a change of course that would take them north along the eastern coast of Freya.

Once the *Terrapin* was settled on her new course, he walked over to join Henry and Mr. Sloan, who were standing at the rail, peering through the mists, trying to catch sight of the coastline.

"If the weather holds—and I think it will, for the wind is from the west— we should reach Haever by morning," Alan told them.

"Now you have jinxed us," said Henry, rounding on him. "Touch wood."

"You have been around Randolph too long," said Alan, but he obligingly ran his fingers along the wooden rail, then rested his hand on Henry's shoulder. "Staring at the coast won't bring us there any sooner. Let us go below for a glass of Calvados before dinner."

"Deck there!" the lookout bellowed. "Dragons!"

At that dread cry, every man on deck stopped what he was doing and turned to look into the sky.

The dragons flew in "wings" of six, flying in "V" formations that allowed them to make eye contact with each other, and thus providing them the means to communicate. The sunlight glittered on their scales. Henry could see the riders in their specially designed saddles and the shining emblems each dragon wore on the chest.

"The Dragon Brigade," said Henry exultantly. He rubbed his gloved hands together. "They came, Mr. Sloan. They came! Kate managed to reach them in time!"

But the sailors watched them with dark and grim expressions, viewing the dragons with suspicion, obviously thinking that the *Terrapin* should be running out her guns.

"Begging your pardon, sir, but do you trust them?" Lieutenant Hobbs asked Alan in an undertone. "Why would the Brigade fight to save us now? They have always sought to destroy us."

Henry overheard the question and replied before Alan could answer.

"A Rosian/Freyan alliance makes sense from the Rosian standpoint, Mr. Hobbs. If King Ullr seized Freya, he would acquire our ships, which are the finest in the world, far better than anything he can build. And once he established himself in Freya, his ambitious gaze would turn to Rosia, where King Renaud calculates that it is in his own best interest to stop Ullr now before he can increase his strength, even if that means coming to the aid of a long-time foe."

"'The enemy of my enemy is not my friend, just the means to an end,'" said Alan, grinning. "Isn't that what you always say, Henry?"

"I do," said Henry. "I fear I will find it very hard from now on to hate the Rosians."

Braving the cold, he leaned over to watch the green of the Freyan coast gradually come into view beneath the keel, seeming to float on the orange mists. As the sun drew nearer the horizon, the reddish glow of twilight set the mists aflame, an image Henry did not find reassuring.

The fiery rays of the setting sun shone on the *Valor*, lighting the way for the ship's boats carrying officers of the Freyan fleet to join their king and their admiral for dinner on board the flagship. Everyone assembled knew they faced overwhelming odds in the upcoming battle, and that many of those seated around the table might be dead before morning.

In spite of that—or perhaps because of it—the meal was cheerful. Thomas led the talk to the *Terrapin*'s astonishing victory over the Guundarans and the officers vowed that Captain Northrop would not have all the glory to himself.

Thomas was aware that these men had initially harbored doubts about their new young king. He was a stranger to Freya, having been raised in Estara. He spoke Freyan with an Estaran accent. But they had heard stories of his heroics in the battle against the Bottom Dwellers, and they knew Queen Mary had named him her heir and given him the ring of King James the night she had died. All that counted in his favor.

Still, they wondered. Their doubts had vanished, however, when Thomas had announced he was going to board the *Valor* and join them in battle. They knew he could have stayed safe in his palace.

"To His Majesty," said Randolph, raising his glass in a toast. "If I were king, I'd rather be on board this ship fighting for my life instead of sitting on my throne waiting for some goddamn Spud to chop off my head."

After dinner, Thomas and the officers retired to the admiral's quarters to formulate their battle plan. They gathered around a chart on which Randolph had marked the Guundarans' latest known position, which was south of Glenham, heading for Haever.

"By sailing all night, the enemy will arrive in Haever near dawn," said Randolph. "Our scouts report sixty enemy ships. Forty of these are ships of the line and five ships are armed with green-beam guns. Scouts in Glenham saw four of these goddamn guns on board sloops that had been refitted to accommodate them, for they have to be mounted on a rotating platform. They could see the green-beam guns on the foredecks."

"Only four, sir?" Thomas questioned. "King Ullr boasted that he had five."

"The discrepancy is troubling, sir," said Randolph. "What is even more troubling is the fact that the four sloops armed with these guns did not sail with the main body. Griffin riders sent to shadow the fleet reported back this afternoon that they could not locate them."

The officers looked grave.

"Perhaps the guns proved too unstable to use," one suggested.

"Or too valuable to risk," said another. "He will use them as reinforcements, wait to see how the fighting goes and send them in only if he is losing."

"Then let us make goddamn sure he is losing," Randolph growled and the officers laughingly agreed.

Thomas looked at the faces of the men around him, resolved to do their duty and fight and die if need be for their country and their king. His eyes dimmed and, fearing that tears of pride might be misconstrued as tears of weakness, he walked over to gaze out the window at the lights of the city of Haever, shining in the darkness.

Randolph went on to lay out the battle plan.

"We are outnumbered, gentlemen, but the Guundarans lost the element of surprise and we have gained it. They have no idea they are sailing into a trap.

"Here is what I propose. The Guundaran ships are bigger than ours, but they are slower and far less maneuverable. We send in our fastest ships to cut the enemy's line and scatter his ships, like a wolf charging into a flock of sheep. We can then pick them off at our leisure."

The officers exchanged glances. All of them knew the battle would not be the least bit "leisurely." It would be hot and heavy and hopeless.

"You sent word that the Dragon Brigade was coming to aid us, sir," one said. "Do you know when they will arrive?"

"They are coming," said Randolph. "But we cannot count on them to arrive in time."

"Can't count on the damn Rosians at all," one officer grumbled to a comrade, who nudged him and glanced at Thomas.

"I have sent a messenger to tell the Brigade that Ullr is preparing to attack tomorrow," said Thomas. "We hope the Brigade arrives in time, but we must rely on ourselves to repel the invasion."

"You should prepare your crews for the possibility that the Brigade will come, make them aware that the goddamn dragons are on our side," said Randolph.

The officers shifted uncomfortably. Thomas could judge the sentiment in the room by the thundering silence. Most of them probably trusted the Guundarans more than they did dragons.

The ship's bell rang seven times. Half past eleven. The officers would be eager to return to their ships. The admiral brought the meeting to a close.

Randolph turned to face Thomas. "One thing I know for certain, Your Majesty. Every soul from the powder monkey to the most senior officer will give his all. If we go down, we will go down fighting."

The officers sailed back to their ships. Since the *Valor* had been refitted to use the crystals of the Breath and could travel inland, Randolph sailed north over the city of Haever to keep watch. The *Valor* would signal when the enemy was in sight. The rest of the fleet took up positions near the harbor, concealed in the mists of the Breath.

"Go to bed, Your Majesty," Randolph advised. "You will need your rest."

Thomas took his advice and lay down on the bed in his small cabin, determined to sleep. He tried closing his eyes, but he could feel Kate's kiss still warm on his lips. She was a member of the Dragon Brigade and presumably she would be going into battle tomorrow. The thought terrified him. He longed to wrap her in cotton wool and tuck her away in a drawer for safekeeping. He smiled in the darkness as he imagined what she would have told him in return.

Thomas expected to sleep fitfully, if he slept at all, and he surprised himself by falling into a deep slumber. He was jolted awake by the sounds of beating drums. Lighting the lamp, he looked at his watch, which he had laid on a shelf near his bed. The hour was five of the clock and this was confirmed by the ship's bells. He hurriedly dressed and ran up on deck, nearly colliding with sailors dashing to their posts. Randolph and the captain were on the quarterdeck, both staring at something through their telescopes.

Midshipmen had hoisted signal lamps warning, "Enemy in sight." The other ships acknowledged the signals with alacrity. Everyone had been waiting for this moment.

"Good morning, Your Majesty," Randolph stated with a broad grin. He handed Thomas the spyglass. "There they are. The Guundaran invasion force. Just as Simon predicted."

The sun had not yet risen. Dawn's glow lit the sky, but the mists were still dark. Thomas could see the ships, their running lights glittering on the horizon, numerous as stars.

Randolph chuckled and rubbed his hands. "King Ullr is going to be in for a nasty shock. Ah! There, sir! They've seen us!"

Thomas could see a flurry of activity among the fleet of enemy ships. Signal flares burst in the sky. Signal lanterns flashed.

"Is King Ullr sailing with his fleet, do you think, Admiral?" Thomas asked.

"The bastard will be somewhere close, you may be sure, sir. Waiting to make his triumphal entry into Haever."

"I would give a great deal to capture him," said Thomas.

"Not likely, I'm afraid, sir," said Randolph. "Ullr will be observing the fight from the comfort of his yacht. He won't venture near. He considers himself too valuable to risk his precious person in battle."

"Unlike me, apparently," said Thomas, grinning as he handed back the spyglass. "You have no compunction about risking my life."

He was teasing, but Randolph regarded him earnestly. "'Those who will not risk cannot win.' You are a true king, sir. You have shown that this day."

Thomas was touched. He turned the collar of his coat against the chill morning wind and watched the lights of the enemy ships draw closer.

The *Valor* signaled to the fleet to prepare for battle. One by one, the other ships responded.

"Too bad there isn't a signal for 'God help us,'" Randolph remarked.

Dalgren landed in front of the cave with a thud that shook the ground.

"Wake up, Kate!" he roared. "I know you're in there!"

"I'm awake," Kate grumbled. She had jumped to her feet in excitement, forgetting about her bruised ribs, and she had to take a moment to wait for the pain to recede. The salve must be wearing off. She slathered more of it on her torso, front and back, then hurried out to meet Dalgren.

"Is the Brigade coming?"

"They are not far behind me. I came ahead to pick you up."

"Then it's time," said Kate softly.

"Climb into the saddle," said Dalgren, with a gleaming-fanged grin. "This day you and I fly with the Dragon Brigade."

Fight for your dreams.

FIFTY-THREE

The Duchess of Welkinstead had converted the wine cellar in her fantastic house to a workshop where she had spent most of her waking hours tinkering with her various inventions. She did not need a wine cellar, she had maintained, because she knew nothing about wine, so why cellar it.

"Doesn't matter to me if I drink a rare, expensive vintage or the local plonk," she had said to Simon. "Especially since most of the time I prefer the plonk."

The walls and ceiling of the workshop were blackened and cracked from the occasional explosion, and the floor was stained with acid and other chemicals. Simon and Albright, Amelia and Sophia had worked all night in the wine cellar to have the Eye ready by dawn. Bandit had refused to join them. He didn't like the cellar. He had slept at the top of the stairs, whiffling in his dreams.

They raided the house for objects they required in the construction of the weapon. The barrel was made from the telescope that Simon had kept for years in his office. Under his direction, Albright cut the telescope into three pieces of differing lengths and trimmed them so that each one fit into the next like a collapsible spyglass.

He melted down one of the duchess's tea sets to obtain silver and, at Sophia's suggestion, Amelia mounted a ladder to remove drop-shaped crystals from one of the chandeliers to serve as a prism.

"We insert two glass rods—one charged with magic, the other with contramagic—into the end of the first chamber," Simon explained. "The switch brings the two rods into contact, releasing the energy and firing the weapon."

Sophia applied magical constructs containing the Seventh Sigil to the silver that coated the walls of the telescope. Simon imbued the chandelier crystals with the same constructs to concentrate the energy obtained from the rods.

"There is just one problem," said Simon, frowning at the Eye. "How do we store the energy?"

"But that's important, isn't it?" Amelia asked, startled.

"Essential. Won't work without it," said Simon.

Sophia regarded him in dismay. "I hope we haven't done all this work for nothing!"

"No, no," said Simon. "The solution will come to me."

Albright spoke up. "If I might make a suggestion, sir. What if we use the duchess's lightning-powered airscrew?"

"That is genius, Albright!" Simon exclaimed. "I haven't thought about that contraption in years! Unfortunately, I have no idea where it is."

"I believe it is in the broom closet, sir," said Albright. "I can fetch it."

"What is a lightning-powered airscrew?" Sophia asked.

"The duchess invented an airscrew that worked off what she termed 'manufactured lightning,' using a 'lightning jar' to store the energy. She hoped to sell her invention to the navy and invited the Lords of the Admiralty to witness a demonstration. Unfortunately, the machine sent an electric shock through one of the admirals, knocking him across the room. That ended the demonstration and the duchess was forced to abandon the idea."

Albright returned with the airscrew and Simon dismantled it. The lightning jar proved to be too large to fit into the telescope. But after studying the design, Simon was able to construct a smaller version using porcelain from a broken dinner plate. He inserted the porcelain into the second chamber to store the magical energy.

"Now, once the switch is thrown, it should complete the circuit and release the energy into the third chamber of the weapon," he stated.

Albright ground down and realigned the lenses from the telescope. Sophia inscribed constructs on them and Simon mounted the lenses in the front of the weapon to focus the energy into a ball of magical fire.

"The Eye is finished," said Simon, regarding the contraption with pride. "I wish we could test it, but while I have a general theory as to its destructive power, I can't be certain if it will work as planned. It might end up blowing a hole in the foundation."

"Where should I mount it, sir?" Albright asked. "Would you like it on the roof?"

"No, Albright. The roof is too exposed, not safe, as we learned the last time the house was attacked. We will place the Eye in the study. Mount it on the tripod I used for the telescope. That will give us an excellent view of the entire city."

Albright ventured a protest. "We will have to break out the magnificent glass windows, sir. They survived the work!"

"Then I won't have to listen to you complain about washing them," Simon returned.

Mr. Albright opened his mouth and shut it again. Bandit suddenly jumped to his feet at the top of the stairs and began to bark and dash about in circles.

Sophia looked up from her work. "Was that thunder? Bandit doesn't like thunder."

They stopped to listen, and above the dog's barking, they could hear muffled booming sounds.

"That is not thunder," Amelia said sharply. "That is cannon fire!"

Simon began hastily gathering up his notes and stuffing them into the pockets attached to his chair.

"Albright, signal the tugboat captains to push the house into position, then carry the weapon to the study," said Simon. "The rest of us will follow."

Albright picked up the weapon and hauled it up the stairs to the second level. Sophia followed, emerging from the cellar, much to Bandit's joy. His happiness at seeing his mistress evaporated when Sophia locked him in the pantry, where he found consolation for his imprisonment by the discovery of a pound cake. Amelia came last, loaded down with a variety of tools Simon thought he might need if he had to make adjustments to the weapon.

They entered the study, which was located in a turret room with enormous glass windows on three sides that provided a panoramic view of the city of Haever.

Albright shielded his eyes with one hand and, with a pained expression, used the fireplace poker to smash out the glass of the center window.

Cold air poured into the room, feeling refreshing after the stuffiness of the cellar. They could hear the sounds of the cannon fire clearly. The sky glowed with the reds and oranges of a brilliant sunrise.

Simon propelled his chair to the window and looked out to see the tugboats pushing the house to a location just above the harbor where he calculated the battle would take place. He looked down to see thick smoke and flashes from the muzzles of the cannons almost directly underneath the house, much closer than he had anticipated.

Albright mounted the weapon on the tripod and positioned it in front of the window. The Eye, which weighed more than the telescope, caused the tripod's legs to wobble unsteadily. Simon frowned at it.

"We can't have that instability. Move the Eye closer to the window so that the barrel rests on the ledge. Miss Amelia, there is a spyglass in the file cabinet that is tipped over on its side, under 'S.' After you locate it, go to the window to search for ships carrying the green-beam guns. You should be able to distinguish them by a blue-green glow."

"And the fact that they are firing green beams," Amelia muttered, setting off in search of the spyglass.

"Albright, since you are a trained marksman, you will fire the weapon," Simon continued. "I will instruct you in how it operates."

He and Albright bent over the weapon, with Simon pointing out the firing mechanism. Amelia located the spyglass. She and Sophia went to the window to observe the battle and search for the guns.

The mists of the Breath mingled with the smoke of the cannons and made it difficult to tell what was happening. Ships would emerge from the smoke for a few minutes and then vanish to be replaced by others. The sound of cannon fire was continual.

"The fighting seems very confused," said Sophia. "The ships are so intermingled, I cannot tell which are ours and which are Guundaran."

"Our ships have broken their line, causing them to scatter, which gives our faster ships the advantage," said Simon. "The only option, really, since we are so badly outnumbered. Any sign of green glows, Miss Amelia?"

"No, sir," she said. "But then I am no crafter."

She handed the spyglass to Sophia. "Isn't that odd?" Sophia asked. "I would think Ullr would send them into battle immediately. Perhaps the magic was too unstable . . . Wait. . . ."

Sophia shifted the spyglass. She stared through it intently a moment, then lowered it to point. "There! To the west. Those four small ships."

She handed the spyglass to Simon.

"Sloops," he stated. "Sound choice. Fast and maneuverable. You are right, Your Highness. I detect a blue-green glow at the front of each."

He studied the four sloops that were floating in the Breath, concealed in the mists. He could catch occasional glimpses of the green-blue glow of guns mounted on the forecastle of each ship.

The tugboat crews must have spotted them as well, for they could all feel the tugboats start to move Welkinstead, setting off in pursuit of the sloops. The tugboats were heavy, snub-nosed boats with no sails, rigging, or balloons that could get tangled, instead relying on large lift tanks to keep them afloat. Each tugboat had six enormous airscrews that propelled them forward, with two additional airscrews that facilitated turning.

The house gained speed. Wind rushed in through the broken glass. Simon found this quite exhilarating.

"I may hire tugboats permanently," he announced.

He handed the spyglass back to Amelia. "Keep watch on them. If I am correct, they will use the cover of the battle to swoop down on the city. When they break free of the pack and swoop in for the kill, we will have them!"

"I count only four green-beam guns," Amelia reported. "Thomas said Ullr talked of five. There they go! They are splitting up."

"Each assigned a different target," said Simon.

"One appears to be sailing toward the palace—"

"They assume the king is there," said Simon. "We need not worry about that one for the moment. We will target the nearest sloop. Are we in range of any of them yet, Albright?"

"Begging your pardon, sir," said Albright deferentially, "but since we have never fired the weapon, I am unfamiliar with the range."

"A valid point, Albright," Simon conceded. "I estimate the range to be about three hundred to five hundred feet."

"Very good, sir," said Mr. Albright. "We are not within range yet. A few more moments."

The house closed in on the sloops. Simon chafed at the delay and he fidgeted in his chair. Amelia lowered the glass to rub her eyes.

"I can take over keeping watch," Sophia offered.

Amelia handed her the glass. Sophia swept the sky, observing the battle. The sun had risen above the mists, providing a much clearer view of the fighting. Sophia suddenly pointed.

"I recognize that yacht! It's King Ullr's royal yacht! He's watching the battle from a safe distance. I don't suppose he is in range of the Eye."

She handed the spyglass to Simon. He searched the sky until he located the yacht—a massive affair with gilt trim, red and black striped balloons marked with the emblem of Guundar, flying the Guundaran flag.

"Too far away," Simon said, shaking his head in disappointment.

"I cannot see the *Valor* for all the smoke and flame," Sophia said worriedly. "I hope Thomas is all right."

Amelia gave her a soothing pat. "Thomas will be fine. I am sure of it. God has not brought His Majesty this far to abandon him now."

Simon was about to refute her claim by informing her that Thomas had brought himself this far. Seeing Sophia gazing unhappily out the window, worried about her friend, Simon kept quiet. He realized that he had come to be quite fond of her. He did not like to see her downcast.

If he had ever had a daughter, which the bullet to his spine had decreed impossible, he would have wanted her to be like Sophia. Not only was she a savant with remarkable skill in magic, she was also brave, quick-thinking, and sensible. She was in his judgment an estimable young woman, aside from what he considered an unaccountable affection for the annoying spaniel.

Simon heard the tugboats' airscrews frantically whirring. The wind whistled through the broken window. Welkinstead was on the move, no longer drifting with panache, but resolutely headed for battle.

He raised the spyglass again to observe the four sloops, each sailing toward what he presumed were their targets. Welkinstead was drawing steadily closer to one of the sloops, which appeared to be taking aim at a row of government office buildings: the Foreign Office, His Majesty's Exchequer, and the Admiralty. He could see the green glow strengthen, which meant the crew was preparing to fire once they were close enough.

The crew had opened the sloop's gun ports, but they had not run out their guns. They had left the battle raging in the sky behind. The Freyan ships were fighting for their lives. If they had noticed the sloops breaking away, they could do nothing to stop them.

"The house will be in range of the first sloop shortly, sir," Albright reported.

"Aim for the green-beam gun," said Simon. "Our goal is to destroy it."

"I will do my best, sir," said Mr. Albright. He cast glances at Sophia and Amelia, who were watching out the window, and said in a quiet aside, "Might I suggest that the women seek refuge in the workshop, sir. I deem that to be the safest room in the house."

Amelia heard him and whipped around to indignantly confront him. "Mrs. Ridgeway of Mrs. Ridgeway's Academy for Young Ladies did not raise cowards, Mr. Albright. 'Women may wear corsets,' she would say to us, 'but we still have spines.'"

"And I am not hiding in the cellar," stated Sophia. "This is my country, or soon will be. Besides, Master Yates might need my help with the magic."

"You have your answer, Albright," said Simon. "I believe we are in range."

Mr. Albright bent down to sight in on the target.

Simon watched him. "You should be aware, Albright, that there is a small chance the weapon could blow up in your face."

Albright straightened to look at him.

"*Small* chance," Simon emphasized. "Fifteen percent. Twenty at the outside. Your death would be instantaneous, if that helps."

"Most comforting, sir," said Albright.

He bent down over the weapon and placed his finger on the triggering mechanism. He made a slight adjustment to the position of the muzzle and fired.

The barrel of the weapon glowed bluish green and started to buzz. Mr. Albright hurriedly stepped away from it.

A ball of white fire burst from the barrel with such force it jarred the tripod, sending it canting sideways. Mr. Albright made a dive for the weapon and caught it before it could hit the floor.

The fireball streaked through the sky like a comet, trailing flame and white sparks, and struck the Guundaran sloop amidships.

"Your aim was way off, Albright," Simon said in reproof. "You did not come anywhere close to the green—"

The sloop exploded with a dazzling flash, split apart, and sank. The destruction was so swift and so complete that it was difficult to comprehend. One moment a ship with some fifty souls had been there and the next it was gone. All that was left was the afterimage of the flash imprinted on their eyes.

"Merciful God in Heaven . . ." Amelia exclaimed.

Sophia gasped and covered her mouth with her hands. Albright stood staring, clutching the weapon in his arms. Simon frowned at the empty space in the sky.

"I knew the Eye would be powerful, but I admit I did not expect *that*."

He raised the spyglass to observe the reaction of the other three sloops. He could see their crews scrambling about in confusion, running to the rails, climbing the masts and the rigging to search for the enemy ship that had wrought such swift and terrible destruction.

They would not see a ship, but they would see Welkinstead. They had not previously viewed the curious house as a threat, but they certainly did now. He observed signal flags soaring up the halyards and saw the remaining sloops change course, abandoning their targets, reacting to this new threat. The green-beam guns on their rotating platforms began to turn in their direction.

"They are preparing to fire on us," said Simon. "We should prevent that, if possible, Albright."

"I am attempting to do so, sir," said Mr. Albright.

He managed after a struggle to reattach the weapon to the tripod and once again rested the barrel of the weapon on the window ledge. Taking aim, he pressed the trigger.

The white ball of fire streaked toward a second Guundaran sloop. The fireball hit the green-beam gun, destroyed the forecastle, ripped open the balloons, and obliterated the forward airscrews. The sloop began to sink, though she did not go down as fast as the first, which was unfortunate for the survivors. The lifeboats had been destroyed and they had no way to escape their fate.

"Perhaps the other two will give up," said Sophia, who was now quite pale. "We can let them go."

"I am afraid not, Your Highness," said Simon. "We cannot allow the Guundarans to escape with these guns in their possession."

"You are right, of course, sir," said Sophia. "I was being foolish."

"It is not foolish to care about the lives of your fellow men," said Simon. "Especially since most of those poor bastards had no choice in the matter. They were probably rounded up by press gangs, torn from their homes and families and forced to work on these ships, enduring bad food, floggings, and intolerable living conditions."

Simon continued to watch the two surviving sloops. "If it makes you feel any better, Sophia, the Guundarans are not going to give up. They appear to be intent on killing us."

The other two Guundaran sloops were bearing down on the house and the one nearest fired a green beam.

Simon had used the Seventh Sigil to strengthen and reinforce the magic on his house. He waited with interest to observe the outcome. Welkinstead shook slightly when the beam hit the north side. He heard a few thuds as sundry objects fell off the walls, but that appeared to be the extent of the damage.

The other Guundaran ship fired. This commander must be smarter than his compatriot, for he was aiming at the airscrews. Judging by a clanking and rattling sound, the beam struck one of them. Simon was incensed; he had gone to considerable expense repairing them.

Albright fired again, but missed. The white fireball blazed harmlessly between the two oncoming frigates.

"Albright, concentrate!" Simon said sternly. "I will guide your aim."

He rolled his chair close to the window and raised the spyglass. He glanced from the target to the Eye and back to the target.

"Shift the muzzle to the right."

Albright moved the weapon as instructed. "The green beam is aimed directly at us, sir."

"Albright, you should duck. I do not want to have to break in a new manservant."

"In a moment, sir. I almost have my aim," Albright returned.

He fired the Eye of God and then dropped to the floor. "I fear I missed, sir."

"Too far to the right," Simon muttered.

He rapidly propelled his chair backward. "Miss Amelia, Sophia, take cover behind the desk. It has magical reinforcements!"

Sophia ran to the desk, but she did not take shelter behind it. She swept up an armful of monographs, treatises, essays, studies, and reports and carried them to the window.

"More papers, Miss Amelia!" she cried. "Toss them outside!"

She flung the papers out the window while Amelia hurled more after them. The gun fired. The green beam lanced toward the window. The breeze caught the papers in a whirlwind, swirling them about. Sophia spoke a word and the papers burst into light, forming a bright, glittering curtain over the window.

The green beam flared, then struck the curtain of blue-green blazing paper. The beam struggled briefly to survive, evaporated, fizzled, and died.

Albright jumped to his feet, aimed the Eye of God, and fired at the sloop that had just fired at them. The ship disintegrated. All that was left was a green glowing dot that trailed down into the Breath and then vanished.

"Well done that time, Albright," said Simon, coughing in the smoke of burning paper. "One more sloop to go."

The flames had died, leaving the air filled with floating cinders and ashes. Albright calmly brushed a few cinders from his eyes, sighted in on his target. "The sloop is attempting to flee, sir."

"Poor bastards," said Simon.

Albright fired. He watched a moment, then turned to report.

"The last ship has been destroyed, sir."

"And that is an end to the green-beam guns, hopefully forever," said Simon. "Well done, Albright."

He regarded Sophia with admiration. "And well done for you, my dear! You held the Seventh Sigil in your mind, allowing you to combine magic with contramagic."

"I had no idea if it would work," said Sophia, flushing at his praise. "I've only cast that spell once before and that was when we were freeing Phillip from prison."

She cast a remorseful glance at the cinders now blanketing the room. "I'm sorry about your work. . . ."

Simon waved his hand. "A small price to pay to witness such exemplary skill in magic."

They heard a plaintive howl drift up from the vicinity of the pantry.

"Poor Bandit is probably terrified," said Sophia. "I must go fetch him."

"Albright, go with her and bring back a bottle of Calvados to celebrate," said Simon.

The two of them departed, descending the stairs, heading for the pantry where Bandit, having finished the pound cake, was complaining about his confinement.

Amelia stood at the window, her arms crossed over her chest, gazing out at the battle that was still raging in the sky below the house. The smoke was thicker now, for some of the ships were ablaze.

"I cannot tell what is happening," she said. "Are we winning the fight or losing?"

Simon rolled his chair to the desk, looked at the cinders and ashes that coated it, and sighed deeply. He fully appreciated Sophia's need to make use of his papers, but he was left without a scrap on which to write down his observations on the Eye's performance.

He was about to go into his bedroom, where he kept writing materials by the side of his bed, when he was stopped by the jangling of the front doorbell, followed by banging on the door itself. Whoever was there was certainly impatient, for the person again tugged on the bell pull while simultaneously banging on the door.

"Who could that be?" Amelia asked, frowning. "Perhaps the police have found Sophia. There is still a warrant for her arrest."

"If it is the constables here to arrest the princess, I doubt they would be so polite as to give us advance notice," said Simon. "Still, it is best to be prepared. Are you armed, Miss Amelia?"

In answer, she picked up her reticule from the desk, shook off the cinders, and retrieved her double-barreled pocket pistol.

"Excellent. Take Sophia and the dog to the cellar. Try to keep the dog quiet, if such a thing is possible."

Amelia checked her pistol to make sure it was loaded, grabbed her umbrella, then hurried down the stairs.

Simon reached into one of the pouches on his chair for his "crackers" and then propelled his chair out onto the landing and floated.

He arrived just as Albright emerged from the kitchen armed with a pistol. Sophia came behind him, carrying Bandit, her hand clamped over his muzzle. She faced Simon defiantly.

"I won't hide in the cellar, sir. I can help."

Simon didn't have time to argue. The banging continued, but at least the bell-ringing had stopped.

"Do you know who is out there, Albright?"

"I have not had a chance to look through the window, sir. I did think I heard a griffin caw, so I deduce whoever it is came by griffin. Should I answer the door?"

Simon flourished the cracker. "No, Albright. I will greet our guest."

Mr. Albright regarded the cracker with consternation. "May I remind you, sir, that the last time you set off one of those devices, you set a ship on fire."

"I have since refined the formula, Albright. I suggest that you escort the ladies to a safe distance."

He propelled his chair toward the door, as Albright, Amelia, and Sophia retreated into the kitchen.

Simon opened the curtain a crack and peered out the window. A griffin perched on the landing, preening itself. The man banging on the door wore a pea coat with the collar turned up against the cold and a stocking hat pulled down around his ears. Simon could not see his face. The man paused in his banging a moment to stamp his feet and peer up anxiously at the house.

He was not a constable, that much was certain. He might be a messenger from Henry.

Simon cautiously opened the door and was about to ask the man his business when he was startled by the sight of Bandit hurtling past him and out the door. The dog flung himself at the man in the pea coat with a joyful bark and began to jump on him in wild excitement.

Sophia came running out of the kitchen.

"I am so sorry, Master Yates, Bandit got away from me—"

The man looked up at the sound of her voice. "Sophia! It's me! Phillip!"

Sophia stopped, stared, then ran past Simon and into Phillip's arms. Bandit jumped on both of them, barking madly.

"I am glad to see you safe, Your Grace," said Simon, replacing the cracker in its pouch. "Please come in. Albright, hot tea for our guest! Drop a splash of Calvados in it."

Phillip and Sophia clung to each other, happily oblivious to everything and everyone. Simon edged his way around them and went out to dismiss the griffin, thanking the beast for its service and making certain it had been paid.

He paused at the door, watching the battle rage over Haever, and reflected on young love.

There had once been a girl in his life. A bookish girl who wore glasses. He had met her in the library at University, where she was studying theology. The two had argued incessantly. They spent most of their time arguing and holding hands across the table. And then he had been shot. She came to visit, but he had refused to see her. He had told the duchess to send her away.

Simon had not thought about the girl in a long time.

He smiled wistfully at the memory and closed the door on the war and the cold.

FIFTY-FOUR

The Battle of Haever began on a clear, bright dawn with the boom of cannons. The Guundaran ships opened fire, finding their range and hoping for a lucky shot in the process. The Freyan ships did not respond. With their smaller twenty-four-pound cannons, they could not hope to match Guundaran seventy-fours, which meant they had to endure the bombardment without answering. They had a long fight ahead of them and they could not afford to waste powder and shot.

Led by the *Valor*, the Freyan ships closed on the enemy to disrupt their battle line and scatter the Guundaran ships in an effort to separate them and take on one or two at a time, instead of facing a solid front.

Thomas had fought in the Bottom Dweller War with the Estaran army at Fort San Estavan. At the time, he had been a student at the Estaran Royal Military Academy. Hearing of the battle, he and his friends had decided to ride to the fort to share in the glory.

Instead of finding glory, they found hell. The fort was besieged and they were outnumbered and surrounded. For three days Thomas lived in terror, thirsty and starving, spattered with the blood of his friends as well as his own, and so exhausted he had once prayed to die just to get some rest. He had deemed those three days the worst in his life, and yet then at least he had found some satisfaction in being able to fight back.

On board the *Valor,* he was helpless as the Guundaran ships fired at them with their long-range cannons. The *Valor* had to endure the punishment. Thomas could do nothing except stand on the quarterdeck and watch cannonballs crash into the hull, tear through the rigging, punch holes in the sails, and reduce men to bloody globs of splintered bone and pulverized flesh.

He was talking to a young midshipman when a ball crashed into him and suddenly the boy—or what was left of him—lay at Thomas's feet in a pool of blood, brains, and entrails.

Admiral Baker keenly observed the battle from the quarterdeck, making himself an excellent target as he paced back and forth and loudly damned their eyes. Thomas admired the coolness of the *Valor*'s captain. Knocked down by a falling spar, he picked himself up, wiped the blood from his face, and continued to calmly issue orders.

At last the *Valor* came into range and Thomas cheered himself hoarse when she sailed between two Guundaran ships of the line and opened fire on both with simultaneous broadsides.

The other Freyan ships were now able to engage the enemy. They were swift wolves among the flock, snapping and snarling at the heavier, more ponderous Guundaran ships. The Freyans fired, then sailed on to fire at the next ship, attacking from seemingly all directions at once.

But even as they fought, the Freyan ships were enduring brutal punishment, battling the much larger fleet. Thomas saw more than one Freyan ship sink in flames into the Breath, and he realized with mingled despair, frustration, and anger that they were fighting a battle they could not hope to win. He did not doubt Kate's promise that the Brigade was coming to help them, but he began to fear that they would arrive in time only to witness the fall of Freya.

The *Valor* had sustained significant damage and was wallowing sluggishly in the Breath. Two of her lift tanks were punctured and leaking gas. One airscrew was a mangled mess of metal and a balloon had caught fire, leaving her unable to escape the Guundaran ship bearing down on her.

"Prepare to repel boarders!" the *Valor*'s captain shouted as the Guundarans hurled grappling hooks over the sides and locked the *Valor* in a deadly embrace.

Rifle and musket fire blazed. Shouting Guundarans armed with swords and cutlasses and pistols poured onto the deck. Thomas and the rest of the crew ran to meet them.

"Sorry, Pip," Thomas apologized, as he locked swords with a Guundaran officer. "It's looking more and more likely you will be king."

FIFTY-FIVE

The morning sun gleamed on the scales of the dragons as Kate and Dalgren flew to join the Brigade in the skies above Haever. The commander of the dragons, Countess Anasi, barked a command at Dalgren, and Captain Thorgrimson acknowledged Kate with a salute as she reported to duty.

"You're with the Blue Flight, Captain," he shouted. "And take off that kerchief!"

Kate flushed. She had forgotten she had tied it around her neck. She took it off and hurriedly thrust it into a pocket.

"Yes, sir. Sorry, sir."

Flights were made up of four to six dragons flying in a "V," keeping each other and the leader of the flight in sight.

The Blue Flight was the last in the formation, or the "tail," as it was known among dragons. Dalgren feared that Kate would protest being stuck in the rear and he cast a warning look at her, reminding her that they were part of the Brigade by sufferance and that she had to obey orders.

Kate gave Dalgren a reassuring smile and a pat on the neck. She had no intention of ruining either his proudest moment or her own. She would have been happy to be flying at the very back with the quartermaster corps—the common dragons who did the hunting and hauled supplies. She was shaking with nervous anticipation and gulping with excitement. Her hands in her leather gloves were sweating, her mouth was dry, and her heart beating fast.

The other dragons in the Flight acknowledged Dalgren. Their helmed riders gave Kate a nod. The Flight Leader pointed and, as Dalgren took his place at the tip of the wing, Kate marveled at the breathtaking sight of the flights of dragons ahead of them, the sunlight of a new day glittering on their scales, gilding their wings.

The dragons soared over the city. People in the streets or standing on the rooftops, who had been watching the battle in the harbor, stared up at them in astonishment and fear. Thomas would not have had either the time or the means to share the news with his people that the Brigade had come to fight for them, and Kate could imagine their terror.

Their fear would change to elation when they saw the Brigade attack Guundaran ships. She waved reassuringly at the people below, though she doubted any could see her.

Kate gloried in the moment, almost giddy with joy. Then the harbor came into view. She saw the smoke and flames of battle, and her joy sank beneath a wave of apprehension. Thomas was somewhere in the midst of that, fighting for his life.

She searched for the *Valor,* raising her visor and standing up in the saddle to try to obtain a better view. She could not find his ship and she earned a reprimand from the Flight Leader, who angrily gestured for her to follow procedure, stay seated, and keep her visor lowered.

Reluctantly, Kate obeyed and continued searching. All the ships—friend and foe—were wreathed in smoke. She saw one ship flying the Freyan flag perish in flames. Even though she knew it hadn't been the *Valor,* she was sick to her stomach at the terrible sight and almost disgraced herself by throwing up over the side of her dragon.

She considered asking Dalgren to break rank and fly off on their own to find Thomas, though she knew Dalgren would refuse to obey her and rightly so. The Brigade's strength was in numbers and being a disciplined fighting force.

Kate was in agony, and wished that their Flight Leader would at least increase their speed. She kicked Dalgren in the flanks, urging him to fly just a little faster, hoping the Flight Leader might take the hint.

Dalgren shot her a grim look and ignored her.

Countess Anasi at last ordered the flights to begin their descent, preparatory to going in to attack. As Dalgren dropped down, Kate had a much clearer view and she found the *Valor,* only to see it captured by a Guundaran warship. The *Valor* had endured severe punishment. Masts were missing, and black smoke billowed out of the gun ports. The flagship was not yet sinking, and some of her cannons continued to fire, but the Guundaran warship seemed determined to end the fight. The enemy cast grappling lines, dragged the *Valor* close, and sent their crew to board her.

Kate urgently pointed to the *Valor,* but the Flight Leader shook his head. Captain Thorgrimson had not yet given the order to attack.

Kate struck Dalgren on the neck with her closed fist to draw his attention.

"I need to talk to Captain Thorgrimson!" she shouted.

"I will not disobey orders!" Dalgren roared.

"Dalgren, please! It's life or death!"

Dalgren snorted flames from his nostrils, heaved a gusty sigh, and left his position, moving up past the other flights to come alongside Countess Anasi.

She hooted at him in ire. Captain Thorgrimson lifted his visor. He looked very grim.

Kate sucked in a lungful of air and yelled, "Sir! His Majesty, King Thomas, is aboard the flagship, *Valor*! We cannot allow His Majesty to fall into enemy hands!"

Thorgrimson's grim expression grew grimmer. He studied the two ships that were about thirty feet below, locked in a death struggle. He shook his head.

"If we attack the Guundaran ship, Captain, we risk taking the *Valor* down with her."

Kate was prepared. "Sir, I have a suggestion. Dalgren and I could land on the *Valor*."

Dalgren hissed at her, reminding her it was not her place to offer suggestions to the captain of the Dragon Brigade. Kate ignored him.

The flights of dragons hovered in the air, waiting for orders. Captain Thorgrimson ruminated a few moments more. He glanced at Kate with a faint smile, as though she had given him an idea, then spoke to Anasi.

"Countess, I need four dragons and riders experienced in landing on board ships."

Anasi nodded in acknowledgment and roared out four names.

Four dragons and their riders flew to within hailing distance of Captain Thorgrimson. He indicated the *Valor* and bellowed his commands.

"King Thomas is on board the *Valor*. His ship has been captured. The king must *not* fall into enemy hands. Lieutenants Merrill and Chambrun will board the *Valor* and rescue the king. Lieutenant Beauchamp, you speak Guundaran. You and Lieutenant Blois board the enemy ship. Cut the grappling lines and disable the helm. If the crew surrenders, let them go, then sink it. Questions?"

"How will we know the king, sir?" Merrill shouted. "None of us have ever met him."

Kate raised her hand, eager to volunteer. "Lord Dalgren and I request permission to join the boarding party, sir. I know the king. I can point him out."

Captain Thorgrimson regarded her with a grave expression. "Have you and Lord Dalgren ever landed on a ship, Captain?"

"Yes, sir," said Kate promptly.

Thorgrimson raised a skeptical eyebrow and Kate amended, more subdued, "Well, no, sir, not really. But he and I have practiced the maneuver many times."

Dalgren blinked at this news, but said nothing. Captain Thorgrimson probably guessed the truth, but he needed her.

"Lieutenants Merrill and Chambrun will land first. Watch them, Captain Kate, and do just what they do. Once you find His Majesty, take him to a place of safety. And keep him there!"

Captain Thorgrimson turned away to explain the situation to Merrill and Chambrun, while their dragons were giving hurried advice to Dalgren on the best way to land on a ship. Dalgren nodded and tried not to look overwhelmed.

Captain Thorgrimson wished them luck, then left to begin his own attack run. Kate watched in fascination to see Anasi swoop down to make the first assault on one of the Guundaran sixty-eights. She breathed a gust of flame on the masts, balloons, and rigging, then pulled up out of her dive to allow the second dragon to swoop down on the hapless ship.

The Guundarans had been certain of victory, relentlessly pounding the beleaguered Freyan ships. Then dragons had appeared, materializing out of the smoke of battle, and now it was the Guundarans who were fighting for their lives.

Merrill and Chambrun conferred briefly, then flew over to speak to Kate.

Merrill was straight-backed in the saddle, rigid, tight-lipped. Chambrun seemed more relaxed. She was younger than Merrill, perhaps new to the Brigade. She gave Kate a reassuring smile.

"What does the king look like?" Merrill asked. "Any distinguishing features?"

"His Majesty has black curly hair and blue eyes," Kate answered, adding without thinking, "Striking blue eyes."

Seeing Chambrun's amusement, Kate asked Merrill hurriedly, "What are your orders, Lieutenant?"

"My dragon and I will land amidships, near the main deck. Lieutenant Chambrun and her dragon will take the stern. You and Dalgren the prow. Are you armed?"

"Yes, sir," said Kate.

"If you find His Majesty, dead or alive, have your dragon call out to let us know."

Kate was chilled. She had never, until that moment, considered the possibility that Thomas might be dead.

"Yes, sir," she said, subdued.

"If the king is not on board, we must assume he has been captured or is lost in the Breath," Merrill continued. "You will go last, behind us."

Merrill and his dragon took the lead with Chambrun and her dragon next in line. Merrill gave the signal to begin their descent. Kate could feel Dalgren quaking with nervousness and she gave him a reassuring pat.

"We can do this," she said.

Dalgren grunted. "Easy for you to say. You don't have to hang onto the side of a ship by your toenails!"

"We practiced—" Kate began.

"—landing on hay bales!" Dalgren roared. "Not on the side of a ship fifty feet above the ground!"

Kate decided it was best to stop being reassuring. She took her pistols from the saddle and thrust them into her belt. Dalgren spread his wings and followed Chambrun's dragon as she began a steep dive. Kate clung desperately to the saddle as Dalgren plunged down on the ship headfirst, flinging her forward. The straps that crisscrossed her chest and fastened over her legs were all that were holding her in the saddle. As the mists of the Breath, the smoke, the flames, and the ships rushed up at her, she clutched the pommel with both hands.

Landing on an enemy ship was one of the most difficult maneuvers a dragon could perform, dangerous for both dragon and rider. A dragon could not land on the deck for fear of getting tangled in the rigging and caught like a fly in a web, unable to defend himself.

Dragons landed by digging their back claws into the hull, gripping the rail with their foreclaws and using their tails for stability. Even this maneuver was dangerous. They could still get tangled in the rigging and they could come under fire from swivel guns or cannons mounted on the upper decks.

Merrill and Chambrun signaled that they were going to land and for Kate to follow. Merrill's dragon dove down on the *Valor* like a hawk stooping on a rabbit. He extended his back claws and drove them into the hull with crushing force, splintering the wood, then rocked forward to grasp the rail with his foreclaws. He hovered a moment, then managed to stabilize himself. Merrill immediately began to free himself of his straps.

Chambrun and her dragon landed next near the stern.

"Here we go!" Dalgren roared with a gulp. "Hold on!"

He dove down with terrifying speed. The *Valor* grew larger as he came nearer, but it still seemed a very small target for him to hit. Kate gripped the straps across her chest with both hands and ducked down in the saddle, holding her breath and squeezing her eyes shut. She felt Dalgren crash into the hull and heard the wood break beneath his claws. The impact flung her with bruising force against the straps, and she banged her head on the front of the saddle.

Dalgren lurched, grabbed hold of the rail, and snagged his horn in the shrouds. He jerked his head and twisted and finally snapped the lines. But his flailing caused him to nearly lose his grip on the rail and he teetered back and forth, trying to find his balance, wings flapping wildly. He scrabbled with his claws and roared at Kate.

"Jump off! I'm not sure how much longer I can hold on!"

Kate fumbled at the straps to free herself, but she was hampered by Dalgren's gyrations.

"Hold still!" she shouted.

Dalgren shot flame from his nose and snarled something in reply.

Kate finally managed to unbuckle the last strap and hoisted herself from the saddle. She remembered at the last moment to grab her cutlass, made sure her pistols were secure in her belt, and then jumped to the deck. Dalgren lost his grip and flew off. He circled around, then returned to the ship, keeping Kate in sight, hovering at eye level.

Kate swept a look around the *Valor*. The quarterdeck was red with blood and littered with bodies of the dead and wounded, fallen spars, and tangled rigging. Smoke swirled, pouring out of the hatches from the decks below. She gave a thought to fire reaching the powder magazine and quickly put that out of her mind.

Merrill's dragon hooted. Kate hoped that meant he had found Thomas. She heard other sounds—swords clashing, pistol shots, men shouting—and she moved toward them. The fight wasn't over, apparently. She drew her pistol and was trying to see through the smoke and the tangled wreckage, not looking where she was going, and almost stepped on the body of a man lying facedown in a pool of blood. The man had curly black hair and he was wearing the uniform of a Freyan officer. Kate recoiled in horror.

Dalgren roared. "Behind you!"

Kate saw out of the corner of her eye a wounded Guundaran sailor aiming his pistol at her. She whipped around and fired first and the sailor collapsed. Kate forced herself to look back at the body with the curly hair and realized with a shudder of relief that the dead man was not Thomas. He was shorter, with a stockier build.

Kate heard Merrill shouting and more pistol shots.

"Find out what's going on!" she yelled at Dalgren.

He nodded and flew off.

Kate was hurrying down the stairs that led from the forecastle to the main deck when she saw that no one was at the helm. The helmsman was lying on the deck underneath it, either dead or unconscious. As desperate as Kate was to find Thomas, she needed to make certain the ship wasn't going to sink beneath their feet.

She ran to the helm and studied the constructs inscribed on the brass plate. The constructs should have been glowing, but the plate was dark. The magic was no longer flowing to the airscrews or the lift tanks.

She placed her hands on the constructs on the helm that sent magic flowing to the lift tanks. If the leather lines had been cut, the ship did not stand a chance. Some of the constructs lit up beneath her fingers, indicating that at least some of the tanks were still working.

Kate shook the helmsman and shouted at him until he groaned and stirred and opened his eyes. He gazed at her in confusion.

"You have to take the helm!" Kate yelled. "Can you manage?"

The man gave a groggy nod and sat up. Kate helped him to his feet. She didn't leave until she was certain he was at least vaguely aware of what he was doing, then she hurried off.

She cast a wary glance at the enemy ship, still grappled alongside the *Valor*, the two ships rubbing hulls. On board the enemy vessel, Lieutenant Beauchamp was wielding his cutlass, slicing through the grappling lines and yelling something in Guundaran. His dragon flew alongside the ship, harrying the enemy crew by spitting fire and gnashing her fangs. Kate decided she didn't need to worry about an attack from that quarter.

Dalgren returned to report. "Merrill landed in the middle of a fight! They're cornered!"

Kate hurried toward the sounds of battle, crawling over debris and bodies, until she came upon a group of Freyan officers under attack, surrounded by Guundarans. The Freyans had their backs against the bulwark. Kate saw Thomas in the thick of the fray, fighting alongside Admiral Baker.

Thomas was pale, his face grimed with gunpowder and wet with sweat. His damp curly hair straggled over his eyes. His right arm hung limp at his side, the sleeve soaked with blood. He kept fighting, holding his sword in his left hand. He wielded the sword awkwardly, but this desperate struggle called for brute force, not finesse. He slashed in all directions, beating back attacks from one side and then the other.

Randolph had braced himself against the bulwark. He favored his left leg, but he was still standing, still fighting, still swearing.

Merrill's dragon and Chambrun's both hovered in the air, helpless to intervene in the fight for fear of harming the Freyans. Kate had to grudgingly credit the Guundarans, who were doing their best to ignore the dragons and were grimly continuing the fight.

Merrill and Chambrun reached the knot of men at the same time as Kate. Merrill flung himself on the Guundarans from behind. Seizing hold of one of them by the shoulder, he spun him around and struck him in the face with the hilt of his cutlass, sending him sprawling onto the deck.

Kate shifted her cutlass to her left hand and drew her second pistol. She was going to try to reach Thomas when she saw the man Merrill had knocked to the deck jump to his feet and grab a knife from his boot. Merrill had his back to him and couldn't see him.

Kate shouted a warning, raised her pistol, and fired. The man flung up his arms and toppled over. Startled, Merrill glanced around. He saw the body, saw Kate holding the pistol. He gave her a swift salute, then turned back to the fighting.

Randolph sagged to the deck, his strength failing. Thomas moved to stand protectively over him. One of the Guundarans lunged at him and Thomas ran him through with his sword. The man slid to the deck, vomiting blood.

The Guundarans had not expected reinforcements and they had certainly not expected dragons. Their enthusiasm for the fight started to wane. They began casting looks in the direction of their own ship and one actually flung down his sword and bolted for it.

Chambrun shot a man wearing a Guundaran lieutenant's uniform, and that ended the fighting. The few Guundarans still standing surrendered. Chambrun rounded them up at gunpoint and ordered them down into the hold, then locked the hatch on them.

Beauchamp and Blois had managed to cut loose the grapples and free the *Valor*. The three dragons attacked the Guundaran ship, gnashing their teeth, slashing at the rigging with their claws, gushing smoke from their nostrils, and spouting jets of flame.

The captain surrendered, handing over his sword to Beauchamp. Blois ordered the captain and the remaining crewmen to pick up their wounded and carry them into the hold. Beauchamp took the helm of the Guundaran ship and steered it safely away from the *Valor*.

Kate ran toward Thomas and found him tending to Randolph, who lay on the deck, groaning in pain as blood gushed from a wound in his thigh. Thomas was trying to stanch the bleeding, applying pressure as best he could with only one hand. Merrill stood by them protectively, keeping watch, pistol drawn.

"I take it this man is His Majesty?" he called, indicating Thomas.

"Yes, sir," Kate answered, breathless.

"Stay with him," Merrill ordered. "I'll see if I can find the surgeon."

Kate knelt down beside the admiral. Thomas was concentrating on his patient and did not see her.

"I need a belt for a tourniquet!" he said urgently, keeping his eyes on the wounded man.

Kate took her kerchief from her pocket and shouldered Thomas aside. "Let me do that."

He glanced up, startled, then recognized her. He gave a faint smile.

"Pip owes you," he said.

Kate had no idea what he was talking about and she didn't take time to ask. She wrapped the kerchief around Randolph's leg, then drew her knife, knotted it into the kerchief, and turned it until the bleeding slowed and finally came to a stop.

"Where is the surgeon? We need him!" Kate looked about, frustrated. "Can you see him?"

"Mr. Goddard!" Thomas shouted, waving his good arm. "Over here! The admiral!"

The surgeon hastened over to them and saw Thomas covered in blood.

"Your Majesty! Where are you hurt—"

"Not me, Mr. Goddard," Thomas said. "See to the admiral."

The surgeon took one look at Randolph and called for help. Thomas watched with concern as Chambrun and the surgeon's mate picked up the admiral and carried him below.

"He'll be all right," said Kate.

"I hope so," said Thomas. "He saved my life."

"Let me tend to your arm—" Kate began.

Thomas stopped her. "Be quiet. Listen!"

Kate listened and heard the wind and the creaking of the dragons' wings, the groans and cries of the wounded, torn sails flapping, gas hissing from a punctured balloon. She didn't know what he meant, and then she understood.

The cannons had stopped firing.

The thundering booms had been so continuous Kate had stopped hearing them. Now the silence seemed to throb in her ears.

Thomas tried to stand, but pain and fatigue were too much. He sagged back against the bulwark, breathing heavily. His face was drawn with concern.

"The fighting is over, but what does it mean? Is the battle won or lost?" Thomas caught hold of her hand. "Help me to my feet, Kate. I have to see for myself."

Kate slid her arm around his back. He draped his good arm over her shoulder and she helped raise him. He grasped the rail with his good hand and stared out into the smoke.

Many of the Guundaran ships were in flames. Some of them had struck their colors and others were slinking away, trying to escape, with dragons in pursuit.

Every Freyan ship had suffered damage and several had gone down. But Freyan flags still flew proudly. The fighting was over.

"We won," said Kate in wonder, scarcely able to believe it. "We have defeated Guundar."

She embraced him. Thomas pulled her closer. They stood together, holding and supporting each other, both of them knowing in this moment without speaking a word that their lives were forever bound together.

"The day is ours," said Thomas.

FIFTY-SIX

Henry Wallace stood on the deck of the *Terrapin,* staring through the spyglass. He was not alone. The ship had arrived in Haever to sounds of cannon fire and the sight of ships wreathed in smoke and dying in flames. Every officer on board was at the rail, spyglass in hand, trying to see the battle.

Gradually the sound of cannon fire ceased. No one spoke; no one moved. They listened tensely and then they heard church bells. The ringing was tentative at first, as though the people could not quite believe it, and then the bells grew louder and more clamorous as every bell in Haever rang, spreading the joyful news.

"We have won!" Henry cried. Overcome with emotion, he lowered the spyglass to take out his handkerchief to wipe his eyes. "We have defeated Guundar! This battle will go down in history!"

"And we missed it!" Alan said bitterly. He snapped his spyglass shut in frustration. "Do you see the *Valor?*"

Henry raised the spyglass and swept the sky, cursing the smoke that obscured his view.

"I see her!" he said, pointing. "The *Valor* is damaged, but still afloat."

He handed the spyglass to Alan.

"Good old Randolph," said Alan. "Let us hope he survived."

He moodily gave the spyglass back to Henry. "The grandest naval victory Freya has ever achieved, and we arrive just in time to witness the surrender."

Henry was in an ebullient mood. He clapped his friend on the shoulder. "My dear fellow, you cannot be the hero of every battle. You must give others a chance."

"You mean Randolph," Alan grumbled. "He will never let me live this down. I can hear him now. 'Where were you during the Battle of Haever, Alan? Enjoying a nap? Taking afternoon tea?'"

Henry laughed. "Tell him you were winning the Battle of Wellinsport. I doubt Randolph sank five enemy ships *and* found a magical well. I just hope he didn't get his fool head blown off in the process."

"You know Randolph. If he didn't lose a little blood, he wouldn't consider he'd been in a fight," said Alan. "And it seems he had help. Unless I am much mistaken, those are members of the Dragon Brigade flying this way. They probably want to make certain we are not a threat."

"I know that man in the lead," said Henry. "He is an old enemy of mine, Dag Thorgrimson."

Captain Thorgrimson brought his dragon to a halt a respectful distance from the ship, not wanting to alarm the crew. He removed his helm.

"Hail the *Terrapin*!" he called. "I would speak with your captain!"

Henry waved. "Dag Thorgrimson! Henry Wallace. Good to see you, sir. How goes the fight?"

"We are victorious, my lord," said Dag, saluting.

Henry asked the question uppermost in his mind. "What happened to King Ullr? Is he dead? Captured?"

"As far as we can tell, the king was not present at the battle, my lord," Thorgrimson returned. "We have questioned the Guundaran prisoners regarding his whereabouts. They claim he was aboard his yacht. The dragons have been searching for it, but we cannot find it. We fear he must have escaped."

"Damnation!" Henry swore.

"What about the ships armed with the green-beam guns, Captain?" Alan asked.

Captain Thorgrimson scratched his beard in bemusement. "I know you will think I have been nipping the Calvados, sir, but the four were attacked by a house and destroyed before they could do any damage."

Alan and Henry both looked at each other.

"Simon!" Henry exclaimed.

"Even he got to take part in the battle," Alan said discontentedly, but he gave a grudging smile.

"I have come to ask you a favor, Captain," said Thorgrimson. "Since your ship is the only one that can sail the Deep Breath, I was hoping you could search for survivors. Several ships went down and may have foundered on rocks, which means men might still be alive. We are also searching for survivors who escaped in lifeboats."

"Certainly, sir," said Alan.

"Wait a moment, Captain," Henry said, realizing what Thorgrimson had said. "You stated four of the green-beam guns were destroyed. I know for a fact that there were five."

"We saw only four, my lord," said Thorgrimson.

He saluted his thanks. His dragon dipped her wings and flew off, heading back to Haever.

Henry scowled, his good mood evaporating. "I do not count this as a victory. Ullr is missing and so is one of the green-beam guns. He could be anywhere."

Henry lowered the spyglass and, remembering their quarrel, deferentially turned to Alan.

"Before you start looking for survivors, would it be possible for the *Terrapin* to convey me to the palace?"

Alan smiled, knowing Henry of old, knowing that in the past he would not have bothered to ask. He would have ordered.

"I should not delay the search," Alan replied, "but I can send you in the pinnace. Why do you want to go to the palace?"

"I must ascertain that His Majesty is safe, of course," Henry replied.

Alan grinned. "I will wager you a case of Calvados, Henry, that you will not find King Thomas anywhere near the palace."

"What are you talking about?" Henry demanded. "Where else would the king be?"

"Thomas Stanford is young. He is a soldier. Do you think he would hide from the Guundarans in the cloak closet? Unless I much mistake our king's character, I will wager six cases of Calvados that Thomas fought in the thick of the battle."

Henry regarded him in horror. "You are not serious! What if something happens to him? I tell you, Alan, I could not survive another succession crisis. I must find him."

"Then I suggest you start by asking Randolph," said Alan. "If anyone will know, he will."

"Deck there!" the lookout bellowed. "Ship off the starboard bow!"

"Likely some poor merchantman who blundered into the fighting," Alan remarked. "Mr. Finch, go aloft. Tell me what you see."

The midshipman scrambled up the shrouds and put his glass to his eye.

"Yacht, sir!" he reported. "A big one. Three masts. I can't see the name through the smoke. The *Stein*-something, sir."

"Stein-*something,* Mr. Finch?" Alan shouted, displeased.

Mr. Finch flushed red, watched intently, and finally managed to get a clear view of the name.

"*Steinadler,* sir," he stated in triumph. "She is sailing east by north, all sail set, sir."

"*Steinadler* . . . !" Henry repeated. "That's King Ullr's yacht! He's sailing east by north for Guundar. The bastard's lost the war and now he's running for home!"

"By God, Henry," Alan said excitedly, "we may get in on this fight yet! Has the *Steinadler* seen us, Mr. Finch?"

The midshipman watched for several moments, keeping them in suspense, then shouted down, "Don't think so, sir. The yacht is maintaining speed, holding her course."

Alan hurried to confer with the helmsman.

"What are you going to do?" Henry asked, going after him.

"Cut her off," said Alan.

"She is faster," said Henry.

"But we do not have as far to sail to intercept her," said Alan. "And she won't know we are chasing her."

He gave orders for the *Terrapin* to sink down into the mists of the Deep Breath. He was taking a risk. The *Steinadler*'s lookouts would have a difficult time seeing the *Terrapin* sneaking up on them. But she risked losing sight of Ullr's yacht in the mists. The *Terrapin* would be sailing blind.

"Are you sure about this, Alan? What if Ullr orders a change in course?" Henry asked nervously. "We will lose him, and we need to capture him! I want to see him stand trial before an international tribunal, humiliated before the world. His utter defeat will serve as a lesson to future despots."

"He won't change course," said Alan with maddening confidence. "He is desperate to reach the safety of home."

Henry conceded Alan had a logical argument, but as he paced the deck, shivering in the cold, he kept thinking of everything that could go wrong.

At last Alan gave the order to bring the *Terrapin* up out of the Deep Breath. The ship cautiously rose out of the mists, moving slowly, giving the lookouts time to see. They immediately sighted the *Steinadler* and reported that the yacht was right where Alan had predicted they would find her, still on course.

The *Terrapin* increased speed, continuing the pursuit with a will, and then the wind died. Not much, but enough to slow the heavy metal-plated warship. Those on board watched in dismay to see the sleek, trim yacht race ahead; it scarcely seemed to notice the drop in the wind. Henry began to swear.

Alan remained calm. He ordered the helmsman to gain altitude in hope of finding more wind. His crew was enthusiastic. Word had gone around that they were pursuing King Ullr and everyone on board ship worked with a will to squeeze every advantage out of even the smallest puff of air.

"It's going to be close," Alan remarked.

Henry had his spyglass trained on the *Steinadler*. He saw a flurry of activity among her crew: men rushing to the rail, sailors scrambling up the shrouds.

"They've seen us," he reported.

The wind was erratic. The breeze that had failed the *Terrapin* continued to breathe on the *Steinadler*. She added more sail, flying through the Breath while the *Terrapin* lumbered along, burdened by her shell.

Henry fumed. "We're going to lose him!"

"Not if I can help it," said Alan.

He gave the order to open the gun ports on the port side and run out the guns.

"We want to cripple her, not sink her," Alan told the gun captain.

Henry watched as several members of the yacht's crew ran to the front of the ship and hauled at a tarp draped over something on the foredeck. He had noticed the tarp before, but thought only that Ullr was trying to protect his comfy deck chairs from the elements. But when the tarp fell off, Henry sucked in his breath.

"Alan! A green-beam gun!"

"So it is," Alan said coolly.

The green-beam gun began to glow with a faint green light. Henry could see the crafter crouched over it, bringing it to terrible life.

Alan watched a moment, then raised his voice. "A hundred silver talons to the gun crew that blows up the green-beam gun!"

"I will double that!" Henry shouted.

The gun crews bent over the cannons, eager to win both the prize and the glory. The *Terrapin* was armed with twenty-four-pound cannons, twelve on each side. The *Steinadler* was also armed, but only with nine-pounders that could do little damage to the *Terrapin*'s iron-clad hull. The green-beam gun made all things equal.

Alan went down to the gun deck and walked along the row of cannons, looking down the sights of each gun, adjusting the aim. The range was long yet, but he gave the order to fire.

"May the devil's luck hold, Alan," Henry said beneath his breath.

He stamped on the deck to warm his feet and felt the ship rock and heave as the cannons fired a salvo. He raised the spyglass to view the trajectory of the balls and watched with disappointment as they fell short.

But then, the devil delivered. The wind that had failed the *Terrapin* now failed the *Steinadler*. Her sails flapped, and her speed slowed. The *Terrapin* began to slowly gain on her.

The gun crews started to find their range. The guns went off sporadically as each crew sighted in on their target and fired.

A single cannonball smashed into the hull of the *Steinadler,* spoiling her gilt trim, but missing the green-beam weapon.

The cannons fired again. Another ball struck the hull, but the rest missed completely. Henry gnashed his teeth in frustration.

The cannonade continued, and finally he saw a ball smash into one of the airscrews that were attached to the keel, two forward and two aft, protected by metal casings. The ball knocked off the casing and destroyed part of the keel.

"A hit!" Henry shouted excitedly. "That will slow the bastard down!"

The green glow of the heinous green-beam gun grew stronger. It must have been mounted on a rotating platform, for as Henry watched, it swiveled about until it was aimed at the *Terrapin,* seeming to stare at him, an evil little eye.

Three cannons boomed simultaneously and the *Steinadler*'s airscrew seemed to dissolve, shattering into fragments. The loss of one airscrew was not particularly significant. The *Steinadler* could continue to sail, though she could no longer hope to outrun them.

The *Terrapin* drew nearer and the green glow of the weapon on board the yacht strengthened. Soon the *Terrapin*'s guns would be close enough to knock down the yacht's masts, disable the remaining airscrews, and puncture her lift tanks.

Unfortunately the green-beam gun would be close enough to destroy the *Terrapin*. The beam could not penetrate the magical steel, but it could heat the plates red hot. Every man on board the *Terrapin* would roast like raw meat thrown on a red-hot gridiron.

The green glow strengthened even more. The crafter was preparing to fire. Henry stood on deck watching with a terrible fascination, unable to move or look away.

He had the joy of witnessing a cannonball smash into the green-beam gun, obliterating it. The green glow vanished.

The lucky gun crew that had fired the shot whooped and cheered. The rest of the *Terrapin*'s guns continued to fire and began to dismantle the yacht, piece by piece.

"Ullr must surrender!" Henry said exultantly as Alan returned to the quarterdeck. "He has no choice."

A blast tore the heart out of the *Steinadler*.

The explosion was powerful, massive. The concussive wave hit the *Terrapin* with such force it nearly sank her. The ship heeled, and men went sprawling. Alan caught hold of the helm and grabbed the helmsman, who had almost been knocked overboard. Henry seized the shrouds and held on for dear life. He feared for a terrifying moment the *Terrapin* might capsize.

The ship righted herself, saved by the weight of the metal plates on her hull. But nothing was left of the magnificent yacht and the one hundred souls who had been on board, except smoke and flaming debris.

No one on board the *Terrapin* spoke. No one cheered or celebrated. They had just seen the lives of one hundred men end in an instant.

Lieutenant Hobbs tried to say something, failed, and had to clear his throat. "Should I send out the boats to search for survivors, sir?"

"No, Mr. Hobbs," said Alan. "No use."

He walked over to stand beside Henry, who was gazing bleakly at the fiery remains raining down into the Breath.

"I guess King Ullr did have a choice," Alan said quietly.

"That was not a lucky hit, was it," said Henry.

"Could have been, but I doubt it," Alan agreed. "Our gunners were targeting the green-beam gun. If I were to hazard a guess, I would say someone on board that yacht went down to the powder magazine and struck a match."

He looked at Henry's bleak face and added, "You have no way of knowing if King Ullr was on board."

"He was," Henry said harshly. "Who do you think scuttled his own ship? He could not face defeat."

"Then he is dead and the war is over," Alan said. "The killing can stop."

"*This* war is over," Henry returned despondently. "There will always be another."

Alan regarded his friend with concern and rested his hand on his shoulder.

"But for now, there is peace, Henry. Our nation has won a glorious victory over a tyrant who sought to enslave us. Freya will soon be prosperous, Simon's well will bring in untold wealth. Thomas Stanford will be a good king. He is young, filled with hope and the optimism of youth. You will help guide him. Our new king will need a spymaster."

"So he will. All kings need spymasters," Henry said. "But it will not be me."

FIFTY-SEVEN

Alan and Henry stood together on the deck of the *Terrapin* as the ship sailed toward Haever's harbor. They could see even from this distance the throngs of cheering people that had gathered on the wharf to welcome them home. The pilot's craft sailed toward them. When the pilot came on board, Alan would have to join him at the helm to guide the *Terrapin* to a safe landing. But for the moment, he and Henry had a brief respite from duty.

"So—our last voyage together," Alan said. "Are you truly determined to submit your resignation? As I recall, you threatened to do so in the past when Queen Mary exasperated you beyond endurance."

"I did resign, on more than one occasion," said Henry, smiling at the memory. "Mary would always tear up my letter and toss it in the fire. One time, she gave it to that damn monkey, who ate it!

"Queen Mary was a wise woman, Alan. We often clashed, but she knew that in a world of danger and threat, we needed each other. But when she needed me most, I was not able to save her. I will live with that regret all my life. At least," Henry added, "I will not let it happen again."

Alan cast him a questioning glance. "Let *what* happen?"

Henry shook his head.

"I still have a few secrets to guard. I have given thirty-five years of my life in service to my country. It is time for me to retire. I hope my legacy to my children will be a world at peace. If so, I will be satisfied with my work."

Alan gave an absent nod. He had seemed preoccupied all morning. He would give an order and forget he had given it. He would start to say something, then fall silent. He had done this several times since the two had been standing here and Henry was growing annoyed.

"Come now, Alan. You have been trying to tell me something this past half hour. What secret are *you* keeping?"

Alan faintly smiled. "I could never hide anything from you."

"My dear fellow, you are so transparent you could not hide anything from a six-year-old," said Henry, smiling. "That is the reason you are a captain and I am a spymaster. Out with it."

"Very well, but you must promise not to tell anyone," said Alan. "I am going to be married. At least, I plan to propose, and I have every reason to believe the lady will accept me."

"You! Married!" Henry scoffed. "You are the most confirmed bachelor I know. I don't believe it."

"You must believe it, for you are responsible," said Alan. "You and Lady Ann invited the lady to the dinner party where we met."

He looked back on that occasion, smiling. "Do you remember? That was a momentous evening! I met my future wife on the same night you and Simon and Randolph and I thwarted Smythe's attempt to steal the *Valor*."

"I remember the *Valor* incident, but I am hazy as to the details of the dinner party," said Henry.

"Lady Ann was so kind as to seat me next to Lord Alfred's charming niece, Lady Annabelle. She and I have been corresponding since then, and we have reached an understanding."

"My wife, the matchmaker," said Henry fondly. "Lady Ann will be pleased, and so am I. If you find the same happiness in marriage that I have found, Alan, you will be fortunate beyond your fondest dreams."

The two men shook hands, then stood quietly for a moment, each reflecting that when the ship docked, they would walk off the gangplank and into new lives.

"But always the same old friendship," said Henry. He gestured to the crowd. "Look, Alan, His Majesty is waiting to greet you. You will be promoted to Commodore, of course, *and* receive a knighthood."

"Good," said Alan, grinning. "As a newly married man, I will need the money. I expect you and Simon and Randolph to stand with me at the altar. I will need the Seconds for support."

"You will need the Seconds to keep you from fleeing," said Henry, laughing.

He added, touched, "I will be proud to stand with you, Alan. We will all be proud."

Moments later, the pilot arrived, and Alan hurried off to join him. Henry leaned against the rail, watching the king, who had come to greet them. Thomas was wearing his ceremonial naval uniform in their honor. He had one arm in a sling. Henry had heard from Randolph that the king had fought valiantly. He reached into the inner pocket of his coat, where he kept the queen's letter. Through all his adventures, Henry had never lost it.

Queen Mary had asked him to show the same loyalty to Thomas he had pledged to her. Henry had made a promise to his queen and he would keep it.

When Henry arrived at his house in Haever, he found it achingly empty without his wife and children, so empty that he left and moved to his rooms in the Naval Club. Henry immediately wrote to Ann, urging her to make arrangements to return home as soon as possible.

He sent his letter by griffin-rider, then had to wait a week for her return letter. He had work enough to do in the interim to keep him busy. He missed Mr. Sloan, who had remained at the site of the White Well, and was apparently still there, according to Simon.

Henry had to make his own arrangements to hire workmen and crafters to start repairs to his house, which had been damaged in the magical fire when Smythe's soldiers had come to arrest him. Henry had to locate his former butler, Jacobs, and bring him back to supervise the staff as they began to set things to rights.

He finally received a letter from Lady Ann. She wrote to tell Henry to express her joy to Alan on his choice of wife and to say that her return would be delayed. The Countess de Marjolaine was sailing for Freya to meet with the king in an effort to establish closer ties between Freya and Rosia. The countess had offered to take them with her on her yacht.

> The children long to see their father, as I long to see my husband. We must be patient a month more, for the countess insists we should wait until the weather improves to sail. She is right, of course, but I do miss you, my dearest.
>
> I remain forever and always your loving, "Mouse."
>
> PS. Wear your flannel waistcoat, Henry. The nights are chill and I know you will not think of it if I am not there to remind you.

Henry smiled and sighed, and went to his dressing room to put on the flannel waistcoat.

He wrote his letter of resignation to the king, but he did not immediately submit it. He shut the letter in the drawer for the time being.

He and Alan and Simon went to the hospital to visit Randolph. Still confined to his bed, he was in a bad mood. He damned all physicians for quacks, complained about the food, and raved that they would allow him nothing to drink except water and small ale.

"Stop grousing, Randolph!" Henry told him. "They saved your leg, and you are to be knighted, along with Alan."

"All that means is that I have to get down on my knees before the king and ruin my stockings," Randolph grumbled, but they could see he was pleased.

"I have no doubt Simon will be knighted also, once news breaks of the White Well," said Henry. "Think of it, friends. All four of us are Seconds—second sons with no prospects—and we four are or soon will be lords of the realm. I can honestly say that in my wildest imaginings, I would never have dreamed it."

"We have you to thank for our success, Henry," said Alan. "You were the brains, as I have always said. Without you, I would have been hanged as a pirate, Randolph would be an aging midshipman, and Simon a clerk in some dingy office."

Henry was touched. He protested, of course, but his friends insisted on giving him credit. Alan had smuggled a jug of Calvados past the healers and he poured them each a glass. The four drank a toast.

"To friends," said Henry simply.

The next day, he visited Simon at Welkinstead to receive his report on the Eye of God and its effectiveness against contramagic weapons.

"I hope and trust all the green-beam guns have been destroyed," said Henry. "Still, it might be adapted to counter some other type of threat. Tell me about the Eye."

"I assume you mean the refocused energy emitter and generator," said Simon, frowning. "There's nothing to tell. I dismantled it and burned the plans. It had serious flaws."

"But you said the weapon was lethal!" Henry protested.

"It was," said Simon. "*That* was the serious flaw. I will not rid the world of one heinous instrument of killing, only to introduce another. Besides, I will be much too busy overseeing the work on my well."

While he was at Welkinstead, Henry greeted Sophia and Phillip and Bandit, who were staying with Simon and Mr. Albright to help them clean up, put the books back to rights, and make adjustments to the lift tanks that were still not working to his satisfaction.

Henry congratulated Sophia and Phillip and promised to attend their wedding.

"I think it will be a double wedding," Sophia said, adding with a sly smile, "But you must ask His Majesty and Kate."

"Truly?" Henry said, amazed. "I have heard nothing!"

"Thomas has not yet made the announcement public, for their union will require an act of the House of Nobles. Still, since Kate is celebrated as a national hero who saved the king's life, I believe the vote to approve the marriage will be unanimous."

Henry was still trying to envision this remarkable pairing as Phillip and Bandit escorted him to the door.

"May I speak to you in confidence, my lord?" Phillip asked.

"Certainly, Your Grace," Henry replied.

"I want you to know that if you ever need him, Pip is always available. I have spoken to Sophia and she is in agreement."

"Thank you, Your Grace," said Henry, smiling. "But as Pip is in truth the Duke of Upper and Lower Milton and His Grace is marrying Her Highness, Princess Sophia of Rosia, I believe our profligate clerk should try to lead a reformed life from now on."

Phillip laughed. "Thank you, my lord. That comes as a relief to my liver."

He and Henry shook hands, and Phillip picked up Bandit, who had been attempting to chew off the buckle of Henry's shoe.

Henry returned to his place of employment, the Foreign Office. He entered the building with considerable trepidation. The night of the queen's death, he had witnessed soldiers of the Army of Royal Retribution storm inside, arresting people and ransacking offices.

He need not have worried. Kings and queens might come and go, nations rise and fall, but the bureaucracy ground on forever. One undersecretary to an undersecretary told Henry in a peeved voice that the soldiers had smashed his favorite teapot, but that appeared to be the only major disruption.

Henry found his own small office untouched. Located in an out-of-the-way corner of the building, it was often mistaken for a closet, and the soldiers had apparently not considered it important. Nor, apparently, had he been missed in all the time he had been gone, for the mail room had thoughtfully continued to deliver his mail, which was piled up on his desk.

As Henry sat down to sort through his correspondence, he reflected that it was well he hadn't died. Years might have passed before anyone noticed.

He was still in the office, reading reports from his various agents, when there came a familiar tap on the door. Mr. Sloan entered and Henry rose to greet him with delight.

"Tell me the news about the White Well."

"Captain Rader and his troops have established a base at Nydrian's Cove to guard it. I spoke to Governor Crichton—"

"He survived, did he?" Henry asked, interrupting.

"He was wounded in the shelling that destroyed his house, but he was able to escape, my lord. He was extremely humble and asked me to convey to you his most sincere apologies for having refused to heed your warning."

"He is a lucky man in more ways than one," said Henry grimly.

"Indeed, my lord. I explained the situation regarding the White Well. The governor was ecstatic, as you can imagine, for this will mean the city of Wellinsport will increase in wealth and importance. Captain Rader will need assistance in guarding the well."

"I have spoken to the Admiralty," said Henry. "Admiral Tower will be receiving orders to send ships to do that very thing. You have the chart that marks the location?"

"I do, my lord. I stopped by the Parrot on my way back." Mr. Sloan removed the chart from his satchel and delivered it to Henry, who wrinkled his nose.

"What is that god-awful smell?"

"Olaf hid the chart in an empty ale barrel for safekeeping, my lord."

Henry laughed, and wondered how he was going to get rid of the smell before delivering the chart to the king.

"Sit down, Mr. Sloan. I have news. I am planning to submit my letter of resignation to His Majesty. I have one more task to do as spymaster and you must help me do it. After that, I mean to retire."

He paused, eyeing his secretary. "You do not look surprised, Mr. Sloan."

"I have been expecting this news, my lord," said Mr. Sloan. "I offer you my very best wishes."

"You know, of course, that you are most welcome to remain in my employment, though I tell you honestly that life as the secretary to a country squire would be a sad waste of your many exceptional talents."

"Thank you, my lord," said Mr. Sloan. "Serving Your Lordship has been an honor and a privilege." He added with a cough, "I was planning to speak to you. . . ."

"Yes, Mr. Sloan?"

"I have been thinking of going into business for myself. You see, sir, I am going to be married. . . ."

"Not you as well, Mr. Sloan!" Henry exclaimed, amazed. "Who is the most fortunate woman who has won your heart?"

"She is Mistress Brown, the owner of a sigil shop, who has done work for you in the past, my lord. She placed the magic on your coat during the Bottom Dweller War that protected you against the contramagic attack."

"She saved my life, Mr. Sloan," said Henry.

"Yes, my lord. Mistress Brown is recently widowed—"

"I am sorry to hear that," Henry interjected.

"Do not be, sir. The late Mr. Brown was a cad," said Mr. Sloan.

"Then good riddance to him," said Henry, smiling.

"Mistress Brown was left to cope with the business and to raise two young boys. She wrote to ask my advice on a matter connected with the shop and I was able to be of some material assistance to her. We have corresponded since then and walked out together on occasion. She and I have formed an understanding."

Mr. Sloan added with some embarrassment, "I am pleased to say that the boys have become quite attached to me, my lord. I find I enjoy fatherhood."

"Congratulations, Mr. Sloan," said Henry, adding with a laugh, "I am to be beset by weddings, it seems. First Alan and now you. The next thing I hear, Randolph will be marching to the altar where he will damn the eyes of the reverend."

Henry grew serious. "And now, Mr. Sloan, I fear we must turn from matters of love to business—a most unpleasant business."

Mr. Sloan rose to check to make certain the door was locked and that no one was loitering in the hall, then resumed his seat.

"I am all attention, my lord."

"I have received disturbing information, Mr. Sloan. I dare not investigate the matter myself for reasons that will soon become apparent to you."

He handed a note to Mr. Sloan, who read it and looked grave. "I am extremely sorry to learn this, my lord. What would you have me do?"

"I need you to procure evidence, however damning."

"I understand, my lord."

Mr. Sloan took his leave. Henry gathered up the documents that he considered important, looked about his office for one last time, smiled, and departed. He would have to remember to tell someone in the mail room.

Mr. Sloan was gone for several days. Immediately on his return, he went to the Naval Club to meet with Henry.

"I have the evidence you require, my lord. I bribed the earl's valet, who has no great regard for his master, and he provided me with documents, as well as several incriminating letters."

Henry read through the letters. His expression darkened. "The damn fool! This is enough to hang him!"

"I am surprised he did not destroy them, my lord."

"He kept them to protect himself from Smythe." Henry grimaced. "I was afraid it would come to this. I must act with dispatch."

"I await your orders, my lord."

"I will not involve you, Mr. Sloan," said Henry. "This could well get *me* hanged."

FIFTY-EIGHT

By the time Mr. Sloan left, the sun had set. Henry reflected that the days were growing longer, the air warmer. Traveling the Breath would be safe now. Lady Ann had written that the countess had ordered her yacht to be ready to sail and that his family would be with him soon. The day could not arrive fast enough.

He put tender, loving thoughts from his mind. He would be venturing into the darkness and they had no place there. Removing the letter of resignation from the drawer, he took a cab to the palace. He was well known to the marines at the gate and they immediately granted him permission to enter. Henry dismissed the cab, saying he would walk from there.

He did not make his way to the palace. Instead, he walked to Offdom Tower.

Henry kept watch in the darkness to make certain he was not followed. He checked more out of force of habit than because he was truly worried. This section of the palace grounds was deserted at night. The tower was undergoing extensive repairs following Dalgren's attack. The top floor of the building had suffered the most damage, and was closed. Only one prisoner occupied the tower: Isaiah Crawford, otherwise known as Jonathan Smythe.

The church bells struck ten of the clock as he walked up the stairs of the

dark and silent tower to the floor where Smythe's cell was located. Two marines stood outside the cell door. They recognized Henry, for both had once
served aboard the *Valor*. They greeted him warmly and inquired anxiously
about Admiral Baker, saying they heard he had been seriously wounded.

Henry was happy to report that Randolph would make a full recovery,
then came down to business.

"I need to speak to the prisoner, gentlemen."

"Very good, my lord," one of the marines replied, adding, "I should accompany you, sir. The bastard is as dangerous as a rabid rat. He's been spewing filth about the king and our late queen, God rest her."

His comrade nodded agreement. "Just tonight, when I took him his meal,
he tried to bribe me to help him escape. He said he had powerful friends
who would reward me well for aiding him."

"Did he happen to name these friends?" Henry asked, trying to appear
nonchalant.

"No, my lord. I wouldn't give him the satisfaction. I told him to rot in
hell, and reported the incident to our commander."

"A proper course of action," Henry replied, vastly relieved. "Thank you
for the offer, gentlemen, but I see no need for you to accompany me. I will
be perfectly safe. Still, you should lock the cell door behind me. We mustn't
take chances."

One of the marines went to fetch the key that hung on a hook on the wall
while the other removed the magical constructs on the door. Henry took off
his greatcoat, folded it, draped it over a chair, and entered the cell.

"Good luck, my lord," the marine said as he shut the door behind him.
"Shout if you need us."

He turned the key in the lock.

Smythe sat at a desk, writing. He looked around when he heard the door
open, saw Henry, and went back to his writing.

"What the devil do you want, Wallace?"

"A moment of your time, Crawford," said Henry. "This won't take long,
I assure you."

"His Majesty sent you, no doubt, to try to convince me to keep silent,"
said Smythe with contempt. "You always were a royal ass-licker. First that
spawn of the Evil One, Queen Mary, and now—"

Henry drew his pistol, placed the barrel against the back of Smythe's
skull, and pulled the trigger. Smythe slumped forward onto the desk, striking
the inkwell and knocking it over. Ink and blood formed a gruesome pool.

One of the marines was hammering on the door.

"We heard a shot, my lord! Are you all right?"

"I am perfectly fine," Henry called. "But I fear there has been a tragedy.

No, don't open the door. Nothing should be disturbed. Fetch your commander."

Henry placed the gun in the corpse's limp hand. He then gathered up the papers on Smythe's desk, including those beneath his head that were soaked in blood. Henry glanced through them and grimaced. He selected several and thrust them into his pocket, then burned the remainder in the grate, stirring them with the toe of his boot to make certain they were entirely consumed.

By that time, the commander had arrived. The marines opened the cell door and he walked inside. He shook hands with Henry, whom he knew from the Naval Club where he had often played whist with Randolph, then glanced at the corpse.

"Bad business, my lord," he said coolly.

"Indeed it is, Captain," said Henry.

"Did you see what happened?"

"I am afraid not, sir," said Henry. "I had walked over to warm myself at the fire. I blame myself. I was careless and he was able to take my gun from my pocket."

The captain grunted. "Good thing he shot himself and not you, my lord."

"I can only suppose he suffered from remorse," said Henry gravely.

"Remorse that he didn't succeed in killing His Majesty," the captain said dourly. "He was as bad as they come. Tried to bribe one of my men."

"So I heard," Henry said.

The captain walked over to examine the body. "Gun in his hand. Hole in his head. Obvious what happened."

He cast a sharp glance at Henry. "I don't see a need for an inquiry, do you, my lord? Those marines are two of my best. I wouldn't want them brought up on charges of dereliction of duty."

"I see no reason, Captain," Henry agreed. "Smythe was a murderer thrice over. An inquiry into his death would stir up trouble at a time when our nation has finally come together in peace. I would suggest your men haul this fiend's carcass to the paupers' graveyard, dump him in the ground, and bury his infamy with him. He deserves no more."

"I'll send up the burial squad," said the captain.

Henry had one last official duty to perform as spymaster. He left the prison and walked to the palace. Organizing his thoughts along the way, he reached inside the pocket of his jacket and touched the queen's letter.

"I have kept my promise, Your Majesty," he said softly.

He asked to see the king, and was told that Thomas had retired to his private chambers to dine with friends.

"I must speak with him upon an urgent matter," said Henry. "This cannot wait."

The footman departed and returned with Henry's elder brother. The two shook hands.

"I heard you were back in the country," said Richard.

"You look well, Richard," said Henry. "Given the severity of your wound, I am surprised to find you have returned to your duties so soon."

"I am fully recovered, thank you," said Richard. "I happened to be visiting with the king when the footman brought your message. A group of us dined with him to discuss his marriage."

"I trust there will be no problem with the House," said Henry. "I happen to know Kate and I cannot praise her highly enough, though I venture to say she will not be a conventional queen. Are there are other guests? I need to speak to His Majesty in private."

"The others have gone and I was just about to take my leave. The king will be glad to see you. He received your report about the White Well. His Majesty is immensely pleased, and has a great many questions."

"His Majesty will have to ask them of Simon," said Henry. "I can tell him only that the well is insufferably cold and smells like rotting fish."

"I wanted a chance to speak to you alone, Henry, if you can spare a moment," said Richard. "I want to tell you I am damnably sorry about Henshaw. I had no idea he planned to betray you. I hope you believe me."

He looked uncertainly at Henry, who hastened to reassure him.

"I know you, Richard. Not as well as I should perhaps, but I know you better than that. What has become of him?"

"He told me he had handed you over to the guards. The wretch was proud of himself. Actually boasted about it! I sacked him immediately. After he was gone, I discovered he had been stealing money from me. The last I heard, he had fled the country, fearing arrest. I have no idea where he has gone and, frankly, I do not care. He will come to a bad end wherever he is."

Richard cast a troubled glance at his brother. "I hope you can forgive me, Henry."

"I could well ask you the same, Richard," said Henry. "We both made mistakes, but we did so out of love for our country."

Richard gave a faint smile. "Thank you, Henry. I will take you to His Majesty."

He escorted Henry into the king's office.

"Good-bye, Henry. Perhaps we could dine together next week."

"I should like nothing better," said Henry.

Richard bowed to the king and departed, shutting and locking the door behind him.

"Please, be seated, Sir Henry," said Thomas. "I am glad to see that you and your brother are once more on friendly terms."

"Thank you, sir," said Henry. "I have come to appreciate the value of family. I trust Your Majesty has recovered from the battle. Randolph told me of your heroism. He praised your skill and courage highly."

"Did he damn my eyes?" Thomas asked, laughing. "Because that would be high praise indeed. We owe our lives, as well as our victory, to the Dragon Brigade."

"And we owe *that* to Captain Kate," said Henry. "Her Highness, the Princess Sophia, hints that Freya will soon have a new queen."

Thomas smiled. "Thanks to Miss Nettleship, who wrote a stirring account of Kate's heroics in the *Gazette*. And now, my lord, I will not keep you. I know your time is valuable. Sir Richard tells me you have come to speak to me on a matter of the utmost urgency."

"I have, Your Majesty," said Henry. "I am here in regard to Isaiah Crawford, also known as Jonathan Smythe. He is dead, sir."

"Dead?" Thomas repeated, shocked. "How did he die?"

"By his own hand, sir," said Henry. "I fear the fault was mine. He removed a pistol I was carrying and used it to shoot himself in the head."

Thomas stared at Henry, who met his gaze and held it.

"The devil he did," Thomas said at last. "You shot him, Sir Henry. Shot him in cold blood and arranged it to look like suicide."

Henry bowed and said nothing.

Thomas slammed his fist on the desk. "Damn it, my lord, I cannot countenance this terrible crime! I cast no aspersions on the late queen, but I intend to rule differently than those who have come before me! I want people to know that their king is a man of honor, that I stand for justice and the rule of law! I intended to do this by putting Smythe on public trial. Show the world that I was not simply going to take my revenge. . . ."

He choked on his rage and had to stop talking to draw breath. Henry reached into his pocket and produced several documents.

"Your Majesty could not put Smythe on trial. You would have done irreparable harm to the monarchy and yourself."

Henry placed one of the documents on the king's desk.

Thomas saw that it was spattered with blood and recoiled. He made no move to touch it.

Henry continued. "That is a speech Smythe intended to deliver at his trial. In it, he names those who had conspired with him to assassinate Your Majesty that day on the dock. The conspirators planned to put Hugh Fitzroy on the throne."

Thomas stared at the document. He read the names and his expression darkened. He looked up at Henry. "These eight people belong to some of the oldest and finest families in the kingdom. I counted them as friends. You are saying they conspired to kill me?"

"No, sir. They had no idea Smythe's intention was to hire an assassin to kill Your Majesty. I have spoken to all of them, sir, and they were shocked and horrified to discover what he plotted. Smythe lied to them in order to convince them to join his conspiracy. Smythe told them that you intended to seize their lands and wealth and claim them for the crown. One person only knew he was going to kill you and that was the Earl of Montford, Hugh Fitzroy. The others realized, too late, that Smythe had duped them."

"They would not be the first," said Thomas in bitter tones.

"These men and women are terrified, sir. They are deeply ashamed and regret their actions," Henry said. "They want the chance to beg Your Majesty's forgiveness and pledge their loyalty. I have no need to add, sir, that if you arrest these noble lords and ladies and bring them to trial as traitors, the scandal would forever cast a dark cloud over the nation and your monarchy."

Thomas picked up the letter and glanced through it, then let it fall to the desk.

"I do not want to put these people on trial, Sir Henry. But neither can I afford to appear weak in the face of my enemies."

"They are not your enemies, sir. Mercy and forbearance are not signs of weakness. They are hallmarks of a strong king doing what he believes to be right. I suggest Your Majesty receive their pledges of fealty in the spirit of new beginnings, to celebrate your wedding and your coronation. In return, you will gain loyal allies for life."

"But I can never trust them," Thomas said in bleak tones.

"No, Your Majesty, you cannot. That is why you have a spymaster," said Henry. "And now, sir, we must decide what to do about the last name on the list, Hugh Fitzroy, Earl of Montford. I have evidence to prove his guilt. Hugh kept letters he received from Smythe. I think he had some crackpot idea of using this plot to turn the Freyan people against you, still hoping to claim the throne for himself."

"And are you saying I must pardon him, my lord?" Thomas asked.

"Hugh is a numbskull, a brute and a lout. But he is Queen Mary's half brother, the son of King Godfrey and an heir to the throne. If you put him on trial, people will whisper that you are attempting to remove your rivals. That being said, Hugh will be a constant source of trouble for you as long as he lives. He continually plotted against Queen Mary and once tried to persuade me to assassinate her sister, Elinor."

"What do you suggest, my lord?"

"Banish the earl from the kingdom. Send him into exile. Hugh has business holdings in Blount. He will be able to eke out a living in that godforsaken country, but he will no longer have the money or the necessary influence to cause mischief. Impress upon Hugh that if he ever sets foot on Freyan soil, you will lock him in prison and toss the key into the Breath. My brother, Richard, knows Hugh. He can make the arrangements."

"It seems you have thought of everything, my lord," Thomas said.

"I try to be of service, sir," said Henry.

Thomas regarded him with cold, glittering blue eyes. "And what about you, Sir Henry? Have you done all this to blackmail me if I put you on trial for murdering Smythe? Will you reveal what you know?"

"If you knew me better, sir, you would not ask that of me, my lord," said Henry with quiet dignity. "I would mount the scaffold in silence. My secrets—and yours—would die with me."

"And why should I believe you?"

"I made a promise to my queen, sir."

Henry drew the queen's letter from his pocket and laid it before the king. "Queen Mary gave this to me to be kept sealed until her death. I opened it the night she was killed. You see the bloodstains on the envelope. That blood is hers. In that letter, she tells me that she has named you her heir. The last time we spoke, she asked me to be the same loyal friend to you that I was to her. I gave her my promise. I consider it to be a deathbed promise."

Thomas reverently touched his fingers to the bloodstained letter, as though it was sacred. Henry picked it up and tucked it back into his pocket.

"What do I say about Smythe's death?" Thomas asked.

"Nothing, sir. There is no need for Your Majesty to acknowledge it. The prison authorities will issue a brief statement saying that he took his own life, a prey to guilt. He will be buried in an unmarked grave in potter's field. The man was a monster, sir. He left a bloody trail of innocent victims behind him. Your Majesty was very nearly one of them."

Thomas fixed Henry with a grim look. "I suppose for the good of the kingdom, I must do as you advise. But I will not have a man such as you in my service."

"I thought that might be the case, Your Majesty." Henry drew the other document from an inner pocket and placed it before the king. "My resignation."

Thomas took it up. "You know I will accept it, Sir Henry. I detest intrigue, scheming, and plotting. I have no more need of spymasters. I will rule in the sunlight, not in the shadows."

"I wish you success, Your Majesty," said Henry. "I look forward to a day when men will find a way to live together in peace. Until that blessed day, I leave you with a word of caution: there is a reason why men and women such as myself and the Countess de Marjolaine work in the shadows. The rats live there."

Thomas was silent for a moment, then said, "I will take your counsel under consideration, my lord."

Henry bowed. He knew he was being dismissed for good, and he would likely never set foot in this room again. He raised his eyes to the portrait of Queen Mary. He remembered persuading her to have her portrait painted, remembered her sitting for it. The sessions had not gone well.

The queen could not sit still. She constantly fidgeted and changed position, complaining that she had lost all feeling in her feet. She would stand up and march off in the middle of a sitting to see her griffins or drink tea and eat biscuits. When the harassed artist had finally shown her the finished portrait, Mary had insulted him by demanding to know who it was he thought he had been painting all this time, because it bore no resemblance to her. Henry had been forced to pay the artist double what they had agreed upon to persuade him not to burn it.

Henry smiled at the memory. His eyes dimmed.

Thomas followed his gaze. His voice softened. "I wish I had known her."

"She was a great lady and a good monarch," said Henry. "As you will be, Thomas Stanford. God bless and keep Your Majesty."

Henry bowed and took his leave.

After he had left the royal presence and the door closed between himself and the king, he realized that he was free. He was no longer called upon to spy, lie and scheme, plot and connive, commit crimes, cover up crimes, or worse. He did not regret what he had been called upon to do in the service of his country. But he was glad that part of his life was behind him. He knew an exhilarating sense of liberty, an absence of care, such as he had not known for many years.

The hour was late. The Long Gallery was dark, save for the light of the moon and stars shining through the windows. No one was about. Henry tossed dignity to the winds and capered down the hall, performing impromptu dance steps and even kicking up his heels. No one was watching except the ever-watchful eyes of the portraits of long dead kings and queens. And what they saw, they would never tell.

By the time he reached the front entrance of the palace, Henry regained his dignity, twitched his cravat into place, and tugged at his flannel waistcoat. A yawning servant summoned his carriage.

Settling back in the seat, Henry smiled in the darkness. He had already made plans for his retirement. He would move his family away from the city to his estate at Staffordshire, a gift from Her Majesty, who knew that one day Henry would need a refuge.

He looked forward to life as a country squire having no more onerous tasks than to settle disputes among his tenants. He would oversee the education of his children, enjoy the simple pleasure of taking tea with his beloved wife, and breed prize hogs.

After dealing in politics for so many years, Henry thought hogs would make a refreshing change.

EPILOGUE

The weddings of Sophia and Phillip, and of Kate and Thomas, were the social event of that century or any century. Amelia's lengthy description of the ceremony and the reception afterward filled the entire *Haever Gazette*. Her description of Sophia's exquisite beaded white lace, silk, and velvet wedding gown took up three columns.

As for Kate's wedding dress, she teased those planning the wedding by insisting she would be married in her slops. Thomas laughed and told her to go ahead, never mind what anyone said. In the end, Kate chose a simple dress of green silk and velvet. People were shocked that Kate didn't wear white. Kate said the green dress was in memory of her father, but she didn't tell anyone why. She and Olaf and Thomas understood. Admiral Baker had returned her red kerchief with his grateful thanks for having helped save his life. Kate carried the red kerchief in her bosom beneath her wedding dress, close to her heart.

The double weddings were held in the springtime. The ceremonies took place in the royal gardens, so that Dalgren and other dragons could attend. Phillip and Thomas had invited the Dragon Brigade and they were represented by the dragons, the Duke of Talwin, Countess Anasi, and Lord Haelgrund, and by humans, Stephano de Guichen and his wife, and Captain Dag Thorgrimson.

Sophia's brother, King Renaud of Rosia, was present, but he did not escort her down the aisle. That honor fell to the Countess de Marjolaine. Upon hearing this, Sophia's mother had taken offense and refused to attend. Olaf and Akiel escorted Kate, who had obtained a pardon for Akiel so that he could come to Freya and not fear arrest.

Thomas's parents, the Marquis and Marchioness of Cavanaugh, were given places of honor as parents of the groom. Constanza was thrilled that her son had fulfilled her dreams by becoming king of Freya, though she was not happy with his choice of queen. She desperately hoped Thomas would change his mind, and until the very morning of the wedding, she made a point of introducing him to every marriageable young woman of noble birth she could find.

Father Jacob traveled from Below to perform the ceremony, and to represent the Rosian church. The Freyan church was represented by the Bishop of Freya, Jeffrey Fitzroy. Hugh Fitzroy did not attend. He had apparently fled the country. Dark rumors abounded, but no one knew why, or where, he had gone. Hugh was not missed, not even by his brother, who had long been fearful that he would do something to disgrace the family. Jeffrey secretly thanked God he was gone.

Kate further scandalized the fashionable world by refusing to select daughters of dukes and barons to be her bridesmaids. She chose two Trundler women, Miri and Gythe McPike, and Amelia Nettleship. Amelia's primary duty was to walk Bandit down the aisle. The spaniel enlivened the ceremony by barking at the bishop and making himself sick on wedding cake. Amelia did honor to the occasion by leaving her umbrella at home, though she insisted on carrying her reticule.

Thomas was at last able to dance with Kate, as he had foretold so long ago after he and Phillip had helped her escape from prison.

"I am glad your dance card was not filled," said Thomas, teasing, remembering their conversation as he had dug a sliver of glass out of her foot.

Kate shook her head, embarrassed. "You and Pip risked your lives to save mine and I repaid you by hurling insults at you. The truth was, I had heard you were going to marry Sophia and I was jealous."

"So you loved me even then?" Thomas asked, pleased.

"I have loved you from the moment I saw your blue eyes," said Kate.

Henry Wallace II, son of Sir Henry and Lady Ann Wallace, niece of the late queen, served as ring bearer. Young Hal acquitted himself well, much to the relief of his mother, who was terrified he would drop the silken pillow or make faces at his father during the ceremony. Following the ceremony, Henry looked for a chance to speak to the Countess de Marjolaine.

He met her in a secluded part of the garden. The two spoke only briefly, aware that eyes were on them.

Cecile gave Henry her hand and said quietly and most earnestly, "Thomas told me you resolved a difficult problem for him, my lord. His Majesty admits the necessity, but he cannot condone the deed."

"I understand, my lady," said Henry. "I would think less of His Majesty if he did."

"Permit me to extend *my* grateful thanks, my lord, for your assistance in this matter."

Henry bowed in response and made no reply. None was needed, nor did Cecile seem to expect one.

She casually opened her lace and gilt-trimmed folding fan and held it before her face to screen her words.

"Thomas tells me that you have retired from the Foreign Office, my lord. I was able to convince His Majesty that your position should not go vacant. You will be interested to hear that the king has appointed an agent who served me, Corporal Ernest Jennings, as your successor."

Henry smiled. "I know Jennings. He is a good man and more than adequate for the task. I am glad Your Ladyship was able to persuade His Majesty."

"Thomas is young and idealistic," said Cecile. She added with a sigh, "He will learn wisdom, more's the pity."

"Let us hope he does not grow too wise," said Henry. "This is a time for youth and idealism."

"Not for old embittered cynics such as ourselves," Cecile said with a smile. She gave him her hand. "I hope you enjoy your retirement, my lord. You have served your country well and earned your rest. Please convey my love to your lady wife and the children."

"Thank you, Countess," said Henry. "I respected you as a foe. I am glad I am now able to esteem you as a friend."

He kissed her hand and the two parted, each going their separate ways.

The dragons stood apart from the humans in a field outside the royal garden in order not to accidentally trample anyone. They gathered to congratulate Dalgren, who had been forced to postpone his decision to do penance by living a solitary life helping Father Jacob in his work Below. He had been invited by the Duke de Bourlet to assist in training young dragons and their riders at the Dragon Brigade academy. Father Jacob had persuaded Dalgren to accept.

"Penance may take different forms, Lord Dalgren. You will spend your life in service to men and dragons, teaching the young what you have learned through your mistakes," Father Jacob told him. "Far better to be part of the world than retreating from it."

Dalgren had agreed at last, but only on the condition that he would spend part of each year helping the Bottom Dwellers.

Father Jacob moved among the dragons, speaking to each, then asked the Duke of Talwin if he could have a private word with him.

The duke agreed, and he and the priest walked across the field. Once they were out of earshot of the others, the two stopped. The dragon settled down in the grass, making himself comfortable and giving the priest his full attention.

"I have a strange story to tell, Your Grace," said Father Jacob. "A bit of a mystery. I was hoping you could help me solve it. Brother Barnaby and I were walking outside of Dunlow when we came across a man who was near death. Every bone in his body was broken and I can only guess as to the extent of his internal injuries.

"He was a stranger. No one Below recognized him. We are therefore certain he comes from Above, although we have no idea how he came to be on Glasearrach. If I were to venture a guess, judging by the extent of his injuries, I would say that he had fallen from a great height."

"Interesting, no doubt, Father," said the duke. "But I fail to see how I can be of assistance. Perhaps he tumbled off the side of a mountain."

"I am coming to that, Your Grace. Brother Barnaby and I were certain the poor man was going to die, and we did what we could to make him comfortable. To our surprise, the man survived. His body appeared to possess magical healing powers to mend itself. I have never seen the like—except among dragons."

"Meaning no disrespect, but isn't that rather a fanciful notion, Father Jacob," said the duke, puffing smoke from his nose.

"Perhaps, Your Grace," said Father Jacob. "As I treated him, I found evidence of old scars on his body, terrible scars that seemed to indicate he had been horribly tortured as a child."

The duke appeared suddenly wary. His mane twitched and his eyes narrowed, though he made an attempt to speak casually, as though he was merely curious.

"What does this strange human have to say for himself, Father? How does he explain what happened?"

"Alas, that is the problem, Your Grace," Father Jacob replied. "All the poor man remembers of his past is that his name is 'Petar.' He is quite adamant about that. He repeats his name over and over. Do you believe it is possible he was taught dragon magic?"

"Preposterous," said the Duke of Talwin, snorting a gout of flame that came near singeing Father Jacob. "You are a learned man, Father, with extensive knowledge of the ways of dragons. I am surprised you could even ask such a foolish question."

He paused, then said, "What will you do with him, Father?"

"He appears to be quite content to remain Below," said Father Jacob. "He is now fully healed, and is a tireless worker. He seems to take comfort in helping others."

"That is good, then," said the Duke of Talwin, seeming relieved. "Given what you say, perhaps it is a blessing the poor man has no memory of his past. Some mysteries are best left mysteries, for the sake of everyone involved. It would never do for some unscrupulous being—human or dragon—to find out that humans were capable of casting dragon magic. And now, if you will excuse me, Father, I must go pay my respects to the Countess Faltihure,

Dalgren's mother. I am glad she was able to attend the ceremony. I have not seen her in many years."

The duke hurriedly lumbered off. Father Jacob looked after him. His question answered, he sighed and walked away.

The wedding celebrations came to an end with the setting of the sun. The couples prepared to leave on their respective honeymoons. Phillip and Sophia were planning to travel to Rosia in company with the Countess de Marjolaine, who said she wanted to come to know Phillip better.

King Thomas and Queen Katherine were spending their honeymoon at Barwich Manor. Kate was having the manor renovated and restored to its former glory. They traveled in company with Olaf and Akiel, who were stopping at the manor on their way back to the Aligoes.

Akiel disconcerted Kate by telling her the house was filled with spirits. "But they are good spirits," he said. "They will bring you good fortune."

Kate and Olaf walked the familiar grounds of her home, the two of them sharing old memories and new dreams. Kate could not help but notice that Olaf walked more slowly, and leaned more heavily on his cane than when she had seen him last.

"I wish you'd come live with me and Tom," Kate said.

"And have me die of the cold!" said Olaf indignantly. "Gert would run the Parrot into ruin and Akiel would be led away by those confounded spirits of his."

He patted her hand. "The Aligoes is my home, Katydid. You and Tom will come visit me often."

Kate promised they would, but she knew differently. She had a sorrowful presentiment that this parting would be their last, and she clung to him as he and Akiel made ready to set sail on her old ship, the *Barwich Rose*.

"You haven't once told me I am my father's daughter," Kate said teasingly, through her tears.

Olaf fondly shook his head. "You are your own woman now, Katydid. And I could not be more proud."

Kate watched the *Barwich Rose* sail into the clouds and seemed to see the old Kate in her slops and red kerchief waving from the helm. She waved back until the ship was lost to sight, disappearing into the orange mists of the Breath.

Kate walked the halls of Barwich Manor and the ghosts walked with her. They were good spirits, as Akiel had said. The spirit of the little girl who had sailed the world with her father and met a dragon and a man who had told her to fight for her dreams. The spirit of the young woman who had been a pirate and had held a future king at gunpoint. The spirit of the woman who had boldly spoken in defense of her friend at his court-martial.

The spirit of the woman who had fought for her dreams and seen them come true and would continue to dream. And to fight.

Thomas came to her and put his arm around her and the two of them left the past to the spirits and walked together into the future.

Amelia Nettleship would later write a book telling the tale of the four friends, Thomas and Kate, Phillip and Sophia. The book would be immensely successful and bring Amelia the fame and fortune she had known would be hers since her days as a student of Mrs. Ridgeway's Academy for Young Ladies.

Amelia's book ended with the sentence: *They lived happily ever after*.

They didn't, of course. No one ever does. But their joys were numerous, while their sorrows were few and strengthened the bonds of love that held them together.

And so, after all, who are we to argue with such an eminent journalist as Amelia Nettleship? We will therefore end our book as she ended hers.

They lived happily ever after.

AUTHORS' NOTE

Alan reminds Henry of Naval Regulations in this quote: "Any captain or other officer, mariner or other, who shall basely desert their duty or station in the ship and run away while the enemy is in fight, or in time of action, or entice others to do so, shall suffer death or such other punishment as a court-martial shall inflict." (*Rules for the Regulation of the Navy of the United Colonies of North America,* November 28, 1775.)

Randolph quotes a naval hero of the American Revolution, John Paul Jones: "It seems to be a law of nature, inflexible and inexorable, that those who will not risk cannot win."